Ancient & Modern:
The Search

David S Hawthorn

First published 2023

ISBN 978-1-9997082-2-1

A CIP catalogue record for this book is available from the British Library

Typeset, printed and bound in Poland

This book is dedicated to
Laura, Rachel and Stewart,
my three wonderful children,
each on their own journey of discovery.

Acknowledgements:

Cover image by David & Irene Bloor
with grateful thanks to the church of
St. Werburgh, Hanbury, Staffordshire

Many thanks to Jill, Gwen and Christine for their insightful,
constructive and extremely helpful comments on the early drafts.

Thanks also to Alan Harris for proofreading the final text.

Preface

When I first had the idea behind this book, it was to answer two interconnected questions.

Firstly, I recognised that despite having been around the Christian world for decades I knew very little about the origins of the church we see today. I knew the basic cast of characters: Wesley, Calvin, Luther and the rest of the boys in the band, but I had little understanding of what they actually did and, more importantly, their motivations. This novel is not meant to be a textbook, many far more learned people have already written hundreds, many of which I have relied on for my research. Of these the most notable is *Protestants: The Faith That Made the Modern World* by Alec Ryrie which I would recommend to anyone wanting a solid grounding on the history of the post-Reformation Church. Don't worry if you are not from a church background, this is just the context. The story is very inclusive and could just as easily have been set in ancient Egypt.

My second question was one with which many Christians wrestle. We know there is a plethora of Christian denominations, some quite similar, others markedly different; and yet more, the Coptic Church, for example, that were so remote in my experience that I had literally no idea who or what they were. Add into the mix the fact that there are several very active pseudo-Christian sects around today and we can see how confusing this hotch-potch of identities must look to the non-church world. And yet the Bible says there is just one Church. Hence the question "How can this be?"

When I set out to answer these questions it was appropriate therefore that the book should take the form of an epic quest, a journey of discovery for our two main protagonists, whom you will meet shortly. There are two carefully intertwined stories awaiting you: one a quest through ancient church history, the other on modern church unity.

But essentially it is the story of two people on the cusp of falling in love; their shared faith unites them but loyalty to their individual traditions, with all the historical baggage that infers, is in danger of preventing them from following their hearts. That is until calamity strikes, forcing them on separate journeys of discovery about faith, foundations and what it means to be part of the Church of Christ.

As the story progresses you will imbibe a lot of important historical facts but, in common with all the best movies, some characters or events have been coalesced, others have been moved in time or location for dramatic effect. In doing so, I have been careful to retain and reflect the religious or political positions and motivations of all the key players and in many cases I have included the actual dialogue that they are recorded as having spoken. If you want to dig deeper or clarify any deviation from recorded events, follow the references to the footnotes where you will find links to source material, my commentary and where I discuss the generally accepted chronology in context. That is what the footnotes are for, but you don't need them to enjoy the story.

And for a bit of fun, each of the core characters has a secret hidden within their name. I hope you manage to decode them all.

Enjoy!

"I have no praise for you, for your meetings do more harm than good...when you come together... there are divisions among you."

Paul's First Epistle to the Corinthians chapter 11 verses 17 & 18.

Cast of Characters

Rector Mashman	Elderly Anglican clergyman who for many years has been the Rector at All Saints' Church, the large edifice that dominates the town centre.
Ralph Shafer M.A.	Educated senior leader of Community Restoration Fellowship, a vibrant and independent charismatic group that meets in a converted cinema.
Joel Whyens	Afro-Caribbean Methodist circuit superintendent, lay-preacher and would-be evangelist.
Rex O. Fogge	Independently wealthy spokesperson for the local Religious Society of Friends gathering, better known as the Quakers.
Jack Fort	Fiery and imposing Northern Irish Presbyterian elder and former Special Constable.
Artur Thelmin	Young, educated, Lutheran priest who recently moved to the town from his native Austria.
Ms. Thea Howlsy	Strong-minded divorcee who is pastor of Broad St. Baptist Church.
Johan 'Bunny' Elstow	Popular church secretary at All Saints' Church, a single lady in her thirties who is a loyal and hard-working Anglican and much-loved by all.
Christian Palmer	Assistant pastor at Community Restoration Fellowship, a gregarious man in his thirties whose inner pain may prevent him from finding love again.

Prologue

BATTLELINES ARE DRAWN

There was blood on the vestry carpet.

"Gentlemen please! Can we please all sit down!" Rector Mashman's status as the oldest person in the room and the de-facto chair of the meeting should have been enough to calm the melee, but passions were too inflamed for him to be heard. It didn't help that his plea came from a kneeling position whilst repeatedly dabbing at three small drips of blood with his monogrammed handkerchief; the unwelcome crimson stain being the result of a spontaneous stress-induced nosebleed. Not his own blood, but that of a now guilt-ridden Rex O. Fogge who swayed over the grovelling clergyman, head back and pinching his nasal bridge. The assurance that this was an oft-recurring ailment did little to assuage the Rector, torn between cleaning the floor and trying to bring the rather unsavoury meeting to a prompt close.

The sight of Rex's distress had begun to quell the worst of the commotion, but no-one in the unyielding group was going to be the first to sit down. The elderly clergyman levered himself upright using the arm of a chair for balance, his aged knees having long since refused him much cooperation in such a manoeuvre. He breathed deeply and forced a barely distinguishable increase in volume to his gentle ecclesiastical tone and tried once more.

"Please, can everyone sit down!"

This time it worked. Largely because he had spoken during a momentary lull as the five-person argument collectively paused for breath. The tensely assembled group, each one a leader of a local congregational flock, simultaneously and somewhat sheepishly looked at him.

"Please, remember where you are."

The Reverend motioned with both hands to indicate that despite being in the vestry of All Saints' Church they were indeed *in church*, and ought to behave in a more dignified manner. The idea of a building inferring a special sanctity didn't fit within the doctrinal interpretation of everyone present, but the point was sufficiently well made to enforce a truce.

They took their seats; Rex was satisfied that the impromptu flow had now ceased. The room fell silent save for the whir of a small Dimplex electric fan-heater that became the dominant noise until the host churchman slid a blood-stained handkerchief into his trouser pocket, folded the fingers of his hands across his chest – thumbs touching each side of his clerical collar – and spoke.

"So, are we really saying that despite..." he looked up at the large cream-faced school clock protruding from the vestry wall, "...despite over two hours, the only thing we can agree upon is that our Lord was crucified on Good Friday and rose again on Easter Sunday?" There was no need to respond to his rhetoric as that was indeed the only fact the assemblage had not contested during that early October afternoon.

Rev. Mashman had invited the ministers, pastors, and priests from the main churches in the town to the vestry of All Saints' Church to explore if they could put on a joint Easter event next Spring. Five centuries of division may have been too much to overcome, and despite the gravitas his age conferred in the group he knew he didn't have the disposition to cope with this level of disagreement any longer.

"So, we have agreed a date!" he announced. As his words hung in the air, the smallest of smiles began to dance upon his lips. Ralph Shafer M.A., leader of the free evangelical Community Restoration Fellowship, was the first to respond to the irony of the statement and, forcing a smirk added,

"It would appear so."

The Anglican chairman turned to his secretary and said,

"Make a note of that Miss Elstow, the date *has* been agreed." Several others joined in with the light-hearted relief of tension as discreet but audible snickers were released.

Miss Elstow, who had been the Anglican parish secretary for several years, did not join the qualified merriment. She didn't look pleased at all. It had been a result of her persistent encouragement that Rev Mashman had issued the invitations to this cross-denominational gathering, the first in living memory.

Miss Johan Elstow, or Bunny as everyone knew her, was arguably one of the most widely known faces in the local church populace. She was in her mid-thirties, although looked much younger, and over the last twenty years had volunteered to help in children's summer camps, on school missions, feeding the homeless as well as visiting the elderly and singing carols in the shopping centre. She had worked part-time in the church bookshop, a popular meeting point on the High Street, and would always be seen fulfilling some important role during any church event. Folks loved Bunny. She was efficient and self-assured although would not hesitate in giving an acerbic rebuke to anyone who didn't come in line with anything that had been *agreed* by her minister. Firmly Anglican in her confession, she was frustrated that the Christian faith was rarely presented harmoniously across the local Protestant churches who each had more than a light dusting of faithful souls upon their pews come Sunday. She knew most, if not all, of the key people at those churches and could see no reason why there couldn't be a well-advertised, well-attended inter-church event that might just *impact the town*, as she put it. Easter was the logical choice and she had been gently twisting the Rector's arm for months to make today's meeting happen.

What she hadn't expected was that so much history, some of it ancient, would be so readily re-ignited to inflame each minister's position. In the last two hours literally every aspect of a generic church service had been scorched: the hymns to be sung, the instruments to be played, the readings to be given and prayers to be offered. The role of women unsurprisingly kindled much discord as did, to her amazement, what people should wear. The temperature began to get really heated when considering the preaching of a sermon - not only *who* would deliver it, and there were many volunteers, but more contentious was whether it should be an evangelistic *outreach message* or an *act of worship*. That led on to the final flashpoint. It was in considering whether to include the simple eucharistic elements of bread and wine that the ancient flames began to roar.

Bunny, not a woman to freely express emotion, could feel herself getting more and more tense as the afternoon progressed, particularly as she had been told that she could only attend in her secretarial capacity and not to offer her own opinions. She snatched at her notepad, drew it onto her lap with a firm slap. Then, as everyone watched, promptly snapped the end of her pencil as she attempted to write the words *Date Agreed*. She felt her cheeks redden so avoided making eye contact around the vestry.

"Gentlemen, as far as I see it, we either give up at this point," Rev. Mashman continued, "or reconvene in a few weeks to see what compromises we are *all* willing to make."

To Bunny's surprise, they all wanted to meet again. Was this just the undercard fight? Next time was there going to be more than just Mr. Fogge's blood on the carpet?

The person who seemed the most surprised was Rev. Mashman, whose audible "Oh!" was expressed with an involuntary air of disappointment. This prompted Ralph Shafer to quickly offer,

"I am happy to host the next meeting, if you prefer."

The timid clergyman was visibly relieved and quickly accepted the offer before any of the others could protest at not being given the option to stage Round Two. Diaries, both leather-bound and electronic, were opened, and amongst the sound of pages turning and digits tapping the next date was agreed. Wednesday October 31st at half-past seven in the evening.

Meanwhile, in a quiet street in an affluent part of London, a handsome young man drew his deep red Mazda MX5 to a rapid halt. On the pavement next to him stood a tall man in a knee-length black leather coat wearing a furry Russian military-style hat. The young driver reached over to open the door for the gentleman, but the would-be passenger had no intention of joining him in the low-slung sports car and firmly closed the half-open door with his two hands. He then leaned over the open top and fixed his gaze on the driver who looked back at him with a mixture of respect and fear.

"The date and time are set as agreed Sluga, so I will see you at the end of this month."

Sluga was not the driver's name. By using the term for *servant* in their shared native tongue, the menacingly imposing man was making clear the nature of their relationship. He pivoted further over the vehicle and closer to the driver's face before delivering,

"Once you have done me this service your family's obligations will have been repaid."

Chapter 1

THREE WEEKS LATER

"There you go, a cappuccino for you and a black americano for me."

Two oversized yellow cups and saucers were slid carefully onto one of the small black circular tables that were scattered around the coffee lounge of the converted cinema building that was now home to Community Restoration Fellowship. The fact that the popular, trendy, charismatic congregation had chosen to name their lounge CROSSTA COFFEE, a clear reference to the Costa Coffee chain, really grated on Bunny who was not known for her sense of humour.

She did, however, take every opportunity to visit as it usually meant a chance to meet up with her long-time friend Christian Palmer. Chris was one of two assistant pastors at C.R.F. and was, in her opinion, the person most likely to be behind the awful Crossta Coffee pun. Bunny appreciated Chris's upbeat personality, not only because it counteracted her occasionally sober demeanour, but also because it was a great testimony to God's grace. Chris's young wife had left him barely four-years into their marriage. Rumours flew around that she had a secret lover, but Chris always attested that she had simply lost her faith and could no longer live with someone who hadn't. Bunny was never sure if Chris had ever come to terms with the devastating, if somewhat clichéd, shock of discovering a hand-written note and finding she had packed all her clothes and gone. His positive outlook might well be his way of coping but nevertheless she enjoyed his company and felt she was, in some way, helping him.

"Rather you than me!" Bunny said as Chris spun a vacant chair over to their table and sat down, neither opposite nor adjacent to her but positioned somewhere between the two.

"Sorry?" he asked for clarification.

"Tonight's meeting. I'm glad you are the one taking notes this time and not me," she admitted. "Last time it was like the Battle of..." she struggled to find a military metaphor.

"Jericho?" Chris offered.

"Definitely not Jericho! Walls were in no danger of coming down! Not from any of them," she said emphatically.

"That bad?"

She nodded as she sipped her frothy cappuccino. She passed Chris a thin manila-coloured folder with the title *Easter Inter-Church Event* handwritten on the front and neatly underlined in red ink. As he flipped it open, he saw that inside was a list of attendees and a single sheet of typed paper with the minutes of their first meeting. How Miss Elstow had indeed produced a page of text from the malaise of non-agreement last time was demonstration of her determination to make the event happen. The page ended with 'Date Agreed – Good Friday' as the single decision.

"Everyone's view of Church is so entrenched, no one can see beyond their own…" she took another drink, "…their own interpretation; their own way of *doing church*. If only they could take a step back and see the Church as the outside world does. People must laugh at us all defending our little areas of sanctity."

"Well, I'm sure they'll see the benefit of working together, especially if they got it out of their system last time," Chris assured her. "By the end of tonight we will have a cohesive and positive result, just you wait and see. Besides, I gather that a couple of additional churches are joining this time, so they all may be better behaved."

"Yes, I had heard…" but before Bunny could get further clarity on who exactly was going to be at the meeting, Chris interrupted her.

"Bunny," he said politely. "If I may… there was another reason I wanted to see you tonight."

He closed the manila folder, placing it back on the table to one side away from their coffee cups. He then carefully lifted his mobile phone and placed it on top of the folder, symbolically sealing the file, and hence the subject, closed.

Bunny looked at him expectantly only to see his line-of-sight remained on the stationery. She tried to see what was arresting his gaze, assuming it to be something displayed on his smart phone's screen. She levered herself up on one elbow, so that she could see the screen, but to her surprise it was blank. For an uncomfortable few moments she watched as he sat uncharacteristically motionless and silent. Had something bad happened to her friend? Was he ill? Had his ex-wife contacted him? Bunny was not blessed with great patience, but something was clearly on Chris's mind. She bit her lip for as long as she could before impatience finally surfaced.

"And the reason you wanted to see me is…?" She spaced the final words out as if coming to a halt.

"Yes, the reason." Chris paused before continuing.

"Yes?" Bunny prompted, slightly irritated.

"I have been thinking, Bunny..." At last, he turned, looking directly at her. She could see moist tears in the reflection of both eyes, "...about us."

"Us?" Bunny said suddenly, now realising she was overly close to his face having remained pivoted forward on one elbow. She rocked back onto her chair.

"I think..." he stammered.

What did he mean *us?* Bunny thought. Surely, he was not assuming there was anything more to *us* than just being friends.

"I think that we have known each other for a while and..." he continued, skirting around whatever subject he was aiming for.

Despite them both being single and of a similar age Bunny had dismissed even considering the prospect of a relationship between them. As far as she was concerned they were from two very different worlds – church worlds, that is.

"I've been thinking, and I think we have known each other for a while, and..." he repeated, pausing.

"Yes, you have said that already. What are you saying?" she protested, but before Chris could answer Rector Mashman arrived at their table. And he wasn't alone, bringing with him someone neither Bunny nor Chris had seen before; a tall, blonde man in his early thirties, or perhaps even younger judging by his distressed stonewashed jeans and Hollister sweatshirt.

"Hello, Miss Elstow, I didn't expect to see you here," the soft-spoken cleric interrupted.

Chris stood up instinctively. "Reverend Mashman," he said to the Rector offering a handshake. "You are early, the meeting doesn't start for another half-hour."

"Yes, you *are* early," Bunny said curtly, desperately wanting Chris to finish his conversation. "*Much,* too early."

"Yes, I know I am. I wanted to go through with you, Chris, all that happened last time, so you are up to speed, so to speak," the Rector explained.

"I've already done that," Bunny complained letting her irritation at his untimely arrival show. All three men now standing at the table towered over her.

As she looked up she realised she had spoken with out-of-character discourtesy, so composed herself, affixed her polite church-smile and said, "Can I get you a hot drink Rector? Tea? Coffee?"

"Tea would be nice, you know how I like it."

As she rose, she leaned over and whispered into Chris's ear,

13

"Weak!"

It wasn't clear if that was a comment on his inability to express whatever was on his mind or simply how the Reverend took his tea.

"And for you?" she addressed the stranger.

"Oh yes, let me introduce Artur Thelmin," Rev Mashman interrupted. "He is the new minister at the Lutheran church in East Gate, at least I think that is right, isn't it? Do you call it *minister* in Lutheran?"

"Strictly speaking I am a priest, but we tend to use pastor," Artur clarified in an English that belied a slight foreign accent. "And no, I don't want a drink, thank you, Miss." Bunny couldn't place the accent. Her instinct was that he was Eastern European, but she wasn't confident, having completely failed to identify accents many times in the past.

"He has recently come over from Austria," the Rector explained.

"Your English is very good," Bunny complimented.

"He speaks six languages," Mashman continued. Then realising he was being rude to speak *about* his guest, rather than include him asked "Isn't that right?"

"Well, I studied languages at Universität," he explained. "I hope to be a missionary in the Balkans one day."

"And he has lots of new ideas, which he would like to share, isn't that right Artur," Rev Mashman prompted.

Bunny didn't wait for an expansion on his *new ideas,* choosing instead to make her way to the counter and order a cup of offensively weak tea. As she waited for the beverage, she looked at the notice board strategically positioned for queueing customers. On the following Wednesday evening C.R.F. were having a 'Releasing Tongues Night.' This was a church where speaking in tongues was the norm. She had never spoken in tongues and, more to the point, wasn't entirely sure if it was even Biblical. Bunny looked over to the three men she had left moments ago: one a conservative Anglican, one a Lutheran and the other a modern charismatic. And if Chris was fumbling about trying to pluck-up the courage to ask her on a date or something, well how would Rector Mashman react. Should she tell him? Would she be considered disloyal if she was going to be associated with one of these tongue-speaking Pentecostalists?

"Is this your cup of tea?" a quiet voice said. Bunny looked back at the poster.

"No, not really," she said distractedly then, realising that the waitress was pointing to the off-white brew on the counter, quickly reversed it to, "Yes that's mine."

Over the next half-hour several more church leaders arrived and began congregating around the table. A little before seven-thirty their host, Ralph Shafer, suggested they should make their way up to the Reformation Room announcing that he would lead the way.

At last, Chris was free. Bunny pounced.

"What did you want to say, Chris?" she demanded.

"There is no time now. Are you going to be around afterwards?" he asked.

"No. Just tell me, please," she insisted.

Chris was clearly getting anxious about being late for the meeting but could see that Bunny was even more concerned. Her uneasiness was his doing, so he reached out and took hold of her arms. Not her hands, not her shoulders, but he put his hands onto the outside of the top of her arms and gently squeezed her triceps. A strange, unnatural posture thought Bunny. He looked her in her eyes and finally said it.

"I like you, and I think I like you a lot, Bunny."

What did he mean, I think I like you a lot? Was this oddly-framed sentence his attempt at a declaration of affection? If it was, what was Bunny's required response supposed to be? Chris was clearly hoping for the requisite, *and I like you too*, but it didn't come. Bunny's reflex reply was simply,

"Oh!"

"Oh? Is that all I get...Oh?" he answered, now emboldening himself with his characteristic humour. "Not even *oh, darling*!"

"Certainly not oh, darling," she replied emphatically before explaining, "It's more of an 'Oh why couldn't you have chosen a better time to say such a thing.'" She didn't want to admit that her honest reaction was actually 'Oh my goodness! what have I done to encourage him?'

Chris's unsolicited semi-declaration of affection had completely broadsided her. When he said 'I think I like you a lot' did he mean what she thought he meant? Was he saying he loved her? As for her, she already knew that she cared for Chris, but had resigned herself that this was the fraternal sort of love between the best of friends. She wasn't looking for romantic love having long since accepted the fact that it was not going to be part of her life story. She was single, in her thirties and whilst that certainly wasn't too old, she had accepted marriage was probably not ever going to be on her horizon.

Acceptance made her strong, she told herself. After all, she'd never really had a proper boyfriend as such. Girlhood expectations of white weddings and happy families had long since been replaced with a passion to live the life she had been given to the fullest possible. Her faith and her church work were a big part of that, as was the sense of satisfaction she attained from her hobby of making pencil sketches of English church buildings. This began when she needed a cover image for a new parish magazine and turned her hand to capturing the front of All Saints' together with the dramatic yew tree that overhung the lychgate. Since then, she had sketched dozens of similar structures, finding peace in the solitude of this casual artistic pursuit.

No, she was settled that her lot in life was to be a celibate servant of the church. Friends with everyone, loved by everyone but not in love with anyone. Nevertheless, she did love Chris and maybe, if she allowed herself, what was the deepest of friendships could potentially blossom into something more.

"Not quite the response I was hoping for," he answered honestly before beginning to graciously concede, "but if you don't have those feelings for me then…"

Bunny was quick to interrupt him.

"No, I mean, yes, I do," she garbled.

"You do?" He said with visible delight.

"Sorry Chris, I do, I do like you too, very much. It is just that…"

"What?" he interrupted.

Bunny didn't know what to say. It was all too sudden for her. She was a thinker, a pragmatist and not one to act instinctively, especially not on such a potentially life-changing subject. She didn't want to slam the door in his face, but she needed time to know if her feelings were deep enough to be reciprocated. Forced to come up with an answer, she hunted her brain for a plausible excuse as to why they couldn't be together, but at the same time she didn't want to be too emphatic in case they could.

"It doesn't matter how much we like each other; we are from such different, you know…" Bunny pointed towards the C.R.F. church sanctuary, through two darkened glass doors at the far side of the coffee shop, highlighting the fact that they were members of different churches. Whilst this was a barrier to her, she was principally just playing for time.

"But we have a lot of common ground, don't we? We both share the same faith, it is just differences in how we express it, that is all it is, isn't it?"

"Yes, but." Bunny didn't know what she was going to say next, fearful of painting herself into a corner and rejecting him outright.

"Chris!" An impatient voice came from the stairwell. Ralph was standing on the half-landing pointing at his watch. Bunny felt a sense of relief and picked up the manilla folder, ushering him to go. Now she would have time to think.

"I'm on my way," Chris assured him as he started to gather his belongings. Ralph disappeared back up the stairs.

"You need to go. You have got some common ground to find upstairs." Bunny dismissed him, placing her manila folder under his armpit.

"Call me when you get home, I mean please call me, I need to know..." Chris insisted, once again failing to articulate his feelings. It was clear from his uncharacteristic fumbling that 'I like you and I think I like you a lot' was indeed his attempt at saying something more substantial.

"I will," she said.

"Promise you will text when you are home safe, it is dark outside and I..." again Chris hesitated to finish the sentence.

"You what?" she teased.

"... and I care about you," he at last admitted.

"Okay, I promise I will text you when I get home. Ring me when you are finished, and we can have a proper conversation."

By then she will at least have had some time to think. Chris smiled and before running up the stairs gave her a peck on the cheek, something he had done many times previously but this time it felt charged with an electricity she had never felt before.

Chapter 2

CONFESSION

It was a cold, autumnal evening. She fastened the oversized buttons of her grey sheepskin coat, put on her grey leather gloves and set off. As she left the building, Bunny slid up her sleeve to look at the large square dial of her digital watch. It was an unusual watch for a woman, but she liked its simplicity and its boldness. The dial displayed 19:39. She smiled noting the time was also the date of the outbreak of hostilities in the Second World War. She hoped that wasn't what was going to be happening in the Reformation Room upstairs.

Thankfully, the earlier rain had stopped, although the dark-grey English sky still looked threatening. As she walked, her mind replayed the stilted conversation that Chris and she had just had. She knew he had been expecting more from her, but she couldn't just say what he wanted, it was all so sudden. It was a *big* question and needed a proper *big* answer. As she walked, a large raindrop landed on her face. Plop! She jolted from the cold impact before noticing several others land around her, the sign of an impending heavy shower. She was still some distance from home so braced herself for a thorough soaking. Then an idea struck her. She was approaching St Mary's Church, or to be more precise The Church of the Blessed Saint Mary, which was the town's main Catholic building. It was an impressive, if a little austere, building on the High Street flanked either side by closed shops and concrete offices. Consequently, the church door opened directly onto the pavement. Locals would often complain that wedding parties would spill-out onto the road as there was little chance to confine the happy crowd upon the pavement. The parish church, like most, remained open during the day. The hand-written invitation to *'Tarry awhile and step aside for quiet contemplation,'* was inscribed in marker-pen upon yellow paper held flat under the Perspex cover of a faded wooden A-frame board whose paint had seen better days. Who was she to refuse such an invitation on a wet October evening?

Bunny had never set foot inside St Mary's Church before. It was probably the only church structure in town that she hadn't entered, that is with the exceptions of the Mormons and the Jehovah's Witnesses which she didn't consider to be part of mainstream Christianity.

She turned the large circular door handle common on so many old churches, and quickly stepped inside, closing the door behind her, the ironmongery clicking loudly back into its place. It didn't take long for her eyes to become accustomed to the dim light levels, it was nearly as dark as it had been outside. Four tall thin windows punctuated the white painted walls on each side, offering some illumination into the nave from two nearby amber streetlights. The original pews had been replaced on each side with ten modern beechwood benches, which didn't particularly look any more comfortable than those at her own church. To her left in the aisle beyond the pews she could see displays from missionary programmes under a large CAFOD poster. In the aisle to her right a small, carpeted area was festooned with children's toys, including a wooden pull-along dog on wheels, identical to the one they had at All Saints'.

"There's always one of those in every church creche," she said to herself.

Directly to her front was the more decorative end of the building, the chancel, with three stained-glass windows surrounding an altar. She could see the rain was now falling heavily on the windows. To their left a large wooden cross filled the wall. It was only when Bunny saw the figure of Christ, in characteristic agonised crucifixion posture, that she realised that this building was different to those she was more familiar with. To its right she could see a statue of Mary, the mother of Jesus, her head bowed towards the crucifix.

Bunny appeared to be alone in St. Mary's. She considered offering a hearty 'Hello?' to announce her arrival to any silent worshippers but instead chose to make a slow walk up the central aisle. As she did, she made her footsteps sound distinctive and purposeful to alert any unsuspecting, kneeling penitent. No one surfaced. She was alone.

At the front, running her hand slowly along the altar rail she tried to make out the images depicted on the windows, but they were too indistinct to be clear in the half-light. She removed one of her gloves to feel the coldness of the marble statue of Mary that stood sentinel atop a white classical columnar plinth that rose as high as her chest. She removed the other glove and put it in her coat pocket, crossed the chancel, absentmindedly leaving the first glove on the plinth, and began to walk up the side aisle toward the children's toys.

Her circumnavigation stopped abruptly when she arrived at a dark wooden structure that she initially considered might be an antique double-wardrobe; two doors each with their own dark velvet curtains, either side of a central decorative panel. It was the confessional. She had never seen one before. Hardly surprising as, other than a visit to the Basilica Santa Maria del Mar whilst on holiday in Barcelona, she couldn't recall ever having set foot inside any Catholic church. Bunny looked around the church to check that she was, as she suspected, alone. She then pulled back the velvet curtain from the left-hand opening and stepped inside. It was dark, very dark. But she felt a sense of peace and calm come over her. She wondered if others might feel a little oppressed in that confined booth, but not her. She liked to be on her own and this little bit of solitude was heavenly. So many heartfelt pleas had been heard over the years inside this tiny space that the very atmosphere invited contrition. She began to pray aloud, processing her own thoughts as she did.

"Dear Lord and Father, what should I do? Chris is a lovely, nice person, and we have been friends for years, but I guess you know that already." She paused. "I do like him, he is many of the things that I am not, and I know we get on really well," she paused again. "But he is from such a different church to what I am used to, to the one I have been brought-up in." Again, she paused, this time remembering the church meeting that was underway back at C.R.F. "You said there was supposed to be One Church, but I don't see it. I see lots of individual churches each defending their own individuality. Each convinced that they are *right* and condescendingly implying that all others are, well...*wrong*. I tried to bring them together, I tried," her voice getting louder as she let her modest anger invade her supplication. "What was the point! I organised that meeting, the first time ever! And what was the point. The whole idea of church unity is completely pointless, actually no, there were lots of points made at that meeting, each one defended to the last. No one was willing to listen to anyone. Why can't they see that there'll need to be some give-and-take for the sake of ... for Your sake, Lord? It makes me mad. If they truly had their eyes on You then they would find a way to make it work, wouldn't they? They are all so small-minded."

Bunny rarely allowed her emotions to be either visible or audible, but here in the quiet solitude of a Catholic confessional she felt she could let it out. She released a long, slow breath to calm herself, an action which she found surprisingly therapeutic, and looked up into the still darkness of the booth.

"And now Chris is there having to pick up the pieces. He will see how impossible it is. Knowing him he will be all upbeat and positive about it." She smiled, thinking of this most appealing quality, which she knew she did not possess. "If I said 'Yes' to him..." she said, almost as a whisper, allowing herself for the first time to imagine life with Chris. "If I said 'Yes' to him, would we be happy? I've come to terms with being single. I'm okay with it... but, You know, I do feel alone...sometimes." She sighed. "Could it work, Lord? Would it? Would it for me? I didn't start this Lord, I didn't ask him, he asked me, well I think that was what he was doing. I'm innocent, I am not looking for…for…for love."

She spoke the final word as though it were a plea from the deepest recess of her heart. An involuntary, confessional appeal. As she did, she felt the enormity of true love rise-up within her. In that very moment, she could feel it, she could taste it. Into her mind's eye came images of them holding hands as they walked in the park, romantic holidays in faraway places and Christmas stockings hung on the fireplace.

"No!" she said out loud shaking her head violently. "That's not reality, that's Hollywood, that's not real love!"

With those images erased from her mind, now she could really feel it, the depth of relationship, the companionship, someone who cared for her and whom she would treasure, forever. She could see the shared laughs *and* the shared tears, arguments and making up, children and grandchildren, aging together and mourning the loss of … a friend? No, the loss of her husband.

"Goodness, he hasn't even asked me out and already I've buried him! Pull yourself together woman." She placed both of her hands on the top frame of the grille, leaned forward and rested her forehead on the back of her hands. Despite the darkness, she instinctively closed her eyes.

"Children would be nice," she whispered. "I'd be a good mum, Lord. I'd bring them up to know You, I'd read them Bible stories and say prayers with them every bedtime. They'll be baptised and we'll take them to church every week." Suddenly, she pushed herself upright from her leaning position letting her hands fall slowly into her lap.

"Which church?" She was stunned at having not considered the obvious, before raising her voice as loud as was appropriate in a place of worship and exclaimed "Which church?"

"It would have to be All Saints'. I couldn't go to C.R.F. – I'm not into all that charismatic stuff. I mean, we believe the same gospel it's just that they do things so…so differently there. I was brought up Anglican, that is what I know. No, if he wants me it will *have* to be All Saints'."

As she said it, she realised the irony that within one prayer she had both castigated denominational intransigence and resolutely refused to consider any compromise herself. She let her head tilt back until it touched the rear of the confessional, a little too far to be comfortable but she left it there.

"Lord, Lord, Lord, you must weep when you see how separate we are. How we all think we're right, that we are the chosen ones, the only ones with the *truth*." She gave out a deep growl of anguish before continuing with a determined prayer. "Dear Lord and Father, I am sorry for my own narrow-mindedness. I confess that I find it so hard to embrace any other type of church other than the one I have been brought up in. Lord, help me understand, show me why we are so fragmented, let me see the Church, truly united, so that we..." she meant herself and Chris but dare not pray that yet, "... can be one."

She stared upwards in silence, in the near darkness as a small glow broke through the top of the heavy velvet curtain.

"I will try..." The sudden sound of a male voice made Bunny leap up from her contorted position, banging her head and giving out an audible yelp as she did. Her immediate thought was that she was hearing the voice of God but before she could speak, it continued. "... but you will have to be open-minded." The voice was coming from the other side of the confessional grille. Presumably a priest had seen her enter and taken up his station.

"Sorry, sorry I just came out of the rain. I am not Catholic, sorry," she flustered.

The priestly voice sounded calm, warm and comforting. He put her at her ease and explained that God heard her prayer whether she was Catholic or not.

"It's just that I have a big question to ask God," she said reticently, hoping to cover her embarrassment. "Well, one big question in two parts. One is about the church, I mean my church, well no, all churches really."

"And the other part?" the voice prompted.

"The other part is... is personal." She leaned back again before continuing, "And as it turns out, it is the same question really."

"God will always answer your questions," the voice continued, "But the question I have for you, Bunny, is are you ready to find the answer?"

"Wait a minute," she said urgently, "I never told you my name? How did you know my name? Who is that?" Bunny leapt to her feet, overbalanced and, for a second time, banged her head heavily on the inside of the confessional.

"Ouch!" she squealed loudly and gingerly felt the top of her head. She could feel moisture on her fingertips. Was that blood? She quickly pushed her way clumsily through the velvet barrier to see her hand in the dim light. It was indeed red; her head was bleeding, badly.

Bang, Bang, Bang. She could hear knocking. Where was that coming from?

Holding her head, she approached the priest-side opening. "Who is in there?" There was no answer. She took hold of the velvet veil but hesitated before she opened it. Was she about to do something terribly sacrilegious?

"I'm going to open this curtain," she announced, hoping to soften the exposure of the occupant. She pulled the curtain back, but the booth was empty. What is more, there was a pile of books on the priest's chair. She pressed the wall of the confessional looking for a backdoor. Nothing.

Bang, Bang.

This was definitely where the voice had come from. She lifted the top book from the pile. It was as large and heavy as the rest of them. She brought it out to read the title in the ray of sunlight that originated from the stained-glass windows above the altar. She could just make out the title, *Assertio Septem Sacramentorum* and it appeared to have been written by King Henry the Eighth.[1] How peculiar?

Bang, Bang, Bang. There it was again; someone was banging on the church door.

"Stop banging, it's open," she shouted, losing her balance briefly as she did. She was losing blood and steadied herself by holding onto the back of the tall dark-wood pews. The relentless pounding started again. She tossed the book back into the confessional and made her way over to the door. She was in no mood for whomever was on the other side and snatched at the brass handle declaring as she did, "It wasn't locked."

Bright daylight hit her eyes and for a moment she couldn't see. As her vision adjusted, through a kaleidoscope of indeterminate shapes, she could just make out a short person dressed in a cloak, staring at her with a hammer in his hand. He had been using it on the other half of the church doorway. No wonder the noise was so loud. They both froze, intent on each other.

As she surveyed the scene, Bunny slowly realised that something wasn't quite right. Firstly, the sunlight, quite a change from the stormy sky minutes earlier; then she noted the lack of traffic on the road as a horse-drawn carriage click-clacked past from left to right. How curious? Next her eye was drawn to the crowd standing looking at her from the front of the church. They stood on

---

[1] Henry VIII wrote "Assertio Septem Sacramentorum" or 'In Defence of the Seven Sacraments' in 1521, a strongly pro-papal tome and for which the Pope awarded him the title 'Defender of the Faith' a title used by every English monarch since. The book would not have been in the Wittenberg church on the day Luther nailed his theses to the church door.

the pavement, but that pavement was now across a small churchyard and beyond a gate that she had no recollection of having entered through. The short man staring at her, hammer in hand, was wearing old-fashioned clerical robes. Any other outfit may have caused her to become understandably anxious - a strange man with a hammer would be menacing in any other situation but here the priestly garb somehow neutralised the scene.

Bunny couldn't speak, she was too confused. As she stood dumbfounded, she felt a hand on her shoulder. The familiar, warm comforting voice in her ear said, "It's all right, just check your watch." In a state of stunned inertia, she looked down at the large square digital display on her wrist which read 15:17. That too made no sense.

The crowd, now filling the road, began to rhythmically chant: "Luther, Luther, Luther."

She looked across at the monk who was now waving and smiling at the crowd; behind him a sheet of paper, or was it parchment, had been nailed to the church door. Bunny felt light-headed. She stepped forward, away from the church, turned around and looked back at the building she had emerged from within. This was not St Mary's; she had never seen this grand church before. Why was this little man pretending to be Martin Luther? Could it be that she was somehow standing outside a church in Wittenberg, Germany, and was the time, or maybe the year, really 1517?

The church bell then gave a hauntingly sombre single toll.

Whether it was due to the loss of blood or simply a reflex to the unbelievable situation she was witnessing wasn't clear, but at that moment, as medieval sunlight reflected from the church windows, for the first time in her life, she fainted.

Chapter 3

MARTIN LUTHER

"I would like to welcome everyone to C.R.F. and an especially warm welcome to the two new faces joining us this evening." Ralph Shafer, pastor of the modern evangelical congregation, glanced down at the yellow post-it stuck conspicuously to his index finger to remind himself of the names of the first timers. "Father Thelmin of the Lutheran Church." Ralph nodded towards the young Austrian.

"Please, call me Artur," he responded, smiling in response to the apparent inclusiveness of the group.

"Artur, welcome to C.R.F." Ralph continued, "And we can also welcome Ms. Thea Howlsy from Broad Street Baptist." It was obvious to all who she was, not only by a process of elimination but because she was the only woman in the room. Rex, who was sitting to her left, offered her a hearty handshake saying, "Welcome, friend." Being a Quaker, he would often refer to a fellow Christian as *friend*. She responded with enthusiasm, then turned to her right to repeat the greeting only to find that Presbyterian minister Jack Fort had turned away from her. His views on the ordination of women prevented him extending her such civility. This clumsy, snubbing manoeuvre was obvious for all to see and instantly infected the atmosphere. Round Two had begun already. Thea fingered the lowest of her oversized wooden necklace beads, as an instinctive comfort reflex.

"Thank you, Ralph." Rev Mashman stepped in quickly to spare Ms. Howlsy her blushes and continued with, "Perhaps we should make a start."

Anxious to avoid a repeat of their first meeting the Rector had decided that they should begin by discussing *how* any potential Easter event should be *promoted*, rather than getting trapped in the format and content as they had last time. This idea had surfaced in his mid-week conversation with the newly assimilated Lutheran minister who had suggested that he could enthuse the group with his ideas for an 'exciting and high-impact campaign.' Reverend Mashman had little idea what his fellow church leader was talking about but felt it might just lift everyone's horizons away from their internal differences and on to how they were collectively viewed from the outside. Besides, as he was a newcomer, they would at least be polite, he thought.

"I would like to invite our new member, Mr. Thelmin to share his thoughts on how an inter-church gathering could be promoted. Artur the floor is yours."

The young Lutheran stood to his feet, a stance that was overly formal for the rather intimate gathering.

"Tweeting, blogging, texting, messaging, video-chatting, posting on Facebook and Instagram. This is how the world communicates today," he announced provocatively. "We need to learn from those who are using social media if we are to communicate with the public."

The room looked at him quizzically as he continued undaunted. "Barak Obama and Donald Trump both came out of nowhere to win the US presidency. What they had in common was an understanding of how to use social media to get their message out to millions..."

As Artur began his well-rehearsed presentation, Chris slipped his phone out of his pocket and placed it face-up on the small table in front of him checking for a second time that the volume was set to silent. Despite the importance of the gathering his mind was elsewhere. He kept replaying the stilted conversation he had just forced Bunny to endure in the coffee shop. He was a confident and charismatic person who was used to speaking to hundreds of churchgoers every Sunday, but face-to-face with someone that mattered he found he had inexplicably become tongue-tied and wooden. Bunny really did matter to him. It had been eight years since the night when his wife had suddenly ejected herself from his life. The list of emotions he now kept safely in a box deep within himself was long. Shock, confusion, sadness, rejection and disappointment were obvious. Under them lay the fact that he felt unloved, unwanted and a failure for not pursuing her and winning her back. Beneath those lurked the fears that would prevent him from ever opening up to another person, trusting anyone, loving anyone. And with them was the terror that those fears would keep him doomed to live alone, forever. Hiding deeper still was the anger, the rage, that he dare not release. Anger at his ex-wife for hurting him, anger at himself for being too passive to not go after her, and, worst of all, anger at God. All these emotions had remained safely stowed away, far enough under the surface to allow him a sane existence free from bitterness and, most importantly, free to maintain his Christian faith. But now the box was rattling and beginning to leak emotions. No wonder he couldn't express himself sensibly as they sat around the coffee table moments earlier. Every emotional sinew had tightened, screaming at him, No! No! but as he felt every heart-beating thump on the lid of his box, he knew he must press on. He had wanted to tell her that for the first time since his wife left him, he had found someone who took him outside of himself. Someone who wasn't taken in by his persona, someone who openly disagreed with him

26

and yet would stay his friend. Someone he felt might stick around if he ever opened his box and allowed himself to be real again. That was what he wanted to say, but all that came out was the embarrassing *'I like you'*. Had he blown it? He needed to speak to her properly, he needed to know. He decided that once she was safely home, he would excuse himself from the meeting and ring her. He checked his phone to see if there was a text from her. Nothing yet, but it was barely minutes since they parted.

Usually when she awakens, Bunny is instantly alert. She is very much a morning person. But not this time. As she opened her eyes, she found herself in an unfamiliar and uncomfortably cold room. The walls were bare stonework, as though she were in a castle. Surely not? The wall to her left, she noticed, was whitewashed but the rest were stark and bare. A large black iron ring hung from the ceiling, suspended on chains like a horizontal cartwheel with a dozen unlit candles evenly spaced around its circumference. The ceiling was a criss-cross of wooden beams and awash with cobwebs. Most of the wall to her right was covered by extensive bookcases. There wasn't a paperback in sight. The shelves were overflowing with intricately bound volumes, hard-backed tomes, rolls of parchment and piles of handwritten paper. The piles continued across the floor, over two small chairs and onto a large ornately carved wooden desk in front of her. The desk was the centrepiece of the room. A grey and white quill feather stood sentry in the inkwell guarding one side of the desk, a large lit candle oversaw the other. She could see the multiple wax trails that had built-up over time, indicating that many candlelit hours had been spent at this desk. Beyond the desk was a large decoratively carved stone and unlit fireplace. More piles, this time of firewood, stood on its hearth and a blackened kettle hung above its cold embers. The man she had seen outside the church was attempting to light the fire. She sat bolt upright.

Bunny was rarely, if ever, in a situation where she was not fully appraised of her surroundings. She didn't like surprises. Friends have, in the past, described her as controlling – something she would baulk at preferring the moniker of Independent – but it was nevertheless true that to find herself in a situation to which she had not acquiesced was totally unacceptable.

"Who are you, where am I?" she asked forcibly as she placed her feet firmly on the floor ready to bolt to the door. She felt confused and vulnerable. She'd just woken in a strange man's room with no recollection of what might have happened whilst she lay unconscious. She instinctively gathered her

27

clothes tight to herself folding her arms across her chest into a defensive stance. The man jumped at the sound of her voice, banging the back of his head on the underside of the stone fireplace.

"Autsch!" he said as he reversed into the room, rubbing his head. Bunny suddenly remembered that she too had suffered a head wound and tentatively felt her own head to assess the scale of the damage, but she could locate neither lump nor scar.

"I banged my head," she said to herself trying to remember the events that had led up to this most distressing of mornings. The strange man was now looking at her, she needed to defend herself and reached for one of the heavy books overhanging the edge of the table in front of her. At least she now had a weapon.

"Ah, you are awake my dear." The man was dressed in a monk's habit. "I was a little worried when you fainted outside the Kirche."

As she looked at him, she suddenly recalled that this was the man who was banging the door of St Mary's... or no, it wasn't St Mary's... it was daylight... and he was holding a hammer.

"Who are you?" she asked again insistently.

She could see that he had managed to light the fire, which was thankfully now beginning to take hold.

"Let me introduce myself properly," he said standing to attention. "I am Doctor Martin Luther, Professor of Theology at the University of Wittenberg; Augustinian Vicar of Saxony and Thuringia."

Not only had she no idea of *where* she was, she also now had the rather more distressing problem that she didn't know *when* she was. Perhaps this is a dream, she thought. That's it! This is a dream, and I will wake up soon. At that realisation, the threat of imminent peril subsided slightly.

"And someone who is rapidly getting a reputation as a troublemaker." An elegantly dressed man had entered the room from the doorway to Bunny's left. Luther laughed at this well-timed interruption. Now there were two of them. Nothing was making any sense.

"Herr Kurfürst Frederick, it is good to see you again. I would indeed be in trouble were it not for your support and, dare I say, your protection."[1] Luther added.

---

[1] Luther's protector was Prince elector (or Kurfürst) Frederick III of Saxony. He had little direct personal contact with Luther, preferring to use his treasurer Degenhart Pfaffinger as his intermediary. Frederick had

"You know that I am an ardent supporter of reform but was there really a need to provoke Archbishop Albert by nailing your latest tract to his door? Apparently, he is furious and has already sent a copy to Pope Leo."

"Let him. I don't care," Luther retorted with a snort of derision. "Leo thinks he can raise money by selling indulgences, allowing the wealthy to get away with sin, bah! His wealth is already greater than anyone else, so let him build the basilica of St. Peter with his own money rather than with that of poor believers."[1]

Bunny was content to sit and observe the conversation this being, in her opinion, no more than a particularly vivid dream. But when Frederick caught sight of her, she froze. The prince was immediately arrested by the presence of a woman in the Friar's private study and his expression of shock was evident. Luther immediately realised that this might look compromising and attempted to allay the concerns of his influential ally.

"Herr Kurfürst, may I introduce you to…" Luther had no idea of her name.

Stop talking to me, stop talking to me was all that Bunny could think. She didn't know where she was or what was happening and regardless of her protestations a medieval drama appeared to be unfolding in front of her eyes. She closed her eyes tightly and prayed that when she opened them, she might be back in her bed, or frankly anywhere other than here. She tentatively opened them only to find Frederick looking expectantly at her awaiting for her to introduce herself.

"Bunny," she said, somewhat reluctantly before she, purely by polite reflex, found herself offering a handshake to the elegant and – she couldn't deny – handsome gentleman.

"Jah, Fräulein Bündchen," Luther continued with relief that she had eased the potentially tense situation. "She was with me as we nailed the ninety-five theses to the door. It all got a bit too much for her, so she was resting here."

Frederick accepted Luther's explanation, took her hand, turned it over and kissed it gently. She felt the hair of his moustache tickle her skin. Still

---

been vocal on the need for church reform since 1500. It was Frederick's support that prevented Luther from being immediately summoned to Rome and tried for heresy.

[1] Point 86 of Luther's 95 Theses states 'Why does not the pope, whose wealth is today greater than the wealth of the richest Crassus, build this one basilica of St. Peter with his own money rather than with the money of poor believers?'

holding it, he looked her in the face, nodded in salute and said slowly and purposefully,

"It is my deepest pleasure to meet you, Fräulein."

Flushed with embarrassment, Bunny momentarily considered giving him a girlish curtsy. No sooner had the thought entered her mind than she stopped herself, a curtsy being something she had told herself she would never do. Bunny withdrew her hand largely out of disgust at her own reaction. Hoping to change the subject and remove the intensity of Frederick's attention, she fixed her gaze on Luther, now searching through the glut of papers, some handwritten but mostly printed, piled across every surface of his study.

"What are all of these, Professor?" she asked, as she replaced the hefty tome that she had weaponised moments earlier. Frederick replied.

"Have you not heard Fräulein, 'Every day it rains Luther-books?' How many have you written Martin? One thousand? Two thousand?"[1]

"Fourteen thousand six hundred and fifty-four if you include all the tracts, books, pamphlets and published articles," Luther admitted.

"There you go, nearly fifteen thousand. This man is the maestro of mass communication. He uses the new printing technology more than every other writer in Germany today – and I mean all of them put together! He knows how to get his message to the people, and this more than anything else is why they are listening."

"The man is an absolute maestro of mass communication." They had to agree that the Lutheran pastor had given them a great example and whether you liked the message or not, both Donald Trump and Barak Obama were prolific communicators.

Chris opened the manila folder and slid out Bunny's notes onto the table as Artur continued.

"He knows how to get his message out there, that is why people listen to him. We need to use the same mentality to get God's message out."

Artur waited for someone to agree. No one spoke and the sound of torrential rain on the window was the only thing that broke the silence in the

---

[1] From 'Martin Luther: Catholic Dissident' by Peter Stanford Chapter 8

room. Chris glanced down at his phone. Still nothing. She will be soaked if she isn't home, he thought.

"Do I agree with you, Artur? I'm not sure I do." Methodist preacher Joel Whyens was the first to speak, prefixing his point, as he tended to, with a question. He was very *anti*-social media and using it to promote the Church felt more than a little sordid. It was all right if you were a personality, he thought, but surely the Church was about Jesus, missing the obvious irony that the personal nature of Christ was the central Christian message. Afro-Caribbean Joel firmly believed that the gospel should be preached the way his hero John Wesley had: loud, proud and on the streets, although thankfully no longer on horseback. He had to let his feelings be known.

"Am I in agreement? Well, whilst the idea has some merit, I couldn't wholeheartedly give your campaign my support," he said leaving Artur uncomfortably stranded on his feet, adding "We should leave mass-media to the masses, we have got a more important message that can't be expressed in one hundred and forty characters."

"I communicate so inexhaustibly, Herr Kurfürst, because the message is so important." Luther stood to his feet ready to preach a message to an imaginary audience inside the large fireplace. He raised his right arm to address the ether.

"Brothers, God's forgiveness is FREE!" he delivered with gravitas almost shouting the final word then, smiling, waved at the make-believe congregation beyond the flames. Bunny considered such behaviour to be very strange and not at all what she had imagined Luther to be like. This dream was getting rather twisted, she thought.

"And free forgiveness is at odds with both the Church's power structure and source of finance. It is a very dangerous message Professor." Frederick interrupted sternly. Luther stopped waving and turned to address him.

"But it *is* the truth." Luther picked up a short log with which to re-charge the fire, but before letting go of it, he prodded it towards Frederick.

"For a long time, I didn't know what to believe, then I came to the verse *the righteous shall live by faith*[1] and at last, by the mercy of God, I began to

---

[1] From Luther's Works, Volume 54, P442. Full text: "For a long time, I went astray [in the monastery] and didn't know what I was about. To be sure, I knew something, but I didn't know what it was until I came to the text in Romans 1:17, 'He who through faith is righteous shall live.' That text helped me. There I saw

understand that righteousness is a *gift* from God. When I realised that, I felt as if I were entirely… born again… and had entered paradise itself through the gates that had been flung open."[1]

Despite her misgivings about where or when she was, Bunny could see why Luther had been so influential; he wasn't just a prolific writer, he was clearly passionate about the transformative truth he had discovered. Luther turned and carefully placed the log into the flames.

"Well, you are going to have a great opportunity to defend that viewpoint." Frederick pulled a folded paper from his coat pocket and continued, "I have here a Papal summons to attend a court hearing at Worms Cathedral and defend yourself. And we need to leave right now."

"The Pope needs to provide arguments not commands,"[2] Luther replied in his reactionary way. He then fell silent as he considered the potential benefit of such a public spectacle. After a few moments he continued, much to the relief of Frederick, "But I *will* go, and people *will* listen."

As Bunny watched, Luther busied himself gathering the necessary accoutrements for this trip into a leather bag, finally collecting his hat and cloak and striding to the doorway. He paused at the heavy oak door and said over his shoulder as he left,

"Come along Fräulein, don't you want to witness my greatest triumph?"

This is just a dream, she kept repeating to herself, but her eyes, ears and indeed every one of her five senses were working fully. Maybe this is a special sort of dream, she wondered. Meanwhile, Luther stood waiting for her.

This was a key moment. She knew that if she followed him, she would somehow have accepted that she was immersed within the most lucid

---

what righteousness Paul was talking about. I learned to distinguish between the righteousness of the law and the righteousness of the gospel. I lacked nothing before this except that I made no distinction between the law and the gospel. I regarded both as the same thing and held that there was no difference between Christ and Moses except the times in which they lived and their degrees of perfection. But when I discovered the proper distinction—namely, that the law is one thing and the gospel is another—I made myself free."

[1] Widely quoted. Taken from '131 Christians Everyone Should Know' by Mark Galli p34. Full text: "At last meditating day and night, by the mercy of God, I … began to understand that the righteousness of God is that through which the righteous live by a gift of God, namely by faith… Here I felt as if I were entirely born again and had entered paradise itself through the gates that had been flung open."

[2] From 'Protestants: The Faith That Made the Modern World' by Alec Ryrie

hallucination imaginable. It was a test to see if she was going to comply. To follow meant to step into an unknown world, one she had no control over, one full of surprises. It may not have seemed much, but to her this was 'One Giant Leap.' A voice behind her whispered,

"Follow him, it will be fine."

She spun around, but no one was there. She turned back to face Luther.

"Shall we?" he prompted, raising his hand toward the door. She swallowed hard and followed him, with no idea what lay ahead.

"I agree, no one wants a Christian celebrity." Jack Fort took some delight in joining in the deflation of Artur's youthful ideas. "The very idea is…is…"

"Worldly?" Joel offered.

"Thank you, yes worldly. I fail to see what benefit there would be to having hundreds, or worse still thousands, of *fans* following your every word. Listening to everything you say. Lining the streets and shouting your name. How would that benefit the Church?"

Artur looked embarrassed, isolated, and defeated as he stood limply next to his chair. He slowly and silently began to slide himself back onto the seat.

"Thank you, Artur. You have certainly given us a lot to consider." Reverend Mashman stepped in before Jack Fort could further puncture the young man's enthusiasm.

Rex Fogge leaned over to Thea Howlsy and whispered that Artur had been led 'like a lamb to the slaughter.'

"Gentlemen… and lady," the Rector added remembering to include Thea, making Jack Fort bristle at the verbal revision. Having failed to use the enthusiastic European to divert the group's attention from their internal differences, by letting them see how the outside world may view them, the Rector cleared his throat and began to deliver what was, in effect, an opening address.

"Before we attend to the matter at hand I wonder if we should take a moment to reflect on why we failed to reach any meaningful agreement last time. Whilst we all represent different expressions of Church, we do share a common desire to see the gospel preached and for people to find faith in our Lord Jesus Christ, so in that sense we are all agreed."

The elderly cleric had spent several hours devising a phrase that he was sure all would agree with. The positive nods around the room confirmed to him that 'Desire to see the gospel preached' and 'Find faith in Jesus' were the common ground they shared.

"Therefore, we gather here as equals with a common goal," he continued. "Rather than focussing on what divides us, we could try to build upon what already unites us, our faith in Christ. As we read in scripture..." He reached for his large black Bible and thumbed the well-worn pages until he found the passage he was looking for. "'If a house be divided against itself, that house cannot stand' and we are, collectively, God's house are we not?" It was difficult for anyone to disagree with his scripture-enforced rhetoric, so again they all nodded. "Dare I even say that, even though the outside world might see us as many churches, God may actually see us as just one Church."

No-one nodded at this rather complex theological proposition, each needing to decode it before assenting to it. Reverend Mashman scanned the room, hoping that he hadn't said anything that might restart the religious warfare of three weeks ago.

Ralph Shafer broke the momentary tightness with a light-hearted observation, "There *actually was* one Church five hundred years ago. That Martin Luther has a lot to answer for!" he said, referencing the domination of the pre-Reformation Catholic Church.

Everyone laughed except Artur. Having only a little grasp of English humour, he wasn't sure if the father of the Reformation and founder of the Lutheran church had just been insulted. For his benefit Ralph added,

"Do you think we should all go back to being Catholic eh, Artur?"

At this, the Lutheran priest understood the joke and momentarily joined in the fun before offering what he felt was a necessary explanation.

"If you came to one of our services you would see few differences to the Catholics. We share the same means of receiving God's grace, that is the Bible, baptism, and Holy Communion; our services are similar, we use much of the same liturgy. Luther just wanted to correct the errors and stop the excesses he saw in the Roman Church. It was only when the Pope rejected them that my church, the Lutheran Church, began."

"So, it wasn't Luther that started the Lutheran Church, it was the Pope," Jack said provocatively.

To his surprise Artur agreed. "If Pope Leo had accepted Martin Luther's reformations there would still be one Church," he postulated, much to the disgruntlement of many of his fellow ministers. "The Church had lost its way since New Testament times and Luther found it again."

The education on Lutheranism came as an unwelcome surprise to many of those in the room, most of whom had little knowledge of the denomination.

"How similar are you to the Catholics, Artur?" Joel asked tentatively, looking, as he did at Jack Fort who had railed against the *Papists* several times at their last gathering. Ralph could see the potential flashpoint rising. He was perhaps the only one present who had a reasonable understanding of the Lutheran faith, acquired on his M.A. in Theology at Oxford University. He quickly stepped-in saying,

"Well, they do not acknowledge the Pope as their leader."

Joel then quipped,

"Lucky that, otherwise the phrase 'Is the Pope a Catholic?' could be answered, 'No, he's a Lutheran.'"

That was enough for any rising tension to be relieved with a laugh - a slightly forced laugh in Jack Fort's case, but a laugh nonetheless.

Chris was the only person in the room who wasn't laughing, there was too much on his mind. He couldn't wait any longer and discreetly slid his phone onto his lap and began to write the message "You home ok?" He then added an X for a kiss, hesitated, then deleted it before pressing Send.

Chapter 4

THE DIET OF WORMS

Bunny, Frederick, Luther and two others whom she didn't know then spent the next hours compacted into an elegant horse-drawn carriage as it made its slow and uncomfortable journey to the city of Worms. With each mile the crowds began to gather. Cheering, waving, blowing kisses, thousands of people – some, clearly peasants, others well-dressed – all lined the route to catch a glimpse of Martin Luther, their hero.

Worms Cathedral was breathtaking, and she instantly wished she had her sketchbook to hand to capture it in eternal pencil. It was the tallest structure for miles around and appeared to rise-up from the ground as they slowly approached the city square, inching their way through the ever-present crowds. Two identical cylindrical towers that, from the perspective of the city square appeared to touch the sky, flanked a bold edifice dominated by four large windows. These windows, each one circular and almost touching the others, gave the appearance of cogwheels at the front of a large clockwork contraption. The church-machine was inside, wound-up to breaking point and ready to dogmatise and humiliate Luther.

As Bunny adjusted herself to descend the two precariously narrow carriage steps, she noticed Frederick's hand offered for her assistance. Despite her self-reliant instincts she nonetheless took hold of it, fearing the alternative might be an embarrassing crashing descent onto the city square, or worse, he might even gallantly catch her as she fell. As she thanked him, she noticed her digital watch, incongruous in this mediaeval setting, said 15:21.

Inside the Cathedral, the visiting party were ushered along several corridors, up stone stairs to arrive in an austere meeting room not in keeping with the ornate decoration of the Cathedral through which they had transited. The room was seething with a colourful array of powerful dignitaries of the Holy-Roman empire intertwined with theologians, scholars and bishops resplendent in their episcopal vestments. They all fell silent as the defendant entered.

The setting was dominated by an elaborate throne, raised a few inches above floor-level on a small, carpeted platform and crowned with red and purple drapes suspended from golden poles. Royalty was clearly present. The grey-bearded man installed upon the throne motioned Luther and his party towards a single line of chairs facing him. They took their seats as the hostile throng either settled into their own chairs or stood expectantly.

The centre of the room was where the action was going to happen and the first to enter the ring was Johann Eck who called the meeting to order, pronouncing that the Imperial Diet of Worms was now in session with his Imperial Majesty, Charles V, Holy Roman Emperor presiding. Eck bowed elaborately towards the Emperor who flicked his left hand in a half-wave of acknowledgment. Eck addressed Luther,

"May I begin by welcoming Doctor Luther to this assembly in order to renounce or reaffirm your views."

Luther arose.

"Here I stand, I can do no other,"[1] he replied to Eck before retaking his seat.

"I have in my hand," Eck waved a paper over his head, "the Papal bull issued by Pope Leo outlining forty-one errors in the venerable Doctor Luther's so-called Ninety-Five Theses as well as his numerous other writings." The assembled crowd gave a cheer.

The titles of twenty-five of Luther's books were then listed. Provocative titles such as 'The Babylonian Captivity of the Church', and 'On the Freedom of a Christian' were met with indignant tuts and over-dramatic gasps from those present. Finally, when the list was complete, Archbishop Eck walked over to stand a few feet in front of Luther's face.

"Two questions, Herr doctor. Firstly, is this collection of books yours?" he asked softly knowing that Luther couldn't deny they were. "And secondly, are you ready to revoke their heresies?"

All eyes were on the diminutive cleric, awaiting his answer. One of the two unknown men who had travelled in the carriage with Bunny quickly stood to his feet and addressed Eck.

"My client requires some time to consider his answer."

"That being the case, we have a consulting room prepared for you," Eck replied motioning to a curtain-covered doorway to the right of the throne, before continuing, "After all we don't want to give you the excuse that we have

---

[1] It is widely quoted that Luther stated this as part of his defence although there is little historic evidence to say that he did as it does not appear in the official transcript of the Diet of Worms.

not conducted this hearing according to canonical law." The crowd murmured in amused agreement.

"It's all right Jeromee." Luther dismissed his lawyer's tactical protest, indicating that he was ready to answer the two principal charges.

"For the first question, they are all mine, but as for the second…" Luther paused for what felt like an age. Was this for dramatic effect or had the showman lost his nerve? Eventually, he was ready. He looked around the room, took a breath and delivered his answer,

"As for the second, unless I am convinced by Scripture and plain reason - I do not accept the authority of the Popes and councils, for they have contradicted each other – my conscience is captive to the Word of God. I cannot and I will not recant anything. For to go against conscience is neither right nor safe. God help me. Amen."[1]

The room erupted with jeers and shouts. Scholars pointed at the papers they held, ministers shouted, bishops waved him away with a dismissive hand, Emperor Charles looked indignant. The civil authorities present feared that a bloodthirsty riot may erupt that may spill out to the crowds outside so ushered Luther's party into the prepared anteroom whilst they tried to calm the ecclesiastical melee.

"That's done it!" Frederick couldn't hide his exasperation as he pulled Luther into the room, holding the door ajar. He pointed at Luther and Bunny. "You two, stay in here and we'll see what damage has been done." Their three travelling companions returned into the hornets' nest to see how big the sting was going to be.

"Hardly the victory I promised you, Fräulein Bündchen." Luther resignedly sat down on one of the chairs near the window.

"But…" she was unsure how to form the encouragement she needed to deliver, "…but it *is* right, you *have to* have faith in what the Scripture says. Not on what others tell you, that's the foundation isn't it."

"Sola Scriptura, Sola Fide." Luther said.

The extent of Bunny's knowledge of classical Latin was limited to the formal genus names of a surprisingly large number of birds and plants; the phrase *Annus Horribilis* that Queen Elizabeth used to describe a disappointing

---

[1] From 'Martin Luther' by Martin Brecht, translated by James L. Schaaf, Philadelphia: Fortress Press, 1985–93, 1:460.

1992; and those expressions now embedded into the English language which few would even recognise as being Latin: *vice versa, carpe diem, alma mater* and *persona non-grata.*

"What does that mean?" she asked.

He smiled at her and tapped the red velvet chair next to the one on which he was already sitting. She took the seat as prompted.

"Solo Fide means Faith Alone," he answered. "I have discovered the simplicity of faith. A passion for God that is at odds with the entire Church structure, form and hierarchy. Their focus on pious good-works and sacred worship differs fundamentally from the simplicity of God's grace to us. It is faith in his love for us alone that matters."

"And Sola Scipt...?" Bunny asked.

"Sola Scriptura simply means, Scripture Alone. No-one, not a priest, an archbishop or Pope Leo himself can tell you what to believe. It is the Bible and the Bible alone that has that authority."

"I agree with you," Bunny said reassuringly.

"Danke schön," he replied as his retinue re-entered the vestibule with the sound of discontent echoing behind them. Luther finished his conversation with Bunny with a heartfelt, "But I fear you may be one of the last to agree." Bunny tried to assure him that this wasn't the end, but her words were drowned by an anxious report from their friends.

"Well, it is not *all* bad news, most of the princes and land-owners in the room are supporting you," Frederick assured him.

"But?" Luther asked for the complete answer which Jeromee duly delivered.

"The papal nuncio from Rome, Girolamo Aleandro, has prepared an edict calling for you to be named as a heretic. If Emperor Charles agrees then you will be arrested, tried and..." He wisely stopped before saying burned alive.

As they waited, the sounds from the meeting room grew softer until eventually a knock at the door signified that it was time. They were summoned to hear the Emperor's ruling.

Jeromee Schurff entered the packed meeting room alone and stood by the central chair where Luther had previously been seated.

"Where's Luther?" Eck demanded.

"Doctor Luther requests the Assembly's gracious tolerance and with respect appeals that I alone hear the ruling on his behalf, avoiding a repeat of the disturbances we witnessed earlier."

Eck was angry, but it was Emperor Charles' hearing and His Majesty quickly concurred to the reasonableness of the argument, not wanting to propagate an uncivil uprising.

Jeromee took the chair as Charles was handed a scroll. As soon as the Emperor read the judgment aloud then the decision would stand. The room fell silent and watched as he took a silk handkerchief from his sleeve, dabbed his upper lip and began,

"I, Charles V, Holy Roman Emperor, in the year of our Lord..."

Jeromee sat patiently as the preamble was read, waiting nervously for the decisive passage to come, which it did, all too soon.

"We forbid anyone from this time forward to dare, either by words or by deeds, to receive, defend, sustain, or favour Doctor Martin Luther who is to be apprehended and punished as a notorious heretic."[1]

As Charles continued to read the edict several armed guards entered the anteroom to affect an arrest, this time without the courtesy of a knock. Moments later they returned as Charles concluded delivering the judgment that Luther was now officially a heretic and liable for arrest.

"They're all gone!" the guard shouted.

Bunny had never felt so exhilarated at any point in her life as she did at this very moment. She held tightly onto Frederick's waist as his horse thundered out of the city gates. Was it divine guidance that had led her to open the small door at the rear of the anteroom to find a stairwell that led to the cloisters? She didn't know, but once outside the Cathedral they were quickly offered horses by their supporters who had gathered outside, awaiting news from the hearing.[2]

Chris could wait no longer so placed his notepad on the table and picked-up his mobile phone. As unobtrusively as he could he stood up and moved toward the door. Ralph looked at him enquiringly, so Chris silently mouthed 'Toilet'. Ralph released his assistant pastor with a nod.

---

[1] The Edict of Worms was signed and issued by Charles V on May 25, 1521 seven days after the Diet of Worms had concluded and Luther had left. It ran for several pages and would have taken over an hour to read aloud.

[2] Whilst Luther had left the Diet of Worms peacefully, he did have to escape into hiding once the Edict of Worms had been passed and spent much of the following years living in disguise.

"There is still one Church and our collective belief in salvation by faith is the first thing that unites us, and the second would be the absolute authority of the Bible." The Rector returned to his address, gaining in confidence.

"Yes, I agree, no one can tell you what Scripture says, no one can interpret it for you, it isn't in Latin anymore, you can read it for yourself and let God speak to you," Presbyterian Jack Fort endorsed.

"Yes, but it is the interpretation of the Bible that can be the biggest source of division." Thea Howlsy couldn't keep quiet any longer. "Don't get me wrong, the point about personal faith in God's grace is absolutely right but that leads to a personal interpretation of Scripture. And if people shouldn't be telling you what to believe or how to express your faith, doesn't that mean we will inevitably all believe something different."

Artur Thelmin raised his hand to speak. Suppressing amusement, several people told him, politely, that he really didn't need to use the classroom gesture and invited him to make his contribution.

"If I may quote Martin Luther, who said 'I acknowledge no fixed rules for the interpretation of the Word of God, since the Word of God, which teaches freedom in all other matters, must not be bound.'[1] So, I agree there will inevitably be many different interpretations."

"The Word of God must not be bound," Ralph said. "I love that, was that really Luther?" Thelmin nodded enthusiastically.

"This is where I must leave you Fraulein." Frederick, ever the charmer, kissed Bunny's hand and gently laid it upon her lap. He turned to address Luther sitting opposite Bunny in the carriage. "You will be under the protection of Philip of Hesse when you arrive in Marburg. He was the one who has asked you to meet with Herr Zwingli. But remember you are now a wanted man, so behave yourself!"

"Thank you, Herr Kurfürst. I am looking forward to showing Herr Zwingli how his interpretation of doctrine needs adjustment," Luther said with a mischievous smile. Frederick looked back at Bunny before releasing a sigh of exasperation. Nodding towards Luther he said to her,

"Great men are rarely great peacemakers, are they Fraulein?"

---

[1] From 'Interpreting Martin Luther: An Introduction to His Life and Thought' By Victor A. Shepherd. P172

Bunny, now conscious that she may have been ever-so-slightly smitten by his elegant allure, was keen to show that as an educated woman she too had opinions. She responded instinctively, contributing to his point with an example of her own,

"You are right, they rarely are. I suppose you could say the same of Winston Churchill."

"Who?" Frederick looked quizzically at her. Instantly she realised she'd made the rookie-mistake of someone having a time-travel dream, or whatever it was she was experiencing. She inwardly castigated herself at being so stupid.

"Never mind," she replied with a blush. Frederick looked back at Luther.

"Now remember, Zwingli is on our side. He has ignited the Reformation that has taken hold across Switzerland." He softly closed the carriage door before concluding, "So don't make any more enemies. I won't be there to rescue you this time and I suspect Philip may be closer to Zwingli than to us."

Chapter 5

LUTHER & ZWINLGI AT MARBURG

It wasn't a lie to have indicated to Ralph that he was going to the toilet as that was the only sensible place to make a private phone call from the first floor of the expansive C.R.F. building. Chris selected Bunny's number from the VIP list on his contacts and pressed the green handset button. After a few moments he could hear that her phone was ringing. His heart missed a beat as he waited to hear her voice. It continued to ring.

Across town in a darkened empty church a phone lay on a stone floor, ringing.

Chris stood impatiently leaning on the hand-dryer in the Gents' toilet not sure what he would say but desperate to undo the confusion he had triggered earlier.

The incongruent sound of a ringing mobile phone continued to echo around the Church of the Blessed St. Mary.

Inevitably the call went to voice mail. Chris's heart sank as he deliberated as to whether to leave a message or not. Before he could decide, the recording started and he blurted out,

"...Erm, hope you're okay...call me, please...it's Chris." He used as upbeat a voice as he could muster before hanging up.

Moments later a mobile phone gave the distinctive beep-beep Message Received alert as it's illuminated screen lit up the side of a confessional. Beside it a heavy velvet curtain lay on the floor and next to that, several large footprints in what appeared to be blood.

The carriage set off into the darkness of evening. They had outmanoeuvred their pursuers and were on their way into the night. The seat next to Luther was a mass of papers but sitting next to Bunny was one of the two people that had accompanied them to Worms. He was dressed largely in black with a gold-rimmed hat resting on his lap. She couldn't remember if he'd spoken on the previous journey but now, with just the three of them in the carriage, she knew she would have to engage with him. She smiled politely, trying to form sensible words of introduction in her mind, words she should have said the first time they met but which felt somewhat redundant now. No such words came, so she was left smiling inanely as he returned her gaze.

"This isn't a dream," he said.

Bunny's jaw dropped. This imaginary character, as far as she was concerned, had broken the fourth wall of her sub-conscious and addressed her directly.

"Don't be afraid," he assured her.

She didn't know what to say. The voice however was very familiar, warm and comforting. She had heard it before, recently. But where? She couldn't place it.

"Do you want to know what is happening?" he asked. Bunny nodded.

"That man Luther, over there." He pointed directly at the doctor who didn't respond to the sound of his name. "He has raised the idea that the relationship between State and Church is now open to debate. Until now there has been a powerful equilibrium. The Church has given rulers legitimacy and in return they keep the people compliant with the law. The Church defines what the law is, and that of course includes collecting tithes, or Church taxes, a proportion of which is paid to the State rulers."

"A co-dependent relationship," Bunny added hesitantly remembering how flat her last educated interjection had landed.

"Indeed." He nodded, much to her relief before continuing.

"As we speak, Frederick, Prince of Saxony, is using Luther's doctrine as the excuse he needs to break free of what he sees as an unfair and oppressive regime. We are on our way to meet Philip of Hesse, who was one of the other princes at Worms and he too is doing likewise. This will spread quickly across Germany, the Netherlands, north into Scandinavia and across to England where King Henry VIII will declare himself the Head of the Church in direct defiance of the Pope. Across Europe rulers and royalty are throwing off their allegiances to the Church of Rome and enjoying the consequential benefits of wealth, increased land ownership and, least importantly to them, freedom of doctrinal interpretation."

"But the Reformation was about discovering God's grace and forgiveness, not about land ownership, not about politics," Bunny protested. "You are making it sound...so sordid."

"I am sorry to be the one to tell you that the sincere beliefs of that most honourable of men has released passions that had been bubbling under the surface for years. What you have witnessed was just the cork being released from the champagne bottle!"

This was not the image of Luther she had held in her heart for years.

She settled back into her seat, her head leaning on the frame of the carriage window. As she began to drift into a liminal half-sleep, she was sure she could see the orange glow of neon streetlights pass overhead. That doesn't make any sense, she thought, before finally dropping off to sleep.

Should the Word of God be bound?" Methodist minister Joel Whyens said. "No, it must not be. But there are lots of people bound to their own way of worshipping and unable to look beyond their own church doors."

"That's a bit harsh," Rex Fogge reacted, in his Quaker understatedly way. "They're good, faithful people and in their own way each doing God's work."

At that Joel Whyens released a broadside emphasising that it is not about doing good works concluding with, "The Bible says, 'Salvation is not a reward for the good things we have done so none of us can boast.'"[1]

Undaunted, Rex then retaliated with a Scripture of his own: "Show me thy faith without works, and I will show you my faith *by* my works. Faith without works is dead."[2]

Ralph jumped in again to diffuse the rising tension.

"Well done chaps, that is an excellent example of how to defend either side of an argument from the Bible. A couple of masters at work!"

Joel had mentally prepared his counter-retort but chose instead to hold his tongue, allowing a tactical chuckle to be released from those not directly involved. Argument successfully averted.

"We have all become experts in using Scripture to defend the intricacies of our positions," Ralph admitted. "Think about how confusing this must be to the un-churched."

Sensing the tension once again rise Rector Mashman offered a consolatory remark.

"We already know that we are all from different strands of the Christian Church, we only need to read the sign outside each of our buildings, the..." he hunted his memory for a useful analogy about branding but only came up with, "...the labels on the jam jars, no less." This might not have been the best of comparisons, but he liked it so continued with the analogy. "But regardless of

---

[1] Ephesians chapter 2 verse 9. New Living Translation

[2] James chapter 2 verses 18 and 26. King James Version

the label on the jam jar, inside we are all…" again he paused considering his next word.

"A bit fruity?" Ralph offered wittily.

"No, that wasn't what I was going to say." The Rector didn't crack a smile at the uninvited remark. Before he could continue Jack Fort added dryly,

"Well preserved!"

At this, everyone, including the Rector, did laugh. The denominational differences between them were indeed *well preserved*. For centuries nothing had changed with each creed having been set in doctrinal aspic, visible to the outsider but unable to be touched.

"Very good, Jack." The chairman enjoyed the witty truism. "What I was saying is that behind the label, inside our buildings we may be different flavours, if you will, but I think we probably share more than we realise. In a very real way, we are all, nonetheless, despite our differences…still just… jam."

"Gentlemen, gentlemen how can it be that having agreed on so much, this last doctrine is causing so much difficulty?"

At twenty-five years of age, Philip was one of the youngest rulers in Germany. He had inherited the Hesse estates at the age of five when his father died, so had little regard for tradition. He was one of those present when Luther gave his defence at Worms and could see the benefits that a Reformed Church, separate from Rome, would mean to a landowner such as himself. He could also see that a fragmented Reformation would be more easily thwarted by the established Church so had invited the two most prominent factions to his home to agree on a single unified set of reformed doctrines.

"Fourteen out of fifteen, gentlemen." Philip was tantalisingly close to successfully agreeing a Protestant theology and could feel the weight of history in the room. "If we can just agree all fifteen then the Colloquy of Marburg…", he had already decided what the resultant agreement would be called, "…will bring about unity between your two great reformations." Both Luther and Zwingli claimed they had independently re-discovered salvation by grace, Luther in Saxony and Zwingli across the border in Switzerland. It would be impossible to prove if either had influenced the other and both were sure of the authenticity of their beliefs.

"Are you asking me to compromise what I believe?" Luther said in his typically obdurate style, hitting the table with the side of his closed fist.

Bunny winced as the room fell silent. Against all the odds, Prince Philip had assembled the ten most prominent reformist scholars and theologians around the grand dining table of his exquisitely ornate state dining-room at Marburg Castle. Conventional wisdom suggested that this would be a recipe for disaster and at best only a half-baked soufflé of an agreement could be achieved. But Philip had the appetite for something juicier. Having gathered the key ingredients, he was just going to keep stirring the pot until every hard-skinned, unpalatable doctrine had softened into an ecumenical stew. Item fifteen, however, was now on the menu and it had stuck in Luther's craw.

Bunny looked down at her watch, it showed 15:29. Everyone else's eyes were firmly upon Luther as he pulled a bottle of black ink towards himself and purposely thrust in a new quill. He stood to his feet, quill in hand and reached over to the centre of the table directly in front of Zwingli. He then carefully inscribed four words onto the oak dining table without care or thought about its owner. The inky sentence slowly took shape as Luther re-dipped the quill nib four times. Soon Zwingli saw that he had written *This is My Body* upside-down so that the Swiss could unquestionably read it.[1]

It was clear to all that this phrase was taken from Jesus' words at His last supper when He took bread, blessed it and said, "This is my body of the new covenant," before instructing his disciples to eat it, 'In remembrance of Him,' and to do so every time they took bread.[2] This was the origin of the Eucharist or Mass that had been faithfully celebrated by the Church for centuries.

When completed, Luther prodded the freshly written message firmly, collecting an ink stain on the tip of his right index finger. He didn't notice the blot however as his eyes were firmly fixed upon Zwingli. The German friar then issued Zwingli the challenge to admit that *this was true.*

Luther believed that when partaking of the bread and wine at the Mass these natural elements would supernaturally transform into the literal body and blood of Jesus who then became physically present and that by joining in His sacrifice the participant, or Communicant, would at that point receive God's free forgiveness. To Luther this was an essential part of salvation by grace.

---

[1] Luther wrote in ink on the table during his meeting with Zwingli. 'Protestants: The Radicals who Made the Modern World' by Alec Ryrie.

[2] Words Jesus spoke at the Last Supper, quoted several times in the Bible including, Luke chapter 22 verses 19 to 20

Zwingli couldn't disagree with Luther's table-top graffiti without denying the authority of the Scripture, something to which both men had already attested. However, he considered the literal interpretation of this passage to be almost tantamount to magic and held, what he considered to be the more commonsense view, that the bread and wine were merely symbols of Christ's sacrifice on the cross and anything more was an unnecessary religious barrier to freely receiving God's forgiveness.

Each unable to back down, they stared at the other in silence for what felt like an age until the hush was finally broken by Prince Philip of Hesse.

"Gentlemen, are we really going to have to give up and say you both agree to disagree?" Philip was once again diplomatically stirring the pot, hoping that both would realise the folly of having to leave the summit without a complete agreement. He clearly hadn't understood that to concede this point challenged each side's understanding of the very nature of Christ's divinity, contrasting His Oneness with His Omnipresence.

Philip was shocked when both men responded, ironically in perfect harmony to his provocation. Turning to him they both said simultaneously, "Yes, there is no other way."

Zwingli then offered Philip an impromptu compromise statement that he had been concocting in his head whilst Luther stood waiting his reply.

"We believe that the spiritual enjoyment of the body and blood is proper and necessary for every Christian." Zwingli rose to his feet as he continued. "...That the practice of the sacrament is given and ordered by God the Almighty." Luther sat down folding his ink-stained fingers across his chin as Zwingli concluded, "...And although we have not been able to agree whether the true body and blood of Christ are corporally present, each party should display towards the other Christian love."[1]

The Swiss smiled across the table, meeting Luther's steely return gaze. The German wasn't happy with the idea of accepting that someone had a different view of grace to himself, but he knew there was no alternative way forward. Despite the wholesale agreements of the day, to Luther this single point meant the two strands of Reformation could never be united. Faced with

---

[1] 'The Marburg Articles (1529), German History in Documents and Images', translated by Ellen Yutzy Glebe, from the German source: 'D. Martin Luthers Werke, Kritische Gesamtausgabe'

the enormity of that realisation he gathered his papers, thanked Prince Philip for his hospitality and left.

Chris thought that two minutes was long enough to leave it, before pressing redial. It was so unusual for Bunny not to answer her phone. Chris could only fear that his verbal clumsiness had done irrevocable damage to their friendship. The text and the voice message were not going to be enough, he *had* to speak to her. The phone rang, once, twice and then at last on the third ring it was answered, but to his surprise Chris heard a man's voice say a tentative, "Hello?"

"Hello?" Chris responded. "Who's that?"

"I've just come to lock the church. Someone must have left their phone. Then it rang." The answer only served to raise more questions.

"Church? What church?" Chris pleaded, "And where's Bun...I mean Johan Elstow?"

There was no immediate answer as his interlocutor appeared to be distracted with the scene he had found. Despite his ardent pleas, all Chris could do was to listen to the voice as it declared, "What's been going on here?" followed by "Who tore down the curtain?" and finally, "Aargh, it's *all over the floor.*"

"Hello, are you still there?' the voice eventually returned to the call before demanding, "Is this *your* doing?" Chris couldn't afford to let the clearly irritated person who had answered Bunny's phone hang-up before he at least found out where he was. Returning her lost phone would give him some credit with Bunny, which he felt he needed right now. Chris courteously explained who he was and to whom the phone belonged, that it was probably lost, and could he come and collect it. Finally he added that he had no idea what had happened *there* because he didn't even know where *there* was.

"St Mary's," the voice answered, followed unnecessarily by the establishment's full postal address and that the person he was talking to was the church deacon.

"And has Miss Elstow left anything else?" Chris asked, hoping that the deacon would spot her, perhaps in prayer, as he looked around the church.

"Someone's put a grey leather glove on the statue of the Blessed Mother, I saw that when I came in, is that hers?" As the deacon went on to describe it, Chris recognised the narrative. It was Bunny's and suddenly Chris began to worry. This was one piece of illogicality too many. Her phone *and* one of her gloves inside a church that admittedly was on her way home but that she had no reason to enter.

"Did I hear you say something was broken?" Chris asked tentatively.

"Yes, someone's pulled the confessional curtain off its pole. I will have to fix that before morning. And there is something all over the floor, and footprints," he answered.

"What's on the floor?" Chris asked. The deacon said he couldn't make it out and would need to put the lights on to see. Minutes later, he hesitantly admitted that it looked very much like blood.

Worry turned into realised fear. Something *had* happened to Bunny.

"Don't move. I am on my way," was all he could say.

Chapter 6

JOHN CALVIN

It wasn't until a while after Luther had departed that Bunny realised she had not left Marburg Castle with him.

"I thought we were going to make l'accord," said the young man sitting next to Bunny, interrupting her thoughts.

"Sorry, I was miles away," she said.

"Mon apologie, Mademoiselle. I said, it is très mauvais that we have not made l'accord today, is it not?" he repeated in a soft French accent.

"Yes," she agreed. "But I can see that unity is going to be difficult when each side has the freedom to believe their own understanding of the Bible. Without the comfort of a definitive papal interpretation there are going to be even more opinions aren't there, each defended to the bitter end." Bunny had grasped the dangerous consequence of freedom of interpretation perfectly.

"But," he responded, "is it faith to understand nothing and merely submit your convictions to the Church?" [1]

"No, I didn't mean that," she protested. "I mean that it is going to be difficult to decide what *the truth* truly is."

"That is why I am going to thoroughly study the Scriptures and find out the absolute correct interprétation. There must be an answer that is absolument correct, and I do not only refer to Christ's presence or not during the Eucharist."

"Transubstantiation," she interrupted.

"Transub..." he attempted.

"Transubstantiation," she repeated.

"Thank you, I will use that," he said scribbling into a notepad he produced from his breast pocket.

"There must be an answer, not just to that issue but to every contentieux question that is yet to appear," he continued. "This is my calling, Mademoiselle;

---

[1] Quotation by John Calvin taken from: 'DTLC: What is Theology for?' by Thomas & Amy Creedy extracted from thomascredy.co.uk

I have to do it. A dog barks when his master is attacked, and I would be a coward if I saw that God's truth is attacked and yet would remain silent."[1]

That was exactly what was going through her mind, there must be a *correct* answer, she surmised. Without thinking, she agreed with the young stranger saying, "Well that is something I would like to discover with you." The young man's face lit up. "I would consider it to be the greatest of honours if you were to accompany me to Switzerland, Mademoiselle," he said with the broadest of smiles.

She hadn't meant to make such an offer but as she had no real idea where she was or what was happening, she agreed.

Remembering the required courtesies of the moment the young man then stood up. "Forgive me, Mademoiselle, I should have introduced myself," he said tilting his head in a short bow. "John Calvin, your servant."

Chris returned from his extended 'toilet' break, collected his coat, keys and notepad announcing, "Sorry everyone but I need to go, I think something might have happened to Bunny."

Most of the people in the room knew Bunny and were suddenly arrested by the anxiety in Chris's voice. Having gathered his things, he launched himself out of the meeting room, followed closely by Ralph. By the time Ralph entered the corridor, Chris was already running so his pastor had to do likewise. When Ralph reached the balcony at the top of the stairs, Chris had made it to the ground floor.

"What's happened?" Ralph shouted over the balcony rail.

Chris halted momentarily, Ralph was his church leader and Chris was at the meeting to do a specific job which he had just abdicated. He owed Ralph an explanation for his hasty departure.

"I don't know, yet..." Chris shouted back at him. "She was at St. Mary's and there is..." Chris couldn't bring himself to shout the end of the sentence. He quickly returned to the foot of the stairway and looked up at Ralph. Chris found tears welling in his eyes as he said, in a hushed tone, "... and there is blood."

Ralph ushered him to go, knowing how special Bunny was to Chris, then shouted his insistence that Chris tell him what had happened as soon as he knew

---

[1] Widely quoted words of John Calvin. Taken from gracequotes.org posted by Andrew Gioulis April 3rd, 2015

anything. Chris charged out through the glass door into the rain, putting on his coat as the door slammed shut behind him.

"Fantastique! Fantastique! Mademoiselle Lapin, come quickly." The heavy front door of Calvin's Geneva home shut with a decisive thud. "It has arrivée, come and see."

Bunny, or as Calvin had taken to call her, Mademoiselle Lapin, bounded down the elegant staircase to see the excited theologian pulling at the string binding on one of five large packages festooned across the tiled hallway floor. As she joined him, her offer of assistance fell on deaf ears, the string now pulled ferociously from under the package and tossed aside. The thin brown paper fell apart to reveal books, or more accurately multiple copies of a single book *The Institutes of the Christian Religion*.[1] Calvin proudly extracted the top-most copy, kissed it, then hugged it passionately. Suddenly realising that Bunny was watching, he turned the heavy volume toward her underlining his name with his index-finger as he did.

"Do ya think he is happy enough eh, Miss? He's like a wee pig in muck?" Bunny turned towards the sound of an unfamiliar, yet distinctively Scottish voice.

"Pardon?" she asked unsure as to whom the well-dressed man now standing beside her was.

"Sorry, I don't speak French," he said slowly and apologetically.

"Nor do I," she replied in an emphasised English accent. They stood in confused silence for a moment. Bunny took the initiative.

"Let me introduce myself, I am Johan Elstow although most people call me Bunny. I have been here for..." She had no idea how long she had been in Geneva; instinctively she looked at her watch.

"Apparently, I've been Mr. Calvin's guest for around five minutes, but I'd swear it feels more like five years," she concluded before raising her eyebrows as a sign for the Scot to reciprocate.

---

[1] "Institutio Christianae Religionis" or "The Institutes of the Christian Religion" was published in 1526 in Latin. It was the first serious attempt at defining a Protestant theology and became the core text for several denominations who later described themselves as Calvinist.

"Aye, is that so," he dutifully replied. "Well, I have just arrived, and at an opportune time it would appear," he said pointing to the pile of books that Calvin had now fully unwrapped. I have come to ask the great man some questions."

"Is he famous in...Scotland?" she asked.

"Famous? Famous? Geneva is the most perfect school of Christ since the days of the Apostles," he replied, adding that people called Geneva "The Protestant Rome". [1]

"What questions do you want to ask him?"

"I have many things I want to put to him," he said dismissively, but Bunny was persistent and asked him for details which he willingly gave.

"Firstly, should church leaders be *elected* from within their congregations, as I believe, and not appointed as from above as so-called bishops?" he answered decisively, continuing with, "And secondly, to ask him whether he thinks godly Christian's should *always* obey ungodly rulers?"[2]

"Is that a problem we have, I mean you have, back in Scotland?" she asked.

"Aye it is, and I am determined to do away with all appointed bishops in Scotland and do whate'er I can to separate the Church from a heathen and papist queen."

"That would be Mary, Queen of Scots?" Bunny stated with confidence, having mentally joined the dots in the somewhat fuzzy recollection of her school history lessons.

"She's nae queen o' mine!" came the indignant retort.

"Sorry, I didn't mean to...." Bunny assuaged.

"Bien, bien, what do you think?" Calvin interrupted, to Bunny's relief. They quickly switched their attention from each other and began exaggeratedly fawning over the pristine publication, much to its author's delight.

Calvin, having now realised that there was a foreigner in his hall, was satisfied that this stranger was sufficiently enthusiastic over *Institutes* that he

---

[1] As the centre of the Calvinistic Reformation, Geneva became known as the Protestant Rome. Taken from the Geneva section of Encyclopaedia Britannica

[2] A great theologian, Knox sought Calvin's advice on two key questions regarding Church governance and the relationship between Church and State. Knox's views went a lot further than Calvin's and fashioned what became a unique form of Church that originated in Scotland, known as Presbyterian.

probably meant them no harm. As soon as the literary plaudits began to subside, Calvin addressed the interloper directly.

"Come now, Monsieur, who are you?" he asked.

"He has come to ask you some questions," Bunny explained before the stranger could even speak. This was a reflex action that probably fulfilled her need to be protective. She would always scrutinise and filter out anyone who wanted to speak to her Rector Mashman.

"Questions, is it? I consider that it is always good to admit you don't know everything! There is no worse screen to block out the Spirit than confidence in our own intelligence."[1]

"Thank you, Monsieur Calvin, I have much to learn from you and the people of Scotland are relying on me to bring them good news."

"Allons-y! Mon bureau awaits and we shall open the Scriptures, as there is no knowing that does not begin with knowing God."[2] Calvin set off, carrying a carefully balanced pile of seven copies of his book. After two steps he turned and demanded, "And bring those with you," motioning to the sprawling pile of literature strewn across the floor.

The Scotsman hurriedly began picking up books, far too many to carry. Bunny stopped him, relieving him of all but eight, saying,

"You go, I'll sort the rest."

He thanked her and departed in the direction of the archway that Calvin had glided through moments earlier. As he reached it, the man stopped and turned back to address Bunny.

"Thank you Miss. I dinna know if you are likely to ever visit Scotland, but if ya do, please be sure tae look me up, now."

"That would be rather difficult, Sir, wouldn't it?"

Her answer was met with surprise, if not indignation, before she qualified that her difficulty was simply that she didn't know his name.

"Ah, my name." He returned across the hallway, peering around the pile of books in his arms, before pivoting the fingers of his right hand out to offer the minimalist of handshakes.

---

[1] Widely quoted words of Calvin extracted from the John Calvin entry of quote.org

[2] The concept of knowledge beginning with knowing God is the opening thesis of "Institutes of the Christian Religion." The quotation stated here is an oft quoted paraphrase.

"My name is John Knox and I'll probably be in Edinburgh, or Dundee." Bunny dutifully squeezed his fingertips and helped him to rebalance the tower to a more manageable angle. "...or in prison," he added before leaving in haste.

Bunny turned her attention to organising the pile of books. At last, something she could do that was well within her comfort zone. She was a born organiser and loved cataloguing, categorising and classifying anything that was disordered. Piles of books would be easy.

"Do you want some help with those?" Bunny knew that voice. The same one she heard in the confessional at St. Mary's, the same one in the coach to Marburg. Was this an angel or her dream-guide? She didn't know, but was glad she had someone to talk to.

"I was hoping you would turn up," she said to him, almost casually.

"And why was that?" he asked, taking a seat in one of the padded and decorated orange chairs at the side of the hall, placing his gold-rimmed hat on his lap.

Bunny, not wanting to sit on the matching chair beside him, surveyed the hall for an alternative place to position herself. The only option was on top of the stack of books she had just assembled. She perched atop them, hoping Calvin wouldn't return any time soon. Having settled her posture she launched into the question that had been preying on her mind.

"When Luther and Zwingli were at Marburg, they were so close to unifying the two main Protestant strands. Surely that can't have been *it*. There must have been, I mean there *will be*, I mean...." Having lost her grasp of tense, she re-scripted the sentence from the start. "1529 in Marburg cannot be the only time that Protestant unity was attempted," she said defiantly, before adding the less confident question, "Can it?"

He looked back at her, a gentle smile on his face. The smile a parent would have as they watched their child attempt to take its first steps. He was leading her, true enough, but every step was her own. "Look at your watch, tell me what time it is now?" he asked.

She slid her sleeve upwards, looked at the large square dial and told him, "15:30."

"Well, in 1530 we have The Strasbourg Confession.[1] Both the Lutheran and the Swiss Reformations have begun to splinter. The Swiss had already ejected a group they termed re-baptisers or as they became, the Anabaptists, who didn't believe in infant baptism. They left to go north, so in Strasbourg Zwingli tries to hold the rest of their group together. Also, in 1530 we have The Augsburg Confession, where the Lutherans attempt to do the same but instead cause a huge divide and they split into two polar opposite groups.[2] Then..." The sentence was unfinished and hung on an upward inflection. He looked at her expectantly, his eyebrows raised. Bunny had no idea what he was waiting for. He softly said the single word "Time?" asking her to relook at her watch. She was surprised to see that her watch now read 15:36.

"Ah, 1536, The Wittenberg Concord,[3] a good attempt to reconnect both the Lutherans and the Swiss. But when Luther claimed victory the Swiss rejected it, not on doctrinal grounds but purely on principle," he said with a sigh before adding, "Time?"

"Hold on," she interrupted. "I haven't heard of any of these...concords or whatever...I don't really know what you are talking about."

He didn't respond to her protest. She looked at her watch and declared that it was, "15:45."

"1545, interesting. The Pope calls for his own ecumenical gathering, the Council of Trent,[4] just over the mountains from here. He wants to instigate changes within the Roman Church that if successful will negate the *need* for a reformed church to even exist... Time?"

---

[1] The Tetrapolitan (four cities) or Strasburg Confession of 1530 consisted of 23 chapters. It was the first confession of the Reformed tradition and despite seeking to prevent any further schism its text was deemed offensive to the Lutherans and was abandoned within a year of its adoption.

[2] Augsburg Confession of 1530 consisted of 28 articles and was the primary confession of faith of the Lutheran Church. It gained political support when the heads of the newly Lutheran principalities used it as the call to arms to oppose the Holy Roman Emperor Charles V.

[3] 1536 Wittenberg Concord sought to unify Lutheran and Reformed traditions over the nature of the Eucharist. It is considered a core text for Lutherans but was later rejected by the Reformed Church.

[4] Council of Trent (Trento, Italy) was held between 1545 and 1563, spanning three separate popes. It was prompted by and denounced the Protestant Reformation, being the start of the Counter-Reformation ushering-in revisions to both doctrine and practice.

"That's the counter-reformation isn't it?" She asked. He nodded dispassionately not commenting on whether he was impressed with her knowledge. Bunny looked at her watch which now displayed 15:48, she was getting the hang of this but had no idea about any of the events he was listing.

"1548 The Leipzig Interim tries to pull the Lutherans together, it won't last. Time?" [1]

The watch had advanced to 15:49.

"1549 The Zurich Consensus. Your host, John Calvin attempts a repeat of Marburg, bringing together the Lutherans and, what are now called the Calvinists."

"Really? Did he, will he, does he succeed?" she asked enthusiastically.

"Well, it became known as the Second Sacramental War, so judge for yourself."[2]

Bunny was getting the picture. Over a protracted period, there had been many attempts to unite the early Protestant factions. All had been lost into antiquity because all appear to have failed.

"I get it," she said hoping the lecture had finished. It hadn't, and he once again asked for a time check. Her watch displayed 15:52.

"You'll like this. Young King Edward invites the key reformists in every country to his palace in England. [3] And do you know who attends?"

"Who?" she asked with genuine curiosity.

"No one, not a single person turns up despite it being By Royal Invitation. The Archbishop of Canterbury was not pleased. Shall we continue?" He looked at her, awaiting her time update.

"15:70," she said, not even noticing that the minutes had now impossibly exceeded sixty.

---

[1] Leipzig interim of 1548 was effectively the text of a ceasefire between Holy Roman Emperor and the Lutheran Princes but managed to cause a major split in the Lutheran Church into the Philippist and Gnesio-Lutherans

[2] The Consensus Tigurinus or Zurich Consensus, of 1548 to 1551, was yet another attempt to unify the two main streams of the Protestant Church over the exact nature of the Eucharist. The description of the consensus as "the innocent occasion of the Second Sacramental War" was not an indication of violence but of the intransigence of the Lutheran side to this Reformed text.

[3] King Henry VIII's son Edward VI was an enthusiastic reformer and invited the heads of all Protestant groups to attend a discussion at his palace. None attended according to: 'Protestants: The Radicals who Made the Modern World' by Alec Ryrie.

"That is the Consensus of Sandomierz. The Polish ruler has more success in bringing people together but no more success in reaching any agreement."[1]

"15:77." She was ready this time.

"The Lutherans finally unite around the Formula of Concord, to patch-up their earlier split. [2] And that brings us to…" he waited for Bunny to say the time but before she could, Calvin returned.

"Mademoiselle Lapin?" Calvin looked somewhat startled to see her. She immediately panicked remembering that she was sitting on a pile of his books and leapt up only to see that she had been sitting on a simple wooden stool and that the books had disappeared.

"Is that you Mademoiselle Lapin? How délicieux to see you again, I haven't seen you for…. and look at you, exactly as I remember. And just in time for the carriage."

Calvin didn't look the same as the person she had been talking to moments earlier. His hair was thin and greying, he'd lost weight and now stood with a marked stoop. He was carrying the same travelling bag she had seen before, but now it looked as old and as weathered as he did. Instantly she understood that time had advanced by decades. She glanced over to her dream-guide-angel in acknowledgement, only to see that he was no longer there.

"You're about to leave, I take it?" she asked Calvin who, to her surprise, shook his head. Bunny instinctively questioned him, "What is with the travelling bag?"

"There is to be a meeting in the city of Dordrecht," he answered.

"And where exactly is Dordrecht?" she asked.

"Oh, that is in The Netherlands," came the answer.

"That is quite a journey from here. Who is going to be at this meeting?" she asked.

"Representatives from the Reformed Churches from all over Europe," he explained, but before he could say any more, she raised her index finger to her lips, a clear signal to arrest his discourse.

---

[1] The Consensus of Sandomierz of 1570 was an attempt to unify the Protestant churches across the Polish-Lithuanian Commonwealth in the face of the Catholic counter-reformation. Initial success ended when the radical Bohemian Brethren joined.

[2] Formula of Concord 1577 became the definitive Lutheran statement of faith although was only adopted by two-thirds of the now fragmented Lutheran Church.

"Don't tell me anything else, I already know that this meeting is going to be more significant than all of the other Concordes, Councils and Consensuses that have been held over the last, wow, several years, and if I am not mistaken, I am supposed to be coming with you."

Remembering her manners, she quickly added the courtesy, "If that is all right with you, Monsieur John."

Looking somewhat surprised at having been stopped mid-flow, he gingerly lifted a bent finger to his own grey lips, repeating Bunny's gesture. Bunny stood silently as Calvin smiled and slowly shook his head from side to side.

"No, Mademoiselle Lapin, you cannot come with me."

She was mortified at the thought of having offended the great theologian. Calvin continued, "No, Miss Bunnee, I have to stay here. You are going alone."

And with that he offered her the battered travelling bag, adding the assurance,

"Franciscus will meet you when you get there. He is the leader of a group that persist in calling themselves Calvinists, much to my vexation. He will look after you, Mademoiselle, he is a good man. Dutch, but a good man nonetheless."

Calvin saw that Bunny's face had dropped at the idea of travelling across Europe, alone. He placed the bag on the floor and rested his frail hand on her shoulder.

"Come, come, Mademoiselle, there is not one blade of grass, there is no colour in this world that is not intended to make us rejoice," [1] he said as he manoeuvred them both toward the door, clearly indicating that this was the time for her departure. Bunny complied, collecting the bag as they walked. As they approached the doorway, he said to her softly,

"Synod!"

Bunny looked at him for clarification.

"Synod," he said again as he opened the heavy door. "This one is a Synod. The Synod of Dort."

The door shut with a solid thud behind them.

---

[1] Quotation by John Calvin taken from the Calvin entry on goodreads.com

Chapter 7

DIRK WILLEMS

Ralph apologised to the group for Christian's rapid departure. Bunny was a well-known and popular figure, and they all expressed their concern that something untoward might have happened to her. As Ralph retook his seat, Rector Mashman suggested they continue. Jack was already primed and ready to jump in.

"I don't know about jam," the Presbyterian said bringing the mood further downwards, "but I know that there are certain Scriptures we will *never* all agree upon." The forceful tone of the Ulsterman and the emphasis he gave to the word *never* left the room in no doubt that he had little appetite for compromise.

Rex Fogge, however, could begin to see the core of the problem they were sharing.

"It's not about changing what we believe so that we can all say we agree," he began. "Obviously, we all believe we have *the truth* and that every other Christian expression is, whilst not exactly false, may be lacking in some way." This was immediately and uniformly rejected by the group as they all rebutted the charge of having called any other church False or Lacking.

"No, no, hear me out," Rex pleaded before continuing over their remonstrations.

"Whether it's fundamental doctrines such as transubstantiation or predestination, or the role of women, or governance, or simply the style of service; we all believe we are *right*. Of course, we do. 'My church is right' is a self-fulfilling statement, if we didn't think it was right, we wouldn't call it *my church*. And if we are *right*, we therefore have to consider all others as..." he didn't want to say the word *wrong* so instead delivered a tentative, "...less right."

Rex's well-argued observation was beginning to ring true as evidenced by the lack of a second verbal rebuttal. Thea Howlsy took the opportunity to contribute to the developing theme,

"We've all maintained an *agree to differ* policy for years, for centuries."

"Quite!" Fogge was pleased with the support, and continued a little more boldly, "We cannot expect anyone in this room to change any of their foundational beliefs. But, and it is a huge but, if we ever use 'This is what I believe' as an excuse to not co-operate on sharing our common confession of salvation by faith, then we have failed."

Jack Fort gave an unhelpful snort. Joel Whyens picked up the baton.

"When we read verses like 'I will build my Church, and the gates of hades will not prevail against it,'[1] I think I am right in saying that the word used for *Church* is singular not plural."

"Yes, it is," Artur Thelmin confirmed. Joel thanked him and continued,

"Then we are left with a problem. Jesus said he is going to build One Church."

"May I point out that when I suggested earlier that we are One Church, you all stared at me as if I had thrown my Bible into the fire," Rector Mashman complained. Joel ignored the Anglican's protestation,

"So, either God meant that He is building one true Church amongst all other false churches..."

"Which is how we have all behaved for centuries," Rex interjected before Joel continued.

"Yes, that is how every denomination has behaved. We have implied, often subtly, that our church alone holds the truth."

This damning accusation was so accurate that no-one had any appetite to be the one to disagree. Then, with a flash of inspiration, Joel added a laboured,

"...*or*..." which he delivered so slowly he could look directly at every person in the room as he did. "Or we accept that there is indeed One Church and we are all part of it. Like it or not."

In that room, in the momentary silence, it felt as though the tectonic plates had begun to move. An infinitesimally small shift, that no one could perceive, but something had started.

"Hmmm, it will be easier to just agree to differ," Thea offered cynically.

The driver needn't have told her that they were approaching her destination as it was obvious to Bunny that they were. As she peered out through the mud-spattered carriage window, the landscape was now markedly flat, a dramatic contrast to the mountains of Switzerland, where her journey had begun some days previously. A layer of snow stretched to the horizon. The branches of trees hung down devoid of leaves but oppressed by layer upon layer of snow. Alone in the carriage, she laid one of the woollen blankets across her

---

[1] Matthew chapter 16 verse 18. New King James Version

lap and tucked each side tight under her seated thighs. I look like an old granny! she thought, but rationally accepted the truth on the basis that anything to retain heat on this bitter morning was going to be worth it. It was almost impossible for her to finish reading Calvin's *Institutes of the Christian Religion* wearing the necessarily thick gloves, but she was pleased that she had already consumed the majority before the freeze set in. She had concluded that there was not a lot in the book she could disagree with and there was plenty she had never even considered. So much of what she took for granted as *Christian*, she now realised had probably been defined somewhere by someone. Everything that Calvin had written was soundly defended from the Bible, but she couldn't help wondering if the Lutherans had their own definitive book of doctrinal interpretations that too were scripturally intact.

She breathed on the glass once more, wiping the condensation away with her glove. As she gazed out across the unspoilt Christmas-card picture the carriage suddenly came to a halt. There was a commotion outside and she could hear the driver objecting.

A single female travelling alone across sixteenth-century Europe should, quite rightly, be anxious for her safety. Stories of highwaymen and bandits were now all too believable from her perspective, seated inside a cold wooden carriage. Whilst Bunny's logical right-brain told her not to worry, this is just a dream or a vision or a whatever; her left-brain was nonetheless completely caught up in the emotion of the moment. A paradox recognised by anyone who had been suddenly awoken from the middle of an intense REM cycle and caught themselves not knowing which side of reality they were in. This was Bunny's reality until she could wake up and return.

She felt the carriage tip over to one side with the weight of a footstep on the doorstep. Someone was coming, and she held her breath as the door was forcibly pulled opened. Thankfully the man who entered wasn't wearing a Dick Turpin mask, nor brandishing pistols or demanding that she should Stand and Deliver. He was large, though not overweight, tall and dressed in military uniform. His blue tunic was buttoned tight against the cold, he had removed his large decorative and wholly impractical hat and was carrying it, together with his gauntlets. His left hand rested on the top of his sheathed sword ready, it would appear, to withdraw it at a moment's prompting.

As soon as he realised the sole occupant of this grand carriage was a lady, he instinctively reached to his forehead to remove his hat, having forgotten he was holding it already. He gave a decisive head-bow instead.

"May I help you?" Bunny asked.

"Pardon, Meisje, I am looking for..." his eyes darted around the small carriage, "...for someone."

As he answered, he lifted the cushion from the seat opposite her, giving it a cursory inspection.

"Whoever it is, we can assume he isn't under there," she said with aplomb.

The officer grunted and looked across at her. Bunny leaned forward, took hold of the bottom of the woollen blanket and lifted it to her chin revealing far more of her legs than would have been customary for the day. Her intent was to show that she was not harbouring a stowaway, but she only succeeded in making the officer blush, emitting a flustered "Pardon!" as he levered himself back out of the doorway.

Realising her unladylike faux-pas Bunny dropped the blanket and asked politely,

"Whom exactly are you seeking, may I ask?"

"Dirk Willems," the soldier replied still halfway inside the vehicle.

Bunny was not expecting the soldier to laugh out loud when she asked what she considered to be the most obvious of questions, whether this Dirk Willems was dangerous or not.

"No, not dangerous at all," he said with a chuckle.

Suddenly the other carriage door was pulled open and into the doorway a less well-dressed man appeared. Bunny felt a cold blast of air rush between the doors and was glad she had lowered her blanket. The man was decidedly out of breath and gasped, as best he could,

"Help me, help me," between strained breaths.

"Willems!" the officer shouted across the carriage floor.

"Ahhhh!" the man gave a terrified reaction. The officer launched himself towards the interloper hoping to catch any part of the fugitive or his clothing as he hastily reversed from the doorway. He missed and was left sprawled at Bunny's feet. He could say nothing but "Pardon!" once again as he proceeded to crawl on all fours across the carriage and out of the door through which his prey had escaped. Bunny could see that Willems had run down an embankment and was cautiously making his way across the small frozen lake that was immediately beside them. By the time the soldier had reached its edge he calculated that Willems had taken a circuitous route and it would be easy to catch him if he went directly across the middle. Bunny watched the action as she closed the carriage doors. Within seconds the sound of ice breaking was unmistakable. Bunny watched helplessly as the young officer who had literally been at her feet, was now standing on thin ice. To her surprise Willems ceased running, looked back at his pursuer, then started to walk towards the stricken soldier shouting something at him. She couldn't make out what it was, but the body-language suggested it was: stand still and don't move.

The soldier thought he knew better and took two further steps towards his quarry. That was a step too far and as he lifted his foot one more time, transferring all his weight onto his standing leg, he disappeared almost silently, beneath the ice.

Bunny gave out a sound that was something between a gasp and a scream and began to re-open the carriage door in an attempt to offer some assistance - not that she had any means by which to help the unfortunate man. As she scrambled down the embankment, she could hear frenetic splashing. At least he was alive, but for how long in this weather? Reaching the water's edge, she stopped and looked up. By now Willems had laid himself across the ice a few feet from where the soldier was struggling. As she watched, the fugitive removed his coat and threw it towards the now desperate man. The soldier caught the sleeve with both hands and Willems began to drag him out.

Within seconds the soldier had his elbows out onto the ice, then a foot, then he'd levered himself out and was on all fours. As she watched, he shuffled slowly over to Willems who placed the coat over the officer and led him carefully to where the ice was thicker. Bunny began to breath normally again and realised that she needed to get him into the carriage as soon as possible.

Once on the safer ice the officer stood to his feet, returned the coat to Willems then drew his sword.

Bunny shouted across,

"Bring him over here into the carriage."

As she did, the scene she saw made no sense. She had meant for Willems to bring the officer over to her so that she could wrap him in a blanket; but now the officer had Willems at sword-point. Who was bringing whom?

Carefully negotiating the ice, they arrived at the carriage. Bunny held the door open as Willems clambered in, military sabre at his back. The officer, teeth chattering and blue-lipped, quickly followed and once seated fumbled with his frozen fingers to secure Willems with the rudimentary lock and chain he carried with him. Bunny wrapped the officer in two heavy blankets and told the driver to make haste to Dordrecht.[1]

The three passengers sat in silence, the carriage rocking them gently as the final miles of their journey passed. It wasn't long before Bunny closed her eyes rather than look at her fellow travellers. She began to drift onto a light sleep, her mind awash with ideas. As she dozed, she became convinced she was travelling not upon the seat of a horse-drawn carriage but that she was being pushed in a wheelchair. Then she could hear voices. A man's voice, indistinct at first, but then she heard him saying clearly,

"It's okay, sir, we'll take her from here."

And what was more, it was a voice with a strong accent. Not Dutch like those in her carriage but Eastern European or Arabic. She opened her eyes, her heart racing, unsure as to where she was.

She was still inside a mediaeval carriage but to her horror the soldier opposite, clearly suffering from exhaustion and shock, had succumbed to the rhythmic motion and had slipped into a semi-conscious state. Bunny and the fugitive Willems looked across at each other. Was she in danger? She quickly deliberated if she should reach over and take control of the soldier's sword to prevent Willems making a lunge for it.

"I mean you no harm," Willems said softly, anticipating her thoughts. He nodded towards the officer saying, "He is just doing his job. He has to take me back to the prison I escaped from earlier."

"What was your crime?" Bunny asked, steeling herself to hear of some hideous evil. She needn't have worried about the gruesomeness of the crime, but she was, nonetheless, shocked by his answer.

"I baptised people," he said. "And I don't mean as kinderen."

This struck a chord with her recent memory. Hadn't she just been told about a group that had left Switzerland due to their stance on what they called *believer's baptism.* They were the re-baptisers she recalled.

"Oh, you are one of those Anabaptists that left Switzerland?" she stated, half-questioningly, but with confidence having congratulated herself on her recall.

---

[1] From 'Compassion for The Enemy' by John S Oyer and Robert Kreider (1995) published in The Mennonite Quarterly Review, Goshen College.

"Not me personally," he answered, "but our leader, Menno Simons, teaches the things rejected by the old Calvinist structures."

How strange, she thought. This is the early days of the Reformation and already Calvin is seen as *old* by some quarters.

"Menno Simons? So, do they call you Simonites?" she asked hoping to fill her knowledge.

"No, they call us Mennonites"

"And, other than the baptism thing, what else do Mennonites believe?" she asked.

"We believe all the same things as all the Reformed Churches. It is mainly just the adult baptism." He thought for a moment before continuing. "And then there is the freedom in worship. We don't have any written-down services..."

"Liturgy!" Bunny couldn't resist correcting him.

"Hmmm," he wasn't impressed with the interruption but continued his train of thought. "Our worship services are very free. One will come with a prayer, another with a scripture. We sing songs of worship then we may sing in tongues..."

As soon as she heard him say tongues, Bunny was instantly transported back, in her memory, to the Crossta Coffee shop at C.R.F., standing next to the 'Releasing Tongues Night' poster and looking over at Chris. It felt like ages since she was there but was it tonight? In one sense, for her at least, ages had passed but her grasp of time and reality was too fuzzy to be sure. But now she could see Chris. Chris who had broken into the normality of her life with one simple fumbled phrase. *I like you*. With all the self-assuredness of a teenager mumbling *I like you* to the object of their pubescent playground infatuation. Of course, he *liked* her - everyone *liked* her, she rationalised. But this was more than just *I like you*; this was packed with the potential of what could be, this was a forward-looking statement, a future-loaded declaration with intent. Why didn't I just say that I liked him back, she thought. *I like you too* would have been so much better than the *Oh!* she had given him in return. What did Oh! mean? Oh, my goodness? Oh no? or could it really have been the precursor to, Oh, yes please? She didn't know, she couldn't let herself consider it. Her rational mind was too quick to point out that they were opposites, different in so many ways. He was funny, upbeat, hopeful, charismatic and she, well she... wasn't. I'm from a more solid background, she thought, and by background she meant church background. Her identity and her church affiliation were completely intertwined, and she knew it. I am used to set services, where I know what is going on, she thought. I need to be able to worship in sincerity, I am content to conform to the way the established national Church does things. But Chris, but them at C.R.F., they all do it all so freely, with everyone taking part, and you never quite know what is going to happen.

"...Freely, with everyone taking part, and you never quite know what is going to happen." Willems concluded his description of a typical Mennonite worship service.

Bunny realised she hadn't been listening to him for the last few minutes and hoped a smile and a nod would suffice at this point. It seemed to, as the fugitive then continued,

"Those beliefs put me at odds with the Dutch Reformed Church. This is supposed to be a nation of religious tolerance since our independence from Spain, but all that means is you have to conform to the way the established national Church does things, with their...liturgy."

This was beginning to get uncomfortable. Bunny could see the clear parallels with her situation. She needed to change the subject.

"How long will you be in prison?" she asked.

Before he could answer another voice said,

"He will be sentenced to death." The soldier had recovered sufficiently to have heard the question and was unequivocal with the answer. Bunny looked at Willems,

"Is that true?" she asked. Willems nodded.[1]

"Hence the knotted rags out of the window," he said with gallows humour.

Bunny was horrified that the sentence for believing something different to the mainstream was going to be death. And the beliefs, from her viewpoint, didn't seem to be too extreme to warrant even imprisonment.

"I have to ask," Bunny addressed Willems. "Why did you save him from drowning?" She pointed directly at the officer, eyes open but still slumped on the bench opposite.

"Ah, yes." Willems sat back against the carriage wall. "I saved him because we Mennonites are committed to the sanctity of life. I therefore couldn't let him die – it is against my religion."

"Really?" she asked.

---

[1] Dirk Willems was martyred on 16 May 1569.

"Yes, and we are also pacifists, another crime of which I am accused."

"Like the Amish?" Bunny offered.

"Who?" both the soldier and Willems replied in unison.

Luckily for Bunny, the carriage came to a halt before she had to once again try to wriggle out of a literally mistimed comment. She had wanted to wish Willems well as they disembarked but she felt it better to keep her own counsel and simply waved a dignified goodbye to her fellow passengers.

By the time he had parked illegally on the kerb outside St. Mary's, Chris had already called Bunny's home phone without success. The lights in the church were on and as Chris dashed inside he was met by two people. The deacon, who was attempting to reaffix the confessional curtain, had been joined by his priest, Father Leonine, who was holding the mobile phone and glove.

"May I?" Chris asked as he took them from the cleric's hand. He didn't know what he expected to achieve in examining them, they were both clearly Bunny's. Chris then saw the footprints. He folded the glove in half and slid it into his hip pocket. He grasped Bunny's phone firmly as he began to investigate the macabre trail. Each footprint was in a distinctive red stain and in an almost perfect crescent shape about six inches between each step. Three partial footprints led away from the stain and looked like they had been made by heavy-soled hiking boots, certainly not what Bunny had been wearing. Each footprint became progressively lighter, as they moved towards the door.

"I think we should call the police." Chris couldn't think of anything more to say, and in doing so felt the pain of admitting that something seriously bad could have happened here.

"Do you think that is necessary?" Father Leonine asked unenthusiastically. "Someone has had an accident with the curtain, to be sure, and dropped their phone, but that is all. No need for the police."

"My...." his mind in such a state of anxiety, Chris stopped himself from saying girlfriend. "My friend is missing, and this is *her* phone and that is her..." Chris looked at the blood-stained floor but couldn't finish the sentence.

"Perhaps she will turn up, I find that people usually turn up," the priest stated in a matter-of-fact manner.

"Well, if you are not going to help find her *I will*," Chris said emphatically.

Chapter 8

THE SYNOD OF DORT

Exactly as Calvin had arranged,[1] the moment her coach arrived in Dordrecht, Bunny was met by Franciscus Gomarus.[2] He was an imposing man, completely bald but sporting a well-groomed beard that was so long it rested upon his chest. Even as his head moved the beard remained curiously affixed to his tunic.

"Meisje?" he asked as he offered his assistance to help her step down from the carriage. She had no idea what he meant but took his hand nonetheless, not that she needed any man's assistance in climbing out of the vehicle, but she was aware that she was the alien in this scene and as such allowed herself the indignity of compliance.

"I think perhaps you have been a little delayed, Meisje," he stated, but before Bunny could relate anything about the excitement of how Willems had rescued a drowning man who then re-arrested him, Gomarus had already started walking briskly, indicating first that she should follow him, which she dutifully did.

Unlike the architectural grandeur of the Cathedral at Worms or the opulent splendour of Marburg Castle, the hall in which the Synod of Dort was being held was austere. Rather than stone, the structure was made entirely of wood. A brass candelabra hung from the apex of the tall ceiling. The sixteen candles were unlit as the evening sunlight streamed in through three large windows that dominated the top half of the two opposing walls. There were no curtains, but the light was softened slightly by stained etchings, the meaning of which she couldn't immediately decode. Beneath the windows were three tiers of wooden pews that extended around three sides of the room. Approximately one hundred people occupied the pews and were busy exchanging pleasantries. The Synod was not in session when they arrived. In the centre of the room there was a large table where, Bunny supposed, the main protagonists were going to

---

[1] Whilst a pivotal event in Calvinism, John Calvin never attended the Council of Dort having died several years earlier.

[2] Franciscus Gomarus (1563-1641) was a prominent member of the Dutch Reformed Church. A strict Calvinist theologian he was opposed to the more liberal views of Jacobus Arminius over the doctrine of predestination and led the Calvinist group at the Council of Dort.

perform. She had no idea who the main players were or indeed what the purpose of this gathering was. She just knew it was going to be important in her understanding of church unity.

She followed a few steps behind Gomarus as they traversed the large room. Their progress was frequently interrupted by people, some wanting to shake his hand or congratulate him, others giving him constructive advice. One thing that Bunny knew of the Dutch, apart from the obvious about windmills and tulips, was that they were natural linguists. Gomarus was no exception. In those few minutes he conversed fluently with people from Germany and Switzerland and at one point addressed a row of empty chairs in French.[1] Eventually, and to Bunny's delight, he deposited her with the British delegation. No sooner had she introduced herself to George, Thomas, John, Samuel and Walter than it was time for proceedings to continue.[2]

"Dames en Heren, Damen und Herren, Ladies and Gentlemen, could we please take our seats." The Master of Ceremonies had a vocal amplitude that belied his stature and soon the room was quiet enough for him to continue, firstly in Dutch, then German and, thankfully, ending with perfect English.

"It is now time to call upon the spokesperson for the opposition, pray silence for Herr Simon Episcopius of the Remonstrants."

As the name was announced an audible murmur of displeasure circulated the packed room like a Mexican wave touring a stadium. Bunny couldn't help but think that Simon Episcopius and the Remonstrants sounded exactly like a sixties rock-and-roll band. Bunny leaned into her neighbour, whom she now knew as George Carleton, and whispered a request for clarification of the term Remonstrant. Carleton, a little taken aback, nonetheless obliged.

"Those thirteen people seated over there," he pointed across the room, "are the ones promoting the Arminian doctrine. They call themselves the Remonstrants, and we are all here to refute every word they say!"

Bunny symbolically circumscribed the room with an outstretched finger and asked,

---

[1] The Synod of Dordecht, or Dort as it was known in English, began on November 13, 1618. 102 men from many countries attended the 154 sessions which concluded on May 9, 1619.

[2] George Carleton, Bishop of Llandaff led the English delegation at Dort. He was joined by Joseph Hall, Thomas Goad, John Davenant, Samuel Ward and Walter Balcanquhall who was the sole representative of the Church of Scotland.

"All of you?" Carleton nodded. As she straightened into her pew, Bunny left him with the cutting observation, "So that is one hundred against fourteen." Carleton didn't answer.

As she watched proceedings unfold, Bunny learned that Jacobus Arminius, who had died some years earlier, had taught on sin, grace, salvation by faith-alone and freewill.[1] As she listened, she couldn't help but see the similarity with Luther's defence at Worms against the established Catholic hierarchy. But now this is the followers of one reformed theologian having to defend what looked like the same position against another reformed Church. Unlike Worms there was no deterioration into civil unrest as Simon Episcopius meticulously began to present the *Five Articles of the Remonstrants*.[2] Despite amusing herself with the thought that *Five Articles* must be the hit album of the fictitious rock-and-roll group of her imagination, Bunny decided she had better concentrate if she was to find out what was causing all the fuss.

Articles One, Two and Three were presented without comment. They covered Original Sin and the need to be Born Again through faith in Christ's sacrifice on the cross. Bunny found no fault in any of the points stated. Two to go, she thought, the fireworks are bound to start soon. She was right, although the phrase that lit the blue touchpaper was buried toward the end of Article Four and to her ears appeared wholly innocuous. *'Grace is not irresistible'*. That was it, as soon as he said it papers were waved, floors were stamped upon, the backs of pews thumped. The dignified became the indignant. Bunny leaned once again towards her nearest neighbour. He took his cue.

"If grace is resistible, then Christ died for everyone, not just the elect," George said, this time not needing to whisper his remarks in the din.

Bunny nearly replied spontaneously, "But *didn't* He die for everyone?" but she managed to stop herself just in time. If this issue was so inflammatory she ought to keep her mouth shut for once. George continued,

"And if true, then it would undermine the faith of all of those who have been martyred, who believed it would have been impossible to recant their confession."

---

[1] Jacobus Arminius opposed Calvin's theology of predestination. His teaching of freewill became much of the basis of the Methodist Movement nearly one hundred years later. He died nine years before the Synod of Dort.

[2] Simon Episcopius was refused the opportunity to present a defence of his doctrines at the Synod. 'The Five Articles of the Remonstrants (1610)' by Dennis Bratcher, ed 2018. Published by CRI Voice Institute

"This is big," Bunny said under her breath as she retook her vertical seated position.

Having just read Calvin's book, she knew that he had taught that Jesus died for mankind, people freely accept that by faith, but as God is outside of time He would already know who would accept that free gift. Therefore, in one sense Jesus died only for those whom he foreknew would accept his sacrifice. They were, as Calvin put it, *predestined* for salvation. But now Arminius was teaching that Jesus died for all people, just the same, and that everyone has a free choice to accept Him or not. Arminianism is therefore opposed to the idea of predestination, saying instead that everyone has a free choice to receive God's forgiveness for their sins, or not. For the first time, Bunny was confronted with the need to make a choice as to what *she* believed. Both arguments made sense. God was outside of time, but she knew people all had freewill.

She had thought that the Synod of Dort was going to be another attempt at unity, but the sad truth had now dawned upon her. Yet another major strand of Protestant Christianity had emerged and whilst she didn't recognise the name Arminianism it was closer to what she was familiar with in the Church of England.

As the church bell gave a single toll that afternoon's session at the Synod was summarily closed, thankfully without weapons being drawn. She remained in her seat, a little stunned, as her fellow English-speaking delegates filed past her. The final Brit, Walter Balcanquhall, stopped momentarily as he attempted to squeeze his obese frame past her and enquired if she was all right.

Bunny, drawn out from the depth of her thoughts, instinctively said,

"I think I need to get back to England."

Walter, equally spontaneously replied,

"Well, Miss, I will be leaving in the morning, and you're welcome to join me. But I will be sailing to Scotland, to Edinburgh and not England."

Bunny looked up at him. He had a kind face and she decided he would pose no threat to her if she were to join him.

"Yes, I will," she answered with a grateful smile. "Thank you. I think I know someone who will be in Edinburgh, and he said I could visit him if I was in the area. If only I could remember his name."

"But in some ways, we *must* agree to differ..." The Lutheran priest, Artur Thelmin, couldn't remain quiet any longer. Not only was he a newcomer to this group, and the youngest, but he was growing uncomfortable with the direction the discussion had taken. He knew it was time to let his views be known whether it made him unpopular or not. Outside of its Germanic homeland the Lutheran Church felt as though it was being held at arms-length from other Protestant denominations, being as it was closer to the Roman Church than most of them. Artur unwittingly already carried this chip on his shoulder. His last few years at seminary had not only given him a thorough biblical grounding but had unintentionally imparted upon him centuries of Lutheran ostracization. Having enthusiastically accepted being appointed to one of the better-attended parishes in the United Kingdom and buoyed by his detailed theological knowledge he felt he was on solid ground to vocalise his discontent.

"Some of the things we each believe are *fundamentally incompatible*," he declared emphatically.

"What do you mean," Joel asked, a little taken aback that his powerfully made point had not been universally accepted.

"He means like singing songs written by your Charles Wesley rather than Graham Kendrick." Jack Fort levelled a divisive remark towards the Methodist Joel, partly in jest but principally because he too was feeling uncomfortable with the rising tide of appeasement.

"What's wrong with Charles Wesley?" Whyens reacted.

"Who is Graham Kendrick?" Rector Mashman asked innocently.

"You know Rector, he wrote *Shine, Jesus, Shine!*" Thea answered, highlighting one of the modern hymn-writer's most popular songs.

"Oh, I like that one," the elderly Anglican replied before beginning to hum the Kendrick tune, a little too loudly to be polite, and waving his finger baton-like as he did.

Ralph released a self-congratulatory snigger and leaned over to Rex Fogge to say,

"We haven't sung *Shine, Jesus Shine* since the nineties."

Joel, much affronted by the slight against the Methodist hymn-writer, stood to his feet and drowned out the Rector's humming by singing the Charles Wesley classic,

"And Can It Be, That I Should Gain..."

Not to be outdone Jack Fort pitched in to the vocal melee with a childishly loud outburst of,

"Amazing Grace, How Sweet the Sound..."

"No, No, that isn't what I meant at all," Artur protested, adding to the noise.

"Quiet! Quiet!" Rex waved his hands violently. The impromptu singing stopped abruptly. "Can't you see, you didn't need any encouragement to leap to the defence of your favourite composers in this ridiculous..." he hunted for the word, "...in this juvenile *hymn-off*. Whether it's Wesley, Newton, Kendrick, or..." he leaned towards Ralph for the composer of one of C.R.F.'s current worship songs. Being put on the spot, he verbally stumbled around before offering Chris Tomlin, a name which meant nothing to most of the group. Rex continued,

"Whether we prefer to sing hymns by Wesley, Kendrick or Tomlin we don't need to look down on those who don't."

The Quaker had not intended to chastise his fellow pastors but that was the positive outcome of his forceful intervention. Joel Whyens, Rev. Mashman and eventually Jack Fort each gave mumbled apologies. Tectonic plates moved again.

Having brought the room to order, everyone was now looking at Rex. The only thing he could say was,

"Thank you," before inviting Artur to continue.

"When I said that there were things on which we fundamentally disagree I didn't mean hymns. I was talking about doctrine. Jack over there and I believe in predestination, don't we Jack," the Presbyterian minister nodded tentatively unsure if he was being led into a trap. Artur continued, "Whereas the rest of you, the rest of you are Arminian."

"Armenian, I'm not Armenian!" Reverend Mashman reacted to the malapropism.

"No Reverend, he means Arminianism." Rex assured him. "It's the belief that salvation is purely a freewill thing."

"Quite right, quite right," the Anglican mumbled to cover his embarrassment.

"You say 'Quite right' but that is my whole point, some of us don't believe that. If we are to find any degree of co-operation we are going to have to *agree to differ*, as you put it."

Chapter 9

JOHN KNOX

It felt good to be back on home soil. Whilst Scotland was still a long way from her actual home, Bunny had nonetheless felt a sense of relief when she stepped ashore in Leith with Walter; despite her apparent sixteenth-century surroundings giving her neither comfort nor familiarity. It was in the bitter cold of the crossing from Rotterdam that she had remembered that it was John Knox who had invited her to visit him in Edinburgh, Dundee or prison. Neither of these was the reality. She soon discovered that he was scheduled to be delivering a sermon in the Scottish university town of St. Andrews and by the time she would get there he would be in full flow.

As she approached the central church, or more correctly the *kirk* of St. Andrews, the doors were suddenly flung wide-open and what appeared to be an angry mob of maybe a hundred or more people ran out. Bunny immediately stopped walking towards the kirk and instead shuffled sideways off the cobbled street and into the doorway of a tavern that was firmly closed, today being a Sunday.

Hidden from view, she peered gingerly around the corner of the doorway, hoping to see the crowd charge in any direction but towards her makeshift refuge. Thankfully, the object of their riotous attention was the university building itself. Several burly men soon forced open a large arched wooden door that she presumed must be the main entrance into the academic institution, and then disappeared inside. Others waited outside as if to receive someone or something that was about to be forcefully ejected. Bunny didn't have the disposition to witness anything macabre, she knew she didn't have the stomach for it. She had resolutely refused to watch the comedy-horror that Chris had suggested they see when he had unexpectedly invited her to the cinema last week, insisting on the latest offering from Richard Curtis instead. Chris didn't seem to mind.

A loud smash jolted her back from her memories. The unmistakable sound of breaking glass was coming from within the university. The crowd was bent on destruction. Was this a civil riot? she wondered, but as it appeared to have originated from the kirk she thought probably not. As the minutes passed, the noise slowly subsided, presumably as there was little inside left to break. She then watched as a large, heavy statue of Mary the mother of Jesus was manoeuvred out of a downstairs window. It took five men to carry it away from the university and onto the steps of the kirk. There it was laid like an offering to a merciful god. Bunny's attention however was drawn up from the supine statue to the person standing at the top of the steps. It was John Knox. The sight of a familiar face was sufficient to entice her from her lair and across the square to hear what he was about to say.

"Men of Scotland!" Knox raised one hand to quieten the throng that had now returned from the university and gathered around the church steps.

"Men of Scotland, I am proud that this day we have joined the likes of Zurich, Geneva, Copenhagen, Augsburg and Münster. The venerated icons and false altars of the evil Papist Church have been destroyed. You have joined the honourable Iconoclasts[1] who, just like the children of Israel entering the Promised Land, did 'Ouerthrowe their alters and breake their pylers and burne their groues with fyre and hewdowne the ymages off theyr goddes, and brynge the names of them to noughte out of that place.'"[2] By now Bunny had appended herself to the rear of the crowd and could hear every word clearly. Knox continued with a passion.

"Know that resistance to tyranny is obedience to God.[3] In this fight, you are on God's side, and the man who stands with God is in the majority."[4] The crowd cheered at this apparent encouragement towards civil disobedience. Taking this as his cue, a heavy-set kilted Scot heaved a substantial stone hammer into the statue of Mary, splintering the top-most part into a thousand shards but leaving her feet hauntingly intact.

Suddenly Bunny felt a searing pain shoot into the back of her right hand. Had one of the porcelain shards flown all the way from the church steps and pierced her skin? She instinctively looked at her hand, prepared to wince at the sight of blood. But to her surprise there was nothing there, just her bare skin.

---

[1] Iconoclasts are those who destroy the religious artefacts of a former outgoing belief system. During the Protestant Reformation significant Iconoclastic riots are recorded as having taken place in Zurich (1523), Basel (1529), Copenhagen (1530), Munster (1534), Geneva (1535), Augsburg (1537), Scotland (1559), Rouen (1560) and La Rochelle (1562). The events depicted here exemplary but fictional.

[2] Deuteronomy chapter 12 verse 3, here presented in the Tyndale translation that would have been the only English language version available to John Knox.

[3] Widely quoted words of John Knox

[4] Ibid.

The pain however was unmistakable. She stared at her hand in confusion. Then, as she looked, in a momentary flash she saw a cannula being taped to her own hand, a thin length of clear PVC tubing being attached to it, and a small stream of her own blood trickle between two of her fingers. Then, as suddenly as it appeared, it vanished, as too did the pain. A familiar Scottish voice brought her back.

"But good souls, we are not here to destroy but to build. To build a new Scotland. For so long as a woman reigns in this nation and the papists are in authority, there Satan must be present.[1] And today is the day we make our declaration. This, the twenty-seventh day of August in the year of our Lord 1560..." Bunny looked at her watch, indeed it showed 15:60,

"...On this day we have completed our Confession of Faith. Come, stand with me bothers."[2]

Knox's commanding position on the top step drew Bunny's eye as she unconsciously framed the scene as if it were one of her church building sketches. No yew tree here, just an austere edifice in Scottish granite, but one she felt she could nonetheless capture.

Knox then invited five men to join him on the top step and introduced each of them to the crowd. As he did so, much to Bunny's amusement, all were named John, which together with Knox made it six Johns in total standing at the top of the church steps.[3] Knox continued his oration, this time holding a substantial parchment above his head.

"Today this *Scots Confession* has been agreed by the parliament in Edinburgh and so we celebrate the birth of the new Church of Scotland. A Church with no government imposed upon it by a heathen queen but free to administer itself from within. Its own congregations, each led by a presbytery of elders, that each attest to the common Confession of Faith I now hold in my

---

[1] Original quote: "That where a woman reigneth and papistes beare authoritie, that there must nedes Satan be prefident of the counfel." From 'The first blast of the trumpet against the monstruous regiment of women.' by John Knox 1558. P32.

[2] The parliament on Edinburgh approved the Scots Confession on 27 August 1560. As it was against the wishes of the monarch, Mary Queen of Scots, it was not ratified until 1567 after her overthrow.

[3] The six people who wrote the Scots Confession of 1560 were John Knox, John Winram, John Spottiswoode, John Willock, John Douglas and John Row. Six Johns, and it was strongly influenced by John Calvin!

hand. The Lord has heard and answered my prayer, 'Give me Scotland, or I die!'"[1] Knox knew how to work a crowd. That final phrase, his well-used rallying cry was the excuse the crowd had been waiting for to release a celebratory cheer. As they did the church bell behind him rang out a single toll. Knox waved as they applauded him before slowly beginning to disperse.

"Ah, *presbytery*, I get it now," Bunny thought. "Presbyterian must mean churches that are ruled from the bottom-up rather than from top-down. There's still a hierarchy but not one imposed from a supreme leader. This is very different from the Anglican Church. We have bishops and archbishops and, I guess, ultimately the Queen as its head. But I can see that this Presbyterian model separates the Church from State control whilst remaining the *official* Church of Scotland. It is a very clever."

"Well, I for one have no intention to deviate one inch from the truth," Jack Fort pronounced emphatically. The Northern Irish Presbyterian minister wasn't having any of the growing air of mollification.

Compromise wasn't part of Jack's DNA. As a child growing up in County Antrim, religion was a normal part of everyday life. His fiercely Presbyterian parents would take him and his older brothers to church every Sunday, often for three services including the Sunday School. But it was at the midweek youth club that he found his personal faith. Sandwiched in the middle of an evening of table-tennis, pool and copious amounts of orange squash, he would sit transfixed, for barely more than twenty minutes each week, in a draughty church hall and listen to Mack, a passionate, God-fearing, Bible-wielding, no-nonsense youth leader. These twenty-minute *God Spots* led him and some of his friends into a revelation of God's love and Jesus's sacrifice for them and before long Jack had committed his life to Christ and was baptised.

As a teenager Jack would be seen on most Saturdays amongst a small group of street-evangelists that congregated beside the statue of King William III in the shadow of the Norman castle that dominated his hometown of Carrickfergus. Mack was their leader, and Jack soon found a niche as their musician. His chosen instrument was the piano accordion whose resounding

---

[1] The prayer-slogan 'Lord give me Scotland, or I die!' is usually attributed to John Knox although there is little historical evidence to the fact. Dr. Marcus Serven, published at www.genevanfoundation.com on February 15, 2016.

timbre and volume would always draw a crowd. Each member of the group would take it in turns to share the testimony of their personal conversion and invite others to do likewise. Jack knew he was doing God's work and admired Mack intensely.

Like many of those of his generation, Jack's family had tasted the bitterness of having lost at least one relative in what was understatedly known as The Troubles. In his case it was both an uncle and a cousin, caught in the blast of an IRA car bomb while they were returning a video they had rented for the evening. Whilst everyone knew that car-bombs were a terrorist tactic of the paramilitary Irish Republican Army, as far as his parents were concerned it was simply *the Catholics*. Few western societies were as polarised as Northern Ireland during those dark days, and Jack was under no illusion as to which side he was expected to be on.

There was a minority Catholic population in Carrickfergus, probably no more than ten or fifteen percent, but that was still around three thousand people. Two of the main Protestant paramilitary groups, the UVF and the UDA, both had a large and visible presence in the town. Consequently, the Catholics would keep a very low profile and didn't interact with anyone else, which was exactly how the paramilitaries insisted it should be.

Mack had a different viewpoint and considered the Catholics to be just as deserving of salvation as anyone else. He had begun to befriend a small group of Catholic boys and was keen to introduce them to his street-evangelists.

"What a coup it'd be to have converted some of the local Catholic kids," Mack told the group with typically infectious evangelical zeal.

After several weeks of careful and surreptitious reeling in of his intended Catholic catch, Mack asked Jack and his friends to meet them. The arrangements were perfectly innocent. Jack and four others would meet Mack at Woodburn playing fields on a Tuesday evening for a game of football against the Catholic boys after which they would share a snack and the gospel. Jack decided not to tell his parents who he was going to meet, they wouldn't approve; he left his accordion but took his football. When Jack and his friends arrived at the rendezvous there was no sign of Mack, nor of an opposing five-a-side football team. As they stood at the side of the park wondering what to do next, seemingly out of nowhere five masked men in military fatigues suddenly appeared. The boys were forcibly dragged away from the park and to the back of a Ford Transit van whose rear doors were wide open. Inside was a kneeling man, hands tied behind his back, a hessian sack over his head. One of the military men stepped into the van to briefly lift the sack just enough to allow the boys to see who it was. It was Mack. He had blood running from his lower lip, a bruise on his cheek and a stream of clear nasal mucus hung from his nostrils. As he caught sight of his small cohort Mack started sobbing. Jack couldn't make out what his mentor was trying to say but in his recollected memory he always assumed it to have been Sorry.

"Take a good look, boys. This is the last you'll see of him," a voice barked at them as they froze to the spot. Jack dropped his football but dare not move to pick it up and heard it bounce twice before rolling away. The hood was firmly replaced, and van doors slammed shut. The disembodied paramilitary voice then turned into a very-real masked face standing in front of them. He held a gun but didn't point it at them. He didn't need to. They were all petrified. Instead, he used his finger as a weapon, pointing and prodding at each in turn as he delivered his mantra,

"No one converts Catholics!"

They never did see Mack again. To this day they have no idea as to who took him. Was it one of the Protestant paramilitary groups delivering a warning that they must not *fraternise with the enemy* or was it an IRA snatch-squad sent to pick him up to protect their Catholic boys? Either was plausible, but the truth wasn't going to bring his mentor back.

Jack resolved that day to stay with what he knew, stay safe within the boundaries of the Presbyterian Church and to never, ever stray outside.

"No deviation," he repeated to his fellow ministers.

"But Jack, we could all say that. In fact, we all do," Rex stressed seeking to help Jack dismount his high horse. "None of us wants to compromise. I would go as far as to say we are the least likely group of people to compromise. It is against *all* of our convictions."

"And some of us would lose our jobs if we did!" As one of the few paid ministers in the gathering, Artur stated the further constraint under which some of them were held.

"But..." The Rector's conjunctive hung in the air like a saggy helium-filled balloon, not sure if it was ever going to land. Everyone looked at him.

"But...," he repeated, "We do have to arrange our Easter..." As he paused, again searching his brain for the next word, a process delayed by his recollection of their previously unsuccessful attempt to agree anything. In the lengthy pause, four people almost simultaneously proposed entirely contradictory endings to his sentence.

81

Methodist Joel offered, "Mission"; Lutheran Artur assumed he was going to say "Service"; Ralph's free-charismatic leanings prompted an instinctive "Celebration"; whereas Baptist Thea suggested the safe "Event".

"Quite." The Rector accepted all contributions equally. Rex laughed and said,

"If we manage to organise anything next year it will have to be a…"

His pause was entirely deliberate. He raised his eyebrows waiting, hoping that he would get a more harmonious conclusion to his sentence. It was only Ralph and Jack who delivered the final,

"Miracle."

Ralph said it because he truly believed in miracles, Jack did because he knew that only divine intervention would change his doctrinal position.

"My, that is a face from the past." Knox had spotted Bunny standing alone as the crowd began to disperse and shouted over to get her attention. Bunny smiled back and walked to where he was standing taking care not to tread on any of the razor-sharp statue fragments.

"And look at you, you haven't aged at all," he continued flatteringly.

"I get that a lot," she replied unaware of the irony of the statement. "Mr. Knox," she started.

"John, please," he corrected.

"John, the model of Church you have instigated here in Scotland, where the State and Church are independent of each other…" she paused trying to form her question accurately, not wanting to embarrass herself again.

"Aye?" he enquired.

"Well, why haven't other countries adopted it?" she asked, satisfied that she had stayed within the time-period constraints with which she now had to comply.

"Ah, an excellent question, lassie. Did ya hear that, John?" Knox and Bunny had been joined by a short, studious looking man who was, once again, named John and for whose benefit Knox repeated the question.

"I have just been asked, why other countries aren't Presbyterian?"

"Ah, that is a good question," the new John concurred before offering Bunny a soft handshake and introducing himself as John Foxe. Knox joined him in the introductions.

"John and I met in Frankfurt a few years ago. He was hiding out there during Bloody Mary's reign," Knox explained.

"Bloody Mary?" Bunny asked for clarity.

"Bloody Mary. The former Queen of England, Catholic and bloodthirsty. Most of the reformers had to escape to the continent otherwise they would have had the same fate as…" Knox waved his hand at Foxe in a gesture to encourage him to finish his sentence.

Foxe duly obliged in a faltering academic style,

"Ah well, too many to name really, but if pressed I would have to say, by way of example, the same fate as Nicholas Ridley, Hugh Latimer and Thomas Cranmer."[1]

Knox leaned over to Bunny and whispered loudly enough to ensure that Foxe could clearly hear him,

"And he knows that because he is writing a history of martyrs."

"Foxe's Book of Martyrs," Bunny blurted out with a satisfied tone of recollection.

"It is *not* my Book of Martyrs; I keep telling everyone." Foxe sounded genuinely irritated at the mistitling of his planned work. "It is to be called *The Actes and Monuments*."[2]

"But everyone is going to call it…" Bunny decided to not complete the sentence for fear of further infuriating the author.

Knox came to the rescue, steering the conversation back to Bunny's question.

"The Church in most countries will need State protection if they are to resist Catholic turnover but that is nae issue up here in Scotland, especially now that our own Catholic Queen Mary is living in France with her fifteen-year-old husband, the heir to the French throne."

---

[1] Bishops Nicholas Ridley and Hugh Latimer together with Thomas Cranmer, Archbishop of Canterbury and the author of the Book of Common Prayer, were all martyred in Oxford during the reign of the Catholic Mary I of England. Burned at the stake Latimer is famously quoted as having encouraged Ridley with the words: "Be of good comfort, and play the man, Master Ridley; we shall this day light such a candle, by God's grace, in England, as I trust shall never be put out."

[2] 'Foxe's Book of Martyrs' or as it is more properly entitled 'The Actes and Monuments of these Latter and Perillous Days, Touching Matters of the Church' was written by John Foxe and published in 1563. Its 1800 pages list every Christian (specifically Protestant) martyr from antiquity to that day, many with detailed wood-carved illustrations. Laws passed in 1571 meant that it was to be placed (literally chained) in every prominent place of worship in England. Several extended editions have been published since Foxe's death in 1587.

"And she is unlikely to return any time soon," Foxe added, "now that she has said she fears the prayers of John Knox more than the army of ten thousand men!"[1]

Knox laughed before continuing, pointing at Foxe,

"And because you English now have a Protestant Queen."

"That would be Elizabeth?" Bunny asked. Neither of the men answered what was to them an obvious fact. Bunny desperately wanted to know how deep the Reformation had taken hold in England and, more importantly, about the origins of the Church of England. She explained that she had been overseas for many years and would they mind bringing her up to date.

"Well, where do we start?" Knox said. Foxe knew exactly.

"England has been swinging backwards and forwards for the last thirty years. Henry VIII split from the Pope so he could marry Anne Boleyn, but he didn't want to change the Church at all. When he died his son, young King Edward VI, on the other hand, removed all the images of saints from churches; altars were replaced with tables; he allowed the clergy to marry, and insisted that services must be in English not Latin, and had his archbishop compose a book of services that they all needed to follow."

"So, England is reformed?" Bunny asked.

"Not really," Knox said before Foxe continued.

"When Edward died his half-sister Mary, Bloody Mary, became queen and reversed everything Edward had done. English Bibles were removed from churches; the clergy were forcibly separated from their wives, and out of nowhere all the old Catholic furniture, icons and vestments suddenly reappeared from their hiding places. Hundreds were executed, most of us fled the country or went into hiding."

"So, England is Catholic now?" Bunny asked.

"No, not really," Knox again said before Foxe continued.

"It would have been if Mary had an heir, but she too died suddenly, allowing her half-sister Elizabeth, Protestant Elizabeth, to take the throne."

"Has everything swung back to where Edward had it?"

"Strangely not. Elizabeth appears to be positioning the Church halfway between the two extremes. While she has overturned much of mainstream

---

[1] Dr. Marcus Serven published at www.genevanfoundation.com on February 15, 2016.

Catholic doctrine, some of Mary's changes to church services have been allowed to remain: priests continue to wear vestments, the confirmation service has continued despite it being a purely Catholic sacrament, church attendance is being made mandatory and you will have to pay a fine if you don't attend. However, she has no desire to enforce any form of personal belief, so rich Catholics will simply pay the fine."

"This sounds like a huge compromise," Bunny conceded.

"It will keep the peace in England, but at the price of true reformation. We have heard that she wants conformity not passion in her new so-called Anglican Church."

The moment Foxe said *Anglican* Bunny was cut to the quick in the realisation that her beloved Church had been born out of compromise. Knox jumped in,

"But don't worry, lass. If she disnae have an heir then our King James will inherit the English throne and bring with him the Presbyterian Church of Scotland into England, aye that would be a glorious day." Foxe agreed.

"Yes, it would certainly be memorable."

Bunny knew that James would indeed unite the two thrones, and yet the Anglican Church that she grew up in seemed to have bishops and archbishops, in no way Presbyterian. She thanked the two Johns for their helpful insights, explaining that she really ought to be getting to England to see what is happening there.

"If you want to know," Foxe said, "you'll need to go to Hampton Court. I think you'll have plenty of time to get there."

"Are you both coming too?" she asked.

"No, we have to stay here, this is for you alone," Foxe answered.

As he said it, Bunny recalled hearing that exact phrase before. Hadn't Calvin said the same thing to her as she left Geneva? Then she realised the inescapable truth. In travelling to Hampton Court time would inevitably move forward again. She looked at Knox, the firebrand Scottish reformer, and Foxe of *Book of Martyrs* fame, and felt a deep sadness well-up inside her, knowing by the time she arrived at her next destination these men would probably both be dead.[1]

---

[1] Both men died peacefully, John Knox in 1572, John Foxe in 1587, several years before the 1604 Hampton Court Conference

Chapter 10

THE HAMPTON COURT CONFERENCE

Chris was in no mood to simply wait for her to turn up. As far as he knew she might be dead. Having been given this second chance, he was going to take decisive action to find the woman he cared for. He stood in the doorway of the church looking at the rain and made the call he knew he had to.

"Emergency, which service do you require?"

It had been many years since Chris had last dialled 999 – that was to request an ambulance for the motorcyclist who had crashed into the garden wall at the front of his parents' house. That call was exciting but this time he was so anxious he garbled that he wanted the police and gave his name and mobile number, before being connected to the duty officer. Chris paused before saying that he wanted to report a missing person. The female officer then courteously and efficiently began a series of carefully structured questions designed to risk-assess this report. As Chris gave his answers, he couldn't help but think that each answer was reinforcing the idea that he was worrying over nothing and that she would probably just *turn-up* after all.

"No, she wasn't a child; No, she hadn't been drinking; No, she wasn't a drug user; No, she wasn't involved with any gangs; No, she wasn't in a violent domestic relationship; No, she had never gone missing before; No, she wasn't in a depressed mental state."

At this answer, Chris momentarily considered outlining the details of their last conversation and how she had left, not so much depressed as angry with him. But before he could speak, the officer asked for the circumstances of her disappearance. Chris described the unusual location, the discarded mobile phone and the bloodstain. Eventually, the officer explained that whilst the apparent blood was concerning, she didn't think that sufficient time had elapsed for the police to take any specific action, that Chris should perhaps ask around to known friends and family and that he should contact them again in the morning if she still hadn't surfaced.

It was going to be up to him. He started with friends and family. Chris at least had Bunny's phone and scrolled through to find the last calls made. She was not a frequent caller as the last ten dialled numbers spanned several days. He was delighted to see that his own number represented four of the ten. Two of the others were to her mother. Chris had met Mrs. Elstow, also a regular at All Saints', several times before and didn't hesitate to press dial.

"Hello darling, you are calling late," came the unexpectedly familiar answer. Chris then realised that Bunny's mother must have her daughter's mobile number on caller I.D. and she could see he was calling from her phone.

"Sorry Mrs. Elstow, this is Christian Palmer," he explained much to the delight of the elderly widow who was always pleased to have someone to talk to. Chris interrupted her to say, "I have found Johan's phone and was wondering if she is with you." Her mother said that her daughter wasn't, so he put her mind at rest, wished her a good night and hung up.

The remaining calls were to the church office, her dentist and a mobile he didn't recognise. He had no idea who else to call so stood in the church doorway, raindrops wetting the bottom half of his Levi jeans, and prayed for direction. If anyone could help him find her, surely it was God.

Bunny had visited Hampton Court Palace once before, as a young girl on a school trip. Standing outside the building in its heyday, rather than as a dormant tourist attraction, was very different. As the main English royal court there was a continual bustle of people moving in and out of the palace. Soldiers stood sentry, carts arrived with provisions, bishops and clerics talked amongst themselves, and immediately in front, three men looked expectantly at her.

"Have you come to add your name to the petition, Madam?" one asked.

Being in her thirties, Bunny was a woman at the awkward age of being somewhere between a *Miss* and a *Madam*. She didn't usually feel offended if greeted as *Madam*, she had sadly become used to that address, but would always try to correct that her status as firmly *Miss* at the first appropriate opportunity. This was especially important to her when, as in this case, the other person was male and of a similar age. The three men who stood in front of her – one in his late-twenties the others perhaps mid-thirties – were all dressed completely in black, except for overly-sized, off-white collars. A very distinctive fashion, she thought. The youngest of them held several large sheets of bound paper covered with many black-inked names each written in elaborate cursive script.

"You must have hundreds of signatures there, Mister...?" she answered noncommittally, requesting as she did, their names.

"Sorry Madam, my name is William Brewster, and this is my friend Richard Clyfton, Rector of All Saints' Church, Babworth, and over there is John Smyth the Vicar of Gainsborough."

Clyfton placed his papers carefully next to the inkwell on the small wooden table that stood beside them before also offering a simple soft handshake.

"We have come down from Nottinghamshire to present this petition to the new King."

"And we have nearly one thousand names already," Brewster added with a smile.[1]

"It is *Miss*, by the way, *Miss* Bunny Elstow." Satisfied that she had managed to give the requisite correction she shook Clyfton's hand and continued the conversation.

"And what is the petition about?"

"It is about the purification of the Church of England, now that the blessed King James has inherited the throne," he explained. "We follow the rules laid out in the Bible for running our church. We gather for prayer and reading the Bible and singing the songs of David, so we expect the King to do away with the awful compromises the old Queen had tolerated."[2]

Bunny smiled, remembering how John Knox had dreamt of such a transformation, seemingly minutes ago. Forty-four minutes ago, to be precise, as her watch now displayed 16:04.

"That does sound like a positive step, but what exactly needs to be purified?" she asked.

Clyfton shuffled through his papers to find the petition's top sheet with the text of their demands. Demands, she read, that were being presented to the King by his *humble and obedient servants*. The list covered, what the signatories considered to be, the seven most intolerable compromises in the English Church.

First was the making of the sign of the cross during baptism; second the confirmation service. This felt a little uncomfortable to Bunny as she had been confirmed in her faith as a teenager. Next was the administration of baptism to

---

[1] The so-called Millenary Petition, as it had one thousand signatures, was orchestrated by unknown Puritan sympathisers and not specifically Clyfton or Brewster.

[2] "We follow the rules laid out in the Bible for running our church" and "We gather for prayer and reading the Bible and singing the songs of David." are both widely attributed to William Brewster.

children by midwives, then the wearing of *rings of marriage*. She had no idea that the wearing of a wedding ring was ever a contentious religious issue. The final three related to kneeling at the altar rail; the wearing of vestments; and the practice where some ministers were paid multiple times for each of the parishes they oversaw, making it a money-making activity for them and their patrons.

Having read the list, Bunny was more confused than before. She didn't like the idea that the Anglican Church has been founded on a compromise, but now some of the things that had been singled out as unendurable she either held dear or at least didn't have a problem with. She decided to change the subject.

"When do you plan to present it to His Majesty?" she asked.

They explained that the King had already received the list of demands and was due to debate them with his bishops at today's conference at Hampton Court. The men were clearly excited at the expected outcome, not only because they had collected so many signatures, but also, they were three of a select few Puritans invited to attend proceedings.[1] The three men bade Bunny a good day and disappeared inside. She made herself comfortable on a low wall, to await their return.

"No need for a miracle..." said Rector Mashman, who was of the opinion that given enough time an equitable solution would surface, concluding, "...provided we all just get along."

In his younger days as a curate to an inner-city parish he was a fiery radical. He remembered leading several banner-strewn marches through the streets, preaching passionately and waving his Bible at the crowd, as much the Billy Graham as any. He knew he had changed a lot since those days. He was in his mid-thirties when his name was put forward for consideration for the tenure of Rector of All Saints', a position which also had responsibility over three neighbouring parishes. As a hard-working curate this was the sort of stress-free posting or *living* that he would dream of on a cold Friday night whilst ministering to drunken teenagers in the city centre. He had assumed that the selection process would be executed entirely within the ecclesiastical structure of the

---

[1] Brewster and Clyfton were the leaders of the separatist group that eventually sailed to America on the Mayflower to establish a religious colony. Neither of them personally attended the Hampton Court Conference but were acutely affected by its outcome.

Church of England. He was unaware that the benefice of All Saints', like many others, was under the patronage of a secular institution or landowner, in this case one Lord Advowson.

The Advowson family owned an extensive country estate including most of the parish land and consequently he, or more accurately his title, had the historical right to nominate the Rector. Without his support no one could be inducted by the Church hierarchy. His church-going forebears had executed this duty with admirable reverence, but the present incumbent was an affirmed atheist. Young Mashman could recall how, at their first meeting, Lord Advowson had enthralled him with the historical importance of his seat - Brennan Hall, the beauty and peacefulness of the parish, and the lavish rectory whose redecoration he had *personally overseen*. The impressionable Mashman was so completely overawed that when the minor noble explained his *terms*, he could do no more than acquiesce. The position was too tempting to turn down, particularly as Mashman's wife was expecting their first child. In accepting Lord Advowson's patronage Mashman had agreed to lay down his youthful passion and adopt the inclusive, non-confrontational, watered-down religion that his patron insisted upon. Mashman never considered that this was compromise, simply that he was *maturing* into the peace-making role expected of him by his Church. The Advowson family not only owned this country seat but also several acres of central London, an historic investment that ensured they would remain exceptionally wealthy. When the title passed to the next generation Mashman maintained the wishes of his appointee despite the present Lord, his wife and their socialite daughter Velia being semi-regular attendees of services, occupying the family pew on the second row. Over the thirty-five years of his tenure Mashman was satisfied that he had been true to his word, accommodating every expression of Anglicanism. The formality and liturgy of high church services; the depth of midweek Bible studies; and the wide inclusion of anyone who crossed his threshold, with no need to challenge their beliefs or their lifestyle. Peace at all costs was the Anglican way he considered and today was no exception.

"Gentlemen. Brothers and sister, I have been thinking," he began. "We are decided that we want to present Christ to our town." Everyone concurred, he was on safe ground. "The only issue is how we do it."

No one nodded this time, despite all assenting to the obvious. The Rector pulled onto his knee an oversized black leather-backed Bible and thumbed through the wafer-thin pages mumbling as he did. Instinctively several others reached for theirs, Artur opened the Bible app on his phone. The clergyman looked up once he had found the passage he was seeking.

"Ah, here I have it. John chapter thirteen and verse thirty-five. 'By this shall all men know ye are my disciples, if ye have love one to another.'"[1]

He didn't need to have his Bible open to quote the passage which he knew by heart, as did most of the others. The act of opening the Scripture was more authoritatively symbolic than textually necessary. He looked intently at the faces of his fellow leaders and repeated the passage, this time more slowly and stopping to emphasise the central *if*. He then concluded,

"As I read this verse, brothers, it appears to me that the *only* way that people will accept anything from us next year is *if* we can demonstrate Christian love for each other."

"And how are we going to do that?" came the riposte, although he didn't know from whom.

Bunny could tell by their faces that it had not gone well. As the three men approached, she knew her moment of tranquillity was over. She chose not to rise to greet them but instead let them collapse haphazard around her. Brewster sat down slowly on the wall next to her, Clyfton dropped himself face-down onto the grass releasing a decisive, Urgh as he landed, Smyth took to the turf, cross-legged and leaning against a small tree. All sat in silence until Brewster eventually broke into their thoughts.

"I cannot believe that King James," he began, "actually said he *liked* the less extreme, passive, middle-way exhibited by the Anglican Church and refused to introduce the Scottish Presbyterian structure."

They murmured in painful agreement.

"What was it he said about elephants?" Smyth asked.

"It was because we said it was wrong to kneel at the altar rail," Brewster explained. "He said, 'Do you think God will have us worship him like elephants, as if we had no joints in our knees?'"[2]

"It was the way he reacted to the word *presbytery* that surprised me." Smyth said, still in shock.

---

[1] John chapter 13 verse 35. King James Version

[2] The, 'King James Bible 1611' by Rev G.D. Campbell, St Andrew's Presbyterian Church, Blackrock published by Saint Patrick's Cathedral Dublin, 13 March 2011

"Yeah, me too," agreed Clyfton. He then stood to his feet, cleared his throat and gave a convincing impression of King James pronouncing that,

"Presbytery agrees as well with monarchy as God and the devil!" ending with the King's decree, "No bishop, no King!"[1]

No one laughed at his accurate depiction. Each understanding that the King's reaction was borne out of a fear that a bottom-up Church structure would undermine his supposed *God-given* authority to appoint only bishops that agreed with him. The King's fear of being over-ruled was emphasised when he had said, "Jack and Tom and Will and Dick shall meet and at their pleasure shall dare to censor me!"[2]

"And as for the petition, agreeing to outlaw baptism by midwives was a small token," Brewster added.

Smyth agreed. "There is little point in us even staying in this country. I have to agree with my friend Thomas who has been saying for some time that we need to leave and find another group that shares our convictions."

"Where will you go to?" Brewster enquired.

"I have heard that the Dutch state is more open to religious freedom than most others," Smyth mused.

Bunny was about to disagree, remembering the conversation she'd had with Dirk Willems as they rode together back to his prison and recalling his likely fate - but she decided to remain quiet.

"Yes, I spent some time in the Netherlands when I was a diplomatic assistant there," Brewster added. "The Dutch state is much more tolerant to the reformed church."

"Perhaps we should move there too." Clyfton's voice was only just audible as he spoke directly into the grass. He repeated himself on Brewster's request.

"I was thinking that if we did move it would be to the New World," Brewster confessed.

At that, Clyfton turned his face to look at him. He then sat up properly on the lawn and asked Brewster directly, "Are you serious?"

"I am," he conceded with a sigh. "There is nothing for us in England anymore. Today has convinced me that the compromise in the Church of

---

[1] ibid.

[2] Attributed to King James by Michael Reeves in 'The English Reformation and the Puritans'

England is going to continue. There is no place for pure believers here. We are being exiled from our own land."

"Do you mean just me and you?" Clyfton asked for clarity.

"No," Brewster answered immediately with an amused laugh, clearly having given the subject much thought. "I mean the whole congregation at Scrooby, or at least all of those willing to go."[1]

"I can't see many of them disagreeing," Clyfton said. "They are already paying hefty fines for meeting in your manor house ever since we were evicted from my church."[2]

"It's the same story at Gainsborough," Smyth added. "I am sure most of the congregation are ready to leave."

"Perhaps we should try Holland first," Clyfton suggested looking directly at Brewster. "And then if that doesn't work out, we can find somewhere else, somewhere... further afield." The thought of traveling across the Atlantic, and presumably not coming back, wasn't sitting well with Clyfton. Netherlands felt like a much more attractive option.

"That's decided then," Smyth said conclusively. "If you two are taking your congregation to the Netherlands then Thomas and I will bring ours as well."

Brewster nodded enthusiastically, Clyfton looked less sure. Brewster then tuned to Bunny.

"Will you join us Madam, er, Miss?" he said correcting himself.

"I would love to come; in fact, I have been there recently and met some... but I am not sure they will still be …. around," she faltered reflecting on the mortality of those whom she had just met.

"Yes, I will sail back to the Netherlands with you," she concluded emphatically. As they began to leave the palace grounds Bunny asked, "Was it a complete failure today?" The only real positive they admitted was that the King had agreed to authorise a new English translation of the Bible.

"Which he will no doubt have the audacity to name after himself," Brewster added with contempt.

"The King James Version," Bunny repeated in recognition. A murmur of disdain filled the air.

---

[1] Much of the church at Scrooby did indeed relocate to the Netherlands before setting sail to establish the Plymouth Colony. Clyfton however died in the Netherlands.

[2] Whilst in Nottinghamshire, the church met in Brewster's manor house rather than the parish church.

"Aye, and I predict there is going to be fireworks soon as a consequence." Clyfton concluded.[1]

No sooner than he had finished his prayer, Chris noticed someone appearing to be waving at him from across the street. Chris pointed to his own chest to confirm that the figure was indeed beckoning him. They nodded. He flipped up the hood of his coat, checked for traffic and strode over to the illuminated entrance porch of the flats opposite. As he approached the functionally spartan lobby, the silhouetted person opened the door and ushered him inside out of the storm.

"I've been watching you," the grey-haired man said.

Throughout Chris's church ministry he had spent time with all classes of humanity. He knew many families who were scraping-by on state benefits and this individual bore all the obvious hallmarks of being in that position. Chris could also see the less-obvious indications that he was a drug user.

"I've seens it all I have, me," the scruffy man repeated, his accent revealing both a lack of education and his out-of-townness. Chris wasn't going to be taken in by what may be an addict's clumsy attempt at asking for money.

"What have you seen, my friend?" Chris asked.

"I've seens it all, the woman and the van, I have," he answered intriguingly.

"What woman?" Chris asked.

"The woman in the grey coat."

"Grey coat?" Chris was now attentive. The man continued.

"I thought it funny cos she's got like only one glove, see. And I goes over to see if she had dropped the other after they'd gone."

"After who'd gone?" Chris was transfixed on every word the man said.

"Them in the van, I telled ya," he said exasperatedly.

"Wait a minute, let me get this right. Are you saying that the lady in the grey coat, with the one glove got into a van earlier this evening?"

"S'what I said!" The man gave out a cough and rubbed his arms for warmth. Chris had seen this signal many times before, it was used as a subtle way of signifying that they felt cold, immediately prior to asking for some money. For once Chris thought this may be money well spent and reached into his trouser pocket to find two pounds in loose change and placed them in the man's

---

[1] The following year saw the foiled Catholic plot to execute King James with gunpowder, an event commemorated in England annually on November 5th with bonfires and fireworks.

hand. Despite uttering the required, "Fanks guv," his look was sufficiently disdainful for Chris to see he may need to part with more. Monetarily lubricated, the eyewitness continued.

"Not got in the van, more carried in."

"You saw someone carry the lady into the van?" Chris asked, the man now shuffling from one foot to the other, nodded. "Was she..." Chris swallowed hard, "Was she struggling with them?"

"Not them, just one man," he answered whilst looking at the floor. "An' no she was like sleeping. He carries her to the passenger side and puts her in, seat-belt and all, then drives off."

Chris's worst fears were suddenly coming true. But what was he to do with this new information? Should he call the police, would they consider this man to be a reliable witness? He did know about the one glove though. Or maybe he was making it all up. As all of this rushed around Chris's mind, the man held out his hand containing the two pound coins that admittedly did look like meagre payment for information supplied. Chris reached for his wallet and began to slide out a five-pound note. As he did, the stranger tempted Chris with what he knew was going to be crucial information.

"I mights know the van," he stammered.

"What do you mean?" Chris asked.

"I mights be able to remember the name on the van." The man's focus was squarely on the wallet. "But my memory...you know... and it is so cold and wet."

Chris had to decide. Was he being played by an experienced drug user or did the man really have information that could lead to Bunny? Chris's instincts would usually be to walk away at this point, but not tonight, not in this pursuit. After all, he had no other clue as to where she was. Chris replaced the fiver, pulling out instead the only higher denomination note he had, a crisp new twenty-pound note. The man's eyes opened wide.

"Tell me everything you know, and I mean everything, and this is yours," Chris demanded, now feeling that he had the upper hand.

The lure of ten times the financial incentive was enough for the whole story to be regurgitated. Chris heard how the man had been looking out of the window in his upstairs flat when he saw a woman in a grey coat enter the church as the rain started. Then how a little while later a man entered on foot and how he ran back out, down the High Street before returning in a small white van, stopping half on the pavement with its hazard warning lights flashing, exactly as Chris's car was currently parked. Then he heard how the woman was carried out by this man and placed carefully in the passenger seat before they drove off at speed. Finally, he revealed that the name on the side of the van was Sam Goode.

"Thank you, Lord," Chris said under his breath as he extinguished the hazard warning lights in his illegally parked vehicle, before adding a thoughtful, "I think."

Chapter 11

All of Bunny's physical senses were reacting violently to her environment, although she tried her dignified best not to let it show. It was a small, dark confined living space, barely ten-feet square. The cold stone floor was glistening, dampened with condensation from the five people that called this room, together with its cramped upstairs chambers, their home. The limited light that broke into the gloom burrowed through two small leaded windows. A man stood silhouetted by the dim light, reading a heavy book and making occasional notes on parchments balanced on the small window ledge. As her eyes grew accustomed to the low light, she could discern that the man was a slightly older William Brewster. The large mediaeval fireplace also served as cooking stove, and the lady of the house was busy preparing supper. The unnecessary source of heat made the room uncomfortably hot. The most incongruous sight was that, despite the limited space, one entire end of the room was dominated by a weaver's loom. Bunny had seen a similar machine when as a child she had visited her wealthy aunt who lived in a house so large there were several such antique machines dotted around the numerous landings and hallways. She would lose herself for hours in an imaginary world of domestic servitude playing on a vintage spinning wheel, mangle, washing dolly, treadle sewing machine and loom. This machine, however, was no decorative curio. It was a full-sized manpowered machine, and the man powering it was an uncomfortably sweaty teenager. He didn't look happy and neither did his mother, and to be honest neither was Bunny. The repetitive click-clack of textile production, the damp heat, and the gloom were oppressive. Bunny made her way over to the door and stepped outside.

Two things happened to her simultaneously, and it was difficult to assess which of these was worse. Firstly, the crowds. The narrow walkway directly outside the room was full of busy people. Half were determined to progress to the left, the rest were equally resolute on going the opposite way. Without intending, she was immediately captured by the haphazard crowd and, face-to-face with infuriated Dutch people, she was bustled and jostled first one way then the next. Her unintended progress, she thought, must look like a microscopic particle subjected to Brownian Motion, as she recalled from a high-school physics experiment. Secondly, was the smell. At the end of the walkway was one of the many canals that interlaced most Dutch towns, and Leiden was no exception. But to describe it as a canal would be misleading – an open sewer would be more accurate. Bunny instinctively tried to raise her hand to cover her nose, but the crush made any upper body movement difficult. The stench was so overpowering that she forced her left arm free and to her relief clasped her nostrils between thumb and forefinger. This helped but the pervading odour was beginning to make her retch. She really didn't want to vomit onto the shoulder of an innocent passer-by, so took the more sensible option to head back indoors. Now she had a preferred direction of travel and joined the melee tactically using her left elbow to plough a course towards the side of the alley and then to slide towards the doorway. Arriving at the wall of Brewster's house she noticed the street name. The sign read *Stincksteeg*. She knew no Dutch but that didn't need any translation; William Brewster lived, appropriately enough, on Stink Street![1]

"Come back inside, ducky my love." Mrs. Brewster had watched her lack of progress and ushered her inside with a firm heave. She shut the door firmly behind them and replaced a heavy roll of fabric across the gap at the bottom of the door, sealing them in from the malodorous local environment.

"Thanks," Bunny said to her hardworking hostess adding, "That quite took my breath away."

"This place stinks!" Mrs. Brewster said firmly. Whilst she said this in response to Bunny, her comment was nevertheless directed towards her husband. Their eldest son Jonathan had just finished working and the loom had now fallen silent just in time for her message to punctuate the calm. Bunny could sense the domestic tension rising. Rather than make eye contact with either of them she occupied herself firstly readjusting her clothes that had been pulled out of position by the throng, then by looking at her watch. It read 16:11. Mister Brewster said nothing and continued his reading.

"And how exactly are we to demonstrate love for each other?" Rector Mashman began to formulate an answer and took a deep unsubtle breath to signify he was about to deliver an important point. Everyone looked at him expectantly, only to see him ultimately let out a slow, laboured exhalation. He may as well have shrugged his shoulders; he had no answer.

---

[1] William Brewster and his family lived in Stincksteeg, Leiden, which translated literally means Stink Street

Ralph's phone vibrated in his pocket; the ringtone may have been switched off, but the vibration was loud enough to make everyone look at him. He slid the offending device from his pocket, offering a pained smile as he did. The display read: Chris Palmer Mobile.

"I'd better take this, it's Chris," he said as he stood to his feet and took the couple of steps towards the door.

"Hi Chris, have you found Bunny?" Ralph asked with a smile as he placed his hand on the door handle. As he listened, he became so distracted that he failed to turn the door handle and exit the room; standing frozen in that pose, much to the chagrin of Rector Mashman who had seen an opportunity to make his own exit for a much-needed toilet break. The Rector was not one to tap anyone on their shoulder to ask them to move out of the way but the combined effect of the earlier weak tea, his now vertical state, and the fact he had told himself he could go, conspired to force him to give the polite, 'Ahem,' of excuse me. Ralph quickly released his grasp of the handle and let the cleric pass. The group could see that Ralph's expression had turned into one of concern.

"What's happened?" Quaker Rex asked him as the call ended.

"Chris has found Bunny's phone at St. Mary's," he answered.

"St. Mary's?" more than one stated incredulously.

"Yes, St. Mary's. But that is not the main thing. There is some blood there and Chris spoke to someone who says he saw someone... but he isn't sure if he was telling the truth or just after some money...but Chris says he'll have to follow it up... and the police won't do anything until the morning." Ralph did his best to deliver a précis of the call but only raised more questions.

"What do you mean someone who saw someone?" Joel asked for clarification.

"Ah. Chris spoke to someone who says he saw someone carry a woman into a van and drive away," Ralph explained.

"Oh my!" Thea said, covering her mouth.

"And does he know if it was Bunny?" Joel pressed.

"That's the thing. He isn't sure, but he is going to find the van," Ralph said.

The Rector returned from his bathroom break and trying to catch up asked, "What van is that?"

"Bunny has been bundled into the back of a van, kidnapped." Joel said over-exaggerating.

"Goodly heavens above!" Mashman said, nearly fainting.

"No-one said kidnapped," Artur clarified.

99

"That's right," Ralph interrupted as he and Rex spun a chair over for the Rector. "There'll be a logical explanation. I can't immediately think of one but let's not jump to conclusions."

"No, no, it is quite right, quite right," the Rector said breathlessly as he lowered himself into the padded meeting room chair. Then, to everyone's surprise, continued, "She'll have been kidnapped, I knew it, I told her something bad was going to happen."

A momentary solemn silence muted the room.

"What do you mean, Rector?" Rex asked, verbalising everyone's thoughts.

"It was that lorry load of aid we sent to Kurdistan," he said cryptically. Over the late summer months his church had sent an aid mission to help the Kurds in Eastern Turkey. Bunny was, unsurprisingly, the person who not only co-ordinated this annual mercy mission but also expertly managed to get most of the church leaders present to contribute. Some donated blankets, tents, simple medicines, toiletries, tinned food, or bottled water while others contributed financially. It was part of Bunny's charm to be able to get such an uncooperative group to park their differences and collaborate for the sake of a worthy cause. And it was partially the success of this venture that gave her the impetus to seek to engineer a unity event next Easter, something she later considered may have been a step too far.

"But what about it?" Ralph asked.

The Rector then explained that three weeks ago the church had received a threatening letter from a group that called themselves the Grey Wolves of Islam, accusing the church of being an agent of the government and sending military intelligence, propaganda and weapons disguised as aid. In faltering words Rector Mashman explained that the letter ended with the ominous threat that 'vengeance would be taken.'

"The little..." Jack Fort blurted out loudly in his fiery Northern Irish twang. His Presbyterian church had fully supported the mission, he himself having done some of the driving on a previous trip several years ago.

"Did you tell the police, Rector?"

"No, we didn't. I wanted to but Bunny insisted it was nothing to worry about. I told her, I told her something bad might happen, but she was adamant that it was nothing."

"Well, we must tell the police now," Joel stated emphatically. A statement joined by multiple murmurs of agreement.

"But Ralph," Artur asked, "didn't Chris say that the police won't do anything?"

"That's right, not until the morning," Ralph confirmed.

"Do they know about this letter? No, they don't, and we need to tell them," Joel rightly countered, but before anyone could comment Artur spoke again.

"But you said that Chris was going to find the van. How is he going to find it?" Artur's clear logical approach had led him to an obvious question.

"Ah yes," the leader of C.R.F remembered the final piece of information and the whole reason for Chris's call.

"He asked if anyone knows of a white van, a tradesman perhaps, of the name Sam Goode."

Many shoulders were shrugged but one female voice spoke.

"Sam Goode?"

Ralph turned toward her and nodded.

"Sam Goode the plasterer?" she expanded.

"Time to get ready for your tea," Mrs. Brewster announced.

Her son clambered out from behind the loom and washed his hands in a small metal basin whose grey-coloured water indicated it had already been used for that purpose several times previously. To the relief of both Bunny and Mr. Brewster the outside door opened, sliding the roll of fabric that provided a makeshift seal with it; in came John Smyth.

"Hello again, Miss." He greeted Bunny politely before turning his attention to the man of the house. Brewster offered Smyth the only comfortable chair in the squalid room, whilst he manoeuvred the wooden stool his son had been using at the loom and seated himself opposite his guest.

"John," Brewster began, "it is good to see you again. It must have been three years since we sailed from England together."[1]

"Indeed, my friend, and so much has happened since then," Smyth replied taking his seat.

"Forgive me, may I offer you something?" Brewster looked at his wife expectant that she would take his lead and provide the required hospitality. His wife however glared back at her husband with an angry stare and pursed lips.

---

[1] Despite originating from nearby parishes in the east of England, and making the same journey, the groups led by Smyth and Brewster did not travel to the Netherlands together.

Given the tense climate, Bunny fully expected that the courtesy would be met with 'And you can get it yourself,' but to her surprise Mrs. Brewster visibly morphed into the epitome of wifely subservience. This must be the Puritan way, thought Bunny, knowing she would never make a good Puritan wife; she would *have* to speak my mind. Smyth declined any refreshment and asked his host,

"How are you finding it here, William?"

"We find that it's quite acceptable here," Brewster replied. As he said it his wife slammed the lid on one of the saucepans she was attending to. Smyth looked startled; Brewster got the message.

"That's more like it my girl," Bunny whispered to herself.

"When I say acceptable, perhaps I should qualify that sentiment, rather." Brewster glanced at his wife before continuing, "The freedom to worship as we choose is wonderful, it was the reason we came to Leiden. And the fact I can teach in the university and have access to a printing press are real blessings, and…"

Mary Brewster dropped a ladle loudly into an empty pot, much to Bunny's amusement. Her husband changed tack.

"To be honest John, life here is not pleasant at all. The only work most of our congregation can get is as textile workers." He nodded across the small room towards the weaving machine looming in the corner. "The pay is poor, so the housing we can get is, well… you know." Smyth nodded in sympathy.

"We are very much in the same situation," his visitor contributed to an increasingly negative air. "Yes, we are free to practise adult baptism, but there is no life for us here. We are country folk; we miss the fields and animals of Lincolnshire. This town life is busy, dirty, grimy, noisy…"

"And smelly," Bunny added uninvited.

Suddenly the door opened again and in ran two boys laughing and shouting excitedly in Dutch. Bunny assumed they were two local street urchins and felt a sense of anxiety, but when they were greeted by a huge maternal hug by Mrs. Brewster, she knew these must be two more Brewster boys.

"English! English! boys," their father said sternly. "And that is another problem, John, our children are turning Dutch."

"Yes, ours too," Smyth agreed. "But it isn't just the language, it's that the Dutch are…" he searched for the word, "…they are a bit too…"

"Liberal?" Brewster offered.

"Exactly!" Smyth agreed. "They accept things that are just not Puritan, and the longer our people stay here the more I fear we will lose our distinctiveness."

Brewster repeated back to Smyth his phrase,

"The longer our people stay." Then added, "It sounds as though you are thinking of leaving."

"We are, well my co-leader Thomas Helwys is going back first, I will stay around for a while and will follow later."

"Back? To England?" Brewster was surprised.

"Yes, to England. Better we take the consequences there than live like peasants here. And another thing..." Smyth leaned towards Brewster and dropped his tone. Brewster leaned closer to hear.

"And Thomas has gained a bit of a reputation with the Dutch authorities. They are threatening to arrest him."

"Why, what crime has he committed?"

"Well, it is all of us. We have all committed, not a crime, but committed something to paper, '*A Declaration of Faith of English People Remaining at Amsterdam in Holland.*'[1] It is our confession of faith; we have documented the core beliefs that our group shares. It amounts to some twenty-seven statements."

"How interesting." The scholarly Brewster looked genuinely intrigued. It was something that the group led by Clyfton and himself had not, as yet, even considered.

"Yes, it is interesting, but a few things have not gone down well with the Dutch Reformed Church," Smyth explained.

"What specifically?"

"Well, when all of us dissenters came over from England, our forty or so from Gainsborough went to Amsterdam, your Nottinghamshire group settled here in Leiden. How many are you?" Smyth asked.

"Just over a hundred," Brewster said with pride.

"Well, we decided to use the time to allow God to shape our understanding of Scripture and to formulate what we actually believed."

---

[1] 'A Declaration of Faith of English People Remaining at Amsterdam in Holland', or as it is sometimes known, the Helwys Confession of 1611, is considered to be one of the foundational documents of the Baptist faith.

Brewster nodded, unsure as to whether Smyth's comments were meant as an insult directed at the group that he, Clyfton and another former Church of England minister, John Robinson, now led. Smyth continued.

"Three of the twenty-seven statements are a little, shall we say, controversial." At this, Brewster raised his eyebrows.

"Firstly, we have taken on board the teachings of an old Dutch theologian, one Jacobus Arminius." Smyth carefully expressed the unusual name, ensuring the correct pronunciation. Brewster had no idea who this was, but Bunny immediately recognised the name.

"Oh, you mean Arminianism," she contributed excitedly.

They both looked at her surprised that a woman would be joining in their semi-private conversation, let alone to claim to have some understanding on the matter. Bunny's indignancy got the better of her so she launched into a definitive statement of the Arminian doctrine.

"Arminianism states that people have freewill to accept God's grace and that salvation is not *predestined* as John Calvin had taught." Bunny enjoyed emphasising predestined, to show her knowledge. Smyth looked amazed at the accurate and succinct explanation. Brewster just looked shocked at the interruption.

"Yes, that is right," Smyth conceded before quickly addressing Brewster saying, "Now, I don't expect you to agree but our group is settled on that doctrine." Brewster said nothing.

"Secondly, we have come to know a small group, somewhat outsiders but they have introduced us to the idea that infant baptism is not scriptural."

"Do you mean the Mennonites?" Bunny added once again, now revelling in her foreknowledge. Both men stared at her, forcing her to be the first to speak. She fumbled her memory to add whatever she could.

"They are pacifist Anabaptists, which means *re-baptisers*," she offered again emphasising for effect.

"Once again, correct, Miss," Smyth said with a grudging nod.

At that moment Mary Brewster could be distinctively heard saying, "Beautiful" as she tasted the warming broth over the fireplace. Brewster looked at her only to be met with a sweet smile as she lifted her wooden spoon to emphasise that she was only addressing the food and in no way revelling in the feminist empowerment that was playing out in her own living room. Brewster looked unconvinced. Smyth continued,

"I don't know where you are on infant baptism, William, but this is fundamental to our group. We are even thinking of calling ourselves *The Baptists*." Brewster was unmoved. "And then there is the third thing."

Brewster's eyebrows were already raised as high as possible, he waited to hear what potential heresy Smyth was going to deliver.

"It is about church governance. We see no place for any office above the local church leader. Which means there are no bishops, no archbishops and ultimately the Church and State are, by definition, separate."

They both looked at Bunny to see if she would, once again, add her own comment on the statement. She had nothing to say on this subject, so just looked away sheepishly.

"I can see that would not go down well," Brewster replied to Smyth, then added enquiringly, "But that will be the same back in England. Whether we agree with it or not the Church of England *is* the solitary Church allowed in England. To go back with the intent to set up a so-called Baptist Church, you will be shut down, imprisoned, and..." Brewster elected to not finish the sentence. Both Smyth and Bunny knew how it would have ended.

"I know, I know," Smyth agreed. "And I have told Thomas that is what would happen."

"What did he say?" Brewster asked. Smyth sat back in his chair and let out an exasperated exhalation.

"He said he is going to write to King James."

"And say what?" Brewster enquired, shocked at the very idea.

"You don't want to know," Smyth said resignedly.

"Oh, but I do," Brewster insisted. Smyth conceded.

"Well, the key phrase that Thomas plans to use is, 'The King is a mortal man and not God. Therefore, he has no power over the mortal soul of his subjects to make laws for them or to set spiritual rulers over them.'"[1]

"So, he wants to get arrested?" Brewster advised sarcastically. Smyth didn't respond.

"What about you and your family? Are you going to stay in Holland much longer?" Smyth asked. Brewster chose his words carefully, knowing that his wife was listening intently. He was getting hungry and didn't want to have to forfeit his meal as the result of an *unfortunate* kitchen mishap.

---

[1] 'The Life and Writings of Thomas Helwys' by Thomas Helwys edited by Joe Early, Jr. Mercer University Press. P156

"I think that if it be the Lord's will, I and my house are ready to move on wherever He leads." To Brewster's relief there were no kitchen sounds to punctuate his dialogue, just the innocent echoes of his two younger sons playing. Brewster continued,

"I know that our John Robinson is itching to leave, but I don't think that Richard Clyfton will be persuaded to move again."

"And are you still set to go to the New World?" Smyth asked.

"I can't see we would ever be welcome in England, and anywhere is better than here, so probably, yes," Brewster reluctantly admitted.

"Boys, it is time to get ready for supper." Mrs. Brewster announced, signalling her desire to bring the conversation to an end. Taking this cue, Smyth rose to his feet.

"I will let you know how Thomas and I get on."

"Thanks. And where are you going to start your first Baptist Church, in the wilds of rural Gainsborough I hope?" Brewster asked as he led his visitor to the door.

"No, Thomas knows of a place in…" Smyth gave his friend a polite but heartfelt embrace as he answered, "a place in Spitalfields."

"That is in the middle of London!" Brewster was amazed at their audacity.

"Yes, on the King's doorstep, right in the heart of London."

And with that remark he disappeared into the crowd. Brewster closed the door, replaced the seal and turned to face Bunny.

"Love wrestling?" he asked her firmly. Bunny was taken aback. Was he angry at her interjections? Had she really overstepped the mark by joining in the conversation? Was she to be the cause of yet more domestic tension? She wasn't going to take this attack on her character lying down. She was no Puritan wife and was going to stand up for herself. The only thing she could instantly think of answering was a mildly sarcastic,

"Not particularly, big men in Lycra is not my thing."

Brewster's face was a maze of befuddlement. He repeated himself slowly, this time articulating his neck to look behind Bunny.

"Love and Wrestling, will you two boys stop playing and get washed up ready for supper."

"Ah!" realised Bunny. "Modern celebrity child names are nothing in comparison with the Puritans. *Love* Brewster and *Wrestling* Brewster."[1]

---

[1] William Brewster's sons were called Love and Wrestling. They both travelled on the Mayflower and became elders in the Plymouth colony. His daughters were named Patience and Fear.

Chapter 12

THE PILGRIM FATHERS

"Yes, I know Sam Goode. He plastered the room conversion I did for my mum last May," Thea explained to the shocked group.

"And did he have a van, a white van?" Ralph asked.

"Of course, most plasterers do, don't they? But I wouldn't have thought... he seemed like such a...normal man. Are you sure he's kidnapped Miss Elstow?" Thea was in obvious confusion at the incongruity of the suggestion that a tradesman she had let in her house now stood accused of the unthinkable. She gave a visible shiver at the thought that she may have allowed a potentially dangerous man into her home.

Plastering was one of the few DIY projects that the middle-aged Ms. Howlsy would not attempt on her own. She had done much of the rest of the work needed to convert a utility room, study and conservatory into a space for her aged and infirm mother. She'd had to learn domestic independence quickly after her now ex-husband was arrested. That was something she took in her stride as she had long since given up relying on others, especially men, to come to her rescue.

No one in the Reformation Room that evening knew her history. She had relocated a few years ago to start a new chapter in her life now that her ex- was safely behind bars, unable to hurt her anymore. She knew she shouldn't blame herself for the subtle isolation he forced her into, but something deep inside her knew what was happening but was powerless to resist. It was not the first time. As a teenager she had been duped by her sixth-form English teacher, whom she admired greatly, but who abused that trust during their after-hours extra-curricular study sessions. She didn't tell anyone about what happened, simply dropped out of her sixth-form class, and started working in an office. She took to work with a passion. Naturally bright, she quickly progressed up the corporate ladder encouraged by the commercial director who made promises of career advancement if she was willing to work hard and *go the extra mile*. She immersed herself in the pursuit of a career working long hours and foregoing the development of any meaningful relationships. She soon discovered that despite her efforts there was a glass-ceiling above which neither women nor non-graduates could progress. When challenged, the commercial director denied he had ever made any such promises. Thea knew she had been tricked into working hard. Her trust once again destroyed, she left and trained to become a Special Needs teacher.

It was around that time she met her husband. She wouldn't have called it love; she just went along with the idea. When he proposed that they moved in together, an offer that morphed into a hastily arranged register office wedding, all she could say was, Why not? The abuse, emotional not physical, began soon after the honeymoon as she was steadily ostracised from each of the small number of friends she had. One friend however refused to comply. Hope Spero was the only born-again Christian that Thea knew and made it her mission to spend as much time with Thea as it was safe to do. Hope told her that Jesus was someone Thea could trust and that He would never let her down. This was a truth she needed to hear and soon made a personal commitment of faith in Jesus. Emboldened with evangelical fervour Thea would, unwisely, take every opportunity to share her new-found faith with her husband. That idea didn't go down well and soon the subtle emotional blackmail turned into foul-mouthed rants and threats. Again and again Thea would pray for him between sobs of tears as she swept up the broken china remnants of their last argument. The only good thing was that he didn't prevent her from attending Hope's church, a lively Baptist gathering. In the church environment Thea felt safe, having found somewhere she was appreciated for being who she was, with no one telling her what she could or couldn't do, and no boss making promises they couldn't keep. In fact, the leadership structure was difficult to pin down. As far as she could see the whole church was run pretty much as a democracy which meant that for the first time ever Thea had a voice.

Their unhealthy domestic co-existence continued for several years. They tried unsuccessfully for a child. When the test result said that they wouldn't be able to, she secretly admitted her relief to Hope.

The final straw came when her husband lost his job. Her assurances that God would look after them were taken as an emasculation and his frustration turned, for the first time, violent towards her. Police intervention was thankfully swift. Within weeks she was in a hostel for vulnerable women, and he had been charged. The decision to relocate closer to her mother was an obvious one, she could easily pick up a new teaching post and once the divorce was finalised she would have enough money to be able to buy her own house.

Broad St. Baptist welcomed her with open arms and it soon became her labour of love. She picked up everything from overseeing the Sunday School to regular midweek hospital visits. In less than a year she had accepted the inevitable, agreed to be their pastor and was duly licensed. No bishop ordained her as there are no bishops in the Baptist Church; she became their leader as much by default as by any sense of calling. But it was a position she felt very comfortable in. At last, she had no one over her, especially not a man, and it felt good.

"No one said kidnapped," Artur again clarified.

"That's right, Artur," Ralph confirmed. He then leant over towards Thea and said forcibly to her,

"If you know who this van belonged to you must tell Chris."

Thea didn't take kindly to this overly-authoritative command, so instinctively stared back at him, unmoved. Ralph didn't know what to do next, so offered her his mobile with which to call Chris offering as he did a conciliatory,

"Please."

She had no justifiable reason to refuse so took the phone and pressed the screen button marked Call Back.

"Are you sure I cannot convince you to go all the way?"

John Robinson's question of Bunny was entirely innocent, but she couldn't help but see the unintentional *double-entendre*. Perhaps it was the sea air, or the thought of at last returning to England, or the fact that her perception of reality had long since left her. Whatever it was, something prompted Bunny to give the austere churchman a somewhat frivolous response, but one she felt was in keeping with his eventual destination.

She placed one hand on her chest, fanning herself with the other as if she were about to faint. She then addressed him in an accent that, she thought was a perfect parody of Scarlett O'Hara,

"Why Sir, whatever do you mean?" with special emphasis on the *ever*.

Bunny wasn't sure if this was even a line from *Gone with the Wind*, but she enjoyed saying it. As she did, she realised that this was completely out of character. She would never had said something so unintentional, something she would even consider slightly risqué. This is the sort of line Chris would have said and at which she would have turned away in embarrassment. But now she had said it, and what was more she said it, *just for fun*! Never mind the fact that she had left poor John Robinson both confused and thoroughly apologetic, she couldn't help but admit to herself that she had changed. She had taken a step outside of herself and was able to see the funny side. Despite being trapped inside an impossible dream sequence, for the first time she felt a sense of freedom to laugh at herself, to laugh at the situation. Something was changing.

"I am so sorry, Mr. Robinson," she pulled herself out of her momentary light-heartedness. "No, I thank you, kind sir, but I will leave you in London to collect your sister ship. I will wish you bon voyage as you cross the ocean."

Robinson thanked her and left her to enjoy the view of each bank of the Thames estuary as they formed on either side of her. It wasn't a landscape she knew particularly well, but she felt sure that in addition to houses, factories and roads, there would be a large container terminal on one shore – she had read that in a newspaper. She took delight in the realisation that what was now a sprawling industrial and cosmopolitan city didn't reach as far as Dartford in, she checked her watch, 1620. She took a deep wholesome breath of fresh English air, sufficient to finally expunge every memory of the putrid Leiden canals.

"We must be passing under the Queen Elizabeth bridge," she murmured as she exhaled.

"What's that? Queen Elizabeth's bridge?" Brewster had joined her on deck and caught the end of her musings. He looked hard at each shore, shielding his eyes from the midday sunlight. "Where is Queen Elizabeth's bridge? I didn't know she had built a bridge."

"It's okay William, you can't see it...yet," she admitted in all honesty. Brewster looked confused then stared to the fore, as if it was still ahead of them. Bunny changed the subject.

"I will be saying goodbye once we land at Rotherhithe."

"Yes, I know." Brewster stopped peering and looked at her and asked, "Now, do you know where you are going? Do you need anyone to look after you?"

Bunny was not offended by what would today be considered a strongly misogynistic sentiment, taking it with the kindness and grace with which it was meant. Once more Bunny noted that she was softening.

"I will be fine on my own, William. I was thinking of visiting the Baptist Church in Spitalfields, to see how Smyth and Thomas Helwys are getting on. What do you think?"

Brewster sucked the air in through his teeth.

"That bad, eh?" Bunny prompted.

"No, you can go of course," Brewster conceded.

"But?' Bunny probed.

111

"When the King received the letter from Thomas Helwys," Brewster explained, "the King immediately had him arrested and placed in the Tower of London…"

Bunny gave a sympathetic, "Ah." But Brewster hadn't finished adding, "And he died four years ago."

They remained in silence for a while as they sailed through the future footprint of the Thames Flood Barrier.

Brewster was the first to speak.

"But the church is still there. Go if you want to but be careful if you do, Miss."

It wasn't long before the ship approached the quayside at Rotherhithe. As they began to come alongside their berth she heard, almost without questioning, a Tannoy speaker announce:

"The train arriving at platform one is the 20:32 to London Victoria."

That's strange she thought, this is a ship not a train. Then she realised that there were no Tannoy speakers in 1620 and whatever she is hearing couldn't be from within her dream.

The housing estate on the edge of town, where Sam Goode's plastering business was listed, was a maze of identical pre-war semi-detached houses. Chris parked across the road, barely fifty yards from number 34. A well-used Vauxhall Vivaro was parked under the yellow glow of an old sodium streetlight that painted the presumably white van in a dirty hue. The only livery visible on the vehicle was the name: Sam Goode. The description, Commercial and Domestic Plastering, beneath it was so small in comparison that it was nearly impossible to see at any distance.

"Well, that meets the description the man in the foyer gave," Chris said to himself.

The rain was still heavy. Chris pulled up his coat, locked his car and approached the van, crossing from the opposite side of the street. It was parked such that the driver's side was away from the house, allowing Chris to make his way to the driver's window. He wiped away the raindrops and casually glanced inside. As far as he could see nothing was unusual. An empty clipboard was wedged under the windscreen together with yesterday's copy of *The Sun* newspaper. The floor had a liberal scattering of Kit-Kat wrappers, Coke cans and Benson & Hedges cigarette packets. Two phone charger cables dangled from the dashboard. This was a typical tradesman's van with nothing to suggest anything untoward may have happened earlier that night.

Chris pulled away from the window, unsure of his next step. He made his way around the rear of the van and tried the door handles. The van was locked. He continued onto the pavement now in full view if anyone from number 34 were to look out. The rain-spattered window of the passenger door was the only other option. Once again, he wiped away the raindrops but this time he couldn't see inside due to the reflection from the streetlight above him. He cupped his hands over his eyes and pressed against the glass. The scene inside was the same as he had just surveyed, only reversed. He looked in the foreground, at the passenger seat that Bunny was supposedly placed upon. There was nothing to suggest she had been inside. Then he saw something. He wasn't sure but there was a dark stain on the passenger headrest. This was not a clean cab, both seats bore the imprint of regular dining on chocolate, cola, and fast food. But a dark stain on the headrest piqued his curiosity. Could it be blood? He stared closer. Was it? He couldn't be sure. He slid his phone out of his trouser pocket and held it up to the window – if he could briefly switch on the inbuilt torch maybe he could see better. He turned and looked straight at the front door of number 34. All was peaceful, and it was unlikely anyone would come out in this rain he thought. He switched on the torch. It was more powerful than he had expected, and its beam filled the cab with light. Chris's attention, however, was focused on the passenger seat headrest. The dark red colour was unmistakable. It certainly looked like blood. And the way it glistened in the light from his phone suggested this was a recent stain. He froze. This was real, something bad *had* happened and he was in the middle of it.

He switched off the light and looked back at the Goode residence. Thankfully, still no movement. His instincts were to run and hide but not this time. Bunny was inside, probably hurt and she needed his help. He rolled himself around to the far side of the van, phone still in hand. What to do next? He scrolled down through his recent calls to find the number for the local police station. Before he pressed Redial, he considered, did he actually have any concrete information to give them? A comment from a drug-user and a stain in a plasterer's van would probably be insufficient. No, he was wasting his time calling them. He was going to have to go into number 34 himself. He scrolled back to Ralph and pressed Dial. At the very least he ought to tell someone what he was about to do.

The walk from the docks at Rotherhithe to Central London was a little over five miles. That journey will take nearly an hour in modern day London regardless of whether you take a taxi; a red London bus; the underground tube; or the least sensible option of driving there yourself. Bunny had fewer choices all of which were going to take her considerably longer, but she had the time and little idea of where exactly she was going. She elected to walk, the leafy tree-lined path tempting her with the prospect of enjoying solitude in the early evening sunshine.

Her solitude lasted a little over an hour before she was joined at the confluence of two city-ward paths by a fellow traveller. Bunny nodded politely at the man before increasing her pace to create the psychological safety buffer that all ladies instinctively employ when circumstances bring strangers into an uncomfortable proximity. As she strode forward, she prayed that he would not speak to her. To her irritation, he did.

"I say, hello there." He may have been simply a polite gentleman looking for nothing more than company along his journey, but Bunny didn't want to take the risk, so ignored him and continued her subtle acceleration.

"I say, hello, again." His voice was louder this time, and if she wasn't mistaken much nearer despite her increase in speed. Again, she didn't stop, having committed herself to this course of action. His apparent persistence did however provoke her to consider a plan of action if it were needed. If he were to make a grab for her, she decided, then he would be quickly disabled with a combination of slap to the face, kick to the shin followed by the unfailing knee to the groin. These were her default moves, although she had no idea if they would be effective. Despite enduring several similarly tense moments as a single, unescorted woman, and having mentally rehearsed the manoeuvre many times, to date she had never used them. As ever, she was ready in case this time the need should arise.

Suddenly a hand landed on her left shoulder, its fingers firmly pressing into the soft flesh below her collarbone, causing her to momentarily wince. Whether such a clench was intended to bring her to a halt or just clumsy, she immediately stopped. Rehearsals over - this was showtime. She stretched out her right arm and brought it around in a wide arc, palm forward ready to strike. As she turned to face her assailant, she saw he had already raised his arm to catch her wrist. His face, barely inches from hers, was smiling at her. Not a menacing smile but one that communicated that he knew what was coming next. As he held her outstretched wrist, she drew her leg back to release the kick. She braced her toes for impact but to her surprise her foot did not make contact and swung vainly into the air. She was now in an impossibly overbalanced position and began to pivot on her standing foot, inevitably falling into his grasp. No chance of the knee coming to her rescue. In desperation she shouted out,

"Lord, help me."

"Calm down Bunny," her would-be attacker said calmly and authoritatively.

Desperately scrambling to regain her balance and push away from the stranger's chest, she suddenly recognised his voice. As soon as she attained a vertical orientation once more, she stepped backwards in order to see the man's face, her free hand now formed into a clenched fist, ready if it were needed. It was the same person she had talked to in Calvin's lobby and on the coach to Marburg. His clothes were different, and he was wearing a hat that was more of the style of the day, but it still had a distinctive golden rim.

"You!" she yelled angrily, adrenalin still pouring through her veins. They stood staring at each other, his eyes smiling, hers displaying a heady mixture of anger and relief.

Bunny looked pointedly at the wrist that he was still holding firmly. She looked back at him and gave him the cold, withering expression that she used to leave people in no doubt that she considered their actions unacceptable. In this case her displeasure was aimed at his prolonged grasp.

"Do you mind?" she said. At once he released her, saying politely,

"Yes, I think it is now safe for me to let go of the tiger's tail."

Bunny regained her composure, straightened her clothes and ended with the predictable dusting-down routine, an action that was more calming than necessary.

"I see you met Brewster and Robinson," her mysterious confidant commented.

"Yes," she answered as they recommenced their London-bound excursion, now shoulder to shoulder.

"They are off to America, and I think I know who they are," she continued before adjusting her tense, "Or were...or will have been? I think."

"Well let's see if you do. They are going to cross the Atlantic on a ship called the..." he paused to allow Bunny to claim a brief trivia victory.

"Hmm. It won't be the Santa Maria, that was Christopher Columbus, so I would have to say the Mayflower."

"The Mayflower," he said in agreement.

"So, they are the leaders of the Pilgrim Fathers, the men who established America… well, the British colony that became America?"

Despite having met Luther, Calvin and several other Protestant heavyweights Bunny, for the first time, sounded genuinely starstruck. These ordinary Nottinghamshire men who were, to her, relatively unknown were on their way to do something truly extraordinary.

"But hold on," she said interrupting herself. "If they were the Pilgrim Fathers, well, pilgrims are going *to* somewhere, they're on a mission *to* a better place, *to* a holy place." He nodded in agreement as she continued.

"But when I listened to them all they wanted to do was go *from* England and then *from* the Netherlands, away from where they were being oppressed or excluded. They are less like Abraham in the Bible, following God's call to travel west, and more like Moses fleeing the Egyptians."

"So?" he prompted.

"So, why do we call them pilgrims, when they are more accurately exiles?" she concluded.

"Probably because *The Self-Imposed Exile Fathers* would be less palatable than *The Pilgrim Fathers* for future generations," he suggested. Bunny nodded in knowing agreement.

"Will I meet them again?" she asked tentatively.

"You will make the same journey in an hour or so, but…" he didn't need to finish the sentence, she knew what he meant. Time was passing so quickly for her that she would probably never meet the same people twice.

The pair continued their journey along the well-trodden lane as the evening sun shone through the oak-leaf canopy above them creating a colourful panoply across the path. The display reminded Bunny of the occasional days when a low evening sun would break through the usually cloudy English sky and decorate the aisle of All Saints' Church through its single stained-glass window.

Several minutes and over a mile of silent onward progress elapsed. It became clear to Bunny that he wasn't going to initiate any dialogue and it was going to be up to her to speak first. This was typical of men, she thought. She could remember the time when she and Chris had driven to the Christian convention, Spring Harvest, together and after three hours in the car together she realised that it was *she* who had started every conversation, not him.

"Let me tell you how I see it," she began.

"Go on," he encouraged.

"We have the Roman Catholics in one hand and then there are three main branches of Protestant, or some would say Reformed, Church in the other. But the Protestants aren't all in the same hand as they are all opposed to each other."

He nodded.

"Firstly," she continued, "there's the Lutherans, largely in Germany and Scandinavia and who believe in salvation by faith. But as they are not dissimilar to the Catholics in most of their other beliefs and the way they conduct their services, many feel they haven't reformed enough."

Again, he nodded.

"Then there are the Calvinists in Switzerland, the Netherlands and Scotland. Less Catholic in appearance and differ from Lutherans in a few doctrines, especially whether Christ turns up in person during the communion service." Bunny's irreverent turn of phrase produced a wry smile on the face of her fellow journeyman.

"And the Scottish version of Calvinism has introduced a unique bottom-up organisational structure that they call Presbyterianism. It means there is a State Church with locally elected regional representatives rather than bishops appointed from above." No sooner had she said this than she wanted to correct the statement that bishops, to her mind, were divinely appointed. "When I say *from above*, I don't mean from God, bishops are of course appointed by God, but I mean appointed by the head of the Church...which I *know* is God, but I mean the State or ...."

At that point she arrested her confused babble allowing her associate to help her out by saying,

"You mean they are not appointed by any earthly authority?" She agreed, and at the same time stored that phrase in her memory banks. *Earthly authority* sounded like an important term.

"And then there's the Anglicans," she continued, emitting an exasperated sigh. "A top-down State Church, part Calvinist and yet part..." she paused trying to remember the group that differed to the Calvinists on their stance on predestination. At last it came back to her mind, "...part Arminian. The Anglicans retain dashes of Catholicism in their rites and the style of some of their services, but not all Anglicans, some are much more Puritanical. It is a real mix-up of beliefs." Bunny suddenly stopped walking.

"What bothers me is that it looks as though the Church of England, *my* Church of England was founded on a compromise designed to maintain peace at all costs." Not quite a nod this time.

"And are there any other groups?" he asked, to lift her from her ponderous gloom.

"A few separatist movements on the fringes, like the Baptists in England and others in the Netherlands, but nothing *official*," she answered.

"Yes, the infant Baptist movement," he said. Bunny began to laugh.

"Whatever is the matter?" he asked irritated.

"You said the infant Baptist movement...!" Bunny waited for the penny to drop. It didn't.

"Yes, it has only just begun," came the reply.

"*Infant* Baptist!" she repeated.

"Oh, I see, what you mean," he gave a wry smile and corrected with, "No pun intended." He started again, this time unambiguously.

"The recently-formed *adult* baptism movement in England will survive as it will become part of a much wider underground movement that call themselves The Seekers. Seekers simply considered that all organised Churches are corrupt and preferred to wait for God's revelation of the truth."

"How long will they wait for?" she asked.

"Well, it's all going to kick off in the next half hour," he teased. Bunny looked down at her watch which now showed 16:37. Her knowledge of history was not good enough to remember what happened in the middle of the seventeenth century, but she was sure she was going to find out soon enough.

118

Chapter 13

PRYNNE, BASTWICK & BURTON

"No one is saying kidnapped," Artur again clarified.

"Well, I hope not. I wouldn't want anything to have happened to Miss Elstow. But I can't help but worry about that letter," the Rector said as he clasped his hand to his chest.

"I assume it is her we have to thank for us all being here," Jack said pointedly. Methodist preacher Joel Whyens ageed,

"Did I think she was the one behind it? Yes, I did," he said. Joel had known Bunny for years and was aware how keen she was to see some expression of inter-church co-operation. He had thought this a little strange, being that she was so embedded within the Anglican Communion, but he was keen on the idea too provided it was some sort of outreach mission.

Rex Fogge too had a lot of respect for the church secretary. He had first met her when All Saints' opened a small bookshop on the High Street, a venture that lasted for less than a year. He was looking for a book on the Quaker businessman George Cadbury and was impressed by Bunny's knowledge of how Cadbury, together with his fellow chocolate pioneers Fry, Rowntree and Terry, brought social reform into newly-industrialised England in the nineteenth century. She had kept in touch with him ever since and Rex too was sure that she had been behind last month's meeting.

Despite his deep-seated doctrinal objection to the Church of England, Bunny was one of the few Anglicans that Jack Fort could tolerate. Not least of which was because of her pivotal role in organising the annual relief truck to Kurdistan. His church was fully behind the effort with several members being personally involved.

Ralph would often chat to Bunny when she was in Crossta Coffee, usually with Chris Palmer whom he had noticed was increasingly finding opportunities to spend time with her. Both Ralph and Jack liked Bunny. Both knew she would have been the driving force behind the attempt to organise next Easter's event, Rector Mashman being, in their opinion, incapable of such decisiveness.

Thea had appreciated Bunny's support with the 'Have a Heart for the Homeless' campaign that the Baptist pastor ran each Christmas. Bunny would call into their chapel to help parcel-up donated provisions and help serve hot food when she had time. Bunny was the only person outside of the Baptist church who was regularly involved in this programme. Thea felt that she owed Bunny and was delighted to have received an invitation to attend the meeting, her only disappointment was to have not been able to make the first one.

It was only Artur Thelmin that didn't know Bunny personally, having been in the town for a comparatively short time. The first and only time he met her was an hour ago in the C.R.F. coffee shop.

Ralph's phone rang again.

"It's Chris," he said as he pressed the green handset key. "Let me put you on speaker Chris, we are all listening." He held out the handset on his extended palm. The group gathered round as Chris told them he had found the van, a bloodstained seat, and that he was about to go inside number 34.

Crossing London Bridge, the *old* London Bridge, was breathtaking. Over a hundred buildings were crammed onto the bridge itself, each one a bustle of mercantile excitement with enthusiastic traders hawking everything from home-grown vegetables to hand-made leather shoes. Political agitators and religious zealots distributed tracts with vocal vigour. Bunny took one of the plain white, single-sided leaflets, written by one Henry Burton. She ought to have been shocked by the headline but was too impressed by the pun: 'English Bishops are stepfathers not fathers and instead of pillars just caterpillars', it declared. The tone got much worse with the first sentence declaring the entire Bishopry to be: 'miscreants, false prophets and antichristian mushrumps.'[1]

Bunny quickly folded the paper, placing it in her pocket. She wasn't expecting to see such antagonism towards her Church and found it deeply troubling. She squeezed her way through the crowds to reach the side of the bridge at one of a handful of open spaces midway across. A dark, muddy Thames flowed toward her, giving her a sense of continuity with the present day. The same river would pass the same spot under a new London Bridge hundreds of years later; a time when all that she was witnessing would be long-forgotten history and yet, somehow, the religious polarisation would live on in deep-rooted predispositions. She slumped over the huge stone wall that edged the

---

[1] Henry Burton wrote of bishops that, "Their fear is more toward an altar of their own invention, an image or crucifix, the sound and syllable of Jesus, than toward the Lord Christ. They are miscreants, traps and wiles of the dragon dogs; like flattering tales, new Babel builders. Blind watchmen, dumb dogs, thieves, robbers of souls, false prophets, ravening wolves, factors for Antichrist, antichristian mushrumps." An Ecclesiastical Biography: Containing the Lives of Ancient Fathers and Modern Divines, Volume 3, Walter Farquhar Hook, page 306.

bridge, letting her hands dangle limply as she stared forward at the approaching waters.

"This was…is…all about how much the Church should be reformed," she said under her breath. "People are outraged, not about abuse or stealing from the offering plate. It's not even really about heresy, just between keeping tradition and…"

Before finishing her sentence, she looked down to see what her fingers had, for the last few moments, been subconsciously tickling. She assumed she had been touching an outcrop of fibrous grasses or a clump of fine-leaved weeds clinging to the outside of the bridge. To her horror she realised that her hand was resting just above the crown of a severed head, staked onto a metal pole fixed to the side of the bridge. All she could see from above were heavy locks of brown hair, some of which she had been absentmindedly touching and now were wound into her fingers. She tried to leap backwards but the crush on the bridge prevented her from easily extricating herself from the ghastly encounter. As she writhed and tugged her fingers free, she caught sight of dozens of the macabre trophies staked along the bridge, some facing the river, but most for the benefit of those crossing the bridge on foot. This was a harsh world, and she didn't like it. Once free of the grisly tresses, she pushed herself back into the safety of what was now a dense crowd moving steadily northward across the bridge. She had no choice but to move with the throng and was soon extruded out of the bridge-gate and into a large city square in Westminster.

Chris rehearsed several scenarios in his mind. There was the police raid scenario, breaking down the front door amid much shouting; there was the tiptoeing through the rear door and sneaking about in the dark scenario; then there was the climbing the drainpipe and in through an upstairs window scenario. None of these felt right. He wasn't a shouty, sneaky or drainpipe-climbing person. There had to be a better way. But whatever he did he knew he had to act quickly; if Bunny was inside, she was hurt, and she needed medical help, which she wasn't going to get at No. 34.

He stood on the highway, leaning as close to the van as he could to maximise the little protection that it gave him from the driving rain. Car headlights then appeared as a vehicle turned into the end of the street. He would have to make a move. He walked purposefully back onto the pavement trying his best to not look suspicious and stopped in the space where a gate would have hung, pausing with one hand on the damp concrete gatepost waiting for the car to pass. The approaching headlights pulled in right behind the van.

Rats, he thought, I can't just hover here, I will have to do something. He started walking slowly up the short pathway. When he reached the front door he looked back over his shoulder at the now parked car. To his shock, the headlights flashed at him. Was this a neighbour or, worse still, someone who lived at 34? Was this Sam Goode in his *other* car? Here was Chris standing at his door with no plausible reason to be there. He had to do something, there was no choice. He reached his now shaking finger towards the bell, said a silent prayer and pressed it. Double-glazing, he thought. I'll be a double-glazing salesman.

The hallway light signalled that someone had heard the chime. He could make out that it was a man scrabbling with the security chain. Chris heard car doors closing behind him but didn't look round.

"Double-glazing, double-glazing," he repeated to himself, "Or maybe changing your energy supplier, that would be better. Who buys double-glazing in October?" Eventually the door opened.

The man was in his early fifties, a little shorter than Chris and overweight. If this turned physical, Chris thought, I bet I could overpower him. But that would have been a particularly out-of-character act, and possibly the first fight he had ever gotten into. Nonetheless, Bunny's safety drove him on. The man stared at him; his unwelcome evening visitor hadn't spoken for at least ten seconds.

"Yes?" the homeowner said impatiently. The heightened levels of adrenalin in Chris's veins took over, completely ignoring the salesman ruse, and before he knew it he had said,

"Mr. Goode? Are you Mr. Sam Goode?"

The homeowner gave a defensive nod with a mumbled, "Uh-huh."

"Is that your van?" Chris asked purposefully pointing behind himself with his thumb over his shoulder. The man followed the direction of Chris's thumb.

"Well, it's got my name on it," he answered sarcastically before adding, "You looking for a plasterer?"

It was such an obvious reason for visiting his house that Chris was annoyed he hadn't thought of it himself. He formulated the word 'Yes,' but as he spoke it all he could hear was an emphatic,

"No!" and that negative expression was delivered in a strong Northern Irish accent. Jack Fort's booming voice was unmistakable in Chris's left ear. Chris turned to see the Ulsterman standing with Rex Fogge. To Chris's right stood Joel, now sporting a grey cap on his bald black head, and Ralph who put a reassuring hand on his assistant pastor's shoulder.

"No, we don't want a plasterer," Jack repeated before demanding, "We want to know what you have done with Miss Elstow." Subtlety wasn't one of his strong points.

Joel, who was now closest to the door, slipped his shoe across the door frame ensuring Goode wasn't going to slam the door shut. The plasterer, now heavily outnumbered, looked panicky.

"Who?" he flustered. Chris's timidity vanished, the presence of four allies standing with him emboldened him. He took the lead in establishing dialogue, but on a more conciliatory manner. He was going to be *good-cop* to Jack's *bad-cop*.

"Mr. Goode," he began. "What my...*brother* is asking is; were you at St. Mary's earlier this evening and did you give anyone..." he swallowed as he said it "...a lift?"

Goode made no protest and replied.

"Oh, you mean the young lady with the blood on 'er head," he confessed, clearly spooked at the multiple door-stepping he was enduring.

"So, you don't deny it," Jack stated loudly. Chris raised his hand across Jack's chest in a hold-back gesture.

"Yes, we mean the lady that *you* were seen taking in *this* van at speed, an hour ago," Chris said calmly.

"Yes." Goode didn't deny it, then asked a curious and seemingly sincere question. "How is she?"

Chris was in no mood to play games. His face dropped from his good-cop demeanour as he leaned forward and said,

"The question is, *where* is she?" Chris looked behind Goode into the hallway and stairs.

"She's at the hospital. I dropped her off at casualty. I've just got back." Goode's explanation did make some sense. Chris hadn't considered ringing the hospital.

Clearly conscious of the disbelief of these five unwelcome *brothers* Goode added,

"She's not here. You can check if you want to."

Before anyone else could respond, Joel had already stepped inside with a cursory,

"Shall we? Yes! Thanks, we will," and disappeared with a bound upstairs.

Chris wanted to test Goode's alibi and insisted that Goode tell them what had happened. Now with someone snooping around upstairs he was in no position to object and invited them to step into his small square hallway out of the rain. He told them how he was doing a plastering job at St. Mary's and went in at around eight o'clock to pick up the last of his gear. How, when he arrived, he found a woman sprawled on the floor, unconscious. He admitted that it might have not been the best idea, but he decided it would be quicker to take her to the hospital himself rather than ring for an ambulance as he had no charge left on his phone. He explained that he had run to get his van, parked it outside exactly as the eyewitness had said, and carried her into the front seat. It was only then he noticed she was bleeding from her head. Their host then gave them a wait-a-minute gesture and disappeared into the lounge just as Joel descended from the first floor.

"Is she upstairs? No," he said.

Goode returned with a set of white overalls that he had put in the utility room, ready to be cleaned. Goode unfolded the workwear to reveal a bloodstain halfway down one arm. That was Bunny's blood. Chris could feel anger well up inside him and clenched his fists. Joel took the opportunity to slip into the lounge to complete his search. Goode continued to explain that when he arrived at the hospital, he was met by an ambulance crew who put her into a wheelchair, said they would 'Take it from here,' and sent him away.

Joel returned shaking his head. Bunny was clearly not in the house. They stood in silence for a few moments. Ralph was no behavioural expert, but he had to admit Goode didn't appear in any way sinister. Chris was too choked-up to speak so Rex broke the silence.

"Thank you, Mr. Goode, for looking after our friend. We'll be sure to come back and see you once we have been to the hospital to check on her." Rex meant it sincerely, but Jack took it as a delivered threat so added a rather menacing,

"Aye!"

The rain was easing as they gathered beside the vehicle the men had arrived in. Now that the headlights weren't dazzling him, Chris could see that Jack drove a rather large 4x4.

"Thank you, guys," Chris said with moist eyes. "But I feel as though I have wasted your time."

"Nonsense, friend, we all want to be sure she is safe and well," Rex assured him.

A dark red Honda Jazz pulled up beside them in the middle of the road. The driver's electric window descended as it came to a halt. It was Rector Mashman and what looked like Artur in the passenger seat and Thea in the rear.

"Have you found Miss Elstow?" the cleric asked.

"Where is she? She's at the hospital," Joel shouted over to him.

"Very good," said the cleric. He then gave both a thumbs-up and a hearty "See you there," as he drove off, electric window retracting as he did. Rex, Joel and Jack were all inside his car when Ralph said to Chris,

"I'll go with you."

"But you don't all need to go," Chris protested.

Ralph shushed him and signalled to Jack to set off, at which he started the engine and pulled away.

"Now, where did you park?"

Perhaps a thousand people had gathered around the perimeter. In the centre stood a small stage barely five feet above street-level and on top were three pillories - wooden crosses with holes designed to hold its victim's head and hands whilst they suffered abuse, and the occasional vegetable missile, from the crowd. When the crowd stopped moving Bunny found she was standing immediately opposite the small staircase up to the platform. She took her place in the expectant audience ready to see events unfold but not in any mood for anything violent and prayed that *pillorying* might turn out to be reasonably civilised.

Surveying the scene – the three elevated pillories, the gathered throng, the air of official menace – Bunny realised something was chillingly familiar. She couldn't place it. It wasn't until the first blood-stained victim was led out that she realised she was witnessing an event that was inadvertently paying homage to Christ's crucifixion at Calvary.

Soon three men had been led, bound, onto the raised platform followed by an official dressed in clerical robes. Was this to be some sort of religious punishment? Bunny wondered. Their names were announced to the crowd along with their crimes. Firstly, William Prynne then John Bastwick and finally Henry Burton. Bunny reached for the provocative paper she had stashed in her pocket to confirm that the name she had just heard was the same as its author. It was. Clearly the mushrumps were fighting back.

As she watched, she heard that all three had been tried and convicted of opposing both the Church and his regal majesty King Charles.

"Ah, King Charles," she said remembering that they must now be on the brink of the English Civil War. This must be the *kicking off* that she was told to expect. Burton had been fined five thousand pounds, stripped of his clerical post and sentenced to life imprisonment without the benefit of pen or paper. They must really have feared his writings.

Bunny's hopes for a civilised punishing didn't materialise. Unable to move from her position she was forced to witness Prynne being branded with a hot metal bar and all three men having their ears ceremonially sliced off.[1] Bunny felt she was going to be sick. She didn't like such barbarism, especially in the name of the Church. This was not her version of Christianity. Bizarrely, she took some comfort in the self-justification that she was right to have refused to watch that grim-looking horror comedy movie that Chris had suggested last week.

Finally, the three men were placed into the pillory stocks ready for the final part of their punishment, *public humiliation* to be administered by the assembled crowd. Was she going to have to take part in this social disgrace? she wondered. As soon as all three victims had been firmly secured, the officiator declared that they were now condemned to public humiliation. He then hastily departed, cowering as he did, in a manner reminiscent of dignitaries hurrying away from a Grand Prix podium to avoid being sprayed with champagne. Champagne was far from the projectile he was expecting. Pillory victims were usually pelted with rotten vegetables, mud and a variety of bodily fluids.

But not this time. The crowd remained silent. Nothing was thrown. Minutes passed with no action from the crowd. The clerical official tentatively tiptoed back onto the stage.

"I said they are now condemned to *public humiliation*," he repeated, ducking as he did. But nothing happened.

The crowd remained silent until one anonymous voice shouted an accusatory, Shame! Several others joined in.

"Shame! Shame on the Church!" rang out. The man standing next to Bunny cupped his mouth and shouted towards the stage,

"We are all proud of you. You'll get a page in Foxe's book of Martyrs."

"It's called Actes and Monuments," Bunny said instinctively correcting him.

---

[1] All three men were sentenced to be pilloried, including having their ears removed, for having spoken out and writing pamphlets attacking the pro-Catholic Archbishop of Canterbury William Laud.

"Eh?" he replied.

"Never mind," she replied sheepishly, hoping that the large man was not offended by her pedantry.

The cries of Shame! and Boo! became increasingly louder. Fearing an outbreak of civil unrest, the cleric was quickly ushered off the stage by his armed guards. As he departed in confusion, Bunny saw him gesture to someone standing at a balconied second-storey window overlooking the square. Was that the King himself? she wondered. And was he witnessing a turning point on his ability to use religion to control the masses.

Chapter 14

THE COVENANTERS

Free of official intervention, several women quickly mounted the stage and began tending to the wounds inflicted upon Prynne, Bastwick and Burton, offering them words of comfort and encouragement. To Bunny's surprise no one attempted to release the men from their stocks. Perhaps to do so would have been a crime and this was to be a peaceful protest. As the three victims were being tended, a smartly dressed man took to the stage and asked for quiet as he had something to say. It wasn't difficult to settle the crowd as the main target of their derision had since exited.

"God is decreeing a new and great period for the Church, the reforming of the Reformation itself," he announced with the confidence of a man who had recently attained an MA from Cambridge University and had already published several books.[1]

As he spoke, Bunny couldn't help but be impressed with his eloquence and passion. Having just seen three men brutalised for nothing more than expressing their opinions, this man was doing likewise. Undaunted, he delivered a venomous tirade against the upper echelons of the Church. The memorable highlight, Bunny thought, was when he called them "The canary-sucking, swan-eating bishops!"[2]

"Hmmm, even better than anti-Christian mushrumps," Bunny whispered to herself.

Was this man Oliver Cromwell? It would make sense as he was going to lead the fight against the King. But she had seen paintings of Cromwell and all she could recall was that his face was covered with several large moles. The man on the stage, however, had the perfect pale smooth skin of the landed gentry. As the gentleman spoke the crowd began to become distracted as the unmistakable sound of marching footsteps began to echo around the square. Anxiety buzzed in the crowd. Bunny too was concerned about the unsettling sound that maybe heralding a military crackdown. The speaker stopped his oration as the military cacophony grew louder and he too looked towards its

---

[1] 'Milton and the English Revolution' by Christopher Hill Verso. p235

[2] Ibid. p260

source, the western side of the square. Most people had already turned their attention from him to see what was happening. The crowd was tense, and several people prepared to make a hasty exit.

Bunny looked, waiting, ready to run, and eventually the crowd parted. There was no screaming, no sound of fighting, just a silent parting to let through the small marching troop. These were not English soldiers, but Scotsmen. Most were bearded, all were wearing kilts in a variety of tartans and each sporting large white-fur sporrans. They continued their march around the pillory stage, stopping beneath the balconied window that the cleric had acknowledged previously.

"Your Majesty, Sire," the leader of the Scots shouted up to the balcony. Nothing happened. He repeated himself, but still no one came to the fore. After a third time the window opened slowly and then, tentatively out stepped the King. The crowd gasped.

"Sire," the burly Scot continued, satisfied that he now had the audience he sought. "We bring you greetings from the Noblemen, Barons, Gentlemen, Burgesses, Ministers and Commoners in your Scottish realms pledging our loyalty to the King."[1] At this apparent good news, the King offered a relieved wave from his elevated position and motioned for the Scot to continue. He unclasped his elaborate sporran and extracted a sizeable scroll, unfurled it and began to read aloud. It took some time to read the allocution, which he did with a determined articulation. It began with a definition of what the Scottish people described as the *true religion*. Bunny remembered that when she had met John Knox, and the other Johns, they had been excited that King James would bring their version of reformed religion into England, but then at Hampton Court he had decided that he rather liked the less firebrand English version of Protestantism; and how that had not gone down well.

Bunny listened carefully to the orally delivered Covenant, which continued with a list of things they had decided were wrong with Catholicism or, as they put it, the Roman Antichrist. She wasn't surprised to hear it described as the 'False doctrine against justification by faith,' she knew enough to expect that. Then came transubstantiation, purgatory, prayers for the dead and many, many more so-called errors including a few surprises such as the 'Baptising of Bells' and the 'Conjuring of Spirits.'

---

[1] The Scottish Covenant of 1638 was signed in Greyfriars Kirk in Edinburgh then toured around Scotland collecting signatures. Some even signed it in blood. It was never read out to King Charles although he undoubtedly knew of its text and implications.

The Covenant then went on to acknowledge the importance of loyalty to the King, at which point he once again smiled and waved. The sting, however, came at the end. The burly Scot paused, looked firstly at his fellow warriors, then turned his gaze to the crowd and finally upwards towards the smiling king, before delivering his coup de gras.

"We declare before God and men, that we have no intention nor desire to attempt anything that may turn to the dishonour of God or to the diminution of the King's greatness and authority," he read it with passion. "But, on the contrary, we promise and swear, that we shall, to the uttermost of our power, with our means and lives, stand to the defence of the King's Majesty in the defence and preservation of the foresaid true religion."[1]

It was a stroke of genius. No one could accuse the Scots of disloyalty. They were swearing their loyalty to protect the King provided he upheld the true religion they had just defined; to defend religion, if needs be, from the King himself. This was the inevitable outcome of the Scots refusing to bow to the new King's watered-down Anglicanism. The crowd took a while to understand the implications of the lengthy decree that had been delivered. The message was explained to the predominantly uneducated throng who responded to the Scots with hearty cheers and backslapping. The King, for his part, quickly disappeared inside.

The multitude began to disperse, several Scots were carried off shoulder-high, the eloquent speaker descended the small staircase and was soon face-to-face with Bunny. She took her chance to introduce herself.

"Mr. Cromwell?" she said offering a handshake.

"I think you have me mistaken, Madam," he answered, nonetheless taking her hand and clasping it between both of his. "Oliver is a good friend of mine, but I am John Milton."

"Ah, Paradise Lost!" she said, again without thinking.[2]

"Paradise lost?" He looked at her quizzically before adding, "I guess that paradise may indeed be lost under this King, but that is a rather thought-

---

[1] The full text of the Covenant is available at www.reformationhistory.org

[2] John Milton was the author in 1667 of the epic poem 'Paradise Lost' one of the most important pieces of classical literature. The work introduces around six hundred and fifty new words (many more than in the combined works of Shakespeare) including terrific, satanic, enjoyable, stunning and famously pandemonium. It has been both banned and been the treatise of revolutionaries; but my personal favourite fact is that it was read by Frankenstein's monster!

provoking way of putting it." He then removed a leather-bound notebook from his breast pocket and with a small pencil inscribed the phrase *paradise lost*, speaking out the words as he did. Bunny bit her lip hoping that having fed him the title of the book for which he would become famous she hadn't inadvertently broken any intrinsic time-travel law, the result of which may cause the universe to implode.

"Sorry, my mistake," she said, attempting to change the subject. "Well, that Covenant thing was a clever twist wasn't it."

"You understood it then," he asked surprised.

Bunny, indignant at this affront to her intellect, retorted,

"Of course, I did. I know all about the Reformation and Luther and transubstantiation and the Council of Trent and Calvin and Luther and John Knox and Presbyterianism and Luther..." she had fallen into a self-imposed defensive rant-loop and didn't know how to get out of it. Milton didn't look at all impressed and decided it was his turn to change the subject.

"Did you hear what happened in St Giles' Kirk in Edinburgh when they imposed the revised Anglican Prayer Book?"

Bunny shook her head, grateful to not have to be talking anymore.

"Well, apparently, when the Bishop of Edinburgh began to conduct the morning service using the new Book of Common Prayer that Archbishop Laud had insisted all Scottish ministers use..." Bunny looked at him attentively as he took great delight in relaying this piece of ecclesiastical gossip. He continued,

'...As he started the service one church member stood up, shouted out in protest and threw a chair at the bishop."

Bunny laughed, then considered that perhaps she should have looked shocked at the reported clerical assault. To her relief, he too laughed.

"That's nothing!" He took her encouragement to share another juicy anecdote. "I heard that in Brechin the bishop had to conduct the service with a pair of loaded pistols aimed squarely at the congregation."[1]

Bunny gave out an involuntary snort as she visualised the incongruous image of a gun-toting bishop. Milton joined her in enjoying the merriment,

---

[1] In 1635, Walter Whitford, the Bishop of Brechin, announced that he was planning to use King Charles' deeply unpopular prayer book. Having been threatened with violence if he did, he took to the pulpit holding a pair of loaded pistols, his family and servant being similarly armed.

performing an impression of an armed-and-dangerous bishop replete with faux-Scottish accent.

It felt good to laugh. Especially on a day when she had literally touched death and been face-to-face with religious brutality.

As she laughed, she closed her eyes and felt herself being laid backwards, upon a bed; gently pressed into a horizontal position which she could only succumb to. As she did, a heavily accented voice whispered in her ear,

"Dobro spavajte, gospodice."

She had no idea what that meant, nor who was saying it. She opened her eyes and saw that she was still standing and face-to-face with John Milton.

A decided chill had filled the air and Bunny noticed that dark clouds had gathered over London.

"Come, let me introduce you to Oliver," he said leading her through the remnants of the crowd. As they left the square, heavy raindrops began to fall. A storm was coming.

Despite being the first to set off, Rector Mashman was the last to arrive in the hospital car park. No one was surprised.

They agreed that eight people would be too many to go to Accident & Emergency reception, so decided that Chris and Ralph would go, while the others waited in the WRVS café, assuming it was still open at that hour. To their collective disappointment it wasn't. As they gathered around two tables that had been pulled together for the purpose, the effervescent Joel Whyens offered to buy everyone a hot drink from the vending machine. With efficient timing he dispensed two cappuccinos, a hot chocolate and a tea. He then took a black americano himself but Rex, who didn't drink coffee and who couldn't be tempted with anything else, declined.

As they waited, several people passed by traversing either in or out of the hospital. Some were clearly patients each in a variety of states of discomfort and undress; others were readily identifiable as staff from the lanyard and laminate that hung from their necks. The rest were presumably visiting patients, although one with a large camera who rushed into the building didn't appear to fit any of those descriptions and caused Thea to remark as such. Once they were all seated Rex asked if he could share a concern.

"Something is bothering me," he said. Mashman asked him to expand, which he did.

"When the plasterer chap said he arrived at the hospital, did he say that the paramedics took Bunny and then sent him away." Jack agreed that was what Goode had relayed.

"But that isn't right. He would have been asked to give some details of the accident and the patient's name, address, details of any medication they were taking," he said.

"But Goode didn't know any of that," Joel pointed out.

"Yes, I know, but the thing is," Rex paused, "...the thing is no one asked him. That never happens, he would have to have given his own contact details at the very least."

No one had an answer to Rex's point. The Rector simply offered a meaningless "I'm sure it will be fine," relieved that they had tracked down Bunny and that his initial fears were unfounded.

They had all finished their drinks by the time Ralph joined them. They could see in his face that something was amiss.

"What's the matter," Thea asked him, adding a sensitive, "Is Bunny all right?"

"That's just it, I don't know," he answered taking the only vacant stool. "No one knows."

"What do you mean?" asked the Rector. Rex then surprised everyone by saying,

"They have no record of her arriving, do they?" Ralph looked at him, shocked.

"How ever did you know that?"

"It was the only explanation," he replied, then repeated his observation that anyone bringing a patient to the hospital would have been asked to leave their details at reception. Goode hadn't.

"That was exactly what the triage nurse said," Ralph explained adding, "Chris is in the toilet, he was very upset."

Jack slammed his fist heavily onto the table, making the Rector jump.

"The little liar," he said, convinced that Sam Goode had duped them. Chris arrived at the WRVS café having homed-in on Jack's booming voice. Ralph told him that he had brought everyone up to speed. Jack stood to his feet clearly intent on returning to No. 34.

"Who's coming with me?" he asked.

Joel started gathering the empty cups, Ralph and Rex put their coats back on. Chris was pleased he wasn't having to go back alone.

133

"Or…"

Artur's voice was almost drowned out by the sound of chair legs sliding roughly over the vinyl flooring. But Chris heard it and looked at him expectantly.

"Or, what he said was the truth. And he did hand her over to some ambulancemen." Everyone had stopped to allow the Lutheran to proffer his alternative theory. "But it wasn't a real ambulance."

"Sorry Artur, but I'm going to see Mr. Up-to-no-Goode," Jack concluded. Rex and Joel said they had better go with him, unsure as to what trouble Jack might get himself into.

Chris was momentarily frozen, unsure whether to follow Jack and the others, or not. Ralph held back with his friend.

"Is there any way to prove if it wasn't a real ambulance?" Chris asked.

"Not without access to the hospital CCTV," Artur conceded. "We are not the police, so I don't suppose they would allow us, even if anyone was here to show us this late at night."

"Hang on," Thea piped-up enthusiastically. "There *are* cameras we can see." The four men looked at her expectantly. Thea enjoyed the position of being needed by men, of having, what she knew was going to be, the answer.

"Every time you arrive at this hospital your car is automatically photographed by the parking machine," she said. "And then again when you leave."

"You're right," Chris said. Thea continued,

"You have to enter your registration number to pay for your parking and it shows you a picture of your car and the time it arrived. So, we could see if an ambulance did indeed arrive or leave at that time."

"Good idea," Artur said, "But there are two problems with that. Firstly, there will be lots of ambulances going in and out of this place, it's a hospital, but more importantly if there were to be a fake one, we don't know which registration number to enter to check it."

"Yes, I know," Thea continued undaunted, "but if you enter the wrong registration number three times it gives you a list of all vehicles that arrived at the time you stated. Pick yours and it will show the picture."

All her male counterparts simultaneously said, "Does it?" Thea was evidently the only person to have forgotten her own car registration number in the past.

It was nonetheless a good idea, and they ran to the bank of four parking machines. Chris, Artur and Ralph each took one machine, Thea the fourth. The

Rector was happy to not have to confront such technology. Thea took the lead role, talking them through the step-by-step process of getting it wrong so that the list was revealed. Goode had said he arrived around eight o'clock, so to cover a wide period they each entered fictitious arrival times staggered by ten minutes, covering over half-an-hour of comings and goings between them. A list of registration numbers did indeed appear.

"That must be Sam Goode's van," Chris exclaimed. "PL45 TRD. It isn't perfect, but doesn't that say plastered to you?" He clicked on the registration number and it was clear. Two pictures proved it, one arrival at 8:05, and one leaving at 8:08. And as he stared at the first picture, he could see the darkened silhouette of someone in the passenger seat. He reached to touch the screen, to connect as if he could with the image of Bunny. As his finger touched the glass, the screen changed to the message, 'No Payment Necessary - First 30 mins Free - Thank you for Visiting.'

"He left at 8:08," Chris told the others. "So, we are looking for a vehicle that left shortly after then."

That wasn't so easy, as you had to input the arrival time, not that of departure. But at least they knew what they were looking for. As the minutes passed, they were getting close to the target: 8:02, 8:27, 8:07. Then Artur hit the bullseye.

"I think I have it," he exclaimed. They all left their terminals to join him.

There it was. Arrival 7:20, Departure 8:09 and, yes, it was an ambulance. The vehicle in the picture had the word Ambulance stencilled across the front, but the tell-tale red and yellow stripes were absent. This was, at best, a private ambulance, the sort you might have at a nursing home, clinic or private hospital, not a regular accident and emergency ambulance at all. The driver was dressed in green paramedic fatigues, but his face was indistinct. The registration number LM02 EAA didn't offer any clues either.

"Goode was telling the truth, but this is a deadend," Chris said. "Unless we know where that ambulance comes from..." he said jabbing at the screen.

As he did, the screen acknowledged his touch and promptly changed to state '1.0 hr Fee Due - paid on Account.' They all looked at the screen to make sense of this additional information. As they watched they followed Chris's finger as he clicked the option Account Settings. The Account Settings screen gave an account reference number and a small menu selection. He pressed each option. Vehicles, Visits and Payment Details were all password protected so offered no clue. Contact Details, however presented a screen with fields for Name, Address,

135

Email and Telephone Number. The problem was that each of these was filled with a string of asterisks except for the last few characters. He tapped the Amend button but that too was password protected. They stared at the meagre data, that was all they had to go on: ****345 the last three digits of a phone number; ****son the last three characters of a name; ****pice.com the last few characters of an email. The end of the address field was easy to decode, but as it was simply the name of the town, it didn't help them.

"So, we need someone called blank-son, who owns an ambulance, has a phone ending in 345 and an email ending in pice.com," Chris said despondently.

"Hospice?" Thea suggested, breaking the momentary silence. "The email could be something-hospice.com. A hospice might have a private ambulance. Mightn't it?"

"That is not a bad idea, Miss," Artur agreed.

"It is all we have to go on. There are two or is it three hospices nearby? It is late so we'd best split up and pay them a visit," Chris suggested.

"First though," Thea insisted, "I think we had best stop Jack paying a visit to a certain Goode Samaritan."

Chapter 15

MILTON & BAREBONE

"It looks like the storm is over, Miss," John Milton said as he shook raindrops from his overcoat.

Bunny nodded in agreement, more concerned about the state of her hair following the intense shower they had just endured. She stepped away from him to use her reflection in a nearby window to make herself presentable. To her surprise there wasn't a hair out of place. As she looked at her reflection she remembered she was in fact dreaming, and perhaps the laws of reality had no jurisdiction here. She was about to say to herself that she quite liked the fact that the rain hadn't wet her hair, even forming the words in her mouth. But, before she could speak, she stopped and let her hands drop from feeling her own hair to hang limply at her side. She looked deep into her own reflected eyes. For an instant she stepped out of her dream, into a moment of lucidity and prayed.

"Dear Lord, I don't like it here. I've seen things, I've touched things, I've smelled things I would rather have not. Violence, death. Is this all so necessary?" She paused, then continued. "I get it, you are taking me through the origins of the Church. I don't know why, but I get it. But I don't like what I've seen; politics, bigotry, brutality, celebrity, it's not what I imagined. I would rather have stayed in blissful ignorance. I knew my church, I knew what it believed, I didn't need to know why. Everything was clean and neat, but now I … I know things… and… I don't have any answers, but…" her prayer had lost momentum. It wasn't a prayer, more of a plea for help. "Lord help me see you in all of this, help me see."

As she said the words, her reflected image changed into the face of an elderly balding man with a long, pointed nose, neatly trimmed moustache and chin-beard. Her eyes opened wider. What was happening? Was she turning into a 17th century Puritan? As she stared at this disturbing image the face came closer and she realised it wasn't her reflection after all, but a face behind the glass, presumably that of the occupant of the building. He reached forward and opened the door.

"Can I help you … Miss?" the man said hanging his sentence in the air and requiring his observer to give her name. Bunny was suddenly very embarrassed to have been caught peering into his room, an emotion that propelled her back into her alternative reality.

"I am so sorry sir, my name is Johan Elstow, but people call me Bunny." She looked at him hoping he would join in with the introductions and not be too angry at her infringement of his privacy.

"Praise God!" he replied with enthusiasm.

"Indeed Sir, praise God, praise the Lord." She didn't know what to say and soon found herself delivering a spontaneous succession of worship clichés ending with "Praise Him in the highest, Praise His holy name."

"No! Praise God!" he said emphatically.

"Praise God?" Bunny replied tentatively as instructed, but no sooner had she said it, John Milton joined in.

"Praise God!" he exclaimed, then briskly walked over to the man and hugged him. As they embraced, they exchanged a sincere, 'It's good to see you again,' whilst patting each other on the back. As the affectionate man-hug parted, Milton turned to Bunny and said with a grin,

"Praise God this is Bunny."

The stranger looked at her, clearly waiting for her to say something. Bunny however was now so confused she couldn't think of anything more to say than,

"Praise Him," which she delivered with uncharacteristic timidity. Milton and his friend looked at each other before Milton said firmly,

"No! Praise God." The stranger stepped towards her, offered his hand and said,

"Praise God Barebone."

Was this an insult? she wondered. No one had ever called her *bare bones* before. What did it mean? And why was she being commanded to offer praise to God by both of these men. She thought it wise to take his hand and shook it carefully, saying as she did,

"And your name is?"

"Praise God!" both men replied in unison. Bunny stopped shaking his hand but kept a firm hold of it. The synapses in her brain began making the requisite connections. After a few seconds of static handholding she tested her hypothesis.

"Your name is Praise God?" she asked hesitantly. He nodded with a smile and said,

"Yes, my name is Praise-God Barebone."[1]

Bunny re-shook his hand vigorously, relieved to have caught up with the conversation, then tried to make light of her embarrassment by quipping,

"And I suppose your brother is called Hallelujah," as the handshake came to an end.

"No," he answered rather puzzled, "My brother is Fear-God Barebone. Have you met him?"

Bunny could feel her cheeks reddening and began to babble.

"Wow, I bet your parents were characters weren't they. Are you going to carry it on and name your children..." she went for broke hoping to get a smile from him, "...erm... for-God-so-loved-the-world?"

She looked at him waiting for a grin. Instead, he looked at Milton then back at her.

"Miss, I don't know who you are, but can I say that my son is not called For-God-so-loved-the-world Barebone. You are mistaken."

"I am so sorry," Bunny said apologising, now fully blushing. "I didn't mean... I wouldn't have..." she tried her best to recover. Finally, she swallowed hard and, trying to compose herself, said,

"What is your son's name, Mr. Barebone?"

Clearly surprised by the direction the conversation had now taken, he nonetheless politely responded.

"If-Christ-Had-Not-Died-for-Thee-Thou-Hads't-Been-Damned," and then added almost as a postscript, "Barebone."

Bunny gave a pronounced, loud, involuntary, embarrassed laugh.

"And I bet you call him *damned* for short," she added, covering her embarrassment with frivolity.

"No, he doesn't like it when we call him damned."

"I'm not surprised," she replied supressing a further laugh.

"So, we call him..." Barebone paused not sure what reaction he would get from the unpredictable woman. Bunny held her breath not knowing what to expect.

"We call him...Nicholas."[2]

---

[1] Praise-God Barebone was appointed as MP for London in Cromwell's Parliament that was made up exclusively of strict Puritans and became known as the Barebone Parliament in his name.

[2] Barebone did indeed name his son 'If-Christ-Had-Not-Died-for-Thee-Thou-Hads't-Been-Damned,' who unsurprisingly chose to be known as Nicholas rather than Damned. He went on to establish the first London

Bunny's eyes widened, her nostrils flared, but before she could say anything further Milton came to her rescue.

"We are on our way to see your new boss," Milton successfully changed tack.

"Oliver?" Barebone's face lit up at the mention of his name.

"Miss Elstow here wants to meet the man who led us to a glorious victory against the Royalist forces and signed the King's execution warrant."

"So soon?" Bunny reacted, surprised that time had moved so quickly: the English Civil War was over, the King was dead, and Oliver Cromwell was running the country as a republic.

"And not before time," Milton replied. "And Praise-God Barebone is a member of the national government."

"He's an elected Member of the Westminster Parliament?" Bunny said regaining her composure and trying to appear intelligent.

"No, that has been disbanded," Barebone protested. "There were no elections, Oliver has appointed us all as the new Parliament of Saints."

"Really?" Bunny enquired.

"Of course, the civil war brought to an end the reign of the antichrist and ushered in the start of the millennial age. You do know that we are living in the thousand years of Christ's glorious reign as prophesied in the book of Revelation?" Barebone asked her.[1]

"But it is..." she looked at her watch whose large square digital dial displayed 16:53. "...it's 1653, the millennium cannot have started."

"Ah, but it has. One thousand years of peace and then Christ will return."

Bunny bit her lip. Knowing fully well that there would be anything but peace over the next few hundred years. But it was clear to her that *they* believed it.

"And what do parliamentarians do during Christ's millennial reign?" she asked cheekily. By way of demonstration, Barebones looked at Milton and asked,

---

Fire Brigade. 'The Weird and Wonderful Names of the English Puritans' published by Findmypast.com 20 Sept 2016

[1] Following the execution of King Charles, a ruling body was proposed based upon the Old Testament Sanhedrin of 70 selected 'Saints.' Cromwell embraced the idea, with some modifications, creating The Nominated Assembly which comprised only strict Puritans in the belief that the rule of the saints would be a prelude to the reign of Christ on Earth. Article: 'The Nominated Assembly' published by BCW Project.

"What is the chief end of Man?"

It wasn't just Milton who answered as Bunny spontaneously joined in the reply,

"Man's chief end is to glorify God, and to enjoy him forever."

"The Westminster Catechism," Bunny noted. "You wrote the Westminster Catechism?"[1]

Barebone confessed that he could not take personal credit for having drafted the Catechism, or the more extensive Westminster Confession, but that the Westminster Assembly was called by Parliament and it was Parliament that had agreed the final text of both of them a few years earlier.[2]

"And have there been any other memorable laws passed?" Bunny asked, genuinely curious.

"We have established total religious freedom in the nation. Everyone is free to practise their religion."

"Including the Baptists?" Bunny asked, keen to know if John Smyth's group would now have a chance to survive.

"Oh yes, as well as many other congregationalist groups."

"Congregationalists?" Bunny asked for clarification.

"Those who do not believe there is any hierarchy above a local church minister. Every individual church is completely independent."

"So, no bishops? no archbishops? no synod?" she asked.

"No. Neither appointed by the State..." Milton began but Bunny quickly interrupted,

"As in the Anglicans, the Church of England."

"Quite." He was slightly irritated by her interruption but nonetheless continued, "Nor elected from within each church."

Bunny completed adding,

"As with the Presbyterian Church of Scotland." Milton nodded before adding,

---

[1] The Shorter Westminster Catechism is a list of 107 questions and answers designed to help those of 'weaker capacity' to understand and learn the core doctrines of the Church.

[2] The Westminster Catechism and Westminster Confession were produced by the Westminster Assembly of the Divines (i.e. bishops and parliamentarians) in 1646, during the period of the Long Parliament, immediately prior to the one Barebones was appointed to.

"Oliver is a Congregationalist, so... you know,"[1] and gave a knowing nod.

"And we have invited the Jews to return," Barebone informed her with some pride. "They've been banished from our shores for over two hundred and fifty years."[2]

"And does this religious freedom including the Catholics?" Bunny asked provocatively. Barebone spat on the floor, just missing Bunny's shoes and causing her to take a large step backwards.

"Never! Never!" he decreed, his anti-Catholic feelings being self-evident. Milton took this cue to suggest they carry on to their meeting with Cromwell and wished his old friend 'many blessings' upon his parliamentary duties.

"Goodbye, Miss," Barebone said as he bade her farewell.

"Bye..." she replied, but, unable to bring herself to call him Praise-God, simply said, "... P.G."

Thea Howlsy would have much preferred to be travelling with Ralph and Chris, or even for that matter with Jack, Rex and Joel. The Rector drove his little Honda far too slowly for her patience. Didn't he realise there was an urgency? But she said nothing and dutifully fastened her seatbelt. The only sense of excitement from Reverend Mashman came as he adjusted his rear-view mirror, now for the third time, before starting the engine.

"I don't know what our bishops would think about us gallivanting around this late at night," he postulated to both Artur, in the passenger seat, and Thea in the rear.

Having firstly sought a translation of the word *gallivanting*, Artur then agreed that his bishop would be both surprised but also pleased they were about God's business. Mashman then asked Thea for her opinion.

"And what of yours, Miss...?" he asked, momentarily forgetting her name.

"I don't have a bishop," she stated simply, hoping the conversation wouldn't delay his departure. Thankfully, he pulled out of the hospital car park and they were at last on their way.

"Is he not? ...or is it a she? ...I mean," Mashman fumbled a reply. "I mean, is the post vacant at the moment?"

---

[1] Congregationalists believe that all churches are entirely independent of each other with no place for bishops or any church hierarchy above the local congregation.

[2] The Edict of Expulsion of 1290 expelled all Jews from England.

"No, we don't have *any* bishops in the Baptist Church. We are congregationalist. I am the pastor and that is all," she explained.

"So, if I may ask," Artur said pivoting a little trying his best to make eye-contact with Thea behind the drivers' seat, "who do you work for?"

"I work for the Church," she said pointedly.

"Yes, yes we all work for the Church," the driver interrupted. "But who is your…your *boss*."

The word *boss* didn't sit right in this context. In their mutual line of employment they all considered Jesus to be *The Boss*. Artur too prickled at the terminology so attempted to re-phrase the question.

"What the Rector meant Thea is, to whom are you accountable?"

"Well, I guess, I would be accountable to the members of my congregation," she explained. "They appointed me so if they were unhappy with anything I was doing I would have to defend myself to them." She thought for a moment as the car engine laboured in third gear. As it was released into fourth, she added, "And I guess that ultimately they would have the power to dismiss me."

"I don't think I would like that, would you Artur?" Mashman said apprehensively. Thea took objection to the condescension of the sentiment.

"If I am not mistaken," she launched, "you two are the *only* people in tonight's meeting who are *not* accountable to the people they serve. The rest of us don't have that luxury."

She sat back pleased with having made her point and having used the word *serve*, clearly evoking 'If anyone wants to be first, he must be the servant of all,' from Mark's gospel. [1]

Milton and Bunny chatted as they continued walking through the cobbled streets of London, the sound of horse-drawn carts occasionally interrupting their discourse.

"With all this freedom, does this mean that the Church of England has been disbanded?"

"No, Oliver was very clear that despite all of its corruption it must remain, as with the Church of Scotland. He doesn't agree with them personally, he being

---

[1] The Gospel according to Mark chapter 9 verse 35. Christian Standard Version

a Congregationalist, but as long as there is no official *national church* he is happy to leave them be."

"So, he is pro-tolerance," Bunny stated.

"I guess you could say that," Milton replied, repeating the previously unknown word *pro-tolerance.*

"That must mean you get some...you know...groups of wackos?" Bunny asked.

"I haven't come across the Wackos. What do they believe?" Milton asked quizzically.

"No, I mean there must be some groups with... questionable beliefs," she clarified.

"Well, it is not up to me to judge," Milton protested, defending his neutral position.

"I am not asking you to pass judgment I just want to know what sorts of groups are now *tolerated*," she said firmly. "Well...," she insisted with mock impatience. He quickly caved in.

"There's the Barrowists, the Behmenists and the Brownists,"[1] he started. "And then there are the Diggers".

"Don't tell me, The Diggers dig things?" Bunny asked amused.

"Yes, they do. They are an agricultural-religious community,"[2] Milton replied before continuing his lexicon of dissenters. "Then there are the Familists and Grindletonians,[3] now both of those can do no wrong as they believe there is no such thing as sin. Then there are the Levellers." Bunny looked at him expectantly.

---

[1] Both the Barrowists (under Henry Barrowe) and the Brownists (under Robert Browne) taught that the entire Church structure was corrupt. Behemists were a more mystical group that emerged from the Lutheran church having rejected salvation by faith.

[2] The Diggers were an agrarian sect started by Gerrard Winstanley in the belief that small egalitarian rural communities would reform the social order and usher in economic equality. Such beliefs continue to this day amongst anti-globalisation and common-welfare activists.

[3] Familists, or the Family of Love, were a secretive sect that believed all things were ruled by nature and not God. The Grindletonians were named after a small Lancastrian town. Both believed there was no such thing as sin and therefore rejected all civil and moral laws.

"They believe everyone is equal, and that all men should be able to vote."[1] Not too extreme, Bunny thought before asking provocatively,

"But is it only men?"

Milton frowned at the idea of female suffrage, and continued,

"And then there's the Muggletonians whose leader says he is a prophet. The Philadelphians, The Sabbatarians.[2] And...oh yes, the Socinians who hold some extreme views including not believing in the trinity."[3]

"And all these groups are now tolerated?" she asked.

"Yes, that is the official policy now," he confirmed. Bunny could tell there was something he wasn't saying. She gave him the look that women expertly use on men that always compels them to speak. It didn't take long and soon he began to confess his personal concerns.

"Hmmm," he began reluctantly. "But it is the Ranters. They are the ones who really put toleration to the test."[4]

"The Ranters? I assume they do more than just rant," Bunny contributed.

Milton explained,

"They say there are many gods, they believe in reincarnation and that old Christianity is dead." Bunny thought for a moment. She had heard that sort of philosophy before. Where was it? she wondered. Then it flashed into her mind.

"That's like New-Age," she said under her breath as Milton continued.

---

[1] The Levellers were more a political movement than a religious one that was very influential during the Civil War and had a particularly strong supporter base within the City of London. They were quashed by Cromwell soon after he came to power. The name had been applied to rural activists several years earlier who 'levelled' hedges.

[2] Muggletonian leader Lodowicke Muggleton and his cousin John Reeve claimed they were the Two Witnesses spoken of in the book of Revelation. Despite being led by Rev. John Pordage, The Philadelphian Society's central theological position came from visions received from the Virgin Sophia by Mrs Jane Lead who considered herself to be the bride of Christ. The Sabbatarians, unsurprisingly, believed that the sabbath should be in line with Jewish tradition.

[3] The Socinians, named after Italian theologians Lelio and Fausto Sozzini held strong anti-trinitarian views as well as rejecting the pre-existence of Christ, original sin and God's omniscience. Their views were taken up by a Polish splinter church and made their way to England where they gained popularity. They are the forerunners of several modern Unitarian movements including the Christadelphians.

[4] In addition to pantheistic doctrine, the most notable feature of the widespread Ranter movement was the amoral belief that man is 'free from all traditional restraints and that sin is a product only of the imagination.' This led to a propensity for nudism and sexual immorality.

145

"But it's the fact that they act like complete sexual and moral libertines that I cannot condone. Orgies and…" He stopped himself continuing the sentence as there was, of course, a lady present.

"That definitely is New-Age philosophy," Bunny said, much to Milton's confusion, adding, "which goes to show, it clearly isn't that *New* after all."

"Here we are." They had arrived at the grand splendour of Whitehall Palace. This enormous building had been the residence of the now former king and, with one and half thousand rooms, was the largest royal palace in Europe, deliberately built to be larger than the Vatican. Now, this ostentatious structure made in Portland stone and decorated with gold and the most elaborate of paintings was where the lowly commoner parliamentarian, turned soldier, turned statesman, Oliver Cromwell now lived and held court. The façade was breathtaking and was protected by high, elaborately crafted metal gates, outside of which two soldiers stood sentry. Milton and Miss Elstow stopped their ingress to seek permission to enter. Bunny held back as Milton approached the guard. As she surveyed the scene, she noticed that a young man, dressed in a black tunic, a white scarf collar and large brimmed hat, departing the building. Milton, much to the irritation of the guard, shouted over to the man.

"George, George, what a lovely surprise." The striding man acknowledged the exclamation and crossed the short courtyard towards them. As he approached, Bunny noticed that his hair was much longer than she would have considered proper in Puritan England. Milton excused himself from the guard and embraced his friend. Bunny coughed politely, reminding Milton of her proximity.

"George, may I introduce you to…" he paused before he and she jointly said, "Bunny".

George said a brief, "Madam," but offered neither bow nor handshake. Bunny had quickly grown accustomed to acting the *lady* in this society and being welcomed with gallant civility. Initially, she was shocked at the lack of courtesy he showed towards her before taking stock of reality, well, as best she could. The modern Johan Elstow would have been aghast at the idea of a man offering to bow at her and would have castigated any individual who had attempted such a gesture; yet now she almost expected it. Milton continued the introduction,

"And this is George Fox. You won't believe it George but only moments earlier I was listing to Bunny here all the different religious groups and hadn't even got to the largest of them... yours George."[1]

Milton returned to the guard to secure permission to enter the palace. Bunny could see that there were tears in Fox's eyes. She immediately asked him if he was all right.

"Thank you for asking, Madam," he looked genuinely touched by her compassion. So much so that Bunny didn't have the heart to correct his second *Madam* into a *Miss*. He continued,

"I couldn't be happier. I have just been with Oliver and I can't believe what he has just said to me. I am most heartened."

Bunny again deployed the look that ensured he would have to tell all. Fox was too emotional to do anything other than comply.

"As I was leaving, Oliver said to me 'Please come again to my house so we can spend an hour together each day' and that he wished me 'No more ill than he did to his own soul.'"[2]

"You clearly must have a good relationship with him," she responded.

"Yes, quite a turnaround considering we refused to bear arms in his war. But praise be to God who has allowed me to *speak the truth to power*,"[3] Fox explained to her with particular emphasis on what sounded like a mission statement.

Bunny was familiar with the concept of 'Speaking the Truth to Power' as a means of affecting political change. She knew that it was one of the core strategies Mahatma Gandhi had used to achieve Indian independence from British rule; how Winston Churchill managed to get the Americans to join the European theatre of the Second World War; and how Nelson Mandela changed the political climate in South Africa. Was this where the concept began? she wondered. Suddenly she was drawn out of her daydream as Fox spoke to her.

"It is time we left. Shall we?" he said, motioning that they depart from the palace entrance.

---

[1] With over 50,000 adherents, the Quakers were by far the largest of the Dissenter groups.

[2] Autobiography of George Fox (1694)

[3] Whilst the Quakers rightly claim provenance of the phrase 'Speaking truth to power', it is unlikely that it originated in the seventeenth century and is more likely to be of twentieth century Quaker origin.

"But I am going to see Oliver, with Milton," Bunny protested turning to locate the author. To her surprise he had vanished. Surely, he couldn't have entered the building that quickly, and why would he have left her outside.

"It is time we left," Fox repeated. The second mention of *time* suddenly reminded her that the laws of physics did not apply in the dream world she was now in. She looked at her watch which clicked over to say 16:58.

"Yes, of course, it is time for me to come with you," she conceded and turned to follow.

Chapter 16

GEORGE FOX

Rex took the call from Chris that explained that Sam Goode had been telling the truth after all, and that they needed to go to The Dame Cicely Hospice to find out if they have an ambulance with the registration number LM02 EAA. Artur, Thea and the Rector were on their way to Sisters of Charity Hospice and he and Ralph were going to St Christopher's. Whoever found the ambulance was to let the others know and they would all rendezvous there. Rex breathed a sigh of relief. As a confirmed pacifist he knew he would have been the one to prevent Jack from doing anything untoward to Goode. An experience he had not been relishing.

Rex had never been one to fight. As a youngster he was very competitive, but that was mainly expressed on the rugby pitch at the fee-paying school that his parents sent him to. He excelled academically both at school and then at Durham University. Before he was twenty-five, he was working for an international investment bank, living in a loft apartment in London's docklands, and earning a six-figure salary. The young Fogge had everything... apart from any sense of contentment. While his peers were revelling in the no-holds-barred, yuppie lifestyle, Rex would take himself away to look for solitude - not an easy task in one of the world's busiest cities. That journey led him inevitably to church. Not just any church – he would frequent several of the capital's vast cathedrals. Like many before him, the emptiness, silence, architecture, and choral worship stirred him deeply. It was during those years he discovered a strong personal faith in Christ that was more meaningful to him than the formality of the Church of England that he had grown up amongst.

At work he was amassing wealth, but in his private life he desperately sought simplicity. Occasional church attendance was helping, but he needed something deeper. His two worlds pulled at him with an ever-increasing tension, a tension that was inevitably going to cause him to snap. There was even a time when, to his shame, he had considered suicide, unable to cope with the disparity between his outer and inner self. Something had to give; and Rex's moment of clarity came in the solitude of St. Dunstan's Chapel, a special part within St. Paul's Cathedral set aside for quiet reflection. Early one morning, his inner turmoil having reached an unbearable point and, being alone in the chapel, he prayed. Unusually for him and unusual for the setting, he did so audibly.

"God, I don't know what I am supposed to do," he prayed. "I cannot be two people anymore. Help me!"

God answered that prayer in a dramatic but unfamiliar way. A young woman had entered the chapel as he was praying and prompted by the earnestness of his plea sat down beside him. She didn't speak, neither did he. They both sat silently for nearly an hour during which time he began to feel tears fill his eyes and slowly trickle down his cheeks. He thought he might be having a nervous breakdown, but the release of tears felt as though they were cleansing his soul. She put her hand on his, an action that only succeeded in releasing more tears.

When they left the chapel, he offered to buy her a coffee to thank her for her support and within a year that girl had become his wife. She introduced him to the Religious Society of Friends, a branch of Christianity that he previously knew nothing about. She taught him to look within himself to find the *inner light*.

As a young couple they spent an extended holiday on the isle of Iona in Scotland. There they lived with the religious community centred around the ancient abbey, and again found a depth of inner peace. This led them to make the easy choice to leave London so that they could bring up a family with a better quality of life. Rex was instrumental in ensuring the Quaker group they subsequently joined held to core Christian theology, some other groups having deviated into seeking an inner light without reference to Christ, which the Fogges knew was tantamount to Buddhism. Rex was not the leader of the congregation, as they had no ordained leaders, but as he had amassed sufficient independent wealth that he no longer needed to work, he devoted his time to the administrative affairs of the group and was selected to be their de-facto spokesperson.

"Welcome, friend." The designated greeter gave a warm and seemingly sincere smile to Bunny as she entered a simple stone-built meeting room in Grace Church Street that was beginning to fill with worshippers.

"This is Miss Elstow."

Bunny recognised the voice of George Fox as he introduced her to the small Welcoming Group before excusing himself and traversing to the other side of the room. Bunny smiled back at the person charged with giving a good impression to visitors then accepted his guidance to a *good* seat.

"I assume that Mr. Fox is the minister here?" Bunny asked her host.

"Oh no, Mistress, there are no ministers. Every believer in Christ is a priest, haven't you heard?" he took pleasure in explaining.[1]

Bunny looked at him quizzically as they reached a small hard-wood chair which Bunny would never have considered in any way *good*; it was nonetheless on the second row and presumably that qualified its status. He responded to her bepuzzlement,

"Miss, let me explain. There is an inner light within all of us. We can all hear from God, we can all speak from God, we don't need someone to give us a ready-made package. Each individual is responsible for themselves spiritually."[2]

Bunny took her seat and began to survey the room. Chairs were organised five or six deep in a square arrangement with no side indicating it was the front. There were none of the telltale religious motifs that she would have expected; neither altar rail nor communion table, no baptismal font, no statues, candles or stained glass, no musical instruments. There was, however, a gathering crowd of clearly excited people. There was a buzz about the place that Bunny had not seen before. This was *austere* Christianity, she thought before correcting herself, or at least it is *simple* Christianity.

The buzz soon dissipated into silence. Bunny could feel the anticipation and waited to see what would happen next. She waited. Her eyes danced across the people on the four front rows, looking to see who was going to open proceedings. No one moved, no one spoke, they all waited – silently. Someone coughed occasionally, but that was the only sound to break the silence. Despite being charged with expectancy the silence was heavy. After what felt like ten painfully long minutes, Bunny looked at her watch to see how much time had indeed elapsed. The square digital dial, of course, still said 16:58. She wanted to say, you're no help! to her watch but rather than break the silence contented herself with just thinking it.

As a single woman, Bunny was not unaccustomed to times of silence. There were days when she would hardly speak at all, but these would tend to be when she was walking on her own in the dales or losing herself in a book.

---

[1] Quakers believe in the 'priesthood of all believers' taken from Peter's first epistle chapter 2 verse 9.

[2] The very centre of the Quaker faith is the concept that there is an 'inner light' within every human soul, where God has implanted an element of His Spirit. 'Meeting the Spirit - An Introduction to Quaker Beliefs and Practices by Hans Weening 1995, published by quaker.org

She had never experienced silence at church. A church service to her was a symphony of sounds, there was a symphonic cadence that let you know where you were and what was happening. The overture would be the peeling of bells, then came the majesty of the pipe organ followed by choral singing. Then came the faltering inflexion of various churchwardens and sidesmen delivering lessons and notices; more singing with more instruments rising to a crescendo of... the drone – there was no better word – of Rector Mashman's sermon; then more singing; and finally, the babble of friendly chatter punctuated by the clink of teacups and the occasional child crying. That was the sound of the church Bunny knew. That was the comforting orchestral score that led her to experience God each week. Silent worship was something new. But this was something of a journey of self-discovery, she thought, so why not give it a go!

She closed her eyes, not quite total sensory deprivation, as the rigidity of the chair was beginning to make her buttocks numb, but it was good to switch off the room visually. She then tried to pray, silently to herself, but nothing came. She tried her best to remember the prayers she had recited hundreds of times each week. She began by mentally saying the prayer of preparation: 'Almighty God, to whom all hearts are open, all desires known, and from whom no secrets are hidden...' but then she couldn't remember anything, no matter how much she concentrated. She changed tack and decided to recall the creed: 'We believe in one God, the Father, the Almighty, maker of heaven and earth, of all that is seen and unseen...' Again, she dried up. Was her memory that poor or was her depth of relationship with the God she professed so shallow that without the familiar sacramental structure she didn't even know how to speak to Him. This was not the self-discovery she was hoping for. She had no choice. For the first time in a church service, she parked the liturgy and began to silently say how she was feeling.

"God, I am not sure what you are doing to me. I don't know what all these encounters are about, but what I do know is that I am losing confidence in Church. I don't just mean the Anglican Church, but I am losing confidence in Church in general. They all seem flawed. You either have politics and bloodshed trying to control what everyone believes, or on the other hand you've got tolerance. I would have said tolerance was a good thing but not if it allows New-Age hippies and sexual deviants to call themselves Christian. Surely you didn't mean for me to react like this. I'm beginning to not know who to trust." She peeped one eye open to make sure nothing had changed. It hadn't, everyone remained earnestly hushed. She closed it again and continued. "And as for this group, whatever they are called... The Mutes... for all I know. Apparently, they are the biggest of the lot. Are you here God? Are you in the silence? Are these people really in touch with you?"

Then, suddenly, Bunny heard a voice speak. It was indistinct but enough for her to open her eyes and prepare for whatever was about to happen. She looked around expectantly to see who had broken the silence. As she waited, she soon realised that no one was speaking; a sporadically repeating dry cough was the only noise in the room. Tentatively, she closed her eyes again.

"God? Was that you?" she spoke to her subconscious.

Once more, a muffled voice came into her head. It seemed to be saying, "Yes, I am here."

She didn't open her eyes this time. For the first time in her Christian experience she was hearing a voice in her head and daring to believe it might be God. This was awesome, she thought. Her logic then kicked in as she realised that she was currently in some sort of protracted comatose dream. She could therefore console herself that such an encounter was no less acceptable than anything else she had experienced.

"Where are you...God?" she asked, not sure of the correct protocol or form of address for the Almighty. "Are you in this place?"

"I don't need a building, I am present inside those who believe," the voice said, now getting clearer.

"So, if you are here, does that mean that all other churches are...wrong?"

That was the nub of her angst, that was the corner she had painted herself into, and without thinking she just blurted it out. Silently, but blurted, nonetheless. The reply she got was more of a feeling than a voice, a deep feeling filled her heart more so than a voice in her imagination.

"What do you mean churches? I only have one." The reply was so perfect that she felt it unequivocally must have been God after all. Her silence was then broken by the sound of a solitary church-bell toll.

"There's nothing here, they don't have an ambulance at all." Artur had considered texting the message to Chris but in the end decided to call him. He was a little confused that Ralph answered but quickly understood that Chris was driving.

"Okay, thanks Artur," Ralph replied disappointedly. "Same story at Dame Cicely's I am afraid. Rex said they have two ambulances, but they are both navy blue and neither have that registration number."

"Are you at St. Christopher's?" Artur asked.

"Just arriving, now and…" Ralph paused. "Well, what do you know…" his tone immediately gave away the sound of good news, if the discovery of an ambulance that had been used to kidnap their friend was indeed good news.

"Yes, Yes, Yes, it is here," he confirmed to Artur, then dictated the registration number over the phone as if to prove the fact.

"Great, we are on our way," Artur replied adding, "I'll let Rex, Jack and Joel know."

Chris parked his car in the small car park opposite the white vehicle. As he did, a security light came on illuminating a faint curtain of misty raindrops in the air, that evening's storm having largely abated. Ralph and Chris both exited his vehicle silently, instinctively closing their car doors softly as they did. This was the second time this evening Chris had approached a parked van in the dark. His heart was beating just as much this time as it had earlier outside Sam Goode's. He tried each door handle, unsure as to what he was going to find inside. All doors were firmly locked.

"Can I help you?" The rather aggressive tone caused both men to look towards the hospice reception. A man stood at the top of the three small steps, to the side of the access ramp, wearing an orange hi-viz coat with the collars turned up for warmth. He had a torch in his right hand but thankfully was not shining the beam into their faces. Neither of them offered a reply. The night-porter-come-security-guard repeated his question as he purposefully walked down the steps and approached them.

"Where is Miss Elstow?" Chris asked, his anxiety dictating his vocabulary.

"Who?" came the unexpected answer.

"The lady who arrived in *this* ambulance this evening," Ralph said adding particular emphasis and tapping the warm bonnet of the vehicle as he did.

"Who are you?" the night-porter asked, stopping a few yards away having realised he was outnumbered two to one. Chris stepped towards him, the man took a step backwards and shone his torch into Chris's face as if to halt his approach. It worked and Chris stopped, raising his hand to shield his eyes.

"My name is Ralph Shafer, and this is Chris Palmer. We are from Community Restoration Fellowship, and we just want to know about the lady who arrived here earlier this evening."

The porter lowered his torch, presumably heartened to hear they were churchmen, and shouted over to them, "The ambulance has not been out all day."

154

"Rubbish!" Chris fumed and started striding past the porter towards the hospice entrance. Ralph hastily followed his friend.

"You can't go inside!" the guard pleaded, beating a hasty retreat in an attempt to get to the entrance first. Chris beat him but as he pulled the door handle towards himself, he found it was locked. As Chris pulled at the door the porter slid his arm across the door saying that he wasn't going to unlock it.

"We *must* see Miss Elstow," Chris demanded. He then spotted a doorbell beside the half-glazed security door and began ringing it repeatedly seven or eight times. He couldn't hear it chime. Either it was broken or was ringing in some distant room, out of earshot. Rector Mashman's car arrived with little sign of urgency, that was until the rear driver-side door burst open and Thea spilled out onto the tarmac. She then rushed over to join Ralph and Chris.

"Stop that!" the porter said, pushing Chris's hand away from the bell.

"Listen, mate," Chris was in no mood to be conciliatory, "that ambulance was at the hospital tonight and brought my friend..." his voice faltered a little as he said it, "...my friend Bunny here and I..."

"No patient has arrived tonight," the guard stated adamantly. Ralph intervened as things were getting out of hand, and gently pulled Chris away from the door.

Thea joined them but before she could ask what had happened, the hospice door was unlocked with a decisive click. As Chris looked, he was surprised to see that it was not the night porter who had unlocked the door, but an older gentleman. The hospice manager standing in the doorway was wearing trousers, shirt, jumper and, most noticeably, carpet slippers.

"Was that you ringing my bell?" he asked Chris, adding to the porter, "Whatever is the matter?"

"Where is Miss Elstow?" Chris repeated, this time directed to the senior person.

The manager, just like the porter, gave him the same neutral replies. Ralph, Thea and then Artur joined in, but to no avail. Clearly irritated with the interruption to an otherwise enjoyable evening, the manager finally asked them to leave, or he would have to call the police.

Chris looked intently into Ralph's face and said,

"He's lying."

"Perhaps, but this is not the way, is it?" Ralph suggested. "Have faith, Chris. God has a way, we'll find her."

"Raise a standard!" a loud woman's voice broke into Bunny's solace, making her grab the seat of the chair she had by now slouched into. As she opened her eyes she could see a long-skirted woman, complete with bonnet, standing on an upturned half-barrel. Whilst Bunny wasn't sure if anyone was going to speak in this meeting, she never expected that they would be addressed by a woman. This was already ticking the right box for Miss Elstow. The fiery woman continued.

"God does not dwell in temples made with hands, but in the hearts of his obedient people. Religious experience is not confined to a building, to a steeple-house filled with ritual..."

The reference to *steeple-house*, a euphemism for church building, brought about hearty cheers that interrupted her flow. Bunny joined in the cheer despite being a loyal and dedicated member of All Saints' steeple-house.[1] The orator continued,

"The ministers in those steeple-houses may be university educated, and have the written Bible, but we have the living word. The qualification for ministry is given by the Holy Spirit, not by ecclesiastical study.[2] Those buildings are filled with ritual and people who do no more than profess faith but whose behaviour is no different to the heathen. We live a life of honesty," she declared as everyone, including Bunny, cheered.

"We pay no tithes," again universal cheers.

"We neither bow nor curtsey to any man," a sentiment to which Bunny now found herself cheerleader.

"And taste no alcohol," all except Bunny joined in this time. The woman ended her impassioned discourse with one final remark,

"Our inner voice says to us that we must forsake all, keep out of all, and be as a stranger to all."[3] And with that final flourish she sat down to rapturous acclaim. As the cheers subsided, another man started to sing. The tune was unfamiliar, but the lyrics were lifted straight from the Bible and Bunny knew them.

"Glory to God in the Highest..." he sang out.

---

[1] The words are those of George Fox. 'The Works of George Fox. Vol III' by George Fox (1659) P442

[2] The words are those of George Fox. 'George Fox' published by the Rowntree Society (2014)

[3] The words are those of George Fox. 'A Journal or Historical Account of the Life, Travels, Sufferings, Christian Experiences and Labour of Love' by George Fox (1765) Page 2

Bunny tried to join in with the acapella hymn but as she did the person to her left gave her foot a gentle tap. She stopped immediately fearing her attempt to join in was sub-standard. She quickly realised however that the only person in the room singing was the man who had started the song. It was a personal song of praise, something Bunny had never encountered in Anglican worship. The song was beautiful and as it reached its climax, much to Bunny's immediate anguish, the man seated behind her suddenly gave out a deafening roar. Others too then joined in the rising cacophony of noise. Several women, including the one to her left, started to cry – not in distress, but in some form of ecstatic religious manifestation. There was real passion in this gathering. It was as though an extended period of silent introspection had opened everyone's heart. There was depth in this place and, despite its format being the antithesis of the traditional services she was used to, Bunny could not deny she too had met with God.

The crying and wailing continued, to the extent that the woman next to her began to shake uncontrollably. Bunny looked at her with concern. She was holding both arms out in supplication and each hand oscillated violently making her fingers appear a complete blur. She had stopped crying but was now muttering unintelligibly under her breath. This was such an alien thing to do in church that Bunny became genuinely worried for her neighbour's wellbeing. Was she having a fit? Bunny couldn't cope with it any longer and placed a concerned hand onto the woman's arm, leaned over and whispered into her ear,

"Are you all right?"

The woman instantly stopped shaking, opened her eyes and looked at Bunny who was by now staring back at her, shocked by the immediacy of her cessation. The woman smiled at Bunny and said,

"Why my friend, of course I am all right. I was just quaking with the Lord." As she said it those in immediate earshot gave a polite chuckle.

"Ah, quaking," Bunny said as the penny finally dropped. "You are Quakers!"

"That is what they are calling us now," the woman added, clearly allowing those around her to hear the remark.

"And that is because you *quake* in your meetings," Bunny stated seeking confirmation.

"No Mistress," came the reply, but not from the woman, rather the handsome young man behind her. Bunny gave him a quizzical look, at which he took the cue to give the correct answer.

"My dear friend, George Fox, the man you arrived with…" he nodded toward the direction of Fox who was now standing and talking as the meeting had come to an end. Bunny followed the young man's gesture thus allowing him to continue.

"When George was first imprisoned for blasphemy, he told the magistrate to 'tremble at the word of the Lord!' at which the judge mocked him, saying that he and his followers were the ones who should quake. What was meant as an insult we have taken as an accolade."[1] At this, several of those in earshot gave a hearty Amen!

---

[1] Article 'George Fox dies in London' by Richard Cavendish published in History Today Volume 66 Issue 1 January 2016

Chapter 17

WILLIAM PENN

"My name is William," the young man said offering her the courtesy handshake that all participants were sharing with each other at the end of the meeting.

"Thank you, I'm Bun…" she stopped and for some reason decided to give herself a more formal introduction. She took his hand and with a smile said, "My name is Miss Johan Elstow."

Whilst she would never have described herself as an ardent feminist, Bunny always considered herself to be equal to any man. This was something that had landed her in trouble in the past, being a position from which she would refuse to back down. She was very much on the pro side of the *ordination of women* debate in the Church of England, despite her Rector being more conservative on the subject. Something would rise up within her whenever she thought that anyone was being excluded or overlooked simply because of their gender. Personally, she never wanted special treatment. She would often eschew using any coquettish charm to get her way and considered those who did so as being manipulative. But she was no tomboy, she enjoyed expressing her femininity in her own modest style. She just wanted equality. And yet, in such a short period of time, she had grown accustomed to having gentlemen politely give her a gallant bow when they were introduced. Unknowingly she found that she enjoyed playing the part. So, the fact that she felt a degree of insult when William made no such gesture didn't make sense. And yet she did and apparently must have let that reaction show in her face.

While still holding her hand, William placed his other palm on top of their clench and gave her a perceptive smile. Somehow, he seemed to know what she was feeling in that precise moment. As their hands remained clasped, she placed her free palm atop his. Whether this was in an expression of female dominance or simply a silent thank-you to a stranger with whom she had momentarily connected was difficult to say. What was clear was that all four hands were now joined, something contemporary propriety would not allow. He released his grip and withdrew his hands.

"Miss Elstow." William repeated her name with a slight cough, revealing emotion in his voice.

159

At that moment Fox joined them and shook William's hand enthusiastically.

"Good to see you free again my friend," Fox said adding, "and I am so sorry to hear of your father's passing."

"Thank you, George. It is indeed good to be out," William explained. "I had begged my father to not pay the fine and purchase my liberty, but I couldn't stop him. But God used it for good as we were finally reconciled. The Admiral said that even though he disagreed with us, he was nonetheless proud that I had stuck to my Quaker principles. Before he died, he reversed his decision to disinherit me."

"Oh my, that is good news," Fox answered clapping his hands.

"Better than you realise, George. In addition to my estates in England and Ireland I now own a significant part of the New World Colonies and have an idea of how to escape the oppression we are now under. I am on my way to the Palace to present my plea.'"

"The Palace! We have just come from there haven't we George," Bunny chipped in, smiling.

Fox looked at her confused,

"Have we?"

"Have you?" asked William.

Bunny nodded but Fox shook his head. William continued,

"I have an appointment to see the King this afternoon."

"King?" Bunny voiced with alarm. "But he was…" She stopped herself from saying beheaded and instead drew her hand to her neck preparing to make a throat-slitting motion.

"Yes, I know, it was my father who brought him out of exile," William said, making a false assumption on the nature of Bunny's protest. His reply, however, only served to confuse her more. She allowed him to continue,

"But that was over ten years ago, and the King still owes me… well, he owed my late father."

"You must go William," Fox decreed, "and we shall be praying for you."

"To see King Charles?" Bunny asked in a state of misperception, her thumb still on her own neck pre-slitting.

"Yes, to King Charles," William replied matter of fact adding, "Would you care to join me?"

"But…" Bunny looked down at her own arm now hovering beneath her chin. To cover her growing embarrassment at the protracted gesture she slowly turned her wrist to see her watch, it flashed 16:70.

"Ah, King Charles the *Second*," she said with relief, again shocked at how quickly time was passing. "Yes, I think I am to come with you," she accepted, much to the delight of her new companion.

"I didn't recognise you in your slippers, Cecil." Rector Mashman's voice, soft as it was, cut like a knife through the negative atmosphere outside the damp hospice entrance. The porter shone his torch in the direction of the voice and illuminated the cleric's face.

"Rector Mashman, I didn't see you there." The hospice manager's tone suddenly changed. "Do you know these people?"

"Yes of course, they are all…." he chose his descriptor carefully, "…my friends."

"Why ever didn't you say, Reverend?" the manager asked.

Rector Mashman was a frequent visitor to St. Christopher's Hospice. It was situated within his extensive parish, and he would regularly attend to the spiritual needs of its terminally-ill residents, as well as officiating at the funerals of too many of them. Over the years he had known several managers before the incumbent, Cecil Robertson. Sensing the change in tone, Ralph gently pulled Chris's arm, signalling that he should hold back. This was the Rector's chance to shine, it was *his* show now.

"Do you want to come inside, Reverend?" the manager offered before adding somewhat reluctantly, "with all your friends."

"Perhaps, but first I would like to know about your fine ambulance here," the Rector said diplomatically taking charge of the situation.

"The ambulance?" Cecil asked puzzled.

"Cecil, may I enquire if perhaps someone arrived in it this evening?" By now all except Thea and the Rector had taken several steps back. But no sooner had the Anglican asked the key question than the manager explained emphatically that no patients had been *received* that day and that he was pretty sure the ambulance hadn't moved from its parking spot all day. The night porter was all too eager to confirm the latter fact.

Chris clenched his fists. Ralph whispered in his ear,

"Patience brother."

"Can we take a little look inside the ambulance?" Thea suggested in a similar diplomatic tone. The manager soon acquiesced to this rather unusual, and in his view pointless, request and asked the night porter for the keys, who complained that this was all highly irregular. In answer to the manager's question for the reason they wanted to look inside, the Rector explained that they wondered if something had been left inside after it was at the hospital this evening. The porter harrumphed as he unhooked the ambulance keys from his unnecessarily bulky keychain, adding,

"It *wasn't at* the hospital this evening."

The manager stepped through the narrow rear door, as the Rector and Thea stood either side, and began to take a look around.

"See, nothing appears to have been left here," he concluded after a few moments of a cursory search.

"Is anything missing?" Thea asked. The manager looked back, and with a furrowed brow soon admitted that the top blanket wasn't there but concluded that it was probably just an oversight from the last people to have transported a patient, something that has happened before, and that he would be *having a word*. Something inside the Rector prompted him to push further.

"Perhaps you would look to see if anything else is missing," he expertly asked, adding a disarming, "Please, if you would, Cecil."

The manager gave an exasperated sigh and began to open and close each drawer, cupboard and box, some of which were locked. It wasn't until he had examined the fourth or fifth place that he let out a surprised,

"Hmm. That's not right."

Thea and Mashman looked at each other, but kept silent. The hospice manager now began a much more thorough investigation, muttering under his breath as he did. Finally, the search came to an end and the ashen-faced manager returned to the ambulance doorway.

"How bad is it, Cecil?" the Rector asked.

"All the morphine has gone," he gulped, "plus two saline drips, needles, some lengths of intravenous tubing and the top blanket."

"And is it likely that these were not replenished by the last person to have transported a patient?" Mashman asked. Cecil looked straight at him and confessed, "Well, I could have excused the blanket, but this stock has to be signed in and out after each journey. But as I was the last person to drive the ambulance then I would have to say, no."

At that moment, the headlights of Jack's 4x4 swept around the car park as it came to a halt. The manager exited the ambulance and instructed the porter to lock it and not let anyone else in it without his say so.

"Is it possible someone might have taken them?" Thea asked him.

"Yes, it looks like they have been stolen from the vehicle whilst it was parked here this evening," he concluded, considering what to do next.

"But this ambulance *has* been out tonight," Chris repeated his original claim, as part of what was now a rather large, assembled group.

"That's impossible," the manager again repeated. "There have been no patient transfers, besides there are no drivers on duty other than me."

"But the engine is still warm," Ralph contributed recalling the warmth he had noticed earlier, adding, "Feel it for yourself if you don't believe me." The manager looked at him incredulously, but as his gaze was met by eight determined faces, he felt obliged to at least humour them. Mr. Robertson strode over to the front of his vehicle, placed his palm on the bonnet preparing to deliver a clear, I-told-you-so message. But to his surprise it was indeed warm. He gave a double-take. It was true, the ambulance had been driven recently and, what was more, there was medical stock missing.

"We'll need to report this to the police," he stated concerned. "Think of the press!"

"Don't worry Cecil." The Rector put his arm on the hospice manager's shoulder. "We'll get to the bottom of this for you."

"May I ask a question?" Artur had been assessing the situation dispassionately. Before anyone granted his request he spoke up, clearing his throat imperceptibly first.

"Is there, by any chance, a tracker on the ambulance? A device that records where it is, perhaps to help you manage your fuel consumption." The mention of fuel consumption was the mental trigger that was needed.

"Yes, we use fuel cards for all staff vehicles. There is a website that logs all of the journeys and separates company mileage from personal, you know for tax purposes," he explained.

"And is the ambulance included in that?" Artur asked. Robertson concurred and immediately suggested they go to his office, log on to the fuel card portal and see if it showed where the ambulance had been that night.

The night porter stayed behind intent on making sure that everything inside the ambulance was tidy. Jack spotted that he was going back inside the vehicle so grabbed Rex's elbow and nodded in the porter's direction. Rex

163

instantly knew that Jack was going to have an exhaustive conversation with the porter and declared himself to be Jack's wingman.

"And my restrainer," Jack added with a knowing smile, appreciating that he would need Rex's calming influence. Jack knew how to handle himself. When he first moved to England from Carrickfergus, he had joined the police force as a volunteer Special Constable, something which made his parents particularly proud. They had wanted him to join what was then known as the Royal Ulster Constabulary, but he could never bring himself to. Republicans considered the RUC's very existence to be a huge part of the problem – not an agent of peacekeeping, but a militarised part of an oppressive regime. But in England he could wear the uniform without fear of being targeted. For seven years Jack wore it for a few hours each week in a variety of civil order duties. He was never required to solve any crime, as his stature leant itself solely to controlling drunken partygoers, unruly teenagers, heated protestors and angry football supporters. He learned self-defence techniques and how to bring down fleeing suspects; he even fired several rounds on a firearms course, but this was never going to be his chosen career and eventually he could no longer afford the time.

Jack stepped inside the ambulance, fifty-percent churchman, fifty-percent ex-copper.

"This is your chance for honesty," he announced loudly in his broadest Ulsterman accent. The night porter jumped, unaware anyone had followed him into the back of the vehicle. Rex, still one-hundred percent churchman, added,

"Be sure your sins will find you out!"

The porter collapsed onto the stretcher bunk, visibly frightened. Jack was an imposing figure in an open space but in the confines of an ambulance eclipsed everything. Rex sat on the bunk next to him and it didn't take long for the orderly to begin to confess. He admitted that someone had indeed asked to borrow the ambulance that evening. Rex asked him what reason they gave for the loan and to their surprise the porter explained it was to be used for a photo shoot for a music video, a plausible if entirely fictitious reason. He went on to say they only needed it for a couple of hours, and that they brought it back on time as promised.

"I never knew they would take any supplies," he pleaded. The identity of the person to whom he gave the ambulance keys was unknown. The porter looked worried and began to mutter that he was sure he was going to lose his job as a result. Jack coldly agreed with him. Rex changed the subject and asked the most obvious question: why had he done it?

"Because they paid him," Jack said. "And handsomely I bet." The porter dropped his head but said nothing.

It was quite a squeeze to fit Thea, Artur, Joel, Chris, Ralph and Rector Mashman into the hospice manager's office, but they all managed to gather behind him as he logged into his account on FuelMgr.com. There were five vehicles listed, the ambulance being the last one. Selecting that vehicle and today's date on a pop-up calendar revealed a journey line overlaid onto Google Maps. The manager used his finger to describe the route: starting from the hospice, driving into town straight to the hospital, and waiting there for around half an hour.

"Look, the time matches with the hospital parking camera," Chris said excitedly.

The manager then continued to outline the route as the vehicle left the hospital, out into the countryside to a remote place marked as *Lane End Farm* according to the text on the onscreen map. Only a short wait there, a little over fifteen minutes, before the ambulance drove back into town, this time to the railway station. Then it went all the way back to the farmhouse before finishing at the hospice. Total journey eleven point seven miles, total time ninety-eight minutes, he concluded.

"Do you want a hard copy?" he asked.

"Yes please," Artur was quick to confirm.

Chris was itching to set off to the farm immediately, but Ralph suggested they meet in the hospice lobby first to decide on a proper course of action. Despite his frustration Chris admitted that this probably did make more sense.

Chapter 18

THE ACT OF UNIFORMITY

The return walk to the Palace was almost unrecognisable from the one she had taken seemingly minutes earlier. The city landscape was now peppered with ash-covered, burnt-out homes everywhere. It was shocking to see so much destruction. The date of the Great Fire of London was one of the few dates that Bunny could easily recall. Four years had passed and much of the centre of London was still uninhabitable with only a few, largely stone-built, buildings remaining. Not that lack of housing appeared to be a problem as few people were to be seen. That'll be the result of the plague, she thought. The Great Plague of London had killed a quarter of the population of the city in the year immediately prior to the fire destroying seventy thousand homes. The Millennium of Peace that P.G. Barebone spoke of was lying, quite literally, in ashes! she thought.

They walked through the blackened streets in silence. Having been fully immersed in the religious zealotry of the times, Bunny was in little doubt as to how these devastating events would probably be construed by the Puritans she now mixed with. This will be interpreted as an act of divine punishment, she thought. Perhaps that was true, her mind having been opened to such an idea in a way it had never been before. But if it was retribution, she had no idea why. She needed to find out so decided to test her theory.

"Tell me William," she asked her companion as they continued their depressing promenade.

"What do *you* think the plague and the great fire were punishment for?"

He stopped in his tracks. Bunny too arrested her march hoping to not have offended him. A few moments passed as they stood in contemplative silence before he shared his thoughts.

"Where do I start, there are too many things to choose from," he mused as they recommenced their walk.

"Such as?" she prompted.

"Well, there is the 1662 Act of Uniformity that re-established the Church of England making it the only legally approved Church. An Act which they expected all the English Presbyterians, Congregationalists, Baptists and we Quakers to duly conform with but ..." [1]

"You didn't, and so you became known as non-conformists," Bunny interjected, pleased to have put two and two together.

"Quite!" he agreed. "Then there's the exclusion of Puritans from holding any high office or receiving any education."

"Ouch!" Bunny exclaimed.

"Then there was the Conventicle Act of '64 which meant that no religious group of more than five people could meet outside of a Church of England building." [2]

"So, any non-conformist gathering would become illegal," she concluded.

"Quite!" he repeated. William then stopped, this time outside one of the churches that had escaped the fire. He turned to face the building.

"But I think the greatest affront to the Almighty was the Five-Mile Act."

"The Five-Mile Act?" she questioned.

"To be more accurate, The Nonconformists Act of 1665," he clarified. Bunny simply deployed her tell-me-more look to which he duly succumbed.

"All clergy had to swear an oath to obey the 1662 Prayer Book. But the days of blindly obeying liturgy are past, even within the Church of England. There were over two thousand ministers who refused to take the oath. Including the vicar of this very parish."

He pointed at the grand façade in front of them.

---

[1] The Act for the Uniformity required all clergy to swear the following oath.' I, ... do here declare my unfeigned assent and consent to all and everything contained in and prescribed in and by the Book entitled The Book of Common Prayer ... and other Rites and Ceremonies of the Church, according to the use of the Church of England...; and the Form and Manner of Making, Ordaining and Consecrating of Bishops, Priests and Deacons.' Many refused and in so doing were to be deprived of their living.

[2] The Act was aimed at preventing non-conformists by outlawing religious assemblies (conventicles) of more than five people outside the auspices of the Church of England. The Jewish community took their objections to the King who granted them an exception from the Act and in so doing indirectly granted them full citizenship.

"All those Godly men lost their jobs, their churches, their homes and, to add insult to injury, were forbidden to *work* anywhere within five miles of their former church." [1]

"Hence the Five-Miles," she said.

"Quite!" he answered once again, this time emphatically.

Her questions had the effect of supressing William's joy-filled enthusiasm. They walked on silently for a while. Bunny's geography of central London wasn't brilliant, but she suspected they should be somewhere close to St. Paul's Cathedral. The difference between this ashen wasteland and the bustling central London that she was more familiar with was stark and understandably depressing. She had clearly sent her companion on an emotionally downward trajectory. Consequently, she felt she had some responsibility to attempt to cheer him, especially as he was about to meet with the King.

"You said you had a plan," she asked, breaking the silence.

"Pardon?"

"You said you had a plan to put to the King? That *is* where we are going, isn't it?" she clarified.

The question managed successfully to pull William out of the negative thought-spiral that she had inadvertently sent him into. He then took delight to share with her his plan to use the land he had inherited in the New World as a Holy Experiment. He planned to set up a community that would be free from religious intolerance. He was totally convinced that the King would agree to back it. As she listened, Bunny couldn't help but think that encouraging thousands of Quakers to relocate over the ocean would, of course, be attractive to the King. It would remove the Puritan irritation from his doorstep. It didn't seem fair to Bunny. She didn't know what the religious version of ethnic cleansing was, but this sounded very much like it. William was so fixated on his colonial experiment that he couldn't see that he was being complicit to triggering a mass emigration with no likelihood of return.

"Assuming the King agrees, have you decided what you are going to call your community?" she asked.

---

[1] Well, the Nonconformists Act of 1665 became widely known as the Five-Mile Act as it forbade clergymen from living, preaching or even setting foot within five miles of the parish from which they had been expelled. Thousands of clergy lost their homes as a consequence.

"I think it only proper to name it after my father the Admiral," he quickly replied.

"Admiral City?" she suggested?

"No, he was Admiral Penn, so I am going to name it Penn Land," he explained with pride.

"Hmmm," she wasn't convinced.

"You don't like Penn Land?"

Bunny shook her head, much to young Mr. Penn's chagrin. "Well, see if you can come up with anything better?"

"Pennsylvania!" she announced with self-confident aplomb. He didn't want to admit it but that was much better.

Presently, they crossed the limit of where the fire had reached. Bunny looked back reviewing the scene they had traversed. Behind them were fire-scorched buildings and gaps where structures once stood. No greenery, just a dark depressing haze of devastation. Looking forward, however, the buildings were all intact, the place was clean and there were even odd flashes of grass, trees and flowers, the starkest of contrasts. The tall fences and gold-leaf gates of the Palace lay but a few yards beyond this dramatic cinder tidemark. Bunny couldn't help but think that if the great fire was an act of divine punishment, then perhaps it had missed its target.

As Rex closed the reception door behind him it was obvious there wasn't going to be anywhere for him to sit. His eyes slowly surveyed the small hospice waiting room looking for a vacant perch. Rector Mashman and Baptist minister Thea Howlsy occupied two of the foam-padded seats to his left; Chris Palmer and Ralph Shafer, both from C.R.F., shared the third, each atop one of the arms. Immediately across from him, beneath an oversized notice board, Methodist Joel Whyens shared a low coffee-table with a lifeless Yucca plant. To his right, Lutheran pastor Artur Thelmin demonstrated his being the youngest of the gathering by folding the printout from Fuelmgr.com into his hip pocket then mounting the reception desk in a single leap. Presbyterian Jack Fort, who had entered from the car park immediately before Quaker Rex Fogge, was already making his way behind the desk to squeeze his large frame into the receptionist's chair. Rex leaned back against the door to complete the circle.

No sooner had he taken his seat, then Jack updated the others on the night porter's confession that someone had paid him to *borrow* the ambulance.

"Goodly heavens above!" Reverend Mashman exclaimed in astonishment.

Everyone assumed that it would have been Jack that had solicited such an admission from the night porter, but he was quick to point out that it was, as he put it,

"Foggie, over there, who got him to spill the beans."

Rex hadn't been called Foggie since his time at boarding school and when he used to play in the school rugby XV. It was an obvious nickname and one he didn't object to but strangely it hadn't followed him into the world of high finance. Everyone looked at him standing in the doorway and promptly gave a repeat chorus of "Foggie! eh!" He smiled back at the group pleased with his new moniker.

Joel then excitedly updated Jack and Rex that they knew exactly where they had taken the ambulance, explaining the route from here to the hospital, then on to a farmhouse, then to the railway station, back to the farmhouse, then back to the hospice.

"Lane End Farm," Artur chipped in for clarity.

It was Ralph who had suggested that they take stock before rushing off, so he assumed the role of convener of this forum.

"I think it would be wise to take a few minutes before we do anything rash," he proposed. Everyone agreed except Chris who was keen to get to the farmhouse, anxious about Bunny's wellbeing. Nevertheless, patience was a virtue and Ralph was his church leader, so he said nothing. Ralph posed the question,

"What do we actually know?" and motioned to Joel to make a note on the bottom right corner of the whiteboard behind him. Joel stood up and searched for a whiteboard marker. He found two, one green the other red. He first checked their labels to assure himself they weren't permanent markers before putting pen to whiteboard.

For a group who had already demonstrated a great skill at ignoring each other and speaking across one another, surprisingly they took it in turns to offer succinct pieces of information and waited for Joel to write them down. There was no logical order but between them they quickly documented that Bunny was taken to the hospital; she was put into the hospice ambulance; the ambulance was borrowed for that purpose; then it was driven to a farmhouse.

"Don't forget the blood stain at the Catholic Church. She was definitely injured," Ralph contributed hoping not to upset his friend. Rector Mashman reminded them that there were medical supplies, morphine and other things missing.

"We could do with knowing exactly what was missing," Artur suggested.

"We'll find out from the night-porter when we are done here," Jack said, adding with a wink, "Won't we Foggie!"

Artur thought this was a good idea,

"If she has been kidnapped then it would make sense she is being sedated."

At this suggestion Chris's emotions got the better of him and he began to rise to his feet, wanting to leave the room. Ralph took his wrist and gently held him down. Everyone was looking at them as tears began to fill Chris's eyes. The group remained silent, not wanting to upset him any further but not knowing what to say. Jack was the first to speak.

"Hobbits, Elves and Dwarves!" he said somewhat cryptically. More than one member of the circle replied with a bewildered,

"What?"

"That's what we are. Hobbits and Elves." Jack's attempt at clarification didn't help as he continued to scramble through his memory. "You know like in the film... you know...with the dwarves."

Thea Howlsy was first to cotton-on to his observation.

"Do you mean *The Lord of the Rings*, Jack?" she asked.

"Yes, that's it," Jack said with relief. "We are like the gathering of the Hobbits and Elves and Dwarves and people, on a mission..."

"Only we are Methodists, Baptists, Lutherans, Anglicans, Quakers, and..." Joel interrupted.

"The fellowship of the ring," Thea entitled as everyone shared a laugh.

"No, no, we are the fellowship of the *King*!" Ralph corrected them emphasising the final word and pointing skywards. They were indeed in fellowship and jointly in the service of King Jesus!

"Amen! to that," Jack echoed.

"So, which one of us is Gandalf?" Rex asked. All eyes looked at Rector Mashman. He may be un-bearded but at his age he was the closest fit.

"By the colour of hair perhaps, but I don't think I am much of a wizard," the Anglican contributed, pleased to be in on the joke.

"I have to disagree Rector," Ralph said firmly. "The way you got the manager here to open up was rather wizardly."

"We all have to do our own bit," he admitted with a grin, rather pleased with having been given the place of honour.

"I wouldn't have thought you'd have seen that movie, Reverend?" Joel asked him.

"Movie?" the Rector replied, "I've read the books, all of them."

The analogy was striking. They were indeed a gathering of different tribes, assembled together in one place for one purpose, for one mission. As the comparison sunk in, thoughts turned to the object of their rescue mission. Chris had by now composed himself sufficiently to declare publicly the fact that everyone was now realising to be the truth.

"Bunny is very precious to me," he said, "and I *am* going to find her." They all assured him they were going to help him find her. Ralph then made an important point.

"I think someone should go to the police and tell them what we now know."

"And we should tell them about the letter from the Grey Wolves of Islam," Joel quickly added. "I've looked them up. They are an extreme right-wing anti-Kurd group from Turkey." The additional factual details didn't go down well. Most would rather have not been reminded about the letter.

It was decided that Rector Gandalf should first collect the letter from the manse and take it to the police station, and that he shouldn't go alone. Thea was desperate to not spend another minute in the Mashman Honda, fearing that if he persisted in travelling so slowly she may eventually crack and take control of the vehicle, leaving the Rector on the pavement. To her relief Joel Whyens volunteered to go with him. A grey-haired white man with a bald-headed black one should make an interesting combination, she thought.

As they left the hospice reception Jack and Rex headed over to the ambulance to make an inventory of missing items. Sadly, both the porter and the ambulance were nowhere to be seen.

"He'll have moved it somewhere more secure," Artur suggested to the two of them.

"Lucky for him," Jack replied with a tut before they all set off for Lane End Farm.

Chapter 19

THE FRENCH PROPHETS

"Thus, sayeth the Lord!"

It was a well-worn trope, an oft-parodied catchphrase, an introduction that was designed to give the endorsement of the Almighty to whatever is about to be delivered; a saying that was so cliché Bunny couldn't remember having ever heard anyone say it other than in jest. But there he was, one of three well-dressed men standing upon a makeshift podium in the centre of a London square.

"Thus, sayeth the Lord!"

They had gathered a crowd, but they weren't entertainers. By the looks of the size of the gathering throng, these three men were popular. Those listening intently appeared to believe that these guys were indeed about to speak from God. There were tears in the eyes of some of these attentive Londoners.

"Thus, sayeth the Lord!"

As she stood, not for the first time in a crowd in the London square, she could hear whispers from the crowd describe them as the French Prophets. Like it or not, Bunny couldn't deny it. These men were about to speak prophetically; were about to deliver a word from God. She was aware that this was something that Community Restoration Fellowship would occasionally dabble in. Bunny had not formed an opinion of whether it was biblical or fanciful, she didn't want to offend Chris. But she was convinced that this was definitely a *modern* phenomenon. In fact, Chris had told her as much saying that the gift of prophesy, as he called it, had only just been *restored* to the Church.

But here she was in - she looked down at her watch to see - here she was in 1706 and three French prophets were commanding a sizeable street audience. If she was ever the sort of person to say she had had her mind blown, this would be an opportunity – but she wasn't – so, as the prophets began their decrees she inched her way to the rear of the crowd.[1]

To her surprise, also at the periphery of the audience she found several people feverishly penning, each with small portable writing desks, ink and quills

---

[1] 'The French Prophets: The History of a Millenarian Group in Eighteenth-Century England' by Hillel Schwartz. Berkeley: University of California Press. (1980)

at the ready. Her curiosity got the better of her, so she manoeuvred her position to be able to look over the shoulder of the nearest one. She half expected to see a page full of indecipherable Latin. Thankfully the scribe was taking an accurate transcription in English of the prophetic words now being released with great authority to the hushed congregation, all seemingly hungry to hear from God.

No sooner had the three Frenchmen finished than two locals took their cue to join in the charismatic proclamation, taking to the mini stage with their own 'Thus sayeth the Lord.' Then four more did likewise. There was a wave of prophecy moving across the London crowd. This was totally bizarre and not the eighteenth-century Church Bunny would ever have imagined.

"Unbelievable!" she said, her surprise palpable. The writer, behind whom she stood, thought she was speaking to him and quickly turned around.

"Miss?" he asked.

"I'm sorry, I didn't mean to disturb you," she pleaded apologetically. He nodded his acceptance.

"It is unbelievable to see..." she struggled to say the word but there was nothing else to call them, "to see prophets... on the streets of London."

"Why is it?" the scribe said before invitingly adding, "It's happening all over Europe, Miss."

Bunny's furrowed brow was enough to demand that he reach down into his leather bag and extract a copy of the *London Gazette* and pass it to her with a cursory "See for yourself."

Bunny thanked him and grasped the inky broadsheet. As she opened the folded paper she noticed the date read 1706. She checked her watch, compliantly it flashed 17:06. The headline and lead article told of several *unnamed* bishops giving their backing to the three French Prophets whose message was 'The Protestant Church in Europe is Asleep.'

She read on and discovered that this prophetic awakening, as it was described, had begun in South-Eastern France a few years earlier when a young shepherdess named Isabel van San began prophesying in her sleep, quoting the book of Joel and warning of coming judgement. Bunny read how the Catholic authorities then had her arrested, at which point other children and teenagers began to prophesy and soon the whole region was covered with child prophets, many of them warning of imminent divine judgement on the nation. People who heard the prophecies would often fall to the ground and howl. Bunny couldn't read it fast enough, this was amazing. She then read how it all turned ugly when Catholic churches started to be attacked. Over 300 prophets were arrested, the girls banished to convents, the boys sentenced to be galley slaves.[1] The article beneath the main one had a similar theme. This time in Silesia children from between five and fourteen started to meet three times every day - not to play, but to worship God and pray. Their parents claimed they were powerless to stop the spontaneous gatherings. Magistrates were at a loss as to how to deal with crowds of *orderly* children.[2] There was an article about fifty psalm-singing Protestants in Camisard, France, who attacked a prison and freed everyone. By the time this rebellion was finally quashed the surviving prophets were no longer children but angry young men, many of whom had fled to London.

Bunny closed the newspaper, her fingers now stained with ink, and handed it back to the scribe with a sincere and slightly bewildered "Thanks."

This was just the good news she needed to hear. She closed her eyes and prayed; not a formal prayer as she would normally have done, more of a Quaker prayer. She felt like being spontaneous.

"Okay God, I get the message..." she began.

Even starting a prayer with such a phrase was a big change for Bunny. She had always begun her prayers with 'Dear Lord and Father.' The thought of saying 'Okay God!' would have been so alien to her and far too familiar. She would have definitely judged anyone who used such a casual divine address. But here she was doing the very thing. Something had shifted in her relationship with her Dear Lord and Father. She continued,

"I get it. Even though I can see that there has been a lot of politics and..." she paused to find the best phrase to sum up her thoughts, "...even from the most well-intentioned and godly of people, there appears to have been a lot of *humanity* in the decisions that have shaped the religious landscape. I get it. You are showing me that despite all of that, you will not be held down and will break out in the most unexpected of places."

She was sure she heard someone give a hearty "Amen," but when she opened her eyes she couldn't be sure whom.

"It was me." The voice was clear and came from her left. She turned to see who had been eavesdropping on her intercession. Some twenty feet away,

---

[1] 'Protestants: The Radicals who Made the Modern World' by Alec Ryrie (2017).

[2] 'Protestants: The Radicals who Made the Modern World' by Alec Ryrie (2017)

just beyond the edge of the crowd stood a carriage, its door open and its two elegant black horses stomping impatiently on the cobbles eager to make away. Leaning towards her from inside the open door was a familiar face. The gold-rimmed hat, warm smile and outstretched arm represented a welcome refuge in an ever-changing world. He beckoned her to come over, she was all too willing to join him.

"Quickly, quickly, we've got a long journey ahead of us," her nameless companion urged.

"I think I'm pleased to see you," Bunny said as she embarked.

This was not the first carriage in which she had recently taken a long journey, but as soon as they set off she could immediately feel the effects of the invention of spring-suspension. This carriage was almost comfortable; certainly, in comparison to the bone-shaking contraption she had endured from Zurich to Dordrecht. The internal panels were painted with the most intricate of floral patterns and above each door there was a golden carved heraldic crest. She could make it out as a shield with a lion to its left and a lamb on its right, but the Latin inscriptions were unclear. She slid her palm lovingly across the plush velvet seat. This was more like it, she thought to herself, then smiled as she realised that, despite this being some sort of dream, she nonetheless knew what she liked.

Once inside, Bunny commented on how surprised she had been to have witnessed prophets in the seventeenth century. Her chaperon explained that if you looked carefully enough you would find that all the gifts of the Holy Spirit had continued ever since the day of Pentecost as God could never be confined within a structure made by man.

"Yes, that was what I said in my prayer," she added, pleased to have been one step ahead of him. He went on to explain that over the next few years many level-headed Protestants across Britain, including one senior bishop, all began to prophesy. Some began to speak in tongues, one even in perfect Latin having never learnt it. And that in all of this the common message was always that the Church establishment was asleep and needed to wake up.

"And did it, I mean, will it?" Bunny asked.

"That is where we are going." He answered cryptically. Bunny gave him her *continue* look. He duly complied. "People call this the Age of Enlightenment."

"Oh, you mean scientists like Isaac Newton and philosophers like Descartes." Those were the only names she could recall from her GCSE history revision, and she was as particularly pleased when he nodded in agreement.

"But for the Church this is the age of Pietism."

"Isn't that just another name for Puritans?" she asked innocently. This time he shook his head sympathetically, then explained that the Puritans' zeal was aimed at *purifying* the State into a godly nation.

"Or set up a new Christian State in the colonies, like in Pennsylvania," she added enthusiastically. Once again, he nodded, much to Bunny's delight.

"Pietists on the other hand just wanted to be left alone by the State," he said. "This thinking allowed the seeds of an awakening to begin across many denominations, especially Lutherans."

"Ah, so are we going to Germany, back to Wittenberg?" she asked.

"Well, I would have to say both 'Yes' and 'No'," he answered smiling. "Yes, we are going to Germany but not to Wittenberg. This time you need to visit Herrnhut in Saxony."

"Herrnhut?" she repeated, sporting a baffled expression and adding categorically "Never heard of it!"

"Few have, but the significance of the small gathering in Herrnhut is easily equal to that of Wittenberg in 1517."

Bunny sat back into the comfort of her seat. As she did, she noticed a large hardback book beside her. She hadn't seen it when she entered and wouldn't be surprised if it had suddenly materialised beside her. She reached for it, laid it on her lap and opened the hardback cover to read the title, *Pious Desires*. She gave out an involuntary snort of amusement, then quickly looked over to her travelling companion.

"Pious Desires!" she said hoping to sound as matter of fact as she could. His expression didn't change. "Pious Desires! It sounds like the sort of title women buy at airports and railway stations. 'Pious Desires' by Jackie Collins, or Jilly Cooper, or Barbara Cartland..." His ungiving demeanour gave her no choice but to look down at the text "...or by Philip Jacob Spener it would appear."

As the miles passed, she began to read. It was clear that this was indeed an age when people were openly questioning the basis of faith. She read that there was a large secular middle-class and the Church was offering them little, but this book was addressing the issue head-on. Spener emphasised the need for a deep and personal relationship with God as more important than theological doctrines or sacramental liturgy. Christianity was not about refuting error but about love, he wrote. This made so much sense to Bunny, particularly in this strange world into which she been involuntarily immersed. Spener was brutally frank when addressing the religious hierarchy of the day. 'If St. Paul were to try to follow a theological debate, he would only understand a little of what our slippery geniuses say,'[1] she read. Bunny wondered if any of the people she had recently met would be classified as 'a slippery genius.' Despite the comparative comfort of her surroundings, the monotonous click-clack of carriage wheels and relentless rocking had a hypnotic effect.

After some time reading, she had a question for her all-knowing companion,

"Are people putting these ideas into practice?"

"Which ideas do you mean?" he asked.

She thumbed-back a few pages to remind herself of the correct expression. She found it and faithfully read aloud the phrase,

"The priesthood of all believers," then gave it her own interpretation. "You don't need a priest or minister to teach you about God, you can get to know him yourself through the Bible."

He thought for a moment then said, "Well, how about Griffith Jones, for example."

"Griffith Jones? That's about as Welsh a name as you could get," she quipped. He ignored the comment and continued.

"Jones was a shepherd turned minister from rural Llanddowror, Wales…" as he said Wales, she wanted to comment but instead remained smugly quiet as he continued. "He set up a school to teach the Bible to the uneducated Welsh-speakers in his community."

"So that they could find their own way to God," Bunny interrupted. He nodded.

"In the following years Jones established schools across the nation and over one hundred and fifty thousand people passed through them. All learned how to read and write, and all developed a good knowledge of the Bible."

"But they weren't all part of his own church in Lland…owy…owy."

"Llanddowror. No, they were from other parishes, some were non-conformists, some were completely unchurched. There was no distinction. This was the pietist way."

---

[1] 'Protestants: The Radicals who Made the Modern World' by Alec Ryrie (2017)

Bunny looked out of the carriage window. She didn't know how she knew it, but they were in France. Perhaps it was the architecture of nearby villages, perhaps it was in the dress of the locals who stood to one side to allow the carriage to thunder past them, or more likely she just knew – the way that you just know things in a dream. The digital display on her watch was continually changing 17:25, 17:26, 17:27. She was transitioning in both place and time. Does this make the carriage a TARDIS, she wondered? No, she concluded, it would be much bigger on the inside if it were. She could begin to feel her eyes getting heavy.

"What have you found out so far?"

She wasn't completely asleep, but his voice jolted her fully awake. She considered for a moment before answering.

"After the Reformation a lot of different versions of Church sprang up. National politics was behind a lot of these, but as time has passed that has given way to ... simplicity."

"Interesting," he answered. "Go on."

"But, and this is what is bothering me, with each new strand of Christianity there is more separation. There is no unity. All of them are in their own little bubbles, at best tolerating each other, but sometimes openly hostile."

"So, what are you going to do about it, Miss Elstow?" he answered.

"Me?" she replied incredulously. "I'm just an observer here," adding hesitantly "...aren't I?"

"What do you *want* to do about it?" he said persistently.

"There's nothing I can do about it, this is H-I-S-T-O-R-Y!" She spelled it out.

"And if I am not mistaken, Miss Elstow, you are part of it. So what are you going to do?" he said emphatically.

"There is nothing I can do..." Bunny hesitated from repeating herself. She knew she wasn't going to succeed in this conversation. She thought for a moment then answered, "Nothing other than pray, I guess."

"What a good idea."

She wasn't sure if his reply was meant to be sarcastic, but she took it that way. Nevertheless, she had to admit that prayer was always a good idea. This was God's problem after all and if there was to be a solution to such a fragmented Church then God would have to be the one to find it. She leaned forward, bowed her head and half-closed her eyes.

"Dear Lord and Fa..."

She had barely begun her supplication when the coach was suddenly filled with an intense brilliant light. As the light shone, she felt a hand, a force, push her back onto her seat. She was so shocked she let out a sudden yelp and closed her eyes firmly for fear of being blinded by the dazzling fluorescence. What was happening? Was this the Shekinah glory of God entering the carriage? Dare she open her eyes, was she having a divine visitation? She was a simple Anglican. We don't do this sort of thing, she thought. She remained frozen somehow, now lying down, unable to move even if she had dared to. The invasive light was trying to pierce her eyelids, but she knew better than to open them.

Momentarily she heard a voice, two voices. Initially they were indistinct but then she began to piece together words and phrases.

"She's coming round ... give her some more ... I don't know how much ... c'mon he'll be here soon ... yeah, that should do it ... there, there, Missy go back to sleep."

Chapter 20

"Ahumm!"

This was the third *ahumm* the desk sergeant had given them since they arrived fifteen minutes earlier. Joel Whyens had suggested that he should do the talking and carefully delivered the facts, occasionally referring to a mobile-phone photograph he had taken of the hospice whiteboard as a reminder. The policeman meticulously transcribed everything that he said but, as he did, it soon became obvious to Joel how limited these *facts* really were:

A missing person who had already been reported and whom the police had already *de-prioritised.* A stain in a church that *may or may not* be blood and whose priest is unconcerned about; a good Samaritan; an ambulance that has *not* been stolen and a hospice which is *not reporting* anything missing. The letter was, to be fair, taken a little more seriously. A photocopy of it was taken and stapled to the missing person's report, but then the sergeant politely thanked them for the additional information and dismissed them without any assurance that they would do anything before the requisite twenty-four hours had elapsed.

"But you must do something!" Joel pleaded in frustration. The officer, however, was unmoved saying,

"Sir, I have no available officers this evening."

"Why haven't you?" Joel asked impertinently.

"Not that it is any of your business, Sir," he explained, "but we have the murder of two unknown males to investigate and, if that wasn't enough, there is some commotion at the hospital and the paparazzi are trying to get the pictures of some celebrity. If I wanted to help I really couldn't, Sir. Give it twenty-four hours and if..." he consulted his notes. "...if Miss Elstow hasn't surfaced by then, come back."

It was pointless to argue. Joel and Rev. Mashman departed. As they arrived at the Rector's car Joel remarked,

"I think we saw a photographer arriving when we were at the hospital earlier."

"I don't remember," the Rector said as they set off to meet the others at the farmhouse.

"Willkommen zu Herrnhut, into the Lord's safekeeping."

Someone had opened the carriage door for her, but all Bunny could hear were cheers, clapping and the occasional blast from the biblical musical instrument, the rams-horn shofar. She had never felt more welcome. Herrnhut was certainly a place she was going to enjoy visiting if this was an indication of how friendly they were. She began to alight from the carriage, taking the hand of the leader of the welcoming committee. She thanked her host and straightened her clothes, a little flustered to be meeting so many people after a long journey and without the benefit of a mirror.

"Rebecca?" her greeter asked her.

"No!" Bunny answered calmly.

"Woher ist Peter?" He ignored her negative answer, instead peering past her into the gloomy interior of the carriage.

Bunny joined him in looking into the carriage, it was devoid of all occupants. Her travelling companion was gone and as for *Peter* he was nowhere to be seen.

"Where is Peter?" he insisted, this time in English.

"Peter who?" Bunny asked politely, conscious of the large audience watching them.

"Vee thought you ver Peter," he protested. "Not you Fraulein, but vee thought this vas Peter's pferdewagen. He is bringing Rebecca here to Herrnhut," he said, very animated and excitedly adding, "She is to be ordained!"

"Well, I am very sorry that I am not Rebecca," Bunny said in her most dignified manner. "My name is Miss Johan Elstow." She considered adding, "And I will not be requiring ordination," but thought she had better not embarrass him further. He looked disappointed, so too did the small crowd.

"Ich bin Christian," he said.

"I assumed you were," Bunny answered. "I am also, but I don't know your name."

He answered to say that his name was David. However, a few minutes of confusion ensued with Bunny understandably addressing him as David. Each time she did, her host tried several times to explain that David was his surname. Eventually the penny dropped, and Bunny began calling him by his correct first name, Christian.[1]

---

[1] Christian David was the co-founder of the refuge at Herrnhut and a Moravian missionary who undertook several missions to the Inuit communities of Greenland, establishing the settlement of New Herrnhut, modern-day Nuuk, the national capital.

It didn't take the welcoming party long to disperse. Christian was at pains to put Bunny at ease and to not make her feel any less welcome, but the cheering crowds were a difficult act to follow.

"I have heard a lot about you," she began. It was a bit of a bluff as she had no real idea where she was or why this group of Christians was so significant, but she had to start somewhere.

"Ah, many have," he replied courteously, clearly not for the first time. "This is God's place of refuge for all Verfolgt..." he paused, hunting his memory for the English translation, "...for all persecuted believers."

It was clear that this was a discourse he had delivered many times before. As they slowly walked towards an assemblage of wooden buildings, he steered them effortlessly towards a large outcrop of stone to one side of the main thoroughfare into the settlement. When they reached it he gestured towards the brass plaque that was affixed to it and waited while Bunny read the inscription.

It commemorated the covenant made by the original founders of the religious community and stated the four foundational tenets it was based upon, each prefixed by ornate Roman numerals. The first line read:

"I. Freedom to Preach the Word of God." That was followed by,

"II. Freedom of the communion of the chalice for all." Bunny presumed that meant no restriction for any believer to take the holy sacraments. Next came,

"III. Exclusion of the clergy from large possessions or civil authority." It was clear that this group was separate from the State, from any civil authority. The final statement ominously stated,

"IV. Strict repression and punishment of mortal sins." That final point did sound a little severe, but she couldn't really find any grounds to disagree with any of these four basic principles. Besides, she had been told that this place mattered, so who was she to question the foundations. Bunny muttered a polite "Very good" and started to walk away.

"Wait a minute!" she suddenly said and made a dramatic double-take as she looked at the bottom of the inscription. Underneath the four foundational creeds was the date this covenant was made. It said July 1420.

"But that is a hundred years before Luther!" she said aghast. "Are you telling me you have been worshipping like this for..." she pulled up her sleeve to look at her watch. Christian had no idea what she was doing and blankly followed her gaze to look at her unusual wrist-jewellery. The display showed

17:36. Thankfully the mental arithmetic required was straightforward enough to allow her to quickly finish the sentence, "…for three hundred and sixteen years!"

"Ja," he answered. "But vee have had to keep moving around, keep in hiding. Vee ver safe for many years in Bohemia. Vee ver der Bohemian Brethren." He gave a protracted sigh, "But Katholisch authorities found us, so for the last hundred years vee have had to go underground in Moravia. Und so vee became der Moravian Brethren."

Talk about a remnant, Bunny thought. She was amazed that this group had remained intact in the remotest parts of the central European highlands throughout all the religious and political upheaval she had witnessed in Germany, Switzerland, Holland, Scotland, England, and soon to be – or was it now? She lost track of the decades – North America. She remained silent and allowed Hr. David to continue.

"But then came Count Nikolaus Ludwig von Zinzendorf und Pottendorf," he said with obvious glee.

"Who?" She couldn't help but react to the excessively grand German nobility title. David repeated the name proudly and pointed to the statue next to them. The face was very distinguished with a fixed grin. Bunny wondered if he was grinning for the statue or whether he genuinely looked like that in real life.

David explained that the Count had bought the land in Herrnhut in 1722 and created a safe place for Protestant refugees. Not only did the underground Moravians find sanctuary there but since then Pietists from all over Europe had joined them.

While he was talking, Bunny couldn't help but be amazed at the longevity, not of the place but of the faithful people. The Church is the people not the building, she remembered Chris from C.R.F. saying to her over coffee. She knew that was true in theory, but this was the first time she had met a congregation that had endured *without* a place of worship. She needed to know more about why they had survived for so long.

"What is so special about…" she wanted to say *you* but that didn't sound polite, so quickly reverted to "…this place?"

He must have half-expected the question as they were already approaching a wooden building from which considerable noise was emanating. He held open the door. Inside Bunny could see around two dozen people ecstatically exclaiming praises, some were dancing, others near to shouting. It was a tumult of heaven-ward activity and joy.

"It was in the summer of twenty-seven," he reminisced, "that twenty-four men und twenty-four frau covenanted to spend one hour each day in prayer. Many others have since joined them." He looked at the dynamic and boisterous gathering before adding, "Prayer has been held here non-stop twenty-four hours a day ever since."

"This is a prayer meeting?" Bunny asked incredulously. He gave a gentle Aa-hm by way of confirmation. She was taken aback. She knew that some of the prayer meetings at C.R.F. would get *lively* but she had never seen anything purporting to be church that was quite so raucous.

"If this prayer meeting is going on continually," Bunny asked, "when is it scheduled to finish?" As a church secretary, the organising of such a long-running event sounded like a nightmare.

"There is no reason it can't continue for at least ein hundred years," he answered confidently.[1] Bunny swallowed hard at the thought of a one-hundred-year prayer meeting.

He quietly closed the door, not that anyone inside would have heard if he had slammed it. Bunny followed almost open-mouthed as he then led them to another building. Inside, benches of smiling folk were enjoying a meal. Bunny had no idea when the last time was that she had eaten and suddenly felt hungry. Hr. David led them to a bench and continued his well-rehearsed tour-guide introduction.

"In this place you vill find Christians from many, many, different confessions," he explained. "Vee all support each other vithout a religious minister's help. In fact, I would say the success of this place vas born from the very lack of any controlling influence."

"So, it's a sort of commune?" Bunny asked.

Hr. David admitted that he didn't understand the word commune but agreed that it was a religious community.

"Yes, vee have communal living in which simplicity of lifestyle and generosity are important to us. As you have seen vee emphasise prayer, worship and Bible study." He collected a small lunch platter for them, then

---

[1] The Prayer meeting did indeed last 100 years according to: "A Prayer Meeting that Lasted 100 Years." Leslie K. Tarr, ChristianityToday.com

added, "And also the confession of sins and mutual accountability." As she followed him to an empty bench-table, Bunny remembered point IV on the brass plaque outside.

"And does it work?" she asked, intrigued.

"If you mean have the divisions between men and women, between social groups and between the extremes of wealth and poverty all been largely eliminated? Then Ja, it works."

Bunny bit into a spicy sausage, not entirely pleasant but it was food nonetheless. Hr. David was so versed in this introduction to Herrnhut that he already knew where Bunny's thoughts had by now taken her.

"But Miss, I don't want you to think vee are in any vay insular."

He was correct. Bunny had already begun to question the benefit of such a religious community if the Christian gospel was not being preached to the unsaved beyond its perimeter.

Thankfully the crisp red apple and coffee were much more to her taste. Hr. David went on to explain that even during their underground years the Moravian Church was continually sending out missionaries. He even described them as the first truly global Protestant Church body, with congregations as far afield as Africa, the Caribbean and, to her great surprise, Greenland. Bunny couldn't fault them.

"In fact, Peter Boehler is due back from Saint Vincent any moment now vith..." He paused.

"With the real Rebecca!" Bunny enjoyed adding the punchline. Hr. David found it amusing also and permitted himself a broad grin.

"Apparently, she is a very accomplished teacher in the things of God," he raved, "und a great preacher also."

"Sounds like my kind of woman," Bunny added lightly.

"And she will be the first female to be ordained in *any church*." His delight at that milestone was palpable.

Just then, someone entered the doorway and shouted what she assumed was German for They're here! causing most of the diners to leave the remnants of their meals and rush toward the doorway. Hr. David stood up and gestured for Bunny to do likewise.

Within moments the welcoming committee had reconvened around a second carriage that had come to a halt in almost the identical position to Bunny's.

Bunny joined the back of the small crowd and began polishing the apple that she had discreetly brought with her from the dining room. As she watched, she saw Peter Boehler emerge first from the carriage, much to the delight of Hr. David and the rest of the crowd who cheered when they saw him. Bunny was unmoved and bit into her apple. A small squirt of apple juice spurted onto her cheek.

Next to alight was a black-coated gentleman with long curly hair who carefully closed the door after he had exited. He was introduced to the crowd as John and to Bunny's relief it was clear that he too was English. Finally, Peter began his impassioned introduction of Rebecca. Even though he spoke in German, Bunny could tell from the intense air of expectation that this had been a long-awaited moment. The crowd grew silent as he re-opened the carriage door, offering his hand and announced,

"Rebecca!"

A modestly dressed but deeply beautiful lady gracefully stepped out of the carriage. As she did Bunny could hear gasps and an occasional Oh! whispered from within the crowd. Bunny looked to her left and right. Most of those gathered were unmoved, but some looked genuinely surprised, maybe even shocked. One even held a hand over their open month. Bunny looked back at Rebecca. What was the problem, if indeed there was a problem? Then she realised. Bunny was so accustomed to modern-day racial integration that she had not even noticed that Rebecca was black. Several in the crowd, however, were clearly expecting that this Caribbean teacher in the things of God was going to be as white as they were. Bunny even wondered if Rebecca might have been the very first ethnic minority that some of these Central Europeans had ever seen.

Chapter 21

JOHN WESLEY

The crowd dispersed, albeit more slowly than it had for Bunny's arrival. She looked-on and finished her apple. Unknowingly, the place where Bunny was standing was directly in the path that Peter, David, Caribbean Rebecca and Englishman John took as they walked into the small township. She watched as they briefly arrested at the brass inscription, clearly the first stop on the tour, before heading in her direction. Soon enough they joined her, and Hr. David was pleased to introduce her to a fellow countryman.

Bunny wasn't sure whether to offer her hand, having been ignored last time. It was a good decision, as John immediately gave a courteous bow and introduced himself.

"John Wesley," he announced somewhat sheepishly.

"Wow!" she replied spontaneously.

"Pardon?" came his understandable query.

"Sorry, Mr. Wesley," she said, quickly covering her faux-pas and introduced herself, unsure as to the level of formality her present surroundings dictated.

"Miss Johan Elstow, but you can call me Bunny," she decided upon, unsure if Wesley would ever use her nickname. It sounded far too familiar for such a famous person.

Bunny inconspicuously followed as the party inspected the prayer room before taking a table in the communal dining hall. In the multi-lingual conversation that followed, Bunny learned that Rebecca had been a former slave. Once freed by her master, she had been instrumental in the conversion of many slaves on the island of St. Thomas and the establishment of a thriving Moravian community on the Danish colony. Bunny couldn't help but be impressed by the confidence and self-evident spiritual authority that this woman carried. If she were to become an ordained minister, she thought, then who was Bunny to argue – a decidedly different position to that which she had held during the somewhat heated debates that had marked the Anglican Communion's decision to allow female ordinands.

After a while, Rebecca left the table with two women who invited her to follow them, intent on making her feel *more comfortable*. Bunny would have appreciated the same offer.

"Peter, can I ask you something?" Wesley took the opportunity to share a question that had been bothering him ever since he and Perter had discussed the matter on their journey. Boehler invited him to share what was on his mind.[1]

Wesley then explained how he had learned about salvation by faith from Peter, and that he had taught him the whole idea of Church was to be small integrated communities, or societies. Peter freely nodded in agreement. Eventually, John arrived at his question.

"But Peter, my brother, I do not have what you have, and I don't know what I should do?"

What a dramatic admission, thought Bunny. Here was a hero of the Christian faith. Someone responsible for thousands, perhaps tens of thousands, of salvations, and with a lasting legacy; and yet he was humbly admitting that he didn't have the intimacy of relationship with God that the Moravians knew. Bunny felt an enormous sense of privilege to have been given a ringside seat to such an intimate moment. Peter replied,

"It is by grace brother, all by grace."

John thought for a moment before answering with a slightly pained expression,

"But I don't have grace, what shall I do? Should I quit preaching?"

Boehler thought for a moment before giving his reply.

"Preach grace because it is in the Bible, and then after you get it, preach it because you have it!" [2]

Over the next half-hour Wesley learned the simple truth. Peter explained that it was not about religion, not about tradition, nor sacraments, nor doctrine. It was all about falling in love with Jesus. The half-hour ended with the chiming of a solitary church bell.

Bunny had never considered whether she had herself fallen in love with Jesus. She had been a committed Christian for as long as she could remember. But whether that was out of a heartfelt relationship with Jesus, she was beginning to question. She was a church-going believer, anyone could see that. She was deeply involved in every aspect of church life; it was a huge part of her

---

[1] Wesley did visit Herrnhut but the pivotal meeting between Boehler and Wesley actually happened in England where Boehler led the Moravian Church. The dialogue shown is accurate according to "Life in the Spirit" by A W Tozer P 159

[2] 'Why I am an Evangelical and a Methodist' by Timothy C Tennent printed in 'Why We Belong: Evangelical Unity and Denominational Diversity' Crossway (2013)

life. Then an awful realisation dawned upon her. Was she more in love with Church than Christ? She loved the structure, the repetition, the security of familiarity, she loved her religion! But now, the protracted liminal narrative that she was immersed within had caused her to question the foundations of her religion. The foundations she had built her Christian life upon were now fatally undermined. Had she fallen in love with Jesus? she wondered. She needed to take stock. No sooner had she admitted to herself that something needed to be reappraised than the very next question boomed into her head; had she fallen in love with Chris? She suddenly realised that this was, to some extent, a very similar question. Her anxiety about a relationship was centred on the doing, about the how, about the practicalities of a life together, not about whether she wanted to be *with* him. For the first time she was beginning to realise that *love* was about sharing your life with someone for no other reason than you wanted to be *with* them. She was ready to admit it. She wanted to be *with* Chris, and at the same time she knew she wanted to be *with* Jesus. Both decisions seemed somehow intertwined. How such a concession would affect her relationship with her Church remained to be seen. She felt confident that whatever happened would now be built upon the new footings she had just laid in the open groundwork of her heart.

"Miss, Miss?" The voice of John Wesley brought her back into the present. Or as it was in her case, the past. Bunny apologised for apparently daydreaming and asked him to repeat himself.

"I said that when I am done here, I am going back to England and am going to take God at his word and allow him to build something new in me; and if you're not staying here, may I offer you a ride to London?" he said.

"I would consider it an honour, Mr. Wesley to accompany you," she replied graciously. "As it happens, I think God is building something new in me too."

The serene peace of Herrnhut was then momentarily shattered by the sound of a violent argument. She looked around for the source of the unrest but couldn't work out where the sound was coming from. Intuitively she closed her eyes and as she did she could make out the figure of a short, balding man seething furiously at two younger men who were both cowering and profusely apologising.

The farm track that led to Lane End Farm began as a tarmacked road but once they crossed a cattle grid, which caused their vehicle to appear to give a shiver of excitement as Jack sped across it, the lane soon deteriorated into a rutted and pot-holed track. Jack knew his 4x4 would easily cope with the terrain and having few chances to go off-road didn't attempt to slow down. As for his passengers, Artur held tight to his seat belt and the rear door handle for safety; Thea on the other hand loved the slight sense of danger. Such a welcome relief. The headlights of Chris's car behind them bounced around as it too traversed the bumpy lane with occasional reflections being caught in the mirror. Ralph and Rex were in the rear of Chris's vehicle. Eventually, Jack slowed his car to a crawl once he spotted the farmhouse. Chris did likewise and momentarily was unsure as to whether they should extinguish their headlights. By the time he had considered it they had both stopped outside the building.

The farmhouse wasn't derelict, but it didn't look as though anyone had lived there for some time. The windows were intact apart from one at the front whose upper left pane was absent. There were curtains in most of the windows, but none were drawn. Instinctively they all exited the vehicles without speaking, closing their doors as quietly as possible – a pointless exercise as the engine noise would have alerted anyone to their arrival. No one spoke. A combination of excitement, adrenalin and fear had struck them all temporarily dumb. Artur switched on the torch app on his mobile phone, Chris and Thea did likewise. Jack collected his torch from the boot of the car, which comfortably outshone all the rest. They split into the two groups they had travelled in. Jack, Artur and Thea would work their way around the rear; Ralph, Rex and Chris had the front door. Neither group knew what to do if the doors were locked.

Before the two parties separated, Rex whispered to everyone,

"Be careful, don't take any risks, and remember 'Greater is He who is in you than he who is in the world'"[1]

It was just the assurance they all needed. In that one sentence, in reminding them of that simple Scripture, Rex had managed to raise the faith of that group of church leaders above their understandable anxieties, above the obvious risks, up to a level that couldn't exist without the danger they were facing.

Ralph placed his hand on the spherical front door handle. Checking first that Chris and Rex were with him, he slowly turned it clockwise. It clicked and opened. As he slid it slowly open Chris shone his phone-torch inside. As the light

---

[1] John's First Epistle chapter 4 verse 4

illuminated the hallway it picked out a frayed red paisley-patterned carpet; no furniture, just a flight of stairs ahead to the right and a passageway on the left. They entered, flicking the torch quickly into each hallway corner to check for anyone waiting in ambush. There was none.

Two rooms led from the hallway to rooms at the front. They took the one on the left first. It too was devoid of any home comforts, not even a carpet covered the bare floorboards. In the silence they could hear each other's breathing. Suddenly there was a loud click from behind them. Ralph and Rex swung round to see Chris with his hand on the light switch. Thankfully the noise came from the aged metal switch that released a solid clunk when it was toggled. Chris, now illuminated in Rex's phone torch, shrugged his shoulders apologetically. The room to the right of the stairs was identically spartan and significantly colder having one of its windowpanes missing. Its light switch was equally as loud.

The passageway snaked around to the right then turned a sharp left before ending at three further doors. Ralph reached for the handle of the central one, this time not the decorative orb that adorned the doors at the front - this was a functional horizontal lever. As Ralph placed his hand above the handle it moved. He held his breath, hovering his hand motionless, frozen in space, as the handle moved downwards away from it. As the handle reached its nadir someone tried to push the door open. It was locked. Rex's finger pointed at the key in the lock on their side of the door.

Ralph looked at Rex and mouthed silently, "Is it Jack?" Rex shrugged his shoulders noncommittally, Chris on the other hand gave a 'probably' nod.

"Jack?" Ralph whispered, but far to quietly for there to be any response.

Suddenly there was a knocking on the door. Five rhythmic taps followed by four quicker ones. Then it was repeated. Five taps followed by four. Neither Ralph not Chris had any idea what this meant. The third time however Rex recognised the rhythm and sang along under his breath.

"Onward Christian So-o-o-oldiers!"

Ralph joined in at the end of the lyric, smiled and turned the key. Jack and Thea were on the other side of the heavy wooden door, Jack with one knuckle poised to repeat his impromptu Christian Morse Code.

The hallway was instantly filled with the light from his torch. Artur stood a few metres behind them peering into the overgrowth on the side of the building. Ralph, Rex and Chris recoiled in the glaring light, shielding their eyes with their hands. Jack apologised as he lowered the beam. The passageway however remained in full light. Artur had spotted the main switch at the electric meter and switched it from off to on. Several lights in the building suddenly came on, including the two rooms at the front of the building.

"Well, I guess if there is anyone here, they know we've arrived," Thea commented.

"There is no one here," Artur said matter of fact. "If there were, the electricity would be on." No one could disagree with his simple logic and collectively breathed a tentative sigh of relief. Now that they were inside, their attention was switched to finding Bunny. Chris tried his best to not fear the worst. If she was still here in this abandoned house, would he find her bound and gagged, drugged, or worse? He couldn't allow himself to think it. The others all knew that these were the only options. Jack split them into three pairs to check every room. He and Thea would check the first floor, Artur and Rex the second, leaving the remainder of the downstairs to Chris and Ralph.

As they climbed the staircase, Jack explained that the toilet should be a giveaway.

"If anyone has been here there will be evidence in the loo!"

"Eww!" Thea said not sure what *evidence* he meant.

The first-floor bathroom had indeed been used, and recently. The sink was dust-free, and a half-used toilet roll sat on the cistern.

On the second floor there were three low-ceilinged bedrooms and a small box room. All were empty with no sign of having been used in years.

Of the two remaining rooms to be checked on the ground-floor, the first was the kitchen. There were clear signs that people had been here too. Cups, spoons and spent teabags littered the worktop. The flip-top bin was overflowing with largely junk-food packaging. Ralph rummaged around the topmost level of trash looking for clues. Not a bad idea, but Chris needed to find Bunny so left him to it and crossed the passage to find out what was behind the other door.

Three out of the four first-floor bedrooms were empty. But in the last one, overlooking the front door, Thea and Jack found what they didn't know they were looking for: two foam sleeping mats – no sleeping bags, just the floor mats. They both had the manufacturer's hanging tags still attached, showing that they had been bought on special offer for £4.99. Two people had slept here and as they had left brand-new sleeping mats they probably weren't homeless squatters.

Rex and Artur joined Thea and Jack, their second-floor search having drawn a blank.

"Hey, what's all this?" Rex said letting his curious excitement show.

"Someone has been here, that's for sure," Jack answered.

Thea picked up the newspaper that lay beside one of the mats. It was this morning's *Daily Mirror*.

"They were here today!" she exclaimed. "This is today's paper."

"Or they still are!" Rex added cautiously. At that moment the unmistakable sound of Christian Palmer's voice filled the empty house.

"Everyone! Come here quickly!" he shouted. The four of them bounded out of the first-floor bedroom, down the stairs, round the passage to the rear of the building. Ralph was stepping through the open doorway - Chris already well inside.

As they arrived, they were confronted by the scene that had caused Chris's outburst. In the centre of the room stood a camp bed, not a simple rolled mat as upstairs but an assembled camp bed with eight evenly positioned legs. A white pillow identified which was to be the head of the bed, and next to it stood an empty intravenous drip stand. Two metal-framed vinyl chairs were positioned on the far side of the bed facing it. There was something laid upon the left chair that seemed to beckon Chris over to it. As he approached, he gasped as he realised that it was Bunny's other glove. Chris reached into his hip pocket and removed the one he had collected from Father Leonine at St. Mary's earlier. There was no doubt, they made a perfect pair. He looked over to the bed visualising Bunny lying there. He reached forward to touch it, as if to touch her, then drew his hand back into a fist. He turned to the rest of the assembled group dumbstruck, unable to comment. He didn't need to, as Ralph had more to share.

"I found packets of morphine in the kitchen bin, and an empty I.V. bag folded inside a pizza box," he said.

"Upstairs, two beds – well, mats actually – but they have been used," Rex added.

"And today's paper," Thea added holding the *Daily Mirror* aloft. As she did several colourful documents fell out from the newspaper. She assumed they were just marketing leaflets distributed free with the paper that had been folded within and had become dislodged as she opened it. She bent down to pick them up.

"Hello, who's this?" she said.

What she had assumed to be leaflets were in fact long-lens photographs of a young woman. She passed the prints around asking if anyone knew who it was. Ralph was the only one to say that he recognised her,

"...but I couldn't identify her."

"I'll tell you who it *isn't*," Chris swung round, picture in one hand and pointing his opposite finger at the camp bed. "She may have the same colour hair, be roughly the same age, but this *isn't* a picture of Bunny."

"That is a good point," Rex agreed. "Whoever this girl is. Who has been...stalked, perhaps? It isn't your Bunny."

"That doesn't help us find her though, does it?" Jack stated the obvious. As curious as this farmhouse was, it appeared to be the end of the trail. Lane End Farm was well named.

Chapter 22

ALDERSGATE

The shoreline along the Thames estuary had hardly changed in the last one hundred years, or from Bunny's perspective in little over an hour. She stood on deck watching it narrow slowly as they approached London. This time however she held John Wesley's hat as he hung limply over their vessel's guard rail, having long since emptied the contents of his stomach, retching continually for the last two hours. Around halfway across from Dunkirk the weather had taken a turn for the worse and in the choppy waves Wesley turned pale.

His reaction didn't surprise Bunny. Before they boarded, Wesley had told her how on his ignominious return from a failed Anglican missionary trip to the English colony in Savannah, Georgia [1] he had feared for his life as a terrible storm struck in mid-Atlantic. He had described how their ship was engulfed in a storm so bad that all the passengers had feared for their lives. But what really struck him had been a small group who in the midst of the peril sang praises to God appearing unafraid to die. [2] He described how he was so deeply moved by these Moravians he decided to follow Peter Boehler to his home in Herrnhut. [3]

"I think the worst of the bad weather has passed John, now we are in the Thames estuary," she said trying to encourage him to reassume a vertical position. Taking her advice, he let go of the handrail and replaced the hat upon his head, thanking her as he did. Bunny suggested they returned inside to shelter from the drizzle. Once inside Bunny decided to engage him in conversation to take his mind off the seasickness.

"Well John, you are an Anglican," she began, "and so am I." He looked nonplussed at this information. She tried again. "Were your parents churchgoers?" she asked. This time he responded.

"I would say so, both were, what one may call, high church," he said as he perched himself on an upturned barrel. "Mind you, my grandparents were dissenters and got themselves into a lot of trouble."

---

[1] Wesley was sent as a young Anglican missionary to Georgia but returned to England having had little success.

[22] Article: 'A storm at Sea' published on Methodist.org.uk

[3] Whilst Wesley did visit Herrnhut, his encounter with Peter actually happened in England.

"That must be where you get it from," Bunny offered light-heartedly, not realising that at this point he had no intention of breaking away from the national religion.

"Whatever do you mean?" he replied sharply. "I am no dissenter."

Bunny tried her best to backtrack.

"I mean you had... have... your own way of doing things... your own... method... don't you?" she said squirming.

"Oh, you mean the Holy Club, as they called it?" he answered, assuming that she must mean his time at Oxford University. Bunny let out a sigh of relief. "Yes, I guess we did behave quite different to the rest of the students," he began reminiscing. "There were about a dozen of us at Christ Church college together, including one of my brothers, Charles. I am one of nineteen, you know?" Bunny gave the required gentle nod of acknowledgment. Wesley continued. "We were mainly all from church families, so we committed to not slip into a life of sinfulness. We just wanted to live a devout Christian life. Like the saying goes..." He looked at Bunny hoping she would indeed quote *the saying* he was referring to. She looked blankly back at him. He tutted and finished his own sentence.

"Theology came from Germany, but devotion comes from England." [1] As he said it Bunny joined in, pretending to know the apparently popular phrase.

Bunny remembered her time at university and how she had tried her best not to slip into the life of excess into which her peers quickly succumbed. In hindsight, she felt that by joining the Christian Union during freshers-week she had nailed her colours to that particular mast early on. The group of friends she subsequently bonded with managed to somehow keep each other on the right course. Whether she would have described herself as a *devout Christian* whilst at university wasn't something she had ever considered.

"What did you do... as a *devout Christian* at Oxford, John?" she asked, as much to judge her own behaviour as his. Outside, she could hear an increase in activity as deckhands prepared the ship for its arrival at London docks.

He began to describe a typical week at Christ Church. She soon discovered that they met daily for three hours of prayer, singing of psalms, and reading the New Testament in Greek. This level of commitment far exceeded anything Bunny could comprehend. She decided she too needed to sit down and joined him on the next barrel. Wesley hadn't finished his description and continued to

---

[1] This was a popular truism of the day. 'Protestants: The Radicals who Made the Modern World' by Alec Ryrie. (2017)

explain that they would pray for a few minutes every hour for *special virtue*. It wasn't the revelation that they took communion every Sunday that impressed Bunny – she did the same herself – but when he said they fasted every Wednesday and Friday until three o'clock she knew she was in the presence of a Godly man.[1]

"I bet that had a dramatic effect, didn't it?" she asked.

"Well, the rest of the students made fun of us... what was that rhyme?" he asked himself, looking to the wooden ceiling above him for inspiration.

"No, I didn't mean a dramatic effect on others..." Bunny interrupted attempting to steer his thoughts to how that decision had changed him; but he was already mumbling the lines of a long-forgotten ditty. She let him finish his recollection. The vessel gave a noticeable judder as it came alongside its jetty.

"I've got it now," he eventually announced:

"By rule they eat, by rule they drink,

By rule do all things but think.

Accuse the priests of loose behaviour.

To get more in the laymen's favour.

Method alone must guide 'em all

When themselves Methodists they call." [2]

"Methodists, eh?" Bunny commented in full knowledge that this was the long-lasting international movement he was to establish.

"Yes, such a silly word," he responded. "As if our devotion was but a method!"

"But such a devoted lifestyle must have had a dramatic effect on you, personally," she enquired.

"I *had* to live a good life. I've always known that God had chosen me. Ever since I was six years old," he was clearly enjoying the storytelling, despite others on the boat preparing to disembark.

Bunny asked what had happened at the age of six and heard how the family home had caught fire with him trapped inside. He was rescued from an

---

[1] 'Watching and Praying: Personality Transformation in Eighteenth Century British Methodism' by Keith Haartman. Rodopi (2004) p172

[2] 'O sing Unto the Lord: A History of English Church Music' by Andrew Gant. University of Chicago Press (2005) p262

upstairs window and consequently had always considered himself as "A brand plucked from the burning."[1]

"Is that why you became a missionary?"

"Ah," he answered thoughtfully. "I went to America to convert the Indians but who shall convert me?" [2]

Just then they heard the sound of a car approaching at the front.

"Quick, off with the lights," Ralph said. Thankfully, the environmentally conscious Rex had already switched off all of them except those at the rear of the ground floor, which in a moment were also extinguished.

"Why are we standing in the dark, Ralph?" Thea asked, adding, "Our cars are parked at the front."

"Good point," Ralph admitted.

Jack quickly took charge. "We had best be ready for them. You two, get behind the front door," he pointed at Rex and Ralph. "Artur and I will be at the rear. When they open the door, grab 'em."

Adrenalin was once again in full supply as they took their posts. Car doors closed; one, two. There were only two of them. Six against two were good odds. Rex and Ralph took their station at the front door. Rex took off his coat and motioned that he was going to throw it over their quarry. Good idea thought Ralph, glad he wasn't going to do any of the wrestling. They listened intently at the front door, but not a sound could be heard. Perhaps they were going to the rear after all, that was where the camp bed was. Ralph stepped away from the door and inclined his ear to listen for any commotion from the rear, preparing to dash to help.

Suddenly, the front door handle started to turn. Rex tapped Ralph's arm to get his attention. Both men swallowed hard and stood out of sight behind the door, waiting for it to open. Rex readied his coat. This was the moment of truth. The door slowly opened and into the darkened hallway two men entered. Rex threw his coat over the first of them and slung his arms firmly around him. Both he and his prey fell to the floor, Rex pinning his flailing arms as the man mumbled

---

[1] 'Brand Plucked from the Fire: The Early Life of John Wesley' by Jonathan Arnold. Gods Missionary Church Inc. (2019)

[2] 'Journal of John Wesley' Chapter 2, 'The voyage to England.' Moody Press (1951)

in anguish. Rex made a grab for the second man, but before he could make contact the man let out a familiar sound.

"Goodly heavens above!" he said. There was only one person that Ralph knew would use that particular phrase when startled. It was the unmistakable sound of an elderly Anglican of his acquaintance.

"Rector?" Ralph enquired.

Thea switched on the hallway lights to reveal that it was indeed Reverend Mashman. All eyes turned to the kerfuffle now rolling on the floor. Thankfully peace-loving Rex was not one to throw punches, but his chin was covered in a fine film of blood as his spontaneous stress-induced nosebleed had started again. He released his grasp, wiped his nose, then pulled down the upturned hood of his coat to reveal a somewhat dishevelled Joel Whyens still wriggling to get free.

Rex clenched his fist, but, instead of a punch, tapped out onto the floor the same five-long four-short Onward Christian Soldiers rhythm that Jack had used earlier.

"Why didn't you use the secret code, Joel?" Rex asked. Joel for his part was totally bemused. He looked first at blood-stained Rex, then Ralph, then the rest of the party standing at the bottom of the stairs. It started slowly and was probably as much from the release of tension as it was from pure amusement, but within a minute all seven of them were doubled-up in hysterical laughter, Joel being the last one to succumb.

The laughter didn't last long, the sight of Chris arriving in the hallway from the rear was stark reminder of what they had discovered in the farmhouse. They took the two latest additions into the rear to show them the camp bed, chairs and the ominous sight of a medical intravenous stand. Thea passed them the photographs in silence, no one speaking for a while to allow everyone to take in the scene. Time to think.

"That's young Velia," Mashman said when he mounted his glasses to focus on the two photographs now in his hand. "Why have you got pictures of her?"

"Velia Advowson, of course," Ralph suddenly remembered. "She is the daughter of Lord Advowson. You know, the socialite. She's... a model or a... something."

"All ashore who's going ashore!" Bunny was delighted to hear the purser make the traditional declaration, telling all passengers to disembark. Bunny helped Wesley gather his not-inconsiderable luggage together; Bunny of course had none.

Once ashore it was clear that Wesley's mind was fixed on the need to visit the nearest Moravian chapel. His mid-Atlantic experience and his conversations with Peter Boehler had stirred something within him that needed to find its fulfilment. It was already evening by the time they arrived at the meeting room in Aldersgate. Bunny took her seat next to Wesley and listened intently to a message about her old friend Martin Luther. It was an impassioned message, nothing like the silent Quaker service she had recently sat through. Just as Peter had said to them both, it was all about falling in love with Jesus. Bunny could feel herself noticeably moved. There was something in this message which was speaking to her deepest soul. She looked across to Wesley to see if he was being similarly affected. Tears were rolling down his cheeks. The sight of this godly, devout man being so tenderly touched by God started Bunny's eyes filling with tears. This was not usual for her; she couldn't recall ever having cried in church before. But now, tears were cascading freely down both of their cheeks.

Neither of them said a word until the service had concluded. Bunny then leaned towards Wesley, who by now had wiped his tears and was sporting a huge grin, and simply said, Amazing!

"It was while he was describing the change God works in the heart through faith in Christ," Wesley replied. "It was then that I felt my heart strangely warmed. I felt I did trust in Christ, Christ alone for my salvation. I had an assurance that he had taken away my sins and saved me from death."[1]

All the talk on the boat about the Holy Club, about fasting and prayer, about trying hard to live a devout life, it all seemed so pointless to Bunny in the face of a personal encounter with a loving God. This is what Luther was really preaching, this is what the reformation was all about and now Wesley had caught it. So too, she wondered, had she.

"This is a special day," Wesley finally added with glee as the church bell rang out a single note. "This is a *very* special day. What day is it Miss Elstow? I should like to remember all that God has done for me this day."

---

[1] 'Journal of John Wesley' Chapter 2, 'I Felt My Heart Strangely Warmed.' Moody Press (1951)

Bunny looked at her watch. There was no date shown, just a time flashing 17:38. She apologised that she couldn't help him.

"Whatever day it is, to me it shall forever be called Aldersgate day," he said.[1]

---

[1] The day was 24th May 1738 and Aldersgate Day continues to be commemorated every year across the Methodist Church.

Chapter 23

HANHAM MOUNT

"Has something happened to Miss Velia?" Mashman asked. No one could give him an answer.

"Do you know Lord and Lady Advowson well, Rector?" Ralph asked.

"I should say so. I know them very well, he appointed me!" the Anglican answered.

"I thought the bishop was the one who appointed you," Jack responded, surprised.

"O yes, he did, but…well… it is more complicated than…" the Rector fumbled for an explanation.

"Could you ring him?" Chris asked anxiously.

"Oh no, I couldn't do that," Mashman replied instantly.

"But Rector, this is a matter of…." Chris couldn't finish the sentence as he planned. Ralph jumped in and added "…of great importance. Velia Advowson might be in danger."

"No, I couldn't telephone him," Mashman protested, "because I don't have his number with me."

Sadly, Mashman kept his telephone numbers in an address book next to his landline, on the hallway table at the Manse. Despite the obvious expressions of surprise that followed this revelation it didn't change the fact that they couldn't make that call. Chris could do no more than exhale his disappointment as they stood in silence contemplating their next move.

"I could visit him though," Mashman interjected belatedly. "If Miss Velia is indeed in danger, I should really let his Lordship know straight-a-wise."

Lane End Farm was one of many farmhouses on the sprawling Advowson estate. The grand Georgian splendour of the Brennan Hall was barely five miles away, although the dark and winding country lanes would not allow for a rapid journey. Mashman said it would be best if he went alone, unsure as to how his Lordship would take to the arrival of a late-night delegation.

Before the Rector left, Artur suggested they all exchange their mobile numbers. Thea took this idea one step further and within seconds had created a WhatsApp group which she entitled Fellowship of the King, referencing the joke they shared earlier. Not only hadn't Rector Mashman heard of WhatsApp, but his Nokia handset was so old it wasn't even a smart phone. Joel suggested they write their numbers onto a piece of paper for him and ripped a section from one of the pages of the *Daily Mirror*.

"Ring us, one of us, as soon as you know something, Rector," was the last message they gave him as he left.

"Where did you say we were going?" Bunny asked Wesley, not entirely convinced that she wanted to mount the horse that he was preparing for her.

Wesley reluctantly stopped what he was doing, rummaged in his bag and produced a folded letter, the wax seal of which had already been broken. He handed it to her and continued to affix noseband and throatlatch to the pale brown horse that had been allocated for her journey.

Bunny opened the letter that had been sent to John Wesley, care of Fetter Lane Moravian Society, the place that John and – as far as he was concerned – she also regularly attended. The letter was an invitation to visit his *friend, fellow Holy Club member and failed missionary*, George Whitefield. The letter explained that he too had recently had a *conversion* experience and had returned from America with the sole purpose to begin to preach the good news of salvation to the poor.

"Bristol!" Wesley belatedly answered. "But I don't know where he is proposing to preach. I can't think any Church of England minister willing to give George his pulpit for an address to the poor."

"Was he in the Holy Club with you at Oxford?" she asked.

"Yes, and with me in Savannah," he expanded.

The journey was not as uncomfortable as she had feared. She had only little experience on horseback as a girl but, to her delight, in this dreamworld she appeared to be quite an accomplished rider. As they approached Bristol, Wesley became more and more agitated about not knowing exactly where Whitefield was going to preach. Bunny could offer little in the way of counterbalance to his anxiety. She ignored them at first but, after the third or fourth, Bunny noticed the simple printed posters that were tied to occasional trees, mileposts, and signs along their route. She steered her mount to enable her to take a closer look.

"At Hanham Mount!" she shouted over to Wesley.

He didn't respond but continued to ride a little way ahead of her. Bunny memorised as much of the poster as she could then geed her horse to walk alongside Wesley's.

"Whitefield is inviting all the 'good people of Bristol' to 'hear the good news' at Hanham Mount this evening," she told him, then pointed out the growing number of posters they were passing.

"Do they say at which church?" Wesley asked. Bunny said they did not.

The closer they got to their destination, they began to be aware that more and more people were on the streets: men, women, children, old people and families. Some, but not many, were well-dressed, most were self-evidently from the working classes. Bunny noted the look of their ingrained soot-stained complexion, all were walking in the same direction as the two of them rode.

Surely all of these aren't going to Hanham Mount, mused Bunny. There must be hundreds on the move. But it was true. By the time they arrived at their destination, several thousand had congregated awaiting to hear the advertised *good news*. Wesley soon spotted Whitefield and led their horses through the bushes to the overhanging outcrop that made this area a natural amphitheatre.

"John, my dear brother." Whitefield sounded genuinely pleased to be reacquainted with his friend, although the etiquette of the day prohibited much more than a hearty handshake. Once they had both dismounted, Bunny was introduced to Whitefield who gave him a polite hello.

Not knowing whether to offer her own hand towards him, or to her disdain to curtsey, she immediately was struck dumb. Whitefield's eyes were permanently crossed,[1] a minor disfigurement but one which trapped her in the predicament of not wanting to stare at him but simultaneously not being able to take her eyes away. Wesley came to her rescue and asked Whitefield the question that had been bugging him ever since they had set off from London, namely, which church was he going to be preaching in? Whitefield laughed, took Wesley by the hand and walked him to the edge of the rocky outcrop.

"No church will have me my friend. The message of *salvation by faith alone* is not acceptable in the Church in which you and I were ordained. So..." he pointed over the gathering throng beneath their vantage point, "... I am going to preach right here, my friend."

Wesley was clearly uncomfortable about the idea but didn't protest. This wasn't his show after all. Soon enough the show began. A short time of surprisingly tuneful communal hymn-singing was the precursor for the main

---

[1] 'George Whitefield – The Cross-Eyed Calvinist Bedevils the Conservative Colonists' New England Historical Society.

event, when George Whitefield took to the stage. Well, not exactly a stage, more of a craggy outcrop.

Bunny listened intently. Of all the great and good of the Christian faith she had met in the last... however long it was, George Whitefield was head and shoulders above them all in his ability to address an audience. The crowd was enraptured by the passion and eloquence of his delivery. Bunny too couldn't help but feel a great stirring within her. The basis of her faith in God had indeed changed, she had begun to encounter God personally, she might even admit to having had the conversion experience that Whitefield was describing. In his words she had been born-again.

"And now let me address all of you, high and low, rich and poor, one with another to accept mercy and grace while it is offered to you;" Whitefield orated fervently as his sermon reached its climax. "Now is the accepted time, now is the day of salvation; will you not accept it now it is offered to you?"[1]

Suddenly, Whitefield turned toward John and without warning, mid-sermon, beckoned him to join him on the natural pulpit. Wesley, quite caught up with the moment, instantly obliged and was soon standing next to Whitefield as he looked across perhaps the largest crowd he had ever seen. When they were both missionaries in Savannah, they would often share a platform but that would be to a congregation of little more than twenty people and would, of course, be inside a church building. But here, all Wesley could see was an ocean of expectant, spiritually hungry faces looking up at him. He was deeply moved. Whitefield leaned over to Wesley and, with a glint in his eye, smiled and said,

"Over to you, my brother!"

Then, before Wesley could protest, he promptly left him standing on his own. Whitefield stood folded-arms next to Bunny, looking back at Wesley who by now was giving him a pained *what-have-you-done-to-me* expression. Whitefield just grinned and motioned back with a *go-on* gesture. Wesley had little choice but to address the crowd.[2]

---

[1] Widely quoted words of George Whitfield, taken from
www.brainyquote.com/quotes/george_whitefield_206603

[2] Whilst not as depicted here, George Whitefield encouraged Wesley, despite his initial reluctance about being outside of the 'proper place', to preach in the open air. Having first done it in Harnham Mount, Wesley continued throughout his life to preach in the open air.

"Brothers, I have seen that giving all my life to God…" he began tentatively, "…supposing it was possible to do this, would profit me nothing unless I gave my heart, yes, all my heart, to Him."[1]

As he delivered his impromptu message Wesley could feel the power of God energise him and whilst he was by no means as dynamic an orator as Whitefield, he knew in that moment that he had discovered his calling. After twenty minutes he brought his sermon to a powerful close. The crowd cheered as hundreds stood to make their personal declaration of faith in Christ. Bunny surveyed the scene and could see several grown men with tears making clean rivulets on their grimy cheeks, a fitting metaphor of the heart-cleansing they were undergoing.

"Still want to preach inside church buildings, John?" Whitefield asked him as soon as the sermon was over.

"No need, I look upon all the world as my parish," Wesley replied. "And I am to declare to all that are willing to hear the good news of salvation."[2]

"I am very pleased that you consider the world to be your parish, John," Whitefield answered, "As I have a surprise for you."

"Another one?" Bunny couldn't help but interject. Whitefield ignored her.

"You see all these good people who have today accepted Christ's salvation?" he pointed out towards the now slowly dispersing crowd. "They need a church to go to. I am going back to America, so all of these souls are my parting gift to you."

Wesley swallowed hard and considered carefully before he replied. He knew this was the moment God had been steering him towards. This was his time to accept his calling.

"Well, if that is the case, then these people can't be left without a guiding hand," he said. "They must all attend their local parish churches, to take the sacraments and to be baptised." He then paused, shook his head and continued, "No, no that won't be enough, they will need to be taught how to live a truly God-centred life." He thought for a moment, then came up with a plan. "I will

---

[1] Widely quoted words of John Wesley, taken from www.brainyquote.com/quotes/john_wesley_789607

[2] 'Journal of John Wesley' Chapter 3, 'All the World My Parish' Moody Press (1951)

travel around and meet with them in small groups. They will be like a church *within* a church." [1]

"Are there not too many?" Whitefield asked.

"Then I will train others," Wesley answered resolutely. "Give me one hundred preachers who fear nothing but sin and desire nothing but God, and I don't care if they are clergymen or not, they will shake the gates of Hell and set up the kingdom of Heaven upon Earth." [2]

"And what of you, Miss?" For the first time Whitefield addressed Bunny directly, causing her to recoil in an out-of-character fluster and garble incoherently. The great preacher continued, "Are you staying here with John to learn his church *method*, or will your time be better spent with me?"

She had become used to just observing history unfold dispassionately, but now she kept being given choices. It was as though she needed to interact with the characters in this lucid dream. It was an easy choice. She was on a *time* journey and as *time* was leaving for America, she was going to follow it.

"Bang!"

Bunny looked up, suddenly startled by the loud sound, and to her surprise the sky had turned dark. "Was that a firework?" she wondered. "Were there celebrations as we leave for America?"

Then suddenly the sound of a second bang filled her ears and she visibly jumped. There was no firework display lighting the sky and no one else appeared to hear it. If anything, it sounded to her more like a couple of gun shots. She closed her eyes to go back to sleep. After all, she had a long journey ahead.

Few were surprised that the sound of the Rector's car leaving the farmhouse failed to have any of the characteristic noises one would associate with a hasty exit. No revving-up, no wheel-spins, no gravel flicked at the building and no skidding down the lane.

---

[1] Wesley never intended on starting a new religious movement. As a committed Anglican he hoped his 'methods' would lead to a passionate church within the Church. It was later when the reluctance of the Church to appoint much needed ministers for the New England colonies forced him to appoint his own that Methodism separated from the Anglican Communion.

[2] Widely quoted words of John Wesley, taken from www.brainyquote.com/quotes/john_wesley_524891.

"I think we need to tell the police about what we have found here," Thea suggested.

The mention of police reminded Joel that he had yet to report back. The subject wasn't high in his priorities after being wrestled to the floor.

"Is there any point? No," he said emphatically. All eyes turned to him as he relayed as accurately as he could the disappointing exchange he and the Rector had just had with a surly desk sergeant. Chris pointed out that they now had some real evidence, pointing at the makeshift hospital bed next to them. Joel could see how desperate Chris was, but he had to be honest with him. Joel had the unenviable task of advising that the police may not regard any of the contents of this room as evidence at all.

"A camp bed and chairs just aren't evidence of a crime. I am sorry. Not even the morphine," he said.

"But we *have* to find Bunny!" Chris was so tearful as he tried to shout an angry response, it only came out as a strangled guttural noise. Rex put a comforting arm on Chris's shoulder.

"Joel is right I am afraid Chris," Ralph said. "It is up to us to find her."

Joel was a glass-half-full person and didn't take too well to being the harbinger of ill news. He had endured enough bad news in his life to know how devastating it can be.

As a child, Joel had received the single most painful news any child should have to endure. He still can recall, and daily does, the afternoon when his father sat with a thirteen-year-old Joel and his elder sister and told them both that their devoted mother had lost her battle with cancer. They had known it was the most likely outcome when she had fallen ill, but that didn't lessen the emptiness and pain that overwhelmed the family at that moment. His father did his best to keep the family together through the remainder of their schooling, but those years felt little more than riding on autopilot as they leaned on a structured daily routine to take them through the remainder of their education. What Joel was unaware of was that the only way his father could cope with the grief of losing his soulmate was through alcohol. Joel and his sister were aware that their dad liked a drink, but it took a few years before they could see that it was more than that. By the time they had both left school their father was regularly spending prolonged periods of time, sometimes days, missing in a haze of ethanol. It was at that time that the second most defining moment of Joel's life occurred.

Joel was one of the 375,000 people to have been privileged to have been in the audience at the last Billy Graham Crusade in London in 1989. He finds it easy to recall how he felt at that time, and why he was one of the first to leave their seats and make the long walk to the area in front of the stage in response to the altar call. He was just one of the 35,000 who made a similar commitment to Christ during that event, but for him it was the turning point of his life. Prior to his encounter with the world-famous evangelist, he knew little of the Christian faith. To him, as a working-class young black man with a big ego, a poor education and few career prospects, Christianity was nowhere on his radar. His friend Kevin had invited him to go with him to the mass rally. Joel had no idea that Kevin was already a Christian as this was never anything he spoke of. As far as Joel was concerned, they were both going to the event to laugh at all the silly religious people. God had other plans.

The transformation to Joel's life was sudden and dramatic. Within days he was already telling his technical college classmates of how he had met Jesus and that they all needed to also. But it was his father that he knew needed Jesus the most. Joel waited patiently for a day when he was sober enough to listen, then told him about his conversion at the Billy Graham Crusade. He pleaded with his father to give his life to Jesus, and if he did, he would find comfort from the pain; but this only inflamed him into an angry tirade aimed at the God who took his wife from him. They never had that conversation again. Joel committed himself to love his increasingly depressed father, hoping that his actions would eventually lead him to faith. Time would tell.

Joel joined the youth group at Kevin's Methodist church and before long was one of their most vocal members. Within a year he had found the girl who was to become his wife, but more importantly, Joel had found his calling – he was going to be the next Billy Graham. As the years progressed, he experimented with a number of career options before discovered an aptitude for selling. He forged a career selling firstly insurance, then utilities, both door-to-door. He loved the social interaction and was forever in trouble for bending the company rules and finding opportunities to share his faith and invite customers to hear him preach. But he was by far the most successful salesperson on their roster and knew his employers would turn a blind eye. It wasn't long before his passion to preach got him a regular position on the regional Methodist circuit, and he would spend almost every Sunday, sometimes twice a day, sharing the gospel to the faithful souls across thirty or so chapels in the district. When the Methodist circuit superintendent announced he was standing down, having been diagnosed with Parkinson's Disease last year, Joel was the obvious replacement. Joel however had never been ordained and whilst this wasn't a barrier it did make him question if he wanted the responsibility for the less enjoyable side of church life. The best he could agree to was to take the role part-time and temporary until they found a proper replacement. That was nearly eighteen months ago, and he was beginning to question if what he considered as a caretaker role was de-facto permanent. Joel loved to share the Good News, what he struggled with was sharing bad news and that included letting Chris know the reality of how little the police were interested in Bunny's disappearance.

"Besides," he continued, "the police said they were far too busy tonight."

"Why, what's happened tonight," Thea asked curiously.

"A double homicide, apparently," he explained using the American expression *homicide* that he was familiar with from television cop shows.

"What?" Chris said, immediately anxious at news that someone had died.

"It's not Bunny, don't worry," Joel said to everyone's relief. "It was two *unknown males* according to the desk sergeant."

Jack immediately began to put the pieces together.

"Two?" he asked for confirmation, which Joel gave in a nod.

"Like the two who slept upstairs," Jack continued logically.

There was an audible gasp around the room, but not from Joel who was the only one of the group unaware of the discovery that they had made on the first floor. Quickly, they made their way back into the previously occupied bedroom where Joel for the first time saw the two sleeping mats. Could it really be true that the people who had spent last night sleeping here were now dead?

Chapter 24

GEORGE WHITEFIELD

"I'm glad you weren't as sea-sick as John Wesley," Bunny remarked as she and Whitefield disembarked from the Dutch schooner that had been their home for the five-week crossing from Bristol to the American Colonies. He didn't reply, his attention being drawn to the gentleman waiting for them at the far end of the steep gang plank they were now descending. Bunny followed closely behind Whitefield, not wanting to become separated from him amid the noisy quayside bustle. Whitefield embraced the gentleman, a marked difference from the greeting he gave Wesley, she thought. Bunny gave a polite feminine cough to remind Whitefield to introduce her to his strikingly handsome friend. He was clearly a wealthy English gentleman as evidenced by his fine clothes, crisp accent and the gold-chained pocketwatch that he promptly opened before suggesting they follow him as there wasn't much time before the tide changed. Instinctively, Bunny checked her own watch which flashed 17:41.

Listening attentively as they traversed the dockyard, she was able to piece together a recent back-story. William Seward was George Whitefield's fundraiser and, for want of a better term, his publicist.[1] Whilst Whitefield had been in England, Seward had orchestrated the publication of Whitefield's personal journals and had furnished booksellers and newspapers with exclusive copies of his writings. During his absence, Seward had cultivated a public image of Whitefield that portrayed him in the best possible light.

"I have great news," Seward teased as they paused to allow a barrel-laden wagon to pass. "The newspapers are adding the results of your preaching to that of Jonathan Edwards…" he continued. Jonathan Edwards, himself a great and charismatic preacher from Massachusetts, had seen numerous dramatic conversions a few years previously.

"… and putting them together they are calling it *The Great Awakening*," Seward announced with some pride at the fruits of his work.

---

[1] 'The Divine Dramatist: George Whitefield and the Rise of Modern Evangelicalism' by Harry S. Stout. Eerdmans Publishing (1991)

Bunny couldn't help but compare Whitefield's use of the newspapers in colonial America with how Martin Luther had used the early printing press to cultivate not only his message but his public profile. Both men used the media of the day, and neither were afraid of becoming celebrities. That has completely changed! The Church would never consider doing that nowadays, she mused. Well, other than American Televangelists, I suppose, she conceded to herself.

"Good work William," Whitefield congratulated his friend adding, "The gospel message is so critically important that I am compelled to use all earthly means to get the word out."[1]

"And talking of Jonathan Edwards," Seward continued. "You have an invitation to speak at his church in Northampton. I have scheduled it as part of the Thirteen Colonies Tour you are about to start."

Whitefield was clearly delighted at this news.

"Although I am not sure what they will make of you there," Seward cautioned. "They aren't as..." he chose his words tactfully, "as vocal as you. Plus, there are all the healings."

"Nonsense!" Whitefield dismissed. "It is a poor sermon that gives no offense; that neither makes the hearer displeased with himself or with the preacher."[2]

Seward suddenly stopped. Not, as Bunny had assumed, a result of Whitefield's bravado, but because they had arrived at Seward's intended destination.

"And here it is," the wealthy benefactor said.

Bunny looked around. They were on the quayside a few hundred yards from the where they had just arrived. Around them were numerous crates, sacks, ropes and people busying themselves with the noisy and perennial task of loading and unloading. Several dockhands had already swerved to avoid them, cursing under their breath as they did.

"Here is what?" the preacher asked, clearly as confused as Bunny.

Seward raised his arm slowly in the direction of the nearest ship, which was currently being readied for sail. It was smaller than the Dutch schooner which had been their recent home, but a sizeable vessel nonetheless.

---

[1] 'George Whitefield: America's Spiritual Founding Father' by Thomas S. Kidd. Yale University Press, (2014), 260.

[2] Words of George Whitefield taken from 'The Westminster Collection of Christian Quotations' by Martin H Manser, P 339

"This is my gift to you George," he whispered. "The crew are getting ready to take *you* on *your* ship, *The Savannah*, on God's mission as soon as you are ready."

Whitefield's protestations fell on deaf ears. It was clear that this was a done deal and he could not refuse it. Bunny was amazed at such generosity, but as she marvelled remembered that Luther too had a wealthy guardian, Prince Frederick, coincidently also dashingly handsome.

Seward then explained that he would not be joining them as he had to return to England to nurse his sick mother.

"Strange he has called it *The Savannah*." Bunny commented to Whitefield as soon as Seward had departed to attend to the stowage of their luggage.

"Why?" Whitefield asked.

"Wasn't that the place where you and John Wesley failed as missionaries?"

Whitefield harrumphed at the thought.

"No, Miss, it is the place where William is building an orphanage."[1]

Bunny said nothing, having been duly chastised.

It didn't matter how long they stared at the two pale-blue foam sleeping mats laid either side of the bricked-up fireplace, the scene yielded no further ideas. It was an empty bedroom. The same was true for each of the rooms the party re-entered in the hunt for anything of significance; they weren't sure what they were looking for, but something might suggest what they should do next.

Other than the bedroom, the only rooms with any sign of occupancy were the upstairs toilet, kitchen and the room with the camp bed and hospital stand. It was here that they silently gathered. Jack and Thea sat in the plastic chairs; Ralph, Artur and Rex perched on the camp bed being careful to not up-end it as they distributed their weight. Chris and Joel stood, Joel with one hand holding the I.V. stand as if he were waiting at a bus stop.

"What next?" Joel asked the pregnant question, but no one had an answer.

---

[1] After returning to England William Seward never made it back to America. He preached around Wales and was martyred a few years later. http://daibach-welldigger.blogspot.com/2011/09/methodist-martyr-william-seward.html

Ralph shrugged his shoulders, a gesture that encapsulated the mood of Lane End farmhouse. There was no obvious way forward; no bread crumb trail to follow.

"We should first consider what we have," Artur proposed. In the absence of any other suggestion, they asked him to continue his line of thought.

"Well, we have a remote farmhouse;" he continued, "and we have two beds, and the police have two bodies."

"And there's the photograph of Miss Velia Advowson," Thea added.

"And someone had been treated here...medically...maybe drugged." Jack didn't shy away from describing the elephant in the room. But this was the paltry sum of disparate facts that they could document. None of which could point them in any direction, none could help them with the one fact that had brought them here in the first place.

Finally, Chris voiced it,

"And Bunny is still missing." His words prompted a murmur of resigned recognition from all present. Was this really the end of the lane?

"We could pray!" a solitary voice said into the resigned silence. By a process of elimination, it became clear that it was Joel who had spoken.

"Well, we are church leaders, aren't we?" he added.

Rector Mashman had suggested they prayed together when they first gathered last month, but that was one of the first subjects that had lit the sparks of aggressively vigorous debate. Was there more value in written prayers versus spontaneous ones; was it better to be kneeling or seated or indeed standing? The entire spectrum of Christian prayer had been debated and defended in the vestry of All Saints' Church, from the Book of Common Prayer to praying in tongues. So, the fact remained that despite being a group of church leaders, they had, in fact, never prayed together. But now things were different. Now they shared a common purpose, now they shared the pressing need to find Bunny, and to their shame they had to acknowledge that prayer was long overdue.

Something quite wonderful then happened in the spartan, irreligious environment of the Lane End farmhouse. Spontaneously, without the need of introduction, they all began to pray. Each one in their own way, each totally sincere and committed. Joel knelt on the floor held his hands together with his eyes firmly closed; Rex bowed over in his seated position; Jack stood and faced the wall; Ralph began to pace across the room momentarily upsetting the camp bed equilibrium as he arose. Artur produced a well-worn copy of the Lutheran Book of Prayer – or, as he called it, his Pocket-LBP – and thumbed through its pages to find an appropriate prayer. Within moments Thea, Jack, Ralph and Joel were all praying aloud, simultaneously and without regard to each other. The cacophony necessitated that Rex place one finger in each ear to hear the whispered prayer he delivered. Chris, also pacing across the room, began babbling in tongues. All were in the most earnest and sincere supplication of their lives. The perilous need of the situation had momentarily united them in this task. After several minutes, the intercession stopped almost as suddenly as it had started.

They all looked at each other, wondering who was going to be the first to speak.

"I've had an idea," Ralph said tentatively.

"Me too," Artur added.

For the first time since they had arrived in the farmhouse Chris smiled, perhaps because now he knew that God was as interested in finding Bunny as he was. Something in hindsight he should never had doubted.

This was perhaps the largest crowd Bunny had ever witnessed. Larger than the gathering at Hanham Mount in Bristol. Larger than those who had thronged into Westminster square to see the public humiliation of Prynne, Bastwick and Burton. And, despite it feeling a world away, larger than any crowd she had been part of in her *real* life.

Whitefield was already in full flow standing atop the courthouse steps, voice booming, tears streaming from his crossed-eyes. These may have been the Philadelphia courthouse steps, but it was a very different scene to the more familiar one of Sylvester Stallone racing up the steps and turning, triumphant, fists aloft, in the definitive scene from *Rocky*. A different context, a different building, but the location was the same, as too was the sense of victory. The crowd was enraptured, to the extent that the very presence of God appeared to be settling over the centre of the modest urban sprawl that was eighteenth century Philadelphia. Earlier that day, as they entered that particular American colony, she permitted herself a private smile when they passed a sign welcoming them to Pennsylvania. That sounds so much better than Penn Land, she thought.

"How many people are here?" she wondered out loud, but to no one in particular.

"That is a rudimentary calculation but one I have already made to a level of precision that I consider to be accurate within acceptable observational

216

error." The unsolicited reply came from a young man standing a few feet to her left. Bunny affixed her attention to him which only served to encourage him to proffer yet more scientific gobbledygook.

"Taking into account that the audible limit of Mr Whitefield's voice is Market Street which is some five-hundred feet from here; and given a one-hundred-and-eighty-degree projection arc; and assuming a footprint of two square feet per person; and adjusting for certain inaccessible spaces; then simple mathematics would suggest around thirty thousand people," he concluded with neither hesitation nor emotion.[1] Bunny decided not to pass any comment, so as not to encourage him further.

Whitefield's sermon was electrifying. Dramatic, eloquent, impassioned, and sincere. And then, within less than half an hour, it was over. A cacophony of sobbing, wailing and cheers accompanied the thousands who responded to an altar call to commit their lives to Christ. This was an encounter unlike anything that Bunny had seen before. This was true evangelism.

Whitefield had already preached to over half-a-million people and was one of the most recognised people in the colonies. Yet despite his fame he left the platform without delay and prepared to move on to his next venue. Bunny was impressed at this level of disciplined humility.

"Who's the nerd?" she asked Whitefield, nodding towards the young maths genius standing to one side. Whitefield clearly didn't understand the word *nerd* but, following the direction of her nod, promptly introduced her to someone he described as his friend, Ben Franklin.

"Benjamin Franklin?" Bunny spurted out. The young man acknowledged that was indeed his name, giving an uncomfortable bow. Before she could stop it coming out of her mouth, Bunny continued in her incredulity with the sentence,

"Future President of the United..." but thankfully stopped when she realised that there was no United States at this time. She checked her watch. True enough it was a few minutes, or a few years, before the Declaration of Independence. Yet here she was in Philadelphia, the birthplace of independence, with one of its signatories. She clumsily tried to change the subject.

---

[1] 'The Autobiography of Benjamin Franklin.' Houghton, Mifflin and Company, (1888), p131

"What do you think of George Whitefield?" she asked whilst castigating herself for such an inane question. Thankfully, his answer was more eloquent.

"If I consider this whole populous, who were indifferent about religion, it now seems as if all the world were growing religious, so that one could not walk through the town in an evening without hearing psalms sung in every street."[1]

As articulate as the reply was, Bunny quickly spotted that it was a factual observation, whereas her question had been personal. Something didn't sound right to her.

"Yes, I can see that there is a great wave of *religion* moving across this place," she began, "But what about *you*, Ben?"

"Me?" he was a little taken aback by the question. "I am one of George's most enthusiastic supporters and have published a lot of his writings." Finally, he added, the smallest token of personal comment. "And I admire that he encourages the people to do good works."

Despite his positive comments, she could sense that he was one step removed from the truth that Whitefield was preaching. She deployed her tell-me-more look at which Franklin soon caved.

"Whilst I don't subscribe to their theology, I do observe that these evangelicals preach liberty of conscience to be an inalienable right of every rational creature, and that I find ... stimulating."[2]

She was convinced. In describing Whitefield as one of 'These evangelicals,' it was clear to her that his friendship with Whitefield was doing little more than help Benjamin Franklin formulate his ideological principles, not his personal faith. Several hugs and handshakes later Whitefield and Bunny had remounted their horses and began a slow walk through the dense crowd that were pleading with him to return soon. Eventually the throng thinned sufficiently for them to pick up the pace and they could make their way to Northampton to meet Jonathan Edwards.

Artur spoke first. He explained that while he was offering his prayer, he had suddenly realised that there had to have been another person involved. As the others listened intently, he began to give a series of logical propositions.

---

[1] Words of Benjamin Franklin. 'John Wesley's Big Impact on America.' Christianity.com

[2] Words of Benjamin Franklin. 'The Ideological Origins of the American Revolution' by Bernard Bailyn (1992) p249

Firstly, he pointed out that if the two bodies are indeed the two who slept upstairs then,

"There had to be someone else who…" Artur instinctively dropped his words to an almost inaudible level as he said "…*killed them.*"

He continued to expand his reasoning that to get to and from the hospice, to collect and return the ambulance, there had to be another vehicle as it was too far to walk. There was another person, or persons, and more to the point there must have been another vehicle. Rex then jumped in to add,

"Didn't the route the ambulance take on the mileage logging website, didn't it go to the station, on the way back to the hospice?" They all agreed with his recollection.

"Yes, and if that was to collect someone, then presumably they've now gone back to the station," Artur added encouraged, before confessing that without access to the station CCTV to see the mystery person arrive, they were no further forward.

"Would it still be parked there? It might be," Joel prompted. Artur looked at him, tilting his head curiously as he repeated himself, this time more confidently. "If the other *person* has taken the train, then the other *vehicle* will still be at the station."

"Unless there is a fourth person," Thea pointed out, unhelpfully.

"Yes, that is true," Artur agreed, adding "But it is a possible, a good possible, that there is a vehicle there and that is all we have at the moment."

"That's it then, we need to go to the station and search the car park," Jack said rattling his keys impatiently.

"Wait a minute," Rex said. "Ralph had an idea too. I want to hear that first."

While Artur had been sharing his hypothesis, Ralph had slipped back into the kitchen and returned with the pizza box they had extracted from the kitchen bin earlier. He then explained that when he was praying, he remembered the pizza box and the morphine pouch he had found folded inside. Now, with all eyes fixed on him, he explained that he never thought about the pizza box itself. He held it up for all to see. It was a generic pizza box, not one from any of the major chains. As he examined it, he soon spotted the message *Lane End Farm* written in black ballpoint ink on the top right corner, followed by *£4.70*.

"This pizza was delivered," Ralph announced proudly.

"So, someone must have ordered it by phone," Chris quickly added.

"But we don't know where from," Thea said. Rex then pointed out that there may have been a flyer menu that came with it.

"Good idea, Foggie," Ralph said as he and Chris rushed back into the kitchen followed swiftly by the rest. Ralph took the lid off the bin, releasing a waft of stale food, and placed it carefully on the worktop. Before he could start the hunt for the flyer in the waste container, Chris upended the entire bin and emptied its contents over the floor and began fingering his way through it. Jack and Rex joined him in the objectionable exploration. Soon, every element of culinary detritus had been pushed and turned on the faded linoleum. There was no pizza menu amongst them.

"There's nothing here," Chris said exasperatedly, hope deferred being the cruellest of blows.

"Wait a minute," Ralph said as he extracted a soggy slip of thermal paper with his fingertips. It was a till receipt.

"Crust Almighty," he announced followed by the price of four pounds seventy and a time stamp that showed it had been delivered around lunchtime that day. No one had heard of that fast-food outlet but within a flash Thea had found their online listing on her smart phone. It was in the next village and offered 'Free delivery within five-miles,' she read.

"Well at least we have a couple of leads and, God willing, we are going to find Bunny before the night is out," Chris declared.

"Amen to that, brother!" Joel echoed the thoughts of many.

Rex's attention however was elsewhere. Having found one receipt, he was now surveying the contents of the bin specifically to see if there were any more. It was an obvious idea but not one anyone else had considered. It didn't take him long before he spotted another, this time screwed up into a ball. He squatted down to pick it up, an action which made everyone look at him. They watched silently as he carefully unwrapped it, a scene reminiscent of a child unwrapping a birthday present witnessed by the family. Expectation was palpable.

"It would appear that they bought: a six-pack of chicken tikka crisps, a bottle of Coke and two bottles of water. Two Pot Noodles... no, make that four Pot Noodles. Chocolate, toilet rolls..." As he listed the items, it was easy to spot the discarded packaging of many of them: the empty Coke bottle; four Pot Noodle lids; a Kit-Kat six-pack wrapper and two pre-packed sandwiches. He didn't read the entire list, it wasn't necessary, simply ending with,

"In fact, a whole load of groceries all from the Co-Op."

The mention of Co-Op prompted Joel to point with his foot to the plastic Co-Op shopping bag also amongst the floor-strewn garbage. Again, an obvious clue that everyone had missed.

"Which Co-Op?" Chris asked.

Rex consulted the receipt, even flipping it over to check, but confessed that it didn't say. There was a store number, but the only address appeared to be head-office. He was able to give them the information that the receipt was dated yesterday and that they paid cash.

"I'm not sure this helps us that much," Thea said, stating the obvious. They had to agree.

"So, we're going to the railway station car park and to …Crust Almighty, is that it?" Ralph asked. The repetition of the clumsy religious pun made all the gathered church-folk wince, but none verbalised the embarrassment they felt.

"You know what this is?" Joel posed. No one responded to his question, not entirely sure what he was saying. This allowed him space to deliver the punchline he had been developing for some time.

"This is a job for Inter-Clerical Rescue," he said, then followed with a few bars of the *Thunderbirds* theme, punctuated by dramatic fist pumps. It was a good line and several of the group laughed. Chris, however, was keen to get moving.

"Yes, let's get a wriggle on!" he said impatiently. "We should split up but keep in touch. We've all got our mobiles, so anything, no matter how small, pop it on WhatsApp." They all agreed and started to leave.

"But not to share it with anyone else?" Thea added questioningly.

"Yeah, that is right, let's just keep this to ourselves for the time being," Chris agreed. "Don't say anything to anyone else."

"Except to the police," Jack added. No one disagreed with him.

The Fellowship then separated. Chris and Ralph would go to Crust Almighty and, assuming they were still open, would try to speak to whomever delivered the pizza. Rector Mashman was already on his way to see Lord Advowson and the rest climbed into Jack's 4x4, Rex, Joel and Artur thankful for the spacious back seat, having insisted that Thea take the passenger seat. They set off for the station with the impossible task of finding an unknown vehicle that may or may not be parked there.

Chapter 25

JONATHAN EDWARDS

"The God that holds you over the pit of hell, much as one holds a loathsome spider over the fire, abhors you."

Jonathan Edwards' sermon was every bit as *hellfire and brimstone* as Bunny had imagined it would be. Whereas Whitefield had been more eloquent and charismatic, Edwards was unapologetic in describing how much his hearers would need to be *saved* in order to avoid the certain and impending damnation.

The chapel in Northampton was a pristine expression of black and white interior design, long before *interior design* had ever been described as such. Walls were whitewashed, as too was the ceiling which was interlaced by black structural beams that traversed the expansive void above the congregation. All of the wooden pews were painted white, a refreshing difference from every ecclesiastical building that, until now, Bunny had seen. The tops and edges of each pew were painted matt black, making a dramatic and stark contrast. Across much of the front of the building there spanned a cascade of organ pipes which gave the only splash of colour in the monotone building; the colour coming not from the soft gunmetal grey of the pipes but an indistinguishable green motif crest on each one. Central was a raised pulpit, also in white with black trim. All eyes were affixed on the man who stood upon it. This was Jonathan Edwards' pulpit and he could preach just the way he wanted. Which was, of course, Black and White!

"His anger towards you burns like fire," Edwards continued. "He looks on you as worthy of nothing but to be cast into the fire. You are ten thousand times as abominable in his eyes as the most hateful, venomous serpent."

At one point in his message Edwards had to stop; the howling and wailing from the audience became so overpoweringly loud that he could no longer be heard. He increased the volume as best he could to counter anymore outbursts.

"O sinner, you hang by a slender thread, with the flames of divine wrath flashing about you." [1]

And yet, the message was clear. God loved mankind enough to send Jesus to die on the cross to save from hell. It was a simple message and dozens

---

[1] 'Jonathan Edwards, The Works of President Edwards, vol. 6' by Burt Franklin New York (1817) pp. 458, 461–62.

responded to his closing altar call. This wasn't the first time. In the last few years so many people made a profession of Christian faith in Northampton, Massachusetts, that Edwards coined a new word to describe the impact it was having upon the city. He called it *revival*, a word which encapsulated the mood across many of the New England colonies at that time; the time being 17:41 according to Bunny's watch.

Whitefield was impressed and didn't hesitate to tell Edwards so as soon as the powerful evangelistic service had concluded. Edwards suggested that they should all retire to his home where he had arranged for some refreshments to be served. Bunny hadn't eaten since Herrnhut but realised that she had no concept of feeling hungry. Another pleasant side-effect of this prolonged hallucination, she thought.

The small group talked enthusiastically as they walked the few yards across the sunny tree-lined street to the house opposite. Bunny learned that over fifty thousand people had joined the churches in the area and over one hundred and fifty new churches had been opened in recent years to accommodate the revival. This was impressive. She began to daydream as they walked in the warm sunshine. She reflected on some of the American pioneers she had recently met. There was Brewster, Clyfton and the others with them that had first left England, then Holland and eventually crossed the Atlantic on their so-called Pilgrimage to find a land that would accept them. Then there was young William Penn and the mandate he was given to establish a Christian colony in the name of his father. Bunny felt sure that these founding fathers must be satisfied with the spiritual foundation they had laid. A safe topic of conversation she thought.

Suddenly the sky turned black and she became instantly afraid. What was happening? Her knees felt weak and could hardly walk another step. Someone grabbed her to steady her, she tried to say thank you, but no words would come out. She tried to walk forwards but her legs weren't cooperating, and inevitably she tumbled forwards, spinning downwards face-first onto the ground. Strangely she felt no impact of landing, no pain, she just lay there with one cheek pressed against the ground. Strange, this wasn't grass she was lying upon, it felt and looked more like bark chippings against her cheek. She felt blood in her mouth. Had she bitten her lip as she fell. Why couldn't she get up?

"C'mon, just a few more steps," the distant voice said as she was lifted from the dirt and ushered forward into the blackest of nights. The voice concluding with,

"Here we are all safe and sound, Missy."

Suddenly the lights came back on, and she was outside Edwards' home. She looked back at the stretch of manicured lawn they had just traversed and could see no sign of bark chippings and no reason why she should have fallen.

"I landed on the ground!" she said loudly, almost involuntarily.

All other conversation instantly stopped as they all turned to look at her. What could she say? She dug deep.

"The ground!" she said, feeling rather foolish as they all stared at her. "The landing ground," she subtly morphed her phrasing, hoping to cover her embarrassment. Then she had an idea.

"This revival must be exactly what the Pilgrim Fathers had hoped for when they *landed* on this *ground*," she contrived.

The group had already stopped walking when she made this statement; but by the look on their faces Bunny felt they would have suddenly come to halt anyway. What had she said? No one spoke, they just looked at her.

"You know, the Pilgrim...Fathers," Bunny began to babble. "Who sailed over on the..." she couldn't remember the name of the vessel but could feel her cheeks redden. She concluded the sentence with a somewhat pained "ship."

"We don't know of whom you speak, Miss," Whitefield offered as the small group began to file through the front door into a simple but pleasantly decorated home. Despite having mused about them only a few yards ago, Bunny now couldn't recall the names of any of the people she had recently met. As cloaks and hats were being removed and placed on hooks and upon an elegant walnut sideboard, she had to say something.

"You know," she began, not sure of where her sentence was going. Then in a flash of inspiration, she found something to say.

"The Puritans!" she gasped. "You know, the Puritans who came over to set up these colonies." Then suddenly added as a grateful postscript "...on the Mayflower!"

She had no idea how badly her well-meaning contribution to the conversation was going to be received but within a short period of time they had all put her straight. Despite being led by religious zeal to settle the colonies, she learned that because they had the legal mandate to govern, the so-called

Puritans soon became more concerned with politics, civic responsibility, and obedience rather than faith. Puritans represented the old order. The Great Awakening was by contrast the New Way and Edwards preached that it would usher in the new millennium. That wasn't the first time Bunny had witnessed someone who was convinced that Christ's thousand-year reign on earth was about to begin.

"They wanted that all citizens should attend church," Edwards explained. "But the doors of the churches of Christ do not stand so open that all sorts of people, good or bad, may freely enter at their pleasure." Adding, "Those seeking admission must be examined first to see that they possess repentance from sin and faith in Jesus Christ."[1]

Edwards and his peers taught that conversion should precede church membership and insisted that new members therefore had to give a personal *testimony* of their conversion before being granted admission. And it was clearly working.

"That's right!" One member of the group, who had remained silent until now, joined in the debate adding his own personal slant on the turn of recent colonial history.

"God has ordained two types of government – Civil and Ecclesiastical. Church is Church, and the State is State," he said. "Who can hear Christ declare that his Kingdom is not of this world, and yet believe that this blending of Church and State together can be pleasing to him"[2]

"Well said, Isaac," Edwards agreed.

It felt strange to Bunny that even in the midst of what Edwards had termed *revival* there was evident antagonism towards the Christian pioneers who had gone before them to pave the way, even though they had themselves been the risk-taking pioneers recoiling against the religious oppression of their day. She wondered if this present group would think any differently about their Puritan forebears had they met them personally.

---

[1] The Cambridge Platform was agreed in 1648 which was the common confession of faith in the Great Awakening. Amongst other tenets it stated that: "The doors of the churches of Christ upon earth do not by God's appointment stand so open that all sorts of people, good or bad, may freely enter therein at their pleasure; those seeking admission must be examined and tried first to see that they possess above all else repentance from sin, and faith in Jesus Christ." Church History in Plain Language: Fourth Edition, Bruce Shelley p359

[2] Taken from 'An Appeal to the Public for Religious Liberty Against the Oppressions of the Present Day', 1773 by Isaac Backus, pastor of Middleborough Baptist church, Norwich, Massachusetts

"Can't you thank the previous generation for anything?" she asked them provocatively. No one answered for a moment. Then, as if to break the slight tension, a voice was heard to say,

"We can thank them that they weren't Lutherans."

At this comment the whole group began to laugh, with the exception of Bunny who recognised that without Martin Luther's stance against the Catholic Church there might not have been any Protestant Reformation at all.

"Without the Lutherans you wouldn't be here!" she spurted without thinking.

"That is certainly true," Isaac said, adding, "Despite the best efforts of Campanius!"

Again, the group chuckled. Bunny however was in no mood to laugh. She had no idea who *Campanius* was, but they had no right to criticise past pioneers of the faith. Whitefield took pity on her and explained patiently that John Campanius was a Lutheran missionary who was sent to establish a Swedish Colony in the New World. He worked tirelessly learning the native language, translating the Lord's Prayer and some of Luther's teachings, and erecting a church building but, after five years of hard work, returned home having won a total of zero converts.[1]

She learned that it was the Anglican and Dutch Reform Churches that quickly became established, with Baptists and Methodists being added soon afterwards but the Lutheran message never really took hold. As he talked, Bunny suddenly had the realisation why. Lutheran doctrine believes in predestination, that those who are to be saved are destined to be so. Consequently, there is little need to preach for salvation. The other groups believed in the Arminianism doctrine that people have the free will to make a choice for Christ. Hence those denominations would preach more passionately and be more expectant of converts. Bunny decided to keep this revelation to herself, not wanting to spark any further debate.

Rector Mashman had visited Brennan Hall several times but hadn't felt this nervous since his first meeting with the present Lord Advowson's father. The

---

[1] Swedish Lutheran missionary Johan Campanius began evangelising the indigenous peoples of Delaware in 1643. He went to great lengths to understand their language, culture and even the local climate and soon gained their trust. Despite having established a church in the colony of New Sweden, he is reported to have had no converts. A statistic that is probably unfair and certainly difficult to verify, he nonetheless gave up and returned home in 1647.

long stately drive through the grounds to the front door was only used for special occasions – visitors used the shorter route from the main road into the stable yard. This was much preferable after dark as there were no lights on the estate drive. The Rector locked his car to the sound of dogs barking, disturbed by the noise of his tyres on gravel and the inevitable illumination of security lights. He made his way to the side-door that the family routinely used, his car keys in one hand and the picture of Velia in the other.

It soon became clear that things were not at all calm at Brennan Hall. A somewhat flustered housekeeper, Ruby, explained that neither Lord nor Lady Advowson were at home. His Lordship had gone to chase off some poachers, having heard some gunshots over in the woods. Ruby explained that poachers had been shooting pheasants for some time and that Lord Advowson was worried they may try to take some of the deer.

"No one shoots birds at night," Ruby explained. "So, he left in a fearful hurry to chase them poachers away."

"And the ma'am is at her bridge club this evening mister Reverend, Sir," Ruby said apologetically.

"And what of Miss Velia?" the cleric asked probingly.

"She is out with her new boyfriend, mister Reverend," Ruby answered, then pursed her lips to add with displeasure, "and I dare say she won't be home tonight."

There was little more he could find out from Ruby. He reluctantly declined her offer of a cup of Earl Grey and bade her goodnight with a promise that he would call back to see them all in the morning. Once safely back in his Honda he found the scrap of newspaper with the list of telephone numbers of the rest of the group. Who to ring, suddenly became a difficult question. He didn't know any of these people any better than the rest. Despite being the Rector of All Saints' for several decades, he hadn't ventured outside of his Anglican structure. Looking at that tatty slip of newspaper it became starkly clear that he had always kept himself at arms-length from non-Anglicans whom, in some way, he had viewed as inferior. None of these people were his friends, and yet tonight they were all working to help find Johan Elstow, someone whom he did consider to be one of his closest friends and a lady he relied upon every day. To his amazement the seven telephone numbers, each written in a different hand on a piece of stained newsprint, represented the best hope of finding Bunny.

Failing to find any logic to help him select which one of them to ring, he dialled the number at the top of the paper.

Chapter 26

MERCY WHEELER

A rather timid and unassuming man hovered close to them holding a pamphlet in his hand. His face proffered the patient urgency of someone waiting outside a toilet cubicle door for it to open. The man's presence was distracting, so Edwards momentarily broke off the conversation to ask the waiting man if he could help him. The visitor introduced himself as Hezekiah Lord, a minister from a nearby church and that he had an unusual problem.

"There is a lady in our church who believes God is going to heal her," he said.

"Hallelujah!" Edwards expressed spontaneously adding, "God does indeed want to heal her!" Edwards then pointed out that all illness ended amongst those who had joined his Church during the peak of the revival. Whitefield didn't comment. Indeed, Bunny could detect the faintest of tightening of his lips as Edwards continued to talk enthusiastically of miraculous healings.

"It was the most remarkable time of health that ever I knew since I have been in the town,"[1] he said before explaining that, "Prayers for the sick that were initially so common became strangely absent from one sabbath to the next."

None of this was helping the visiting minister who patiently waited for the great preacher to finish.

"The problem is," Hezekiah Lord politely interrupted, "is that it is *this* woman." He passed Edwards the pamphlet he had been holding. It was entitled 'An Address to Young People.' It had been published some ten years previously and was written by a Mercy Wheeler.

"Ah, Mercy Wheeler," Edwards said in recognition. Whitefield too knew the name as he scanned the pamphlet before passing it to Bunny. Mercy Wheeler could not walk. She had never been able to walk and it had been medically diagnosed that her ankles were 'loose'. Consequently, she needed to be carried by two people wherever she went and spent most of her time in bed. The short tract was an exhortation to young people that despite her disability

---

[1] 'The Healing of Mercy Wheeler: Illness and Miracles among Early American Evangelicals.' by Thomas S. Kidd. (2006)

she nonetheless had a deep and sincere faith and that they should not look upon her with pity but as an example of what was in important in life and how God had sustained her. This was a well-known, well-distributed and oft quoted publication that had inspired many people to a deepening of their faith. If Mercy Wheeler was healed, it would be impossible to deny it as anything short of a miracle.

Her minister, Hezekiah, was clearly sceptical about the whole concept of healing and had come for advice. George Whitfield, also a sceptic, couldn't help himself and offered what amounted to a somewhat negative comment.

"I am no Enthusiast," he said defiantly, *Enthusiast* being a term used to describe those in New England who claimed to have access to miraculous powers and who spoke in tongues. Despite preaching fervently about all of Christ's miracles, Whitefield didn't believe that healings were of his time and emphatically claimed to have not healed anyone.[1] Jonathan Edwards however was very much pro-healing, having already seen the evidence of miraculous divine interventions within his city.

"You should go and pray for her. When God is about to do a mighty new thing, he always sets his people praying. Then if God wills it, she shall be healed," Edwards said.[2] Whitefield bit his lip.

"But..." Hezekiah Lord began. Edwards held up his hand to politely stop his protestations.

"You don't need to have faith," Edwards said to the questioning minister. "She clearly has enough for both of you," he said as he handed the pamphlet back. "But if it would help you, would you like one of us to come with you?" Lord nodded thankfully.

In that moment, all three men, Edwards, Whitefield and Lord simultaneously looked at Bunny. This protracted dreamscape was now beginning to make demands upon her. She was having to participate in ways she hadn't expected, but she also knew that it would be pointless to protest. She couldn't claim that this wasn't what she had signed up for as she clearly wasn't here by her own volition. Besides, if she didn't comply her guiding angel with the gold-rimmed hat would no doubt suddenly appear and chastise her.

"That'll be me then," she said with begrudging acceptance.

---

[1] 'A vindication of the Reverend Mr. Whitfield.' Anon, (1745)

[2] Widely quoted words of Jonathan Edwards. Taken from https://quotefancy.com/quote/1173793

"That's my phone," Rex said rummaging through his pockets, releasing the central seat belt to help him extricate the impatient device from his hip pocket. The car filled with an irritating 'Bing' that persisted until he re-connected his safety belt. Despite all listening intently, his fellow passengers had difficulty in piecing together the whole conversation Rex was having, based solely on a random sprinkling of 'Yes,' 'No,' and 'Ah-hum.' They had to wait for a fuller explanation once the call was finished. Rex then explained that Rector Mashman had found that neither Lord nor Lady were at the Hall and that Velia was out with her boyfriend.

"Sadly, I don't think any of that helps us," Rex said, then added, "You know, I've been thinking." Jack glanced at Rex in the rear-view mirror as he re-clipped his seat belt. "We know the farmhouse is linked to Bunny's disappearance and that she was in St. Christopher's ambulance, but the other place we know she has been tonight, in the ambulance, is the hospital. Perhaps one of us should try to see if we can find out anything more of what happened there."

The station car park was itself a long shot, so sending part of the group to the hospital was at least doubling their slim chances of finding anything helpful.

"I'll go," said Thea, explaining that she regularly did a lot of hospital visits and that she gets on well with the chaplain. Then suddenly she realised that all the other occupants of the car, being church leaders too, probably also did *lots of hospital visits*. Thankfully, no one objected, and she was allocated that task. For the first time she felt she was amongst a group of equals. None of them were over her, they were just her equals, and she felt a sense of satisfaction to be part of this group.

The immediate problem was that they now needed to be in two places at the same time, but only had one car. As they had almost arrived at the station, they decided to first drop Artur there, then take Thea to the hospital and let her see what she could find out. Jack would then drive Joel and Rex back to C.R.F. so they could pick up their vehicles and return to the station and the hospital for Thea and Artur.

Mercy Wheeler was a formidable woman – a little older than Bunny, who immediately recognised a kindred spirit. She was a woman confined to her home and yet so passionately in love with Christ that it shone out of her. And she wasn't going to take no for an answer. She was determined that God was going to heal her, that it was going to be instantaneous, and it was going to be

230

today. No amount of reasonable dissuasion from Hezekiah Lord was going to shake her. She had been reading from chapter five of John's gospel, about a man who had been disabled for thirty-eight years and Jesus met him by the Pool of Bethesda.[1] That man was healed instantly and so would she be.

Hezekiah was at a loss as to what to do. This was going to look bad on him and he was going to be the one responsible for upsetting the faith of one of the most well-known people in the colonies. In desperation he opened his Bible and read a passage from the prophet Isaiah saying God would 'Revive the spirit of the humble and the heart of the contrite ones.'[2] But it was when he began to pray for her and said that God would bring her out of the furnace that things began to manifest. Mercy suddenly began to tremble, shake and speak gibberish. Lord immediately panicked and tried to console her.

Mercy screamed,

"Noooooo!" and insisted that she *would* be healed. She then described that she could feel a strange and irresistible motion and shaking beginning with her hands, then her arms and moving to her whole body. She said she felt a weight press upon her as if every joint was being squeezed together. She screamed in agony. Bunny didn't know if she should intervene, but decided not. Then suddenly the weight left her, the pain with it and she said she felt strong. Strong enough to stand. The minister was dumbfounded and speechless, frozen to the spot. Bunny stepped forward to take Mercy's hand and help her rise. This was going to be the moment of truth. Either she was going to collapse in an agonising heap and Bunny would have to lie her back in her bed, or, and Bunny couldn't believe that she herself was now believing in the *or*... or she would stand.

A bare foot slipped out from under the bed clothes. It was pale and gnarled and overly thin. Almost too thin to hold a person upright. Then a second foot joined it. Mercy sat up unaided, her upper body was strong to compensate

---

[1] The Gospel according to John chapter 5 verses 5-9: "And a certain man was there, which had an infirmity thirty and eight years. When Jesus saw him lie, and knew that he had been now a long time in that case, he saith unto him, Wilt thou be made whole? The impotent man answered him, Sir, I have no man, when the water is troubled, to put me into the pool: but while I am coming, another steppeth down before me. Jesus saith unto him, Rise, take up thy bed, and walk. And immediately the man was made whole, and took up his bed, and walked." KJV

[2] Hezekiah read Isaiah 57:15 to Mercy Wheeler: 'For thus saith the high and lofty One that inhabiteth eternity, whose name is Holy; I dwell in the high and holy place, with him also that is of a contrite and humble spirit, to revive the spirit of the humble, and to revive the heart of the contrite ones'. KJV

for her years of lack of movement. She prepared herself for the literal step of faith. Bunny offered her a hand which Mercy gladly accepted. The next moment seemed to last an eternity. Motionless, Mercy and Bunny made eye-contact. They looked deep into each other's eyes, both looking to see if there was anything in the other person that would make this next, and first step, any easier. Both searching for any one of a number of negative emotions that would be entirely justified in this situation. Was there any fear? Any doubt? Maybe anxiety? No. Neither of them had any of those emotions. They both had placed their faith in the ...'or'. They were invested in the 'or', in the face of overwhelming odds, in the face of opposing logic, to the contrary of any well-argued doctrinal stance. None of this mattered. This moment was about Mercy and the God of mercy. And Bunny could feel it. Bunny's faith was a continual, steady, rock-solid foundation which her life had been built upon. But that was before this ridiculous dream, she thought. Before speaking to God in a silent Quaker meeting and hearing him reply, before feeling her heart change in a Moravian meeting in London, before seeing thousands upon thousands commit themselves to Christ, and before this moment when Bunny, for the first time in her life, was convinced, absolutely convinced, she was about to witness a miracle of biblical proportions. This lady to whose eyes she was affixed was about to 'take up her bed and walk!' Bunny raised her head a fraction of an inch as if to indicate, Are you ready? Mercy nodded then pulled with all her might. Bunny held tight to her hand and stepped slowly backwards. Once vertical Mercy let her hand drop. This first step had to be unaided. She had held an assisting hand for too long. This was the moment for her first step. And then she did it. Not only baby-steps but confident solid strides, a brisk turn at the side of the room and five steps back. She had risen from her bed for the first time in seventeen years, fully healed.

"Bless the Lord Jesus who has healed me," she exclaimed then screamed in joy. Bunny joined her, the loud emotional release being as much praise as it was relief.

Hezekiah Lord was convinced that the pair of them were in some form of a frenzy and physically forced Mercy to sit down, at which both women began to laugh uncontrollably.[1]

---

[1] 'The Healing of Mercy Wheeler: Illness and Miracles among Early American Evangelicals.' by Thomas S. Kidd. (2006)

"I don't think you are helping, Miss; I think you should leave!" he said accusatorily to Bunny, unsure as to what had indeed happened in this room. Bunny was, quite understandably, offended at his sharp rebuke but when Mercy then took hold of her hand and whispered,

"It's all right, Miss, it is time you moved on," then Bunny knew it was safe to go.

She hugged Mercy and said goodbye to Hezekiah Lord and stepped outside into the cold Connecticut air. An open-topped buggy was waiting outside. One door had been left open, presumably for her. She stepped in and closed the door carefully behind her. She was on her own and felt a little vulnerable. No sooner had she taken her seat than she heard the cry of a newspaper street-vendor. She was a little disappointed that he didn't deliver the traditional, 'Extra, Extra, read all about it!' but the mention of Miracle Healing did focus her attention. She beckoned the young man over who gave her a copy but asked her for no payment. I like the price of newspapers in dreamland, she thought.

"Where to, Miss?" A driver had appeared at the front of the buggy. She had no idea where she was meant to go.

"I don't know?" she admitted.

"Do you know where you came from?" he asked.

That was a question that had only one answer. She closed her eyes and could see her home, her church, Rector Mashman and, of course, she could see Chris. But for some reason he looked worried. He looked troubled, and she didn't know why. Chris was always upbeat; he was the happy one of the pair. If they were indeed a pair, a couple now. She was the dour, careful, sensible one. He was the fun, gregarious, spontaneous one. But now he looked worried about something, he looked worried about *her*, she felt. She could see him mouth some words over and over. What was he saying? She stared at his fading face trying desperately to lip read as he said, "Bunny, where are you?"

"Where are you from, Miss?" the driver repeated. Bunny re-opened her eyes suddenly. All she could think of saying was,

"Jonathan Edwards in Northampton." That was sufficient for the driver who simply looked forward and with a flick of the reins urge the single black horse into its stride.

The lead article in the *Boston Gazette* described the healing she had witnessed seconds earlier. It said how the healing was, "Well known and attested" pointing out that it was difficult to challenge this as a miracle, based on the medical diagnosis printed in her pamphlet ten years prior. The article then referred to the similar healing in England at the time of the French Prophets. Bunny's jaw dropped unconsciously as she realised that she had personally witnessed three Huguenot Christians prophesying in London. She hadn't realised that they were accompanied by healings. She read on about the report of a Mary Malliard who also had been lame in her left leg from birth. Then in 1690 at the height of the London prophetic movement prayed for healing. She felt a great pressure on her leg, followed by an audible snap as the bones reconnected and then said she heard a voice saying, "Thou are healed." The leg was fully restored, and the healing publicly attested.[1]

Why have I never heard of these things? Bunny wondered. This is all so true it is being written about in the newspapers here in... she looked for the date at the top of the page, 1744. The article finished with a comment from a prominent Protestant minister, Cotton Mather,

"There seems as if there were an age of miracles now dawning upon us," he said. "Just as the miracles had ceased due to the rise of the Antichristian apostasy so also miracles might resume with Catholicism's destruction."[2]

It was clear, from this preacher at least, that the blame for the lack of any miraculous healings since Bible times was being laid squarely at the doorstep of the Catholic Church.

It was indeed less than five miles to the village whose late-night culinary needs were met by Crust Almighty. The fast-food outlet wasn't the only retailer still to be plying their trade late into the evening as directly opposite its frontage there was a modestly sized branch of the Co-Op with a small car park for customers. They pulled in to take one of the half-dozen spaces, all of which were vacant, directly opposite Crust Almighty.

"I bet they did their shopping here," Chris said. "They took a menu and then phoned in their order the next day."

"Yeah, when their Pot Noodles had run out," Ralph added. It was an entirely plausible scenario. Ralph began to head off across the road, but as soon as Chris had locked the car, he shouted over to him that he wanted to look inside

---

[1] Hillel Schwartz, The French Prophets: The History of a Millenarian Group in Eighteenth Century England. 1980 p68-69

[2] This quote from the prominent preacher Cotton Mather was not published in a newspaper but delivered from the pulpit.

the grocery store first. Ralph spun around obligingly. As they entered the store a man hurried past them carrying a single bottle of milk, the signature late-night purchase of the disorganised.

The inside of the village Co-Op store was pretty much the same as the inside of every other. Chris began to slowly wander along the first aisle, nonchalantly glancing over the shelves of produce. Baskets of loose fruit and vegetables flowed into tins of the same. Two wall chillers displayed all the essential dairy and meat options. There was no freezer, Chris assumed that would be around the next aisle. Then came the preserves, sauces and ready meals. Chris paused momentarily as he spotted the Pot Noodles. At the end of the first aisle the end wall held shelves devoid of its stock of bread, bar a solitary white loaf and two six-packs of brown rolls. After the bread were the cakes, an alarmingly diverse and brightly coloured selection of largely chocolate-based bakery. The breakfast cereals and soft drinks marked either side of his route along the return aisle. Again, he paused when he noted the two-litre Coke bottle that he had last seen on the farmhouse kitchen floor. Sure enough, a glass-lidded chest-freezer stood back-to-back with the chillers and provided everything from ice creams to oven chips. Opposite the freezer was an array of soap powders, dishwasher tablets, toilet rolls, toothpaste and shampoos. Chris had no idea what he hoped to achieve by walking through this store in this way but, lacking any reason not to do it, at least it made him feel he was doing something. He glanced back at Ralph who had just turned the corner at the end of the store and was bizarrely holding an empty shopping basket. It was clear there were no customers in the store - not surprising for so late in the evening. The shopkeeper was kneeling just a few paces onwards replenishing his stock of several lines of confectionary. The retailer met his gaze, Chris smiled in return and offered a muted, "Evening," as he turned his face towards the produce. The shopkeeper nodded in reply, but Chris's attention had moved on to the diverse display of housewares including firelighters, frying pans, mops and buckets. Then he saw it. There at the bottom of the shelf, a solitary one, rolled up, tied with a blue cardboard sleeve extolling its virtues, and with a manufacturer's label displaying the special price of £4.99. It was one of the sleeping mats that he had seen in the bedroom at Lane End Farm.

"Oh!" he exclaimed, loud enough to attract the attention of both Ralph and the shopkeeper.

"Is everything all right?" the shopkeeper asked from his kneeling position.

Ralph followed Chris's gaze and he too saw the mat. They were identical, the same shade of pale blue, with the same label. Chris was frozen to the spot, so Ralph answered the shopkeeper with the only off-the-cuff remark he could think of,

"It's a surprise to see sleeping mats here," he proffered. The owner didn't reply. Ralph then added the cleverly inquisitorial,

"I bet you don't sell many of these do you?" The shopkeeper took the bait.

"Sold two this week, as it happens," he said, confirming Chris's suspicions.

"Really?" Ralph continued. "Who would buy sleeping mats in October?"

The shopkeeper pursed his lips as he began to think. It was a very good point and one he hadn't considered until asked the question.

"S'pose not," was his considered, although succinct, reply. "But a chap bought two a couple of days ago."

"Really?" Ralph added with overly stressed enthusiasm. "Well, I never!"

"And did he buy anything else...strange?" Chris quickly added, hoping to find out something, anything that might prove useful.

The retailer stood up from his kneeling position, taking a moment to stretch his aching back, as he did.

"Well, now you mention it, there was something."

Chapter 27

Bunny was still elated when she arrived back in Northampton. Jonathan Edwards' suburban home was a stone's throw from the church building at which he would preach almost every Sunday.

Bunny walked across the neat front garden and gave a gentle tap on the door to announce her arrival, followed by a tentative, "Hello." No one answered so, emboldened with her new-found faith, she entered. Once in the hallway the sound of angry voices focussed her attention on the direction of Jonathan's office.

Jonathan was seated behind his desk; a small delegation was scattered around the room — two standing, two seated — and the atmosphere was decidedly negative. Edwards acknowledged Bunny's arrival as the leader of the visiting group made his point.

"You and your so-called New Light followers are upsetting the established Churches, Mister Edwards," he said. They had come to accuse Edwards of being behind a degree of religious unrest but to Bunny's ears it sounded identical to several other such accusations she had witnessed. Whether it was Luther at Worms or the Arminians at Dort, the established Church reacted with suspicion to anything that was outside of their own core beliefs.

This just keeps happening over and over again, she thought. Something new comes along and no matter how good or how worthy it is, it's immediately rejected by the established Church of the day. Jonathan Edwards, for his part, sat quietly as they read their list of indictments.

"People have convulsions, they wail, they cry and laugh uncontrollably. Some fall over in your services claiming to have been slain by the Holy Spirit himself. Others claim to see visions and hear voices."

Edwards nodded as it was read but otherwise listened dispassionately as they continued. The principal accuser, an austere looking elderly man, looked up from his prepared list and stared at Edwards.

"All of this is just made up, hysterical, a purely natural phenomena," he said hoping to goad the evangelist into an angry response.

They had delivered the case for the prosecution, now it was time for Edwards to defend himself. They waited, silently, ready to hear his counterclaims which they would then pick apart with their prepared doctrinal arguments. Edwards thought, and prayed, for a while before speaking.

"Yes, of course, they are natural," he said much to everyone's surprise. "After all, that is what people do when faced with great danger." The accusers looked uncomfortably at each other; they had no recourse for his agreement. Edwards continued,

"Anyone who stood on the brink of hell and showed no signs of terror, surely they are the irrational ones."

Bunny couldn't help but be impressed with the confident eloquence and simplicity of his reply.

"But what about the visions and voices?" he was asked by a young challenger seeking to ignite controversy. Once again, Edwards thought for a moment before replying.

"None of these manifestations prove anything about whether the Holy Spirit is at work or not. The only proof has to be paid in the orthodox Protestant currency: sober and enduring conversions, regenerate lives, honest affirmation of doctrine and quiet obedience to lawful authority."[1] And with that, the wind had well and truly been taken out of their sails.

With a confident: "Now if you don't mind, I have another meeting about to start," Edwards dismissed this delegation who gathered their Bibles and duly left.

Once they had departed Bunny relayed with great excitement the healing that she had witnessed at Mercy Wheeler's bedside, an encounter Edwards lapped up. It was clear to Bunny that miraculous healings were part and parcel of this so-called Great Awakening. Bunny and Jonathan stopped their excited interchange at the sound of a polite but firm knock on the study doorframe.

"Would it be acceptable if we were to enter now, Father Jonathan?"

The man leaning to one side in the doorway was clearly also a minister. He was dressed in the black cassock, white-collared shirt, heavy shoes and crowned by the traditional wide-brimmed black hat that Bunny associated with colonial times. But most noticeably, she could see that dangling heavily from a substantial chain around his neck was perhaps the largest cross she had ever seen anyone wear. Edwards gestured that the visitor, and his small party, should

---

[1] Taken from a sermon by Jonathan Edwards. 'Protestants: The Faith That Made the Modern World' by Alec Ryrie (2019)

come in and make themselves comfortable. Bunny vacated the padded guest chair and allowed the female member of this next delegation to take the place of comfort. It soon became clear that this woman, one Bethesda Kingsley, was the reason for the meeting. She was joined by her husband, a tall burly man who did not look at ease with being in the room and stood with his arms resolutely folded, visually disengaged.

Over the next few minutes Bunny learned with fascination that Jonathan Edwards was being asked to intervene in a case of church discipline being brought against the *unruly* Mrs. Kingsley. Bunny looked at Bethesda, intrigued as to how unruly a woman could be in colonial America, and keen to discover what she had done that required the intervention of the revered Mr. Edwards.

The minister did all the talking, neither Bethesda nor her husband said a word. She sat confidently in the red armchair; he stood indignantly in front of the window. The minister explained that she was being disciplined by her church for a number of infractions.

Firstly, it was claimed that she would go around from door-to-door and share the gospel with her neighbours. No crime there, thought Bunny. Next, they heard that certain ministers took objection to her *preaching* in public. Clearly it was not the *done thing* to have a woman share her faith so openly. But that wasn't all. She would travel to nearby towns in order to visit those who had voiced opposition to her preaching, and having found her target detractors would then denounce their specific personal sins, 'As God revealed them to her', often shouting about them in front of their neighbours.

Bethesda's husband audibly harrumphed at the notion of *God revealing* anything. Mrs. Kingsley on the other hand remained dispassionate. Bunny couldn't help but like this feisty woman's style and couldn't suppress a smile, but thought it best to raise her hand to politely cover her grin.

Bunny began to wonder what was meant by 'As God revealed them to her.' Her knowledge of God's revelation was limited to an inner conviction she experienced sometimes when she was reading her Bible. Sometimes a specific verse would seem to leap off the page and have a special significance to her current situation. She knew that God spoke to her in this way. But then there was that moment she felt she could hear God's voice in her head in the silence of the Quaker meeting. But again, this was personal to her and very ... internal. Bethesda here was setting off on a journey to find a specific person in the full knowledge that when she found them God was going to whisper in her ear a juicy piece of tabloid gossip. Suddenly, Bunny wasn't sure about the ethics of what Mrs. Kingsley had done. Surely this wasn't very ...Christian. But then, if it truly was God who had exposed personal sins amongst the clergy, then maybe it was. Finally, a further charge was levelled at her.

"In order to visit these places," the minister began, "she took her husband's horse without his permission." Ridiculous, thought Bunny, thankful that she hadn't said so out loud.

At this charge, the simmering kettle that was Mr. Kingsley began to boil. For years he had stomached much of the embarrassment his wife had caused him, but this was too much. He unfolded his arms and stepped closer to her, casting an immense shadow into the room, the only source of light being the window behind him. His frame towering above her as she sat, he looked down upon her and said with disdain,

"Why did you do it?"

She didn't make eye contact with him, but matter of fact gave her reason.

"God gave me an immediacy of revelation to go and spread the word!" she said.

Incensed at what he took to be a further attack on his domestic authority, her husband snapped. Bunny couldn't make out what he said, she was so shocked to see a man, a large man at that, hit his wife across the face. If this were modern times he would be arrested, but this was colonial America. She couldn't help herself.

"No!" Bunny screamed at him, "You can't do that."

Bethesda held her right hand to her left cheek, nursing a rapidly developing bruise. By the look of resignation in her eyes this wasn't the first time she had been victimised in this way. Mr. Kingsley spun round to look at Bunny, fury raging in his eyes. For a moment she feared she too might be on the receiving end of a slap. She looked at Jonathan Edwards who instantly saw the terror in Bunny's eyes.

"No, Sir, you cannot," Edwards said adding, "Not in my house," as if to give some legitimacy to the enforced imposition of restraint. Kingsley stepped back to his position, refolded his arms, but said nothing.

Having been asked to give a ruling on this woman's actions, Edwards brought the meeting to a conclusion. To Bunny's delight, he said that whilst he could not endorse her public ministry, she should nonetheless continue to visit her friends and neighbours to spread the word. As a token to her husband, she promised to ask permission before taking his horse again.

Bunny was impressed. Despite the societal norms, there appeared to be no desire to supress the female voice in the Great Awakening.

Chapter 28

JOHN WESLEY, AGAIN

It wasn't just the name of the eatery that suggested poor taste, everything about Crust Almighty indicated that this was not a place that either Chris or Ralph would willingly choose to frequent. Even in the dim light of the distant streetlight the place looked dirty on the outside, the windows still damp with raindrops from the downpour earlier that evening. The state of cleanliness was no better inside, nor too was the temperature. This wasn't specifically a pizza shop but a multi-national takeaway offering Turkish kebabs, American fried chicken, Indian curries and British fish & chips alongside the Italian pizzas that had framed the outlet's name. Their arrival prompted the overweight balding person behind the counter wearing an ill-fitting and grease-spattered woollen pullover to reach for a pen, collect a dog-eared order pad and stare at them expectantly. Whether it was reflex or the unmistakable chip-shop smell, Chris suddenly felt incredibly hungry. Luckily, Ralph spoke first, otherwise Chris would have probably ordered battered sausage, large chips, and mushy peas.

"Hello," he started. "You delivered a pizza to Lane End Farm at lunchtime today."

The proprietor looked at him suspiciously but said nothing. Sensing that he might be assuming a complaint was coming, Chris jumped in.

"No, don't worry, there wasn't anything the matter with it, in fact it was..." he didn't want to finish the sentence with a lie.

"It was eaten!" Ralph added.

"Yes, it was all eaten," Chris joined in adding a final, uncomfortable, and in no way convincing "Yum! Yum!"

"So?" the takeaway owner said.

"Could we please speak to whomever delivered the pizza?" Chris asked, unsure if he should have used the word *whomever* in a shop with someone who looked as though they might have a rather limited vocabulary.

"Why?" came the answer, doubling the number of words that Chris now knew was in the proprietor's lexicon. Again, they reassured him there wasn't a problem, but the owner didn't look convinced. Chris then had an idea.

"We didn't give him a tip and ..." he offered. Ralph took the bait adding,

"Yes, and as we are church leaders, we've come to give him one."

"You can give it me and I will give it 'em," he unsurprisingly answered. They both instantly replied that it would be better to give it to the deliverer personally. "Church leaders, eh?" he asked, unsure if he could trust them.

They explained that they were from Community Restoration Fellowship and then kept talking passionately about it hoping he wouldn't question them further. They continued, and when their staged banter morphed into why everyone needs to believe in Jesus, the grease-stained worker promptly disappeared into the back room saying,

"I'll get her."

"I hope you have got the *tip* with you?" Ralph said out of the side of his mouth to Chris while they were waiting. Chris felt into his trouser pockets and pulled out twelve pence, hardly enough to justify their visit.

"It'll have to be a note!" he replied.

"She's going to love you!" Ralph joked.

The delivery had been made by a young woman in her early twenties and by the looks of the black Belstaff jacket and waterproof trousers she was wearing, such deliveries were made by motorbike.

Chris pulled out his wallet and withdrew the five-pound note that he had nearly given to his first informant of the evening before they had upped the stakes to twenty. Hopefully this time it would stay at just a fiver.

"Miss," he asked, "Do you remember delivering to Lane End Farm today, around lunchtime."

She glanced at the owner to check if she should answer or not. He nodded that she was free to talk. She admitted she had made the delivery, adding that it was unusual as she had never been to that address before; thinking it to have been abandoned. She clearly didn't have any of the vocal limitations exhibited by her employer.

Chris asked if she remembered what was parked in the drive at the time. Again, she looked to check with the owner, but he was taking an order from a middle-aged woman who had just entered the shop.

"I didn't do nuffin," she said defensively. Chris gave her the five-pound note.

"I know you didn't, but I really need to know if you remember what was parked there at lunchtime."

She looked at the fiver in her hand, then at her two beneficiaries, then at her boss. He hadn't seen the cash change hands, so she quickly scrunched the note into her hand and then into her jacket pocket. She suggested they move

243

away from the end of the counter and stepped towards a large, framed picture showing the unlikely scene of a handsome couple lovingly sharing a Pukka Pie in bed. They gathered around the delivery girl.

"I thought it were unusual, in like an abandoned farm, you know, I would have expected a Land Rover or summut. But there was like this sports car, deep red one it was, can't tell you the make, but it was a nice colour, all glittery but like spattered wiv mud."

"A sports car?" Ralph repeated.

"Yeah, little two-seater with a soft top. And there was like an older one too. Didn't notice that as much but there was another."

"Can you remember anything about that one, Miss," Chris implored her. "Please think!"

"Are you's the police?" She asked. They both shook their heads and Ralph pulled one of his business cards from his wallet and showed it her as proof he was indeed a churchman. The assurance worked.

"I remember one of you was angry that they'd ordered pizza."

"One of us?" Ralph queried.

"Yes," Chris said continuing the ruse that they were the recipients of her delivery. "In the farmhouse at lunchtime, remember?" Ralph said nothing.

"Yeah, someone shouts 'what the eff,' when I shows up at the door. He was none too 'appy."

"Who answered the door?" Ralph asked.

She looked at both of them, as if to check if it was either of them.

"All I know is that he had no 'air and paid cash."

"He was bald?" he clarified. She nodded adding,

"As a badger."

Ralph had never heard anyone use the phrase as *bald as a badger* before. Surely badgers aren't bald? He thought.

"And the car?" Chris asked again.

She closed her eyes reimagining her visit earlier that day. As she did, she leaned first to the left, then right as if re-enacting her motorbike journey in a way similar to a bobsleigh pilot rehearsing the Cresta Run. Ralph and Chris gave her as much time as she needed, the chip-shop owner on the other hand was growing impatient. She was due a delivery and this conversation was taking far too long for his liking. He gave a loud "Oi" at which she opened her eyes.

"It was a long one and dark blue," she said.

"Long, like an estate car," Chris asked as she began to brush past them to return to her duties.

"Yep," she said replacing the hinged counter back into position with a decisive click.

"And dark blue?" Chris asked as she stepped through the coloured beads hanging in the rear doorway.

"Yep," she answered confidently, before returning briefly to say "Or black."

"I didn't expect to see you again."

Bunny had grown so accustomed to only meet people fleetingly in her whistle-stop tour of Christendom that when she saw John Wesley enter Jonathan Edwards' study, she couldn't help but express her surprise.

"No, and I wasn't sure if I was going to be let back into this new country," he said in jest as he shook her hand courteously.

New country? Bunny thought. That must mean that time has now progressed passed the Declaration of Independence. She checked her watch which confirmed that they were now no longer in the American colonies but in the United States of America. Bunny looked around for Edwards but for some reason he was no longer there.

"What a pleasure it is to see you again, Miss Elstow," Wesley said.

He had certainly aged by several years since their last meeting. She didn't want to ask but she guessed that he was well into his seventies, perhaps even older. But he was still distinctively John Wesley. Bunny appreciated being addressed personally. She had begun to feel as though she was no more than a fly on an ancient ecclesiastical wall. Moments like this, where she had some one-on-one time, were most welcome, particularly as she had a host of questions to ask.

"What brings you back to America, Mr Wesley?" It was the obvious, if overly polite opening question, and one he answered with typical eloquence.

"A problem not of my own making brought me here," he said. Bunny was unsure as to whether she should look concerned, so she gestured that he take the seat next to her, an offer he didn't hesitate to accept.

"For the past forty-five years," he said, as he settled himself into the padded chair, "I have preached thousands of sermons, I have taught: 'Do all the good you can, by all the means you can, in all the ways you can, in all the places you can, at all the times you can, to all the people you can, as long as ever you can.'" Bunny looked at him expectantly, needing him to continue.

"I have seen tens of thousands of people in England transformed by the power of the gospel. And even more here in America."

Bunny smiled compassionately as the great preacher reflected on his life's mission. It was clear that he had a strong sense of contentment and yet something was troubling him. She waited, allowing him time to verbalise what was on his mind.

"Everyone who responded to the message of the cross and joined one of our Societies," he continued, "were all, to a man, members of the Church of England. But now there are so many here in America we desperately need more ministers."

Bunny nodded dispassionately as Wesley continued.

"And despite my most earnest of appeals the Archbishop of Canterbury has refused to do so, denouncing us as merely *religious enthusiasts*." He delivered the phrase with disdain before reaching his painful conclusion. "And so, he has left me with no choice but to ordain my own ministers and in so doing they will have to be separate from the Church of England."

Bunny had always assumed that Wesley's Methodists had been a breakaway movement from the outset. She had no idea that throughout most of Wesley's life he considered it to be *within* the Anglican mainstream.

"And I fear that having done so here, England will soon follow," he added. It was time for Bunny to offer some consolation that he was doing the right thing.

"I wouldn't worry about that, John. I am sure your followers will thrive. In fact, I can imagine that little Methodist chapels will be built all over England and folk from every town and every village will gather, free from the strictures of the established Church."

No sooner had she said the words than she realised that she was talking about freedom from *her* Church. In offering encouragement to the founder of the Methodist Church she had casually painted the Anglican establishment as the bad guys. Her continual observation of history repeating itself was making things become ever clearer. Why should each new move of God react so badly towards the previous one? Without those foundations laid the new move wouldn't have anything to be built upon! In that very room some hours earlier – no, it would be years – she had criticised Jonathan Edwards and George Whitefield of the very same thing. She needed to change the subject.

"Will you be seeing your old friend George Whitefield during your visit?" she asked innocently, but to her surprise Wesley then said something that shocked her.

"While I admire George Whitefield and how God is using him, I wouldn't say that he was a friend."

"But I thought..." she sputtered.

"No, Miss, we disagreed on so many points of doctrine, fundamental doctrine, that we could never be united. We talked and talked but neither of us was going to change what we believe."

Once again, history was repeating itself. This was Luther vs Zwingli all over again but without scribbling on someone else's table; it was Calvinism vs Arminianism at the Council of Dort; it was top-down bishops vs bottom-up Presbyterianism at the Hampton Court conference. So many times great changes in the Church had become mired in fundamental disagreements, forcing both parties to spin-off into disunited factions. Then, as if to bring some clarity into the midst of her thoughts, Wesley spoke a profound truth,

"So, we came up with a new doctrine of Christian unity," he said.

Bunny looked straight at him, what was he talking about? What was the solution he had found that had eluded so many others over the centuries?

"As neither of us were prepared to change our views, we came up with a new way of thinking. We decided to *Agree to Disagree!*"

That didn't feel particularly revolutionary to Bunny but perhaps this was where the idea of accepting that the beliefs of another denomination were equally as valid as one's own had first begun.

"And on that subject, I have a rather disagreeable message to preach in the chapel across the street," he said as he began to rise from his chair. "Will you join me, Miss?"

Bunny enthusiastically agreed as she helped the elderly preacher to his feet.

'Look for a dark blue/black estate car and small red sports car.' Chris posted the WhatsApp message, assuming Artur, Thea, Joel, Rex and Jack would by now all be touring the railway station car park looking for an unknown abandoned car. It was only Artur who sent a reply, 'OK will do. Thanx.'

The official railway parking stretched away from the station concourse for about quarter of a mile, parallel to the tracks, on land that had formerly been railway sidings. It allowed for four lines of diagonally parked cars, one each on either side and two face-to-face down a central aisle. Six bright LED streetlights were interspersed in tandem along the linear expanse. They gave near-daylight illumination to the Pay-and-Display machines mounted on their pillars as well as a dozen or so vehicles clustered closest to them, but beyond that did little to assist evening travellers condemned to park in the dark.

Artur had already completed his first pass of the vehicles parked nearest the railway tracks. Chris's message came at just the right time, as he had already started to question the value in this exercise. With renewed purpose he replaced his phone into the pocket of his stone-washed jeans and started the search in earnest. The further away from the entrance he walked, the more cars became clustered around the lamps. Only a handful of vehicles were in the dark zone. He presumed that these must have been parked earlier in the day when artificial illumination didn't matter. But now he realised that if someone wanted to abandon a car at night, then instinct, if nothing else, would draw them to use these least visible public areas.

Silver Mercedes after grey Audi after white Ford, he soon discovered that over half of the parked vehicles were either silver, grey or white and easily ignored them in his search. The other colours however were much harder to distinguish, especially in the darker zones. The headlamps of two cars that slowly drove past him, one arriving the other departing, did so at just the right time to provide him with a useful flash of light and allow another batch of suspects to be removed from his search. In the absence of any other vehicle, the torch on his phone proved necessary, although he was very conscious that snooping around a car park with a torch did make him appear suspicious. 'Lutheran minister arrested for suspected car theft!' was the headline he could easily imagine.

The far end of the enclosure deteriorated into wasteland. The tarmac had ended and the gravelly red soil was pot-holed and muddy. Nettles, dandelions, and wild grasses spilled through the wire fence lining the railway embankment and covered most of one side, rendering it unusable. No-one would park here unless there was no choice. As he peered into the darkness Artur could make out the silhouettes of two vehicles parked in the opposite corner. One was a small rusty white van with a very flat tyre, the other a dark-coloured estate car. His heart jumped.

This was a moment to take stock. He was alone in a remote dark place. As far as he knew the car in front of him was linked to a kidnapping and maybe a double murder. Someone might be waiting inside it, his arrival might disturb someone, was he in real danger?

He couldn't be one hundred percent sure, but the car looked empty. Why would anyone be seated in a car in such an isolated place? No. He decided the risk of being attacked was small and so began to walk towards the car. He took a couple of steps forward then suddenly stopped. The more awful, and more likely, realisation hit him. Bunny could be inside it. This would be an obvious place to abandon a car with a body inside. Was he ready to see a dead body? In his short career as a Lutheran minister he had so far officiated at only two funerals and had no cause to see either body. If she was slumped across the back seat, or under a blanket in the boot would he even recognise her? He had only met her once, earlier that evening in Crossta Coffee at C.R.F. If she was there and he reported it to the police, how would he explain why he was snooping around the car park late at night? The newspaper headline he was imagining suddenly morphed into 'Lutheran minister arrested for kidnapping and murder!' No. He couldn't allow fear to stop him. He continued his slow progress, reciting the words of the twenty-third psalm as he did.

"Yeah, though I walk through the shadow of... a dark car park... I will fear no evil," he declared with uncharacteristic paraphrasing. "For thou art with me, thy rod and thy staff they comfort me," he continued before stubbing his toe. It was neither rod nor a staff but a piece of black metal tubing that he had kicked.

"Thank you, Lord," he said as he picked up the improvised weapon and slapped it into the palm of his hand as if warning any would-be assailant that he was now armed and dangerous. Emboldened he arrived at the bonnet of what he now saw was a Volkswagen. It was certainly a dark colour, but he was unsure whether he should use his torch-phone to verify the exact tone. He decided not but instead to approach the driver-side window. All was still. No one else was about. The darkness of his surroundings was compounded into impenetrable darkness inside the car. He leaned closer to the glass but his eyes, now fully adjusted to the dim illumination, couldn't distinguish anything within. Nothing became any clearer. There was going to be no choice, he was going to have to light up the inside using his mobile phone. He reached into his jean pocket, not taking his eyes off the window, hoping that they might acclimatise yet more to the dark and then he could see empty seats. But no, he could see nothing at all – just blackness. He knew that the moment he switched on his light he would suddenly and irrevocable know the scene within this vehicle. That sight was going to be scarred into his memory forever. He expertly manoeuvred the phone around his hand without breaking his empty stare. He was ready, one press and the light would come on. He held his breath.

Chapter 29

TWO CHURCHES

Bunny was shocked to see what had happened to the church building directly opposite Jonathan Edwards' home. Instead of one church there were now two, somehow welded together side-by-side. Both buildings were identical in every respect. There were two gates, two paths, two front doors, two steeples and an equal number of people were filing into each. If she were to sketch it, she could have done so by folding the paper on top of a heavily pencilled sketch of one half and capture an outline of the other perfectly. Bunny had never seen anything as incongruous and wondered how she could ever sketch it. Was it a historical fact that two churches shared a joining wall, or had she stumbled into some dream-addled metaphor? She wasn't sure. Despite his age, Wesley had already made it across the road and through the right-hand entrance gate. Bunny followed shortly behind him, her mind now awash with confused questions, observations and opinions.

She couldn't be sure which of the two identical churches was the one she had previously been inside. The black and white interior was entirely familiar as too were the rows of faithful pilgrims who sat neatly in the pews waiting for the preacher to begin. One thing however was very different. A hole in the wall! To be more precise, the large archway that appeared to connect this chapel with its sibling next-door. The archway was two thirds towards the front of the sanctuary, it was larger than a doorway but not so big as to allow much of the other church to be easily visible. Her eye was drawn to an inscription above the archway which she tried to make out, but she needed to get closer for it to become legible. She detoured towards the archway, and as she approached saw that PSALM CXXXIII was carved into the brickwork. Her inability to readily decode Roman numerals gave her a convenient excuse, as she suspected that her Bible knowledge was probably not good enough to recall that particular chapter of the Bible.

As she looked down from the inscription her gaze fell upon a familiar face. The clothes were different, updated in keeping with the period, but the gold-rimmed hat was the giveaway. At last, she thought, I can get some answers.

"Thank goodness you are here…" she began, but as she spoke he put a finger to his lips to signal that she should remain silent. She instinctively obliged and followed the direction of his arm inviting her to look inside the other building.

It looked exactly the same. The same black and white décor, the same grey organ pipes with green crests, the same pulpit, but wait…! She looked back at the first church then into the second. She couldn't believe it. Not only were the buildings identical but the same people were seated in each. An elderly gentleman with white hair, a young lady in blue, two children, a man holding his hat. She described every person on the front row and saw that the self-same people were in each place. Now she knew it, this had to be a metaphor. Her guide leaned towards her and whispered,

"This isn't a good chapter."

What did he mean? She looked upwards at the inscription. Did he mean that Psalm CXXXIII wasn't a good chapter in the Bible? At last, she realised that the conversion from Roman numerals was much easier than she initially feared and worked out that it was Psalm one hundred and thirty-three.[1]

"I mean this is not a good chapter in the history of the Church,' he clarified adding sincerely, 'And I am so sorry you have to see this."

Accident & Emergency reception never closed. Every hour, day or night, the waiting room was filled with the perennial assortment of broken bones; cuts and scrapes; burns; infections and road traffic accidents. Thea's previous pastoral visits had always been to the long-term wards, so this was in no way as familiar as she had implied; but she had volunteered and now she had to see it through. The receptionist was very skilled at preventing people wasting her time. Despite explaining that she was a chaplaincy visitor and was looking to visit Ms. Advowson the triage nurse would not divulge any information other than she had been admitted earlier that evening. She wasn't getting anywhere.

"Lord," she prayed as she left the hubbub of the casualty department for the empty serenity that is a hospital at night. "What now? This is going to be a complete waste of time."

She had nowhere specific to go, so began to wander the near-deserted corridors, vaguely, instinctively following her usual route to the chaplain's office.

The post of hospital chaplain had been occupied by Rabbi Pascal Tikvah for as long as Thea had lived in the town. He was a very genuine, honest and

---

[1] Psalm 133 begins, "Behold, how good and how pleasant it is for brethren to dwell together in unity!" KJV

sincere person and someone for whom she had the greatest of admiration. She had never asked him about his faith, preferring to avoid any such confrontation for the sake of a working friendship. Rabbi Pascal worked part-time for the hospital trust and would be in his office one or two afternoons per week. When Thea arrived outside the chaplaincy door, she was alarmed to find it unlocked and ajar. She slowly pushed it open and to her great surprise he was seated inside.

"What are you doing here so late at night, Pascal?" she exclaimed in relief. The Rabbi almost jumped out of his skin at the sudden voice in the doorway but smiled when he saw who had disturbed him.

"Thea, it is you, is it so," he greeted her in his usual and rather linguistically curious way.

"Why are you working so late?" she repeated as they shared a polite embrace in the confines of the small multi-faith office.

"That is a peculiar question is it not," he began. "I was praying at home this evening and my heart could not be at peace. I had a strong feeling that I needed to come down to the office here for some reason. So, I did, and it is so."

Thea looked at him.

"And now I know it must be because you needed me," he concluded rather matter of fact.

Thea's expression didn't change.

"Well, you do need me," he pried. "Do you not?"

Thea snapped out of her momentarily perplexed state and admitted that yes, she really did need his help. She explained that she wanted to get into the Casualty Observation Ward to see Miss Velia Advowson. Having said that much, she held her breath. If he asked her the most obvious question, why? she had no answer other than recapping the entirety of all that had happened that evening, and she didn't know if she ought to, having promised her Fellowship members to not tell anyone. Thankfully, he nodded, unlocked a desk drawer and removed an over-sized white laminate on a blue lanyard. CHAPLAINCY PASS was the bold inscription across the whole top of the front of the plastic sleeve. The bottom-half appeared to hold a tiny microchip not dissimilar to the one Thea was familiar with seeing embedded within her credit card.

"Put this on," he said passing it to her, "and we'll see if we can find your Velia."

A few minutes later they had both scanned their passes at the electronic reader and gained entry to the Casualty Observation Ward, using the internal door at the opposite end from reception, thus avoiding the triage nurse. The Rabbi knew his way around and immediately walked the two of them over to the ward sister's station. He was greeted with a broad and welcoming smile and the acknowledgement that he 'Must be working the late shift.' Pleasantries exchanged, he soon had read Velia's bed number from the whiteboard behind the ward sister's desk. He turned his back to the nursing staff to allow him to communicate in private with the Baptist pastor.

"She's in bed twelve," he told her. Then with a couple of head-nods and eye-movements he subtly communicated that she should go to bed twelve whilst he continued chatting to the nurses. Charged with sudden excitement Thea started walking slowly and counting beds.

"Four, six, eight..." The perimeter of each bed was delimited by a heavy clinical curtain sporting blue flowers and butterflies - a touch of delicacy unrequired in such a setting, she thought. Most of the curtains were closed, but number eight stood open to reveal that across the bed there was a wheeled table holding a water jug, a plastic beaker, a box of tissues and several cardboard nausea bowls. To one side there was a small empty cabinet and a solitary visitor's chair; to the other side was a heart-rate monitor, currently switched off. She didn't need a monitor to convince her that her own heartrate was elevated. She was in the deep-end and unsure if she was going to be able to swim. Next to the monitor there stood an empty intravenous drip stand. The sight of the I.V. stand made her suddenly stop. It was almost identical to the one they had found at Lane End Farm. Here it made innocent sense, but at the farmhouse it was a frightening and sinister reminder that Bunny was in grave danger. Thea had her own part to play in finding her, she couldn't back out. She took a couple more steps.

"Ten, twelve!" She stood silently outside the curtain and reached her fingers forward trying to find the edge of the drapery, part of her secretly hoping she wouldn't find the way in as she had little idea what she was going to say.

"Stick to the facts," she whispered to herself. But what facts did she know? The picture in the farmhouse! That was the only link after all. She rehearsed her opening statement in her head: we found your picture in a deserted farmhouse and wanted to know if you knew why it was there. It didn't sound in any way convincing. She had to admit it, she had said she would go and find out what she could, but she was no Miss Marple. She was a Baptist Church minister, maybe that was all she should say. Yes, that would work. She grasped the corner of her

Chaplaincy Pass, yes this was the way in, she was *just visiting!* Suddenly the curtain opened in front of her causing her to inhale violently.

"Can I help you?"

A smartly dressed young man had pulled back the curtain from inside. He was roughly the same height as her but there any similarity ended. His perfectly coiffured black locks and deeply tanned olive-coloured skin contrasted with her decidedly English rose appearance. His understatedly designer look could have been lifted from the casual-wear collection from any of the Paris or Milan fashion shows. Thea's floral dress, oversized bead necklace, brown tights and off-white trainers, which had been visible underneath the curtain for too long for his patience, was certainly not the outfit of a nurse, she thought.

"Good evening..." she began. "I was looking for..." she leaned to one side in order to see past him. The bed was empty.

"She isn't here, who are you?" he retorted irascibly.

Thea returned her attention to meet his gaze noting that his eyes showed all the anxiety of a loved-one in the emergency ward. She turned on her pastoral charm, explaining who she was, exhibiting proudly her access-all-areas pass as proof. The man gave an atheistic tut but accepted her unwelcome intrusion politely. Slowly Thea teased out of him that Velia had been taken to X-Ray to have her head wound examined. He was clearly anxious and kept stressing the sole fact that she was unconscious. Once Thea considered that she may have overcome his initial imposition, she gently and innocently asked how Velia had received her injury. At this the well-dressed young man suddenly became defensive, refusing to answer, clearly suspicious of her questioning. He even accused her of being a reporter with a stolen chaplain's pass. Thea quickly changed tack and asked how the young man was coping with the stress of being at hospital with a *loved one*. That phrase didn't go down well either. He explained that whilst the newspapers described him as her boyfriend, they hadn't been dating long enough to be called loved ones. But he really did *care* for Velia. An oddly unnecessary admission, Thea thought as he looked, for the third time, at his watch.

"Don't worry, they will bring her back soon," Thea said attempting to assure him.

"Yes, they will," he replied. "And you don't need to be here when they do. In fact, please don't come back, she's unconscious, you see," his manner was becoming increasingly resolute.

"Anyway, I'm fine, really I am fine, and when she wakes up I will tell her that you stopped by," he said as he reached for the edge of the curtain.

There was nothing more Thea was going to wring out of this conversation. How could she ask about the pictures in the farmhouse? Velia wasn't here. Her boyfriend had said all he was going to; and clearly, he didn't want her to hang around any longer. Miss Marple would not be impressed at all, she thought. She wished him well and offered to pray for them both, as if to underline her credentials as a genuine chaplaincy visitor.

"Please don't, I am past redemption," he said as he pointedly re-closed the curtain.

Thankfully, being such a slow and careful driver meant that Rector Mashman had already slowed down to almost walking pace by the time he arrived at the torch-brandishing person ahead of him. As he lowered his driver-side window to speak to the late-night explorer and offer any assistance they may require, he was surprised to discover that it was someone he had been talking to barely an hour previously.

"Cecil? What are you doing out on the lane this late at night?" he asked the manager of St. Christopher's Hospice.

"Rector?" he replied with notable surprise. "I am so pleased to see you." Initially dazzling the clergyman, he lowered the torch-beam to a more polite focal-point before adding cryptically, "At least I think I am or is this more than just a coincidence?" The events of the night had caused such a disquiet in the hospice administrator's mind that two-plus-two was now adding up to a sum that made him suspicious of even this well-known, inoffensive and harmless churchman.

"Whatever do you mean, Cecil?" Mashman pleaded as he switched on his hazard warning lights, conscious he was stationary on a country lane. It was then he realised that they were just a few yards from the rear driveway into St. Christopher's, a seldom used cut-through.

"I'm sorry Reverend, I don't really know what's happening," he said, then began to recap the events that had led him onto the lane with a torch.

"Not long after you and your friends had left, our night-porter staggered into my office, bleeding, saying it had gone again and that it was nothing to do with him this time."

"What had?" Mashman asked.

"The ambulance. It was missing...again. He said someone had jumped him and taken it, stolen it, he said. I didn't know if I could believe him, I had already told him that he would have to attend a disciplinary hearing tomorrow. So, I wondered if it was him, but it was a nasty bang on the head," Cecil tapped his forehead to indicate the location of the night-porter's wound. "Needed five stitches from the duty nurse." Mashman winced at the thought. The hospice manager continued his recap.

"Anyway, before he had his stiches done, he took me outside to where it was parked and, true enough, it was gone. Someone had snuck up behind him, coshed him, taken his keys and the van. And we could see by the tyre tracks they had driven it along the back lane, here. No one drives up this lane anymore, it's too narrow, especially for the ambulance. We always take it out the main drive."

"Have you reported it to the police yet?" Mashman asked.

"Not yet, but I think I am going to have to," he said, adding with a sigh, "Goodness knows what sort of investigation that will lead to."

"But why are you out here? On your own?"

"Well, I thought the ambulance might get stuck on the back lane and if I was quick I might find it," Cecil explained. He was then at pains to express that he knew it was foolish to have gone on his own, especially in light of the assault on the night-porter, but he was so keen to find his ambulance and avoid a fuss, he didn't think about his personal safety until after he had reached the end of the lane and bumped into the Rector.

"I take it there was no sign of the ambulance?" the Rector asked.

Cecil shook his head. Then, in a moment of inspired recollection, glanced back at the entrance of the lane, pointing his torch into the dark void.

"But there was something..." he said pondering, looking into the direction of the light.

"Something?" Mashman prompted. The hospice manager spun round to face him, momentarily blinding him again.

"Sorry. Yes, there was something unusual at The Woodshed, at the top of the lane, but I ignored it as I was intent on finding the ambulance. But maybe..." he said distractedly inching back towards the lane.

"Well, you had best not go alone Cecil," Mashman advised, adding an insistent "Jump in." Within moments the Honda Jazz had started to crawl ponderously along the dirt track that meandered through the densely wooded area surrounding the hospice; a lane that had not been regularly used by vehicles for many years. After little more then quarter of a mile Cecil asked Mashman to stop. For the first time that evening the elderly Rector felt a rush of adrenalin pass through his veins.

To their left stood a wooden cabin, known to the residents as The Woodshed. Not a storage area for wood, as the Rector initially assumed, but a substantial wooden structure that acted as a destination for patients and visitors taking a walk into the woods. The Woodshed was more of a pleasant summer house albeit without any view to speak of. Some tools were stored towards the rear of the building which is locked overnight and remained so now. What had struck the hospice manager as unusual during his first pass was that the oversized flowerpot that usually stood next to The Woodshed was missing. He

257

explained to the cleric that a large plastic circular planter should be "Just there!" he pointed, but now it was gone. Cecil unclipped his seat belt. Mashman did likewise, asking the question,

"Where are we going?" too embarrassed to say the question he really wanted to ask, "Do I really have to come?"

"To find a flowerpot," was the unsurprising answer.

The hospice manager led them to the exact spot where the planter had been, and immediately they could see a groove in the loose soil and bark chippings where it had been dragged. They followed the groove which began to turn and then disappeared behind The Woodshed. At the apex of the turn, there it was – a grey plastic plant pot almost a meter in diameter and now lying on its side, badly cracked, with soil, compost and daffodil bulbs spilled from its guts like a macabre floral death scene. The planter was huge and would have been extremely heavy.

"It would have taken a few people to have dragged that flowerpot over to here," Mashman declared.

"No, not dragged..." the manager disagreed, finishing his point with the word "...*pushed*!"

Mashman looked up at him, but Cecil's attention was already fixed on something behind The Woodshed. Following the direction of his torch beam the Rector could see that there, embedded in the dense bracken, two grooves in the bark chipping ended at the rear of a car.

"And pushed by *that* car," Cecil said with satisfaction at his discovery. His high-powered torch lit up the abandoned vehicle, a black Ford Mondeo estate.

Chapter 30

SEISMIC SHIFTS

The man in the gold-rimmed hat ushered her to look towards the front of the right-hand church where Wesley had by now joined Whitefield at the pulpit. The elderly Methodist cleared his throat, the congregation waited expectantly for him to speak. So too did Bunny despite having no idea what was about to happen.

"Liberty is the right of every human creature as soon as he breathes the vital air," the Methodist founder bellowed. "And I say to the slaveholders 'The blood of your brother cries against you from the earth.'"[1]

"Is that what this is about, slavery?" Bunny said as she looked at her guide. He said nothing, just motioned for her to look back at the pulpit as, by now, Whitefield had taken the stage.

"To the planters of South Carolina, Virginia, and Maryland, I think God has a quarrel with you for your abuse of and cruelty to the poor negroes,"[2] he decreed. "Your dogs are caressed and fondled at your tables; but your slaves who are frequently styled dogs or beasts, have not an equal privilege."[3]

She repeated her question to the man in the gold-brimmed hat.

"So, this *is* about slavery? Everyone knows that slavery is wrong. The Bible teaches so... doesn't it?"

But he said nothing, just turned to face the second, left-hand, church and indicated that Bunny needed to do likewise. She didn't recognise the man who took to the pulpit but discovered, when he introduced himself to the congregation, that his name was Richard Furman.

---

[1] 'The Works of the Reverend John Wesley. Vol VI' John Wesley, J Emory and B Waugh (1831) p292

[2] In 1740, during his second visit to America, Whitefield published an open letter to the planters of South Carolina, Virginia, and Maryland chastising them for their cruelty to their slaves. He wrote, "I think God has a quarrel with you for your abuse of and cruelty to the poor Negroes." Taken from Jessica M. Parr, Inventing George Whitefield: Race, Revivalism, and the Making of a Religious Icon (University Press of Mississippi, 2015), 67.

[3] George Whitefield wrote: "Your dogs are caressed and fondled at your tables; but your slaves who are frequently styled dogs or beasts, have not an equal privilege." From 'George Whitefield on Slavery: Some New Evidence' by Stephen J. Stein (Church History Vol. 42, No. 2, June 1973), p. 244.

"Brothers and sisters, as a Baptist minister I can tell you that the Bible makes it very clear that God has no quarrel with slaveholders. Does not Leviticus 25:46 say that the Israelites were directed to purchase their bondmen and once purchased they were to be bondsmen forever. And similarly, in the New Testament neither Jesus himself nor the apostles ever demand the emancipation of slaves. They refer to slaves and masters and in the very same breath talk of male and female. If we do away with slaves, should we also do away with marriage? Why, didn't Paul himself return the slave Philemon back to his master! Brothers and sisters, the Bible never condemned slavery." [1]

"What?" Bunny said incredulously. Suddenly someone in the congregation stood to their feet and shouted out.

"Amen brother, and what's more, Christian slaves would be better slaves, more loyal and honest and hard-working."

Again, Bunny could say no more than,

"What?" as she looked back at her guide who had by now turned to face the right-hand church. She followed his direction. Wesley and Whitefield were nowhere to be seen. A different person was at the pulpit addressing the people.

"In Bible-times the apostles kept silent on the subject," he said, "because they knew that an anti-slavery message, in an era that tolerated the practice, would drown the message of salvation they came to preach. Revelation was a progressive thing. Only now do we understand that enslaving our fellow man is evil." *Progressive revelation* thought Bunny, that's an interesting concept. The passionate orator continued his discourse.

"Consider the ancient practice of polygamy, where a man would take several wives. That too was the practice in Old Testament times – King Solomon himself had seven hundred wives and three hundred concubines – and yet today we now know that to be wrong. The same progressive revelation is true of slavery."

Then, just as had happened in the other church, a man stood to his feet from the body of the congregation. Stirred by the preacher he was compelled to add enthusiastically,

"Those slaveowners may say that they want their slaves to become Christian, but that would come as a surprise to my friend Abraham."

---

[1] Richard Furman was one of the main Christian apologists for the pro-slavery lobby.

Without hesitation he then described how a slave named Abraham had been attacked, beaten, tied-up then dumped outside the Moravian church which he wanted to attend. And then how, with steely determination, Abraham took the ropes used to bind him and sent them back to his captors, one-by-one, each with a hand-written apology for any damage their property may have suffered whilst upon his person.[1]

"Tell me who is the true Christian, the one who does the beating or the one who forgives his abusers?" he ended. It was a powerful message that brought the reality of slavery alive to the audience who gasped at the beating and stood to applaud Abraham's selfless act of forgiveness. Bunny too began to applaud but then noticed that her fellow onlooker had already turned within the small vestibule they shared to face the other sanctuary. She too pivoted while still applauding. She did, however, reduce the sound of her handclaps to hear a new voice address this congregation.

"Ladies and gentlemen, it is my great pleasure to introduce to you," he began, "the first black African ordained minister of the Church. A former slave himself, Jacobus Capitein."

Once the audience was applauding, Bunny, who had not stopped, turned up the volume of her clapping to welcome the speaker. Capitein was a short black man, quite chubby in appearance with a wide African nose. He wore dark ecclesiastical robes which included a square of off-white fabric fixed to his chest just beneath his chin. Bunny couldn't help but think that this embellishment looked suspiciously like a baby's bib. In his right hand he carried the obligatory large black Bible, in his left he held another book. The Bible was placed on the lectern. He opened it at his chosen text and without looking up he began to read aloud,

"With freedom did Christ set us free, stand fast therefore and be not entangled again to the yoke of bondage," he read to an audience who had replaced their applause with silence.[2]

"This isn't going to go down well with the folks on this side," Bunny whispered to the man in the gold-brimmed hat, adding with a thumb-pointing gesture, "He ought to be next-door."

---

[1] 'Protestants: The Radicals who Made the Modern World' by Alec Ryrie (2017).

[2] Galatians chapter 5 verse 1. English Revised Version

Her guide remained unmoved, ignoring her comment. Capitein spoke with, not an African nor American accent, but that of a Dutchman. After concluding his reading, he addressed the congregation, thanking them for his welcome and saying that he had just arrived from Leiden where he had been ordained into the Dutch Reformed Church.

As soon as he said Leiden, Bunny remembered her brief time at Leiden at Mary Brewster's house. She remembered the cramped living conditions, the smell, the sense of alienation and hopelessness that the few Puritan pioneers were feeling. And yet here, in the land they had eventually settled, was an ordained former slave. In going to Leiden, the very place where the freedom gospel seed had first been sown, it was as though a salmon had returned to its spawning grounds. Bunny looked at her watch to work out how long it had been since she was in Leiden. The large square dial flashed 17:42. She recalled that it was around 16:12 when she returned to England from Leiden, so an hour and thirty minutes ago, or more precisely one hundred and thirty years.

Capitein raised his left-hand, holding aloft his second book. He opened the front cover, cleared his throat dramatically and read the title:

"In Defence of Slavery by Jacobus Capitein."[1] All his listeners instantly cheered. This was very curious. A freed slave writing a book that *defends* the practice of slavery. He had certainly got her attention.

"Slavery is not in conflict with Christian liberty," he began before launching into a detailed exposition of how the Bible taught freedom, not of the body but of the spirit. He referenced Bible verse after Bible verse to underscore this point. His preaching, he explained, was to reassure slaveholders that God was only interested in their slaves' souls not their bodies. In reaching the conclusion of his short Bible study people stood to their feet, once again to applaud him. Then a curious thing happened. From within the heart of the congregation a chant began; a simple refrain repeated, over-and-over again. It took a few iterations before Bunny could make out the impromptu lyrics. Then she had it,

"His skin is black, but his soul is white since Jesus prays for him," they sang.[2] Bunny was shocked. This freed slave was being lauded as an honorary

---

[1] The title of Capitein's thesis was: 'Politico-Theological Dissertation on Slavery as not being opposed to Christian Freedom' Published in 17242 by G. de Groot, Amsterdam.

[2] 'The Atlantic in Global History: 1500-2000' by Jorge Calzares-Esguerra

white man because of his Christian teaching. This was so totally racist to her ears.

However, she couldn't fault his teaching. He made a good case that the Bible spoke of freedom of the spirit not the body, plus he was a former slave. His words and in particular his book seemed to carry a great deal of weight. Bunny spun around to see if those in the other sanctuary had also committed their message to print. Yes, was the answer, in the shape of one Quaker minister called Anthony Benezet whose pamphlet *The Case of our fellow-creatures, the oppressed Africans*, she learned, had run to eleven thousand copies. She turned to the pro-slavery side only to see, to her surprise, another Quaker minister. Quakers to the left of me, Quakers to the right! she thought.

She didn't know his name but learned he had written to a slaveholder to say that whilst the Church taught that slaves should be free, what that meant was that they should be *free to worship* as the soul's freedom was more important than bodily freedom.

"Why should they be Satan's slaves as well as man's?" he asked.

"Enough!" a loud, angry, male voice bellowed from behind her, in the anti-slavery chapel.

Bunny turned to see the incongruous sight of a rather short man, less than five feet tall, dressed in a military grey coat. It was unlikely that he was in fact a soldier, not only was he far too short to be enlisted, a fact confounded by his slightly hunchbacked stance, but he also had a profoundly large bushy beard that was certainly not regulation. Nonetheless he was clearly angry and released a second exclamation.

"Enough!" he said again as he took hold of his Bible and placed it firmly and squarely atop the communion table. He unbuttoned his grey coat to reveal full military uniform, albeit a couple of sizes too large, including a most serviceable sword which he ceremoniously unsheathed as he spoke.

"Thus, shall God shed the blood of those persons who enslave their fellow creatures," he proclaimed and raised the sword above his head, then stabbed it down upon his Bible piercing it completely through. As he did blood appeared to spurt out from its pages in an arterial fountain covering himself, the sacred table and those members of the congregation unfortunate enough to be nearest. Bunny's jaw dropped. For a moment she was unsure if anyone had been hurt. In the commotion that ensued it became clear that the diminutive Quaker, one Benjamin Lay, had carefully planned the dramatic stunt, having first hollowed-out a Bible and inserted a bladder of red pokeberry juice. Also,

263

this wasn't the first dramatic act he had orchestrated. He proudly told of how he had temporarily kidnapped slaveowners' children to show them how slave families must have felt when their children were stolen.[1] An impressive and memorable stunt, Bunny thought.

The noise from each side had become rowdy. Bunny turned towards the pro-slavery church, worried that things might be turning into a riot, but there was no anger on that side. The place had become a serene haven of rationality. The battle lines had suddenly and significantly changed. Several men were already on their feet, not in an angry stance but open, conciliatory and smiling. The epitome of reasonableness. One read from his Bible a passage in Genesis chapter nine that spoke of Noah's grandson Canaan. He read that God cursed Canaan and his family saying they would be *forever slaves*. Hence a tribe of slaves was instigated by God himself. Bunny knew that passage but would always have considered it should be taken figuratively and not literally, but then again that was the same argument that the pro-slavery lobby was making to the whole concept of *freedom*. For the first time Bunny began to doubt what she believed on this subject.

Another man, who introduced himself as William Knox, joined the discourse. He was a slaveholder and talked at length of the dull stupidity of slaves concluding with the question,

"Wasn't it better to rescue natives from pagan Africa, was this not a kind of liberation?" A third joined in the subtle de-humanising rhetoric.

"Of course, we want every man to come to Christ whether slave or free," he said. "But Africans are a childish race that needs to be matured. Slaves must be civilised *before* they can be converted."[2]

This prompted a fourth to recall a recent encounter with a Baptist minister who had asked if he may give communion to his slaves. The slaveowner then challenged the priest saying that it would be as much use as giving communion to his horse! The argument had changed from fierce outright opposition to a much more understated movement. Some of those arguments had landed. Bunny shook herself and turned to see how the anti-side would respond.

---

[1] Article in the Smithsonian magazine by Marcus Rediker September 2017

[2] Ama, A Story of the Atlantic Slave Trade by Manu Herbstein

Taking the pulpit was a smartly dressed black African who was introduced as Philip Quaque. Bunny had assumed that he too would be a former slave, but to her surprise she discovered that he had converted to Christianity as a child in his native Gold Coast. He was then taken to England by missionaries to be educated and trained for the ministry and became the first African to be ordained into the Church of England. He therefore sat uniquely at the intersection of both worlds, a position of great influence and insight.[1]

At the climax of his short yet eloquent presentation, Quaque opened his collar and pulled out what looked like a ceramic brooch on a gold chain around his neck. Unprompted, several others, perhaps even the majority of the congregation, did likewise. They were all wearing the same ceramic brooch, and all displayed it with corporate pride. Bunny could see that this jewellery piece was significant but had no idea what it depicted, so approached the nearest individual who was proudly exhibiting their trophy. The medallion had a contoured relief of a kneeling black man in chains with the inscription 'Am I not a man and a brother?' [2]

So, we've now moved on from public relations stunts to merchandise, thought Bunny. The parishioner who had shown Bunny her brooch then offered to give her one of her own. Bunny tried to decline the gift but before she could escape, the porcelain insignia had been pressed into the palm of her hand. She considered slipping it around her own neck but, in catching the eye of the man in the gold-brimmed hat, decided she had better wait to see how the growing debate turned out and looked to see what was happening in the pro-slavery church.

This time there was someone at the front whom Bunny was sure she recognised. He was older than she recalled, but that was a common experience for her now. It was the distinguished look and fixed grin that sparked something in her memory.

"I know him," she said softly to her guide, adding tentatively, "Don't I?"

"That is Count Nicholas Zinzendorf und Pottendorf," her fellow time-travelling compatriot explained. Bunny mentally paused for a moment to allow

---

[1] Article 'Philip Quaque 1741-Oct 17, 1816' The Colonial Williamsburg Foundation. (2020) taken from slaveryandremembrance.org

[2] Decorative pottery maker Josiah Wedgwood was a campaigner for the abolition of slavery and his plaque depicting a kneeling man in chains with the inscription 'Am I not a man and a brother?' became a prominent image in the abolitionist campaign.

her synapses to make all the necessary connections. It didn't take her too long before she had worked it out.

"I've got it," she announced to him. "The Moravians in Herrnhut; he was their leader, founder, bishop-type person, wasn't he?" He nodded.

"I thought he was dead," she added. "All I saw was a statue of him and with time... you know... moving on so quickly I thought..." But her guide wasn't looking at her, his attention was already focussed on the Count.

"Whether you are a king, a master, a servant or a slave," he declared, "you must endure in the state into which God has placed you."

Bunny was shocked. Weren't the Moravians the good guys? And yet their leader is here making a point, albeit an oblique one, that appears to be in defence of slavery. Another man then took to his feet to add to the point that the Count had made. He stressed that slavery was a time-honoured institution working within the God-given inequality and racial difference. He said that all Protestants believed that God had ordained a well-ordered hierarchical society where everyone knew their place, adding finally that abolitionists were fanatics seeking to upturn God's structure. Bunny had not expected that the pro-slavery camp could take the moral high-ground and unashamedly claim that God was on their side. And yet that was what was unfolding in front of her eyes and ears. She was not a flaky person. She had been sure of her convictions for as long as she could remember, but now she was, for the first-time, genuinely unsure of what she believed on such a fundamental thing as slavery. What did God's word really say on the subject? She turned back anti-side for help.

"Do unto others as you would have them do unto you," she heard.[1] Yes. that was it, a simple and strong message. Now she was sure... at least she thought she was.

"Do unto others as you would have them do unto you!" Confusingly, she heard the exact same verse now being used by the pro-side. She turned to see how that could be.

"Those saying 'Do unto others as you would have them do unto you' fail to point out that it means *in their situation.* A father may still treat a child as a child - they are not equal, are they. Likewise, a master should treat a slave as a slave; the way he would want to be treated if he were a slave."

"Is that what *do unto others* really means?" Bunny began to wonder.

---

[1] Matthew chapter 7 verse 12

"Slaves are not property, but a sacred trust," the speaker continued. "Slaveholders have a God-given responsibility over them. Slave and slaveholder are bound together under God."[1]

Bunny's head was spinning, both figuratively and literally as she returned to hear the next anti-side message.

"The lack of any legal status flies in the face of any so-called *sacred trust*," she heard.

Back to the pro-side.

The unambiguous message she heard was, "If God is opposed to slavery, then why has no Church banned it?"

"Was that true?" she said under her breath, puzzled to discover the shocking truth. Was the Church complicit in agreeing to slavery? she wondered.

Back to the anti-side.

A white-haired black man was astride the pulpit holding, not a Bible, but a newspaper in his hand.

"Pro-slavery clergymen within the American Church have stripped the love of God of its beauty," he decreed. As he continued, Bunny learned the speaker was called Frederick Douglass. He said he was a slave who had escaped to Massachusetts in 1838 but when he went into the Methodist Church he found it to be *segregated* and was forced to leave and join a black church.[2]

The Church is definitely at fault, Bunny was beginning to conclude. Douglass went on to say that he considered himself a freeman but when he refused to sit on the segregated seats on the Eastern Railroad he was thrown off the train. Bunny was amazed, that was years before Rosa Parks refused to give up her seat on that Alabama bus!

The newspaper in his hand was an edition of the *North Star*, a paper that he was prompted to publish and whose motto included the phrase *Truth has no Color – God is the Father of us all.*

Bunny turned to the pro-side where she heard an impassioned plea to *work with* slavery in order to improve it and that the abolitionists were getting in the way of reform amongst slave *households*. This was too much for her to comprehend.

---

[1] 'Protestants: The Radicals who Made the Modern World' by Alec Ryrie (2017).

[2] ibid

On the anti-side, that earnest plea was countered with the matter-of-fact reality that despite claims to the contrary no actual reform was happening and that many would say slavery was unreformable.

Back on the pro-side the message attempted to undermine the abolitionist gospel by saying it was one of their own invention.

Like a spectator in the middle of a protracted table-tennis rally, Bunny's vision was by now blurring as she bounced back and forth rhythmically, no longer in control, praying that somehow the lunacy would end.

"This is the age-old battle of the *spirit* of the Bible versus the *letter* of it," a speaker on the anti-side offered. "Some Christians make virtues of *suffering* and *patience* in order to keep slaves in their place. And they emphasise the glories of the afterlife so that slaves will endure evil treatment in this present age."

Ping-pong to the pro-side.

"Reformed slavery would be America's gift to the world."[1]

"Please God make it stop," Bunny prayed.

Ping-pong to the anti-side where William Wilberforce had now taken to the pulpit.

"I consider slavery a national sin," he declared with the authority of a man speaking prophetically as though on God's very behalf.[2]

The moment he said it the whole building began to shake. The sound of women screaming and chairs moving accentuated the sense of panic. The ground beneath Bunny's feet began to move as dust from falling plaster filled the air. To steady herself Bunny reached out and took hold of the arm of the man in the gold-rimmed hat. His presence gave her a sense of security amidst the developing earthquake. Bunny was the only person standing astride the two church buildings and so felt her feet begin to move in opposite directions. Looking down she saw a sudden crack appear beneath her like a well-worn cartoon cliché. She had to make a choice... she had to step in one direction or the other. The tectonic crack was widening. She had to make a move, which was now going to be difficult as her hesitancy had left her in an unbalanced state and in danger of falling into oblivion. She pulled on her fellow traveller's arm and with an almighty wrench yanked herself into the anti-slavery church. As she

---

[1] 'Protestants: The Radicals who Made the Modern World' by Alec Ryrie (2017).

[2] 'Out of Slavery: Abolition and After' by Jack Hayward. Frank Cass (1985) p50

did, the crack widened and with an enormous crash the archway gap between the two identical chapels sealed shut, as if the other one had never been there at all. Bunny's mind was a rage of confused theology, her body a rush of adrenalin.

"Thanks," she said as she released the sleeve she had used for leverage. To her shock the owner of the arm she had been holding was not that of her fellow traveller. In her sudden panic she had grabbed the arm of a second gentleman standing to his side.

"What just happened?" she said to them both as she simultaneously steadied herself and thanked the stranger for his assistance. As she gathered her composure, she realised that he was no stranger but rather one of the most recognisable people in history, Abraham Lincoln.

Bunny was in serious danger of losing her English reserve and well-honed Anglican decorum. Her mind was racing with all that she had just witnessed, so too was her heart rate. And now she was face-to-face with yet another American President. Thankfully, she had already asked a simple question, to which Mr. Lincoln duly and courteously responded.

"Well, Miss," he began, "in great contests each party claims to act in accordance with the will of God. Both read the same Bible and pray to the same God, and each invokes his aid against the other. But the prayers of both cannot be answered, the Almighty has His own purposes."[1]

That was exactly what was buzzing around her head. Both parties were using the Bible to defend their positions, and both cannot be right. She needed to have this out with someone, but perhaps not Mr. Lincoln.

She turned back to look into the great chasm that moments earlier she narrowly escaped, only to see it wasn't there. There was no crack in the earth, the arch that connected the two chapels too was gone; completely sealed, plastered and re-painted. In fact, there was no sign of any division at all. She looked over at the people in their pews as the church bell chimed a solitary note. Some were singing, others praying, some chatting, but all oblivious of the earth-splitting division that had just happened.[2]

---

[1] Words of Abraham Lincoln. 'The Religion Factor: An Introduction to how Religion Matters' by William Green and Jacob Neusner. Westminster John Knox Press (1996) p26

[2] The American Baptist, Presbyterian and Methodist churches all split into two factions, those promoting slavery (often taking the identifier 'Southern') and those against it.

It felt like ages since they were last at Community Restoration Fellowship, but it was less than five hours since they had each parked in their allocated visitor's space behind the former cinema. So much had happened that no one showed any signs of fatigue. As they pulled into the neatly tarmacked space, they agreed that Rex was going to return to the station to find Artur while Joel was going to head to the hospital for Thea. As they each placed a hand on the rear door handles, ready to step out into the darkness, Jack stopped them, saying,

"Hey, you two."

They both paused beside their half-open car doors and looked at him.

"Please be careful, and look after the others, we don't know what we are getting into here, but it is... you know." He didn't need to finish the sentence; they knew what he meant.

Both Rex and Joel nodded solemnly back at him and said simultaneously,

"You, too!"

Having closed their car doors, Joel gave a hearty double-slap onto the roof of the 4x4 as if slapping the hindquarters of a horse to usher it on its way. Jack said nothing but was quietly gratified with the sense of camaraderie that it evoked. Something he had not experienced since he was a Special Constable.

Chapter 31

WILLIAM MILLER

"You are not going anywhere," Bunny insisted, wagging her index finger at the man in the gold-rimmed hat. He looked shocked.

"I've got some questions and you had better have the answers!" she stressed as she suggested they move outside so as not to disturb the now tranquil surroundings in the black and white chapel. As they exited, she instinctively looked to see if the second structure was still attached. Unsurprisingly there was no sign of it. As she suspected, she had been party to a dramatic and powerful metaphor and one which had left her particularly disquieted.

"What was all that about, eh?" she demanded. He said nothing. She knew she needed to unload, and he was the only constant figure in this lucid dream. He was going to get both barrels.

"I don't like it. Both, them..." she said pointing with her thumb back at the chapel they had just vacated, 'And them!' she wanted to point at the pro-slavery chapel, but she knew it was no longer there so waved her hand indistinctively in its former direction.

"Both of them were using the Bible to defend their positions, and what's worse is that I began to believe both of their arguments." Bunny was emotional. For the first time in her life the static solidity of her faith had been loosened and she was feeling vulnerable.

"I mean, I know what I believe, at least I thought I did, but with all that going on, for a moment I seemed to lose.... to lose my footing. I didn't know what I believed and it... scared me. I know I believe the Bible; I know it is true, but..." she wasn't sure how to continue the sentence so gathered her emotions and decided to launch a second front.

"And another thing, what is with each group of faithful believers being actively hostile towards any new group of equally faithful believers. And for that matter, every new movement wanting to distance themselves from all the previous ones!" The accelerated nature of her journey had brought into clear focus the fact that Church history appeared to repeat itself, again and again.

"I don't like it," she pleaded. "When I see how every Church strand begins, it looks like good people start it and then..." Again she couldn't finish it.

271

She knew enough to be able to express her inner angst but insufficient as to know why she was feeling that way.

"And what is the deal with all the violence and bloodshed in the name of The Church. I say *The Church* as I cannot believe it could ever be in the name of God – he would have no part of it, I am sure."

Her guide remained dispassionate. She had one further irritation to scratch.

"And then they all believe they are *the right ones*, the final ones. That all of Christendom had been awaiting the revelation of one last perfect group, their group. The final perfect denomination to end all denominations had arrived. And what's more they talk as though the New Millennium is about to begin, or already has, and that Christ is about to return."

At this final complaint he raised a single eyebrow, the only visible reaction he had made since she began her heartfelt plea.

"People say that Christ is about to return?" he asked, reflecting her last comment.

"Yes, but only for *their* particular group," she stressed.

"You have discerned this wisely, Miss Elstow. But what you have seen so far is only a fraction of what is to come."

"Oh great!" Bunny responded with uncharacteristic but uninhibited sarcasm.

The man in the gold-rimmed hat raised his arm to invite her to look to the right of the quiet avenue in front of the chapel. As she did, she saw a large-wheeled open-topped buggy arrive and stop beside them. Her heart sank. She wasn't sure she wanted to find out anything more about Church history until she had answers to the questions she had just asked him. She was going to stand her ground and demand an explanation. She swung back towards him, loudly venting her anguish.

"I need to get some answers first!"

But he had, once again, disappeared from sight. She turned back to the buggy, whose smiling driver simply asked if she was the person he needed to take to Exeter, Massachusetts. She compliantly nodded and began to climb on board.

As she did, she felt a man's hands pushing her inside the carriage. One hand was on each of her hips pushing her inwards. This was a gross invasion of her dignity.

"Surely no one was this physical in the nineteenth century?" she puzzled.

She tried to turn around to see who was giving her such unwelcome assistance, but her body didn't seem to be able to move. With concentrated effort she forced herself to reach behind her and took hold of whatever she could find to try and stop him. All she could feel was fabric which she pulled with all the strength she could muster. Suddenly she flopped down onto a plastic vinyl bench seat, cheek first with the fabric in her hand following her. Thankfully the hands removed themselves from her hips and she heard the sound of a car door closing. She pulled the fabric to her face to see what she had collected. It was black, woollen and inlaid with an intricate yellow pattern.

"Why did you leave in such a rush?" Ralph asked Chris once he had caught up with him in the street outside Crust Almighty.

Minutes earlier, while he was composing the message to alert his fellow church leaders about the type and colour of car to look for, Chris had suddenly dashed out of the eatery. Ralph had no idea what had spooked his friend and half-assumed he was just impatient to get back to the car and move on. By the time he had pressed Send and stepped outside, Chris was nowhere to be seen. Firstly, he checked Chris's car; it was still locked. Next, he peered along both Co-Op aisles they had circumnavigated minutes earlier. Again, he wasn't there. Ralph was at a loss to know where his friend was.

The village high street was deserted. Other than the two stores across the road from each other, the only illumination was a single orange sodium streetlamp, eighty yards away where the road took a sharp bend. Evidently, the move to replacement LED lighting had not yet made it to this village. The imperfect light reflected off the damp road, ripples dancing in the puddles that had gathered in its numerous potholes. Several cars were parked outside darkened homes, but there were no signs of life other than the two storekeepers both busying themselves behind their glazed frontages. The street was dark, it was damp, it was cold, and it was quiet, the only sound being the whirr of an extractor fan whose ducting dominated the side of the fast-food outlet.

Where had he gone? Ralph puzzled as he looked down the street, toward the streetlamp, then back the other way. There was no sign of him. There was no sign of anyone. Given the choice of which way to walk he elected to go towards the light. It was a fifty-fifty toss-up, but something urged him that would be the right direction. He had already traversed almost half of the distance to the aged concrete light-pillar before he realised that it would make a lot more sense to simply ring Chris on his mobile. Inwardly tutting at himself for not having thought of it sooner, he scrolled to find Chris's number amongst the favourites on his phone. Despite it being one of those he called most frequently, Ralph had no idea what Chris's number was. As he pressed dial, he was struck by the sound of a ringtone chiming nearby. He lifted his own handset to his ear; the ringing coincided, Chris must be in the vicinity. Following the sound of ringing, within a few steps Ralph soon found his friend.

Chris was sitting on the wet pavement, his feet either side of a rather deep puddle in the road. The knees of his trousers were both blackened with damp patches, as too was one ankle and shoe that by all accounts had already been immersed in that puddle. His forehead and eyes were covered by the palm of one hand, its elbow anchored upon his left knee. His other hand had extricated a now loudly ringing handset from his pocket. The hand holding the phone was shaking uncontrollably. Ralph cancelled the call. Chris caught sight of Ralph's feet in the reflection of the puddle in front of him and removed his covering palm. Even in the indistinct orange glow, Ralph could see that his eyes were just as damp as the rest of him. Two near-perpendicular tracks glistened down each cheek and as he lifted his face a tear spilled out from his right eye and rapidly navigated the predefined salty waterway to his chin. The sensation prompted Chris to wipe this tear away.

Chris was clearly in an emotionally distressed state as well as thoroughly wet. Ralph knew which of these two concerns he could deal with the easiest, so reached out a hand to pull his assistant pastor back to his feet. He would attend to Chris's anguish once he had him off the cold, damp pavement.

"Why did you leave in such a rush?" was the obvious question, which Ralph repeated in the dim light.

Chris took Ralph's hand and stood, carefully avoiding placing his foot, once again, in the puddle. His voice initially faltering, Chris explained that whilst Ralph was posting the WhatsApp message, he had seen a dark car drive past the chip shop and instinctively ran after it. He knew it was a pointless exercise, it being almost impossible that Bunny would be inside that particular vehicle, but something primordial overtook him. It wasn't even an estate car, he confessed. Unsurprisingly he didn't catch up with it, but rather caught his foot in a waterlogged pothole which cascaded him onto all fours on the greasy tarmac. Chris ended his pitiful recollection with a sincere, Sorry. The pastor waved the unnecessary apology away.

"We need to get you warmed-up and dried-out, mate," Ralph instructed as he started walking back towards the shops, indicating with his thumb that

Chris should follow. He duly obliged, gingerly testing his weight on a slightly twisted ankle as he set off.

Whilst the temperature inside Crust Almighty was little warmer than in the street, it was nonetheless dry and had a selection of colourful plastic tables and chairs that allowed somewhere for Chris to sit down, take off his shoe and wring out a rather sodden sock. Despite his protestations, Ralph convinced Chris that they should have something to eat before they left. Primarily this was to allow Chris to calm down and begin to act rationally; besides they had no idea where they were going to go anyway. Ralph cleverly used the moral excuse of needing to thank the shopkeeper for his co-operation in allowing them to question his delivery girl. Chris chose not to argue.

It had been several years since Ralph had seen Chris this energised, not since the immediate aftermath of his wife walking out. There, amongst the obvious emotional trauma, he had seen a determination rise up within his assistant pastor who had confided that he was going to find his wife and bring her back. At the time Ralph had only known Chris for a short while and as far as he knew that was exactly what was going to happen. After all, Chris had a plan and the apparent resolve to see it through. But then something happened, Ralph never knew what. That determination suddenly waned, replaced with a thin veneer of positivity. Within days Chris had somehow given up on his marriage and even when the divorce papers eventually came through he raised no protest. Since then, any setback, any problem, any disagreement, was met with humour and conciliation. But not tonight. Tonight, he was serious; tonight, he was determined; and, it would appear, he was driven by something vitally important to him. Ralph knew that Chris and Bunny were close, but seeing how passionately he was behaving tonight revealed that Chris's feelings for Bunny were much stronger than Ralph had realised.

It was perhaps the largest tent she had ever seen.[1] Several times larger than any of the circus tents that used to visit the local recreation fields when she was a child. Bigger even than the tent crusade that she and Chris had attended a few years previously. Chris had invited her to go with him to hear a charismatic American faith-healer – she had long since allowed the name to slip

---

[1] William Miller's meeting tent was the largest ever constructed and is said to have been the inspiration behind P.T. Barnum's travelling circus which became known as the Greatest Show on Earth. The tent was used for several years, eventually collapsing in 1843.

from her memory, as she wasn't particularly enamoured at the event. But now, her recollection of that highly charged evening felt quite different. At the time she had bristled uncomfortably, stating several times that this wasn't *her kind of church*. But now, having a much broader appreciation of the diversity of *Church*, she felt she was becoming more open-minded.

After all, she mused, I've witnessed prophets on the streets of London, I bet Chris has never seen that. Mind you, it was in seventeen-o-six! The thought prompted her to update herself on the current time. The large square dial of her digital watch flashed 18:44.

"This can't still be The Great Awakening, can it?" she said under her breath. "That was around a hundred years ago. Wesley, Whitefield and Edwards will all be long gone by now, I guess."

The giant tent had alternate green and red stripes, although the red had faded to near orange. Dozens of people poured inside through openings that were evenly spaced across the end which Bunny assumed must be the rear. The buggy continued past the obvious points of ingress and halted outside a single entrance at the head of the enormous structure. She thanked her driver, exited the horse-drawn taxi, and headed for the entrance, once again unsure as to what lay ahead.

Her assumed layout of the tent was correct. She soon found herself in the wings of a relatively modest stage area, beyond which she could see that a huge audience was waiting patiently and excitedly. A few feet in front of her there stood two people whose demeanour were polar opposites. One was a buzz of efficient organisation, issuing polite but firm orders to an enduring tide of underlings who would silently dissolve into the background to accomplish their instructions. The other, a robust, well-dressed gentleman in his sixties looked as though he was without a care in the world and was playing with, what she assumed to be, two of his grandchildren. As one child ran towards Bunny, she caught the gentleman's eye.

"Hello, Miss," he said, adding to her surprise, "I've been expecting you."

"You have?" she spurted, before quickly re-conforming to the unwritten rules of her enforced dream. "Yes, of course, you *have* been expecting me!"

He introduced himself as William Miller, a name of which she had no recollection. He then introduced his grandson, granddaughter and then his son-in-law who had arrived to take the two little ones away.[1]

After the obligatory kisses and wails of 'Not now Papa,' Miller's attention was eventually brought round to the reason four thousand people had gathered in the tent, specifically to hear him.

"It's almost time, William!" The efficient man joined them, straightened Miller's tie, and brushed the lapels of his jacket. He was introduced to Bunny as Joshua Himes, again a name unknown to her and of whom Miller gave the plaudit that all this was his doing and he would still be farming in Vermont without his publication of the magazine he passed her. It was entitled *The Signs of the Times*. Bunny politely flicked through it only to see it contained an almost incomprehensible exposition of the Old Testament prophet Daniel and the Apostle John's Revelation. This was not the popular reading material she would have expected would draw such a large crowd. Upon closing, she noticed that she was holding issue number Twenty. Surely there weren't another nineteen of these, she wondered.[2]

"Now remember, William," Himes coached him, "today's the day. They have come for you to tell them..." he hung the sentence in the air between them requiring Miller to provide the punchline.

"I know, they've come to hear the date," he said in mock irritation. Then turning to Bunny, he added,

"I was a lot happier when I had narrowed it down to a full year. But they want an exact date... so a date they will have!"[3]

Bunny had no idea what he was talking about, so just smiled and gave a polite laugh of affirmation. Before she had any chance to question him, he had turned and mounted the small stage.

---

[1] Captain William Miller, a gentleman farmer and veteran of the war of 1812 was the founder of the Millerites or as it is sometimes known the Adventist movement, whose main focus was the Second Coming of Christ.

[2] Joshua Himes was an early follower of Miller's teaching and published over 4 million copies of Millerite teachings, principally in the form of The Signs of the Times, which is still in print to this day.

[3] Miller first postulated that the Second Coming of Christ would be between 21 Mar 1843 and 21 Mar 1844. When this period passed without incident he was encouraged by additional teaching by Samuel Snow to revise the date to 22nd October 1844. For simplicity, only this latter and more significant date has been presented here.

He was far from the most dynamic of preachers she had heard. In her mind she began to collate a league table of power preachers: Whitefield would be top, then John Wesley, then perhaps John Knox or would it be Calvin? The fact she was distractedly making a Top Ten was evidence itself that Miller was somewhere near the bottom. And yet the huge audience sat transfixed. What's the big draw? she wondered.

Miller explained that a study of Daniel chapter eight had shown him that the cleansing of the sanctuary would take place at the end of a 2300-day period. He went on to say that when the Bible said a day it really meant a year. Counting from the accepted date that the children of Israel were led into captivity and the temple sanctuary was desecrated, then 2300 years later Christ would return.

Then it came. Like a bolt of lightning. Like a slap in the face. The moment the audience had been waiting for. With neither emotion nor fanfare Miller simply continued his discourse to say,

"I can confidently tell you my friends that Jesus Christ will return again to Earth on the Twenty Second of October 1844!"

Bunny's jaw dropped open, literally. She couldn't believe what she heard. This cannot be right! she thought. Doesn't the Bible say that no man shall know the day nor the hour of His return?[1] The whole audience on the other hand cheered and applauded, they were totally caught-up with this theology, particularly the confidence with which he had calculated the date of the Second Coming, or as Miller called it *The Second Advent*. History had already told Bunny that such an event never happened. She looked at her watch wishing she could set an alarm for 23rd October 1844, the day *after* the supposed Second Coming. The display then suddenly lit up with the message: 'Alarm Set: 23/10/44'. This is going to be interesting, she thought.

---

[1] "But of that day and hour knoweth no man, no, not the angels of heaven, but my Father only." Matthew 24:36 KJV

Chapter 32

THE GREAT DISAPPOINTMENT

Everyone knew that the logical meeting point at the hospital was the WRVS café. Joel headed there hoping to find Thea brimming full of useful information, but when he arrived he found two people in the late-night rendezvous, both male. He sent Thea a simple WhatsApp message to alert her of his location but asserted that she need not rush. This was as much to give her a chance to maximise her interrogative powers as it was to give him time for his second coffee of the evening.

Of the two other people in the café, one sat hunched over a table, either asleep or comatose. Joel decided he was best avoided. The other was seated at the table next to the vending machine. On the circular melamine covered table, he had placed a large professional-looking camera. Joel remembered that Thea had remarked that they'd seen someone rush in with a large camera when they were there earlier. This was presumably the same person. Joel inserted his coins, pressed the button marked cappuccino, and waited as the machine began to whirr and sputter.

"Is that a nice camera? I think it is!" Joel said in his unusual question and answer way. The man looked up over the rim of his own drink allowing Joel to ask him, "Local newspaper?"

"Freelance for the tabloids mate," came the world-weary reply.

"What brings you out here then?" Joel continued as he waited for the final black drips to descend into his cup.

"A wild goose-chase, that's what," he answered. Joel said nothing, simply extracted his cup from the machine and pulled out the chair opposite the stranger. It was a bit forward, but Joel had always been a natural connector with people; he even considered it to be a key part of his ministry as an evangelist.

"My name is Joel Whyens," he said offering his hand as he sat down. "I am the local Methodist minister, and which particular goose were you chasing?"

The photojournalist weighed his options. He could spend a few minutes having a sensible conversation with an unknown churchman whom, if nothing else, would allow him to moan about his wasted evening, or he could finish his drink and set off on the long drive home. He also knew that conversations sometimes lead to stories, a healthy trait in any journalist.

"Tonight's golden goose was going to be Miss Velia Advowson," he said lifting his paper cup as if toasting his lack of success.

Joel was amazed to hear the same name mentioned as was on his, and his friends', list of loose ends. He said nothing nor let his face change from the sympathetic expression he gave the reporter who duly began to vent his angst.

"I gets this tip-off right, that there was gonna be a big story in this 'ere hospital tonight involving Miss Velia Advowson," he began. "Well, she sells copy and I could get a few hundred for an exclusive, spesh if she's like injured. Could be front page. But nothing serious like, just her with like a bandage over 'er eye or 'er arm in a sling, say."

"You got a tip-off to be here because she was going to be admitted to hospital?" Joel clarified.

"Yeah, and what a waste of a journey – not for the first time, but I really thought I had something. Spesh when I rang and heard she was in casualty. But you've got no chance of getting anything out of them. No names, no details."

Joel asked, "But you got the pictures in the end?"

"Nah, she was taken straight into the back ward. Celeb privileges as usual. Couldn't get through," he said exasperatedly. "Hey, I did try, it is my livelihood after all, but this copper threw me out. I'm on a bit of a final warning with the boys in blue, so thought I had best hang back."

"Can I ask you a question?" Joel interjected. "When exactly did you get the tip-off?"

"This afternoon and that I needed to be 'ere soon after 8:30," he admitted, adding frustratedly, "I had to drive up from London."

Joel sipped his coffee and asked,

"Isn't that a little strange?"

The photojournalist looked back at him. Joel expanded his point.

"Someone told you this afternoon that she was going to be admitted by 8:30."

The journalist nodded.

"So, they had to know in advance," Joel explained.

"Yep, as I said a tip-off, although they only said it was going to be a story, not that she was going to be admitted or stuff."

Joel didn't think he was being completely honest so gently but firmly challenged him.

"But you just said you expected to get an *injured celebrity* picture."

The reporter clearly didn't like being corrected and when Joel then asked about who he got the tip-off from, he was brushed aside with the usual mantra about reporters never revealing their sources. However, Joel's sensible observation had put a very different spin on the goose he had come to chase, and the weary professional pulled out his phone to scroll back through his Call Received list, to check the time of the tip-off himself.

A few minutes of uncomfortable silence passed. Joel was the first to break it, as he usually was.

"Shall I tell you about another story happening tonight? I think so," he said wanting to engage with the journalist and all he could offer was the potential of a new lead. He added "Two bodies!"

"Yep," the reporter said emptying the last of his drink. "Missed that one too. Local news are already there at..." he looked at his phone to check the details, "Sanguine Wood and I expect the TV news crews will be on the way. No, all I get, for my sins, is to scratch out a living from celebrity gossip."

The photojournalist swung around and reached behind him to the vending machine and without standing up inserted the exact coins and pressed black americano. Joel made use of the momentary distraction to add a brief WhatsApp message to the group saying the bodies had been found in Sanguine Wood. Jack, still in the car park of C.R.F., looked at his phone and immediately started the engine of his Japanese 4x4.

Meanwhile, Joel at the hospital café was struggling with personal internal conflict. The group had agreed to keep quiet about the events of the evening; and yet here was someone who might be able to help them locate Bunny. After all, his business was to ask questions, Joel thought, so he decided to offer the smallest piece of information he dared. As the unshaven news hack blew across the top of his coffee to cool it, Joel distractedly added,

"And there's a missing lady also."

The journalist admitted he hadn't heard about a missing person and without taking his eyes off Joel slipped a small notebook from inside his jacket. Before Joel noticed, he was already flicking shorthand characters as the churchman explained whom Bunny was, with only spartan details on her disappearance. He didn't mention the blood in the church, the plasterer's van or the borrowed ambulance. He didn't want to say anything about the farmhouse but almost unknowingly the professional questioner had conveyed to Joel that he was genuinely interested and perhaps he could offer something that might help them find her. The mental process that Joel went through at that table was

281

completely irrational. So many internal trade-offs were being played out in his brain that he couldn't justify any of them. He knew he oughtn't say anything more about Bunny, but the farmhouse did have a link to the two bodies, and besides, the journalist already knew about them. Then Joel heard himself say something he immediately regretted. He told the reporter that he knew where the 'bodies' had slept last night and that the police didn't know the location yet.

Beep, beep, beep!

To Bunny's knowledge she had never set the alarm on her watch, she wasn't even sure it had an alarm. However, the unambiguous beep, beep, beep, demanded that it was now October 23rd 1844, the morning after William Miller's predicted Second Coming of Christ.

It was daybreak. The tent was gone from the field and in the dim early morning light Bunny could discern figures surrounding her. Many, many, figures. Some were fumbling about in the half-light, the entire scene the literal embodiment of the-morning-after-the-night-before. As the first rays of sun released its unwelcome motivation, Bunny could distinguish that there were hundreds, maybe even thousands of people. As theatrical as this visual panorama was, what was even more dramatic was the unmistakable background sound of weeping. A collective mournful lamentation on a biblical scale. The sound of uncontrollable crying became an alternative dawn chorus, drowning out any bird song. The field was populated by the distraught faithful whose faith was now considerably less *full*. These were loyal people who had waited all day and all night for their miracle; when the morning eventually came, and it had failed to materialise – then came the tears. This morning of mourning was indeed The Great Disappointment [1]

Bunny kept silent. She certainly didn't want to gloat at what she considered to be the foolishness of so many. As the sun slowly rose, she could eventually make out the facial details of those nearest to her, tear-stained and red-eyed, but not one of them familiar to her. She looked around hoping to identify William Miller, but he was, perhaps unsurprisingly, nowhere to be seen. Then, at last, she spotted someone she thought she recognised.

"Mr. Himes?" she asked softly.

---

[1] The 22nd of October 1844 became known as The Great Disappointment.

The mastermind of the Millerite publicity campaign looked as grief-stricken as the rest. Bunny didn't really know what to say. She knew that Christ had not planned to return yesterday, but she certainly didn't want to sound too supportive to one of the leaders whom, she considered, had led so many astray. She plumped on asking a purely factual question.

"Were there a lot of disappointed people?" she asked. Himes exhaled dramatically before answering,

"Well, I'd say at least a hundred thousand, and that included over two hundred church ministers."[1] As they continued this factual discourse for a few minutes, some tear-stained people began to gravitate towards the sound of Himes' voice. Bunny watched them carefully, unsure if any might allow their disappointment to turn into violence directed at one of the most recognisable people in this failed movement.

"So, what happens now?" she asked, genuinely curious and trying not to be provocative. Bunny half assumed Himes would just give a shrug of his shoulders and walk away but, ever the efficient one, he decided to take the initiative.

The group that had gathered around him were clearly known to him, Bunny assumed they were an inner-circle or a representative body of some sort. Himes began by simply asking them for their opinions. Tears were dried and sensible, objective comments began to be made. They all agreed that the vast majority of the Millerite followers would probably just abandon their faith and would have to find their own way back to mainstream religion if that was what they wanted. They, however, considered themselves to be the faithful *remnant* and as such were determined to 'keep the faith alive.' Bunny couldn't help herself but react to that idea.

"How?" she said spontaneously, incredulous to understand how you can *keep the faith alive* when the impending apocalypse had passed by without a whimper. Several of the group turned to her suspiciously. Despite her personal scepticism she smoothly turned her outburst into a positive question and deflected any accusation.

"How are you planning to keep the faith alive?" she asked.

Several said they were going to form communes and begin to worship God away from prying eyes. One even said he was going to move his group to Jerusalem. Bunny thought it quite understandable to go into hiding after you

---

[1] 'The Great Disappointment and the Birth of Adventism' by Professor Walter J. Veith, PhD. (2011)

had told all your friends the world was about to end. Then a woman spoke up. Himes acknowledged her as Ellen and invited her to share her thoughts and the group turned to listen.

"There is an *alternative* interpretation," she said. "I have been speaking to someone and they pointed out that the date may well have been correct." At this point the group released a simultaneous collective murmur built upon an amalgamation of 'What?', 'How?' and 'Eh?' Ellen continued,

"I believe that Christ did indeed return to the sanctuary yesterday, exactly as prophesied." No one spoke, allowing her to continue. "But it was not the Second Advent we were expecting. Christ is in the Sanctuary now and has started a time of cleansing. Once that has been completed, He will return for the faithful."

Bunny bit her lip. This sounded so much like papering over the cracks and making up doctrine on the spot in order to fit the undeniable contrary evidence. As far as Bunny could make out, there was no biblical justification for what she was saying. *Can't they all just admit they got it wrong?* she thought, yet dare not say out loud.

"That sounds like a very... satisfactory explanation," Himes admitted. Righteous indignation welled-up in Bunny. She couldn't hold it in any longer.

"Of course, it is a *satisfactory explanation*!" she released. Immediately attracting everyone's focus. She continued, "It's a very satisfactory way to save face and still think you were right all along."

Everyone was looking at her. Bunny scanned every face looking for someone who saw the logic in what she had said. Surely someone would. But no, nothing, no one; the whole group stood looking at her, cold and unemotional. Bunny's heart sank. She couldn't believe what she was hearing. A totally implausible doctrine whose entire existence was borne out of the fact that William Miller, and his puppet-master Joshua Himes, had recklessly promoted a patently false doctrine about the imminent return of Christ. She needed to break eye-contact with these crazy people. Rather than try to push her way out of the circle around her, she squatted down, covered her face with the palms of her hands. This is madness, she thought.

"Did you find anything?" Rex asked Artur through the driver-side window of his car as he pulled into the drop-off zone in front of the railway station. Artur, walking back from the main car park, hands in pockets to keep warm, shook his head.

"I thought I had found the car, but it was just an abandoned VW," he admitted, thankful to have not been the one to have discovered Bunny's body. Before Artur could approach his car, Rex raised the electric window then swung his car into one of four parking spaces at the front of the station concourse and promptly got out.

"I don't know about you, but I am starving," he said as he pressed the lock door button on his key-fob. They both walked across the street to the station entrance under the exterior Tannoy speaker that thankfully was silent after hours. The small station plaza was deserted. The ticket desks were all sealed shut — each had a small brown roller-blind printed with CLOSED, pulled down across their locked windows. The digital matrix signs next to five pedestrian turnstiles all displayed the decisive red X that prohibited unwanted ingress onto the platforms. A metal retail bin for the free *Metro* newspaper, much loved by travellers, stood empty awaiting its daily refill ready for the morning commute. A Photo-Me booth and a children's Postman Pat ride had both been switched off, presumably to prevent Pat from issuing a ghostly invitation to, 'Come and Ride!' throughout the dark and lonely night hours. Thankfully, the solitary vending machine which stood at the opposite side of the foyer remained on, invitingly illuminating its needs-must offering to late-night passers-by such as Rex and Artur.

Rex selected a four finger Kit-Kat for himself and bought Artur a cereal bar. As they unwrapped their welcome snack, Artur asked Rex how well he knew Bunny. Rex explained that he had a lot of respect for her and that she was someone who *for an Anglican*, as he put it, knew a lot about the Quakers. He went on to relate how they had met in the short-lived bookshop but how since then they had kept in touch and how he considered her to be on a *strong intellectual level*, whatever that meant. Once Rex had reached the end of his anecdotal recollections Artur shared what was bothering him.

"I thought I was about to find her," he said.

Rex failed to grasp the significance of Artur's confession, so the young Austrian restated it, only to find that this time he couldn't prevent his voice from faltering emotionally.

"I honestly thought I was about to find her body laid in the back seat of that Volkswagen."

Rex heard the plea of his fellow church leader's heart and placed a comforting arm on his shoulder. This, Rex had found, was the most acceptable form of physical consolatory connection acceptable to men. He wasn't a naturally tactile person, more comfortable with logical argument than pastoring. He was at home in a church that focussed on the internal relationship with God more than any outward expression of emotion. However, on feeling Rex's hand on his shoulder, Artur immediately began to cry uncontrollably. Rex had no choice; his controlled and dignified stance gave way to a fatherly hug which itself induced further sobs. There they stood in the brightly illuminated yet abandoned station concourse, Artur's head cradled in Rex's shoulder. Rex's left arm wrapped around Artur and there in his left hand the half-eaten Kit-Kat beckoned to him.

Rex pondered, is it acceptable to take a bite of a Kit-Kat whilst someone is crying and hugging you? He considered that he could probably bite it silently and chew it *really* slowly, limiting any sudden jaw movements such that Artur wouldn't notice. And as any owner of half-eaten confectionary knows, it is impossible to even contemplate not finishing the bar once started. Rex brought his hand closer to his lips, moving the Kit-Kat within range. Artur interpreted this as a tightening of the hug and gave a further sob at which Rex came to his senses and gave the Lutheran a series of comforting pats upon his back. The chocolate would have to wait.

"Hey, what are you two up to?" the semi-official voice brought an abrupt end to the moment of inter-church humanity. As soon as they separated, Rex took a large bite of the Kit-Kat then looked over his shoulder toward the source of the voice. A security guard had approached them. Rex tried to assure the guard of their innocence, but a mouthful of chocolate and wafers made him almost intelligible, and he motioned to wait a moment while he finished eating. Artur, having wiped his eyes, came to the rescue of the situation.

"Jó estét," he said to the guard adding, "Ön Magyar?"

The security guard's face immediately lit up with the broadest of smiles. He nodded profusely, taking Artur by the hand and shaking it vigorously. Artur then began to speak to him in a language that Rex did not understand. Rex had a smattering of German from his time working in the City of London, but Artur was not speaking in his native German tongue. Momentarily Rex was introduced to Artur's new friend, Karoly according to his security badge, and was required to shake his hand equally as vigorously. Clearly now redundant, Rex gave his attention to the final two fingers of his Kit-Kat, savouring every mouthful.

Having initially said, multiple times, 'Nem!' which Rex assumed was No, Karoly and Artur eventually appeared to reach an agreement. The guard then furtively set off towards a door marked Private and beckoned them to follow.

"Do you know this chap?" Rex asked.

"I never met him before," Artur replied. "Karoly is a traditional Hungarian name and I speak a little..."

"A little!" Rex interrupted as they began to follow the official. "You sounded fluent, friend. Anyway, what's happening now?"

"Ah, he is going to show us tonight's CCTV," Artur replied proudly. Rex stopped suddenly, dropped his voice to a pronounced whisper and asked,

"And how exactly did you get him to agree to that?" Artur joined him in a whispered reply,

"I told him we were two priests who had been sent by God to him tonight and he had a choice." Rex waited for him to explain the nature of the choice God had apparently given the Hungarian.

"Either he lets us see the CCTV so we can find something..."

Rex added a forced,

"Or?"

"Or, we would be staying all night praying for him."

Rex gave a chuckle which Artur joined in. Rex patted the young Lutheran on the back as they entered the security office saying,

"Genius, my friend, genius."

Inside the office the guard was already rewinding that evening's footage. Six individual pictures were on a large monitor all playing in reverse. The time counter on the lower left of the screen scrolled backwards in time like the dials on H.G. Wells' Time Machine.

"Mikor?' Karoly asked Artur

"What time?" Artur translated. "He wants to know what time we want to see."

"Yes, what tiyem?" the guard said in imperfect English.

Artur pursed his lips and admitted, "I don't know."

"If only we knew when the ambulance arrived here," Rex pondered.

"Aha!" Artur said as he pulled a folded sheet of paper from his hip pocket. It was the report printed from FuelMgr.com that the hospice manager had given them earlier. He placed it in front of the guard and pointed at the exact time the ambulance should have arrived at the station. He typed the timestamp into the system then suddenly there it was: first on one small screen, then another and finally a perfect rear view of the same ambulance they'd seen at the hospice, now waiting in the railway station drop-off zone.

"Let it run," Rex said as they both leaned towards the screen. At the click of a mouse Karoly selected the viewpoint of interest which then expanded to fill the entire monitor. There it was, parked at the front of the railway station as the minutes passed by. They couldn't see any occupants, and no one got out of it. It just stood parked there, waiting, eerily still.

"They are waiting for a train," was Rex's unnecessary comment to which no one replied.

Soon people began to stream from the railway entrance, some with laptops, others with rucksacks, two with suitcases and one with a bicycle. They filed past the ambulance at haste, each one busying themselves with their onward journeys. After the initial rush had subsided a solitary man emerged and headed straight toward the passenger door of the ambulance. This was a much better picture than the ANPR record taken by the hospital parking machine, where they had first seen the borrowed ambulance earlier that evening. They could clearly see that the man was wearing a thigh-length black leather coat under which was what looked like a black and yellow scarf. What was most distinctive was the hat. It was a Russian style ushanka hat with flaps that could be folded down to cover the ears. Karoly paused the playback to help them. The freeze-frame was not as good quality as the recording, so they asked him to just let it continue. The man wore spectacles, had a neat black beard and a very pallid complexion. As they watched, he held a brief conversation through the passenger-door window before the door opened and a passenger emerged. The occupant wasn't wearing the familiar green ambulance crew fatigues but jeans and a heavy brown jumper over which was a sleeveless tabard that was orange on both front and back, green on the shoulders with a black and white checkers across the chest and a circular motif on the front. It conveyed a vaguely medical chic but was not a uniform either of them had seen before.

The passenger acted demonstrably subservient to the man in the leather coat, holding the door as he took the seat he had just vacated. The passenger, duly relegated to ride in the back, rushed to the rear door and as he opened it Rex and Artur peered inside. As best as they could make out from this oblique angle the ambulance was empty. The rear door then shut as the ambulance began to move away.

Chapter 33

THE HERESY EXPRESS PART ONE

Bunny stood up and removed her hand from her face. The New England field was devoid of people. The small post-non-apocalypse committee meeting that she had gate-crashed had disappeared together with the mournful thousands. The only person who remained in that field was the woman, Ellen, who had the alternative explanation of why William Miller's prediction had failed, the woman whom Bunny had publicly criticised. Ellen had her back to Bunny and was busy packing a satchel. When she turned around, she simply looked past Bunny as if she wasn't there, then began to walk hurriedly towards her. I really ought to say something, Bunny thought. But I think her idea is ridiculous and I don't really want to have anything to do with her. Ellen brushed past Bunny without even acknowledging her existence. Perhaps she can't see me, she thought, allowing herself an exhalation of relief.

Bunny turned to see where the woman was heading in such a rush only to see her climb aboard the single red carriage that was coupled to the rear of an enormous steam locomotive, barely twenty feet away from where she was standing, and which was now assaulting every one of Bunny's senses. Her eyes feasted on a bewildering concoction of gleaming wheels, spokes, rods and pulleys that underpinned a cylindrical body painted in vivid and vibrant red. Above, a black funnel opened to the sky like an ebony vase and from its mouth sprouted a bouquet of grey and white steam clouds that both lifted heavenward and also swirled towards where she stood, leaving her with a momentary warm kiss of moisture upon her cheeks. Through the mist she could see leather-clad railroad engineers busying themselves for an imminent departure. The smell of ash and hot oil was so strong that she could almost taste it. For the briefest of moments, she could understand the fascination that compels some people – she had to admit, usually middle-aged men – to be captivated by the visceral sight of these mechanical marvels.

Her thoughts were suddenly interrupted by the deafening sound of a train whistle at which she involuntarily stooped and covered her head as if to avoid an incoming attack.

"Time!" the conductor shouted, somehow expressing the single word in multiple syllables and using all of the vowels. She slowly unfolded herself from her defensive crouch and looked towards the train. She could see no conductor through the swirling steam but heard his voice a second time, now directed towards her.

"It's time to go, Miss," he said.

Ah, time! I know what *time* means, she admitted to herself and, despite having no desire to follow Ellen, headed toward the carriage that she had disappeared within.

The railway carriage was itself a work of grandeur with ornately painted decals embellishing the red painted exterior. Then something quite curious caught her eye. Along the side of the carriage, beneath the windows, in the place where she may have expected to have read *Union Pacific* or the title of some other such early American railroad company, large gold cursive letters spelled out, 'Second Peter 2 v 1.'[1] For the second time, Bunny wished her mental recall of Bible verses was better. She had no idea what that verse said, but its inscription was sufficient to confirm she needed to be on that train. As she placed her foot on the first of two metal steps the reassuringly stereotypical sound of a distant conductor announced,

"All aboard!"

As Thea approached the WRVS café Joel spotted her and immediately leapt to his feet declaring to the photojournalist that it was 'Nice to chat,' but he really had to leave now that his friend had arrived. It didn't matter that Thea may have wanted another coffee; she had no choice as Joel seemed intent on bundling her away in unnecessary haste. Thea obliged and they headed for the exit until suddenly she remembered that she still had the Chaplaincy Pass around her neck.

"Wait, Joel, I need to..." she halted, lifting the blue laminated lanyard. She really ought to have taken it back to the Rabbi, but Joel's haste meant she had to consider an alternative. Directly opposite the WRVS café was a small administration zone comprising an unmanned desk with a telephone, behind which was a series of wooden pigeonholes used to distribute internal hospital correspondence. The top row of makeshift letter boxes each had black labels with white writing on them displaying X-RAY, ONCOLOGY, MATERNITY and OUT-PATIENTS. Thea's eye was drawn to the bottom-left-corner slot headed,

---

[1] "But there were false prophets also among the people, even as there shall be false teachers among you, who privily shall bring in damnable heresies, even denying the Lord that bought them, and bring upon themselves swift destruction." 2 Peter 2:1 King James Version.

somewhat amusingly CHAPL.IN, some wag having filled in the 'A' with black marker pen. She had used this pigeonhole once before when she needed to correspond with Rabbi Pascal and his office had been locked. It wasn't ideal but this would have to do. She stepped behind the desk and pushed the pass into the slot and stepped away. Had she looked back she would have seen that it was not lying discreetly flat as she had intended, but had become folded, displaying its credentials to any passer-by.

After a journey of barely ten minutes the train pulled into the first station. Bunny looked out of the carriage window to see a sign indicating that they were in Battle Creek, Michigan. She had no idea why. As the metal beast came to a final halt, the ear-piercing sounds of vented steam and screeching brakes was eventually supplanted by the conductor's voice proclaiming several times as he traversed the carriage that this was the,

"18:63 at Battle Creek."

Despite it being, once again, a numerically impossible time, Bunny nonetheless noted that the time agreed with that shown on her square digital watch. Ellen was already disembarking so Bunny followed behind her. Whatever buildings and landmarks existed in Battle Creek, Michigan, all Bunny could see was the single wooden shack, inside which Ellen promptly disappeared. It was a stoutly made timber construction with its framing covered with horizontally affixed wooden planks, although several had slipped out of their fixings, making angular imperfections that blemished the otherwise uniform appearance. There were no windows, just a simple doorway and porch above which Bunny could see was affixed a large number *Seven*.

Whether it was the inner pull of her curiosity, or the lack of any other options, Bunny decided to follow Miss Ellen. No sooner had she started to tentatively make her way inside the shack than she was unapologetically bundled out of the way by a man pushing past her to enter with great haste. He hardly noticed that he had connected with her, carrying as he was a large, orange-coloured box under one arm. Bunny ignored his unmannerly haste and followed him inside.

Despite its small-scale the building was laid out as a plain religious meeting house. A simple pulpit stood at the far end, behind which Ellen stood ready to address her flock. It was clear that the rather ungallant latecomer was well known to her as she acknowledged him as he took a seat near the front.

"Well, her ideas must have garnered some followers," Bunny said under her breath as she took one of the rear-most chairs.

For the next few minutes, she listened as the speaker expounded the virtues of healthy living: how God insisted that they must have a healthy diet and not partake in eating pork, drinking alcohol or smoking tobacco. This was nothing new to Bunny, the Puritans she had met previously were equally as prohibitionist. What surprised her, however, was when Ellen seamlessly and equally vocally began to rail against the perils of sexual immorality. This wasn't a subject the Puritans dare to express and was certainly never one that Rector Mashman would have included in a sermon. She began to feel her cheeks starting to redden as her maidenly innocence was being put to the test. She consoled her embarrassment with a rather matter-of-fact recognition that it was relatively common for churches to preach against the perils of promiscuity and adultery. But as soon as she had accepted that position Ellen turned to marriage, advising her married followers to abstain from any form of nakedness with their spouse and to perform nothing more than the most perfunctory of sexual acts required to procreate. Bunny, now fully blushing, was shocked and couldn't help but think that this lady must have had some bad experiences in the bedroom.[1]

Whatever level of self-conscious discomfiture Bunny had endured in that broken wooden shack was about to reach its crescendo when Henry, the man carrying the large orange box, was invited to join Ellen at the pulpit. Bunny's Anglican sensibilities were insufficient to prepare her for the mortification that hit her as Henry explained that he had invented a cure for *illicit private sexual urges*, proudly tapping the box under his arm. If she had been drinking a cup of tea, this would have been the moment she would have spat it out; if she had been holding a tray, she would have dropped it; if she were reading a book, she would have slammed it shut. But this was real! Here was a man announcing in church – well, some sort of church – that he had invented a *cure* for something she couldn't even bring herself to even think about, let alone hear from the pulpit. But the shocks hadn't finished. Henry proudly held the orange box aloft and read his hand-made label: 'Henry Kellogg's Toasted Corn Flakes,' he

_____

[1] 'Ellen White and Marital Excess' by Dirk Anderson. Nonsda.org (2009)

announced to the enraptured audience. Bunny was flabbergasted. Surely that wasn't the real story behind the invention of Kellogg's Corn Flakes. Was it?[1]

Mr. Kellogg thanked his leader by name, Ellen Gould White, who then concluded her message by saying that in addition to the Adventist teaching that they had all enjoyed as their Millerite foundation, they were now going to change their day of worship from the first to the seventh day of the week, Saturday. At that moment Bunny suddenly understood the significance of the numeral seven above the door.

"This must be the origins of the Seventh Day Adventists," she said, again to no one in particular.

The realisation gave Bunny a renewed vigour. If Ellen Gould White's interpretation of the Millerite failure had led to the Seventh Day Adventist movement, which held to some doctrines she could not agree with, then she was satisfied that her initial reticence had been justified. Bunny immediately exited to see the train was waiting for her. She ran over to it and no sooner had she settled herself in than it pulled away.

Barely another ten minutes passed.

"Pittsburgh, Pittsburgh, this is the 18:76 at Pittsburgh," the conductor declared. Bunny looked through the carriage window to confirm that they were indeed pulling into Pittsburgh Station and as soon as they had come to a halt, stepped outside. Scanning the immediate cityscape, she marvelled at the beautiful array of pristine timber-lapped buildings. This is so authentic, she thought, it is as though I am standing in a Hollywood film set of colonial Midwest America. One building, however, caught her attention. A less-than-perfect shack with wooden slats that had slipped from horizontal and looked identical to the one she'd entered next to Battle Creek station. This shack was in exactly the same place as Shed Seven had been, thus leaving her in no doubt this was where she needed to go. As she approached, she noticed above the door, not a numeral but a small pictograph of a tower, somewhat similar to a lighthouse but without the lamp.

Inside the layout was pretty much identical as the previous shack, which strangely came as no surprise to her. This time a man was addressing the group. Bunny didn't take a seat and just stood at the back not wanting to stay any longer than she needed.

---

[1] A passionate seventh Day Adventist, Henry Kellogg invented his world-famous Corn Flakes as a cure for sexual urges. He offered the brand and patent to the church who declined ownership in what was surely the biggest commercial mistake of any religious group.

The man was in mid-flow promoting the wonders of his *miracle wheat* which, he claimed, grew five times faster than regular wheat. He was offering to sell it at sixty dollars a bushel. Bunny could tell by the audience's reaction this must have been particularly expensive, but nonetheless a show of hands indicated he had some takers. Seamlessly he went on to describe his wonder cure for cancer. Bunny allowed herself a suppressed smile as he explained how his *millennial bean* offered cures not only for cancer but a whole host of other ailments, also available for sale at a ridiculously elevated price.[1]

"What a quack," Bunny whispered, adding derogatively, "Magic beans indeed!"

It didn't take long before the same man turned to doctrinal points. Annoyingly, he talked of himself in the third person as both Charles and Mr. Russell. He explained how as a child he had met Jonas Wendell, a follower of William Miller. Charles told of how he had realised that Miller had misinterpreted his end-time prediction and explained that the date had been wrong because Christ's *presence* had already returned several years earlier, and that God was now busy *harvesting* his faithful followers. He then went on to postulate that Scripture said the faithful would only number a total of one hundred and forty-four thousand. When Bunny heard Charles state categorically that 'Jesus was not God,' that was enough for her, she didn't want to stay any longer. As she turned to leave, she was confronted by an elderly lady with a forced smile that was both intimidating and comical; and whose positioning was designed to block her escape route.

"Can I help you, Miss?" she said, tilting her head empathetically to forty-five degrees.

Before Bunny could answer, the woman thrust a small magazine into Bunny's palm. She looked down at it with unguarded disdain. The title read: 'Zions Watchtower and Herald of Christs Presence.' The author, Charles Taze Russell.

"Watchtower! I get it! It's not a lighthouse, it's a watchtower. And you are the J.W.s."

"J.W.s?" the smiling woman asked somewhat indignantly, assuming it to be an insult.

"Yes, Jehovah's Witnesses," Bunny expanded.

---

[1] Charles Taze Russell was sued for selling Miracle Wheat which was proved to be worse than regular wheat. 'History of the Jehovah's Witnesses'. www.catholic.com

"No, we are the Watchtower Bible and Tract Society, but I do like the term *Jehovah's Witnesses*. In fact, that might even be a better name."[1]

Bunny returned the tract to the woman, said a firm goodbye and left the building.

"Have I just named the Jehovah's Witnesses?" she muttered to herself as she re-boarded the waiting railcar. As she settled in her seat, she mused on the fact that two major pseudo-Christian sects had both emerged from the remnants of the Great Disappointment. And whilst she previously had no idea about their origins, now she could see how the foundation had been laid by William Miller's heresy.

He didn't need to check if anyone was watching as that part of the hospital was completely empty. Nevertheless, as much as by instinct than necessity the man looked around in all directions before stepping behind the administration desk, taking the electronic pass from the CHAPL.IN pigeon-hole, and secreting it in his paramedic uniform pocket.

"Boston, Boston," the conductor's voice echoed around her, "18:79 at Boston."

This time she knew what to expect. She stood in the carriage doorway as it pulled to a halt and looked over in the same direction as at Pittsburgh Station. Yes, it was there, the same broken-down shack.

Inside it resembled part therapy clinic, part lecture theatre and seemingly part séance. The audience sat spellbound, perhaps literally. A woman was speaking and told of how she had sought help for her constant pain from a Phineas Quimby who had advocated what she called *magnetic healing*. Bunny had no idea what she meant by magnetic, but as she listened it became clear that Mr. Quimby was a traveling showman who performed hypnotism to *cure* various ailments. The woman explained that she wasn't convinced by this cure.

That's a relief, thought Bunny, neither am I.

The speaker, however, hadn't finished and told of how she had slipped on ice several years ago and had been left an invalid. Remembering Quimby's

---

[1] The Watchtower Bible and Tract Society changed its name to The Jehovah's Witnesses in 1931

ideas and combining them with her Calvinist upbringing she discovered the New Thought that brought about her instant and complete healing.[1]

"I've got to hear this," Bunny said to herself, admittedly sarcastically but tinged with an element of genuine curiosity.

"Sickness is an illusion," the woman pronounced. "All matter is an illusion, death is an illusion."[2] Bunny wasn't impressed.

"Sin is acceptance of those illusions, healing comes when you become aware of this reality," she continued.

"Don't tell me," Bunny whispered to herself, "There is no spoon!"

The famous line came from the movie *The Matrix* in a pivotal scene when a bewildered Keanu Reeves has to embrace the fact that the entire world as he knows it, is not reality. The idea makes for great Sci-Fi but poor religion, she decided.

Bunny had seen miraculous healings performed in front of her eyes, not least of which was the rising of Mercy Wheeler. But that was all through faith in Jesus Christ. This, whatever it was, was fantasy. The biggest shock, however, came when the speaker went one step further to explain that the false reality can be manipulated through the power of the mind. What she was endorsing was the casting of curses designed to wreak harm on others. Bunny had heard enough and turned to leave. Again, her egress was prevented by a smiling woman, no tract in her hand this time.

"Who... and what... is this?" Bunny said indignantly gesturing towards the woman and then the room. The smiler responded to say that the speaker was Mary Baker Eddy and that they called themselves the Church of Christ, Scientist. Bunny quickly returned to the train.

Flopping into the red-leather padded seat of the train carriage, she closed her eyes in mental exhaustion. Her dream had started out as an accelerated adventure through Church history. She had learned about famous people and seen how mainstream Christian denominations were founded. But in the last... however long... it had all got messy. She hadn't got over the fact that both sides in the slavery debate had used the Bible to defend their position and how she had almost lost her footing, doctrinally as well as literally. Then there was Miller

---

[1] Church of Christ, Scientist (not to be confused with Scientology) was founded in 1875 with the publication of 'Science and Health with Key to the Scriptures' by Mary Baker Eddy.

[2] 'Why Do Bad Things Happen If God Is Good?' by Ron Rhodes. Harvest House Publisher (2004) p186

and the huge following he had. And since then it had felt as though she hadn't met anyone other than heretics. And still the train continued. The Heretic Express had more stops to make. She needed some good news.

As she sat there, eyes closed listening to the rhythmic clickety-clack of wheels on track, she fleetingly thought she heard people singing. The more she listened, the more she heard it. A tune she hadn't heard for years. It was faint and indistinct but steadily grew louder. She began to hum along, the distant familiar tune dancing on her memory. What was it? The rhythm of the train began to slow as it approached its next sacrilegious encounter; but the distant singing grew louder. As the melody returned to its chorus Bunny spontaneously joined in.

"Dance, then, wherever you may be, I am the Lord of the Dance said he!" she sang.

It was such a pleasant and uplifting surprise to remember a familiar tune. The song immediately took her back to her weekly childhood attendance at Sunday School. She loved Sunday School: the Bible stories depicted with Velcro and flannelgraph; the running races and quizzes; the cacophony of tambourines, triangles, rattles and other instruments; the copious amounts of orange squash and ginger-nut biscuits. Bunny was the child who was always ready to answer any question and who had meticulously remembered the weekly Memory Verse. In fact, she could probably still remember most, if not all, of them. But then again, that is the whole point of a Memory Verse. Pity we never learned second Peter two verse one, she thought.

She opened her eyes as the train stopped, to see that the station platform was filled with people singing, twirling and pirouetting enthusiastically, very enthusiastically. The joyously familiar song tempted her out of the train in, according to the conductor,

"Logan County, Kentucky."

She stood on the lower step, unsure whether to join them on the platform, not wanting to be engulfed in people dancing wildly, passionately, and much to her discomfort, sweatily. Not one to dance in public, she contented herself with humming along with the twirling dervishes around her. As she listened, she realised the words were not the same as she'd remembered from her childhood. Not the 'Lord of the Dance' but different lyrics. She listened carefully as they sang:

"'Tis the gift to be simple, 'tis the gift to be free,

297

'Tis the gift to come down where we ought to be,
And when we find ourselves in the place just right,
'Twill be in the valley of love and delight.

When true simplicity is gain'd,
To bow and to bend we shan't be asham'd,
To turn, turn will be our delight,
Till by turning, turning we come round right."[1]

As they sang the line, 'Turning, turning,' they rotated with such speed she was sure someone would be bound to fall over. None did. These must be the original lyrics, she thought as she watched the group continue to twirl and rotate with never-ending vigour. Despite not being one to express herself in dance, she couldn't help but tap her foot and pat her thigh as they moved past her along the platform and begin to file into a building. Bunny froze as she caught sight of the building, all thoughts of song and dance instantly falling from her. The joyous crowd were filing into the same tumble-down wooden shack, with sloping horizontal planks, as she had seen at each of the previous stops.

"Oh no, not another dodgy group," she said as she clasped hard onto the handrail. "I used to love that song."

As the final few Shakers disappeared inside the shack, she slowly reversed her steps into the carriage, turned and retook her seat.

As she rested her forehead on the widow the loud chug-chug of the train beginning to move drowned any sound of the familiar tune. She exhaled disappointedly as the train began to gather momentum before saying to her reflection,

"It's sad that *Lord of the Dance* wasn't a Christian song after all."[2]

As the minutes passed, she stared absentmindedly out of the window. Fields, farms, homesteads, cows, horses and towns passed with a monotonous frequency as the train pressed westwards. She had no idea what doubtful

---

[1] These are the lyrics of the first verse of 'Simple Gifts' 1848 by Elder Joseph Bracket (1797–1882)

[2] The Shaker hymn, 'Simple Gifts' was later rewritten as 'Lord of the Dance' by British Folk singer Sydney Carter (1915-2004). Carter openly admitted that the song was non-religious saying "By Lord I mean not only Jesus; in other times and places, other planets, there may be other Lords of the Dance." 'Lord of the Dance - a simple song that has danced its way around the world' by Tony McGregor. Hubpages.com (2009)

doctrines and dubious practices still lay ahead but resigned herself to the fact that this was all part of her *education*.

As she watched the landscape unfold, she became increasingly aware of people walking, riding and driving wagons along the trail that lay parallel to the rail tracks. The snake-like procession of humanity reminded Bunny of the lines of immigrants she'd seen on the news, fleeing natural disasters. What was this mass exodus? she wondered.

"This is the 18:47 at Salt Lake City," the conductor's voice confirmed.

"Ah, I think I do know this one," Bunny said as she begrudgingly headed outside, along the platform and into the now familiar wooden shack. As she entered, she noticed that once again there was a symbol above the door. This time it was a pair of reading glasses. Was this the Spectacle Cult? She was about to find out.

The inside was, again, a rudimentary chapel with a man addressing his congregation; giving a recap on why he had moved them all to Utah. Bunny listened as he presented the curious story of how his friend Joseph had received a visitation from the angel Moroni. The angel had then led Joseph to find golden plates inscribed with a language he couldn't understand; and then how he had also received some *seer stones* on a wire frame which he could place over his eyes.

Aha, the spectacles, Bunny thought.

The fantastical saga went on to explain how the stones could be used to translate the writing on the golden plates, which told the story of how indigenous Americans were the true Church of God. The plates and stones had since disappeared, but Joseph had written the message down in a book before he died. The audience was lapping it up, but Bunny was amazed that anyone could believe what she considered to be farcical rot.

She'd heard enough and turned to leave only to be, once again, blocked. This time by two young men, each smartly dressed in white shirts and black ties, both smiling inanely. One offered her a copy of the *Book of Mormon* by Joseph Smith Jr.[1]

Bunny pointed at the name on the front of the book, then towards the speaker as if to ask, is that him? The two young men shook their heads and whispered,

---

[1] Article: 'Church of Jesus Christ of Latter-day Saints' by J. Gordon Melton. Encyclopaedia Britannica.

"No, that's Brigham Young."

"And you are the Church of Jesus Christ of Latter-day Saints, aren't you?" Bunny asked. They both gave a familiar empty smile back at her and nodded. She declined to take the book choosing rather to swiftly make her way outside and back to the train.

As she approached, she noticed that the conductor, who had previously been present in voice only, was now standing on the platform next to the carriage door.

Bunny wasn't immediately sure, but she thought she recognised him. The closer she got the more certain she became until finally she spotted that the conductor's hat was rimmed in gold. It was him, her travelling confidant, her personal angel, her dream guide. Whoever he was, she was simultaneously relieved and annoyed that he had left her previously with unanswered questions, something she now had even more of. As emotions go in Miss Elstow's psyche, annoyance would always trump relief, so she played it very cool. As she reached the carriage door, she stopped with one foot on the lower step, turned to the conductor and simply said,

"You've got a lot of explaining to do, Mister... erm... whatever your name is."

Chapter 34

THE HERESY EXPRESS PART TWO

"I needed this!" Chris said licking the salty, vinegary grease from the fingers of his right hand. "It's something about that chip-shop smell that is so ..."

"Irresistible?" Ralph suggested. Chris nodded in agreement.

This was more than just a late-night pitstop that Ralph had initiated. Concerned for his friend, he had insisted they spent a few moments taking stock before they dashed off to who knows where. While Ralph collected the order, Chris laid a single damp sock on an adjacent storage heater that was marginally warmer than the square plastic table he sat at in a draughty corner of the eatery. The small television fixed to the wall above their heads was thankfully muted.

Ralph had forged a close friendship with Chris when he helped him come to terms with the sudden departure of his wife. Most people knew Chris as the upbeat, positive and charismatic assistant pastor of C.R.F. but Ralph had seen him when he was at his lowest ebb. Chris had confided that his first wife had *stolen his heart* and that he would never be able to love anyone ever again. There was not a lot that Ralph could say other than 'The right woman would come along when the time was right.' Prior to this evening Ralph had no idea that the *right woman* might indeed be Bunny. He was not unaware that Chris thought a lot of the secretary of All Saints' Church, after all, it was he who was particularly keen to have C.R.F participate in the inter-church planning meeting last month. But Ralph was oblivious that this friendship might have developed into anything more. So, over a late-night feast of battered sausage and chips, Ralph bit the bullet and asked his friend, in the typically ineloquent and painfully circuitous way that most men, even church men, approach conversations about matters of the heart,

"So," he began, having swallowed his first wooden forkful of chips. "You and Bunny...?"

Chris didn't make eye contact, choosing instead to pile several chips into his mouth, preferring to use his fingers. Ralph waited for an answer.

"I hoped so, I *hope* so," Chris answered correcting himself.

"And does she...?" Ralph posed the obvious follow-up question. Chris started to shrug his shoulders but stopped himself and answered,

"Honestly, I don't know. You see tonight I was going to tell her and, well I tried, but then everyone came and…" Chris bit into a sausage and finished his sentence with a large piece of processed meat masticating in his jaws.

"Well, I made a complete pigs-breakfast of trying to tell her."

The owner of the chippie walked over to the door and flipped over the OPEN sign to CLOSED but gestured that they were fine to remain inside until they finished their meal. Ralph responded with a clumsy thumbs-up. He too had bitten into his sausage but chose not to speak until he had swallowed the piece.

"So, you don't know if she…?" This was the third statement that Ralph had made at the table, none of which were full sentences. Chris knew exactly what his friend was asking and shook his head disappointedly. They sat in silence awhile as they both consumed more food. Before Ralph could make a further half-statement, Chris spoke.

"The thing is Ralph," he said holding an over-sized potato chip between his thumb and forefinger.

"The thing is…" he repeated, sitting back in the cheap plastic chair and, to Ralph's relief, not putting the chip in his mouth before he spoke.

"…I can't help but think that it is all my fault. If I hadn't started to say anything to her then she wouldn't have marched off in a …"

The chip began to droop markedly and then cracked in half, dangling precariously above his lap.

"…and wouldn't have gone into St Mary's and…"

Chris paid no attention to the greasy timebomb now hanging from his fingers, his focus entirely taken on disgorging the aching apprehension that had been growing since he found the bloodstains on the floor of the Catholic church.

"…and disappeared."

Chris suddenly leaned forwards, elbow on the table, and pivoted his hand towards his Pastor. The chip began to swing violently with the movement. Chris didn't care, his face was a torment of determination. Ralph on the other hand was becoming fixated on the risk of fried potato landing on his own lap.

"I've already lost one woman I loved," he said, tears forming once more in his eyes, "so I'm not going to…"

Whether he would have finished his sentence had the chip not split in two and fallen, is impossible to know, but Ralph's adept skill in catching the stray fried potato before it hit the table was impressive. Ralph used the symbolism to make his point.

"Chris, my friend. You may have thought you were doing this on your own, but you are not."

He looked at the cold potato now greasing his own hand, before continuing,

"I've got the other end with you, mate. We are in this together." And with that he popped the lukewarm half-chip into his own mouth. Chris smiled in gratitude and consumed the other half.

"In fact, I am not the only one," Ralph continued, having swallowed. "There is the oddest, most incompatible, incongruous, unexpected collection of church leaders scattered across the town, tonight, currently searching for her too. And the one thing that is forcing them to rise above their differences is your..." he paused a moment before stating the obvious, "...your *love* for Bunny."

Chris didn't deny the truth that Ralph had spoken. He did indeed love Bunny and wasn't ashamed to let it be known. He wiped the tears from his eyes with his non-greasy left hand before adding,

"Well, I am not sharing any more chips. They will have to get their own!"

They both laughed as the shopkeeper began upending unused chairs onto the tables, a clear sign that their welcome was soon to run out. They quickly finished their feast as he started sweeping the floor. Nothing that resembled a potato chip remained in the grease-stained polystyrene trays, so, as they hoovered-up the final mouthfuls of fried crumbs that they understatedly knew as *bits*, they turned their attention to where they were going to go next. They had no idea where anyone else was as they had all left so hastily. They hadn't arranged any sort of rendezvous. They'd have to ring around and find out where everyone was.

"Have you got their phone number?" Ralph asked Chris, without indicating which of their fellow church leaders he meant.

To his surprise it wasn't Chris but the shopkeeper, sweeping directly behind Ralph, who answered.

"Of course, we always do," he said. They both looked at him, confused.

"The number that called from Lane House Farm," he explained. "Jeannie told me there was an argument over who placed the order. I figured you'd want to know who rang."

"Yes, we do," Chris replied thrilled with the idea. The shopkeeper returned to his side of the counter and lifted a hardbound manuscript book that he presumably used as their order book. He began shouting over the digits of a mobile number. The two friends fumbled about for a pen before asking him to repeat it. Satisfied that they had transcribed it correctly Chris stood up and made for the door. Ralph raised his hand to stop his hasty getaway. Chris looked up to see Ralph pointing at the solitary sock adorning the storage heater. Chris looked down at his own feet, one in a shoe, one decidedly not.

"Good point," Chris said, as he dressed himself.

Ralph thanked the owner and they left to allow him to sweep under their table and lock up.

"Are you going to ring it, or shall I?" Ralph asked as they returned to the car, but before he got an answer Chris was already punching the digits into his mobile phone. It rang several times before it was answered. Chris's heart stopped as he waited to hear who was on the other end. No one spoke, and an uncomfortable silent stand-off ensued. Ralph froze to the spot half-in and half-out of the car, not wanting to distract him. Chris was desperate to not let the caller hang up, so it was up to him to break the silence which he did with a simple,

"Hello!"

After a short pause a male voice answered, in a strong accent,

"Who is that?"

Once she began to unload her angst, there was no stopping her. Bunny was frustrated, so the conductor sat silently opposite her as she let it all out with the train trundling on. Not only did she have all the unanswered questions following the pro/anti-slavery debate; then more questions on how William Miller could have had such a huge following for such a flawed idea; now she had seen how the seeds of disappointment had grown into serious error. She had symbolically witnessed the birth of some of the world's major sects: the Seventh Day Adventists; The Jehovah's Witnesses; Christian Science; and the Church of Jesus Christ of Latter-Day Saints, or, as most people would know them, the Mormons. All of which had taken advantage of the spiritual frailty of the nation in the aftermath of the Great Disappointment, each one tapping into a vacant spiritual need in the people of the day. Each one purporting to have supplemented the Christian faith. And yet all this had come about so soon, well soon in *her* timeline, after the national revival and miracles of The Great Awakening. It almost looked like a negative spiritual backlash had been released to neutralise all the good that had happened previously. Eventually, her verbal tirade came to an end and they both sat silently, listening to the soothing rail-rhythms.

"And what is your interpretation of these events?" the conductor asked her as the sound changed to a chatter-chatter as the carriage crossed a set of points.

"My interpretation?" Bunny retorted angrily. "I don't have an interpretation; I need *you* to tell me why this is happening; I need *you* to explain to me exactly why..." She couldn't finish the sentence. As her words hung in the air, she realised she couldn't put her finger on exactly what was making her so emotional. She sat back in her seat, crossed her arms, and exhaled with a growl.

"Look, I don't know why you've brought me here, or what all this is about but I've had it with the history lesson," she pleaded, adding defiantly, "My head is full, okay?"

He smiled compassionately at her before replying with a simple play on her words.

"And is your heart full, also?" he asked.

She looked him deep into his eyes wanting to be angry. His eyes were warm and kind, and as she looked into them, she could feel her frustrations partially subside. She had no reason to be angry, her heart had indeed been stirred, she had to admit it. She dropped her gaze and spoke.

"I get it, alright, I get it. I admit something happened when I was with John Wesley at Aldersgate." As she said it, she laughed at the hilarity of nonchalantly admitting to having been at a church service in London with John Wesley. Then at the potential double-entendre of *something happened.*

"No, I don't mean something happened. I mean... I met with God... in a deep, deep, special way at that Quaker service. Something... new happened inside of me," she admitted. "I too felt my heart strangely warmed, just like John said. And from that moment I was... I am... completely sure that my sins have been forgiven."

"And?" the conductor asked.

"And..." she considered before she answered, "then thousands of working men responded likewise with tears in their eyes. I get it." The conductor nodded, but Bunny wasn't looking at him. Her eyes were fixed to the floor.

"And... so, when Mercy Wheeler stood up out of her bed, completely healed..." she looked up at him, "I wasn't surprised. In fact, I expected it."

The conductor smiled, but she hadn't finished.

"And... when I had to go into all of these God-forsaken shacks." The conductor raised an eyebrow at the expression God-forsaken, to which she repeated herself,

"When I had to go into these… places, I instantly knew that something was wrong. It was as if I *just knew* it on the inside."

"Looking further back, what else do you *just know*?" he asked.

Without thinking, she replied with a couple of things that had become so obvious to her over the last three hours or three hundred years whichever way you look at it.

"I just know that every new Christian movement will distance themselves from the previous one. No matter how inspired or worthy or faithful the previous one was, they are destined to be, *the old way*."

It was an unmistakable truth, she wasn't wrong.

"And the daft thing is that in a few years the *next* movement will do exactly the same to them!"

Again, he nodded in agreement. Bunny was on a roll which encouraged her to make another point.

"And then there's the fact that when things do go well, and there is religious…well, success, however you measure it," she was now gesticulating pointedly, "why is it that they always think it's a clear sign that they are in the End Times; Christ is about to return; or the millennial reign has begun?"

"Why indeed?" he responded. After it became clear that Bunny had finished making her points, he added, "So it's not all in your head, is it?"

"No, it isn't all in my head," she confessed. "It's also in my heart. But why…" He raised his hand to his lips prompting her to stop.

"The *why* comes later. Soon, but later," he said cryptically. "For now, go with your heart, or should I say, the Holy Spirit within you." This time it was Bunny who nodded in agreement as the train began to slow down, preparing for its arrival at the next station.

"But!" she said emphatically, causing him to look at her curiously. "But, no more shacks!"

He smiled, looked back at her, and simply said,

"But you have already told me that you will *just know* if there is any heresy at…"

He stood up and announced loudly in his train-conductor voice,

"Topeka, Kansas, all change. This is the 19:00 at Topeka, Kansas." Adding, with a final flourish, "This is the end of the line, the end of the line."

Chapter 35

Sanguine Wood was one of several large copses spread across the Advowson estate and lay approximately halfway between Lane End farmhouse and St. Christopher's Hospice. It was a densely covered ancient wood popular with dog-walkers and those looking for a not-too-energetic countryside ramble. With no specifically designated car parking, Jack had always used a little-known foresters' track whenever he had brought his chestnut Labradors for some exercise and so did the same tonight.

Why exactly Jack had driven to Sanguine Wood and what he hoped to achieve when he got there wasn't that easy to define. Jack desperately wanted to help in the hunt for Ms. Elstow. Rex and Artur were at the station; Thea and Joel at the hospital; Rector Mashman was at Brennan Hall; and Ralph and Chris were busy chasing a pizza delivery. As for himself he had nowhere to be and as he had sat in the car park behind the converted cinema that was now C.R.F. he had done the only thing he felt he could; he began to pray for help to find Bunny. No sooner had he made his supplication than he had received the WhatsApp message saying the bodies were at Sanguine Wood. Jack had taken it as a sign that he should go there but it wasn't until he was well en route that he embraced the stark reality that one of the bodies that had been discovered might be Bunny's.

The torch which Jack kept amongst a few tools in the spare-wheel compartment of his car had rarely ever been used but now, for the second time that evening, he held it in his hand. He locked the car and set off along his familiar, although dark, route. The minimal night-time woodland sounds were soon encroached upon by the disembodied sound of walkie-talkie voices. Jack deviated from his usual route towards the crackle and babble of a site of police interest. As he tramped through the bracken-covered thicket the trees ahead of him appeared to take on an eerie life of their own. In moving his torch away from them the trees would remain illuminated by a vivid and intermittent blue light. He must be getting close to the scene of the action, he thought. He switched off his torch, now able to make out his steps in the flash of azure half-light.

He had no reason to tread silently, he was committing no crime, but instinctively he placed each footstep with a delicacy that belied his size-thirteen shoes. The direction of travel was dictated by the lights and sounds of police activity ahead, tempered by the challenge of, firstly, a moss-covered tree that had fallen some years ago across the seldom-used path and necessitated a detour; then a boggy stream with no obvious means of crossing without getting wet. He briefly considered putting his torch on but decided not. Rather, he inched his way firstly left then right, until he found a collection of three large stones that someone had placed in the water for means of traverse. The stream covered the middle of the three, but this was his only realistic option. He securely stepped onto the first but was unsure as to how slippery the second was going to be. He cautiously tested putting his weight onto the flattened boulder and leaned forward.

"That's far enough."

Body-armour clad police officers appeared from behind two of the larger trees ahead, each holding a handgun in their outstretched hands aimed directly at Jack's face. Suddenly, he was a child holding a football looking at the back of a van as its rear door opens to reveal his friend Mack, hooded and sobbing. He dropped his football, or the torch, an action which made his assailants even more nervous. Amidst much insistent shouting, his mental van door was slammed shut and Jack stood petrified in a dark wood, hands aloft. He then realised that his left foot was in the stream and getting increasingly wetter and colder. Despite his size, his willing compliance meant that within moments he had been handcuffed and was being frog-marched to the detective inspector in charge of the murders in Sanguine Wood. In leading him by the most direct route to their commanding officer, the apprehending constables walked Jack past the main area of activity. Three bright LED lamps on tripods flooded the area with light. A blue and white incident tent was carefully being erected around a scene where four officers in white disposable forensic suits knelt examining what Jack assumed must be bodies. As he got closer it was clear that there were just two. Both were face down and were wearing sleeveless orange and green jackets. There was a lot of blood around, and Jack assumed they had been shot in the head. Even with his County Antrim childhood, this was far more gruesome than anything he had encountered before, and he had no idea how he was going to explain why he was there.

"Who the hell is this and, more importantly, why have you brought him straight through my crime scene, you idiots?"

Thankfully the D.I.'s first question wasn't directed at Jack but the two constables that had apprehended him and who, in their enthusiasm, hadn't considered where they were walking. They quickly explained that he was a suspect they found *snooping* in the woods. The detective, unimpressed, pointed out that *he* was the one who decided if someone was a suspect, not them. Having further verbally belittled them both he then turned his attention to Jack. He looked him up and down and asked succinctly,

"Journalist?"

Jack was expecting the more direct, 'What are you doing?' or 'Who are you?' type of questions, but clearly this particular detective must have had prior experience of story-hungry reporters crashing his crime scenes and consequently that had become his default assumption. Jack took delight in replying with an equally succinct,

"Church minister!"

It is difficult to describe the detective's resultant facial expression. Somewhere between surprise and resignation. If there was a sub-title to his look it would read, 'Of course you are, that is all I need tonight.' Undaunted, the battle-weary policeman enjoyed a spontaneous retort.

"Well, you're too late to give the last rites to these poor fellas, padre."

Jack ignored the fact that he was neither a padre, a priest in the armed services, nor authorised to administer the last rites – a sacrament to be shared with those of the Catholic faith in their dying moments. All Jack heard was that the officer described the unfortunate victims as *fellows*. By inference they were both male – so neither of them was Bunny – and in Jack's opinion both were likely to be the occupants of the first floor of the farmhouse. That fact, at least, was a relief. The officer's demeanour, understandably, changed.

"Well perhaps you would care to explain what exactly you are doing in this wood, so late at night... Mister church minister?" he said with professional sarcasm.

Bunny had grown used to seeing the same tumble-down shack at the end of each of the platforms at which the Heresy Express had stopped. Topeka, Kansas, was the first time it was missing. Bunny breathed a sigh of relief, believing that perhaps her time of having to endure teachers of falsehood had concluded. But why was she in Topeka, Kansas? The place held no significance in her memory. She cautiously lowered herself down the two metal carriage steps onto the platform then immediately paused, unsure as to what to do next. A voice behind her, on the carriage steps, asked that she excuse them as they needed to get out. Bunny unconsciously apologised and stepped to the side to allow the person to alight. To her surprise the person was the first of a steady stream of passengers. Bunny had been the only person aboard the train. Where had all these people come from?

Bunny took a few steps forward then spun around to look at the carriage she had just exited. To her amazement it was no longer red, but green and with the inscription UNION PACIFIC RAILROAD proudly displayed where previously the biblical reference Second Peter chapter Two verse One had been written. She looked to her left, away from the engine, and saw there wasn't just the one carriage but now at least five or six, all disgorging men, women, children, and baggage onto a now bustling railway platform.

"Well, at least I am out of the travelling metaphor and back into reality," she said to herself, then tilted her head, pursed her lips and reprimanded herself with, If you think this is reality you definitely need to wake up!

"Miss, Miss, over here." A voice brought her out of her self-chastisement. A man was beckoning her as he slalomed towards her, effortlessly side-stepping the transit hubbub around them both. She had no idea who he was, but that wasn't the first time she'd had to bluff her way through a one-sided familiar welcome, a skill she considered she had mastered.

"Hello," she said, greeting the ardent stranger who warmly took the hand she had offered. Not a kiss this time, society had clearly moved on from that required etiquette. He gave her a hearty double-handed handshake and introduced himself as Charles Fox Parham, and said he had a buggy waiting to take them to Stone's Folly.

Stone's Folly was a grand mansion, modelled as a fairytale English castle, on the outskirts of Topeka. The outside was a mix of red brick and white stone and the whole structure was overlooked by an observatory toward the front and two domed towers at either side of the rear, each topped with ornate cupolas. Inside she was greeted by a beautifully carved staircase and exquisite panelled woodwork. As he showed her around, Parham explained that they had rented Stone's Folly since last October in order to house the Bethel Bible School, of which he was principal. No two rooms had the same combination of cedar, spotted pine, cherry wood, butterwood, oak and birds-eye maple.[1]

"We invited all ministers and Christians who were willing to forsake all, sell what they had, give it away, and enter the school for study, and prayer, where all of us together might trust God for food, fuel, rent, and clothing," he said.[2]

---

[1] 'The Topeka Outpouring' from M.E. Golder Research Centre extracted from www.ApostolicArchives.com Article number 173161

[2] These words were actually spoken by Parham's wife Sarah according to the book 'Apostolic Faith' (1951)

There were around forty students, including several ministers, occupying the dormitories and it was clear that a place had been prepared for Bunny. Finally, they climbed to the top of one of the vaulted towers. This was known as the Prayer Tower and was the crescendo of his introductory tour. Inside the venerable space some people stood, others were seated and a few lay prostrate. All were praying fervently.

"People pray here in three-hour watches twenty-four hours a day," he explained. This activity was not unfamiliar to her.

"Just like at Herrnhut," she said. He didn't connect with her observation and just looked back at her.

"The Moravians in Herrnhut," she expanded. "They prayed for twenty-four hours a day for a hundred years." Her point fell on deaf ears.

Parham went on to explain that as it was December, students had already just sat their exams in Repentance, Consecration, Sanctification and Healing. Bunny almost laughed at the concept of sitting an exam in Repentance or Healing and couldn't imagine how the Religious Education teacher at her former school might have marked such a paper. Parham was clearly excited about the final exam, looking forward to hearing the students report back on the challenge he had set them prior to his recent trip out of town. Today was feedback day prior to this evening's Watch Night Service that would mark the start of the New Year, 1901.[1]

"What was the question you set them?" Bunny asked.

"To investigate the biblical evidence of the Baptism of the Holy Spirit," he replied. "I have heard so much talk about it whilst on my travels, but I am not wholly convinced there is a basis scripturally."

Baptism of the Holy Spirit was a phrase that Chris had used liberally. He said it was a transformational moment in his Christian life when one gave themself fully and totally to God and, Chris said, the power of the Holy Spirit came powerfully upon them. Bunny wasn't entirely sure what this meant so the idea of sitting-in on a thorough biblical exposition sounded both timely and interesting. Just so long as she didn't have to sit an exam on the subject.

The feedback session was held in the main meeting room in the afternoon. Each student took it in turns to present. Amazingly, every one of

---

[1] The Revival Library, quoting James R Goff, 'Fields White unto Harvest: Charles F Parham and the Missionary Origins of Pentecostalism' 1988

them declared that, in their opinion, there was undeniable proof in Scripture that God, the Holy Spirit, desired to indwell people in an overwhelmingly powerful way... and added that to call this a *baptism* experience was entirely justified. Bunny was, much to her surprise, convinced. The problem she faced was when the students, without exception, said that the demonstration that such a Baptism of the Holy Spirit had occurred was that the recipient would begin to *Speak in Tongues*. To Bunny's disappointment, it became clear that not one of the students, nor Charles Parham, admitted to speaking in tongues. The entire exercise had been purely academic. Whilst she accepted the argument, she felt that without the reality it was just an idea. Yet she was nonetheless open-minded. After all, she had already witnessed miraculous healings, so why not a spot of glossolalia.

Chapter 36

AGNES OZMAN

By the time the evening Watch Night service began the forty students had been joined by over seventy locals and the room was packed. Vibrant worship, prayers, Bible readings and a short sermon from their leader took them to midnight. Shortly afterwards, one of the students, Agnes Ozman, shouted out from her position towards the rear. She was addressing Mr Parham but clearly wanting everyone to hear.

"I want to be filled in the Holy Spirit" she said. "Just like we talked about this afternoon, just like it happened in the New Testament." Charles was momentarily wrong-footed. He wasn't expecting this at all and tried to dissuade her.

"We all agreed it was real," Agnes went on, "but unless we see it actually happening... well, there is no point is there?"

"I agree," Bunny blurted out without thinking. That was precisely the same conclusion that she had come to.

"Unless it actually happens," Bunny added emphatically, "what is the point in talking about it."

It was hard for anyone to disagree. Buoyed by the support, Agnes pushed forward towards the centre of the group and insisted that Charles and others laid hands on her and pray that she would be baptised in the Holy Spirit and speak in tongues. It was clear that saying such a prayer had never been done before. The entire group had no option but to back up their theory with practice. This was going to be a step of faith for everyone in the room, not just Ms Ozman.

Hands were laid and prayers began, softly at first and with a broad generality but slowly those praying began to step out. As the minutes passed the volume, pace, passion and – above all – authority of the prayers increased. One after another, students began to outdo each other in their faith-building, overconfident, declarations.

"Be filled," "Be baptised," "Receive," were spoken over her again and again. Bunny couldn't help but join in. She was on the edge of her seat, albeit she was standing. Suddenly, without anyone's prompting the room grew silent. It was as though the bowls of prayer were now filled; the prayer quota had been met and all eyes were now transfixed on Agnes Ozman. There she stood, eyes tight shut, both her palms outstretched in front of her in a *receiving* stance. This was the moment. The one hundred and twenty or so people in that room held their collective breath.

Agnes opened her mouth and tentatively said, 'Yēsū.' It was a word that meant nothing to her, but, as she stood in the silence it came to her again.

"Yēsū shì zhǔ," she said as people began to beam at each other. "Yēsū shì zhǔ, wǒ shì tā de púrén."

It wasn't completely distinct, but someone said a visible glow could be seen around her head and face; some described it as a halo, others as tongues of fire.[1] What was unmistakable was that Agnes was now speaking in what appeared to be Chinese. But that wasn't all. When she was asked how she felt, she could no longer speak in English. She motioned for someone to bring her paper and a pencil and to everyone's absolute astonishment she began writing in Chinese script. This was more than speaking in tongues, this was *writing in tongues!*[2]

Spontaneously, someone started to sing the hymn, 'Jesus Lover of my Soul,' but, to everyone's amazement, it was being sung in at least six different languages each part in angelic harmony. Parham himself was enraptured with the Spiritual outpouring around him. He leapt to his feet and prayed vehemently,

"Lord, I am willing to suffer all the persecutions, hardships, trials, slander, scandal that it will entail if You will just give me this blessing." Then he remarked that he felt a slight twist in his throat, a glory fell over him and he began to worship God in Swedish.[3] A church bell rang out a single chime indicating that it was now well past midnight. Regardless of the time, no one wanted to leave. Students started bringing their bedding down from the dormitories into the meeting room and declared they were going to stay there until they received the same infilling.

"Pentecost! Pentecost!"

---

[1] 'Tongues of Fire' were visible upon the apostles on the day of Pentecost when they too began to speak in tongues., according to Acts chapter 2 verse 3.

[2] Examples of Agnes Ozman's Chinese writing are readily viewable online.

[3] This spontaneous multi-lingual singing and Parham's first speaking in tongues happened three days later at Topeka Free Methodist Church where he was scheduled to preach and during which dozens were baptised in the Holy Spirit. 'The Latter Rain' from M.E. Golder Research Centre extracted from www.ApostolicArchives.com Article number 173163

Bunny's attention was distracted by a voice coming from the hallway outside the meeting room. She looked around but no one appeared to hear it, being as they were caught up in worship. The voice repeated so she stepped into the vestibule, then toward the open front door and finally outside into daylight where a young newspaper vendor stood.

"Read all about the Pentecost," he chimed as he gave Bunny a copy of the *Topeka Capital* newspaper, once again not waiting for payment. The date on the masthead stated it was 3rd January 1901. Already days had passed in the blink of an eye. The events she had witnessed at Bethel Bible School were headline news. She read that around half the student body were now 'Revelling in the Baptism of the Holy Spirit, speaking in tongues, praying, trembling, laughing and singing.' She also read that the Prayer Tower was miraculously illuminated so that 'No gas lamps needed to be lit.' The newspaper had sent language experts to investigate, and government officials had also been consulted. All testified that people were indeed speaking in other earthly languages and, what was more amazing, with the proper intonation and accent. Poor Agnes Ozman, Bunny read, after three days was still unable to speak anything other than Chinese.

Her reading was interrupted by the intrusion of a besuited man who demanded to speak to Parham immediately. The visitor did not look happy. Charles soon arrived and as Bunny eavesdropped upon their heated exchange, she discovered that the landlord had come to evict Parham. He had sold Stone's Folly to someone who was going to turn it into a *pleasure resort*. Bunny's first reaction was that a pleasure resort was somewhat akin to Centre Parcs or Alton Towers but soon the realisation hit her that it was more likely to involve dancing girls and illicit alcohol. Sadly, Parham had no alternative but to comply. However, he did leave the landlord with a prophetic warning:

"If the new owners use the building, which God has honoured with His presence, for secular reasons, it will be destroyed by fire."

Bunny had never heard such a thing. This was like an Old Testament prophesy of doom and was fascinated to see if it was going to be fulfilled.[1]

"Looks like we are moving on," Charles said to Bunny as he led her outside to a waiting horse-drawn wagon.

---

[1] The initial lease of Stone's Folly ended in July 1901 by which point it had been sold to bootlegger Harry Croft. Parham's prophetic warning came true on 6th Dec 1901 when the building mysteriously burned to the ground. The site is now a Catholic church. See Kansas Historical Society extracted from www.kansasmemory.org article number 216406.

"So, soon?" she protested. "Where are we going?"

"I think it is time to go to Houston, Texas," he replied, then began to load the waiting wagon. Bunny offered to assist him but within moments the whole area was full of willing helpers, so she stood by and watched. Once the wagon was laden with luggage, supplies and small pieces of furniture it was time for the family to board. Firstly, Parham's wife Sarah took her seat; then the children with their governess, an African American woman named Lucy; then Bunny; and finally, Parham himself who said his emotional goodbyes to all those who had gathered for the departure. It was such a tight fit in that over-filled wagon that as they click-clacked away down the drive, the position Bunny had to perch in meant she only had a rearward view. She had to turn her head around in order to speak to Parham.

"Why Houston?" she asked.

"I have preached there many times. In fact that is where we met Lucy here, isn't it?" he said gesturing at the governess who nodded politely.[1]

"Lucy was the pastor at a small black church there."

The phrase *black church* didn't sit right with Bunny. Immediately she remembered the divisive trauma she had witnessed as the Church split between pro- and anti- slavery doctrines. Naïvely she had hoped that racial division had now long-since subsided.

"Black church?" she responded by reflex.

"Yes," he replied, adding matter-of-factly, "There are black churches and there are white churches."

Bunny looked at Lucy who was pointedly not allowing her gaze to be engaged with the developing conversation. They had a long drive ahead of them, so Bunny decided that, despite her reservations, it was perhaps best to let the subject lie for now. Besides, it was also rather uncomfortable trying to hold a conversation over her shoulder on a moving vehicle. She turned rearwards again and watched as Stone's Folly grew smaller and smaller as they slowly made their way to Texas.

She had witnessed something special happen in that building. She had many remarkable encounters over the last...however long it was, but something about Agnes Ozman's determined faith, and the spontaneity shown by all was staying with Bunny. Perhaps she found this flavour of vibrant energetic

---

[1] Lucy F. Farrow was indeed governess to the Parham children although not in the time period depicted here.

316

Christianity so unfamiliar that her natural curiosity was heightened. Perhaps she wanted to discover what it was about the Pentecostal charismatic movement that caused it to grow exponentially when all other denominations, her own included, were in mortal decline. But probably it was because this was the type of church that Chris belonged to and if she was ever going to agree to be with him, if she ever woke up from this unrelenting dream, she was no doubt going to have to embrace the fire and passion of this alien church-world.

As she looked in the distance to the mock castle they had recently left, she saw a column of smoke begin to rise above it and then, within moments, the unmistakable flash of flames licking from the now remote windows. Don't mess with the Prophet of God, she thought as the flames lit the distant sky.

Chapter 37

WILLIAM SEYMOUR

"You will have to look inside, Cecil, I can't do it," the Rector said as he sat on the top of The Woodshed steps. "I am afraid of what I might find."

"Why? What do you think is in there?" the hospice manager replied.

"Not what," Mashman said exhaling, "but whom?"

Cecil looked at the car, then back at the elderly churchman. It was clear that of the two of them he was the only one going to approach the car that was, after all, on his property and had damaged his flowerpot. From a few paces away, he shone his torch through the rear window to satisfy himself no one was sitting in any of the seats.

What did he mean, whom? Cecil thought as he began his approach.

Two steps further and he could see through the glass that the large estate-car boot was empty, completely empty. The passenger side was pressed hard into foliage and he could see that several branches had been broken by the vehicle's forced intrusion. He moved slowly along the driver's side and reached forward to the handle of the rear door.

Who would be in an abandoned car at night? he pondered.

He lifted it up to see if it was locked. It opened with a solid clunk. He looked back at the Rector who was nervously monitoring his progress.

Unless they were tied up or... Cecil considered.

One more step forward and he would be able to tentatively shine his torch across the rear seats.

...or dead! he concluded.

As the manager of a hospice, death was a regular occurrence and the sight of the motionless body of the recently departed didn't concern him. What he didn't want to see was a body in any state of trauma. All of his deceased were neatly prepared ready for their loved-ones to grieve over, usually with a single flower neatly positioned on the pillow next to their peaceful faces, now in eternal sleep. He held his breath and looked inside. There was no one lying across the back seat and, as far as he could see, nor in the front. He allowed himself a brief exhalation of relief.

"There is no one inside, Rector," he shouted over to Mashman, much to their mutual relief.

"Wait a minute though," Cecil added. "There *is* something inside."

318

He placed his torch on the rear seat and forced himself through the narrowest of door openings, and with numerous groans and puffs spent the best part of a minute extracting two finds: one from the nearest rear footwell which had caught his eye from outside; the other, he discovered, wedged into the space where the seat-belt clips into the rear seat. Something had been caught by the buckle, a discovery which was met with a distinctive,

"Well, I never!"

"What have you found?" the Rector asked, now having walked over to the rear of the stranded Mondeo. The hospice manager de-corked himself from the vehicle and presented the elderly cleric with a black and yellow scarf. Mashman held it. It was a high-quality piece of fabric. Black silk with what looked like yellow-gold lettering running down the length in four stripes. Cecil shone his torch while the Anglican tried to read the lettering. It was impossible, they were in Cyrillic script with characters he didn't recognise.

"And then there was *this* stuck in the rear seat," Cecil declared as he held up a lady's wristwatch, gold-framed with a square digital dial.

"Goodly heavens above!" Mashman exclaimed. "That's Miss Elstow's watch."

The Apostolic Faith Bible School in Houston was based in a large but more modestly styled building. This was hardly surprising as Stone's Folly was perhaps the most overly ornate building Bunny had ever seen. The sound of people worshipping, praying and, most markedly, singing in tongues was evident even through the permanently open windows that Bunny found herself outside.

According to her watch it was 19:05. Parham was in full flow inside but on the outside two people were standing next to the white-painted wooden frame of the closed mosquito screen. Bunny could see that one was Lucy, the Parham's governess, but she was with a man, also African American, who was intently peering inside. As she approached them Bunny realised that Lucy too was fully engaged in the worship and she too was singing in tongues.[1] *Why are they outside?* she wondered.

"Don't you want to go inside?" she asked innocently. Neither of them had seen Bunny approaching and jumped suddenly, as if to attention.

---

[1] An accomplished preacher Lucy Farrow is popularly considered to be the first African American to speak in tongues.

"No, Miss," Lucy replied timidly.

"But I heard you singing in tongues, surely you would want to be in the...." Bunny's sentence ended prematurely as the man interrupted her.

"It doesn't matter if we want to, we cannot, Mistress," he said firmly.

"Why ever not?" Bunny asked. Lucy looked at her friend to see if he was going to give Bunny an answer. Clearly not, as he had already turned back to look into the room. It fell on her to explain.

"It is because we are black, Miss," she said. "We are allowed to listen to the preaching, but only through the windows."

As she said these words, Bunny suddenly realised that everyone she had met at Stone's Folly, Topeka – all the students, all those who had been so gloriously Baptised in the Holy Spirit – were white. She wanted to say, 'But!' to register her protest, to emphasise the injustice, to simply say that it was wrong, but she knew in her heart that such a remonstration was going to be fruitless.

"This is my friend William Seymour," Lucy said introducing the man. As he turned to face Bunny, she was momentarily shocked when noticing that one of his eyes didn't move. It was glass. He nodded graciously at Bunny but didn't offer her a handshake; neither did she, unsure of the prevailing racial etiquette.

"I would not be here were it not for the evident and glorious manifestation of the Spirit of God," he emphasised. In the absence of anything else to say, Bunny released the pent-up 'But!' that she had been storing up inside. Slightly taken aback, Seymour thought for a moment then responded,

"But wherever God can get a people that will come together in one accord and one mind then the Baptism of the Holy Ghost will fall like as at Cornelius' house."[1]

The reference to Cornelius' House from the book of Acts[2] was powerful. This was the time God declared that we should not call unclean anything that He had already cleansed. In the Bible this was about the integration of Jew and Gentile. By making this reference Seymour was cleverly emphasising the need to integrate black and white believers and in so doing then the *tongues of fire* revolution might really take light.

"I agree," Bunny declared boldly, much to Seymour's delight. He responded by saying that having listened and learned through this window, he

---

[1] Words attributed to William J Seymour, extracted from www.christianquotes.info

[2] The story of the Apostle Peter's visit to Cornelius' House is written in Acts chapter 10

thought it was now the right time to put this teaching into practice. He explained that he had received an invitation to become the pastor of Santa Fe Street Holiness Mission in Los Angeles, and if he went he could preach about racial integration *and* the Baptism of the Holy Spirit. But, he conceded, he could not afford the rail fare to Los Angeles. Bunny wanted to help him. She patted her pockets, but they were empty. She had zero reserves of dream currency. Every purchase she had needed previously had just magically happened. Now, for the first time, she wanted to give but had no means to do so. Shortly afterwards Parham appeared in the open window. In what was clearly a pause between Bible-study sessions, he wanted to speak to Lucy regarding the children, but before he could speak Bunny jumped in.

"Charles, this is William Seymour."

"Yes, I know," Parham answered. "We have spoken at length over recent weeks." Bunny was surprised that this William had spent so long faithfully listening and learning.

"And despite only being able to listen through the window," she continued, "he has been really inspired by your teaching." Parham smiled.

"The anointing of the Holy Spirit is given to illuminate His word. To open the Scriptures, and to place the spiritual man in direct communication with the mind of God," Parham pronounced with pride.[1] Bunny continued,

"And now, he is ready to leave for Los Angeles."

"Is that true, William?" Parham asked. Seymour nodded in agreement. Bunny pounced.

"But he needs the rail fare... you need to give him the fare... for the rail," she said. As with many of her interjections she had not thought through the potential outcome and was now in a position where she, and probably Seymour, were both likely to be humiliated. To her delight Parham reached into his hip pocket, opened his wallet, and passed several notes to Seymour.

It was a moment that would have deserved a well-wishing hug, but Charles' racial intransigence prevented him from showing William any sense of affection. Having then concluded his short domestic exchange with Lucy, Parham returned inside.

"Thank you, Miss," Mr. Seymour said sincerely. "Thank you, thank you, thank you."

---

[1] 'The sermons of Charles Parham' by Charles F Parham Chapter 2

"You are welcome," she replied. 'I hope you'll see tongues of fire in Los Angeles."

"Why don't you come and see the whole city set aflame," he enticed. Who was she to refuse?

"Thank you for rescuing me," Joel whispered to Thea as they headed into the hospital car park.

"Rescuing you?" Thea repeated. "From whom?"

"From that…" he had intended saying from the journalist but stopped himself and finished the sentence "… well, from myself, really."

"Why, what have you done?" Thea's question was understandable if a little pointed. Joel confessed.

"Was there a journalist there? Yes, there was. And do you know, someone had given him a tip-off to be here at 8:30 saying that Velia was going to be injured," he said changing the subject. "And isn't that curious. How can anyone know that someone is going to have an accident…"

"Unless they are the one giving them it!" Thea finished. "Yes, I agree that is strange. Did he say who gave him the tip-off?"

Joel shook his head as he paid his parking fee on the machines that she had shown Chris, Artur and Ralph how to use to find the hospice ambulance. It felt like a place of minor victory for her, a welcome alternative to the feeling of failure she had following her fruitless conversation in the emergency ward.

They stepped outside to see the rain had finally stopped. It made the walk back to Joel's car more pleasant than the dash that Thea had made when she jumped out of Jack's earlier.

"That doesn't explain why I was saving you from yourself," she said as they reached the car.

"Aaaherm… surry!"

The indistinct noise that Joel made reminded Thea of the sound a child would make when caught with their hand in a tin of Quality Street, having already been told to keep the lid on it. Involuntary confession, she decided.

Joel pressed the central locking and they both climbed in and shut the doors. Joel didn't start the engine. Using the headrest for support he looked vacantly at the ceiling.

"I think… I mean, I know… I said too much to him."

"The reporter?" Thea asked. Whyens nodded.

322

"But we all agreed to not say anything to anyone!" Thea was annoyed, she had been the one to suggest they kept quiet about Bunny's disappearance, and now one of her fellow ministers had broken that pact in less than an hour.

"I know, I know, it's a failing I have." Joel was sincerely sorry. "I haven't been able to tell anyone this before Thea, but..." She wasn't expecting a late-night counselling session, but emotions were running high this night.

"... I know I come across all confident, but it is just that I want to be in the centre of what is happening. I don't want to miss anything, and ... you know... I just let it slip out."

Joel looked over at Thea in the passenger seat. She parked her irritation and smiled sympathetically back at him. Then, without warning, Joel Whyens said something that completely floored Thea,

"Are you the right person for me to ask? Yes, you are. Ms. Howlsy, I must ask then. Ms. Howlsy, will you please forgive me for letting you, and the group, down."

Thea was taken aback. Here was a seasoned Methodist minister asking for forgiveness from a Baptist minister whom she barely knew. Did she have the right to forgive him? What were the implications of this act? Could she forgive him on behalf of the whole the group? All these thoughts rushed into her mind. Joel just looked at her expectantly, hopefully, vulnerably.

"Don't worry about it..." she said, pulling her seatbelt strap across her body, hoping to change the subject.

Whyens reached over and gently took her wrist, preventing her from fastening her seatbelt.

"No, Thea," he interrupted. "I need you to forgive me. I have wronged you all."

Slightly shocked, Thea let go of the buckle which slid slowly back across her chest, clanked against the glass of the passenger window, and re-seated itself into the inertia reel. They sat in silence for at least a minute.

"I can think of all the reasons why I shouldn't," she began. As she did, Joel's face dropped markedly.

"No, not because it was such a bad... sin," she recovered. "It's just because you're Methodist and I'm Baptist. So, what right do I have to forgive you?"

Joel knew his Bible and rather than answer her question, simply shared Ephesians chapter four verse thirty-two,

"Be compassionate to one another, forgiving each other, just as Christ God forgave you."

"All right then, Joel. I forgive you!" she said retaking the seat-belt buckle and emphatically fixing it in place.

He thanked her, fixed his own safety belt and started the engine. The car headlights suddenly illuminated the side of the car parked directly opposite.

"Wait a minute, Joel," Thea reached for her smart phone. She opened WhatsApp and scrolled back through the last couple of posts to find the one she needed.

"Look for a dark blue/black estate car and small red sports car," she read Chris's message out loud, but Joel had no idea why until she pointed through the front windscreen at the car now clearly identified by their headlights. It was a deep red, Mazda MX5. And what was more, the sides were splattered with mud. This city roadster had either been off-road or at least in a farmyard recently. Joel opened his door and began to get out.

"What are you going to do?" Thea asked with a whisper. Joel leaned back into the car and whispered back at his new Baptist confidante, "What am I doing? I'm going to redeem myself!"

Thea watched as he walked over to the low sports car which had its canvas soft-top roof up but both side windows open. It only took a few steps for him to be looking through the open driver-side window. He then looked over both shoulders, checked above for security cameras, then much to Thea's shock, whilst standing with his back to the car, reached one arm inside the cockpit and pulled something out from on top of the dashboard. Was it a phone? He fiddled with it briefly then put it back on the dashboard, then hurried back to his car. Before getting back inside Joel collected something from under a coat on the back seat. Once safely back in the driver's seat Thea saw he now had a laptop computer and, before she could say anything, had powered it up.

"Should I ask?" she enquired.

"I need my laptop..." he laboured, waiting for it to finish its booting sequence, "so that I can read... this."

He opened his left hand to show her a Micro SD card, the sort of memory card she was familiar with inside her camera. He spun the card around in his fingers and slid it carefully into the slot on the side of his laptop, firmly pushing it into place with his thumbnail.

"Did you just nick that from that car?" she scolded.

"No ... not at all," he said with mock innocence. "I borrowed it from out of that car's dashcam. And will put it back just as soon as we... ah, there it is."

Joel slid the laptop screen into the centre of the car. File manager showed a list of around twenty files, each filename being the date and time of a short recording. All were dated today but the times were varied as it only recorded when the vehicle was moving, and hence appeared in consecutive blocks. Joel clicked on the most recent file timed at 21:50. They both watched the red bonnet of the car drive the last few hundred yards into the hospital car park into the very slot it was now parked in. Back at the menu they watched the rest of the files that came immediately before, which showed the car had come from facing a blue garage door below an apartment block in the town centre – nothing suspicious at all. The next block of timestamps were all around eight o'clock that evening and they decided to watch them in the proper sequence rather than backwards. Again, the journey began from the same blue garage door, only this time the occasional flick of wipers showed that it was raining. As they watched the red bonnet snake its way through traffic lights and junctions it became apparent that the exact same route was being followed. Joel fast-forwarded it several minutes until it pulled into the hospital car park. But this time it didn't stop, but made its way up the ramp at the rear of the car park which led to Accident & Emergency drop-off. Once stationary it was clear from the rocking side-to-side that someone was getting out. Thankfully, the driver had left the ignition on and the recording continued. Soon a figure appeared pushing someone in a wheelchair away from the vehicle, then they suddenly stopped as if remembering something. He left the wheelchair and came back to the car before the recording terminated.

"The driver must have remembered they'd left their keys in the ignition," Joel explained.

"Can you just play that last bit again?" Thea asked. Joel obliged and watched as Thea peered at the 12" screen.

"Stop it! Freeze it there!" she said and again Joel did exactly as he was instructed. Thea looked closely at the figure returning to retrieve their keys before declaring with some satisfaction,

"I know who that is."

There was no doubt in her mind, it was Velia Advowson's boyfriend, whom she had been talking to barely half-an-hour ago. Whilst this was interesting, they already knew that the heiress had been admitted to hospital earlier that evening. Back on file manager there was a third batch of recordings. As they watched, they followed the route down the elegant drive of Brennan Hall, into town and then to the blue garage door that they will depart from later. The next set of recordings – the last few files to view – was the journey to Brennan Hall early that afternoon. They took these in reverse presuming nothing more than a simple journey from blue door to the Hall. However, it became quickly apparent that the red sports car, and Velia's boyfriend, had spent the afternoon somewhere decidedly more rural. Joel clicked on the final, earliest file only to see the vehicle reversing then departing along the rough, muddy terrain of Lane End farmhouse.

"Velia's boyfriend was at the farmhouse today," Joel said. "Now that is suspicious... isn't it?" Thea nodded thoughtfully.

"Quick, turn off your lights," she said, prompting Joel to ask her why.

"We are going to wait for him to come out," she explained. "Then we are going to follow him, and he is going to lead us straight to Bunny."

Joel pressed the ignition button under his steering wheel. The lights went out, the car fell silent. They were now on stake-out.

Chapter 38

William Seymour's first sermon in Los Angeles had been electrifying. He would most definitely be on Bunny's top ten list, but she was too captivated to even consider rankings. He had ingeniously woven themes of racial integration into a powerful holiness message to an enraptured audience in the Mission Hall on Santa Fe Street. However, when he seamlessly moved his topic into the Baptism of the Holy Spirit and the importance of speaking in tongues the audience became split. The majority responded positively, but a minority clearly baulked at this teaching. Sadly, the minority included Julia Hutchens, the leader of the mission and the person who had extended the invitation for William to move to Los Angeles. That is why, after just one sermon, William Seymour found himself outside the padlocked door of the chapel reading a note saying his services were no longer required.[1]

As they both stood there in the warm Californian afternoon sunshine, Bunny could see he was shocked. It wasn't the most auspicious of starts to a ministerial career, but she had no idea what she could say to console him. Multiple options spun around her mind but before her mental fruit-machine had rung up triple cherries she was spared the need to embarrass herself.

"Don't worry, you can preach in our house," an unfamiliar voice broke the heaviness. Richard and Ruth Asberry were a young couple who had been in the audience to hear Seymour's first sermon and were convinced that what he was saying was right. Modestly affluent for the area, their home on North Bonnie Brae Street had a large front verandah, ideal they said, to preach to people gathered on their front lawn. William wasn't entirely convinced but, short of options, agreed to take a look. The house was only a few streets away and by the time they arrived a crowd had already begun to gather.

William, Bunny, the Asberrys and a few others climbed the steps onto the front porch. As she looked out over the assembled, expectant faces, Bunny couldn't help but recall the similar view from Hanham Mount in Bristol where she had first witnessed John Wesley's dramatic preaching. That sermon had been unashamedly about salvation from a fiery hell, but William Seymour was

---

[1] Despite initially rejecting Seymour's teachings, Julia Hutchins later repented and joined the new movement, and eventually received the Baptism of the Holy Spirit herself.

going one step further. Having been locked out due to teaching on the Baptism of the Holy Spirit, he felt that had given him license to speak on that very subject with a fiery passion. It wasn't long before people had responded and were soon speaking in tongues, singing and dancing. The intoxication of the Holy Spirit was so infectious that Bunny couldn't help herself and soon began to join in the dancing. This was perhaps the first time she had danced *in church* if a verandah can be considered as church. She rarely, if ever, danced. Early clumsy attempts at school discos had morphed into a collection of awkward movements that she would self-consciously deploy when required to do so at wedding parties and other times she was required to *join in*. This time the desire to move her body was entirely voluntary and, to her great surprise, came from within. Several joy-filled worshippers clambered onto the porch and soon everyone was bouncing up and down.

Suddenly the ground began to shake. Bunny froze. She had already encountered one earthquake, one seismic shift that had split the Church. Was it happening again? The ground was definitely moving but not back-and-forth but slowly and steadily sliding sideways. Then with an almighty crash, the porch collapsed from under their feet. Splintering wood, dust and several hanging plants landed amongst those who had been on the make-shift stage and who now were desperately clinging on to whatever they could in an attempt to steady themselves. Thankfully, no one was injured.[1]

Then it began. Laughing! Everyone was laughing, Bunny included. Seymour eventually composed himself, stood to his feet and asked,

"Does anyone know of anywhere we could meet?" but this only served to increase the ironic hilarity. Eventually the mirth subsided and as it did a solitary hand was raised. A voice was heard to say she knew of a disused Methodist chapel nearby. But, she emphasised, it was quite tumble-down.

When Seymour and the others laid eyes on the former chapel at 312 Azusa Street, they agreed that it certainly was in need of repair. Its ecclesiastical heritage was clear from the weathered, white-washed clapboards and single Gothic style window over the entrance. But for some time, it had been used as a warehouse and livery stable, and consequently had been left infested with the sights, sounds and smells that didn't lend itself to being used for worship.

"This is the place!" Seymour announced.

---

[1] The collapse of the Asberry's porch happened five weeks after William Seymour began using it as a make-shift platform.

Cecil, the manager of St. Christopher's Hospice had made both Rev. Mashman and himself mugs of hot cocoa to warm themselves. When Cecil had showed him Bunny's wristwatch, the Rector became so queasy he had to steady himself on the wooden verandah rail at the front of The Woodshed. Cecil hurried him inside the hospice, and not wanting to heighten his anguish, suggested they had both grown chilly rummaging outside on such a cold autumnal night. The warmth of the hospice lobby did indeed provide a much welcome respite for the two elderly gentlemen. Having finished his drink and regained his composure the Rector knew he must let his fellow churchmen know what had happened. The concept of posting on WhatsApp was far beyond his ability to comprehend. The last time he had anything to report, he simply rang Rex Fogge so that was going to be the logical thing to do this time.

"Hallo, is that you Reverend Fogge?" Mashman spoke loudly at his mobile phone.

"Please, Rector, call me Rex," he replied.

"All right then Rex. Well, I have to tell you that I have found something." And with that introduction the Rector unloaded onto Rex, firstly the discovery of the abandoned Mondeo in the hospice grounds and the items they had found inside. When the cleric said they had found Bunny's watch, Rex could tell he was quite distressed. The fact was even more obvious to Cecil who could see tears welling up in the Reverend's eyes. Cecil laid a comforting hand upon Mashman's shoulder, just as he had reciprocated more than once before.

"Listen, Reverend, my friend, Artur and I are finished here at the railway station." Rex looked over to the young Austrian for confirmation. Artur nodded in agreement. "So why don't we come over to join you now and we can decide what to do next. Would that help, Sir?"

Mashman agreed and said he would wait at the hospice until they arrived.

Bunny had lost track of how many cathedrals, churches, chapels and meeting places she had visited in the last… few hours. But it was evident that out of all of them 312 Azusa Street was by far the most basic. The pulpit was made from two large wooden crates nailed together. The benches, laid out in a rectangle, were simply planks resting on empty nail kegs. The oppressive heat wasn't helped by the low roof. Little attempt had been made on decoration save for the lettering of *Apostolic Faith Mission* inscribed upon the wall in black paint. The floor was bare and whatever purported to have been a thorough clean had failed to eradicate the seemingly perpetual haze of flies that hovered in the centre of the room.[1] It didn't seem to matter. Over three hundred people were crammed within, others gathered peacefully outside for a chance to take someone's place should they leave. The racial mix was notable. Bunny had been shocked by Parham's segregationist leanings, but Seymour was vehemently pro-integration and it showed. A wide diversity of people filled those benches. Men, women and children; black, white, Hispanic and Asian; rich and poor; illiterate and educated. All were present and welcome.[2]

The atmosphere was electric. Bunny closed her eyes to take it in but as she did a faint waft of antiseptic filled her nostrils. It reminded her of being in a hospital. Strange, she thought, one thing I wouldn't have used to describe this place would have been clinically clean. She allowed her mind to wander into medical reminiscences until she was suddenly startled by the loud two-tone siren of a passing ambulance. She opened her eyes and, unsurprisingly, there was no ambulance to be seen.

It was a bit of a squeeze on the front bench to the left of the pulpit, where Bunny found herself seated. The constricted elbow-space was relieved only when those next to her rose to their feet, an action which frequently happened. To her surprise, one of those whom she was in hip-to-hip contact with came from England and, judging by the accent, Alex was a Northerner.

To her right she could see that the portly frame of William Seymour was virtually obscured by the makeshift pulpit, his balding yet bearded black head almost completely inside the top-most pulpit-crate as he leant forward in prayer.

Next to him sat the Parham's governess, Lucy Farrow, and to Bunny's delight it was she who first stood to speak. The room fell to a hush and as they listened Lucy explained that she was sorry she hadn't been able to arrive in time for the grand opening earlier that week, but when she received Pastor Seymour's invitation to come and help she left as soon as she could. She then introduced Mr. Seymour as their *leader*. Seymour thanked her but reacted to the term of her introduction.

---

[1] 'The Azusa Street Revival.' from M.E. Golder Research Centre extracted from www.ApostolicArchives.com Article number 173190

[2] 'The Black Roots and White Racism of Early Pentecostalism in the USA.' By Iain MacRobert. Macmillan Press. (1988).

"All who are in touch with God realise as soon as they enter that the Holy Ghost is the leader," he corrected then reached for the newspaper he had folded on the floor next to him.

"I have in my hand a copy of the *Los Angeles Daily Times* dated today, April 18th," he said waiving the broadsheet dramatically. Bunny glanced at her watch which flashed 19:06. Seymour then read the headline. 'Weird Babel of Tongues,' he said questioningly. The gathered crowd murmured, clearly unsure if they wanted to be called *weird*. Seymour had his punchline ready. He raised a hand to quieten the congregation then read the subheading with punctuated emphasis,

"New Sect of Fanatics is Breaking Loose!"[1] The whole group cheered. Apparently, *fanatic* must be better than *weird*, Bunny concluded. Seymour went on to read snippets from the newspaper article, which was not in any way flattering. This prompted him to announce that he intended to write their own newspaper and that he would call it: *The Apostolic Faith.* [2]

The level of expectation in the room was high. For every negative comment that Seymour read from the LA Times, he would then produce a hand-written letter which accentuated the alternative positive.

"A visiting Baptist minister sent me the following," he announced, removing a missive from its envelope and delivering its contents.

"The Holy Spirit fell upon me and, as it seemed, lifted me up, for I was in the air in an instant, shouting 'Praise God,' and instantly I began to speak in another language. I could not have been more surprised if at the same moment someone had handed me a million dollars."[3]

Once again, the crowd began to cheer, and those cheers soon turned into heavenward praises. The whole meeting continued in this ad hoc spontaneous way. There was no order of service, no address, no collection, there were no musicians, no choir and yet the singing was so powerful some even claimed they could hear angels. As Bunny basked in the effervescent worship, people flocked in and out of what felt like a non-stop worship service. Some arrived as sceptics

---

[1] Copies of the front cover of the Los Angeles Daily Times for 18th April 1906 are readily available online.

[2] The Apostolic Faith was first published in September 1906 and at its height had a circulation of 50,000. It is believed by many that it was disputes over the ownership of this mailing list alone that ushered the demise of the Azusa Street revival.

[3] 'William J. Seymour and the Azusa Street Revival' by Gary B. McGee extracted from Enrichment Journal article 199904.

and left singing, dancing and speaking in tongues. Bunny couldn't begin to calculate how many people were passing through that small inornate chapel, but it was a continual stream.[1] Suddenly she heard a church bell ring out a single chime. Funny, she thought, I know this isn't a church building, there is no steeple and no bell. What just tolled? What's more, she was sure she had heard that single church bell tolling before – several times in fact, although she wasn't sure where or when.

"Brothers and sisters," Seymour bellowed, hoping to be able to speak to the assembly. Most paid attention to him, but not all.

"Many come here in order to catch the fire and then take it home," he continued, "and today we are sending home..." he consulted a small piece of paper that had up until that point been folded into his Bible, "Jonathan Paul from Germany and... Alexander Boddy from Sunderland, England."[2] She had been correct. The Alex she had been conjoined to on that front bench was indeed from the North of England, and according to his introduction was ready to take the Azusa Street awakening back to England. It gave Bunny a warm feeling of completeness that having followed what was the *current* move of God from Germany through Switzerland and Scotland into England that here it was on its way back to England, and for that matter Germany too.

Without specific invitation, two groups quickly formed around the international visitors once they had responded to William's bidding to come forward. Hands were laid upon and prayers said for the safe passage and faithful ignition of the Holy Spirit's fire in each of their nations. Prayers for these two Pentecostal missionaries morphed seamlessly into prayers for the American nation and before long a cry could be heard to,

"Shake the nation out if its complacency!"

No sooner had that heartfelt decree been made, than the building literally began to shake. This was not the first earthquake Bunny had witnessed first-hand, but this was no metaphor. This was the real deal. The distinctive side-to-side swaying of the earth felt as though they were back onboard ship crossing the Atlantic and it initiated an immediate yet orderly evacuation of the building.

---

[1] At the height of the awakening, it was said that a thousand people visited the Azusa Street chapel every day.

[2] Alexander Boddy is credited with taking the Pentecostal revival to England.

The fluid ground movement was very strong but insufficient to cause any serious structural damage and within a few minutes it had subsided.

The requisite amount of time that one should wait in the street before returning inside after a 'quake isn't that easy to define. It was in some way preferable to be outside rather than in the rather restricted confines of the chapel, but the ardent worship and prayer had briefly been replaced by the speculative chit-chat of a slightly dazed crowd milling around post-tremor. It wasn't long before news reached them that the epicentre had been some three hundred and fifty miles away in central San Francisco and that, unlike Los Angeles, there had been structural damage, fires and significant loss of life.[1]

On hearing the sobering news several worshipers immediately began to make plans to go north and offer whatever help they could. This was the kind of Christianity that Bunny was more at home with, and she too was quick to volunteer. She hadn't realised it but ever since this time-accelerated journey began all she had witnessed were debates on doctrinal differences, passionate preaching and, she had to admit it, some inspired intimate times of personal encounter with her maker. What she hadn't seen was any help for the poor, the needy, or the homeless. Help for those whom the Church, she believed, was especially called upon to support. She had never been part of a disaster relief effort, but the chance to get her hands stuck into fixing some real problems excited her.

---

[1] The 1906 San Francisco Earthquake struck at 5:12am on 18th April, the same day as the Azusa St revival made the front pages and as such cemented the link between the two events in many people's minds. The earthquake, still the most devastating in American history, would have been easily felt at Azusa Street had anyone been in the building at the time.

Chapter 39

THE SALVATION ARMY

It didn't take Rex and Artur long to get to St. Christopher's Hospice for the second time that evening. The roads by now were quite empty that late at night. When the two church leaders entered the hospice lobby, they immediately saw the black and yellow scarf laid out neatly on the coffee table next to the dead yucca plant. Cecil had slipped the wristwatch safely in his pocket knowing that the sight of it would probably upset the Rector. Artur picked up the scarf and slid the silk slowly between his fingers.

"This is the one we saw on the railway CCTV," the young Lutheran stated confidently. Rex nodded his confirmation. Cecil removed the wristwatch from his pocket and discreetly gave it to Rex. The Quaker thanked him, taking the hint and placed it into his own pocket. Artur replaced the scarf onto the table in a coiled heap.

Rev. Mashman sat next to the low coffee table on one of the two padded chairs. Artur could see that he was staring into space and presumed he was in a state of mild shock. He sat down in the chair next to him and placed his hand comfortingly onto the Rector's forearm which was resting limply on the arm of the chair. The Anglican broke his stare and turned to the Lutheran whom he had met for only second time this evening. The Rector smiled and placed a thankful hand atop Artur's, tapping it gently as he did.

"How did you get to be here, again?" Artur asked him. "We thought you were at Brennan Hall."

"Ah, yes, Brennan Hall," the Rector said, thankful for the reminder. He then told him of how both Lord and Lady Advowson weren't at home and that his Lordship was hunting poachers in the woods on the estate.

"In the woods?" Rex asked.

The Rector turned to Rex, who was now seated on the coffee table, and nodded.

"Did they say which wood?" Rex couldn't mention that the police had found two bodies in Sanguine Wood earlier that evening. He knew it would probably be more of a shock than the elderly churchman could take. The Rector said he didn't know which part of the vast estate his Lordship was in but thought it might be a good idea to try to find him.

"That's probably a good idea, Rector," Rex agreed. "But you shouldn't go alone." Rex was about to suggest that he would go with him, but before he could speak, Artur jumped in.

"I'll go with him. After all, I don't have my car here, and you do." The Quaker couldn't disagree; they had one car too many for them all to go together.

"If that is all right with you, Rector?" Rex asked. Mashman nodded and squeezed Artur's hand, still resting on his forearm.

"Well, perhaps a good place to start looking, Artur, might be Sanguine Wood," Rex suggested animatedly as though the idea had just occurred to him. Thelmin took the bait and replied with equally bad acting,

"That's a good idea, let's go to Sanguine Wood, Rector."

The clergyman had no idea why they were heading to that specific wooded copse but agreed anyway. He and Artur then made their way to the Rector's Honda Jazz. As they did, the young Lutheran's heart sank, remembering how impossibly slow the Mashmanmobile travelled.

"As it is so late, Sir," he asked tentatively, "perhaps you would let me drive?" Both the Rector and the young Austrian were relieved when the keys were placed into Artur's hand.

Meanwhile, in the hospice lobby Rex thanked the manager for looking after Mashman. He then asked if he wouldn't mind going through the events of the evening once again for him.

"Why don't I show you?" Cecil suggested. Rex agreed and they set off down the tree-covered back lane towards The Woodshed.

The banner reading 'FREE HOT MEALS HERE' was stretched on high poles between two white canvas tents, well above the wooden tables where grateful men, women and children sat with bowls of soup and hot drinks. There were upwards of two hundred people at this feeding station and Bunny could see in several of the diners' eyes the vacant stare that only those bereft of homes, possessions or kin could replicate.

When she arrived in San Francisco earlier that day, Bunny had seen the extent of the damage. Whole city blocks lay in rubble and fires continued to rage out of control. Over three hundred thousand residents had been made homeless, a full three-quarters of the entire population of the city. The death toll had already surpassed two thousand and was continuing its ominous march upwards.

Yet amid the devastation there was a very visible Christian presence. Many feeding stations, like the one at which she had just arrived, as well as dormitory shelters, had sprung up almost instantaneously right across the city. Keen to help, Bunny looked around for someone in charge and her eye was soon drawn to the uniformed officials orchestrating the soup production and seating arrangements.

"Hello, my name is Bun… Miss Elstow," she said to the bonneted woman in the black tunic, black knee-length skirt and thick black stockings, adding, "How can I be of assistance?"

Bunny assumed this official was either police or military, but the large silver letter 'S' insignia on her collar was very distinctive. Bunny was sure she had seen it before.

"Thank you, Ma'am," came the reply from the official, whom Bunny was now beside. Being in close proximity Bunny could see a shield-shaped badge on the left breast of her buttoned tunic. The penny suddenly dropped, and she realised what was familiar about the uniform.

"You're Salvationists, aren't you," Bunny blurted out without thinking. She had seen the Salvation Army many times before and had assumed it was a British institution. Here she was in San Francisco, on a journey to meet, it would appear, every significant person in Church history. In genuine curiosity she asked,

"Is this where you all began?"

The bonneted woman looked at her dismissively, clearly too fatigued to engage in such banal conversation and passed Bunny a folded white apron. Bunny slipped the protective garment around her waist and attempted a recovery with, "I mean, you are from The Salvation Army. That must be why you're here… I mean."

"Yes dear, we are The Salvation Army and you had better look lively and get to your station. We are to have a visit from the General soon."

Bunny's station was a large copper soup pan and, much to the relief of the young Chinese man who handed her his ladle, she was to be his respite.

The one thing Bunny knew enough about The Salvation Army – aside from the uniforms, the Christmas bands and collecting tins – was that they were founded by William Booth. He was their General and if he was arriving soon she was sure she would get the chance to meet him. In the meantime, she would attend to her serving duties for the sake of the hungry and homeless of San Francisco. There were several serving stations, each manned by two or three people, one of which was fully uniformed, the others, like Bunny, just aproned volunteers. The people changed periodically and each time she got a chance to survey her surroundings new faces would have appeared.

People often speak of the eerie stillness that descends upon an area following a disaster. The lack of traffic and machinery, together with the absence of the general day-to-day hubbub, conspires to create a pervading sombre mood that permeates the atmosphere. This was certainly true of San Francisco following the earthquake of 1906. Despite the solemnity, Bunny felt she was, at last, helping people. It was against this backdrop that the sound of a beating drum and shouting caused Bunny to pause her soup serving mid-ladle and look towards the source of the sound with sudden anxiety.

"What's that noise?" she asked the woman who had just arrived at her station. It was Bunny's turn to take a break as part of the ongoing rotation of duties, so she ceremonially passed the ladle and stood back.

"What noise, my dear?" the uniformed Salvationist responded as she started to serve the next grateful family. "I didn't hear anything."

Satisfied with her contribution, Bunny untied her apron, folded it neatly and laid it on the table ready for the next volunteer.

"Do you think he's arrived yet?" she asked whilst looking around from the feeding station, trying to identify where William Booth might be. There was no obvious sign of him.

"Sorry?" the newest server asked whilst mid-spoon, clearly adept at multi-tasking. "Who are you expecting?"

"The General," Bunny replied, scanning the horizon. "I am looking to see if he's arrived yet." The Salvationist smiled.

"And why are you looking for *him*?" she asked emphasising the final word.

Bunny, replied distractedly,

"I assume I am supposed to meet him," quoting the rules of engagement of the never-ending dream she was trapped in.

"And what makes you think that, Miss...?" she said.

Bunny snapped herself out of her fruitless camp-wide gaze to focus on the server.

"Sorry, I should have introduced myself," Bunny said politely. "I am Johan Elstow, but most people just call me Bunny."

"Pleased to meet you, Bunny," she replied. "I am Evangeline Booth, but most people just call me..." Bunny's attention was immediately concentrated upon the uniformed server as she delivered the punchline "... General!" she said with a smile.

Mortified that she may have unwittingly caused offence, Bunny began to apologise profusely. Miss Booth was having none of it, seeing nothing but the funny side of Bunny's discomfort. Evangeline then went on to explain that her parents, William and Catherine Booth, were still in England, and that she headed up their operations in American and Canada.[1] Whilst Miss Booth was talking, Bunny was sure she could hear the sound of drums again but didn't comment, intent on making the most of this latest encounter.

"It's nice to hear an English accent," Evangeline commented. Bunny described where she was from and, when asked, that her church affiliation was Church of England. Evangeline explained that her father left the Church of England because it was so wedded to the past. She said her father considered that the Church was blind to the needs around them. Bunny was a little taken aback at this insult directed toward her Church.

"What needs?"

The statistics were on Evangeline's lips before Bunny had even asked the question. Two thousand suicides per year; thirty thousand living in prostitution; one hundred and sixty thousand convicted drunkards; nine hundred thousand paupers. And this was in London alone.[2]

"So, do you see that as your main mission, Miss Booth?" Bunny asked her sincerely, "To help the poor and needy?"

Bunny was not expecting the reply.

"Of course not!" Evangeline said incredulously. "That is not enough. To give a man a new pair of trousers, to give him regular work, or even a university education... if the inside remains unchanged you have wasted your effort."[3]

---

[1] Evangeline Booth was William and Catherine Booths seventh child. She headed the Salvation Army in America and Canada from 1904 and was instrumental in co-ordinating relief, and in particular, fundraising in the aftermath of the San Francisco earthquake. She became the fourth head of the Salvation Army, and as such The General, in 1934.

[2] Statistics taken from Church History in Plain Language, Bruce L Shelley.

[3] Said by William Booth, not his daughter. The exact quote being "To get a man soundly saved it is not enough to put on him a pair of new breeches, to give him regular work, or even to give him a university education. These things are all outside a man, and if the inside remains unchanged you have wasted your labour. You must in some way or other graft upon the man's nature a new nature, which has in it the element of the Divine."

Bunny nodded. She could see the sense in there being a need to renew the person inside rather than just meet their external needs.

"So that is why we preach the three S's," Evangeline said as she ladled another bowl of soup. Bunny looked at her quizzically prompting her to explain what the three S's were.

"*Soup, Soap and Salvation*," she said with assertion.

Suddenly the sound of drums began again, only this time louder and much closer. Bunny turned her head towards the direction of the rhythmic cacophony only to hear a barrage of shouting and jeering. A group of men stood at the edge of the woods, next to the makeshift refugee camp. They looked angry and their offensive gestures were clearly aimed towards them. Then Bunny saw one of the men arch his arm backwards as if preparing to throw something. He launched it with an almighty heave, and she watched its trajectory as it came towards them. It was long, larger than a stone, and spun slowly in the air as it came closer. His aim was good, and the projectile looked likely to hit Miss Booth. The General was unaware of the approaching missile, so Bunny quickly pulled her towards herself as it landed with a crashing 'plop' into the large soup pot next to them, knocking it off the table and spilling the contents over the mudded grass beneath their feet. The hand-launched grenade was in fact a dead brown rat that now lay smothered in vegetable soup.

Bunny didn't know what to say. Evangeline on the other hand, quickly assessed the situation, then shouted over to the men, ironically thanking them for their kind gift and inviting them to collect the rat at their leisure.

"What was that?" Bunny asked.

"That, Miss Bunny, was a calling card from the Skeleton Army."

"And who is...?" Bunny didn't need to finish her sentence. Miss Booth explained that the Skeleton Army actively seek to disrupt the Salvation Army. Drums, shouting and dead rats today, other days it will be marches, rotten eggs and "if we are not careful, beatings".

"I had no idea," Bunny admitted, impressed by the dignity with which The General was continuing her mission despite active opposition.

"But why are they opposing you?" Bunny asked the obvious question. "You are doing good work here, there is nothing to object to in helping the poor... is there?"

Evangeline explained that it wasn't a protest about what the Salvation Army did, it was all about their so-called *temperance* leanings. Alcohol abuse was a major cause of poverty both in England and here in America, so it made a lot of sense to encourage abstinence. A small but vociferous group quickly arose intent on suppressing this opinion, violently if needed. The group called themselves the Skeleton Army and their mantra was the defence of the three B's, *'Beef, Beer and 'bacca!'*[1]

The commotion brought several uniformed officers to their immediate assistance, together with a replacement soup pot, much to the delight of the never-ending queue. Miss Booth passed the ladle to the next willing volunteer.

"If you are really interested in helping the poor, I'm going to New York to try to raise the funds we need to sustain the work here," she said to Bunny, then unexpectedly invited her to join her. Bunny immediately accepted. Evangeline looked over towards the men still loitering at the edge of the woods and said loudly, 'We are not sent to minister to a congregation and just keep things going. We are sent to make war!'[2] Bunny liked this sort of fighting talk, especially from a strong woman, but the overt opposition was rather disconcerting.

As they left the feeding station, Bunny heard the man at the front of the line ask the volunteer server,

"If it's all the same with you, Miss, would you mind if I didn't have rat in my soup!"

Artur confessed that he didn't have any idea how to get to Sanguine Wood. In common with much of his generation he relied solely on the map function built into a mobile phone or by using a sat nav, but that meant he had to be able to type in a destination and Sanguine Wood was too small to be listed and had no postcode. Most millennials don't own a map and Artur was no exception. He was greatly relieved to discover that, unsurprisingly, Mashman kept a collection of maps folded neatly in the pocket behind the passenger seat. The Rector placed the local Ordnance Survey map on his lap, switched on the interior light and quickly pointed out both where the wood was situated and, just as importantly, where they were currently parked. Artur looked closer, then

---

[1] The Skeleton Army operated in England not America, between 1880 and 1893. Over six hundred and fifty Salvationists were assaulted, some of whom sadly died, while the authorities largely looked the other way. One leading Skeleton Army member, Charles Jeffries, later found faith and joined the Salvation Army.

[2] Said by William Booth, not his daughter. The exact quote being "We are not sent to minister to a congregation and be content if we keep things going, we are sent to make war and to stop short of nothing but the subjugation of the world to the sway of the Lord Jesus."

pointed to what he thought must be Lane End farmhouse. The Rector looked and confirmed that he was correct. Interestingly, Artur could see that the best way to drive to the wood was along a lane that began almost halfway between the hospice and the farmhouse. As they turned into the lane that approached the wood, they could immediately see something was amiss. The flashing of blue lights interrupting the night grew brighter as did the umbra of LED lights that illuminated the incident scene. Within a few hundred yards a ribbon of yellow and black tape stretched across the lane, looped around a tree at one side and tied to the top of a metal stake at the other. A uniformed constable stepped out of the shadows and, hand aloft, brought them to a halt before approaching the driver-side window, one hand on his weapon. Artur fumbled around the dashboard trying to locate the button that lowered his electric window. Mashman politely coughed and pointed to the switch on the internal door handle.

"It is my duty to inform you, Sir, that you have entered a live crime scene," the constable announced ominously to Artur. "You must now exit the vehicle, together with all your passengers, and come with me and answer a few routine questions." Within moments Mashman and Artur were compliantly following the officer as he led them to the detective in charge who was busy talking with his sergeant.

"Well, well, what do we have here?" the detective inspector said at the sight of two people being led towards him. One elderly, white-haired and having difficulty walking; the other in his late twenties, well-dressed and allowing the older one to lean on him. Father and son? Grandfather and Grandson? The constable explained that they had been stopped, approaching the crime scene in a vehicle.

"Is that so?" the D.I. said. "And have you, perchance asked them their names?"

The constable erm'd and ahh'd until the detective dismissed him with a disdainful wave of the back of his hand. The sergeant took out his notebook and began the *routine questioning* with the one-word request,

"Names?"

The two churchmen looked at each other, then back at the sergeant and said,

"Rector Mashman of All Saints' Parish Church."

"Father Thelmin from Our Saviour's Lutheran Church."

The sergeant began to write their details down but rapidly trailed off at their unsuspected identities. The inspector, who had been looking intently at these latest suspects to see their reactions, couldn't help but emit a profanity which he then immediately tried to withdraw.

"Bloody hell, is there a vicar's tea party going on tonight? Sorry vicar... vicars, I didn't mean..."

Before the churchmen could even begin to assure him that they weren't offended by his outburst and had indeed heard much worse, the investigating office addressed his colleague,

"Where's the other one, bring him here."

Within seconds a bulky silhouette appeared beyond the LED lights.

"Rector Mashman?" the indistinct silhouette said.

"Jack?" Artur tentatively replied, his eyes being younger and better than the Anglican's.

As the Presbyterian stepped into the light, the only thing that the Rector could say was,

"Goodly heavens above!"

Chapter 40

WALTER RAUSCHENBUSCH

New York was by no means the sprawling metropolis that Bunny knew it would become. Only a few of the familiar buildings that would go on to punctuate the skyline were there. The Statue of Liberty and Brooklyn Bridge were impressive landmark structures, but even the Empire State and Chrysler buildings were decades away, let alone the dozens of modern concrete skyscrapers. Union Square, between Broadway and Park Avenue, was the focal point of the growing city and it was here that Evangeline Booth was planning to hold a mass meeting to raise much-needed funds for the victims of the San Francisco 'quake. Miss Booth was waiting for several of her specially invited high-profile guests to arrive later that afternoon, at which point she would deliver her address. Until then the growing crowd was enjoying the inspirational sounds of one of several Salvation Army bands charged with the task of entertaining them.

'O God of Burning Cleansing Flame, Send the Fire,' one song rang out much to Bunny's delight as she joined in with a familiar tune.[1] Bunny surveyed the audience. She had faced several large crowds recently, having stood with Wesley at Harham Mount; Whitefield at Philadelphia; and of course, with Miller in his enormous tent. The people here in New York weren't gathering to hear a dynamic preacher, this had been billed as a fund-raising event.

But it wasn't someone in the crowd that caught Bunny's eye, but a young woman who was standing beyond the perimeter of the gathering. The prim, long-haired and bonneted lass stood sheepishly as if unsure whether to join or not. Bunny felt moved to talk to the girl but, before she could take the few steps towards her, a bearded gentleman in a three-piece suit, sporting a fob watch and folded handkerchief, placed himself squarely in front of the Salvation Army General, obscuring Bunny's view of the girl.

"I am a great admirer of your father, Miss Evangeline," he said, raising his hat as he did. Bunny had no idea who Walter Rauschenbusch was, but on the assumption that he must be someone significant whom she really ought to know about, she adjusted her attention to him. As Bunny listened to the

---

[1] General William Booth wrote the hugely popular hymn 'O God of Burning Cleansing Flame, Send the Fire.'

conversation between Evangeline Booth and Mr Rauschenbusch it became clear that he had recently returned from England. He had spent time in Liverpool, Birmingham and London seeing how the Church in general, and the Salvation Army in particular, was affecting the social needs of the nation. Miss Booth introduced Bunny as someone who was part of the relief effort at the San Francisco earthquake. Bunny felt a little guilty that serving a few bowls of soup could be considered as being part of the relief effort. She shook the rather limp hand he offered. Over the past few hours, she'd had gentlemen bow towards her in greeting and had the back of her hand kissed several times. A simple handshake seemed rather impersonal by comparison.

"I am impressed by how you and your father are helping those trapped in poverty," he said to the General. Evangeline thanked him and stressed it was a seemingly never-ending battle, and that even some in the Church opposed what they were doing.

"Indeed," he agreed. "They don't understand that we are called to establish the *Kingdom of God*, and to affect every aspect of society."

Bunny had heard that idea several times in the past. The concept of establishing The Kingdom was something that Chris talked about a lot. He would say how the Church had to *invade* all the *spheres* of society. She couldn't remember the list he would give but was sure it included: education; politics; business; media; and the arts. *Is this where such a concept began?* she wondered. Is this the point where Church stepped outside of the… well…, outside of the church?

"I couldn't agree more," Evangeline said. "That is why I am here in New York to do something that has never been done before. I am going to gather all the top businesspeople, the politicians, the wealthy elite and get them, as well as the open-hearted church folk, to contribute to the disaster relief in San Francisco."[1] Rauschenbusch's expression towards Evangeline cast doubt on her chances of success.

"They ought to contribute, they are the ones with blood on their hands," he said dismissively. This time it was Miss Booth's turn to look quizzical. Rauschenbusch continued, expanding his thesis.

---

[1] Evangeline Booth held a mass meeting at Union Square, New York and raised $12,000 (equivalent to around $350,000 in 2019) towards their work in the aftermath of the San Francisco Earthquake. This is said to have been the first large scale disaster relief fund-raiser in history.

"It is the self-same wealthy and powerful people who will put a dollar in your collecting tin, Miss Booth, that have allowed society to slip so far from Eden. We need to tackle some of the great sins of our age."

There may have only been a couple of people listening to him, but it was sufficient a platform for him to continue. Bunny hadn't expected that in his short, polite discourse he would list: long working hours; child labour; selective education; poor housing and workplace safety as some of the *great sins* he had in mind. He sounded more like a social reformer than a church man, she thought.

"The individualistic gospel has taught us to see the sinfulness of every human heart and has inspired us with faith in the willingness and power of God to save every soul that comes to Him. But it has not given us an adequate understanding of the sinfulness of the social order and its share in the sins of all individuals within it."[1]

Bunny could see the solitary shy girl looking at them, only a few feet away, probably able to hear every word. As she met her gaze the girl looked away. Bunny focussed back on the conversation in hand and, as she digested his last statement, warning bells began to ring in her mind.

"Are you saying that society as a whole is sinful, not the individuals within it?" she asked. Rauschenbusch looked at her, clearly annoyed at her interjection, and tried to placate her,

"Yes, of course," adding derisively, "...my dear." He reached into the small leather bag he had with him and produced a single volume hardback book.

"You will find it all in here," he said condescendingly as he patted the cover with his palm and passed it to her. Bunny received it graciously. The book was entitled *Christianity and the Social Crisis* by Walter Rauschenbusch, Principal of Rochester Theology Seminary, 1907. Bunny looked at her wristwatch, she didn't need to see that it read 19:07, but it was reassuring that it did. Having dismissed Bunny's interruption, he turned his attention back to Evangeline Booth.

"Man's salvation is impossible until that Kingdom of God is established," he implored. "And that cannot happen without an end to the sinful capitalist system."

---

[1] Integrative Approaches to Psychology and Christianity, Third Edition' by David N. Entwistle. Cascade (2015) p75

Bunny was shocked. This was pure socialism dressed up as religion. He hadn't finished. It became clear that his purpose in meeting Evangeline today was to offer her an invitation for The Salvation Army to attend an inter-church gathering he was helping to organise the following year. The Federal Council of Churches, he claimed, would bring together churches from many different communions to agree a common mission.[1]

"Surely the common mission, as you put it, is to save souls, to *make disciples of all nations*," Bunny interrupted. Rauschenbusch ignored her but Bunny caught sight of the eavesdropping girl nodding in agreement.

"Ever since the Reformation..." he began. Bunny's ears pricked up. She didn't know what he was about to say but this was a subject she had first-hand experience of. "The Church has been progressively stripped of having any political platform." Bunny thought for a moment. She was going to take great pleasure in countering this patronising theologian with an insightful, opposing argument that would take the wind out of his bloated sails.

'But what about...' she constructed in her mind.

No name immediately popped into her subconscious to fill the gap. The Church had moved further and further way from the State, and therefore from affecting society. Great preachers had gathered thousands *into* church, but the Church had not made it into the outside world. There were some high points of influence with Oliver Cromwell and the Puritans; and the early colonial pioneers like Penn, but these all ended up seeking to impose Church rules onto society rather than help society to be better. The more she thought the more irritated she was with the inevitability that she wasn't going to be able to burst his pompous bubble. Irritatingly he may be correct.

Initially Evangeline wasn't convinced. Despite the Salvation Army being a major player in social action, she wasn't sure about the overtly political stance he was proposing. Rauschenbusch gently applied a little leverage.

"Have you read Charles Sheldon's novel *In His Steps*?" he asked. They both shook their heads.

"In it he continually poses the question 'What Would Jesus Do?' So, I ask you the same question Miss Booth, 'What Would Jesus Do?'"

"W.W.J.D!" Bunny blurted out without thinking. They both looked at her.

"W.W.J.D.," she repeated. "What Would Jesus Do?"

---

[1] The Federal Council of Churches was one of the key forerunner organisations that became The World Council of Churches in 1948. Thirty-two churches gathered in Philadelphia in 1908 and agreed: 'The Social Creed of the Churches' a mandate largely about social impact.

Again, she got nothing from either of them. This must be where the phrase came from, she thought, but clearly it hadn't gained its popularity yet.

"I'd copyright those four initials if I were you, they're going to be huge," she said adding as a final plea, "Trust me."[1]

Again, Rauschenbusch ignored her unwelcome disruption, instead he played his ace card.

"One of our key demands will be the prohibition of the sale of alcohol!" he said directly to Miss Booth.[2] Evangeline thought for a moment. He had hit upon one of the key ills that her parents had fought against in England, and that she could see dragging America downwards also.

"In that case consider us in," she agreed. He was delighted.[3]

"Is it something about Range Rovers that are incapable of parking in a designated spot?" Joel commented as a dark green Vogue swung into the car park and parked diagonally across two spaces, only a few yards from where they were waiting and watching.

"I think it is the type of people who *drive* Range Rovers," Thea remarked dryly. Joel agreed. The driver who had made such a poor attempt at parking was someone they both thought they recognised.

"Isn't that Lady Advowson?" Thea tested, looking at the woman attempting to lock her car, put a jacket on, and find her mobile phone.

"I think it is," Joel confirmed. "And she is in a frightful panic it would appear." The minor aristocrat rushed into the hospital at a canter, whilst simultaneously making a phone call on her mobile.

"I'm not surprised she is in a hurry, her daughter is inside having an X-ray of her head," Thea deduced.

---

[1] Charles Sheldon's religious fiction 'In His Steps, What Would Jesus Do' was published in 1896 and has sold over 50 million copies making it one of the best-selling books of all time. The popular WWJD acronym was first used in 1989 at Calvary Reformed Church, Holland, Michigan after their youth group discussed the book and subsequently wore friendship bracelets sporting the slogan. The idea soon took off amongst teenagers worldwide in the 1990's.

[2] The Federal Council of Churches was one of the most influential advocates lobbying for a total ban on the sale of alcohol in the United Sates. The Prohibition Act eventually came into force in 1920 until it was revoked in 1933.

[3] The Salvation Army didn't attend the first meeting of the Federal Council of Churches but soon became fully participative members of the organisation as it evolved.

"X-ray? … of her head?" Joel said puzzled. Thea nodded but Joel was unconvinced.

"That doesn't sound right," he said. "They don't do head X-rays here; it's all C.T. scans now. I know, 'cos I've had one. Are you sure it was X-ray?"

Thea thought carefully, replaying the conversation she had with Velia's boyfriend in her mind.

"No, that is what her boyfriend said, for sure." They thought for a while as they stared again into the near-deserted hospital car park, trying to make sense of what it might mean.

"Still doesn't excuse the parking," Joel said, prompting a welcome laugh.

Chapter 41

THE BRETHREN

Rauschenbusch's departure was the opportunity Bunny needed to sidle over to the girl who had been loitering at the fringes of the crowd.

"Hello," Bunny said.

The shyness of the girl, who looked at the floor, was obvious. Bunny tried to open up a conversation with her.

"Are you here to support the Salvation Army?" sounded like an obvious opening question. The girl shook her head. Bunny stood in silence, subconsciously forcing the girl to speak.

"We're not allowed to mix with others."

"Others? What do you mean others?" Bunny asked.

"Christians from other churches," came the unexpected reply.

"Well, I am a Christian. Maybe I'm from another church to you?" Bunny teased. "And perhaps you shouldn't be talking to me either." The girl looked at her, concerned.

"Don't, Miss," she pleaded. "You have a kind face. I knew when I saw you that you were going to be kind to me."

Bunny really didn't know what say next so reached out and put her hand on the girl's shoulder. She didn't recoil.

"What's the matter? You can tell me," Bunny said. She then leaned towards the girl and whispered in her ear, "I'm not really here anyway." The girl didn't know what to make of that comment. She looked at the floor for a while considering her words carefully. It took Bunny to ask,

"What happened?" for her to speak out.

"I shouldn't be talking to you..." she faltered, "because I've been Shut In."

Bunny had no idea what she meant by *Shut In*, so asked her to explain. The girl said her church elders had deemed her Shut In, which meant she was supposed to stay indoors and was certainly not allowed to talk to anyone else. Bunny asked her why she was suffering such punishment. Her reply inevitably led Bunny to ask what rules she was accused of having broken. At this, the girl rolled her eyes and resignedly said,

"Most of them!" Bunny pressed her for the specifics. In reply, the girl listed a litany of infraction after infraction. As the list unfolded Bunny's jaw began to drop.

"Cutting my hair; listening to music; having a friend who goes to the Baptist church; asking to visit the theatre; wanting a pet cat; not wearing a head-scarf outside," adding, "I wore one always at the assembly, but why do I have to wear it outside?"

"None of those seem like punishable offences, to me." Bunny offered a consoling hand on the girl's shoulder. The girl clearly wanted to continue to unload.

"I can't go to university, nor join a union, become a nurse, nor vote or stand for political office," she protested. Bunny didn't know what to say. Her life-long feminine independence was the antithesis of what she was hearing from this young lady. She needed to say something, but what? Suddenly her attention was arrested by a man's voice calling her name.

"Hello, Miss Elstow. Do you remember me?" the voice behind her said.

The idea of meeting someone more than once in this whistle-stop history tour was always welcome. Every meeting, she was finding, was tinged with a hint of sadness knowing that as soon as she had said goodbye to a person, they would have passed-away, been buried, and become part of the fabric of Church history forever. A 'Do you remember me?' greeting was very welcome. She turned to see to whom the voice belonged. The man who now stood in front of her in Union Square New York was vaguely familiar, but not enough for her to attempt to put a name to. She smiled sweetly, offered her hand and said a somewhat unconvincing,

"Ye...es!"

He shook her hand enthusiastically, clearly delighted to have met her again. She hunted his face, his clothing, his shoes, anything for a clue as to whom he was. Nothing! She let his hand go and hoped, desperately, that he would re-introduce himself. He didn't.

"Aye, its well canny to see tha' lass," he said in a broad northern accent that Bunny had no hope of locating precisely.

"Ye...es, isn't it just."

"Are yas heading back across tha' poond, Miss?" he asked. Bunny however failed to understand the question and found herself staring at him, puzzled.

"Ah mean, issa lang way frim Los Angeles," he added by way of attempted explanation. Los Angeles was the first clue Bunny had. When was I in Los Angeles? Not the earthquake, not the big old house in Kansas. Ah, it must be...

"Azusa Street?" she said to him, as much guessing as agreeing. Thankfully he nodded.

"Has yae gotta boot?" he asked. This was the worst part of bluffing your way through a conversation with someone you didn't really know. Eventually you were going to be asked a question that required a yes/no answer. She didn't expect it to be about footwear.

"A boot?" she asked looking at her shoes.

"Aye, if ya nae gotta boot, wic'd gae together, like," he added digging Bunny ever deeper into her hole of dialectal confusion.

"Wicked?" Bunny asked, repeating one of the few words she picked up.

"Aye we cu'd. Best we gan soon," he said clearly delighted at Bunny's acceptance of his offer to travel back to England together. Bunny on the other hand had no idea that was what she was agreeing to.

"Ah'll gets tha a ticket tae Plymouth, lass," he said picking up the suitcase and coat he had with him and motioning that Bunny should do likewise.

"Plymouth?" she repeated, now beginning to realise that her onward journey was unfolding before her eyes.

"Unless yas come tae Sonland, wi' me?" Sonland was not a place Bunny had ever heard of.

"Sonland?" she asked.

"Aye, Sonderlan."

"Sunderland!" she said relieved. Suddenly the penny dropped. She remembered that two of the people on the front row of the Azusa Street Mission had been singled out and *sent home* with the anointing. And one of them, she remembered, came from Sunderland, England. Was this unassuming northerner really responsible for the whole Pentecostal revival that swept through Great Britain?

"Yes, I will come with you," she answered, confident that this was her next step.

"But..." She remembered the timid girl she had been talking to. "Let me finish talking to this young lady."

Bunny turned around but the girl had vanished from sight.

"I don't even know which church or denomination she came from," she said aloud but to no one in particular, masking a sense of having failed, for the first time, to understand the significance of that brief encounter.

"Who is that?" the unknown voice on the other end of Chris's phone call repeated. Chris had all too hastily dialled the number of the person who had ordered the pizza to be delivered to the Lane End farmhouse and now had only seconds to think.

What have you done with Bunny? Where is she? You had better not have touched her? If you have... were some of the phrases that rushed through his mind. He desperately wanted to say them and yet he knew he couldn't. He knew the voice would simply hang-up and then they would be no closer to finding her. He didn't possess the *very particular set of skills* that Liam Neeson told the abductor of his loved one in the movie *Taken*. No, Chris knew he needed to play it softly, very softly, and say something that would be plausible enough for this person to talk and hopefully give something away.

"Hi, this is Chris," he said in as upbeat a voice as he could muster, then waited for a response. All he got in return was the sound of a car engine. Whoever this voice belonged to was evidently driving. Chris got into his car and switched on the ignition but didn't start the engine. The call quickly transferred to the hands-free allowing Ralph to listen in to the conversation.

"Sorry, have I caught you driving?" Chris asked trying his best to sound innocent. Still nothing in return. He needed to open up some dialogue but what could he say? Then he had a flash of inspiration.

"You ordered a pizza earlier today," he stated. Ralph gave him a thumbs-up gesture by way of encouragement.

"I don't think so!" the voice replied. At least it was an answer, but then it followed with, "I need to go, goodbye."

Chris jumped in,

"Yes, you did, for delivery to *Lane End Farm*." He gave special emphasis to the destination hoping the mention of the farm would work. It did. The voice didn't hang up and they could clearly hear the sound of a car indicator clicking on-and-off as the driver waited at a junction. Then there was the sound of an engine revving-up followed by the awful crunch of someone failing to find the right gear. Both Chris and Ralph winced at the sound.

"What if they did?" the voice answered unconsciously changing *you* into *they*. Whilst this was interesting, Chris knew he needed a reason to have called someone late at night. What possible excuse could he give? Now, it was Chris's turn to listen in silence while he thought. Ralph tried to come to the rescue by rubbing his fingers together to symbolise *money*. Chris couldn't make sense of his friend's suggestion but launched in anyway.

"I have some money for you…erm…we overcharged you earlier…yes, that's it I need to give you some money back," adding finally and confidently, "Where would you like me to bring it to?"

They both held their breath, listening to the unmistakable accompaniment of road sounds as the voice's vehicle traversed noisily. They waited. Hoping against hope that the promise of money might be enough to lure this person to say where he was going… and perhaps Bunny would be there.

"Keep the change," he said menacingly, then hung up.

Chris dropped his forehead onto the steering wheel. All he could think was that he had failed. That was their only lead and he'd blown it. Finished, utterly, finished. He felt wretched.

Suddenly the car was filled with the sound of Chris's own voice,

"Where would you like me to bring it?"

Chris looked over to Ralph who had recorded much of the call on his own mobile phone and was now playing it back. Chris began to speak but Ralph shushed him. They both listened to the recording which ended with 'Keep the change.'

"Did you hear that?" Ralph asked.

"What?"

He rewound the voice memo and replayed the same section.

"There! did you hear it? In the background, that *badum badum* sound?"

Ralph played it for Chris a third time at which point he did indeed hear a distinct badum badum sound. Despite it appearing familiar to Chris, he wasn't sure what it was, but Ralph had already worked it out.

"It's a cattle-grid." Ralph played the clip a fourth time until Chris agreed.

"But there must be dozens of cattle grids scattered over this area," Chris protested.

"Yes, dozens, but we are looking for one that comes shortly after a turning. Remember the sound of an indicator?" Then, almost simultaneously, they both remembered at least one place that met that requirement exactly.

"Lane End Farm!" they said in unison.

This was the second time Bunny had arrived in England by sailboat. The first time she had returned from Holland and landed in London with one of the Pilgrim Fathers; this time her passage was from New York and she docked in Plymouth, the very port that he had set sail from many years earlier.

353

Her travelling companion, whom she now knew as Alexander Boddy, was fascinating company. Having tuned herself into his accent she had discovered that he, like his father before him, was an ordained Anglican minister. He was returning to his parish at Monkwearmouth, on the coast near Sunderland, to host a series of conventions modelled on what he had experienced in Azusa Street. She also learned that Azusa Street wasn't the first *revival* he had visited. A few years earlier he had travelled to the Rhondda Valley to experience the outpouring that was happening in South Wales under Evan Roberts; and then he had travelled to Oslo to see the same that was happening under T.B. Barratt. This man was clearly hungry to experience all that God had for his Church and was willing to travel across the world to find it.

Plymouth harbour was a bustling place with several ships simultaneously disgorging their passengers and cargo. The walk to the railway station took them through the middle of the south-coast city. The next train that would take Bunny and Alexander to Sunderland was not due to leave until much later that day which gave Bunny some time to kill in the city centre.

It wasn't just the absence of motor cars that emphasised to Bunny that she was walking in a world more than a hundred years before her time. The grand buildings lining either side of the streets retained the striking honey-coloured stonework that their architects originally designed; years of smoke, traffic grime not yet having given them its signature grey coating. Shops were few and far between and announced their presence with intricate and ornate signs above their doors; none being so garish to broadcast their wares with roof-to-floor glazing. The roads carried an incongruent combination of horse-drawn carriages and electric trams, with pedestrians seemingly free to wander haphazardly as the mood took them; a visual depiction of the massive transitions to come into society over the coming century. There in the centre of Plymouth, Bunny's attention was drawn to small church building nestled between larger Georgian homes, and to the small stream of people filing inside. Curiosity led her towards the front door. Then to her immense surprise, she saw someone she knew. There walking toward the entrance was a young woman. The exact same girl she had been talking to in New York. 'She must have been on the same ship,' Bunny thought. Then, determined to finish the conversation she had started, Bunny ran over towards her.

"Miss!" she exclaimed. The girl ignored her. Bunny repeated her shout, this time a little louder but, again, she gave no reaction. Finally, she was close enough to touch the girl, so tapped her shoulder and once again said, "Miss!"

The young woman stopped in her tracks, a little startled to have been the subject of a stranger's attention.

"It's me..." Bunny began. The girl looked at her with no recollection of having ever met her before. It was now Bunny's turn to be on the wrong end of a conversation where the other party had no idea who she was.

"It's me," she repeated tapping her own chest. "...from New York." Still, no response. A third time she attempted to make the connection.

"We spoke in New York, you told me about your church," Bunny pointed to the building they were about to enter. "Not this church... *your* church in New York," she emphasised.

"Madam," she eventually replied, "I fear you may have me confused with somebody else."

Bunny began to say, "But..." which faded as quickly as it began. The stark realisation then kicked in. This was a dream. Normal rules of recognition didn't apply. Nothing normal applied! But this was not a chance encounter, there had to be an important reason that she had met the same girl twice.

"Besides, Madam," the girl continued, "I do not go to what you call *church*, this is my *assembly*."

"Assembly! That's the same word that you, I mean not you, used in New York." Bunny was convinced she was on to something now.

"Before you go inside, Miss," Bunny continued, "may I ask you a few questions?"

The girl reluctantly agreed and stepped out of the modest flow of people arriving at the assembly.

"How may I help you?" she politely asked.

"Am I correct in saying that in your... assembly... the leaders can forbid you from meeting with anyone else?" The girl thought for a moment then shook her head.

"That they don't allow you to..." Bunny had to think hard to remember the list that she, or at least her transatlantic twin, had given her. "They don't allow you to go to university, nor join a union, or become a doctor or nurse; you can't vote or stand for office; or go to the theatre or listen to music; you can't have friends who go to other churches or have a pet." Bunny was impressed at her powers of recollection. Again, the girl thought for a moment before giving her answer.

"Well, Madam, we *are* told that as God's people we are meant to be separate, and to not let the evil of the world taint us, but no, none of the things you say are forbidden." Bunny was now really confused.

"But I have heard the exact opposite from…. well, one of you!" she exclaimed.

"One of us?" the girl repeated, making Bunny nod at her, exasperated, lips pursed and brow furrowed.

"Ah, when you say one of us, what do you mean?" Now it was Bunny's turn to think before replying. Honesty, she decided, was going to be the best policy.

"I don't know what I mean," she began. "But I met someone like you who told me her chur… her assembly, rather, would stop her from doing those things and punish her if she failed, by keeping her indoors. How can two of…*you*… have such different experiences?" The girl began to smile, having realised what was likely to be causing Bunny's confusion.

"That's the difference between Open and Closed," she explained. Bunny, however, was none the wiser and asked her to expand on her pronouncement.

"We are the Open or, as some people call us, the Plymouth Brethren," she said, "whereas the other person you spoke to must have been from the Closed, or Exclusive Brethren." Bunny had heard of the Brethren but knew very little about them other than they kept themselves to themselves. There was a small Gospel Hall in the town, and when Rector Mashman wrote to them, at her behest, they politely wrote back to say they did not get involved in any form of inter-church activities. It was clear from this brief conversation that, regardless as to how open or how closed they were, separation was a key belief.

"How can two such different, well… types of church… be included within the same denomination?" Bunny asked. The answer was clear and well-rehearsed, as the girl emphasised that they were not a denomination but a collection of individual assemblies, not churches. Each assembly was led by elders, not a priest or vicar – they have no central structure, no clergy, and no hierarchy.

"Well, what is it based upon?"

"This," she said raising her black Bible and waving it gently at Bunny.

"It's all about the Bible," she decreed. Bunny hadn't noticed that while they had been talking, Alexander Boddy had joined them and was also listening intently to their conversation.

"And thee Baptism of the Harly Spirit too," Boddy added in his Wearside accent, fired up with revivalist zeal. The girl, however, looked at him aghast.

"Most certainly not!" she said indignantly. "The gifts of the Holy Spirit were for the time of the early Church and most decidedly *not* for today." Somewhat flustered she bade them farewell.

"I beg to differ!" Boddy whispered quietly as the girl disappeared inside the Gospel Hall. As she did, Bunny heard a single church bell ring out.

"There it is again!" she said to Boddy. He hadn't heard it.

He and Bunny silently made their way to the railway station and caught the next train to Sunderland.

"And this is pretty much how we found it." Cecil concluded his overview of how they found the abandoned Mondeo behind The Woodshed, the rolled flowerpot, and the discovery of the scarf and watch that Rex now had safely in his pockets.

Rex approached the car wedged into the bushes, holding one of two powerful torches that the hospice manager had brought to facilitate their exploration. He opened the rear door, just as his compatriot had done some time earlier, and squeezed his head and arms inside. He peered around, his torch illuminating every part.

"Was it unlocked?" Rex projected his voice back at Cecil who affirmed the car wasn't locked when they had found it. Rex shone the torch at the dashboard.

"Where are the keys?" Rex then shouted.

"The keys?" Cecil queried. "Aren't they in the ignition? I didn't take them out?" The keys were not in the ignition.

Rex was a very logical person, a quality that had helped him progress rapidly in his city career. He immediately surmised that the keys must be in one of three places: either with the person who had abandoned the car; or secondly, they had been discarded deep into the undergrowth impossible to find without daylight and a metal detector; or thirdly, they had been stashed ready to be collected later. In this latter scenario the car wasn't abandoned, just hidden here as some kind of a getaway car. This option was the only one they could do anything about. Rex instructed Cecil to begin looking around for a hiding place nearby where the keys might be, and he would search inside the vehicle.

Having quickly checked the back seat he lifted the central compartment between the front seats. With the lid tipped open it was awkward to position himself to see inside and had to push further into the car in order to peer over the top. Inside there was a copy of the Crust Almighty menu, evidence if needed that this was the car used by the two men at Lane End Farm. As he shut the box it closed with a thud, and he found himself leaning heavily upon it. It was only a short push further to force his chest between the front seats, a position that allowed him to reach the sun visors and lower them to find nothing hidden behind them. Then he opened the glove box, which held nothing more than two used packets of cigarettes. He was now squashed firmly between the seats with his arms in the front compartment and his legs in the rear. He pulled himself further forward, his feet now off the ground, and reached over to the passenger door pocket. Again it was empty. In order to reach the driver's door pocket, he needed to bend himself through ninety degrees, a difficult manoeuvre that meant his feet were now on the rear seat and the steering wheel was in his face. His fingers probed into the pocket but it too was empty. Before he began the awkward process of reversing himself out of the car, he relaxed a little and propped himself with one hand in the driver's foot well and his forehead on the driver's seat. For a brief moment, thoughts of all the bottoms that had been in that same position flashed into his mind, but he quickly took control of his stray thoughts – as all Quakers are taught to do – and focussed on the task in hand. The keys clearly weren't in the car, unless perhaps they might be under the seats. He slid his supporting hand under the driver's seat, shifting his weight on his head. There was something there, but it didn't feel like keys. Neither did it feel like part of the sliding mechanism under the seat, chiefly because with his outstretched fingers he could move it. It felt cold and it was heavy, so he presumed it was something metallic. With a little persuasion he slowly coaxed it out from under the seat. He turned his head to see what it was, but the foot well was too dark. The torch was above him in his other hand, so he spun it around to fill the footwell with light. To his shock his fingers were caressing a black Glock 19 nine-millimetre compact semi-automatic pistol.

Chapter 42

MONKWEARMOUTH

The conference in Sunderland, or more accurately in the small church hall of All Saints', Monkwearmouth, wasn't particularly well attended. Nothing like the throng she had seen squeezed inside the equally compact Azusa Street Mission Hall in Los Angeles. The sense of expectation, however, was almost identical.

Once again, Bunny had a front-row seat and she too was waiting expectantly to see what was about to unfold. She knew that something about this meeting will have been significant in the history of the Church.

In every meeting she had attended on her protracted, virtual journey, it was clear why she was there and, more importantly, who she was to meet. All around her people were having a dramatic encounter with the Holy Spirit, the singing and dancing was energetic and impassioned, but she had a sense that this wasn't *it*. She had no idea what the 'it' would be but consoled herself that she would be sure when she finally saw it.

At one point, Alexander testified that as a result of the generous offering that had been taken up, the outstanding loan needed to build the hall they were gathered in could now be paid off in full. A great cheer went up when he said he was going to get a stone carved into the building inscribed with 'WHEN THE FIRE OF THE LORD FELL IT BURNED UP THE DEBT,' as testimony of God's blessing. [1]

Alexander had invited T.B. Barratt, whom he had met on his travels in Norway, to be the main speaker and he proved to be a charismatic and gifted minister. The service showed no sign of ending as evening turned into night, such was the dramatic power being released in that modest northern gathering. As midnight passed Barratt declared,

"The eyes of the religious millions of Great Britain are now fixed on Sunderland."[2]

---

[1] A stone with the inscription '1907: WHEN THE FIRE OF THE LORD FELL IT BURNED UP THE DEBT' remains to this day on the wall of the church hall in Monkwearmouth. Interestingly it is now juxtapose to a similar one attesting to the repeated miracle in 1996 when the Anglican Church sold the hall to a small group of Pentecostal believers who raised the asking price in full.

[2] From the 'Pensketch biography of Alexander Boddy' by Tony Cauchi, 2005. Published by revival-library.org

He went on to explain that of the estimated twenty-thousand people recorded as having spoken in tongues, only six were in Great Britain but that this number was rapidly changing.[1] Boddy said he had received letters from several people who had spoken in tongues in earlier years and who, having been accused of being mad, were thrown out of their churches.[2] This came as little surprise to Bunny who was now well versed in the polarisation that she had witnessed caused by an emphasis on the Holy Spirit, divine healings and, above all, speaking in tongues.

A final altar call was given that brought several folk to the front who knelt for Barratt and Boddy to lay their hands upon them for the impartation of the Holy Spirit.

By 4am the meeting eventually came to an end and people began to drift away, each one aglow with their new-found spiritual indwelling. One or two milled about intent upon thanking one of the ministers. Bunny's eye was caught by a scruffy, yet sincere looking man who appeared to have little desire to leave. Bunny wandered over to where he was seated, head bowed, and took the chair next to him.

"Don't you have a home to go to, Sir?" she asked, then quietly castigated herself for asking such an inane question. The man looked up at her, nodded, then said,

"I'll be going back to Bradford when I'm ready, but I'm in no rush to leave." He then suffixed his statement, clearly as an after-thought with, "Perhaps you should come with me." This was the unmistakable next-step invitation that Bunny had become used to spotting.

"The secret of spiritual success is persistent hunger," the man added thoughtfully. "God is looking for hungry people. It's an awful condition to be satisfied."[3] Bunny wasn't sure how to reply, so simply asked the most obvious question,

"Are you hungry... for God I mean?" He adjusted himself in his chair, sitting uprightly as if to engage in conversation. Bunny knew she ought to be

---

[1] Ibid.

[2] From 'All Saints Parish Hall (1907)' by Andy Williamson published by ukwells.org

[3] The full quotation attributed to Smith Wigglesworth is "The secret of spiritual success is a hunger that persists...It is an awful condition to be satisfied with one's spiritual attainments...God was and is looking for hungry, thirsty people."

tired but felt drawn to hear what this man was going to say. He explained that since his conversion he had been an Anglican, a Methodist, a Baptist, had been in the Salvation Army, and attended a Brethren assembly. Bunny was pleased that the list he gave included all denominations she had personally had an encounter with. She felt as though, in some way, she *knew* each of these Church streams.

"I've left all of these," he said, explaining that ever since he had been left in charge of his church when the ministers went to the Keswick Convention, things had changed.

"Oh dear," Bunny uttered. "Whatever happened?'

"I preached a simple sermon, I cannot even remember about what, then asked people to come out to the front if they wanted God to heal them," he explained. "And fifteen did. One of them on crutches!" Bunny immediately diagnosed what must have happened. The disappointment he must have felt when those people weren't immediately healed must have knocked him, she surmised. Swelling with compassion, she jumped in, hoping to re-build his faith.

"Don't worry, Sir," she began, "sometimes divine healing takes time to work out." This was something Rector Mashman had said several times. It was almost the go-to stock phrase to give at the end of any prayer for a miraculous healing. She knew how this worked.

"I am sure you did your best," she added for good measure.

To her surprise, this was the wrong diagnosis.

"No, Miss, you don't understand." Bunny bit her lip apologetically.

"When I prayed for those people, they were all healed," he said. "The man left with his crutches in his hands."

Bunny let out an involuntary "Oh!" her genuine surprise tangible.

"All of them?" she asked.

"Yes, Miss. Every single one of them. One had a severe bite on their tongue, another a weeping sore on their ankle. All were completely and instantly healed."[1]

Bunny did not know what to say. Here was a quiet and unassuming man who appeared to have an amazing healing gift with a one hundred percent success rate. Why was he here? What else could he be possibly looking for?

"Hello, there!"

---

[1] These healings were part of his early ministry, although not all at the very first meeting. Taken from Stanley Frodsham's 'Smith Wigglesworth - Apostle of Faith,' chapter 3.

A new voice broke into the momentary lull in conversation – it was Alexander's wife, Mary. The man instantly stood up to greet her. Bunny ignored the fact that he hadn't stood for her, consoling herself with the fact that she was seated next to him, so that must have been the reason.

"Mrs Boddy," he said. "Would you please lay your hand upon me that I might receive this Baptism in the Holy Spirit and speak in tongues."[1]

Bunny was surprised. Here was someone through whom God had clearly been working in a miraculous way, and yet he wanted more of the Holy Spirit to empower his life, his ministry. In the humility of his request to Mary Boddy, Bunny suddenly understood the importance of being *persistently hungry*, as he had put it.

The man knelt. The vicar's wife laid her left hand upon the top of his head and began to pray that the Holy Spirit would fall upon him. Bunny could see that he began to shake violently and uncontrollably. His lips began to move in thankful prayers which almost imperceptably morphed into the incoherent heavenly babbling that Bunny had now witnessed several times before.

"Simple, childlike faith is powerful!"

Another new voice. A man had seated himself next to Bunny and, rather impolitely, taken the opportunity to offer his commentary on the prayer taking place in front of them.

Bunny turned to address the late-night interloper. He was dressed in a simple dark suit and, as she turned, he lifted his trilby hat to politely greet her. A glint of faint light reflected in a thin line of gold decorative trim that encircled the brim of his hat. It was her fellow traveller, her guide, her angel. She didn't know who he was, but she knew he had answers. His arrival was met with a sense of relief and a resigned smile on Bunny's lips.

"Why am I in Sunderland?" she asked, then not wishing to insult her hosts added, "I mean, why is this particular meeting so important?"

He then pointed across the room to three separate individuals each busy saying their goodbyes with hearty handshakes and hugs. Identifying the specific people, he announced that one would start the Elim Pentecostal Church; another the Assemblies of God; and the third The Apostolic Faith Church.

---

[1] From 'Smith Wigglesworth: The Apostle of Faith' by Jonas Clark.

"Every Pentecostal tradition can trace its roots to either this place or to Azusa Street," he concluded with satisfaction.[1]

Bunny failed to be impressed with the statistic.

"So, all that means is that yet more denominations have been birthed from this one move of God."

The point she was making was accurate. She had seen that every outpouring of faith, no matter how dramatic or exciting, whether motivated by the doctrinal or the miraculous, has nonetheless ended by producing more and more reasons for disunity.

"It may be a cliché," she said, "but history, Church history, keeps repeating itself."

He didn't disagree with her. Instead, he nodded towards the man kneeling a few feet away from them.

"Do you want to go with him, to see where that leads?" he asked.

"Leeds? I thought he was from Bradford," she answered cheekily. "Anyway, who is he?"

"His name is Smith Wigglesworth, and many, many people will be healed when he prays for them," he explained, adding dramatically, "Plus, several will be verifiably raised from the dead."

"Wow! That sounds amazing." Bunny had become so spiritually open that she was prepared for, and able to believe for, anything. Her time-travelling companion added that many say Smith Wigglesworth was the father of the Faith movement, widely influential across the global Church. Bunny was too distracted to notice the sound of a church bell once again giving a single chime. She thought for a moment while he was speaking then added a polite but firm negation.

"No, I've seen enough."

The man in the gold-rimmed hat immediately stopped talking. This wasn't the answer he was expecting. Bunny gave her reasoning.

"It's clear to me that since I was with Martin Luther, all that has happened is the Church has splintered. Every time it has been for a justifiable reason, but it's fragmentation nonetheless, with no desire to unite."

Again, he didn't disagree.

"So, what do you want to do?" he asked.

---

[1] Taken from 'Sunderland's Legacy in New Denominations' by William K Kay, Journal of the European Pentecostal Theological Association, Vol. XXVIII No. 2 (2008)

"I want to go back," Bunny requested. The man smiled.

"Are you sure?" he said. Bunny nodded.

"Yes! I don't think I need to see any more to understand just how disunited God's Church is. I'm ready to go back now."

He didn't waste any time.

"If you are sure you want to go back, stand up and hold out your arm in front of your face so you can look at your watch," he instructed.

She too didn't hesitate and took to her feet, moving a few strides away in order to give some room to the now ecstatic Mr Wigglesworth. She lifted her arm, the square black dial of her watch flashed 19:08. That's been nearly four hours, she noted to herself. The man in the gold-rimmed hat placed his right hand over both of her eyes. Bunny's instinct was to pull away, but she resisted the impulse and leaned-in to his warm palm.

How will I even begin to explain all this to Chris? she began to wonder as the present light disappeared from view. As she did, thoughts of Chris flooded into her memory. How he had blundered his way into an atypically self-conscious declaration of affection; how she had left him hanging while she walked away; how she had decided, yes, she HAD decided that she too had feelings for him; how she now understood that their different church backgrounds needn't prevent them from making a life together; and how the differences between them didn't seem to matter so much now. She had seen that her Anglican tradition, as well as his Pentecostal one, despite both being founded on passionate and well-meaning zeal, nonetheless they were both imperfect. And that sad fact was true with every single group, denomination or tradition she had met. I think we should be able to find a compromise that will work for the pair of us, she said to herself as she waited to wake up. Maybe she would see Chris when she opened her eyes. Wouldn't it be perfect if she awoke in, perhaps, a hospital bed and there he was on the visitor's chair?

Chapter 43

THE BROWN SYNOD

Suddenly the hand was removed from over her eyes and the dim Sunderland chapel light had been transformed into stunning daylight.

Where am I? she thought. Arm still outstretched, her focus was immediately drawn to the fact that she was standing afront a church. Not just any church! Before her were the unmistakable doors of Castle Church, Wittenberg. She had been here earlier, much earlier, with Martin Luther hammering his ninety-five theses to these very doors.

"When I said I wanted to *go back*, I didn't mean back to Wittenberg!" Bunny complained loudly, but her words fell on deaf ears. Her occasional travelling companion had, once more, deserted her. I don't need to see Martin Luther again, she thought angrily.

The surprising sound of a heavy vehicle suddenly drew her attention and she spun round to follow the sound. The sight was indeed familiar, but the last time she was here the road was filled with sixteenth-century townsfolk and the occasional horse-drawn carriage. Now the gentle click-clack of hooves had given way to the exclusive roar of the internal combustion engine. The pavements were a bustle of besuited men, some in overcoats and several of whom were making their way up the church path towards her. The large-wheeled vehicle roaring past, with a tarpaulin-covered rear, was a heavy, grey military transport and there above the front wheel arches Bunny zoomed-in on the unmistakable and chillingly familiar red, black and white insignia. A swastika.

Bunny's arm was still outstretched, she drew her focus away from the street to look at the dial. She might have expected it to say 15:17 as it had the last time she stood here, but now it ominously flashed 19:33.

"This is not where... or when... I wanted to be," she pleaded skywards, as she allowed her arm to fall limply by her side. Perhaps I have to walk back inside to end the dream, she thought, but before she could reach the door the small crowd had already caught up with her and she felt herself being gently but firmly ushered inside.

"Do you want me to put the engine on?" Joel offered, seeing Thea give a reflex shiver as they sat alone in the hospital car park waiting for the owner of the car in front of them to return. "It is pretty cold, isn't it?"

"No, it's fine," she answered. "Thanks anyway, but we don't want him to know we are here, should he ever come out."

They continued their secluded lookout, like biblical watchmen on the ancient walls of Jerusalem, ready to raise the alarm if needed.

"Do you think we should let the others know what we are doing?" Joel asked softly.

"I was just thinking the same," Thea admitted, then stated emphatically that she would post a message and reached for her phone.

As soon as the words came out of her mouth, she had a sudden twinge in her conscience. Ever since her divorce she had become more self-assured, more self-determined and much more confident. Without consciously knowing it, she had refused to put herself in any position where a man had any claim on her decisions. She was an independent woman now and enjoyed the freedom of that status. Being a Baptist minister was part of that, the absolute authority in the area, with no hierarchy to answer to. But now, sitting in a darkened car with a Methodist minister, for the first time in years she felt she needed to ask for someone's agreement. This was a strange feeling and not one she was used to. It wasn't permission she needed, just to know that he too agreed with the trivial matter of the fact she was going to compose and post a message. If she had thought about it any longer it would probably have been much harder to say, so she just gave voice to her conscience.

"Assuming that is okay with you, Joel."

He had no idea about the seismic shift that had suddenly happened in Thea Howlsy's heart as evidenced by his simple,

"Yeah, 'course."

As she composed the message, she couldn't help but smile. Inside she knew that the simple question she had asked Joel was evidence she was finally over her break-up.

The message she composed read: 'Velia is in hospital having head X-ray? We've found the red sports car (her b/f's) parked at hospital. Joel and I plan to follow it. Will update later.' Before pressing Send, she again asked Joel to comment on it. He offered no corrections, but to Thea that was never the point.

Joel put the car radio on softly. The lateness of the hour, the darkness and the gentle sounds of Radio Two conspired to have a soporific effect on them, who both had to fight hard to keep both eyes open.

Suddenly they were lurched out of their half-trance by the simultaneous beep-beep and flash of indicators as the owner of the red Mazda MX5 pressed the remote unlock on his key fob, as much to help him locate his car in the darkness. Joel and Thea, now fully awake, instinctively slid down in their seats, so as not to be seen – not that the dim glow of distant streetlights would have penetrated enough into their vehicle to allow anyone to spot them.

"Let him pull away first, don't start your engine until he is moving," Thea whispered.

Joel didn't answer but did exactly as suggested. When the red Mazda reached the exit, Joel pressed the ignition, having switched off the headlights before he started the car.

"Good idea," Thea congratulated, "with the lights, I mean." They slowly rolled towards the exit as the Mazda turned right. Now it was time to speed up and pursue.

Joel switched his headlights on as they too turned right. Glancing in his rear-view mirror he saw a pair of headlights suddenly switch on behind them, as another vehicle also emerged from the hospital car park. Was someone following *them*? he wondered.

The meeting room inside the church in Wittenberg was surprisingly informal and functional, the oak panelling on three of the four walls being the only attempt at ornamentation. Around the room dozens of men, and they were exclusively men, were loosely scattered about. Some stood, some were seated, a few were alone, but most were in small groups. By the look of the empty chairs only around a third of the expected attendees had so far arrived. Bunny waited for a few moments, but she was ignored. No one came to greet her; no one attempted to connect with her in the way that by now she had grown accustomed to. She looked around uncomfortably self-conscious. All she would be able to do would be to stand and observe, and as the only woman present she felt decidedly out of place. She made her way to the rearmost wall and positioned herself inside the frame of a locked door, out of line-of-sight of most, and hoping no one would see her.

A rather officious man, clearly irritated by the non-arrivals, stood to address those who had gathered on time. The sight of him standing caused all to quickly finish their conversations and take their seats.

"Brothers, this is a great day for Germany," he began. "Having already united twenty-seven out of the twenty-eight Landeskirchen regions, the national church elections last week will have taken unity one step further."[1] His words were met with a chorus of approval, some adding an ecclesiastical "Amen" for good measure.

"What?" thought Bunny. "Did he say that the German churches had actually found a degree of unity?" She remembered how she had seen previous attempts at unity collapse, especially when Luther scrawled *This is My Body* on the oak table at Marburg. She had no idea that in pre-war Germany there had, at long last, been a reversal of disunity. My guide must have sent me here for some encouragement before I go home, she concluded.

"The National Awakening has brought an unprecedented unity amongst the German Evangelical Church. Lutheran, Reformed, United, Methodist and Baptist are all in agreement," the official declared much to Bunny's delight.

"This will allow us to stand united against the great evil threatening to take over our nation," he continued. "As soon as the rest of our number of newly-elected ministers have taken their seats, then we shall get this synod formally underway, elect our leader and agree the points that have already been circulated."

That must be the reason, Bunny thought. The rise of Nazi-ism has forced the Church to unite and take a stand against it. A common enemy, of course!

"Well done, Church in Germany," she whispered to herself, conscious to not let anyone hear her.

Much to the relief of the chairman, the door finally opened, and men began to file inside. Much to Bunny's amusement the first few that entered were all wearing the same-coloured clothes. More and more entered also dressed in identical brown shirts. Not just the same shirts, this was more like a uniform. Dozens more continued to join. This wasn't just a *same dress nightmare*; this was a much worse nightmare. The room was rapidly filling with brown-shirted members of the *Sturmabteilung*, or simply the SA, feared across Germany in the years when Hitler rose to power. They were the ones responsible for the *Night of the Long Knives*, when Hitler purged all his political opponents. Now they were filling the church hall and soon outnumbered the churchmen waiting for their colleagues.

---

[1] A politically motivated move to force all German churches to unite was agreed by 27 of the 28 regional Protestant groups, or Landeskirchen. In so doing this represented 3000 out of 17,000 national pastors. From this base there followed, on 23rd July 1933, national church elections which were heavily biased by the Nazi party. And won by a landslide by pro-Nazi churchmen.

The others must have stayed away, half expecting this invasion, Bunny thought worriedly. There's going to be mass arrests, or worse. She feared she was going to witness a bloodbath. But it quickly became clear that the brown-shirted arrivals were not the object of fear she had supposed. In fact, they were being warmly greeted by the rest of the gathered group. As she watched, she saw every SA member take one of the vacant seats. To her immense shock she realised the awful truth. The others hadn't stayed away; these stormtroopers were indeed the remainder of the synod.[1]

Every seat was now filled, the nearest being less than six feet from where she was standing. An air of foreboding filled the room and Bunny pressed herself into the wood panelling, hoping it would somehow swallow her up. It didn't. She would have to silently watch the proceedings.

Item one on the agenda was the election of Ludwig Mueller as their *Reichsbischof* or national leader. In his address he proudly admitted his membership of the Nationalist Socialist, or Nazi, party and the conversations he had that morning with Der Furher. That went down particularly well with the assembled churchmen.

Next, there came a doctrinal presentation. Again, with the enthusiastic agreement of apparently all, a theologian Emil Brunner introduced the concept of Natural Theology, the idea being that if you see it in nature then it must be of God. Seeing God through a human lens gave reason to reject anything in the Bible that didn't fit with this naturally focused understanding of God.[2]

"God not only likes us – he is like us!" he concluded to rapturous applause. Bunny couldn't help but think this sounded totally upside down. Bishop Muller then took to his feet to introduce the next order of business, *The Paragraph*, as he put it.

"We stand on the ground of positive Christianity," he began. "We profess an affirmative faith in Christ, but mere compassion is charity and effeminates

---

[1] On 27 September 1933 what became known as the Brown Synod was held where more than half of the newly-elected minsters wore the brown shirts of the SA. Many reports say it was held in Berlin though some say Wittenberg.

[2] The doctrine of Natural Theology had been around for centuries, being used during the period of the enlightenment as an attempt to rationalise Darwinism and Creationism. The idea returned through Emil Brunner, a Nazi supporter, and became an important and dangerous precursor to the developing theology that paved the way for the adoption of firm antisemitic views. Church History in Plain Language: Fourth Edition by Bruce Shelley p440

the nation. We know something about Christian obligation and charity towards the helpless, but we also demand the protection of the nation from the unfit and inferior."[1]

Bunny held her breath as the awful reality of what she was hearing unfolded. The Paragraph, she discovered, was the Aryan Paragraph that all German institutions were obliged to adopt. It specifically vilified the Jews and those of Jewish mixed-race descent and forbade them from holding any public position, effectively excluding them from society.[2]

How can the Church agree to this? Bunny thought. Putting to one side the rampant antisemitism, even I know that Jesus *was* Jewish!

Mueller then introduced Ernst Bergman who had published an essay entitled *Twenty-Five Points of the German Religion*.[3] He opened by denying the canonicity of the entire Jewish Old Testament,[4] and said that parts of the New Testament were not suitable for the new German Reich Church and will be re-written.[5]

He then addressed head-on the obvious misnomer of the Jewish Jesus, stating that Jesus was actually a Nordic martyr put to death by the Jews, a warrior whose death rescued the world from Jewish influence. Bunny was all but expecting them to agree that Adolf Hitler was the new Messiah sent to earth to save the world from the Jews.[6]

Finally, it was announced that the Catholic Church had endorsed the new Nazi republic and the concordat that Hitler had signed with the Pope guaranteed the freedom of the Catholic Church and excluded them from any interference in politics.[7]

---

[1] Speech by Bishop Ludwig Müller, taken from Spartacus-educational.com by John Simkin, September 1997

[2] The Aryan Paragraph was formally adopted by the German Church at the synod of 27 September 1933

[3] 'Twenty-Five Points of the German Religion' by Ernst Bergmann (1934).

[4] Doris Bergen, Twisted Cross: The German Christian Movement Inside the Third Reich, (Chapel Hill, NC: The University of North Carolina Press, 1996) page 143

[5] In 1940 Walter Grundmann published a version of the Bible, called The Message of God (Die Botschaft Gottes) excluding the Old Testament, John's Gospel, and all references to Jesus as the lamb of God.

[6] The German Church did indeed begin to preach that Adolf Hitler was the Messiah.

[7] On July 20, 1933 Cardinal Eugenio Pacelli, the Vatican secretary of state and future Pope Pius XII, formally signed a concordat with Germany's vice-chancellor, Franz von Papen, thus excluding the Church from any

"This is so wrong. Isn't anyone going to stand up against this?" Bunny whispered. At least she *thought* she had whispered, but as soon as she said it the man seated directly in front of her turned around and looked at her. Bunny froze to the spot. She held her breath and stared into space, as if lack of movement might somehow accentuate her invisibility. It didn't work. He had seen her. The man, not one wearing the brown-shirt of the SA, began to make his way to the nearest end of the aisle intent on getting to her. Bunny's heart began to race. She had dreamed herself into some dangerous places, but for the first time she felt afraid. He kept looking directly at her as he excused his sideways passage. Bunny was unsure whether to run. But to where? Soon he was walking toward her. She started to clench both fists but soon realised the probable futility of any resistance. Not only did he tower above her, and by the look of him clearly had a military background, but the whole room was full of equally Aryan stock. She stood in the darkened doorway, rigid with fear.

"Come with me," he said as he grabbed her forearm with his strong left hand. She didn't move, just looked at him square in the eyes. He met her gaze and rather than drag her off he leaned towards her and whispered,

"My name is Martin, and we can't keep silent when God commands us to speak, we must obey God rather than man."[1]

Bunny instantly knew she had found at least one person who dissented against the travesty of church she had just witnessed, and the two of them quietly slipped out of the rear of the meeting room.

"Rector Mashman? What are you doing in my wood so late at night?" Lord Advowson's surprise at seeing the clergyman in such an incongruous setting was palpable.

"Hey, I'm the one asking the questions," the detective inspector protested. No one paid attention.

---

interference with Nazi ambitions. Four years later, on March 14, 1937 Pope Pius XI reversed this, issuing an encyclical condemning the Nazi regime. Pius XII however took papal office in 1939 inevitably earning him the probably unfair moniker of *Hitler's Pope*.

[1] This is a paraphrase of the last sermon Martin Niemoeller preached before his imprisonment in June 1937. The full text being "We have no more thought of using our own powers to escape the arm of authorities than had the Apostles of old. No more are we ready to keep silent at man's behest when God commands us to speak. For it is, and must remain, the case that we must obey God rather than man." Taken from 'Religion in the Reich' by Michael Power (1939) p142

"Your Lordship!" Mashman replied, relieved at seeing yet another friendly face. "I called in to see you earlier, but Ruby said you were out catching poachers?"

The Reverend's choice of words may have been both innocent and accurate but was possibly the worst thing he could have said at the scene of a double shooting. The D.I. suddenly had both a suspect and a motive. In the scenario now playing out in his mind the two victims were poachers executed by a landowner who considered himself above the law.

"Lord Advowson," the detective quickly followed-up, "Are you the owner of a firearm?"

The aristocrat admitted that he did in fact own a single-barrel 12-bore shotgun; that he used it to control rabbits as the law required him to; and that it was fully legal. He then added, rather irritated by the question, that the Section 2 licence had been issued by the commanding officer of the self-same police force that his present interrogator worked for, adding for good measure that he was also a *close personal friend*. Undaunted the detective continued,

"And where exactly is the said firearm now, Sir?"

"Well, it's in my Land Rover," Advowson said pointing towards his vehicle, parked a short distance away.

"Sergeant!" was all the officer needed to say to instruct his number two to request the keys of the Land Rover, to then give them to one of several constables nearby, with specific instructions to seize the weapon as evidence. The investigating officer then turned his attention to the latest two additions to the gathered group.

"As for the God Squad 'ere," he began, "Mr. Fort informs me that you churchmen were tasked with finding a missing woman... a Miss Elstow." He consulted his sergeant's notes, "and that he thought she might be in this 'ere wood."

"Yes, that is correct," Artur pitched in, keen to be associated with an innocent reason for being there.

"The thing that puzzles me, though... is why?" the police investigator asked. "Why this particular wood?"

The three ministers looked at each other. Jack then admitted they had been told there had been a shooting in this wood and they feared it may have been Miss Elstow.

"Who told you there had been a shooting here? The press only arrived the same time we found you sneaking about." Jack thought it best to not challenge

372

the accusation that he had been sneaking about as that was exactly what he had been doing. He thought for a moment, then explained truthfully,

"It was our friend Joel Whyens who told us there had been shooting here."

The sergeant, who was by now busy making notes, asked,

"And who is this Mr. Joel Whyens?"

Artur, Jack and the Rector all replied in unison.

"The Methodist Minister!"

"Of course, he is, I should have guessed!" the detective said sarcastically throwing his hands skywards. "And how in God's name did he know? Don't tell me, don't tell me, you're going to say it was Divine Inspiration, I suppose." They chose not to join in his rhetoric.

Suddenly a mobile phone began ringing, causing everyone to pat their pockets to see if their handset was the offending device. Rev. Mashman was the only person to not join in the ritual – his cell phone rang so infrequently it had yet to engender such a reflex response. The guilty party this time was Lord Advowson who waved his ringing phone towards the officer and asked if he would be permitted to take the call, saying it was his wife and it was unusual for her to ring. The detective nodded his agreement but determined to keep one ear on the call. Despite trying to answer his mobile call quietly Lord Advowson's voice soon became louder the more agitated he became.

"Velia's where?" he said anxiously.

Jack leaned sideways towards the detective and said to him, "She's in the hospital!" He looked over towards Artur, gave him a knowing wink and nodded for him to join in.

Artur immediately understood what Jack was doing and grinned back at him. Artur too leaned toward the detective, on his other side, and said, as nonchalantly as he could,

"She's having an X-ray for a head injury."

Lord Advowson finished his call, looked worriedly at the policeman and said,

"It's our daughter, Velia, she's in the hospital. She's had some sort of head injury and is having it X-rayed right now. My wife has just arrived at the hospital. She'll let me know as soon as she knows how Velia is."

The detective looked first at Jack, then at Artur.

"And I suppose your friend Joel told you that, too?" he provoked sarcastically.

"No, not Joel," Jack said dismissively, allowing Artur to deliver the punchline,

"It was Thea," Artur submitted with a disguised grin.

"And who, might I ask, is Thea?"

To the detective's surprise it was Rector Mashman who answered his question.

"Thea? Thea Howlsy? Well. She's the Baptist minister. A lovely lady," he said.

Chapter 44

DIETRICH BONHOEFFER

There were stark differences between the Brown Synod from which she and Martin Niemöller had quietly left, and the alternative gathering held discreetly in the German town of Barmen. Bunny was much happier in the latter. Niemöller, she discovered, was a veteran of the Great War, a former U-Boat captain, but more importantly was instrumental in setting up the opposition to the Nazification of the German Church. He had initially been, like most Germans, pro-Nazi and was an active supporter of Hitler. It was, however, the introduction of the Aryan Paragraph that had brought him to his senses. He, and a small group of followers, began to promote an alternative confession. One of those was the short bespectacled gentleman that Niemöller was in the process of introducing to Bunny.

"I am most charmed to make yar acquaintance, Fraulein," he said in a soft German accent, shaking her hand and giving a firm nod of his head. Bunny had half expected a simultaneous click of the heels but decided that was probably the result of having watched too many old war films.

"And your name is..." she asked.

"Dietrich, Fraulein. Dietrich Bonhoeffer," he replied releasing her hand. Bunny had heard of the name but wasn't exactly sure who he was. Bonhoeffer explained that over seven thousand churches had already signed up to their alternative Confession, an opposition to the Aryan Paragraph.

"What is this alternative Confession?" Bunny asked curiously. Bonhoeffer could recite it verbatim without notes and immediately stated:

"We confess our faith in the Holy Spirit, and therefore reject, as a matter of principle, the exclusion of non-Aryans from the Church, because it is based on confusion between State and Church. The State is supposed to judge, and the Church is supposed to save."[1] As he spoke a church bell rang out a solitary note. Bunny noticed it this time but didn't remark about it.

"That is pretty unambiguous," Bunny conceded, impressed with the lack of subtlety in the text. "Have many pastors signed up to it?"

---

[1] There were 12 points to the Confession that Niemoeller and Bonhoeffer requested church leaders to give their assent to. Point 7 is shown here. Taken from 'Berlin: 1932-1933: Dietrich Bonhoeffer Works', Volume 12 by Dietrich Bonhoeffer p107/8

"Seven thousand so far," then added, "and zey are across Lutheran, Reformed und other denominations."[1]

"It is as though there are now just *two* churches in Germany," Bunny said encapsulating her realisation that a major change had happened to the Church in this nation.

"Ja, the Reich Church und our... Confessing Church," he agreed.

"No, I mean there are *only* two churches," she clarified. "All the old liturgical, doctrinal, historical differences don't seem to matter anymore, in the face of this opposition." Bonhoeffer nodded,

"Ja, zat is correct, Fraulein. As it says in the Bible, he who is not with us, is against us!"[2]

Despite the ominous cloud hanging over the Church, Bunny could see that in the face of opposition – the figurative *call to arms* – all the entrenched differences could be put to one side. Doctrinal positions, that she knew only too well people had defended – sometimes with their lives – were suddenly diminished in importance when faced with a wholesale sell-out of the Christian faith.

"The need to defend the Jews has suddenly produced unity," Bunny said to herself. "It wasn't the ominous threat of persecution, but the Jewish thing that has actually pulled them all together."

Bonhoeffer didn't hear her aside and said, with resignation, "Ah, but seven thousand is but a fraction. I fear there are too many already going in the wrong direction." Bunny snapped back into the conversation with,

"But some of them may turn around, surely."

"If you board the wrong train, it is no use running along the corridor in the other direction," he said determinedly.

"He may well be right," Bunny thought.[3]

Their conversation was suddenly brought to a halt as the door burst open, swinging hard back onto its hinges. Everyone in the room turned in shock as dozens of brown-shirted stormtroopers forced their way inside. These men in uniform were no church ministers, but heavily armed troopers who forcefully

---

[1] 'Holocaust and human behaviour.' Chapter 5. Taken from www.facinghistory.org

[2] This is based on Matthew chapter twelve verse thirty: "He who is not with Me is against Me, and he who does not gather with Me scatters abroad." NKJV

[3] Taken from 'Bonhoeffer: Pastor, Martyr, Prophet, Spy' by Eric Metaxas, p187

made their way to the front of the room to take hold of both Niemöller and Bonhoeffer.[1] The leader of the raiding party, very satisfied with having snared his prey, declared the terms of their arrest with authority, then condescendingly asked if either of the ringleaders had anything to say in their defence. Niemöller thought for only the briefest of moments before replying, not to the arresting officer, but to his fellow clergymen,

"First, they came for the communists, and I did not speak out because I was not a communist," he said. "Then they came for the trade unionists, and I did not speak out because I was not a trade unionist; then they came for the Jews and I did not speak out because I was not a Jew. Finally, they came for me but there was no one left to speak out for me."[2]

The lane that led to the farmhouse was unlit and the cloud-filled night sky obscured any assistance from moonlight. Chris had tried to inch his way along with no lights on at all, but that proved to be nearly impossible and at one point they veered off the lane and nearly into the small gushing gully that flowed to its left. Ralph insisted that he at least put his side lights on, which he did. Their progress remained cautiously slow as bump after bump shook them sideways. Before it arrived at its destination the lane became a broken concrete yard as they passed discarded and rusty farm machinery; a water trough inside of which stood three unopened plastic sacks labelled Wynnstay; several large mounds of unknown provenance each now overgrown with nettles, grass and in one case polythene sheeting and two old tractor tyres; and finally, it cornered around an empty barn to reveal Lane End farmhouse. Chris switched off the meagre illumination before stopping at the final turn.

He was surprised to see that lights were on inside the building, a faint glow emanating from two of the downstairs windows. More startling though was that the only vehicle parked outside was an ambulance. The light from one of the windows at the front of the farmhouse meant they could just make out the registration number: LM02 EAA. This was the self-same vehicle they had investigated at St. Christopher's Hospice hours earlier.

---

[1] Bonhoeffer was arrested in April 1943 then tried and imprisoned. Niemoeller was imprisoned, without trial in 1938.

[2] Widely quoted, this is the most well-known statement to come from the Confessing Church movement. It was delivered by Niemoeller as a sermon, not at his arrest.

"Pull the car into the barn, Chris," Ralph suggested.

It was a good idea. Chris slipped it into reverse and arced right until the car was hidden behind the barn wall, unseen from both the farmhouse and the lane. He switched off the engine.

"How did that ambulance get here?" Ralph asked rhetorically.

"I don't know." Chris thought for a moment, as if working out the most plausible of scenarios in his mind. Conclusion reached, he postulated the truism,

"Last time, there was no ambulance and no Bunny. So, if the ambulance is here then Bunny must be also." Ralph wasn't so sure, but there was some logic in Chris's statement.

"That means..." Chris said unbuckling his seatbelt and reaching for the door handle "...that I'm going in."

"Wait a minute!" Ralph tried to grab his arm to stop him, but Chris was already outside.

"Wait! You can't go in there on your own," Ralph insisted as he too jumped out of the car, leaving his door open. "You don't know who's in there with her, and by all accounts he's already killed two people tonight."

"Yes, you are right," Chris answered continuing unabashed towards the entrance of the barn, "and I'm not going to let Bunny be next on his list." Ralph hurried over to his friend and managed to grasp his sleeve. Chris stopped and turned.

"You don't have to come with me if you don't want to. But I *have to* do this," he said.

"I'm coming with you. We are probably both completely crazy, but I am coming with you," Ralph assured him. Chris clasped his hand over Ralph's which was still holding his sleeve.

"Thanks," he said.

"But..." Ralph cautioned, "before we launch this rescue, we should at least let the others know first."

Chris could see the sense in that suggestion. He pulled his phone out, opened WhatsApp and typed, 'Ambulance and Bunny are at Lane End Farm. Come quickly.' He pressed Enter, then wished he had added a further remark. He typed a short second message immediately after the first which simply read, 'Be careful!'

"Eins, zwei, eins zwei!"

378

Only the most rudimentary knowledge of the German language was required to understand the numerical accompaniment to forced marching. It was only a narrow corridor. Bunny pressed herself hard against one of the damp walls to allow two guards to pass. As they did, she was shocked to see that their black uniforms were sporting the unmistakable lightning-bolt epaulets of the SS. Between them they carried a solitary, frail, pathetic example of mistreated humanity wearing the tell-tale stained, frayed and striped uniform of a Nazi concentration camp.[1]

"You must be Fraulein... erm."

From seemingly out of nowhere a short, bespectacled man had appeared, his attention fixed on a clipboard, continually lifting and lowering the top page and exasperatedly tutting. He wore an off-white overall that was far from clean, having stains, maybe even blood stains, liberally daubed across his rather rotund abdomen. This was a medical man, although she could have been forgiven for mistaking him for a butcher. Most doctors wear the stethoscopic signature of their profession proudly around their necks – a symbol of their status in the establishment – but Bunny could see that he kept his stethoscope neatly folded in his side pocket.

"Ahh yes, Fraulein Hase," he concluded, tucking his clipboard under his arm and instructing her to follow. They set off in the same direction she had seen the prisoner frog-marched moments earlier. Bunny was too frightened to point out she was not the Fraulein Hase he was expecting.

As they walked, briskly, she was momentarily overcome by the smell of cleaning fluids, bleach principally. The smell was particularly strong, but she couldn't see any clean surface, the whole place being dark and grimy. She felt a hand on her shoulder and then the strongly accented voice whispered very close to her ear,

"You need to keep quiet." The intrusion sent a chill across her whole body and she stopped suddenly to turn and see who had spoken to her. No one was there.

"Come, come, Fraulein Hase," the doctor reacted to her momentary pause. "It is very unusual to allow condemned prisoners to have any visitors," he said, talking loudly over his shoulder as they continued to stride forwards. Bunny replied only by making an indistinct sound.

---

[1] Bonhoeffer was moved to Flossenbürg Concentration Camp prior to his execution.

"But you appear to have clearance from the highest authority, Fraulein Hase," he conceded.

Bunny remained silent. He strode on, pushing through several sets of spring-hinged double-doors which swung back into her face. She chose not to complain. Behind the third set of doors the passageway continued along the side of a larger open space. The doctor maintained his forward trajectory and as Bunny followed she couldn't help but glance into the large room on their right. As they walked past, she witnessed a scene so dramatically staged it could have been the pre-interval moment in a West-End play, held in freeze-frame as the curtain fell. They had caught up with the guards and etched indelibly onto her defenceless memory was one of them tightening a noose around the neck of the prisoner who stood blind-folded and facing a wide, open pit. The other guard rested one hand on the prisoner's back ready to swing him over the pit once the noose was tightened. No town-square gallows here, no chance to address the crowds, just a gaping pit and a rough rope looped over a ceiling pulley. Efficient execution, SS style. No one moved, they became a frozen cameo, until the doctor led Bunny past them. She knew that scene would stay with her forever.

"In here, Fraulein." The doctor checked that the cell number matched that of the key he had been given. "Cell 92! You have fünf minuten with Herr Bonhoeffer. No more!" he demanded. [1]

---

[1] Before being transferred to Flossenbürg, Bonhoeffer was held for several years in Cell 92 of Tegel prison. Guards here illegally allowed him writing materials and amongst his many writings from prison were those to his fiancé Maria von Wedemeyer later published as 'Love Letters from Cell 92'

Chapter 45

"I SHOULDN'T BE HERE"

It was almost impossible for Rex, in a near upside-down position straddled between rear and front seats of the abandoned Ford, to be able look at his mobile phone. The Message Received chime was sufficient a prompt for him to smoothly disentangle himself, finally re-emerging through the rear door.

"Did you find the keys?" Cecil, the hospice manager asked from his safe position a few yards to the rear of the vehicle, at the corner of The Woodshed. Rex was too light-headed to reply immediately, steadying himself by grasping the open rear door and pausing to allow the blood flow in his body to return to its normal non-inverted equilibrium. Once stability had returned to his legs, Rex responded. He slid his right hand back onto the rear seat to collect the item he had left there while he clambered out.

"No keys, only this!" he said, holding aloft the handgun, dangling precariously between two fingers as he held it by the end of the barrel, conscious to not add any unnecessary fingerprints. Cecil gasped, covering his mouth with both hands in an involuntary reflex. Rex reached into his pocket and consulted his phone.

"Sorry, but I have to go," he announced to the shocked manager who then immediately began to protest about what they ought to do about the discovery they had just made.

"Don't worry," Rex assured him, "I'll let the police know just as soon as I see them."

Both Thea and Joel's phones responded simultaneously to the message being received. Joel's, being linked by Bluetooth to his car, initiated a sudden cacophony of sound; Thea's buzzed discreetly in her jacket pocket, having left it on silent mode since the start of the meeting at C.R.F. earlier.

Joel could do nothing about it, he was following the red soft-top Mazda, carefully trying to maintain the optimum distance. Not too close so as to be noticed; not so far back as to get trapped behind a changing red light or allow another vehicle to pull out between them. He found judging the distance a bit of a challenge as his natural driving style was always to go as fast as he thought appropriate. Years spent travelling the motorways as a sales representative had made him rather blasé to the national speed limits. He knew he really ought to be more law-abiding, especially as a Methodist preacher, but 50,000 miles each year without prosecution did little to adjust his theology.

"That'll be the..." Thea said as she reached for her own phone, unsure of the correct collective term for their group.

"The other elves!" Joel finished, a reference to their discussion in the hospice reception where they compared themselves to Tolkien's incongruent assortment of Middle-Earth tribes. Thea smiled at the recollection of the amusing and somewhat accurate comparison. She read aloud both of Chris's messages.

"Ambulance and Bunny are at Lane End Farm, come quickly, be careful!"

"That is roughly the direction that we are heading," Joel said, adding his opinion, "I vote we keep following the red car for now."

"Agreed," Thea said.

Joel looked again in his mirror. The headlights of the car that had exited the hospital car park immediately behind them were still behind them. He hadn't said anything to his passenger so far, but Chris's instruction to *be careful* was all he needed to share his concern.

"Thea, don't turn around, but I think... well, I am pretty sure... we are being followed," he said soberly.

Thea looked dead ahead.

"Since when?" she asked.

"Out of the hospital," Joel explained. Thea then asked for a second level of confirmation to his assertion to which Joel replied emphatically that he was, *really* sure.

Neither Artur nor Jack had left their phones on silent so when they were simultaneously alerted to the arrival of a new message, it raised a curious eyebrow with the detective inspector trying his best to make sense of the murder scene.

He had released his only suspect, Lord Advowson, on a mercy dash to the hospital to see his daughter, but only if he was accompanied by a detective constable. Rector Mashman had offered to go with them but the D.I. refused, wanting rather to get to the bottom of what he proudly described, in somewhat grim police humour, as 'The Holy Body's involvement with these holey bodies.'

So far, from his initial interrogation, not only did he have three churchmen at the scene of the crime – one Anglican, one Lutheran and one Presbyterian – but he also had reason to believe that a Baptist and a Methodist were also somehow involved.

In response to the WhatsApp alert, both Artur and Jack took out their handsets, although only Jack asked for permission to read it.

"Let me see that," the detective demanded of Mr. Thelmin as he opened the application and began to read. Artur compliantly gave him his handset.

"Ambulance and Bunny are at Lane End Farm, come quickly," he read out, followed by, "Be careful!"

Rector Mashman couldn't help but respond,

"Oh, that is good news, Bunny has been found."

Artur and Jack were more circumspect, having interpreted the *Be careful* instruction as an indication, as it was meant, that Bunny is still very much in danger. The detective then asked for Jack's phone and saw that he had received the same message.

"And who, might I ask, gentlemen, is this Chris Palmer," he said, then added much for his own amusement, "A Jehovah's Witness? or one of those from the Church of the Latter Day whatever they are?"

"Certainly not!" Jack said indignantly. "The J.W.'s and Mormons are cults, we are Christians. We follow the true and living God and would have no truck with the followers of the spirit of error."

The detective ignored the unwelcome doctrinal put-down, still waiting for an explanation of who had sent the message. Jack stopped himself in mid-rant and Artur chipped in to spare his new friend's blushes.

"Mr Palmer is the assistant pastor of C.R.F." Artur said. The detective did not recognise the acronym and so asked for an explanation. Artur attempted to explain but quickly painted himself into a verbal corner when, instead of correctly saying Community Restoration Fellowship, he began with 'Christian Resource...' Jack came to the Austrian's rescue, as he was searching his memory for the F word.

"C.R.F. is Community Restoration Fellowship, the big free church," Jack interrupted, adding by way of explanation, "Or you might call it Pentecostal."

For a painful few seconds no one spoke. The detective sergeant finished recording the incomprehensible facts in his notebook while the inspector looked over his shoulder, then flipped back a page or two before addressing the three churchmen.

"Bingo!" the inspector said. No one replied. "Bingo!" he repeated, "Or is it *House!* you say?" Again no one commented. The officer continued,

"It would appear, Sergeant, does it not, that we have a full house of churches involved, somehow, in this crime."

The sergeant then read out the names of six denominations that now appeared in the pages of his notebook, struggling as he did to articulate the word Presbyterian.

"Yes Sir, I would call that it's a full house," the sergeant agreed.

"Any others you would like to admit to?" the D.I. provoked the churchmen. All three immediately thought of Quaker Rex Fogge but none spoke, knowing that it would add little to the direction of investigation that the detective was now pursuing.

"Sir, may I say something?" Jack proffered. The detective was more than happy for anything that might help him unravel what was going on and made that sentiment clear.

Jack then gently explained that all they were doing here was trying to locate Miss Elstow, or the 'Bunny' referred to in the WhatsApp message. And now that they have been told she is at Lane End Farm, perhaps some officers might be deployed there to help rescue her. The detective could not see beyond the murder scene he was confronted with and refused to waste any of his limited resource on any worthless errand for them, insisting they must have something to do with the killings.

"We don't," Rector Mashman interjected with perfect timing, causing the policemen to stop his oration. The Anglican then added, as if it were a cleverly constructed punchline, "But Lane End Farm might."

"What do you mean?" the sergeant asked suspiciously.

Unsure about how much information they ought to give, Artur jumped in and spoke across the Rector.

"Lane End Farm is not too far away from here," he said, "There might be something there that is linked to this crime, so you should really send some officers."

Again the D.I. refused. No sooner had he done so than they were all distracted by the sound of the first of two body bags being zipped up ready to be stretchered towards a waiting ambulance, ominously devoid of its flashing blue lights. It was a sobering sight.

"I think they know more than they're letting on," the sergeant stated rhetorically, his professional interrogation senses working overtime. It was now Jack's turn to try to take control of the situation. He had spent enough time as a Special Constable to have a good grasp of their rights, so directed his comments directly at the senior officer.

"Sir, if you're not going to go to the farmhouse, and if you are not going to arrest us..."

The Rector gasped at the idea of being arrested. Jack continued,

"Then you will have no objection if we *do* go to Lane End Farm to find Miss Elstow. You have all our details, and we shall be at the station tomorrow to make our formal statements."

Jack had delivered a statement of intent, not a request, and it would be up to the D.I. to stop them. He looked at his sergeant but they both knew they had no grounds to hold the churchmen right now so released them, having first repeated that they must give their statements in the morning.

The Rector's car was nearby. Jack's was on the other side of the wooded copse, beyond the police line. He asked if Mashman might drop him off at his car before going to the farmhouse. Jack had never ridden with the elderly Anglican and could feel impatience rise within him as he dithered and delayed before setting off. Patience is one of the fruits of the Christian life so, despite wanting to grab hold of the wheel, Jack said nothing as the Honda Jazz crawled along the deserted lanes. After what felt like an age, he directed him left, left and left again towards his abandoned 4x4, and Jack eventually unbuckled himself from the rear seat and thanked his chauffeur.

"Wait," Artur said as Jack departed, "I'm coming with you!"

Evidently, he couldn't cope with the gentle pace any longer either.

"Ah, danke for coming, Miss," Bonhoeffer said as he offered Bunny the only chair in the small dark cell, "especially at such short notice."

He retreated to the middle of his thin bunk, which hardly registered any movement as he sat down. Bunny didn't know what to say. Here was a man who had dared to stand up to Hitler and had mobilised thousands to do likewise. Here in this dank cell was a man of the church, who had put his faith into action, standing up against the Jewish persecution. Clearly malnourished and bruised, he was nonetheless a picture of saintly serenity. Bunny knew she was in the presence of a great man, albeit one she hadn't really heard of. With this level of conviction, she surmised, perhaps he was going to be one of those who rebuild post-war Germany. Bonhoeffer reached under a dirty pillow and extricated a small, well-worn Bible. Bunny felt she had to say something in her allotted five minutes.

"There will be a better Germany, a better society, after this war is over," she said in part to offer the detainee a glint of hope.

"I am sure there vil be, Fraulein. Ze ultimate test of a society is the kind of world that it leaves to its kinderen," Bonhoeffer replied flipping open the Bible and pulling from within, a single piece of paper folded in half. He passed it towards Bunny.

"Could you give this to Archbishop George Bell when you return to England?" She reached out a hand and took the missive, sliding her thumb into the fold so that it half-opened.

"May I?" she asked. Bonhoeffer nodded his agreement, so she opened it fully. Inside, just ten words were inscribed. Ten words so poignant and telling it made tears instantaneously well-up in her eyes. It simply read: 'This is the end – for me the beginning of life.'[1]

Bunny didn't know what to say. She had already witnessed the stark brutality of the SS. Was she about to see, not for the first time on this endless evening, a man of God martyred for his faith.

"This is the end," he echoed. Bunny glanced at her watch, it flashed 19:45.

"No, it isn't," she said hurriedly. "But it's 1945. The war will end in 1945!" she pleaded.

Bonhoeffer raised a hand to quieten her. "We know the Americans will be here in one or two weeks," he said calmly. "That is why zey have to eliminate all we conspirators."

"Conspirators?" Bunny asked surprised. "But you are a minister, a churchman," she protested, "not part of any conspiracy."

"Well, they think I was part of the attempt to assassinate Hitler last July," he said, very matter of fact.

"But you were in prison at the time?" Bunny postulated. He nodded then leaned forward and dropped his voice, not that anyone was listening.

"But this church minister has been eine dopple-agent, working for the resistance for years," he confessed. He then tapped the now folded paper in Bunny's hand, "And ve owe a lot to my good friend Archbishop Bell."[2]

Bunny looked down at the paper in her hand.

---

[1] This was Bonhoeffers final message from prison. 'The History of the German Resistance, 1933–1945' by Peter Hoffman, 1996. McGill-Queen's Press.

[2] Prior to his arrest Bonhoeffer was a double-agent and exchanged secret messages with Archbishop George Bell, who was in a position to pass them on to the authorities in England. Bell was an important voice in England in the pre-war and wartime periods and tried, in vain, to make a separation in people's minds between Nazis and the wider German population.

"Is this a coded message?" she asked without thinking. He smiled at the thought. The sound of the key re-entering the lock was instantly chilling. Bunny folded the paper into a quarter of its size and slipped it into her pocket. The door opened to reveal, not only the doctor, but the same stone-faced SS guards she had avoided earlier; their sombre intent clear to see. She wanted to object, to protest, to state how this was such an injustice. But she found herself unable to move from her chair. Struck dumb in fear. All she could do was watch as Bonhoeffer compliantly followed the guards. The doctor closed the door behind them leaving Bunny alone in the cell. The key turned in the lock. Bunny, now finding herself free to move, rushed to the door.

"Let me out, let me out!" she screamed as she pointlessly pulled at the handle. She thumped the heavy door with the side of her fist. It was useless, no one was going to hear her, let alone release her. She allowed her forehead to rest against the cold steel as her arms fell limply to her side.

"I shouldn't be here!" she shouted. It was meant to be a plea to her impromptu jailors, but she knew inside that she was talking to herself. She repeated it loudly,

"I shouldn't be here!"

This time it had become a complaint levelled toward her angelic dream-guide. When she'd said she was ready to 'Go back' he'd sent her back to Wittenberg. A third time she said it,

"I shouldn't be here!" This time, rather than a plea or protest, it became more of a prayer.

"Lord, what am I doing here?" She pivoted around, with her back to the door, eyes firmly closed. "I get it, I get it. You wanted to show me the origins of every Christian denomination, how they all claimed to be the special ones; that they were better than those who came before, even though their predecessors had thought that they too had been just as special; how they all believed they were living in the final generation; how they all used the Bible as a weapon to justify their position; I get it! Hey, I was able to spot the heretics a mile off!"

She stood silent for a moment.

"I've seen healings, miracles, heard prophesy and speaking in tongues, seen thousands having their lives changed by encountering..." She paused briefly. "Encountering... not church, but you God... that is what it is all about, isn't it?"

Reflective memories began to flood in.

"Even me! I heard you... for the first time... in the silence of that Quaker chapel; I opened my heart to you in that Moravian meeting with Wesley; and despite all my misgivings I became open to the Baptism of the Holy Spirit in Topeka. I have changed, Lord, really, I have. I am ready to go back to Chris and, if he still wants me, I am willing to start a life with him."

She kicked the door with her heel in frustration.

"So why have you brought me here? Just to see all this awful, awful, brutal, injustice!" She paused; she needed a breath. Still eyes-closed she continued, "Okay, let's think about this logically," unsure as to whether she was still praying or now just verbally processing her thoughts. "Let's see... what's so special about the story of the wartime Confessing Church?" she asked herself again out loud.

"Well, they ignored all of their differences to become a united opposition to the Nazis." She thought for a moment.

"No, that's not strictly accurate. The unifying *Confession* wasn't about opposition to the Nazis, that would have just been politics, the same as happened over and over again in mediaeval times. No, this was different. This was about resisting the expulsion of the Jews. How bizarre! The thing that united the Christian Church was its treatment of another religion!"

Bunny knew little about the Jewish religion, other than what she read in her own Bible, largely in the Old Testament. She knew Jesus and his disciples were all Jews, and that the early Church was mainly full of Jews. Like most Christians, she had no idea when this Jewish-heavy version of Christianity had ended. She continued to explore her thoughts verbally, in the privacy of a Nazi prison cell.

"The whole thing started with a split from another religion, well sort of," she mused aloud. "Luther's Reformation started the Protestant Church, as opposed to the Catholic one. That is fact. But does that mean that disunity also began with Luther? Was the Reformation a bad thing?"

Every time she got any level of clarity in her thoughts, more confusion surfaced. Then an important question popped into her mind. A question that would test an assumption she had all along. An assumption which she was now willing to consider might not have been right after all. She tentatively spoke it aloud, eyes still firmly closed, into the empty atmosphere of the prison cell,

"There was just one Church before Luther, wasn't there?"

The sound of a solitary slow handclap jolted her out of her soul-searching. Clearly, she was no longer alone in the cell. She opened her eyes to see the man in the gold-brimmed hat, smiling and offering her an almost congratulatory handclap. What was most startling, however, was the fact that they were no longer in the prison cell she had been in a few moments earlier.

Ralph had watched enough war films to know that you never approach an enemy position in a direct line but take as wide a circuitous route as you can, hugging the treeline and sprinting from one position of cover to another. Having rehearsed such an approach many times as a child, playing with his elder brothers, the reality held little of the excitement and much more genuine peril than he had hitherto experienced. Finally reaching their initial objective, they both stood with their backs firmly pressed against the slightly damp red brick of the farmhouse, unable to speak. It wasn't that they were out of breath, their short sprints being well within the ability of two men who each considered themselves to be reasonably fit, but it was pure adrenalin that had robbed them of the capability of discourse. After a full minute of heavy but silent breathing, Ralph managed to half-whisper, the simplest of one-word questions to be asked in such a situation.

"You'kay?"

Chris nodded his reply, then swallowed hard. They had made it undetected to the side of the remote building. The ambulance was parked at the front, now out of their view. All they could see was the end of the lane curving past the barn where they had left their car. To their left, towards the rear of the building, a few feet away was the dim illumination emanating from a window that Chris felt sure would be the rear room, where they had found a camp bed and intravenous stand; and where Bunny might be right now. They had gone this far, he had to look closer and tapping Ralph's arm indicated he was going to try to look inside. It was Ralph's turn to nod in reply. Chris swivelled round to face the brickwork then began to inch his way along. No need to look back to see if Ralph was following him, he knew he would be. Slowly and silently he approached the window. As soon as his fingers touched the flaking paintwork of the wooden window frame, he squatted down to position his body such that only his eyes and forehead would be above the height of the windowsill. Thin paisley-print curtains were drawn. Light was pouring through the fabric, but it was impossible to see anything distinguishable inside. There was little chance to find a viewpoint at the edge or the bottom – the curtains descended well below the window. There was, however, a glint of light where the curtains had not been closed together properly. Presumably, someone had drawn them in haste and had left a narrow slit which might afford Chris a view. He rocked his now squat body left then right, moving with the inelegance of the Star Wars droid R2-D2. Within a couple of oscillations, he was ready; his head under the sill, positioned to slowly raise himself and behold the scene inside. This was the moment, he thought. The single most risky and yet most important thing he had ever done. Whatever he was about to see inside was probably going to define his future. Whether positive or – he dared not think – negative, this scene was going to be indelibly etched upon his mind.

Chris glanced up at Ralph, still standing back to the wall but now close to the window. He looked down at his friend and colleague, and gave a reassuring nod whilst forming the word 'Believe.' It was a strange thing for someone to say by way of reassurance at such a moment, but it was also the right thing to say. Chris was a man of faith, as were all of those who were seeking to find Bunny on that cold October night. But here, at his moment of greatest need, not only did he have a belief, but this was also the moment where a step of faith was needed and only such a step should be taken if you truly do believe. As he shivered below the windowsill, he needed to be sure.

Do I believe? Do I really believe that I can do this? Chris stared at the mouldy bricks beneath the window. Suddenly he remembered a verse of Scripture, one he knew well but which seemed to just fly into his mind unprompted.

I can do all things through Christ who strengthens me, he remembered, then whispered it as if making a declaration of his intent. He was sure and with a final nod back to Ralph he began his ascension.

The good news was that it was indeed the correct room. The medical apparatus was there, the empty chair and of course the camp bed. The bad news was that the bed was now occupied. Chris's heart skipped a beat when he saw her lying on the bed. It was Bunny. She was covered with a blanket, presumably one of those missing from the hospice ambulance, but thankfully not covering her face. "She's still alive..." he said to himself. Two saline bags hung from the stand, one connected to a clear silicone tube that disappeared from his viewpoint but presumably entered her left arm to administer its anaesthetic charge. "... alive but sedated," he ended his silent sentence.

There was no-one else in the room, well, certainly not within his limited field of vision. Chris beckoned Ralph over to squat down, shuffle over, and take a look. No sooner had Ralph joined Chris's viewing gallery, than a man entered the room. The two men froze to the spot, convinced that any movement would give away their snooping. The man walked straight over to the camp bed, stooped over Bunny and peeled back each eyelid as if to check on her health. Chris could feel rage rise within him, but dare not move. The man then checked that the saline drip was delivering the correct flow rate. They were barely six feet from this man and had an excellent view of him. He was tall, pale-skinned and sported a neat beard. He wore spectacles and most notably had black hair on either side of his head but was bald in the middle. This wasn't typical male-pattern-baldness but a completely bald streak from front to back making his pale white skin look like a white stripe. Checks completed he then turned and left the room. Chris and Ralph both breathed again, neither conscious they had been holding their breath for the duration of his bedside visit.

"The Badger!" Ralph whispered.

Chris didn't cotton on to why Ralph was calling the stranger by this name until he reminded him of the description the delivery girl had given.

"Ah yes, bald as a badger!" Chris echoed.

Chapter 46

TWO POPES

"You?" she exclaimed, seeing the man with the gold-rimmed hat sarcastically applauding her from the opposite side of the room. "How did you get..." she started. Then quickly adjusted her logic to fit the ethereal world she now inhabited and finished with a perfunctory, "Never mind."

He stopped his muted clapping to speak.

"So, you are asking if there was just one Church before Luther, are you?"

"Well...," she began. "Well, I don't know. I do know that there are hundreds of different Churches *after* Luther. And, I have seen first-hand how many of them began," she told him with an air of satisfaction.

"I know," he replied, "I am the one who showed you!" Bunny didn't respond.

"If you want to know if there was more than one Church before Martin Luther then come and sit down over here and watch." He motioned for her to join him at one of two simple wooden chairs that now faced the door. Compliantly, she began to slowly cross the room. He hurried her with an anxious,

"Quickly!" at which she instinctively jumped forward and took the chair next to his. Leaning slightly towards her, he whispered,

"Just watch and see." He then tapped his wrist and repeated the phrase, this time with special emphasis on the word *watch*. Bunny looked down at her own wrist, pulled up her sleeve and saw the digital dial flash 12:94. For the first time she had travelled backwards across the centuries. And no small jump. She had travelled over six hundred and fifty years, taking her to a moment two hundred years before Luther. No sooner had she looked down, than the door burst open with such force that the sound of splintering wood underlined the fact that the steel door she had kicked moments earlier had now morphed into wood. The room was still a prison cell, albeit now a cold damp mediaeval one. Two large men squeezed through the open door dragging with them a man, perhaps in his eighties, and dressed in the simple grey habit of a Benedictine monk. They didn't need to throw him into the cell; simply letting him go had the effect of causing him to crumple into a heap in the middle of the floor. The scene was eerily reminiscent of those she had just witnessed in Nazi Germany, centuries apart.

392

Bunny was shocked, she had no idea what the old man's crime must have been but, surely, they should be treating him better, after all he was a monk too. Not only did a sense of injustice began to rise within her, but she too began to stand to her feet in protest. As she did, her guide held her wrist and gently lowered her back into the chair, again repeating his instruction to just, 'Watch.'

The guards were dressed in distinctively mediaeval costumes, flamboyant and colourful, a stark change from the austere clean lines of the SS still etched upon her mind. One of them looked down at the crumpled ecclesiastical heap.

"So, you want to retire do you, Pope Celestine," he said in a distinctly Italian accent. Bunny gasped involuntarily. "Want to return to the tranquillo life of a hermit. Molto Bene! You can stay here and rot, tutto solo."[1]

With that he kicked the monk heavily in the stomach, adding as he did,

"Complimenti, from good Pope Boniface VIII." Bunny winced at the sight. Once the men departed, locking the door from the outside, Celestine began to sit up, his face already badly bruised, with blood evident from his upper lip and his nose. Again, Bunny recoiled at the sight. He groaned as he manoeuvred himself into a seated position before looking toward the door. He breathed deeply, as though charging himself with the energy required to speak.

"Good Pope? It is impossible for someone to be both Pope and be good at the same time,"[2] he said vicariously to his successor Boniface, before slumping back to the floor.

Bunny felt a tap on her arm. Her guide pointed to a pair of large purple velvet curtains that had appeared across much of the right side of the cell wall. No sooner had she spotted the curtains than they slowly opened to reveal a large glass-less window frame. The side wall of the room now had a huge opening that reached from three- or four-feet above floor-level to well above head height; and stretched two-thirds of the width of the room. Above the opening an inscription, carved into the lintel read 'ROME.' Through the opening she could see an opulently decorated room. Two enormous gold-trimmed tapestries hung at the rear, between them a small ornate stained-glass window.

---

[1] A former hermit and monk, Celestine V knew he was not cut out for the papacy. In 1294 after just 5 months, he became the first Pope to resign, having passed a decree to give himself the right to do so. The next Pope to use this right was Benedict XVI some 719 years later in 2013. Celestine's successor, however, was suspicious of having another potential powerbase around and had him imprisoned. Some reports say Boniface had him beaten; others deny this. Either way Celestine's retirement only lasted 10 months.

[2] Quotation taken from 'The Western Schism of 1378' by Charles River Editors, May 2017.

Seated on a large oak chair sat a man in lavish silken priestly garments as three marble statues stood silently watching. At the very top she could just make out an ornately painted ceiling.

Bunny whispered to her guide through the side of her mouth,

"I didn't really need the inscription above!"

This was obviously a window into the papal palace in Rome. Her guide whispered back,

"Oh, you *will* need the inscriptions."

Meanwhile, in the window, the central figure, she presumed to be Pope Boniface, was in a rage.

"I have the authority of the King of kings," he screamed spitting over those unfortunate enough to be in close proximity. "I am all in all, and above all so that God himself and I are but one. I am able to do almost all that God can do," he thundered.[1] This was self-evident blasphemy to Bunny's ears, and she started to turn to look at her fellow viewer when her attention fell on the centre of the room. Poor old Pope Celestine was gone and in his place a man sat alone at a desk writing under the light of three candles. The scratching of the quill soon ended as he returned it to its inkwell and leaned back in his chair in satisfaction.

"There you go Boniface, I've consigned you, and all your immoral evil-doers, to the eighth circle of Hell," he said before reaching for his final piece of parchment upon which he wrote a bold title in elaborate cursive script; *Inferno*, followed by his name: Dante Alighieri.[2]

Her guide then drew her attention to a second set of curtains, this time on the left side of the room. They were identical to those on the right in every way apart from the colour, these being azure blue. They too opened slowly to reveal another, similarly decorated, opulent room above which the carved inscription read, FRANCE. Upon the ornate French throne sat what Bunny had

---

[1] The full quote, taken from the text of the November 18 1302 Bull sanctum reads: "I have the authority of the king of kings, I am all in all and above all, so that God, Himself and I, the vicar of God, have but one consistory, and I am able to do almost all that God can do, what therefore can you make of me but God."

[2] Dante Aligheiri's poetic masterpiece 'Inferno' (1308 to 1320) imagined layers of increasing torment in damnation for sinners of ever-worsening degrees. Nine circles of Hell were described, and Pope Boniface VIII had a place in circle 8 reserved for those who committed Simony, i.e. those who made money out of what belonged to God. Inferno Cantus XIX Bolgia 3

to assume was the French King. Although she had no idea which one was on the throne in... she checked her watch ...1296.

"King Philippe le Bel," an attendant helpfully announced, addressing his monarch. "Your decree, to raise taxes on all French bishops, has now been issued."[1]

"What!" a loud voice thundered from the opposite side of the room. Bunny spun her head to see. "How dare you try to tax the Church!" he screamed. Boniface was standing at the open window, one hand grasping the gilded wooden frame and foaming at the mouth with rage. With his other hand he produced a document, a rolled parchment that he waved decisively at the French sovereign.

"Clericis laicos," Boniface said cryptically before pointing an angry index finger several times at the scroll and shouting, "Only the papacy has the right to tax the Church."[2]

Bunny turned to see if King Philippe was going to respond. This was like watching a tennis match, she thought. Philippe was having none of it and, addressing his attendant, issued a counter-declaration,

"I hereby impose an embargo on any and all money moving from France to Rome," he said loud enough such that Boniface could easily hear.[3]

Bunny spun back around. If nothing else, this was entertaining. Boniface harrumphed. Clearly, he needed the money. As she watched he exchanged one scroll for a another, and shouted,

"Listen son..."[4] Bunny gasped. No matter how acrimonious, that was no way to address a monarch. Boniface then took the scroll, entitled *Unam*

---

[1] King Philippe the IV, also known as Philippe le Bel (the fair, due to his good looks), ruled France from 1285 to 1314. France was the most powerful single realm of its day, Italy being largely a collection of city states, Germany likewise an amalgam of allied independent territories known as the Holy Roman Empire. In need of raising funds for the ongoing war with England he sought to tax the French Church. He would soon arrest the Knights Templar and confiscate their wealth.

[2] Boniface VIII issued the Papal bull 'Clericis laicos' in 1296 outlawing the taxing of the Church without papal permission. Any king doing so would be promptly excommunicated.

[3] Philippe passed an embargo on the movement of French coinage to Italy.

[4] In December 1301 Boniface VIII issued the Papal Bull to King Philippe IV of France entitled 'Ausculta Fili' which simply translates as 'Listen Son!' Perhaps the most insulting title to any diplomatic communication in history.

Sanctam. "It is necessary for salvation that every human creature be subject to the Roman pontificate," he read. Bunny was not impressed.

"The Pope is the lord over the spiritual souls of Europe," he continued, "and as the soul is superior to the body, then spiritual authority is superior to political authority. Therefore, the Pope alone has the right to decree what happens in nations."[1]

Unam Sanctam amounted to a threat to undermine Philippe's right to rule France. Bunny had already learned that it was the Church alone that appointed kings. So, if gone unchecked, this would seriously undermine Philippe's sovereignty. Boniface continued, his voice increasingly animated as his rage became self-evident,

"I am the descendant of the apostle Peter, I am Caesar, I am Emperor." [2]

Over in the FRANCE window Philippe said nothing. He just leaned towards one of the guards and whispered in his ear. The soldier nodded then quickly departed. Bunny looked back at ROME but to her surprise Boniface was no longer there.

Suddenly, the cell door burst open. Once again, a prisoner was being ushered in against his will, but this time by French soldiers. The prisoner, Pope Boniface VIII, snarled at them,

"I would rather die than rescind Unam Sanctam."

Up to this point, the soldiers had treated him with respect, but this defiance prompted one to remove his leather glove and ceremoniously slap it across Boniface's cheek.[3] This afront to his dignity immediately caused Boniface to stop. The soldier replaced his glove, and he and his colleagues left the cell where Boniface remained, a broken man.

Back in the ROME window, Bunny could see that around twenty cardinals had gathered to elect an elderly, docile looking man to be the new Pope. He

---

[1] The 'Unam Sanctam' was arguably the most controversial papal bull ever given. Issued in November 1302 it unashamedly stated that 'Outside of the Church, there is no salvation,' and that 'It belongs to spiritual power to establish the terrestrial power.' Seeking to position the Pope as being above all earthly kings.

[2] Quotation taken from 'The Western Schism of 1378' by Charles River Editors, May 2017.

[3] In September 1303, two of Philippe's advisors led a party of 2000 troops who broke into Boniface's summer retreat at Anagni. The place was plundered, and Boniface held without food or water for 3-days. According to legend one of the leaders, Sciarra Colonna, struck Boniface with his gauntlet in what became known as the 'Schiaffo di Anagni' (the Anagni Slap). 'The Slap of Anagni' by Alberto Carosa taken from Catholic World News, Oct 01, 2003

took the name Benedict XI and his first order of business was to revoke Unam Sanctam. As she watched, the same French soldiers began picking off Italian cardinals and replacing them with French ones. By her reckoning, more than half were now French. Suddenly, Benedict grabbed his stomach, then his throat. With an unearthly cry of "Poison!" he then collapsed out of sight beneath the window.[1] Curiously, the cardinals began to file away, leaving the ROME window completely empty. Bunny looked to her left to see them arrive in the French throne room where they quickly elected Clement V as the new Pope and announced that the papal headquarters would henceforth be in France. At this, the inscription above the French window morphed to read AVIGNON. Clement took his seat in the new papal throne room.[2] Bunny looked at her watch, it now read 13:05.

"I didn't know that the Vatican moved to Avignon," Bunny admitted to her guide. He didn't reply. When she looked up, Clement had been joined by a rather prurient lady wearing heavy make-up and a low-cut bodice that left little to the imagination. She was perched on the arm of the papal throne, much to his evident delight. Two lowly peasants soon entered to petition the pontifex on some matter of importance to them. In passing judgment Clement instructed them, with a huge grin, to place their offerings into the silky white bosom of his voluptuous lover.[3] Even as a non-Catholic, Bunny could see this was highly inappropriate.

"Weren't they all supposed to be celibate?" she remarked to her guide.

"That's nothing," he replied. "Would you like to buy a *Pearly Gate Pass*?" he jested nodding in the direction of Avignon.

---

[1] Barely eight months into his papacy Benedict XI died suddenly. Most suspect he was poisoned although no definitive historic proof exists. 'Pope Benedict XI' by Charles Herbermann (1913) taken from Catholic Encyclopaedia.

[2] Pope Clement V was elected to the papacy whilst in France and never moved to Rome, choosing instead to relocate the papal throne, its court and bureaucracy (known as the Curia) to Avignon in 1309 where it remained until 1377 - a period termed by some as the Babylon Captivity. In the early 14th century Avignon was not part of France, but the Kingdom of Naples; later it became a papal state. Finally, it changed hands during the French revolution in 1791.

[3] Many believe that Pope Clement's move to Avignon was as much to be close to his mistress, Brunissende de Foix, the Countess of Perigord. Quotation taken from 'The Western Schism of 1378' by Charles River Editors, May 2017

"Surely not?" Bunny said in horror as her guide nodded. "They're selling tickets to heaven?"[1]

Bunny looked back at the AVIGNON window to see the face of the Pope had changed. So too had the woman next to him.

"Pope Gregory," the woman said, "I have been sent by the Almighty who has disclosed to me the secret vow you made on the eve of your coronation to bring the papacy back to Rome." [2]

"How could you possibly know that, Catherine?" he replied.

Bunny could see that this truncated metaphor was being staged for her benefit, but she couldn't help but think that the dialogue was no better than a badly scripted amateur dramatic production. Nevertheless, she got the point and continued watching as Pope Gregory arose from his throne, exited stage left, with all his cardinals, arrived in the ROME window, and promptly died. The year was 1377 and once again, the French cardinals, now in Rome, had to elect a new Pope. This time the *Am Dram* performance turned into a *Farce*. The off-stage sound of drunken rioters chanting "We want a Roman or an Italian!"[3] filled the cardinals with such fear for their lives if they failed to do so, they selected one of their number, despite his vocal protestations that he didn't want the job! The fearful cardinals were having none of it, and as they led him to his throne, the new Pope Urban VI, began to kick, spit and swear at his former colleagues. Bunny found this plot twist hilarious, irony worthy of Oscar Wilde, and within moments of taking his seat the Pope started accusing the cardinals of being in league with the devil. Leaving Urban on his throne they exited in haste, stage right, promptly reappearing in Avignon where they rescinded the vote that had elected him.

"Come over here Urban, let us talk," the cardinals shouted across the room, now a safe distance away from an increasingly paranoid maniac. Bunny was no psychiatrist but could see that Pope Urban was someone showing visible

---

[1] Financial impropriety was rife during the Avignon Papacy, and included Pearly Gates passes. 'The Western Schism of 1378' by Charles River Editors, May 2017.

[2] Catherine of Siena spent several months trying to convince Pope Gregory XI to return the papacy to Rome, to no avail until she said that she had been sent by God and to prove it disclosed the details of a secret vow he had made. 'The Saintly Politics of Catherine of Siena' by Francis Thomas Luongo, 2006

[3] Quotation taken from 'The Middle Sea: A History of the Mediterranean' by Viscount John Julius Norwich p215.

signs of mental instability[1]. Urban crudely swore back at them then appointed twenty-six of his own cardinals, who stood behind him. Back in the Avignon window, the original cardinals elected Clément VII, and stood behind him. Now both Rome and Avignon had fully functional Popes in place.

"Two Popes!" Bunny said to her fellow observer.

---

[1] Pope Urban VI was mentally unstable. ibid

Chapter 47

THREE POPES

"Keep watching, it gets better," he replied. Urban screamed across the room saying that Clement's cardinals were nothing more than devils in human form. Clement, in reply, accused Urban of being the Antichrist.[1] The tennis is back, Bunny thought as she pivoted her head during the tit-for-tat exchanges. Flags of every nation of Europe then began to appear in the background of each of the two rooms as each realm had to decide which of these competing popes was the real one.[2] First, Bunny could see behind Clement's throne in Avignon the flag of France. Alongside it, others quickly appeared. She recognised the flags of Scotland, Wales, Spain and Cyprus; the others she hadn't ever seen before but somehow knew them to be Naples, Aragon, Burgundy, Savoy, Sicily as well as several others. Turning her attention to Rome, Urban VI was flanked by the flags of England, Ireland, Hungary, Poland, Denmark, Norway, Portugal, Sweden, Flanders and The Holy Roman Empire. The whole of Europe was split over the election of a madman.

The door in front of them suddenly opened. Bunny half expected to see one of the two popes forcefully thrown into prison, but instead a small group of learned men entered, deep in discussion. A small assembly of theologians had gathered to propose a solution and were soon ready to speak.

"Your holiness...es," their spokesman began. "We have decided that one of you will have to be the bigger man and accept the 'Way of Resignation'". Unsurprisingly both immediately refused.[3]

Bunny felt a gentle tap on her shoulder. Her guide was pointing with his thumb suggesting she should look behind where they were seated. She spun round to see a third set of curtains, this time dark brown, slowly opening to

---

[1] Urban VI was called "the Antichrist" by the French Pope; Catherine of Siena called the Avignon cardinals "Devils in human form."

[2] The breakdown of which nation followed each pope is widely reported. Taken from 'The Western Schism of 1378' by Charles River Editors, May 2017.

[3] Efforts to find a theological position to settle the two-pope dispute was the main topic debated across all European universities, most notably Paris. A number of solutions were proposed with the so-called 'Way of Resignation' being the most workable outcome. Unsurprisingly, neither sitting pope agreed.

reveal yet another ecclesiastical scene. The inscription on the lintel this time read PISA, and according to Bunny's watch it was 14:09. Barely five feet from where she was seated Bunny watched, frozen to her seat, as the group of scholars now entered the scene. Their spokesman took to his feet and said that as neither Pope had accepted the invitation to attend, the case against them had been heard in their absence. Having heard convincing testimony, they all agreed that neither was fit to remain in office. They had therefore unanimously elected Alexander V as the rightful Pope.[1] Bunny spun around to look at the other two popes. Both were still there, both defiantly looking angry. In turning back Bunny caught the eye of her guide, who smilingly raised three fingers. Bunny acknowledged the obvious truth and raised three fingers likewise. As she did a church bell rang out.

"There it is again," she said. "I keep hearing it."

The relief of having located Bunny, and seeing that she was most likely still alive, did little to assuage Chris of any of his anxiety. She was alone inside a farmhouse with a man who had not only kidnapped her in a stolen ambulance but had, most probably, killed two of his former associates. Bunny was far from safe. They were going to have to tread very carefully – if they did anything to spook him, he might well do the same to helpless Bunny as she lay there in a state of morphinic ignorance. Chris and Ralph slid themselves away from the exposure of the window opening, back to the seclusion of the brickwork.

"Any ideas?" Ralph asked softly.

"One to the front door... the other... round the back," was the best Chris could come up with. Ralph gave an exhale of disappointment, knowing he would most likely be the one to go to the front door. What would he say? What possible reason could he give to knocking on a remote deserted farmhouse this late at night. He had no idea, but Chris was one step ahead of him.

"You've come to give him his change," he suggested with a smile, referencing the spontaneous idea Ralph had come up with when they made the

---

[1] After many failed attempts to bring the papacy together, most notably when subsequent popes died, it was eventually agreed that a general council would be held at Pisa on 25-28 March 1409 to settle the matter. The council comprised: 24 cardinals, 89 abbots, 80 bishops, 41 priors, representatives of every nation state as well as theologians from all universities. Neither pope attended so they were both tried 'in absentia' and found incapable of holding the papacy. The council unanimously elected a new Pope Alexander V to replace them.

earlier call to the man they had now christened The Badger. Ralph frowned at the idea.

"It'll be fine," Chris encouraged. Ralph might have been Chris's superior in the church workplace, but that didn't seem to matter much now. Chris was determined in the task at hand and nudged Ralph gently towards the front of the building with a slightly dismissive, "Off you go." Reluctantly he started to move.

"Wait, what's that?" Chris said urgently as he grasped Ralph's sleeve. There was the distant sound of an approaching car. They both froze, it must be one of their group responding to his 'Come to Lane End Farm' message. Whoever it was, they were going to make such a commotion any attempt at a surprise rescue would be gone. Worse still, The Badger may react, and if so in an unthinkable way. The reflection of headlights began to dance on the tyre-covered polythene heap at the end of the lane. Someone was definitely coming; all Chris knew was that they had to stop them.

"Quick, we need to head them off into the barn," Chris said in a forced whisper as he began to sprint directly across the farmyard, making no attempt to hide behind any cover. Ralph followed. He had no choice!

The headlights were getting brighter, and the deep baritone of the internal combustion engine was puncturing the silence. Thankfully those on foot arrived at a point which gave them line of sight to the car before it had reached the apex of the turning at the barn. Ralph raised the palm of one hand whilst simultaneously placing the index finger of his other hand across his lips, signifying both 'Stop' and 'Be quiet.' Chris pointed into the barn, anxiously looking over his shoulder at the farmhouse hoping the sound had not made it through its thick walls.

The car instantly drew to a halt, skidding slightly in the wet mud of the lane, and both Ralph and Chris breathed a sigh of relief. They had caught it just in time. Chris gestured that they should extinguish their headlights and turn into the barn, but to his surprise they didn't. Independently both Ralph and Chris raised a visor like palm to shield much of the dazzling headlight glare, hoping to see which of their group was failing to understand their urgent sign language. As they stared, the driver slipped into gear and began to drive at speed straight at them.

"No, no, stop!" Chris pleaded placing both palms forward. The vehicle headed straight at him and then, to his horror, began to sound its horn. Beep, Beep, Beeeeeeep! it sounded as it relentlessly drove towards Chris. What on earth were they doing? He had to stop them, determined not to move aside. The car accelerated still sounding its horn. Just before the headlights crashed into Chris's knees Ralph grabbed him, pulling him with an almighty heave towards himself, clear of the car as it sped through the very spot where Chris had been standing. Ralph and Chris both fell to the ground and as they landed, saw that it wasn't Jack's 4x4 nor the Rector's Honda Jazz. Their assailant was a red soft-top sports car, just like the one the delivery girl had said she had seen.

The momentum of Ralph's last-minute rescue caused them both to skid face down onto the dirty, leaf-covered and damp farmyard. Half-expecting the car to spin around and make a second thrust towards them, they were relieved when it skidded to halt and extinguished its lights. Chris lay there in the unwelcome embrace of cheek-to-yard as his mind raced trying to make sense of what had just happened. Soon, the sound of engine and horn were replaced by that of shouting and approaching footsteps. Chris feared the worst. He pulled himself onto all fours then rocked back onto his haunches and as he did he could see Ralph a few feet away in the same submissive stance. And standing in front of them both was The Badger, pointing a gun first at Ralph, then Chris, then back at Ralph. He did not look happy.

All three curtains were now closed, and Bunny was once again alone with the man in the gold-rimmed hat.

"I get it, I get it, the Catholic Church wasn't perfect," Bunny said. "It was just as ready to split as the Protestants have been."

"Tell me." Her guide asked, motioning towards each of the three closed curtains. "What do you think is the cause of all these divisions?"

Bunny thought for a moment. This was an important question, perhaps *the* most important question, and she wanted to give a considered answer. Some splits she had seen were triggered by different interpretations of biblical doctrine; some had been more about politics and power; but this wasn't the cause she suspected. She placed her head in her hands, elbows on the simple table in front of where they were seated. Was she going to be trapped inside this lucid dream until she gave him the right answer? Her guide gave her as much time as she needed. Eventually she had an insight, admittedly not entirely sure if she was right but confident enough to offer it as her first answer.

"I think that, perhaps most of the splits – if not all of them – might have had their origin rooted in... personal ambition." Her guide said nothing.

"I mean," she continued, "we should all be forgiving and loving towards each other, and accepting of differences, not defending our own positions at the other's expense... is that it?" Still her guide said nothing. Bunny sat back upright in her chair.

"Are there still three branches of the Catholic Church today? I mean in the *real* today?" she asked him as she pointed at the purple, blue and brown curtains.

"No, give it a few years and all three will be replaced by Martin V whose line endures in Rome until your day."[1]

"So, you haven't answered my question then, have you," she challenged him. He looked back at her quizzically.

"I asked if there was one Church before the Reformation. You said no but, as entertaining as this three-pope farce has been, it would appear you're wrong. There was one Church pre-Luther."

Her guide began to laugh as he stood to his feet and turned towards the brown curtains a few steps behind their chairs. With one hand he grasped the join in the floor-length drapes and with the other beckoned that Bunny should follow him. She rose and stood beside him as he pulled the heavy fabric to one side and they stepped through.

Moments earlier, Joel couldn't help but keep glancing in his rear-view mirror. The relentless sight of the same headlights behind him remained an ever-present threat that someone was following them. What's more, he couldn't make any of the dramatic U-turns favoured in spy films or crime novels. For the first time in his life he had the reason to 'shake-off his tail' and couldn't do it as he had to maintain a discreet position behind his own quarry oblivious to the small procession behind him.

Thea, now convinced of the veracity of Joel's suspicions, asked all the obvious questions. 'Who could be following them? Should they take evasive action? Should they ignore Chris's message and avoid leading them to the farmhouse?' and as built-up area turned into open countryside they discussed every possible scenario. The question they didn't verbalise was 'Are we in danger?'

---

[1] Under continued pressure, all competing lineages came to an end. John XXIII (Pisa) was deposed in May 1415, Gregory XII (Rome) resigned in July 1415 and Benedict XIII (Avignon) was deposed July 1417. With all three papal lineages now terminated a new conclave met in 1417 and elected Pope Martin V.

When it became clear that the red sports car they were following was indeed heading for Lane End Farm, Joel and Thea had a decision to make. The plan they hatched was to allow the sports car to drive on ahead, confident that they knew where it was going. They would hold back, slow down and see if they could tempt their pursuer to overtake them. Once they were in the countryside, Joel moved down into second gear and watched the rear of their prey disappear into the dark distance ahead. From nearly sixty miles per hour, Joel slowed down to twenty, then ten. Thea lowered the passenger side sun visor so she too had a rear-facing view in its small vanity mirror. The pursuant headlights slowed also. Joel spotted a field gate opening ahead, switched on his left indicator and pulled two wheels onto the rough grassy verge and stopped.

"Will this do it? Yes, it will," he said. "Now he'll have to pass us."

Sadly, the car behind also pulled to a halt. The reality of their situation suddenly sank in. They were alone on a deserted country lane, it was dark and late. Over the last few hours they had unearthed the evidence of an array of nefarious actions from theft and kidnapping to murder, and as far as they knew one of the miscreants was now a few yards away, waiting for them. Joel's mind was paralysed in indecision. Thea began to pray, aloud. As she interceded a passage from the Bible, from the book of James chapter four, suddenly came into her mind,

"Resist the devil, and he will flee from you..." she said, determined to implore the Almighty's assistance.

Resist! Flee! That was the idea Joel needed. Suddenly he opened the driver's side door. He then leaned out, without unbuckling his seat belt. To Thea's horror Joel then beckoned for the driver behind to come to them.

"What are you doing?" Thea asked anxiously.

The lights of the car behind switched off as the driver's door opened and a man exited. It was too dark to distinguish who it was, but he was large and imposing. Thankfully, no one got out of the passenger side.

"Just as you prayed, Thea," Joel said. "I'm resisting the devil..."

Thea let out a pained "But...!" as she watched the man close his door and begin to walk towards them. She swallowed hard.

Joel kept looking backwards, trying his best to smile disarmingly at the silhouette now barely four yards behind his car. With his outstretched left-hand he reached into the car and without breaking his rearward gaze managed to subtly slip the car into first gear.

"And now..." he said to Thea under his breath.

Joel then swung back into his seat, released the clutch and floored the accelerator. The engine revved furiously as the wheels began to spin, cascading mud and leaves backwards directly at the man now stranded between the two cars.

"Now we flee from him!" Joel announced as his car lurched into the road swerving first to the right then the left. There was no way the unknown pursuer could get back to his car fast enough in order to follow. But that didn't stop him making a valiant attempt. In seconds Joel and Thea had turned the first corner and were rapidly approaching the start of the lane leading to the farmhouse. Thea pointed to it feverishly, concerned Joel might overshoot it. He swung the car hard right into the lane, skidding on the cattle grid. He just managed to keep control of the vehicle, avoiding the boggy ditch on the left side of the lane. Thea instructed him, for the second time that night, to switch off the car's lights, which he did as the car righted itself back into the centre of the lane. Thea abandoned the subtlety of the sun visor and swung herself around just in time to see a white Ford rush past the end of the lane. They had done it.

They sat in silence for a few moments.

"Well done," Thea said, thankful not only for Joel having out-witted their pursuer but also having not dumped them both in the ditch.

"It was your idea," Joel said returning the compliment. It made sense to continue the journey down the track slowly and with the car lights still off. They had no idea what lay ahead.

Chapter 48

THE GREAT SCHISM

Beyond the curtain, a whole new mediaeval world greeted Bunny. The papal palaces she had seen through her virtual windows were clearly from antiquity, but the place she had now landed in felt even older. This is the era of Robin Hood, she thought, as she tried to find a reference point with which to orientate herself. The walls were castle-like, made from solid grey stone, but were decorated with enormous paintings whose colours somehow reflected magically in the light of the naked-flame torches held securely to the walls. She had assumed at first glance that they were paintings; but as she stepped closer to one she realised they were the most elaborately made mosaics she had ever seen. She'd only ever seen mosaics as part of the dusty floor of some ancient archaeological site she visited when she was at school, and then they were at best patchwork representations of a bygone age. Not only were the mosaics full of vivid colour, but they were also complete and filled the walls in the wide and deserted hallway in which she found herself alone. The image represented by the thousands of individually and meticulously crafted pieces of coloured ceramic was obvious. It was Christ, seated and robed in a blue cloak with golden trim. In his left hand he held a closed book, presumably the Bible. It had an elaborately decorated front cover and clasp, with five or six off-white slices representing closed pages. As she looked at it, she realised that the book's cover appeared to be smaller than the rest of the pages. They haven't quite got the perspective right, she thought. In his other hand he made a strange gesture touching his thumb to the tip of his fourth finger with his palm facing forwards. That must mean something significant, she wondered unknowingly. Behind and above him, Christ had the familiar halo she had seen in other paintings; not just a hollow golden ring, this included a bejewelled cross within its centre, giving it the impression of a small decorative cartwheel hovering behind his head. The mosaic included text on either side of the image of Christ, but to her surprise not in Latin but Greek. The more she let her eyes traverse this elaborate work of art something began to stir inside her, something she hadn't felt before. She took three steps towards the wall and let her fingers softly touch the smooth cold tiles.

"This is more than just decoration," she said aloud. "This is more than art. This is somebody's act of worship… and I can feel the worship calling to me."[1]

She looked around the hallway, her eyes now fully adjusted to the half-light. Three further mosaics adorned the space, as did several marble statues. This was a royal palace of some description, but she had no idea where or when. With a note of self-chastisement, she looked at her watch. At least she could always know *when* she was. The dial pulsed at 10:45 – nearly a thousand years ago.

"And about time too!" an angry male voice thundered towards her from a distance. It occurred to Bunny that whatever time or country she was visiting, in her dream everyone spoke English. So far, she had conversed eloquently in German, French and Dutch. Her school language teacher would have been very impressed. In fact, the only language she struggled to understand had been the Wearside accent of Alexander Boddy. As for now… was she in Greece?

"It is totally unacceptable for a legate from His Excellency Pope Leo IX to be kept waiting for so long," he thundered. The angry man, and his small retinue, were now close enough to be addressing his angst towards Bunny. She looked behind her to see if there was anyone else to take the flak, but she stood alone. Within moments she could see him clearly. Flame-haired and bearded, he was dressed in a long white robe trimmed elegantly befitting his office. His face was red with rage as he demanded an explanation for being kept waiting. Bunny said nothing. After all, she had nothing to say. Whether it was her silence, or simply her gender, something began to abate his fury. Having allowed his pressure-cooker to vent, he could now give Bunny the customary nod of greeting.

"Madam," he began in a more conciliatory air, "would you be so kind as to ask if His Excellency, Michael Cerularius, Patriarch of Constantinople, plans to keep us waiting any longer? If so, we must return to Pope Leo and convey this slight to his authority."

"Constantinople," Bunny said by reflex, having now located herself.

"Yes, Patriarch of Constantinople," he repeated impatiently.

"And you are…?" she asked innocently, but he did not appreciate her ignorance and thundered in reply, "I am Cardinal Humbert of Silva Candida,

---

[1] The 11ᵗʰ century image represented here is held within the Hagia Sophia Museum in Istanbul. Iconography is an important act of worship within the Eastern Orthodox Church, not that the icons themselves are worshipped - a common misconception - but that through them one can enter into an act of worship.

papal legate of Pope Leo IX, and I am here to offer correction of the errors of the Constantinople patriarchy."

"Which errors?"

Once again, Bunny's curiosity was getting her into trouble. In the following three minutes she endured a non-stop hairdryer blast of incredulity from legate Humbert, the likes of which would have adequately graced any corporate boardroom or the post-match dressing down of a well-beaten football team. She let much of his indignant verbosity pass her by but managed to extract a handful of topics that were keeping him on the boil. Using *unleavened bread* in the eucharist was one of those, as was *priestly celibacy* as Constantinople apparently allowed their priests to marry. Then there were issues of *tonsure* which she knew was the curious looking haircut worn by some monks. Once his irate monologue ended Humbert stared at Bunny, clearly expecting her to do something. Her motionless response prompted him to add sarcastically,

"Perhaps you would be so kind as to ask His Excellency if he would at last honour us with his presence."

He pointed at the curtain from which she had emerged moments earlier, obviously expecting her to return within to fulfil his errand. Bunny looked at the curtain.

"I'll see what I can do," she said.

Logic would have given her to expect to re-enter the same cell she occupied earlier, but she had learnt enough to know that logic, and for that matter all the laws of physics, no longer applied. She was on a rollercoaster of discovery and one without rails. She was therefore not in the slightest surprised to step into a papal throne room, upon which sat Michael Cerularius, who too was not surprised at her arrival and beckoned her towards him. Bunny gave a clumsily uncomfortable bow-cum-curtsy, having never made such a gesture before, before walking over to him.

"How angry is he?" Cerularius asked. Bunny confirmed that Humbert was most indignant at being kept waiting.

"So he should be," he replied sharply. "What makes him think that the Patriarch of Rome has any higher authority amongst the five of us?"

"Five?" Bunny asked. Cerularius stopped in mid flow, irked at having to explain something he considered to be patently obvious.

"Yes, yes, five!" he snapped. "Constantinople, Antioch, Jerusalem, Alexandria and Rome – the five patriarchies, or the five *popes* if you prefer. All

409

equal, all in communion together, doctrine to be agreed only when we five agree."[1]

Bunny hadn't any concept that there were five leaders of the Church in the eleventh century. This was yet more new information for her, and she was hungry to understand more. She knew she would have to tread carefully. Michael Cerularius and Humber of Silva both looked like the sort of people who could start an argument on their own. For now, Cerularius was more than happy to vent his spleen directly at her as some sort of proxy of Humbert.

"The Bishop of Rome had no right to amend the Nicaean Creed. The five patriarchs of the time agreed the wording exactly at the First Council back in the year three hundred and twenty-five, and it has been unchanged ever since then... until Rome thinks it can add The Filioque."

Bunny deployed her well-used *tell me more* look. Despite his antipathy, the patriarch of Constantinople could not resist, quoting the offending part of the Nicaean Creed.

"'...the Holy Spirit the Lord, the giver of life, who proceeds from the Father... *and the Son.'* The audacity of Rome to add *'and the Son'* or *filioque* as they say in their Latin. How dare they think they have the authority to rewrite the creed just to counter some local heresy."[2]

Bunny had faithfully declared the Nicaean Creed thousands of times during her Anglican worship, but try as she may she couldn't bring to mind whether she recited the version with 'and the Son.' In church, they would always just read it from the Order of Service and so, just like the Lord's Prayer, by repetition it had become some sort of ecclesiastical muscle-memory, impossible to think of what you were saying unless you started from the beginning.

"We believe in one God, the Father Almighty, maker of heaven and earth..." she began in her head.

"This is an absolute violation of Canon VII of the Council of Constantinople, 'That no words can be added to the text,' and what's more they

---

[1] The five patriarchies - or as they are sometimes known, the Pentarchy - were established in the 6th century under Emperor Justinian I. The Sees of Jerusalem, Antioch, Alexandria, Constantinople and Rome were decreed as equal, but Rome always considered itself to be the 'first amongst equals.' The fall of Jerusalem, Antioch and Alexandria to the Muslims put Constantinople and Rome on an inevitable collision course.

[2] 'What is the filioque clause controversy?' By Matt Slick, extracted from Christian Apologetics & Research Ministry website.

know it!" he screamed. "And just because three out of the five patriarchies have fallen to the Muslim invaders, Rome thinks it has become somehow pre-eminent. Well, it is time I told him, No!" He delivered his defiance with a shout, adding a direct instruction to Bunny to "Send Humbert in!"

Bunny tentatively stepped back through the curtain, where the indignant Roman papal legate was pacing.

"He will see you now," she said falteringly, holding the curtain to allow the visiting party ingress.

She hadn't intended to remain outside, but having dropped the curtain behind them, thought it best to refrain from opening it, as the shouting immediately began. What quickly unfolded was a playground-esque slanging match. Claims of doctrinal and ritual shortcomings were met by accusations of authority usurpation. Bunny had only just learnt what was behind this disagreement, but the verbal missiles that were launched so vehemently, vociferously and viciously at each other were evidence of the time the issues had festered unresolved. This wasn't about to be solved any time soon and it would probably be better to stay outside, she concluded.[1]

She was beginning to feel tired, so took the opportunity to sit down and close her eyes. As soon as she did, she immediately felt as though someone was wrestling her from her seated position, lifting her up and lying her on a cold hard bed. She desperately wanted to open her eyes to see who was assaulting her but, try as she could, they were firmly shut. Then the wrestling stopped, and she was lying horizontal. A metal door then slammed shut so loudly that the noised made her jump, at which her eyes opened again.

The last time Rex held a gun was at a shooting weekend he attended with his parents during his time at university. The hospitality of the country estate was most convivial, but he still remembers the nervous dread he felt knowing he was going to have to shoot some birds in the morning. When they arrived at the designated section of moorland bracken, dampened by the morning dew, the shoot captain who greeted them was as stereotypical as was humanly possible. Bearded, ruddy and sporting plentiful tweed, he wore plus-four shooting breeks, deerstalker hat, a chequered twill shirt and shooting jacket having countless

---

[1] Having rumbled on for centuries the filioque issue came to climax largely because of the arrogance and intransigence of both Michael Cerularius and Humbert of Silva. See the video 'The Eastern Schism' by Dr Ryan M Reeves, Gordon of Conwell Theological Seminary.

pockets teeming with cartridges. Rex was in jeans. Once the initial pleasantries were concluded the shoot captain came over to Rex and, without warning, placed an unloaded 12-bore shotgun in the shoot-virgin's hands. Some people would feel a sense of empowerment, a thrill, at handling their first weapon. Not Rex. As a piece of engineering, it was beautiful. He appreciated the four different colours of wood inlaid throughout the stock and fore end; the soft leather padding of the recoil pad; the exquisite carvings in the stainless steel of the receiver; and the long cold metal double-barrel. The shoot captain lifted it lovingly from Rex's hands, gave the mandatory safety briefing then demonstrated how to hold, aim and fire the weapon. Finally, now loaded, he passed it back to his latest recruit, a young Rex who was now expected to join the line alongside his parents, uncles and their friends and bring down several members of the feathery Phasianus family which had been bred for this specific purpose. Rex couldn't do it. He had no doubt in his technical ability to shoot a moving object. Despite inbuilt fairground bias, he would often hit the required number of targets, cans or rubber ducks to take home a large stuffed teddy bear. But this was different. This wasn't shooting as a skill; this was shooting to kill. Of the thirty or so discharges of his gun, at no time did he aim at a living creature and willingly became the butt of the *bad shot* jokes for the rest of the day.

And now, he sat in the driver's seat of his car, for the second time in his life, resting a firearm in his hands. It was a less elegant piece of craftmanship: completely black, no inlaid wood on the handle just a moulded plastic grip, no barrel just a short muzzle etched with the words 17 Gen4, Austria and 9x19. On the left side of the grip, at the place where the shooter's thumb would rest, there was a small button. Rex pressed it and the magazine popped out from the bottom of the handgrip. He carefully slid it out just enough to see that it was charged with bullets, although it was impossible to see how many were in the cartridge. He snapped the magazine back into the handgrip and placed the pistol carefully onto the centre of the front passenger seat. Looking down at it he then turned the gun so that the muzzle was pointing away from him, in some way neutralising its power over him.

Rex wasn't the only person sitting contemplatively in their car late into the evening. Having watched Jack and Artur speed away in Jack's 4x4, Rector Mashman sat for a moment, conflicted. The evening had not gone at all as he had expected with this gathering of disparate church leaders at C.R.F. which he was going to do his best to steer into a certain unified direction, before returning

412

home for a warm cup of Horlicks before bed. Most days held little surprise for the elderly Anglican, but tonight was different. Rather than allow him to steer the ecumenical collective towards a healthy compromise, they had flatly refused to move in any direction. Then the disappearance of Bunny seemed to have galvanised them to snatch the figurative steering wheel out of his hands and accelerate along a path of unfolding twists and turns, each one seemingly ghastlier than the last. At best he felt as though he had been a passenger, now feeling increasingly superfluous with his slow progress. The sight of Lord Advowson in Sanguine Wood and his distressed agitation over Miss Velia tugged at the Rector's heartstrings. This was at least something he could help with, this was something he could do, he thought. So rather than follow the same route Jack had taken a few moments earlier, the Rector determined that he would go to the hospital and offer some comfort to his benefactors in their time of need. The others can rescue Bunny. At least he wouldn't be slowing them down anymore.

Bunny had visited Saint Paul's Cathedral in London on more than one occasion. At the forefront of its nave, midway between the north and south transepts, there is always a bustle of tourists jostling to stand under the exact epicentre of the dome. She had never understood the appeal of that particular spot and she never had any intention of joining the rather unseemly yet silent rumpus. There were no tourists inside the Church of the Holy Wisdom, or Hagia Sophia as it is better known, but as it happened Bunny's seat was at that much-sought-after central point known as The Crossing. The immense dome above her was supported by two semi-domes, themselves giving way to numerous quarter-domes creating a multi-layered scalloped structure the likes of which she had never seen before. The central dome was probably no bigger than that of Saint Paul's, but these supporting structures opened the space up markedly. Some say it was the largest building in the world; it was certainly large enough to comfortably accommodate the fifteen thousand or so faithful worshippers who had gathered to celebrate the Eucharist on Easter Sunday morning. Bunny rubbed her arms to try and solicit some warmth, the atmosphere having decidedly turned chilly.

She looked directly upwards. The distant face she saw staring back was that of Christ – again depicted in a blue robe holding a Bible and with his distinctive cartwheel halo. It wasn't the exact same pose as she had seen in the hallway but unmistakably the same stylised figure. From this distance she could

413

only surmise that the artwork was a mosaic rather than a painting. That thought however made her fear the descent of small pieces of ceramic if the glue holding them should fail. That was enough to turn her gaze away from upwards, directly forwards to the altar and Michael Cerularius, bedecked in all his ecclesiastical finery. As he spoke, however, it was almost incomprehensible to understand what he was saying, the ten-second reverberation playing tricks with her ears. The choir began to sing. Bunny feared that this protracted echo would make the worship descend into choral chaos but to her surprise the opposite was true. The hymns and chants must have been written for the specific church space with the acoustics adding to, not detracting from, the choral veneration. Everywhere she looked she saw icons and golden crosses reflecting the cascading sunlight. The altar glinted in silver and gold, rich with jewels and pearls. Silver censers of perfumed incense filled the air.[1] This was *high church* at the highest she had ever experienced, and she loved it. Simply listening to the choral masterpieces transported her to a deep place of worship. She wouldn't have been surprised if she had looked up and seen angels flying in the semi-domes. This was the closest thing she had ever experienced to what she imagined heavenly worship to be like.

As the final chords of one song rang to a close the dominant sound in the church changed to something more sinister. A small party of armoured men marched along the central aisle, the echoes of their boots seemingly multiplying the size of the incursive force. At the head of the delegation strode papal legate Humbert of Silva Candida, a tightly bound scroll in his right hand, held afore him as if a weapon. He had clearly waited for the singing to end to maximise the impact of their arrival. Bunny assumed they were guests and, despite the disruptive nature of their late arrival, they would take their seats on the front row. To her surprise they marched directly to the altar, Humbert face-to-face with Cerularius across the elaborately laid table prepared for the Eucharist.

Despite the imperfect acoustics, it was perfectly clear to all what happened next. The scroll Humbert had been carrying was a papal bull from Leo IX and as he thrust it toward Cerularius, Humbert declared that the Patriarch of Constantinople was hereby excommunicated from the Church. He then clarified what *he* meant by Church saying,

"The true, widely-recognised, universal, *Catholic* Church."

---

[1] 'History of Hagia Sophia - the Church of Holy Wisdom' by Bob Atchison extracted from www.pallasweb.com

An audible gasp travelled like a Mexican wave across the huge auditorium. As she watched, Bunny saw Cerularius slowly take the scroll from Humbert's hand and, without breaking his eye-to-eye gaze, slid the parchment over one of the eucharistic candles, allowing it to instantly become engulfed in flames. After dropping it onto the table one of the sidesmen dowsed the ashes with communion wine.[1]

"On behalf of the apostolic authority of the pentarchy I hereby excommunicate the Bishop of Rome from the Church," Cerularius replied calmly, then clarified what *he* meant by Church.

"From the true, mainstream, traditional, *Orthodox* Church."[2]

"Ah ha!" Bunny's heart jumped. "I had forgotten about the Orthodox Church," she said under her breath as a solitary church bell rang out a chime. It was the same single bell chime she had heard before, but this was a higher-toned note. Then it all began to fall into place in her mind. Orthodox means normal in the sense of traditional or standard, whereas Catholic means normal as in universally accepted. Both sides of this divide can claim to be the true Church. But it was a shock to learn that it was the Roman Church that had broken away from the rest of the five patriarchies. She had assumed the Church of Rome had unquestionable history going back to Saint Peter, but now that was thrown into doubt.

Her meandering journey through post-Reformation Protestant Christianity had failed to answer the basic *question* that had filled her mind. It wasn't a question she could easily verbalise as to do so would force her to admit that her own expression of Church wasn't the be-all-and-end-all, and in many ways was as flawed as all the others. But the lack of discovering any definitive answer on her unintended expedition, any eureka moment, had done no more than add fuel to the smouldering kindling of disquiet. And as it caught hold, *The Question* kept growing. It was no longer a question of, how come there are so many churches? No, it was something much more fundamental that she needed to understand. Churches come and churches go, but now she needed to find what *real* Church was. She threw her head back and looked skywards and made eye-contact with the mosaic of Christ, seemingly smiling lovingly back at her.

"Okay, take me further back!" she spoke into the expanse.

---

[1] 'The great schism of 1054' article on www.historyforkids.net

[2] Cerularius' excommunication of Rome actually happened some months later.

Suddenly she felt her chair begin to move. She instinctively grasped the arms of the chair, realising that those very arms had not been there before. The chair then began to move. Not an erratic movement but a smooth gentle glide as though it were on wheels. Despite her attempts to focus on her surroundings her vision was too blurred to make out anything more than bright lights passing overhead and people – some dressed in white, others in green – walking past her. The moving chair turned first to the left, then the right, and she felt her heavy body slump in either direction as it cornered. Eventually she stopped in a room full of doors, hundreds of doors surrounding her. Small metal doors on top of small metal doors as far as her blurry eyes could make out. This was exhausting, she thought, and closed her eyes again.

Chapter 49

THE COUNCIL OF CHALCEDON

All Chris could think of was that he was so near but still so far away from Bunny. He and Ralph sat cross-legged on the floor of one of the front rooms of Lane End farmhouse with their arms on their heads; the posture of naughty schoolchildren caught in the act. Bunny was in the next room, but standing between them and her was the handsome Mazda driver, uncomfortably holding a revolver towards their general direction. Their guard was not seated, but stood anxiously over them, his demeanour a mixture of 'I never signed up for this' and a dutiful 'I must do what I am told.'

For their part Chris and Ralph were calm. Ralph hadn't spoken since they had been taken captive, Chris had attempted a variety of protestations that all fell on deaf ears. Chris knew he was no action hero – no Bruce Willis in *Die Hard* – just an average man, a churchman at that. But he had managed to find Bunny and one way or another he was going to rescue her from whatever fate this evil pair intended for her. Then the realisation hit him. Bruce Willis may have single-handedly fought the terrorists keeping his wife hostage in the Nakatomi Tower, but Chris didn't have to be single handed. He had Ralph and the others. Rex, Jack, Joel, Thea, Artur and even Rector Mashman were all on their way to help. Eight against two sounded like much better odds, but the *two* did have firearms with them.

Suddenly Ralph and Chris saw a figure move past the window. The floral curtains had been drawn but they were so thin that the light from the room illuminated the outline of the figure now standing at the window. None of the careful tiptoeing they had painstakingly executed earlier; no, this was someone standing outside the window and by the looks of the outline Chris was pretty sure it was Joel Whyens.

Ralph was the first to react and attempted to launch into a largely meaningless conversation with their handsome captor. Bizarrely, the subject matter that came to his mind was the difficulties of driving a soft-top convertible in the cold English winter climate. Amazingly, the olive-skinned millennial took the bait and replied, probably thankful of the distraction from the tenseness of their mutual situation. Joel slid his hand through the small space where the broken glass pane had been, took hold of the curtain edge in his fingertips and slid it slowly open. As he did Ralph's impromptu conversation turned into a forced laugh hoping to cover any noise. Thankfully, there was none. Joel was suddenly confronted with the scene. Chris and Ralph were seated on the bare floorboards, backs against the wall and a man stood over them holding a handgun at his side. Joel froze as he made eye contact with Chris who couldn't do anything that might cause the young man to be suspicious. Chris needed to tell Joel what to do, so joined Ralph in his inane winter-motoring conversation, carefully highlighting certain of his own words by raising the index finger of one of his hands, still on his head.

"I guess you have to store the soft-top in the rear..." Chris began, highlighting the word 'rear.' He continued, "...before you switch-off the power." Underlining much of that phrase.

Joel just stared at Chris, bemused. Frustrated, Chris repeated his statement.

'You have to store the soft-top in the *rear* don't you and fold it down before you *switch-off the power*.' He repeated now giving some emphasis to his key words. The guard replied to the repeated question.

"Of course, it will not fold away if the engine is switched off."

Chris looked over the man's shoulder directly at Joel. Something was working in the Methodist preacher's mind, but Chris wasn't sure he had grasped the plan. Chris added one final phrase.

"And when you switch the engine off, all the *lights go out*," Chris added with yet more emphasis staring directly at Joel. The guard looked at Chris and saw that his attention was not towards him but looking over his shoulder at the window. The guard swung round to see what was taking his prisoner's interest. The window was empty. Only seconds earlier Joel had slipped away with a knowing grin and a tactful thumbs-up.

"The wind has blown the curtain open," Chris said, then tactically added, "Do you want me to close it?"

Ralph joined in by saying that it needed to be closed as it was cold. The guard refused their help saying he would do it. He tucked the gun in the back of his trousers and stepped towards the window. As he turned around Chris tapped Ralph's arm and motioned that they should both stand up. Chris rehearsed in his mind the manoeuvre where he would grab the man around the neck, pull the gun from within his belt then push him to the ground. One man would be overpowered, just The Badger to go.

This would be the perfect moment for the lights to go out, Chris thought. C'mon Joel, do it now!

The Mazda driver took hold of each curtain but, before he pulled them together, for some reason he looked back over his shoulder to see the two men now standing and both having taken one pace away from the wall. He immediately let go of the drapery and retrieved the handgun from its temporary holster and began to shout animatedly at them,

"Get back, sit down, what are you doing?"

"What's going on in there?" came a voice from the rear of the farmhouse. That was the worst thing, now The Badger would come through.

"It is okay, Majstore, I have it," the driver replied, jabbing his gun pointedly at the pair.

Suddenly the room fell into darkness. It may have not been the ideal moment, but the die had now been cast and they needed to act. Spontaneously they both leapt at the young man in the knowledge that if his gun fired one of them would certainly be shot. Thankfully, in the initial brawl there was no gunshot sound, just that of two untrained but enthusiastic amateurs attempting to wrestle a firearm from an equally inexperienced captor. The combined weight of the two Pentecostals easily overwhelmed him. Chris had him by the neck, as he had visualised moments earlier, hoping that Ralph had the gun. Ralph had charged at him and made a classic rugby tackle around the waist and was pushing him steadily towards the window, hoping Chris had the gun.

Bang! The noise of the discharge was ear-shattering. The flash of light from the gun filled the room with a momentary photoflash snapshot of the action scene. Chris and Ralph momentarily both froze. Clearly neither of them had the gun. Chris was the first to move. In the solitary strobe he caught sight of the handgun inches from his face and pointing downwards towards Ralph grappling around the man's waist. Chris made an instantaneous lunge for the firearm, successfully snatching it.

"I've got the gun!" he announced.

Ralph didn't answer. Chris now had the gun so took two full steps away from the melee but all he could make out was the sound of someone falling to the floor. Had Ralph been shot? The intense sounds of wrestling had now ominously stopped. It was clear that Ralph had released the man from his tackle, but who was on the floor? A cold sense of dread filled Chris's mind. Was Ralph... dead? It was impossible to know. He needed to see what had happened. All he could think was to use the torch app on his mobile phone, which he pulled out from his trouser pocket with his left hand. Before he could switch on the torch function, simply accessing his phone caused Chris's face to become illuminated.

This was not what he had intended, and, in the half-light, he suddenly felt very vulnerable. He turned the phone around to cast a dim illumination across two bodies hunched on the wooden floor. As he stared, he watched in horror as a trickle of blood began to flow from the assorted legs and arms directly towards him before disappearing between an overly large gap in the floorboards. The trickle began to widen. Someone evidently had been shot.

"Ralph, Ralph, you okay?" was all that Chris could say.

Ralph looked at Chris but said nothing. He just raised his left hand, looked at it and saw that it was covered in blood to the extent that a crimson rivulet cascaded from his palm to the floor without breaking into droplets.

"Ralph?" Chris repeated.

Opening her eyes, the blurriness had abated. She was still looking at the mosaic of Christ high above her, a momentary reflection of sunlight glinted from the gold-leaf gilding into her eyes causing a reflex squint. She lowered her head from its vertically upwards gaze only to see that her environment had indeed metamorphosed around her. She was now in a smaller church, which wasn't difficult as the Hagia Sophia was such a vast expanse, although this was just as elaborately decorated. She felt that this was perhaps a building she could have sketched, whereas the Hagia Sophia was beyond her amateur skills. The room was full of people seated in a broadly circular arrangement on raked benches forming three or four tiers. The circle was broken by the presence of an ornate throne at one end. At her own church, All Saints', Bunny would routinely count the size of the congregation each week and became quite adept at estimating the number of people present. There was more in this sanctuary than she would ever have seen at All Saints', even at the ever-popular carol service. She began a quick headcount of one section, then multiplied it to find that there were around five hundred people present. What was most striking was that they were all wearing robes; mainly white with a variety of ecclesiastical insignia, sashes, belts and headgear. Her last encounter had been in the eleventh century but, judging by the clothing, she guessed she was now several centuries earlier. She pulled-back her sleeve for confirmation as the digits on her watch flashed 04:51. She had no idea where she was. It was clearly a gathering of diverse church leaders, some sort of council, maybe it was the five patriarchies gathering to decide something. Momentarily her heart jumped at the thought that this might be at Nicaea, the only ecumenical council she had ever heard of, but then she recalled that Cerularius had said the wording had remained intact since three-twenty-five. She looked back at her watch; this wasn't Nicaea.

Bunny was on the back row, opposite the throne, and as far as she could identify she was the only woman present. This was a time to stay in the background, she decided, and settled herself into her hard chair and adopted spectator-mode.

As she watched from her vantage point, the whole event faded into some sort of time-lapse movie montage. Before proceedings could get underway there ensued a hilarious medley of seat shuffling. Some people refused to be in the same room as others; some were relegated to sit in the outer nave of the church; then there were others who had been excluded who were now reinstated. It was a canonical comedy but eventually the speeded-up pastiche paused just in time hear the announcement that,

"The Council of *Chalcedon* is now in session." Bunny had never heard of it.[1]

She once again zoned-out as the somewhat boring debates played out before her. She heard little apart from what were, presumably, key snippets. This included them officially confirming the creed decided at Nicaea. That was over one hundred years ago! How long does it take to make a decision? She thought incredulously, then countered herself thoughtfully with, I suppose the pace of life must be that much slower. Then there was much mention of Eutyches of Constantinople, the local hero, she having discovered that Chalcedon was in Constantinople; and of Leo of Rome, who had written a definitive text which they called Leo's Tome; and of Cyril of Alexandria who had died a few years earlier. It was nearly impossible for her to keep track of the detail so she let it wash over her, knowing that when the important bit came she would be ready. The subject being debated, she gleaned, was about Christ being both divine and human at the same time and how can that be and what does it mean. This wasn't anything that she had thought about herself. For her it was simply something she could accept by faith. She didn't need to understand how it worked. But people were getting hot under the clerical collar

---

[1] The fourth ecumenical council was held in Chalcedon, a district of Constantinople, between October and November 451.

about the precise wording of a doctrinal statement and arguing over words like: *Person* and *Nature* and what they mean in multiple languages.[1]

Bunny felt a tap on her knee which jolted her back into the room.

"You'll need to pay attention to this bit," the man next to her said. She was embarrassed to have been so obviously disengaged and turned to thank him politely. It was *him* again.

"Have you been sitting there all the time?" she asked. He didn't answer, just nodded for her to pay attention. She focussed on the person reading from a prepared parchment that he described as the Chalcedonian definition of the nature of Christ. Bunny was not an unintelligent woman but what followed was difficult to comprehend.

"Truly God and truly Man; the Self-same of a rational soul and body..." then "Two natures inconfusedly, unchangeably, indivisibly, inseparable..." then finally "Concurring into One Person and One Hypostasis."

She was sure it was much easier to just accept such a truth by faith than to try and define it in writing.[2] What then happened surprised her. Each Church or group of Churches present signified their agreement with the statement, but two groups refused. The Coptic Church of Alexandria chose to hold to the definition proposed by Cyril. The second group to voice opposition was the Armenian Apostolic Church who stated that,

"The Lord Jesus Christ is God the Incarnate Word. He possesses the perfect Godhead and the perfect manhood. His fully divine nature is united with His fully human nature yet without mixing, blending or alteration." As far as

---

[1] Much of the discourse at the Council of Chalcedon centred around the dual nature of the Christ, hoping to agree a definition that would be acceptable to all and counteract various heresies of the day. As with most ecumenical councils each party tended to defend the doctrinal stance proposed by their local favourite.

[2] The Chalcedon Definition was written in Greek, the full English translation is as follows: "We, then, following the holy Fathers, all with one consent, teach men to confess one and the same Son, our Lord Jesus Christ, the same perfect in Godhead and also perfect in manhood; truly God and truly man, of a reasonable soul and body; consubstantial with us according to the manhood; in all things like unto us, without sin; begotten before all ages of the Father according to the Godhead, and in these latter days, for us and for our salvation, born of the virgin Mary, the mother of God, according to the manhood; one and the same Christ, Son, Lord, Only-begotten, to be acknowledged in two natures, inconfusedly, unchangeably, indivisibly, inseparably; the distinction of natures being by no means taken away by the union, but rather the property of each nature being preserved, and concurring in one Person and one Subsistence, not parted or divided into two persons, but one and the same Son, and only begotten, God the Word, the Lord Jesus Christ, as the prophets from the beginning have declared concerning him, and the Lord Jesus Christ himself taught us, and the Creed of the holy Fathers has handed down to us." Creeds of Christendom extracted from www.ccel.org

Bunny could discern there was no discernible difference between their statement and the more elaborate Chalcedonian Definition.

And then it was over. Those who disagreed embraced their fellow bishops and departed to the sound of a solitary church bell, never to attend such a gathering again.

"Questions?" Bunny's travelling companion posed.

"Plenty," she admitted. First on her lips was to ask for clarification on who exactly the Coptic and Armenian Churches were or, more to the point, still are.

"They are just other parts of the overall Church of Christ. The Coptic Church will grow from strength to strength from Alexandria across north Africa. They will keep the Christian flame burning despite centuries of Muslim oppression so that in your day there will be around thirty million Coptic Christians."[1]

"Thirty million?" she reacted with amazement. He just nodded.

"And a further forty million in the Armenian Church," he added. "Although, there will be several splits, so I ought to say in the Syriac rite... or across Oriental Orthodoxy, but whatever they become, these all originate from today and grow to cover most of north and east Africa, Arabia, Syria and southern Asia. You know, the lands that apostles Thomas, Bartholomew and Thaddeus planted."

Bunny had never considered that there would have been any missionary journeys other than those she knew well from reading about them in the Book of Acts. But of course, there were many apostles so it made sense that there would be church-planting journeys other than those of Paul. Presumably all of them were peppered with great sermons, healings, miracles and mass conversions.

"These two groups make up much of the patriarchies of Alexandria, Antioch and Jerusalem," he said pointing at the dissenting parties leaving the building.

The mention of Jerusalem suddenly made a figurative lightbulb flash above Bunny's head. She had visited Israel as part of an organised church holiday a few years previously. Her tour guide had explained that the historic Old City of Jerusalem was divided into four quarters: one each for Jews, Muslims, Christians and Armenians. She had been too polite to ask why such a

---

[1] Taken from the section: "List of Christian denominations by number of members." Wikipedia.org

small country as Armenia got to have a quarter of Jerusalem, but now she had a reason.

"Are these the ones who have a quarter of the old city of Jerusalem?" Bunny asked.

"Interesting that you call it the Armenian *quarter*," he replied. "They consider that they are part of the Christian *half* of the Old City." [1]

"So, does that mean they are just as much Christian as..." she thought for a moment, "Well, as I am?"

"Perhaps that would be a good question to ask them when you meet them in heaven," he replied mischievously.

---

[1] The Armenian patriarchy backs the statement: "We regard the Christian and Armenian Quarters of the Old City as inseparable and contiguous entities that are firmly united by the same faith," from 'Dividing Jerusalem: Armenians on the line of confrontation' by Hratch Tchilingirian, published on Armeniapedia.org

Chapter 50

QUESTIONS

"That was a gunshot," Thea said to Joel as they stood silently next to the electrical consumer unit inside the rear porch. When Joel heard the loud bang his initial assumption was that something electrical had fused. That was clearly impossible as he was the one who had disconnected the power moments earlier.

"Gunshot?" he queried. Thea nodded, then set off towards the front of the building concerned about what might have happened to Chris, Ralph or Bunny.

"Šta se dešava?"

The expression for What's going on? was shouted from behind the closed door of the back room of the farmhouse. The moment he heard the gunshot The Badger calmly closed himself into the room where Bunny helplessly lay. He was not inexperienced in being in life-threatening situations and knew the wisdom of only communicating with your accomplice in their native tongue.

"Šta se dešava?" he repeated then added, "Da li si dobro?" asking of the young man's wellbeing.

The lack of a reply suggested they were under attack, and he knew he might have to come out fighting.

Joel hadn't yet tried the handle of the backdoor. He liked to consider himself as a confident person but knew it was as much a smokescreen covering his inner anxieties. But now he had the opportunity to do something decisive. If it had been a gunshot, Chris, Ralph and Bunny were inside and he needed to play his part. He reached out and grasped the decorative solid brass orb. It was bitterly cold to his touch, but he clasped his fingers tightly around it, making his whole hand feel decidedly numb. Slowly, ever so slowly, he applied angular momentum, pivoting the spherical ornament in its housing. It moved, but was this just the natural play in a locked door? He didn't know and continued with its tentative arc. What he needed to hear was a... click!

There it was. They must have left the door unlocked from their visit earlier and all it needed was to be turned open. He pushed the door forwards barely more than an inch before reversing his slow wrist revolution to return the handle to its original position. Finally, he released his grasp and quickly replaced his cold hand into his pocket. The backdoor was now open.

As a special-needs teacher Thea had received a wealth of training in student care and safety. Whilst none of it was nursing, it did cover some of the basic principles, including more than rudimentary first aid. She had found it useful, not only in her employment but also throughout the years she cared for her invalid mother. But she had never had to be the first responder on the scene of a gunshot wound and had no idea if she would cope. Stop the bleeding first; then C.P.R. would be the plan. She feared as to whom the victim might be. In haste, she turned the front corner of the farmhouse and ran straight into the chest of a man. The impact not only stopped her progress but provoked a spontaneous fight-back reflex by which she placed both hands on the chest of her assailant, pushing him as hard as she could. The man was no larger than she, and the combination of both her haste and her instinctive self-defence propelled him backwards, clear off the ground. As he became airborne – as if in slow-motion – Thea realised she had just launched Artur Thelmin, the diminutive Lutheran she had met for the first time earlier that evening. There was nothing she could do about it now and could only watch as he sailed backwards, landing on his back with both feet flailing in the air.

"I am so sorry, Artur," she whispered, but he didn't hear her.

She then noticed that Jack was standing against the wall beside the front window. Having grown-up in Carrickfergus during a decade of paramilitary insurrection, he was already familiar with the sound of gunshots, but it was his police training that had taught him to never stand in front of the window of the person shooting at you. He stood as close to the wall as possible and beckoned Thea to come next to him. She immediately took a long stride to join him.

"Please don't do that to me, will you," Jack whispered having watched Artur despatched so uncompromisingly onto the farmyard. Thea didn't answer.

Jack explained in a combination of whispers and gestures that they had just arrived and heard a gun fire inside the room next to where they were now standing. Thea looked past Jack to the window and could see that the curtain was still parted in the middle, just as Joel had left it minutes earlier. She dropped to all fours and began moving beneath the window. Jack considered stopping her but held back. Thea was a determined and capable woman, and he could she what she was planning. It was dangerous, but made sense. Artur had by now rolled himself onto his hands and knees and began to shuffle towards the wall. Thea, now at his eye level, mouthed another, "Sorry." Artur gave a silent, "Okay," before disappearing around the side of the building away from her.

Squatting beneath the window she tentatively lifted her head, hoping to assess the situation inside. There wasn't a lot of light, but her eyes had already adjusted sufficiently to the darkness to allow her to make out a blood-stained Ralph kneeling on the floor and Chris, frozen to the spot, holding a gun.

Bunny didn't know what had launched her onto this crazy journey. Reality seemed such a long time ago. She had been instrumental in organising a meeting of local church leaders, but that had gone so badly it had both shocked and upset her. How could people, supposedly on the *same side*, be so uncooperative and antagonistic towards each other. And then there was Chris and the fact that he, a fervent Charismatic, had made his feelings known towards her, an ardent Anglican. Well, he hadn't really said anything, but she knew that was what he was trying so badly to express. The reason she knew it was that she now accepted she had the same feelings for him, despite never allowing herself to even consider them. The thought of letting those emotions surface had sent her into such a spin that she found herself inside, of all things, a Catholic confessional. Since then, everything was difficult to understand. Was she still in the confessional? Was this a dream? Was she dead?

"Are you any closer to knowing the question?" the man in the gold-rimmed hat asked her.

"Pardon?" she answered.

"You won't find an answer as to why you are on this journey until you know the question, will you?"

"Stop being in my head!" she stated, firmly irritated. The point he was making was nonetheless wisely provocative. What was the answer she was looking for?

"When this started it was... interesting to find out where all the Churches began," she said, partly to him but mainly thinking out loud. "But that is all it was. I was binge-watching the Church-History Channel. But then something happened. I found that I was changing, I was able to embrace other types of worship. I could see that God was present in the silence of the Quakers, the evangelical zeal of the Methodists, the worshipful charisma of the Pentecostals as well as the melodic chants, mosaics and incense of the Orthodox. So many folk of differing persuasions all striving to find and speak the truth. Calvin, Wesley, Parham and even today at Chalcedon, all about finding the truth. And all able to use the Bible to defend whichever position they take. The defence of slavery was shocking... and then there was the Confessing Church in Nazi

Germany." She gave a shudder. "But, I guess, God is present in all of them." She paused for a moment before continuing, checking her thought process.

"Even though some fought and died for their personal view of Church, God was not only with them but *also* with those they were opposing, who had a different understanding of Church. Some were just plain wrong, though! It was strange how when I was on the Heresy Express, I sort of *just knew* that those other groups were… well, just not part of the same… Church. I suppose that's the Holy Spirit inside me, isn't it." He said nothing, he knew she had more to unload.

"When I twisted Rector Mashman's arm about Church unity I was only thinking of co-operation between we Anglicans and, you know, the Methodists, Baptists, Pentecostals and so on. I hadn't even thought of the Lutheran minister that he invited and certainly not the Catholics. But now you've thrown me a curveball with the Orthodox, the Coptics and the Armenians. Are they all part of the same…?" She stopped herself finishing the question. They patently weren't the same *Church*, that was the whole point. She thought for a moment before repeating herself.

"Are they all on the same side?" she said tactfully before answering the question herself. "I guess they are, that is what you are showing me, isn't it?" Still, he said nothing.

"Okay, okay," she turned to face him. "You say in order to get the answer I first need to know the question I am asking. Well, I don't know if you are giving me three wishes," she said playfully, "but like it or not this is my first question."

"Let's hear it then," he said smiling.

"I accept that every Church, every denomination is different, and that those differences might be about doctrine, worship, style, government, inclusion or simply architecture… but the question I have is this." He looked at her expectantly.

"Is God happy with such a fragmented Church?" she asked.

He paused for a moment, his smile remaining, before saying, "Now, that is a very good question."

Bunny wasn't going to be satisfied with that for an answer so immediately deployed her tell-me-more look which soon yielded the desired result. His answer, however, appeared to be so tangential to her question that it came as a huge surprise.

"What can you tell me about the Children of Israel," he asked. "The people you read of in, what you call, the Old Testament?" Unable to think why on earth he was asking her this, she began to list all the facts she knew about God's chosen people.

"The Children of Israel? Well, they are a nation that had been promised to Abraham and were named after his grandson Jacob whom God renamed Israel. Jacob then had twelve sons," she decided not to attempt to list them by name, unsure of the likelihood of her success. "They were all captive in Egypt for years before Moses led them across the Red Sea, through the wilderness, and into the Promised Land." This exposition would have been fine in any Sunday School, but it wasn't unlocking any key truth for her. He was no help, and kept just smiling back, patiently. She took a breath, praying for insight.

"They all settled in the Promised Land," she continued, "where each tribe was allotted a ..."

She stopped suddenly in mid-sentence. Something clicked into place. Something so obvious she had never seen it before.

"Each tribe!" she repeated. "Simeon, Levi, Rueben, Benjamin, Asher, Dan, Zebu..." she began without thinking and, as expected, quickly gave up listing names.

"Never mind what they were called. They were each one a different tribe. They were *one nation* made up of *twelve tribes*!"

"Indeed," he confirmed with a satisfied nod.

"So, God is fine with the Church, His Church, being made up thousands of tribes," she postulated.

"Well, perhaps just twelve," he clarified with a chuckle.

"Okay, I can go with that," Bunny sparked. "Coptic, Armenian, Orthodox, Catholic, Anglican, Pentecostal..." She stopped herself trying to complete a list. "That's the point isn't it. It isn't up to us to decide." She realised that this had been the mistake she'd seen repeated over and over again across the centuries, each group trying to decide who is *in* and who is *out*.

"We just need to know which tribe we are part of and celebrate the fact that other tribes are all part of the same... *nation*. No one better than any other, none with a monopoly on knowing what truth is." All of a sudden, she could see that even the attempt to decide who was right and who was wrong, this was the very act that fuels the seed of division.

"In a sense all Churches are equally right," she postulated, before adding the caveat, "apart from those teaching heresy of course."

But how can I know which ones are teaching heresy? she thought, realising that to pass judgment on others was the very thing she had just seen was the spark of discord. Before the full insecurity of this circular argument could take hold of her, he came to her rescue.

"That is why we need the Holy Spirit to guide us, to warn us of dangers."

"Just like when I was on the Heresy Express," she said. "I somehow *just knew* something was amiss."

"Yes, that is right. If you are mature enough to hear the Holy Spirit, He will always help you discern rightly," he said graciously before standing to his feet and offering his hand to help Bunny up. She briefly considered taking it but had no need of it. Besides, she found this guide to be both helpful and irritating at the same time.

"Come with me," he said. "There is someone I think you would like to meet."

They shuffled sideways out of their allotted seats on the back row of what was now a near-empty church hall and headed to the door. As the daylight hit them, he waited momentarily so she could walk beside him.

"Did you get your first wish?" he asked cheekily.

"Yes," Bunny replied laughing. "Know your tribe!"

The only problem would be to know which tribe she and Chris were going to join when he plucked up the courage to actually form a coherent sentence and ask her.

Joel slowly, cautiously pushed the door forwards. He fully expected that the old heavy door, as it opened, would make the loud protracted and somewhat comical creak that was the staple of all classic Hammer Horror films. Thankfully, it opened near silently. Peering inside, he could see that to his right the kitchen door was still open, and he could see the large pile of trash they had left upended on its linoleum floor. Ahead was the corridor that led to the front of the farmhouse, although there was no clear line of sight as it first turned a corner around the stairs; its walls marked only by faded paisley print wallpaper and flaking paint. To his left was the door within which they had gathered around a camp bed and prayed a few hours earlier. That door was ajar but as he looked, it slowly closed tight shut. It could have been the breeze, caused by opening the backdoor but then, as the handle turned, he knew someone was the other side of the yellow six-panel door. In common with most buildings of that vintage most doors had a keyhole; the absence of the sound of a lock turning assured him that at least this door had no key.

Joel reached one foot forward as far as was comfortable, adjusted his balance and stepped inside, pulling his trailing foot with him. This silent arrival reminded him of the times, as a teenager, he had to creep home from the church youth group without waking his father from a drunken stupor. The fear of reprisal then was a fraction of the fear he felt now. He carefully let the door swing to a near closed position behind him; subconsciously he needed to leave an escape route open.

"Ralph!" Chris said trying to make sense of what had happened. He couldn't make out whose blood was on the floor, but there was a substantial amount. Ralph was seated on the floor with their captor kneeling face-down slumped across his lap. Chris held his breath. This was the moment at the end of the movies when the hero expired, having delivered the memorably dramatic last word.

"Speak to me, brother!" Chris insisted.

His pastor said nothing, but just stared at the blood covering his palm. What was notable though was he showed no sign of being about to fall pitifully backwards as the final credits began to roll. He was fully conscious. Chris's attention then went to the third man in the room. Without thinking, Chris reached forward and pulled his shoulder firmly enough to dislodge him from on top of his friend. Chris half-expected that the good-looking stranger would keel over, dead on the floor, but to his muted relief he was still alive and gave an incoherent mumble as he rolled onto his back.

There was the wound. Chris had never seen a gunshot wound before and to look at it was both disturbing and fascinating. Almost half of the young man's shirt was red, the focal point of which was the small, neat hole a couple of inches to the left of his navel. It was from this hole that blood pulsated with the rhythm of his heartbeat. The movement onto his back caused a wave of blood to descend from below the hem of his shirt and spill across his trousers as an incoming crimson tide. In their grapple Ralph had unknowingly collected a handful of the man's warm life-force, covering his own clothes. At last Ralph spoke.

"He shot himself, he shot himself!"

That much was self-evident. In a panic-ridden attempt to release himself from his assailant's body-tackle he must have pointed the pistol downwards and, in the dark, missed Ralph and punctured his own abdomen.

"He's shot you too, Ralph!" A woman's voice broke the tense stillness. "Can't you see?"

They both turned to the window where Thea, now standing, was gesturing that they look at Ralph's left arm, at the back just above his elbow. Ralph held up the required arm and attempted to turn it to see what she meant. Chris swung his phone toward him and immediately saw what Thea had spotted in the dim light. Blood was dripping from his triceps. Evidently, the gunshot had not entirely missed its intended target.

It is a well-known fact that some people suffering the most horrendous injuries report no feelings of pain until they are made aware of the extent of the wounds. This was exactly the case here. Ralph hadn't felt even the slightest discomfort until he was confronted by the sight of his own blood. He too let out an incoherent moan.

"What do I do?" Chris said to Thea.

"Go to the front door," she said calmly, "and let me and Jack in."

Suddenly the darkness behind Thea lit up with a growing bright light that made her look almost angelic. Her halo, however, was nothing more than a pair of headlights approaching the front of the farmhouse. Unlike Chris, Joel and Jack, this vehicle made no attempt to approach discreetly nor to divert into the barn. Someone else was coming.

Chapter 51

AUGUSTINE

Not previously known for her sea legs, Bunny had found that she'd enjoyed her numerous crossings of the English Channel and the Atlantic Ocean during this longest of nights. She was surprised therefore to discover how similar it was to cross the Mediterranean in a simple fifth century sailing vessel. This was one mode of transport that stood the test of time. She had left the major port city of Constantinople, within which the Council of Chalcedon, a district of the city, had been held. The truncation of time was particularly poignant as the marvellous Orthodox cathedral, Hagia Sophia, later to dominate the city's skyline and within which she had experienced such a wonderful sense of worship, hadn't even been built yet. Rapid time travel was at best confusing, but even more so now she was doing it backwards. The sea crossing ended on the north African coast in a small city whose name she couldn't help but find amusing, Hippo Regius. They were visiting an African Hippo. There was, however, no one with whom she could share the joke, the man in the gold-rimmed hat having, once again, mysteriously disappeared not long after they set sail.

Clambering down the rickety wooden gangplank and setting foot for the first time in her life in Africa she was taken by the fact that the landscape was in no way barren or arid but lush and fruitful, well, at least it was around the coast. As soon as she was safely clear of the quayside bustle, she looked along the shoreline hoping to catch the eye of someone who might be expecting her. No one returned her gaze and for a moment she felt invisible. Unsure as to what to do next she slid up her sleeve for a date check. At least that was something she could do in this new place. She had no idea why she was here but had to presume it must be important. Her last stop had been in 451 in prosperous Constantinople, but she had no reference points in this era of antiquity to have any idea when she was. The large square digital dial came to her rescue, 4:10, only forty years earlier.

"The world is a book and those who do not travel read only one page."[1]

---

[1] Words attributed to St. Augustine, widely cited.

The somewhat philosophical statement took her by surprise. She immediately covered her historically impossible watch and turned to see who had spoken. He was dressed in light ankle-length robes with an animal skin cloak over his shoulders. He had a short soft beard that was just beginning to turn grey, and short dark hair that she couldn't quite tell if it had been cut into a monk's tonsure. He had kind eyes – that was the only way to describe him – deep dark eyes that seemed to portray calm, humility and, for a woman travelling alone in a strange place, safety.

"God provides the wind, man must raise the sail,"[1] he said, pointing to the vessel she had just disembarked from, in yet one more truism. Bunny was not one for trading axiomatic clichés even with such a friendly looking person, and chose to ignore his statements and politely introduced herself, adding a question that would normally be considered arrogant but in the context of her lucid dream she'd now learnt to expect.

"I assume you are expecting me?" He nodded politely and indicated the direction they should walk, offering to carry her jacket as they set off. Bunny declined, preferring to keep her coat on but did ask him to tell her his name.

"Aurelius Augustinus Hipponensis," he confirmed with an apology for not having done so. Bunny was none the wiser as to who he was. It wasn't long before he had led her to a small table and chairs under a large acacia tree that gave him 'thankful shade from the African sun', as he put it. Bunny didn't seem to feel the effect of the sun. If anything she felt quite cool, surprisingly so for Africa. They were outside what she assumed must be his home, inside which he briefly disappeared before returning with two wooden goblets of lightly fermented grape juice. It was up to her to open the conversation.

"Good Sir," she started, not knowing why she used that phrase, but as it sounded sufficiently old to be justified she continued, "I assume you are a follower of the Nazarene?"

She had never before described being a Christian as *following the Nazarene*, but the antiquity of her surroundings somehow demanded a change to her vocabulary.

"Yes, but not always," he said. "In my youth I lived such a life of sin that my only prayer would be 'Lord give me chastity, but not just yet!'[2] but then one

---

[1] Words attributed to St. Augustine, widely cited.

[2] The actual quote widely attributed to St. Augustine is: "Give me chastity and continence, but not yet."

day, as I lay contemplating in my garden, I heard God himself speak to me. 'Take up and read'[1] He said, so I did just that, I reached for a Bible and found what I had been searching for all my life, Christ. I had read in Plato and Cicero sayings that were wise and very beautiful; but I had never read in either of them: Come unto me all ye that labour and are heavy laden."[2] That was as succinct and heartfelt a testimony of a conversion experience as she had ever heard. Whoever this person was, she was sure he was genuine.

"And as for you, dear lady, what is the question that brought you on this journey?"

What a startling thing to say. It was almost exactly as the gold-rimmed guide had provoked her moments earlier, or years later. And what did he mean by journey? Was he referring to crossing the Mediterranean or did he mean my *journey*?

"Well, I think..." she began, not entirely sure how she was going to express her thoughts. "I think I am looking to find out why the Church has... or will... or whatever... never mind." Not for the first time she lost her sense of past, present and future. She re-collected her thoughts and tried again.

"Church divisions. That's pretty much it. Why do they happen?"

"Ah, there is nothing more serious than the sacrilege of schism, because there is no just cause for severing the unity of the Church," he said sympathetically.[3] She took a small sip of the lukewarm grape juice and nodded in agreement. He then went on to briefly describe that there are two types of Church: the first being the visible, with its sacraments, buildings and hierarchy; the second invisible – the souls of its members both living and dead. A heavenly City of God.[4]

"Yes, I get that," she said almost dismissively. This wasn't a new concept to her but suddenly she realised that this person might have been the first to

---

[1] Augustine reported that when he was in the garden during his time in Milan, he heard a voice say "Tolle, lege" or "Take up and read" which he took to be a prompt to re-read the Bible he had just put down.

[2] Words attributed to St. Augustine, widely cited.

[3] Words attributed to St. Augustine, widely cited.

[4] St Augustine published his 28-volume "City of God" in 426 partly as a response to the growing anxiety caused by the collapse of the Roman Empire. His other masterpiece "Confessions" had been published in 397.

express that truth. She apologised and asked him to explain how different groups could be united. He thought for a moment before replying.

"In essentials, unity; in non-essentials, liberty; in all things, charity."[1]

She quickly picked up on the *in non-essentials, liberty* clause and jumped in excitedly, "Yes, that is what I said." She had rudely cut across him, so tried to cover her faux pas with some seamless flattery,

"But not as eloquently as you, Sir."

She wasn't sure if it worked. He had stopped speaking, so she had to continue with her interruption.

"I said, 'Know your tribe' and give all the other tribes freedom to be what they are."

"Tribes?" he asked, understandably a little confused as to her unrequested contribution.

"Yes, like the tribes of Israel," she tried to explain, but he just looked back at her blankly prompting her to add firmly, "The Jews!"

"Ah, of course, the Jews," he answered, thankful to now have a connection with his house guest and added, "God's special people."

This prompted him to arise from his seat, asking Bunny to remain and that he would return momentarily, which he duly did, this time holding a collection of opened scrolls. The first of these, he explained, had been sent by Jerome. At least that was a name Bunny had heard, although with little idea of whom he was. The missive Jerome had sent was apparently attacking him for being 'dangerously Jewish.' The second scroll was from a Faustus, again accusing him, and in the particular passage which he chose to read to her expressed that,

"Christianity is based on the belief that Christ came to destroy the Law and the prophets."

That did not sound correct to Bunny's ears who immediately let out a reflex 'No!' as she inwardly classified this unknown Faustus as a heretic.[2]

"No, indeed," her host echoed.

The third scroll was a copy of the reply he had sent to Jerome. He then took great delight in reading a passage from it:

---

[1] Words attributed to St. Augustine, widely cited.

[2] 'Augustine and Thinking with Jews: Rhetoric Pro- and Contra Iudaeos' by Paula Fredriksen

"Did Peter and also Paul not live according to Jewish law? Both apostles would have maintained their traditional practices even after becoming Christian since God himself had ordained these practices, they had no reason not to."[1]

Bunny had never really considered whether Peter and Paul, the New Testament apostles, had continued to practise their Jewish rituals after their conversion to Christianity. Her instinct would have been simply to ignore this minor point of historical detail, but she had learnt that every conversation she was having must be vital for her *journey* of discovery. More importantly, she had no idea why her question about Church division had now moved to whether Jewish converts still practised their *Jewishness*. She then had an idea as to perhaps why.

"Sir," she asked tentatively, "Are you a Jew?"

Her host smiled, rolled-up the scrolls and placed them carefully on the table in front of them, sat back and shook his head and smiled at her.

"Let me explain, my child" he began, "Our Lord and his apostles all lived as Torah-observant Jews the whole of their lives and so there must be space for Jewishness in the Church. After all, the Church and the Jews stand as one community, especially against the pagans and heretics."[2]

"One community?" Bunny reacted with surprise. "But I thought..." He raised a hand to politely calm her sudden disquiet.

"I can see you are seeking truth, Miss," he assured her. "If you believe what you like in the Gospel and reject what you do not like, then it is not the Gospel you believe, but yourself."

"I don't want to reject any of it," she protested. "I just thought, you know, Christians and Jews are... well they are two whole different religions." Suddenly filled with an uncomfortable degree of self-doubt she could do no more than ask a question she never thought would have been necessary. She leaned over toward the table, nervously grasping the edge of it with her hand, looked him in the eye and asked,

"Aren't they?"

He made no attempt to give her an answer which only served to disquiet her even more. He gathered up the scrolls from the table and together with the

---

[1] Ibid.

[2] A review of 'Augustine and the Jews' by Paula Fredriksen Yale University Press 2010 entitled 'Was Saint Augustine Good for the Jews?' by David Van Biema, Time Magazine 7 Dec. 2008.

now empty goblets tidied them away inside. What had this all been about? She had no idea. In her quest for a simple answer to her questions about Christian unity she was now even doubting what Christianity was. This was most uncomfortable. He returned from inside and announced that her return ship would soon be setting sail and that they should begin the short walk back to the quayside. Bunny agitatedly repeated her question, this time with a deliberately impolite forcefulness. She *needed* an answer.

"Aren't they different?" she insisted as he set off for the harbour area. She began to follow, reluctantly at first, then gave a short sprint to catch up with him.

"Aren't they different?" she repeated. This time he stopped.

"Let me ask you a question," he said.

"More questions! Why can't anyone give me a straight answer," Bunny complained, then promptly apologised and bade him ask his question.

"Is the God that you and I pray to," he began, "is He the same God that the Old Testament Jews prayed to?"

Bunny gave him no answer, and he didn't expect to get one. The truism he had posed was profound. Whichever way you look at it, Jews and Christians are praying to the same God.

Within seconds they were beside the same ship ready to set off back to Constantinople.

"It was nice to meet you, Miss Bunny," he said as she stepped onto the rough gangplank. She turned to shake his hand,

"And it was nice to meet you Mr Hipponen..."

He interrupted her poor attempt to remember his name.

"Most people call me Augustine."

Bunny's jaw dropped at the realisation that she had just spent precious one-on-one time with one of the world's greatest thinkers and the father of Christian doctrine. This was the person who had first articulated so many concepts that much of Christendom now take as settled. As for her, he had helped settle the idea that differences should be tolerated in love not judged or resisted. But he had planted yet more questions in her mind.

It was impossible to tell if the driver of the white Ford that swung onto the gravel driveway had seen Jack and Thea entering the front door, before they slammed it shut, turned the key in the lock and slid one of the two bolts shut.

"That was the car that was following us," Thea said momentarily out of breath.

"What?" Chris asked, shocked at the new information.

"It followed Joel and I from the hospital," she explained, but couldn't offer an answer to any of Chris's subsequent questions about who or why.

Meanwhile, Jack rushed into the front room to make an initial assessment on the state of the two wounded men on the floor.

"I could do with some light in here," he shouted at Thea and Chris, promptly terminating their discourse.

Within moments Chris was shining his mobile phone torch over the blood-soaked scene. It was patently obvious; Ralph's injury was serious but not life-threatening whereas the other man's gunshot wound was most likely going to be terminal. Ralph's police training allowed him to take charge of the situation calmly as he instructed Chris to tie a belt around Ralph's upper arm to stop the bleeding, whilst he and Thea would try to seal the gaping abdominal puncture through which the young man's lifeblood continued to flow. Thea knew who this man was. She had spoken to him in the hospital barely an hour ago and she and Joel had followed his sports car all the way to Lane End farmhouse. The urgency of the life-threatening situation, however, made the need to share that fact with the others slip from her attention.

Joel heard the commotion in the wake of the slamming of the front door, and Jack's voice which carried in the stillness of the building. Intensely aware that someone was inside the back room, presumably with Bunny, he didn't want to alert them to his presence inches away, outside the door. Joel began a silent step towards the corridor to the front of the building, taking a huge stride away from the door. The parquet flooring, laid upon concrete, didn't creak under his weight so encouraged a second giant stride. As he completed this second step suddenly a sound froze him to the spot. Not a creaky floorboard, but the sound of the back door opening with a click. He was a full six feet away from the door which now began to swing towards him. He had no idea that another car had arrived at the front so had to assume it must be one of his compatriots entering the building. As the door swung towards him, he grabbed hold of it as it reached a position perpendicular to the hinge. It was going to be imperative to tell the person, whoever they are, to be silent. Joel then swung himself around the door, rapidly pivoting with long arms in a manoeuvre that ended with him clasping a hand firmly over the mouth of the intruder.

439

"There is such a loss of blood, if we don't get him to hospital quickly he's going to die on us," Jack admitted with sombre composure. "Someone needs to ring for an ambulance."

"We already have an ambulance," Thea pointed out.

It was true. The hospice ambulance was parked outside and, assuming the keys were in the ignition, it would be a much quicker and potentially more life-saving option than waiting for paramedics to arrive. Jack nodded his assent at Thea's suggestion. Chris and Ralph did likewise. There was, however, someone else outside.

Inside the rear door, Artur looked stunned, his small eyes peering over Joel's large black hand. Joel raised a finger to his lips to ensure he got the message before releasing his palm gag. Artur nodded compliantly then beckoned to Joel that he needed to whisper something in his ear.

"Someone has arrived at the front, in a white car. I had to dash round here to hide."

The description of a white car made it clear to Joel that it must be the car whose headlights had followed them. Joel pulled Artur into the rear lobby then silently closed the back door, this time turning the key in the lock. They both held their breath as it locked with a firm clunk.

"Drrrriiiiing!"

The last thing anyone expected was for the front doorbell to ring. Ralph, who had by now made it to his feet, was closest to the front door and stooped involuntarily at the resonant sound. Jack and Chris were about to attempt to move the young man as Thea retained pressure on his stomach wound. Everyone froze as if buffering. Foreign tones then suddenly filled the silence.

"Šta se dešava," came loudly from the rear room. Its occupant, clearly getting more agitated, needed to know what was happening, adding,

"Ko je na vratima?" to ask who was at the door.

Jack and Thea had no idea anyone else was in the building, neither did Artur. Joel froze beside the young Lutheran, the voice having come from inside a room barely four feet from where they both stood. Then, much to Joel's amazement, something most surprising happened. Artur replied,

"U redu je," he said in perfect Serbian, pointedly at the closed door, followed by, "Rekao sam im da odu."

Joel's eyelids widened to such an extent that the entirety of his pupils became encircled by the cool yellow of his eyes. A large grin then followed.

440

"You speak Turkish?" Joel whispered assuming that their adversary was part of the Grey Wolves of Islam. Artur looked puzzled and simply whispered back,

"No. Serbian."

Joel was now totally confused. Who on earth had kidnapped Bunny?

The sound of a second Serbian voice inside the building had the effect of spooking the churchmen at the front of the building to such an extent they had to act quickly. This was a choice of priorities. The wounded man was barely conscious but was at least on his feet being supported by Jack and Chris. Chris still had the gun tucked into the rear of his trousers so drew it out.

Three firm knocks at the front door convinced Ralph that the driver of the white Ford was still outside. Ralph had line of sight down the corridor and could see it was clear to make their way to the front door and, if he could get the man out of the way, they could make a dash to the ambulance.

"Go 'round the back!" Ralph said loudly through the front door, as matter of fact as he could. Adding an unnecessary, "Please," for good measure.

A disembodied voice said, "Okay."

Thea could see through the crack in the curtain the exact moment he passed by and signalled to Ralph that it was safe to open the front door. Within less than a minute the young man was lying in the rear of the unlocked ambulance, Ralph beside him holding pressure onto the wound.

Jack opened the driver's door but before he could step inside Thea grabbed his forearm.

"I've got this," she said. Jack looked at her. Earlier that evening he had objected to Thea's attendance at their meeting but here he was being asked to give way to her. As they looked at each other it was as if something switched in his heart.

"You're needed here, with Chris and the others," she insisted. Jack knew she was right. Important as it was to get this man to the hospital, he knew he had to face up to the unknown, to willingly step into the firing line, for the sake of, not just Bunny, but his own self-respect. He stepped back and held the door open for Thea. Seconds later the ambulance sped off into the darkness.

Chris and Jack, both bloodstained, returned behind the security of the locked front door. Artur and Joel were likewise secure at the rear of the farmhouse but, as they stood silently, the handle of the back door began to turn.

Chapter 52

THE COUNCIL OF NICAEA

Constantinople had hardly changed in the one hundred and twenty-something years that had elapsed since she was last there. Or as she was now travelling back in time, she thought, it shouldn't be *elapsed*, but she couldn't think what the opposite of elapsed would be... *relapsed* perhaps? She slid her sleeve back over the square face of her watch, hiding the flashing 3:25, and disembarked. The most noticeable thing about the quayside and roads leading into the city were that they appeared to be full of people. This wasn't the first busy dockside she had experienced on this mind-trip but the difference here was that instead of being full of ship-hands, stevedores and dockers, the crowd she was immersed within comprised almost exclusively men in ecclesiastical robes. Robes were the fashion of the day; this was evidently Roman Constantinople, but the religious iconography adorning most of the garments – some elaborately ostentatious, others modestly simple – left no one in any doubt of their provenance.

The throng, once they had disgorged from the dozens of vessels double-parked in the harbour, began to slowly funnel toward a fleet of waiting carriages. Bunny had ridden in several carriages over the course of the last few hours, or centuries. She was perhaps the only person to have had first-hand experience of the evolution of carriage design, upholstery and most importantly suspension. She had accidentally become something of a carriage nerd, to the extent this could be her specialist subject if she were ever on the TV quiz show *Mastermind*. These present carriages, however, were of the most rudimentary design; little more than a glorified platform on wheels behind one, or in some cases two, horses. They were in some way reminiscent of the chariots raced by Charlton Heston in the movie *Ben Hur* (thankfully minus the spikes on the wheel hubs). Evidently, the dignitaries were to be taken by carriage whereas their entourage would, presumably, follow on foot.

Bunny allowed herself to gently flow with the human tide, moving slowly towards the waiting chariot-taxi-rank. As they slowly moved, it didn't take her long to sample the emotional flavour of the day. To her surprise, and there were few things that surprised her anymore, everyone appeared to be happy. Occasional cheers and whoops rang out; people greeted each other with hugs and kisses as if they were long-lost friends, reunited after years apart. Perhaps

442

they were. The unmistakable sound of spontaneous worshipful songs painted an audible backdrop across the distant air. This was a day of unbridled joy. Something must have triggered it and she felt compelled to find out why. Not for the first time, she spoke without really thinking.

"Excuse me!" Her interjection was directed at the group nearest to her, a party of six whose focal point was a short olive-skinned man whom she soon discovered was the Bishop of Caesarea. On hearing her interruption, the small group came to a sudden stop, causing the party of six following behind to execute an abrupt bypassing manoeuvre.[1]

"Yes, Madam?" the Bishop addressed her, much to the surprise of his retinue. Despite knowing that she too often would speak when she shouldn't, Bunny nonetheless balanced this with a strong sense of decorum. She knew her manners.

"Sorry to interrupt you, Your Highness…, Your Grace…, Your…" she offered a polite bow by way of apology. The clerical grandee walked towards her.

"I am Eusebius Pamphilli, Bishop of Caesarea," he replied graciously. Bunny thanked him then introduced herself,

"My name is Johan, but most people call me Bunny."

Then she asked, what was to her the most obvious question, why is everyone so joyful? A huge grin came across Eusebius' face.

"Why, 'tis the day of God's great victory. The day of our freedom." Bunny deployed her *tell-me-more* look, to which he, as many a man before him, complied.

"The Emperor, having signed the Edict of Milan, has decreed an end to the persecution of Christians." He gave a spontaneous "Hallelujah!" raising his hands and looking skyward. "For the first time the bishops of every church may gather in one place without fear of arrest. So here we are, at last together by the grace of the architect of our freedom."[2] She would have liked to have

---

[1] Every bishop who attended the Council at Nicaea had permission to bring with them two priests or elders and three deacons, hence every delegate brought a group of six.

[2] The Edict of Milan had been issued some 12 years earlier by emperors Lucinius, who ruled the Western Roman Empire, and Constantine I, who ruled the Eastern half. It ended Christian persecution and decreed that all possessions confiscated from them should be returned. By 325 Constantine had become the ruler of both halves of the empire.

thought that the architect of their freedom would have been God, but it was clear that Eusebius was speaking about the Emperor.

"Yes, we owe it all to Emperor Constantine," he continued, "to whom our Lord chose to reveal Himself at the Milvian Bridge and through whose intervention wrought a great victory." Not for the first time Bunny wasn't aware of the historical events being described, but she was pretty sure God wouldn't have intervened in any military victory.

"Well, that is how I shall tell the story," he added, immediately casting doubt on the validity of any heavenly encounter the Emperor was supposed to have had.[1]

By now they had reached the waiting chariot and to her surprise Eusebius invited her to join him on board, which she courteously accepted. Not for the first time, she was glad she got special treatment in this dream – she was sure she would have had to have walked had it been real life.

There were only a handful of cars parked in the hospital car park, night-shift workers and the relatives of late-night accidents. For Rector Mashman there was something rather satisfying to park in the space between Lady Advowson's badly parked Range Rover and his Lordship's Land Rover Defender. He felt safe between nobility, this was where he belonged, he assured himself. As a regular pastoral visitor, the Rector knew his way around the hospital. He didn't have the access-all-areas pass of the hospital chaplain, in fact he had no idea such a permit existed. The clergyman's visits were confined to his scheduled chaplaincy times, his slot being Thursday afternoons between two and four.

Two triage nurses manned the A&E reception and one of them recognised the Rector and initially assumed he might be in need of treatment. Having assured herself to the contrary she then replied to his request for information on Velia Advowson.

"Lady Advowson arrived a while ago," she explained. "But we told her she'd have to wait."

"Then Lord Advowson arrived," the other nurse chipped-in, thankful to momentarily not have a line of incoming patients to deal with. "Then it all started

---

[1] The authenticity of Constantine's conversion to Christianity is one of the most debated events in Church history with many claiming that he never renounced his personal pagan sun-worship and that the change of fortunes for the Church was principally a politically expedient move.

kicking off," she added with a rather unprofessional air of gossip. Her senior colleague stopped her saying anything else.

"What do you mean?" Mashman asked. The nurses looked uncomfortably at each other. The churchman repeated his question and waited patiently, smiling disarmingly at them.

"I've been thinking," Chris said quietly to Jack as they stood with their backs to the stairs. Jack didn't respond. "I don't think he's got a gun in there."

"What makes you so sure?" Jack asked. Chris held up the gun which he had snatched from the mortally wounded young man.

"This was The Badger's gun. He gave it to the other one to guard Ralph and me," he explained.

"The Badger?" Jack understandably queried, to which Chris responded with an irritated "Never mind!" pointing with his thumb to the rear room to clarify whom he meant.

"Well, if you are sure that is something in our favour," Jack said reassuringly, then crushed any sense of confidence, saying, "But there is someone outside and by the sounds of it another accomplice in the rear. And as far as we know they are both armed."

Joel and Artur had made it to the start of the corridor towards the front of the farmhouse and were breathing very heavily. They had heard the front door open, close and then a vehicle speed away. It couldn't be the owner of the white car as his rough silhouette was visible through the two opaque floral glass panes in the back door. None of the sights and sounds around them made any sense. As far as they knew they were alone with Bunny's captor and others closing in on them, the figure at the back door being the focus of their attention.

"Is it Rex?" Artur whispered. Joel shook his head convinced the frame of the silhouette wasn't right. Artur wasn't so sure. Knock, knock, knock! The stranger gave three firm raps on the rear door, the same as he had at the front. Artur had an idea. He clenched his fist and, using the wainscot panelling at the bottom half of the corridor as a sounding board, he tapped out five-long followed by four-short taps in the Onward Christian Soldiers rhythm they had used earlier. If it was Rex outside the door he would respond in kind.

Artur repeated the coded message. The figure outside gave nothing in reply which was little relief to either of them. Then all of a sudden, they heard the distinctive Christian-code-rhythm echo in the stillness, but it didn't come

445

from the back door, but the sound originated along the corridor towards the front door.

"Who's there?" Joel spoke in a projected whispered around the corner.

"Chris and Jack," came the reply followed by the reciprocal, "Who's there?"

"Me and Artur," Joel continued in his strained whisper.

"Who's *me*?" Chris asked for clarification.

"Joel," came the reply, perhaps a little too loudly, prompting the man outside the rear door to speak.

"Joel? Joel! I need to speak to you," the mystery man said. Joel had given away his name. He held his breath not knowing what to do next. Then to his horror, as he and Artur stared at the door, neither could have guessed what the sinister voice would say.

"Mr. Whyens?... Methodist minister? ... I need to speak to you," he said pointedly.

"How does he know who I am?" Joel puzzled, frozen in fear.

Bunny hadn't connected the year with the Council of Nicaea until they arrived in the lakeside resort town of that name, a few miles outside Constantinople. The town itself was dominated by a magnificent imperial palace, a truly immense structure in marble and white stone with slated orange tiles. Bunny had seen many Roman ruins in her time but to see one in its heyday, fully intact, painted and gilded with gold leaf was genuinely breathtaking. The procession of chariots deposited their luminaries outside the main entrance, each one met by a glamorous dark-haired and overtly curvaceous hostess. They were led along a pristine corridor which opened out into a cavernous central hall at whose entrance they were greeted by an official whose job it was to formally announce their arrival. The Bishop spoke his credentials to the official who then declared in a booming voice,

"His excellency the most noble Eusebius Pamphilli, Bishop of Caesarea." But the doorman hadn't finished and to her embarrassment announced the arrival of,

"The most noble Lady Johania Bunnicus."

The hall was a wide near-circular theatre, surrounded by dozens, maybe even a hundred, elaborate columns supporting a roof that didn't reach across the whole structure but encircled them. Bunny made a full three-sixty-degree turn – the room somehow invited it – and as she did the curved arches around the perimeter oscillated up and down like waves on the lake they had just passed. The centre of the hall was open to the elements allowing the warm Mediterranean sun to stream through the large oculus onto a central altar table.[1] Bunny felt she could do with some warm Mediterranean sun on her right now. Eusebius paused on entry. It was indeed a magnificent sight but what it prompted him to declare came as quite a surprise to Bunny.

"As the sun liberally imparts his rays of light to all, so does Constantine proceed from the imperial palace and impart the rays of his own beneficence to all who come into his presence."[2] She tried her best to give him the benefit of the doubt, but he was beginning to sound overly sycophantic, a quality that Bunny found most objectionable in people. She decided to change the subject.

"It's a big place isn't it," she remarked. "How many people do you think there are here?" Simple chairs were laid out in curves from the centre, most of which were now filled. He looked around them.

"Two hundred, two hundred and fifty maybe more," he said indifferently. "But I will write that there were three hundred and eighteen mighty men gathered in this place."

"Why that specific number?" Bunny asked.

"That was the number of mighty men Abraham had around him,"[3] he explained.

"So, you will say that was the number regardless of how many are actually here?" she said incredulously, waving her hand over the seated assembly. Eusebius just gave an indifferent nod.[4] At that point the Emperor entered the hall through a side archway. He was fully bedecked in his imperial regalia as the occasion demanded. The sight of Constantine electrified the gathered clerics, none more so than Eusebius.

---

[1] 'The Meeting-Place of the First Ecumenical Council and the Church of the Holy Fathers at Nicaea' by Cyril Mango extracted from deltionchae.org

[2] 'Constantine's Sword: The Church and the Jews – A History' by James Carroll, p 179.

[3] Genesis chapter 14 verse 14

[4] The commonly quoted number of 318 participants is entirely apocryphal. None of the eye-witness accounts, including Eusebius, quote that exact number.

"Ah, see how he sits upon his golden throne in his purple robes like a heavenly messenger of God," he exclaimed with glee, adding that Constantine was "The tallest man in the room."[1]

The Roman Emperor patently wasn't any taller than anyone else. Eusebius was taking hero-worship to a new level and the sight of his idol prompted him to hurry towards the front and take his seat. Bunny used the opportunity to turn away and find an inconspicuous seat at the rear from which to view proceedings.

As she sat contemplating her surroundings, the lights (not that there were any lights) suddenly went out and she was plunged into complete darkness. Momentarily afraid, she didn't know what was happening. This couldn't be happening; it was the middle of the day, and the great hall and Nicaea had an open roof through which the sun had been shining. Was it an eclipse? The only thing more surprising than the sudden emersion into darkness was that she realised she felt very, very, cold. Again, it made no sense, this was the Mediterranean summer. And then, almost as suddenly as the black had engulfed her, it vanished and she was back, seated at the rear of the great hall at Nicaea watching and waiting.

The council began with Eusebius addressing the crowd and thanking God for the Emperor. Constantine then spoke to say how distressed he was that having united the empire he now found it divided within over what he called 'A serious issue of religious doctrine.' As Bunny listened carefully, she managed to piece together that the divisive issue at stake was *the nature of Christ's substance*. Beyond that statement she had little idea. Constantine went on to give an impassioned plea that they should all be united. Once the Emperor had finished, Eusebius thanked him, creepily, then invited the gathered throng to begin to debate the issue at hand, at which point everyone completely ignored the Emperor's plea and began to argue. Chaos ensued across the entire hall as dozens of impromptu bearpits formed, each a hotbed of argument and rancour.

Bunny became aware of the young man she had randomly seated herself beside. He wasn't participating in any part of the verbal melee but was getting increasingly agitated at the behaviour of the bishops whom, he considered, should know better. Suddenly, he stood to his feet and shouted out. No one heard him, there was just too much noise in the room. Then purely by

---

[1] 'Decoding Nicaea' by Paul F Pavao

coincidence a momentary collective lull happened as everyone seemed to take their breath at the same time. It only lasted for a few seconds, but as it coincided with his vocal entreaty, momentarily he had the attention of the entire audience.

"Christ and the apostles did not teach us dialectics nor useless subtleties... but simple-mindedness which is preserved by faith and good works," he stated vigorously.

"Yes, that is right," said a somewhat rotund bishop a few yards in front of Bunny. "And as for your heresy..." he raised his right arm and slapped one of the other bishops firmly across the face, whilst giving a loud and notable laugh. There were audible gasps as the room quickly fell silent.

The overweight bishop was promptly escorted from the room, guards dragging him by his red cassock as he was told his attendance would no longer be required.

The young man next to Bunny half-leaned over to her and whispered,

"You can always tell him by his laugh, can't you?"

Bunny had to confess she didn't know who the rather portly cleric was.

"Nicholas of Myra," he replied. "Or as most folk call him, Ol' Saint Nick."[1]

Bunny spun around. Firstly, to look at the young man, then across to the departing kerfuffle. She could no longer see the bishop, but the sound of his laughter was indeed unmistakable.

"Ho, Ho, Ho."

Now that much of the furore had calmed down a more orderly and constructive mood surfaced. Before long a simple statement of belief had been agreed. One which she began to recognise as the Nicene Creed which she had faithfully regurgitated every week at All Saints'. The first draft was opposed by many as they felt it didn't go far enough to state that Jesus was of the same nature of God and would not expose some heretics. At this point Constantine called order and indicated that they must introduce the word *Homo-ousios* which meant *the same substance.* Several bishops objected to the inclusion of this non-biblical word but nonetheless it was enough for the masses. So, it was agreed and signified by the ringing of a single bell. The Nicene Creed was written and would stay intact until, well, until the Great Schism of 1045 when the

---

[1] The attendance of Nicholas of Myra (the original Father Christmas) is contested, his name only appearing on some of the later lists. He did live at the time, would have been invited, but wasn't fat and didn't wear red. The questionable legend of him assaulting one of the heretics surfaced in the fourteenth century.

introduction of another word, *Filioque* would result in the split with the Orthodox Church.

Chapter 53

HEBREW ROOTS

"We have to do something," Chris whispered in Joel's ear, snapping him out of his momentary paralysis. "He has got Bunny in there."

With so much anxiety filling the back corridor of Lane End farmhouse, it was good to have one thing to focus on. Bunny was, after all, the reason they were all in this predicament. Chris pulled the other three towards himself in the centre of the main corridor and, keeping his voice to a minimum, swallowed hard then stated the obvious.

"We are going to have to storm the room," he whispered. "He already knows we are in the building. He knows he is cornered so could be doing all sorts of... anything... to her. We have no choice." He was right, they knew it, but it didn't make the prospect any more appealing and their hesitation prompted Chris to offer them an option.

"Well, brothers, I'm going in. You don't have to if you..."

"I'm with you," Jack interrupted. Having been forced to abandon his friend and mentor, Mack, all those years ago in militant Carrickfergus, he wasn't going to stand idly by now.

"Me too," Artur added determined to cement his inclusion within his new group of friends. All eyes then turned to Joel.

Joel knew that if he had not found faith his life could have taken the same direction as several of his former schoolfriends. They all grew up in broken families and, as an Afro-Caribbean with an alcoholic father, Joel could easily have found his place in a world where violence begets violence. But that was not *his* story and he was always ready to testify as to how he had been saved from sliding into that life. His life now was characterised by hope, love, and happiness. He had long ago cut himself off from such negative influence in all its guises. But tonight, in the dim light of Lane End Farm, he was going to have to embrace who he might have been. He couldn't speak, so just gave a nod of acceptance.

Chris asked for ideas to which Jack already had given some thought and explained that, as he was the largest of them, he would break the door down with his shoulder. It wasn't the first door he had forcibly entered, he explained, adding that this experience came from his time in the police, not as part of his Presbyterian pastoral duties. He then advised that as soon as the door was open, they should all rush in, one to the left, one to the right, and one in the middle.

Whoever confronts the occupant should then stand still while the others circle around behind him.

"Won't it be too dark to see him?" Artur pointed out.

"We could switch the lights back on," Chris suggested.

Joel, conscious of the figure still standing outside the rear door who mysteriously knew who he was, explained that wasn't an option.

"We'll have to use our phone-torches," he suggested. They all agreed this would work, but not to switch them on until the last possible minute.

Knock, knock, knock. Three more firm raps on the rear door were followed by the unknown figure grabbing the door handle and attempting several firm twists, but to no avail.

The sudden, loud intrusion to their quiet scheming made Chris jump.

"Is that the driver?" he asked. Artur nodded.

"Mr Whyens, please let me in," the voice from outside repeated. Chris turned to Joel for an explanation, but the Methodist preacher simply shrugged his shoulders masking his unease.

Jack ushered them forwards, ignoring the intruder. They gathered around the door of the back room. Artur lined himself for the left channel, Joel the right. Chris stood behind Jack, ready to burst into the centre of the room. Despite Jack's clear instruction Chris had already decided he was going to make his way straight to the camp bed and release Bunny. He closed his eyes and visualised where the bed was situated within the room based on their time inside earlier. In his hand, hanging by his side, he held the gun unsure if he had the wherewithal to use it. At least it would be a threat to get Bunny free.

"Onward Christian Soldiers!" Jack whispered before beginning to count down from five by progressively lowering each finger of his right hand which he stretched out in front of them all. Artur and Joel prepared the handheld illumination.

"All of this debate is so wrong!" The young man sitting next to Bunny at the rear of the Nicaean palace sighed. Bunny looked empathetically at him, thus making herself a safe place on which to unload his angst.

"All of these elders and bishops have just one theological function," he protested, "to preserve the truth that they had received from the apostles unchanged."

"But sometimes there is a need to debate and decide what..." Bunny began only to be interrupted.

"They need to understand that their position is that of witnesses not as exegetes." Bunny didn't know what an exegete was but assumed it must mean a *decider of theology.*

"They have one duty, Lady Bunnicus," he continued, "to pass down to faithful men what they had received. Their first requirement is not learning, but honesty. The question is not what do I think probable but what have I been taught."[1]

Bunny decided to not risk further interruption. He then went on to explain that the second agenda item was to decide when Passover was to be celebrated and how he expected them all to cave in to the doctrine of Athanasius and abandon that which all the holy fathers practised.

"Passover?" Bunny queried.

"Yes, the day we celebrate the death of our Lord," he explained.

"Ah, you mean Good Friday."

"Good Friday?" he puzzled. "I don't know what that means. We celebrate our Lord's crucifixion at Passover as He decreed. The debate today is to decide if Passover is to be on the day of Passover as it has been ever since... well, since Passover, or if we are to artificially move it to be a fixed holy week."

"Yes, Good Friday and Easter Sunday... I mean *Passover Sunday.*" As she verbalised it, the phrase *Passover Sunday* sounded clumsy and ludicrous to her ears. She had always marked Easter on a Sunday, but Passover, well that was a Jewish thing. But then the words of Augustine rang in her ears: 'Is the God that we pray to the same as that of the Jews?'

She felt she might be on to something... something important. She spun round in her small seat to face the young man.

"Jesus died at..." she hung her phrase in the air seeking clarity.

"Calvary?" he answered tentatively unsure why she was asking. She clarified her question to be the date not the place of the execution of Jesus Christ.

"Passover, as the sacrificial Lamb of God," he answered, a little more confidently this time. As he said it, she knew it was correct. She had read the gospels so many times and yet had never actually seen it. Jesus was crucified at the feast of Passover. It was staring her squarely in the face, it was literally

---

[1] Philip Schaff. 'Nicene and the post Nicene Fathers' Series II Volume XIV

gospel truth. But she also knew that her Bible said that Christ rose again on the first day of the week, which would be on a Sunday.

"And He rose again on…" she posed seeking agreement, but to her surprise the answer he gave wasn't at all what she was expecting.

"On the Feast of First Fruits," he confirmed. "As the apostle Paul wrote: 'Christ has been raised from the dead, the *first fruits* of those who are asleep.'"[1]

"What?" she exclaimed in confusion having confidently expected 'Sunday' to have been his answer.

She had little concept of there being a feast called First Fruits. Indeed, she had no real understanding of the Old Testament Hebrew feasts at all. She did however know the Passover story from the Book of Exodus. In it, God would protect his people from death if they sacrificed a spotless lamb and daubed its blood on their doorposts. She knew that Jesus' death on the cross was the final sacrifice for mankind and that is why he is sometime called the Lamb of God. The parallels were strong. What she hadn't embraced was that the date to remember this was indeed Passover. How had she not seen this before?

"When is… was… Passover?" she asked.

"The fourteenth of Nisan," he answered. That didn't help. Clearly the Gregorian calendar hadn't yet been instituted.

"And when is … First Fruits?"

"That is the day after the first Sabbath after Passover."

She thought for a moment doing the mental arithmetic.

"So, some years it may be a couple of days after Passover, but other times maybe up to a week later." The young man nodded in agreement.

"But when Jesus died it was on a Friday and he rose on a Sun…" she paused for a moment before reframing her question in terms that would be era-appropriate.

"When Jesus died, Passover would have been the day before the Sabbath and First Fruits was the day after?"

He looked sympathetically at her seeing she was confused.

"Passover *is* a sabbath, Lady Bunnicus," he answered. "Most of the feast days are extra sabbaths." Bunny made no expression other than deploy her *tell me more* look. He complied.

---

[1] Paul's First epistle to the Corinthians chapter fifteen verse twenty.

"In Jerusalem that year, Passover fell two days before the weekly Sabbath. It had to be that way otherwise he could not have laid in the tomb for three-days and three nights as he had prophesied."[1]

Bunny fell silent trying in vain to compute three days and three nights between the traditional crucifixion date of Good Friday and the resurrection on Easter Sunday.

"It doesn't add up," she said with a shock. "Friday to Sunday just doesn't add up. It's a day-and-a-half at best."

As she tentatively let go of her traditional Easter timeline, things began to slot into place.

"If Passover was a Sabbath, then His body would have been taken down before *that* Sabbath..."

He nodded in agreement.

"... and then there would have been the normal weekly sabbath two days later..."

Again, he nodded.

"Before he rose again on the first day of the week, which was..." She was going to say Sunday but before she could speak he quickly jumped in again with,

"First Fruits!"

It was as if, not a sacrificial Passover Lamb, but a sacred religious calendar cow had been slaughtered right in front of her, and it felt liberating. This was huge.

"We should be marking Christ's sacrifice on Passover," she said.

"Exactly," he said with delight that she was now agreeing with him. "On the fourteenth of Nisan just as the Holy fathers did."

Then it struck her. This was the year...she checked her watch, Three Twenty-Five. That is less than three-hundred years after the holy fathers, the apostles, had died. How many generations would that be? Would any of these elderly bishops gathered here have known someone who had met the apostles? She looked upwards, out of the open oculus, as she did the mental arithmetic. She gave the answer to her calculation audibly, much to the confusion of the young man.

"No, it's too long a gap, this is six or more generations. I'd need to be in the year one hundred and something." The young man, quite understandably,

---

[1] The Gospel of Matthew chapter 12 verse 40

looked at her with a puzzled expression. A voice from behind, however, knew exactly what she was talking about.

"Well, if that is what you want, Aladdin …. 'Your wish is my command.'" She spun around but no sooner had she caught sight of a gold-rimmed hat than her eyes were blinded by a dazzling white light, and suddenly she was filled with a sense of foreboding.

For at least the second time that evening, the private ambulance of St. Christopher's Hospice arrived outside the emergency reception of the hospital. This time it was making a genuine delivery, not a faked collection. There were two entrances to the emergency room: one for the walking wounded, the other for more serious cases. Thea pulled up outside the latter and, leaping out of the driving seat, pressed the large red button marked *Urgent Assistance* next to the automatic doors. Rotating yellow lights began to flash both inside and outside, and before she had even moved away to return to the ambulance, she could already see two people rapidly approaching.

Ralph managed to open the rear door of the ambulance with his one good hand. When Thea returned to the ambulance and saw him, he looked grey with shock. She helped him out of the vehicle and into one of four waiting wheelchairs positioned for such an arrival. Thea directed the two nursing auxiliaries who by now had arrived to attend to the patient inside the ambulance.

"He's been shot," Thea added constructively.

"My goodness!" one of the men exclaimed as he stepped inside the rear door, adding a rather telling, "So I see."

Within moments all that is great about the NHS clicked into gear. Medical terminology was shouted, nurses arrived, devices and clinical appliances were quickly assembled as the seemingly lifeless, blood-soaked young man was quickly stretchered inside. Thea waited for the flurry of activity to disappear inside before wheeling Ralph after them and heading to the reception desk to check in her patients.

"Miss Howlsy?" a voice queried behind her. Thea turned to see a bewildered Rector Mashman rising to his feet from one of the blue plastic reception chairs.

"Whatever are you doing here?" they both said in unison.

Chapter 54

IRENAEUS

"Where am I?" Bunny said as the blinding light faded. She formed the outline of a figure in front of her dressed in white robes. For a moment, she had considered she might be in heaven. The blurred luminescence, the white robes, this was stereotypical heaven minus the clouds and harps. She knew enough of her Bible to be sure that such a view was a work of fiction. Anyway, the floor wasn't made of clouds but sand-coloured dirt. She was in a rather rudimentary room, devoid of the palatial splendour of Nicaea – straw and mud walls with open spaces for windows. The figure, a man, was standing with his back to her leaning over a writing desk that stood so tall no chair was needed, which was handy as the only chair in the room was behind her. Hearing her plaintiff voice, he replaced a quill into a simple inkpot and turned to see who had interrupted his studies.

"Madam," he greeted her.

"Who are you?" Bunny asked her second question, ignoring the fact that she hadn't had an answer to the first.

"My name is Irenaeus," he said with a nod of the head. He then opened both arms and welcomed her saying, "And this is my humble home in the heart of Smyrna." Bunny's heart jumped. Smyrna was one of the seven churches to whom part of the book of Revelation is written. She couldn't believe it, was she in New Testament times? Tentatively she looked down at her watch and slowly tugged her sleeve upwards to reveal the digits 1:77. Once again her watch was displaying an impossible time with the minutes exceeding sixty, but that didn't seem to matter anymore. Not quite New Testament times but only one or two generations thereafter, just as she had *wished for*.

"But it will not be my home for much longer," he said. Bunny noticed that her host was busy sorting his meagre belongings ready to pack them into a small selection of wooden boxes and rudimentary leather bags. His attention moved away from his sudden guest, back to his organisational dilemmas. Bunny, as ever, required more information and spontaneously asked where he was moving to and why. He had been appointed to be the Bishop of Lugdunum, he explained, but he couldn't leave until he had finished his writing as it was going to be a long, and presumably one-way, journey. Bunny had no idea where

Lugdunum was but decided to ask about his literary composition rather than geography.

"It is called Adversus Haereses," he said quoting the Latin title of the manuscript. [1]

"Heresies?" Bunny responded, mishearing the Latin expression but in so doing correctly translating it. She remembered her time on the Heresy Express and was pleased with how successful she was at spotting false doctrine.

"What specific heresies are you ...adver...sus about?" she asked fumbling linguistically. Irenaeus explained that the main focus of his writings was to counter the dangerous teachings of someone named Marcion of Sinope. Bunny couldn't help but smile at the thought that there was a heretic who was also a *Martian*! Thankfully, Irenaeus took the time to explain that rather than being an extra-terrestrial, Marcion was a fellow church leader, from the city of Sinope on the Black Sea coast. Despite having been universally excommunicated by every church, except the one that Marcion led, his teachings were still growing in popularity.

"What are these *dangerous teachings*?" she asked, frankly unsure as to whether she would find them to be dangerous at all. Her mind had been so stimulated over the last few...centuries ...she found herself to be far more open-minded than she had ever been. As it happened, she came down squarely on Irenaeus' side.

"Marcion taught that there are two Gods: the God of the Old Testament who was blood-thirsty and bad; and the God of the New Testament who is loving and good. In order to accept Christ, he taught that the Church must reject the Old Testament God. That would, of course, mean discarding all of the Hebrew Scriptures, large parts of the gospels and all of the apostolic writings except for Paul's."[2]

"That's very wrong, isn't it," she agreed. "And I assume you are writing to him to tell him." Irenaeus laughed.

"That would be difficult. He died nearly twenty years ago."

---

[1] Adversus Haereses (Against Heresies) or more properly, "On the Detection and Overthrow of the So-Called Gnosis" is a five-volume work written around 180 by Irenaeus, Bishop of Lugdunum (modern-day Lyon). Amongst other things it is also the oldest ancient text to list most of the books to be included in the New Testament canon.

[2] "The New Marcion" (by Jason BeDuhn, (2015). Forum. 3 (Fall 2015): 163–179.

"Then why do you need to write about it now?" she asked, curious to know how such an outlandish doctrinal position was being maintained years after its originator's death.

"Because there are those who seek to disconnect the Church from its roots," he said. With that he returned to his writing desk and shuffled through the neat pile of scrolls, bound ready to be packed, clearly looking for a specific one. At last, he found the correct one and loosened the binding.

"Ah, here it is, Paul's letter to Ephesus," he said. "A lovely group of people. I've visited them many, many times."

Bunny couldn't believe it. In her mind she was standing with her jaw wide open. Thankfully in reality she maintained a dignified propriety. Was he really holding in his hands a copy of the apostle Paul's Letter to the Ephesians? This was amazing. Irenaeus rolled open the scroll and scanned down it with his index finger to find the section he was looking for, announcing its discovery with a satisfied clearing of the throat.

"Therefore, remember that you, the Gentiles, were excluded from Israel and strangers to the covenants of promise, having no hope and without God in the world. But now in Christ Jesus you who formerly were far off have been brought near by the blood of Christ. For He made both groups into one and broke down the barrier of the dividing wall so that in Himself He might make the two into one new man."[1]

"Two into one new man?" Bunny couldn't help herself from repeating the last phrase. Irenaeus signed this agreement with a muted,

"Ahum!"

"And by that you mean Jews and non-Jews?" she said. Once more greeted with an,

"Ahum!"

"As one?" Bunny was incredulous.

"Yes of course," Irenaeus retorted. "Everyone knows that the Church is the wild olive branch that has been grafted into the true olive tree our Lord spoke of."

Bunny looked puzzle, prompting Irenaeus to clarify what he was saying.

"Some, like Marcion, would teach that the Church has replaced the nation of Israel in God's affections. Whereas Scripture teaches that the Church

---

[1] Taken from Paul's Epistle to the Ephesians Chapter 2 verses 11 to 15. English Standard Version.

has been firmly connected into the nation so that the blessings promised to Israel may be inherited by we gentiles.[1] This dangerous teaching needs to be stamped out. If we do not deal with these heresies, who knows, we may have a Church that didn't even celebrate Passover."

A great sadness came over Bunny as she realised that in one hundred and fifty years that is exactly what was going to happen.

"Or agree a statement of faith that doesn't even make mention of Passover," she confessed "...or Israel for that matter." The ironic truth sank in. She was so excited about being at Nicaea that she hadn't even considered what was being left out of the final Nicaean Creed. By the time Constantine had made Christianity the official state religion it had been sanitised of any reference to its cultural origins, losing a whole part of its doctrinal relevance.

"But how can you be sure that the Church is..." she chose her words tactfully, "supposed to have Hebrew roots?"

He smiled pastorally at her.

"Because that is what every bishop across all the churches teaches," he answered. "That is what my bishop, Polycarp, taught and, of course, you know who taught him?" he asked rhetorically. Sadly, Bunny had no idea and sheepishly shook her head.

"Why the apostle John himself," he explained.

Bunny gulped.

"Are you saying that John taught Polycarp, and Polycarp taught you?" Again he gave his signature "Ahum!"

"And the same is true for the other bishops – I mean not all from John, but from one or other of the apostles."

He replaced the letter to the Ephesians and picked up one of the scrolls of his Adversus Haereses and scanned through it to find the requisite section. Once located, he read it carefully to her,

"We refer those who oppose us to that tradition which originated with the apostles, and which is preserved by the succession of elders in the churches. All doctrine which agrees with the apostolic churches must be considered truth as it undoubtedly contains that which the Church received from the apostles.

---

[1] Paul's epistle to the Romans chapter 11 verses 17 and 24

Whereas all doctrine must be judged as false which smells of dissimilarity to the truth of the churches and apostles."[1]

It was beginning to become clear to Bunny. If there was such a thing as true Church unity, it would have to be where every church, despite being independent, nonetheless believed the same... truth; and was not based on a new or spurious revelation, but the same truth as had been handed down. She had already seen how divisive *new* truth had been. Every church can be different in their own way, have their own style of worship, their own governance, they can identify as their own *tribe*, but they *must* all agree on the core truths as passed down.

Old farmhouse doors are solid and heavy; old farmhouse door frames, however, are riddled with various forms of decay and offer little in the way of resistance to a sudden and concerted application of force – in this case Jack with a four-step run-up and a commitment worthy of an international rugby full-back. The door swung open and slammed back on its hinges, hitting the wall with a loud crash as Jack tumbled onto his knees unable to stop his momentum.

The light from two mobile phones was surprisingly bright as Artur and Joel pointed them into the room at arm's length. Before either of them could make their required incursions, Chris barged between them both and vaulted over Jack, gun in hand, intent on one purpose – to get to Bunny.

Artur's phone swung to the left as he entered, Joel's to the right, both men hoping to find their section of the room empty. To their relief they both were. All Artur could see was the single chair, Joel just the wall and window. Chris, heading straight for the makeshift hospital bed in the centre of the room, found more than he bargained for. Before he had taken even two rapid steps into the room he was already face to face with their adversary. Had Chris had proper firearms training he wouldn't have held the weapon at arms-length, allowing it to be easily apprehended by someone familiar with basic self-defence. Before he knew it, Chris was on his knees, somehow having had his arm twisted backwards forcing him to release his grip on the gun. He felt such a fool.

From his knees he could see that Bunny lay unconscious under a blanket, the very one stolen from the ambulance; a tube from the intravenous drip disappearing under it and into her arm. The Badger quickly retreated to the far

---

[1] Against Heresies' Irenaeus (184) III: 2:2 (slight paraphrasing)

end of the bed, gun in hand, and stood over Bunny's motionless body smiling menacingly back at Chris. Joel swung the beam of his phone torch in a smooth arc around the room, allowing all to survey the sombre scene. As he did the piercing LED light reflected off the stainless-steel blade of a large hunting knife that The Badger produced from his belt and laid menacingly across the throat of his comatose victim.

The noise of the door having been forced open was enough to convince the silhouette outside the backdoor to do the same. Within seconds it too gave way under modest applied pressure and swung open, hitting a floor-mounted rubber doorstop which caused it to vibrate uncontrollably. The four churchmen's rear was now exposed.

The last scroll had to be wound up extra tightly in order for it to fit neatly in the last space in the box.

"There we are. Packed and ready to go," Irenaeus said with an air of both satisfaction and sadness. The last box was taken outside by two young men who for the last few minutes had been facilitating the removal of their pastor's belongings. Both had noticeable tears in their eyes.

"Weep not for me," he chastised them lovingly as he hugged each in turn in gratitude for their assistance. There was one final package left; a small parcel wrapped in cloth and tied loosely with two intersecting strings. Irenaeus had asked the boys to leave that one. He picked it up and passed it to Bunny.

"May I ask you to complete a favour for me?" he asked. Bunny assured him that she would be honoured to help in any way she could. She had no idea what the next part of her unfolding saga was going to be anyway.

"Please give this to Hegesippus when you see him." Bunny of course agreed, after which Irenaeus bade her farewell and began his final journey.

Bunny stood alone and repeated to herself,

"Give this to Hegesippus when you see him." It was a simple request, but as a standalone phrase taken out of context it sounded completely incongruous. She repeated it again, this time as a direct impression of how Irenaeus had said it. Then she said it using a variety of poor-quality regional British accents ending with one much akin to an angry Basil Fawlty. The more she said it the funnier it sounded. She slid into movie references as she sat down.

"Give this to Hegesippus when you see him" became a line from *The Godfather*; then, placing the package on her knee, she spoke the line again this time preceded by "My momma always said..." as if she were Forrest Gump. Next she went down on one knee and proposed with it as foppishly as Hugh Grant may have in *Four Weddings and a Funeral*; finally on both knees Gollum said, in a gravelly non-human voice, "Give the precious to Hegesippus when you see him!"

"Give me what, exactly?" the somewhat puzzled voice asked. A man, presumably Hegesippus, now occupied the doorway. Bunny froze in embarrassment, staring straight ahead so as not to look at him. The man, unsure about the alarming voice this kneeling creature had just used, sought clarification by adding an interrogative "Miss?"

Chapter 55

UNITY DISCOVERED

Time stood still. Jack had made it back to his feet but knew better than to approach; Artur and Joel were both illuminating the camp bed from opposite sides; Chris knelt a few feet short of the bed looking intently at the shape of Bunny's body lying there peaceful, still, unaware of the mortal danger she was in. He couldn't see her face beyond the huge knife held threateningly millimetres from her skin. He could feel the emotion of her vulnerability rise within him, but he was powerless to do anything. He had given up the gun, their only means of defence. But they had found her, and at least she was still breathing.

"Stay back!" was the first instruction her captor issued followed by "No pictures!" which he quickly insisted upon when he saw the two phones pointing at him. Joel instinctively raised his arms in surrender and said,

"It's only a torch, I haven't taken any pictures." Artur confirmed that he hadn't either.

"Let her go!" Chris shouted up at him.

"Or what?" The Badger replied. "What are you going to do? I have the gun."

Chris started to get up from his cowered position, but that movement was taken as hostile.

"One move and I will bleed her," he said threateningly as he straightened the knife to a horizontal stance as if about to slice a gateau. Chris compliantly reversed his actions. No one spoke, no one moved, in fear of what might happen next. Finally, The Badger broke the silence that, despite being seconds, had felt like minutes.

"I'll tell you what you are going to do," he said. "You are going to stand by that wall," he pointed with the gun to the area away from the door that he wanted them to move to. "You are going to drop your phones and car keys on the floor, and then I am going to leave." This arrangement didn't sound too bad to Chris, Jack, Artur or Joel who all nodded their acceptance.

"But no pictures!" he insisted once again. "One picture and I kill you all!"

Clearly, he was hoping his anonymity would allow him a successful getaway. Joel laid his phone on the floor face down so that the upwards torch beam continued to illuminate the room. Artur did the same, smiling to himself, as he remembered he had already seen a picture of this man on the railway station CCTV earlier. Chris and Jack carefully reached into their pockets to withdraw their keys and then tossed them onto the bare floorboards in front of them. They all then began to make slow movements towards the wall, Chris doing so on his knees.

Suddenly, multiple flashes of light filled the room together with the unmistakable whirring sound of camera shutters taking a stream of photographs in quick succession. The Badger stood up and screamed at the top of his voice,

"I said no photographs!"

He pointed his gun and pulled the trigger. Bang! Bang! Two shots rang out.

"I am so sorry," Bunny said for what felt like the fourth time. Her attempt to try to explain who or what Gollum was only added to her embarrassment. She stopped herself in mid-flow and, not for the first time, started over.

"Good Sir, my name is Johan Elstow, but most people call me Bunny," she said offering him a micro-curtsy whilst avoiding making eye contact.

"And I, Hegesippus of Nazareth," he replied. Bunny had met so many people, only some of whom she had heard of, and again this time she drew a complete blank.

"And what brings you to …" Bunny wasn't sure if she was still in Smyrna, or if she had once again suddenly translocated, so elected to end the sentence with a neutral "…here?"

"I am visiting *all* of the churches of Christ," he said with special emphasis on the word *all*.

"*All* of them?" Bunny echoed inquisitively. "And what are you hoping to find?"

"I have already found that in every city, the state of affairs is in accordance with the teaching of the Law and of the Prophets and of the Lord."[1]

The significance of his statement hit her. Was he saying that he had visited *every* church and had found that in *every* one of them the *state of affairs* was the same?

"Are you some sort of church auditor?" she asked. He didn't understand the question, which she rephrased: "Is it your job to make sure all churches are… behaving? That they are teaching the same thing?"

---

[1] Hegesippus 'Fragments from His Five Books of Commentaries on the Acts of the Church' extracted from EarlyChristianWritings,com

465

"No, no," he protested. "All churches are independent. I am recording the names of all the elders, all the bishops to produce a chronicle of the Church of Christ. It is a happy bonus to see how every church from Jerusalem to Rome all believe the same, teach the same, worship the same."

"*All* of them?" she asked for clarity, as excitement rose within her.

"Well, except for the heretic at Sinope."

"Ah, the Martian," Bunny interjected. She was about to comment about the fact he was dead, but then remembered she was travelling backwards in time. A swift glance at her watch confirmed it was now 1:55.

"Yes, Marcion," he agreed. "The only one to deny the Law and the Prophets. But other than him *every* church believes the same." [1]

Bunny couldn't believe it. Had she at last found a time when there really was unity.

It was self-evident that this was not the first time The Badger had fired a gun. His first shot hit its mark, but his target was none of the churchmen but the intruder who had broken open the rear door. His body fell forward through the doorway, landed on his side, and spun onto his back. As he lay there, Joel saw that it was the photojournalist he had met at the WRVS café in the hospital. Now it made sense. That must be who had followed Thea and him from the hospital, and that was why he knew all about him. He had taken what might have been his last photograph and lay on the floor with a single gunshot wound in his shoulder.

What of the second shot? Had it too hit its target?

All eyes turned toward the holder of the gun. To their surprise his eyes were bulging wildly as he stood at the head of the camp bed. He dropped the gun and looked down at his chest as blood began to seep through his clothing. He had been shot, and it appeared to have been, not in the front, but the back.

Who had shot him? He had the only weapon in the room. Eyes moved to the wall behind him, and then window through which they could see a handgun being pointed through the faded curtain. The Badger began to sway uncontrollably as he gasped for breath. He still held the knife in one hand and slashed it pointedly at the churchmen who all stood too far away to be caught by its blade.

Artur spun his phone torch at the window. The dim light picked out the figure holding the gun. It was an ashen-faced Rex, a single trickle of blood running

---

[1] There were a handful of other heresies around at the time. For brevity I have omitted them here.

from his left nostril. He had witnessed the whole stand-off through the window and, faced with the risk of someone being shot, had pulled the trigger of the gun he had found in the abandoned Ford.

Rex hadn't deliberately missed his target this time. The Badger somehow knew that his time was almost up. His ability to stand upright was nearly over. He had just one final barbarous act. He looked down at the helpless sleeping form on the bed in front of him and spun the knife ready to strike downwards. Chris could see what was about to happen and, from his kneeling position, tried to reach forwards to stop him.

"Nooooo!" Chris shouted as he sprawled the final few feet, arms outstretched to prevent the knife harming his love. But he was too far away, his intervention came too late. As the tyrannical captor fell, he plunged the hunting knife deep into her abdomen before releasing its handle as he fell to the floor and breathed his last.

Suddenly, everything went black. This was the second time that the lights (not that there were any actual lights) had inexplicably all turned off and she was plunged into deep, impenetrable darkness. She was gripped with a sudden sense of foreboding, the realisation that in reality she may be in a coma. Would she ever wake? Would she ever see her family, her church, Rector Mashman again? More importantly would she ever get to see Chris and tell him? And how cruel it was, she had, at last, found what she had been looking for – evidence of real Church unity.

She tried to speak, but no words came. She tried to move, but nothing seemed to be connected. She focussed all her concentration on moving something, anything. A leg? An arm? Anything. Her limbs felt too heavy, but a finger, yes that might be possible. The index finger of her right hand became the centre of her attention as she channelled all of her mental and physical resources into trying to make it move.

Chris was stretched out on the floor beside the camp bed, his head on his outstretched arm. His fingers pulled at the only thing he could reach, the ambulance blanket, under which he could see a finger. The index finger of her right hand.

Blood began to pour in rivulets down the fold in the blanket and dripped profusely onto his own hand.

"Don't leave me," he screamed as he stared at her finger.

It was no use. She couldn't make her finger move at all. The facts were incontrovertible – she was paralysed, dumb and blind.

Maybe, she thought for the first time in this endless night, maybe... I'm actually dead.

"Quick, call an ambulance," Artur shouted. Joel was first to react and lifted his phone from the floor to dial 999.

Any hope that the knife had not punctured her abdomen was immediately dashed as she recoiled in agony, causing more blood to ooze across the ambulance blanket through which the knife protruded vertically.

Chris clambered onto his knees and placed his fingers around the knife preparing to withdraw it.

"Stop!" Jack insisted. "You must leave it in. If you remove it there will be more bleeding. We need to get her to hospital straight away."

At the same time that Joel announced the ambulance was on its way, blue lights began to flash through the window as sirens approached.

"Wow, that was quick!" he said.

She wasn't the only one in need of urgent medical attention. The photojournalist lay in the doorway clasping his shoulder and groaning in pain. At least that shot hadn't been fatal. Rex's on the other hand had pierced Bunny's captor centrally in the back and floored him in a single shot, like a fairground duck.

In the window, Rex held the gun, his arm remaining outstretched. Jack looked over at the window. Having spent the evening with him he knew that Rex was, like most Quakers, a pacifist. The thought of harming anyone, let alone shooting them, would have been a huge challenge for him. Artur too looked over at the window. Earlier that evening Rex had comforted him at his lowest point, now was the time for him to repay that support and he walked over to the window and lowered Rex's arm as it still gripped the pistol. Rex remained motionless as Artur put a single hand on his new friend's arm and as he did a tear ran down Rex's cheek and mixed with the blood now flowing freely from his nose.

"Wait a minute!" Chris's voice sounded anxious. They all looked across at him to see him tenderly brush soft auburn hair from her forehead.

He looked up at them and said,

"This isn't Bunny!"

Chapter 56

CHURCH VISIT

"Don't you have something for me?"

The question hung in the air as Bunny tried to make sense of what was happening to her. She opened her eyes and to her relief the darkness lifted. It took a few moments for the face in front of her to come into focus. It was Hegesippus, once again, but this time he looked somehow different. She couldn't decide how exactly, but something was not the same.

"Don't you have something for me?" he repeated, at which point she remembered the package Irenaeus had given her. She looked down at her hands and there was the cloth-covered package neatly wrapped with two strings; she whispered to herself,

"Give this to Hegesippus when you see him." She sat back into the chair and passed him the parcel. He thanked her and carefully laid it on the tall table that Irenaeus had use to roll each of his scrolls before packing them away ready for transport. Firstly, one string was pulled, slowly, deliberately until it fell loose. Then the second string was untied with a tug. Hegesippus smiled at her as his hands slowly unfolded both ends of the cloth to reveal the contents. It was a hat. Not any hat. This was a hat with a distinctive and unmistakable gold embroidered rim. Hegesippus lifted the headgear with two hands as if lifting a trophy and ceremoniously placed it upon his brow.

There was no mistaking it. This was her guide, her travelling companion, her angel, the chaperon of her hallucination, her trance guardian. She had assumed he was just some ethereal narratorly character, but now he had a name, he was... or had been... a real person.

"Hegesippus?" she asked tentatively.

"Ah yes, that is I," he confessed. For the first time in his acquaintance Bunny was lost for words. "It was your prayer," he explained. Bunny had no recollection what he was talking about.

"Back in the confessional of St. Mary's, you prayed a very specific prayer and it would seem that I was the answer."

"You may think you are the answer to my prayers," Bunny retorted, "but as far as I am concerned you have been the most irritating, unhelpful..." she stopped herself mid-rant and changed tack. "What did I say in this prayer?"

"You said, 'Let me see the Church, truly united,'" he accurately quoted Bunny's prayer. Bunny didn't speak. "And so, I was sent to bring you here to see the united Church."

"But," she said, adding politely, "and please don't take this the wrong way," Hegesippus braced himself, "but I don't know who you are." He laughed.

"Few people do! I was the first chronicler of the Church and have maintained a detailed record ever since, right up to your time and beyond, but don't let that trouble you. All but a few of my earthly writings have since been lost. All that remains is the fact that I documented that *all* churches were … as you put it… united."

It was as if she had reached a finishing line. A sense of satisfaction welled up within her. All the trauma, disappointment, frustration didn't seem to matter now. She knew there was a time and a place when the Church was, indeed… one.

"Hegesippus," she suddenly asked decisively. "Take me to church, I want to see this for myself."

"I'll take you to where my church meets," he replied. "But let me warn you, it will not be anything like church as you would recognise it."

Thea explained to the Rector what had happened at their second visit to the farmhouse. How Ralph had been shot in the arm when a young man had shot himself accidently. It was when she said that the young man was in fact Velia's boyfriend that Mashman suddenly stood up in a fitful state.

"Whatever's the matter, Rector?" the Baptist pastor asked.

Mashman explained that he had known one of the nurses on reception for several years and how she had confided in him that there had been, 'such a kerfuffle as they had lost her.' Thea quizzed him but that was all he knew. It would appear that Velia Advowson had been admitted to casualty earlier in the evening, but she was now nowhere to be seen.

"I visited her a while ago," Thea said before correcting herself. "Actually, I didn't *see* her, only her boyfriend. And he was very agitated at the time. I just put it down to hospital anxiety… but maybe."

"Goodly heavens above," Mashman said clutching a handkerchief to his lips.

Even though the room in Hegesippus' home was obviously first century, something about it felt almost up to date. It was a large family room whose centrepiece was a dining table laid for a meal for the dozen or so people present. Around the table people were seated, some on rather rudimentary chairs, but most were at ease upon seats that were padded at one end, and looked more like chaise-longues. She wasn't sure if this was church, first century style, or a dinner party prior to them leaving for the service.

"Everyone, this is my long-term travelling companion, Bunny," he said by way of introduction.

The reception was sincere and warm, with several rising to greet her with an embrace, several of whom kissed her on the cheeks. Bunny's English reserve, having been forcibly removed earlier on her centuries-long journey, allowed her to receive their heartfelt affection. In fact, she felt strangely at home in this setting.

"You have chosen a very special day to visit us," a young woman said, her face full of a smile. Bunny's uncomprehending expression prompted the girl to conclude, "Today we celebrate the Lord's Day."

Did that mean it was Sunday? Bunny wondered.

Hegesippus wasn't the leader of the group; that fell to a man who was seated almost opposite. Once a chair for Bunny had been found and she had taken her place at the table next to Hegesippus, the leader stood and spoke.

"Our God loves to help us by using symbolism, today's service is full of symbolism."

He had said *service* so this really must be church, Bunny noted.

"Symbolism that has been repeated in Jewish families for centuries. It is only through our Messiah Yeshua that such symbolism is revealed."

Hegesippus leaned over to Bunny to explain,

"Yeshua is the Hebrew name of whom the Western Church call Jesus."

Bunny could see that there were four large empty goblets on the table next to a large pitcher which she presumed was full of wine. The leader then explained that these four cups stood for the four promises that Father God made to His people in Exodus and which Yeshua has fulfilled. He then went on to make the point that the Hebrew number four is the letter Dalet which itself is a picture of a door.

"Yeshua said 'I am the door; if anyone enters through Me, he will be saved,'"[1] he concluded to a chorus of Amens and Hallelujahs. Finally, he prayed a blessing before stretching his hands out and announcing,

"Let all who are hungry come and eat."[2]

Bunny looked around for the food. Little did she know that the *eating* was to be firstly spiritual before physical. The leader then lifted a pitcher of wine and filed the first cup, almost to the brim.

"This is the Cup of Sanctification," he announced. "God promised to the Children of Israel that He would 'Bring them out from under the burdens of the Egyptians.'[3] And we have the fulfilment of this promise, being sanctified through the offering of the body of Yeshua."[4]

The cup was then passed around. When it came to Bunny's turn, she first wiped the cup with her fingers before taking the tiniest of sips, just as she would for her Anglican Eucharist. However, when she attempted to pass the cup to Hegesippus he wouldn't take it from her, gesturing that rather than a sip, she needed to take a mouthful. This didn't feel right. This is a holy act not a booze-up, surely only a sip was proper. But everyone was staring at her, and she knew she would have to comply. She brought the cup back to her lips and tipped it sufficiently to allow the sweet taste of the fine wine to pour over her tongue and swill around her mouth. A gentle cheer went up as she did, which prompted her to swallow, principally a result of her embarrassment reflex. The taste was amazing. This was high quality wine, the warmth of which seemed to wash back over her as she passed the cup onwards. Once the cup had made a full revolution of the table and everyone had taken a drink, to Bunny's surprise it continued being passed around with people taking a second dink, until it was empty.

Whilst her attention was on the ever-approaching cup, she nearly missed what happened next. Someone at the far end of the table appeared to take some flat square items and place each of them into a small elegant black bag declaring them to represent God the Father, God the Son and God the Holy

---

[1] The Gospel according to John chapter 10 verse 9

[2] For centuries, this Invitation has announced the commencement of the Jewish Seder Passover meal

[3] Exodus chapter 6 verse 6

[4] The Epistle to the Hebrews chapter 10 verse 10

Spirit. He then removed the middle of them, broke it in half before replacing one of the halves back into the middle of the bag. The remaining half was then wrapped in a white linen cloth before he then took it and hid it behind the curtain in the corner of the room. Curious! She thought. Next, the leader asked Hegesippus to read part of the letter to the Ephesians. He stood to his feet ready to speak, receiving as he did the scroll passed to him.

"Become a choir," he read, "being harmonious in love, and taking up the song of God in unison, you may with one voice sing to the Father. So that He may perceive by your works that you are indeed the members of His Son. It is profitable, therefore, that you should live in an unblameable unity."[1]

Bunny knew her Bible and had read the apostle Paul's letter to the Ephesians many times before. What Hegesippus had just read, as good as it was, sounded very different to the Ephesians she knew. As Hegesippus continued to speak, he placed the scroll on the table which allowed Bunny to read that this was the Epistle to the Ephesian Church from Ignatius of Antioch.

"Who is Ignatius?" she asked him once he had retaken his seat.

"One of the disciples of the apostle John," he said.

"Is this part of your..." as she began to ask him, she was suddenly filled with anxiety at the thought that the Holy Scriptures might have been undermined. "Is it part of your Bible?"

"Of course not. The Holy Scriptures are set apart," he reassured her. "But we do not allow just anyone to bring their own interpretation, or individual preferences into the Church. That is why we share letters from those whom God has appointed as teachers and bishops in the Church."

This made some sense to her. She had sat through far too many sermons at All Saints' from people she hardly knew and whose message was clearly part of their personal agenda.

No sooner had she begun to digest the first century Church's attitude to teaching than the wine pitcher was used to pour another brimful into the second cup.

This is The Cup of Deliverance," was the decree that went along with it.

---

[1] The Epistle of Ignatius to Ephesians chapter 4

God promised, 'I will rescue you from bondage,'[1] and now we say with Yeshua, 'You shall know the truth, and the truth shall make you free.'"[2]

Bunny was pleased to recognise a verse from John's gospel.

"And that truth is the gospel which is the power of God for salvation to everyone who believes, to the Jew first and also to the Greek," the leader concluded.[3]

Bunny was ready for the wine this time, and was quite looking forward to a second taste, but before the cup began its journey a wooden bowl was brought around the table and everyone was required to wash their hands. Strange to not do the handwashing before we started, she thought.

"This is the point where our Lord broke with tradition and washed his disciples' feet," the leader said.[4]

Bunny leaned over to Hegesippus.

"So, let me get this right. This service is one which has been around for a long, long time," she asked. He nodded.

"And one which Jesus... Yeshua... would have taken part in?"

"Yes, many times but specifically it is the Last Supper meal,"[5] he explained. Bunny was amazed, she had no idea that the Last Supper was a regular Jewish service. As the time came for her to wash her own hands, the realisation dawned on her. The feet washing wasn't just an act of servitude, it was also a break with established tradition. No wonder Peter initially refused to allow him to do it.

With clean hands, the cup was then passed around, after which the group began to spontaneously pray. Most of the prayers were for those of their number who had been arrested and imprisoned and for the families of those who had been martyred. This was very sobering. It soon became clear that one of the women around the table had recently been widowed. Bunny presumed that her husband may have been martyred, but the important thing was that she had a young family to feed and no means of income. She was in great need,

---

[1] Exodus chapter 6 verse 6

[2] The Gospel according to John chapter 8 verse 22

[3] Paul's Epistle to the Romans chapter 1 verse 16

[4] The Gospel according to John chapter 13 verses 3 to 5 and 12 to 17

[5] "Was Jesus' Last Supper a Passover Seder?" Rich Robinson April 11 2017. Extracted from jewsforjesus.org

but the others had come prepared. Bunny watched as this tearful young widow was showered with an abundance of food, clothes, money and promises of practical assistance. What Bunny found most remarkable was that these gifts were given directly to her, not to the church first who then would give them, but literally straight into her hands. Earnest tears were shed but the sight of the material support she received in her time of great need was powerful.

At last, it was time to eat – a modest meal of lamb and herbs, which Bunny thought delicious. While they ate, she learnt that even the food was significant. It was pointed out that just as the blood of the Lamb protected the Israelites from death back in Egypt,[1] so the blood of Jesus, the Lamb of God, protected both Jewish and gentile believers today.

After the meal, the linen-wrapped item that had earlier been secreted behind the curtain was retrieved and laid in the centre of the table. Bunny could now clearly see as the linen cloth was carefully unfolded to reveal what looked like a large cracker.

"The bread which we break is a partaking of the body of Messiah,"[2] the leader said as he smashed it into several pieces before inviting all of those present to,

"Take and eat for this is His body."[3]

Each person, including Bunny, rose from their seats to collect a piece of the now broken cracker. But before she placed it into her mouth, she would need further clarification.

"What is this? I haven't ever seen anything like it before," she asked Hegesippus.

"It is called matzah, or unleavened bread," he explained, then showed his own piece to Bunny.

"Look closely at it, can you see how it is both pierced and bruised...."

Bunny looked at the rows of holes and the discoloration on each ridge.

"He was *pierced* for our transgressions *bruised* for our iniquities,"[4] he said and as he did it was as though scales were falling from Bunny's eyes.

---

[1] Exodus chapter 12

[2] Paul's First Epistle to the Corinthians chapter 10 verse 16

[3] Paul's First Epistle to the Corinthians chapter 11 verse 24

[4] Isaiah chapter 53 verse 5

"What was all that at the beginning of the meal?" she asked. "With the three pieces in a bag and hiding one of them behind the curtain?"

Hegesippus then explained that at the beginning of the meal, three matzah are placed in a bag, symbolising the trinity. Then the middle matzah is broken, wrapped in a linen cloth, and hidden. He then asked Bunny,

"If the middle matzah symbolised God the Son, then what does it mean that it was broken, wrapped and hidden?"

This was an easy question; it was just like being back in Sunday School.

"Jesus, I mean Yeshua, was killed, his body wrapped in linen and then buried."

"Yes," he agreed. "And this is a tradition that Jews have perpetuated for centuries and still do in your day."

"Really?" she asked surprised. Again, he nodded.

"Can't they see that it so obviously talks about Jesus?"

Hegesippus just shook his head.

Bunny took the matzah and as she did prayed a simple prayer, thanking God for opening her eyes.

"Are you saying that the Breaking of Bread, Holy Communion, The Eucharist, is something that the Jews have been doing for centuries?" she asked her host. "And it wasn't a new thing that... Yeshua instigated at the Last Supper?"

"Correct. Remember he came to fulfil, not to replace."

The third cup, the Cup of Redemption, was then poured, during which the leader quoted the Gospel of Luke before explaining the significance of the Church's relationship with Israel.

"After they had eaten, Yeshua took the cup saying, 'This cup is the new covenant in my blood, which is shed for you.'[1] God sent forth His Son to redeem those who were under the Law and that we might receive the adoption as sons.[2] Remember that you gentiles," he said pointing around the table, including Bunny, "you were at that time separated from the Messiah, alienated from Israel and strangers to the covenants of promise, having no hope and without

---

[1] The Gospel according to Luke chapter 22 verse 20

[2] Paul's Epistle to the Galatians chapter 4 verses 4 to 5

God in the world. But now in Yeshua we have all been brought near, by His blood.[1]

As she gratefully imbibed her third drink, she closed her eyes and thanked Jesus for the blood he shed on the cross and the many blessings promised to her in the Bible. As she did, for the first time, she realised that those blessings were promised to Israel and that the only way they could be hers was because she had been spiritually *adopted* into the Jewish nation. Without Israel, I have nothing, she suddenly realised.

The fourth and final cup, the Cup of Completion, was then filled. The leader explained that this is the cup of which Yeshua said, 'I will never again drink of the fruit of the vine until that day when I drink it new in the Kingdom of God.'[2] A prophetic statement looking toward his return.

"While Yeshua only drank three cups, we can drink all four and rejoice as His joy remains in us and our joy is complete,"[3] he said to much cheering.

Then the singing began. She wasn't sure which Psalm they were singing, but the relevance of these Old Testament truths became significant in a whole new way.

"The Lord has become my salvation…I will not die but live… You have become my salvation…The stone the builders rejected has become the capstone…Blessed is He who comes in the name of the Lord."[4]

As best she could, she joined in and as she worshipped her mind replayed all that she had just witnessed.

Firstly, it was a meeting in someone's house, around a meal, and at a time when to meet outside would have meant arrest. There was no liturgy, and yet there was structure. Everyone took part. There was no collection plate, but when someone was in need, they all gave freely. There was no sermon, but the word was shared and held in great reverence. There were earnest prayers all spontaneous and sincere. And songs of joy without accompaniment. And there, right in the centre, lay broken bread and wine. Not established as a new sacrament but the fulfilment of a very old, very Hebrew, one.

---

[1] Paul's Epistle to the Ephesians chapter 2 verse 12 to 13

[2] The Gospel according to Matthew chapter 26 verse 29

[3] The Gospel according to John chapter 15 verse 11

[4] Psalm 118

The roots of the Christian Church were self-evident, and appeared obvious to her – these roots were Hebraic. This must be what Augustine meant when he asked her to consider if she prayed to the same God as the Jews.

Sadly, she then realised, it was probably when the Church was severed from its Hebraic roots that Church unity began to wither.

Chapter 57

HELP ME, PLEASE

Blue lights flashed through the windows and illuminated half of Rex's face as he remained statuesque outside the rear window, unable or unwilling to move, and still clutching at his side the pistol with which he had shot The Badger. It wasn't the ambulance that Joel had dialled for seconds earlier, but instead five police cars pulled into the gravel yard in front of Lane End farmhouse. The sight of a gun-wielding man was sufficient for them to rapidly deploy into a defensive arc behind the sanctuary of their open car doors. The officer in charge shouted his demand for compliance from the suspected perpetrator as several police firearms officers took aim.

"It's okay Mr. Inspector, Sir." Artur leaned out of the window next to Rex's motionless frame as he shouted over to the officer, "He's with us."

Artur saw that Rex was still holding the gun so, whilst assuring the assembled law-enforcement cordon that it was 'Okay,' reached down and carefully lifted the pistol with his thumb and forefinger and tossed it to the ground. As arresting officers cautiously approached the scene with their own guns outstretched, Artur attempted to ease the situation.

"We forgot to tell you about Mr Fogge..." he said as handcuffs were forcibly snapped on to Rex's wrists now pulled behind his back. Artur spotted the detective inspector he had met an hour ago in Sanguine Wood and fired the end of his sentence in his direction, "He's the Quaker minister.'"

The DI stopped in his tracks.

"Are the rest of you Hallelujahs inside?"

Artur looked back into the room needlessly to make a quick headcount. Jack and Joel were there but no sign of Chris. The sight brought back to the forefront of his mind the seriousness of the casualties within.

"There are two more of us, but there are three others, all casualties. You'll need to come quickly. A young lady who's been stabbed and is bleeding badly; a man who has been shot in the shoulder," as he said it, he realised the implication and quickly pointed at Rex, "Not by him. And there is a kidnapper person who is... well, I think he is... most probably... dead." As he said it, he looked into Rex's eyes, now both filled with tears.

As the service ended and people began to slowly depart, she knew she was in a protracted fantasy, moving through time and space, witnessing pivotal events, decoding metaphors, spotting heresy, and hearing from the great and the good of Church history. And through it all his guiding hand had steered her to see for herself the internal self-destruction that the Church has brought upon itself, and to discover the roots from which it had become disconnected.

Once she was alone again with Hegesippus she stated clearly to him,

"The Church might be united *now*...I meant *then*... I mean in your now, but I have seen what happens next," she added angrily.

"*And yet?*" His gentle and sincere enquiry had the effect of, once again, causing Bunny to look within herself for the answer.

"*And yet...*" Bunny took the bait, "And yet the Church, across all of its ...*tribes*, has grown and grown from country to continent. It could have been the single most positively influential organisation in the world." She was on a roll. "And what is more, an organisation who, unlike any other, exists for the betterment of those people who are *not* its members! By bringing people back to God all of society's ills could be solved. The world would truly be a better place, it would be... Eden, once more."

"And will be," he added. Bunny wasn't sure about this particular eschatological theology so chose not to be distracted by it, rather pausing for a moment before continuing to share her personal revelations.

"*And yet...* despite its growth and influence, it is more fragmented than ever. It isn't one Church, but hundreds, thousands, and as far as I can see... or have seen... there aren't many real differences between them all. Apart from obvious differences in style and emphasis, they all serve the same Jesus, worship the same God. Apart from the heretics that is. Heresy is obvious. But beyond that, our differences are largely just arguments over words."

He chose not to interrupt her.

"*And yet...* today, in 155AD, the Church isn't in a mess. And that is without anyone organising it, no one in charge, no creeds or confessions, no five-volume expositions or printed pamphlets, no synods, no councils, no patriarch, no pope. Independent churches that are, in essence, all the same. Everyone singing from the same hymn sheet... literally." She enjoyed the joke. He just nodded, smiled and allowed her to continue.

"*And yet...*despite it all being exactly as God intended, it begins to deteriorate as different parts go off and do their own thing, go their own way, disconnect from..." It was then that the realisation hit her. The roots that it was disconnected from were Hebraic.

Her mind was abuzz. Despite all that she had witnessed in her liminal adventure, she seemed to be able to hold every experience, every conversation, every challenge to her traditional religion in her mind simultaneously. It was no longer a linear sequence of events but a three-hundred-and-sixty-degree subconscious immersion. She stood as if in the epicentre of all of Church history. Around her she could see face after face as they appeared and disappeared in a fast-paced montage. As they did, voices came into her head.

"Miscreants, false prophets and antichristian mushrumps!" one thundered. Then the voice of a sycophantic Eusebius of Caesarea announced, 'Well that is how I shall record it!'

Suddenly Bunny was standing at a table. As she looked an ink bottle was tipped over across it. Bunny's field of vision pulled-back to see that the words 'This is My Body' had been etched across the wood. As she stared into the black ink puddle, its surface began to ripple and bubble as if it were boiling. Suddenly an enormous splash made her recoil as droplets cascaded toward her. A dead rat had landed in the ink soup.

"I am no enthusiast!" An indignant voice demanded.

Bunny looked up. The table had gone and in front of her three men stood with their heads and arms in pillories. Slam! Slam! Slam! They each closed shut on their victims, Prynne, Bastwick and Burton who lifted their heads to look directly at Bunny, their expressions not one of resolution but of sadness. A sweet little girl's voice pleaded,

"I've been shut in, Miss."

The crowd around her began to press in on her. It was oppressive. Some seemed to be moving in one direction, the rest opposing them. Try as she may, she found herself bundled and jostled in one direction then another. The voice of John Wesley pleaded,

"But who shall convert me?"

Ahead she caught sight of a sign on the wall displaying that she was in Stink Street. She started to walk towards the sign and as she did the crowd began to thin. She had to stop when her foot hit something on the floor. She looked down to see a statue of the virgin Mary laid down on the floor as if sleeping. A plummy-voiced minister accused,

"She took her husband's horse without his permission."

As Bunny looked into the Madonna's face a hammer was brought down onto it and it instantly disintegrated into a thousand shards. She turned her face to protect it from flying pottery. When she looked back it was gone. Ahead she could see William Seymour standing outside the window of Charles Parham's charismatic meeting. He turned to look directly at Bunny, his eyes full of disappointment from being excluded because of the colour of his skin. Bunny continued towards him hoping to speak to him, but as she approached he pulled open the heavy curtain and indicated that she should look inside. To her surprise, behind the curtain she found she was looking inside the same Catholic confessional she had opened earlier looking for the priest. The same chair was there, again piled high with books. The topmost one was again, *Assertio Septem Sacramentorum* by Henry VIII. Beneath it this time she spotted Calvin's *The Institutes of the Christian Religion* and below it *Actes and Monuments*.

"Foxes Book of Martyrs," she said knowing how much he hated its popular title. She placed the top three books on the floor so as to inspect those beneath. They were Dante's *Inferno*, Milton's *Paradise Lost*, Rauschebush's *Christianity and the Social Crisis* and Spener's *Pious Desires*, the title of which again solicited a raised eyebrow. At the very bottom she could see wedged in the join of the seat-back and the cushion a tightly rolled scroll. She picked it up but the light in the confessional was too dim to read the hand-written title. She stepped back out of the confessional, unrolling the first portion to reveal the title, *Adversus Haereses*, its author Iranaeus. She quickly rolled the parchment up only to find a hand taking it from hers.

Her eyes followed the scroll. To her shock it was drawn right over a lit candle, igniting it instantly. Bunny looked up to see who was holding it. It was Michael Cerularius, who had burned the papal decree of excommunication. He dropped the burning parchment onto the table whilst smiling sarcastically, not at Bunny but behind her. She turned around to see that the confessional had vanished. Looking back at them was Humbert of Silva Candida fuming at Cerularius. Suddenly the ground beneath her feet began to vibrate. She was in the middle of the unmistakable seismic distress of an earthquake of some magnitude and looked down at her feet just in time to see a split fissure between her shoes. Once again, she was astride a divide.

She looked up and to her left, no longer Cerularius but now the short, stooped figure of Martin Luther. She smiled at him. His was the first face she had seen on this life-changing vision. He didn't smile back but gave a cold, empty stare. Bunny looked away and caught sight of Zwingli staring back at him.

The gap beneath her feet opened wider. Now on her left stood John Calvin and an indignant Franciscus Gromarius, her host at the Council of Dort. Opposite him stood Simon Episcobus, the Arminian. The ground began to move, a slow but unrelentingly drift apart. Looking to her left she watched William Brewster, Richard Clyfton and John Robinson coldly turn their back on her and walk away. The gap beneath her was now getting uncomfortably wide but she had no idea which side she should take. Face after face appeared on each side as she pivoted: Christian David and Peter Boehler from Herrnhut; John Wesley, then George Whitefield and Jonathan Edwards. She had to adjust her feet, moving each one to the edge of the widening fissure. Charles Parham, Alexander Boddy and Smith Wigglesworth surfaced but Bunny's attention was largely upon the fact that she really couldn't stretch her legs much further apart. Something was going to have to give. But how could she make a choice as to which side to take?

Enough of the left and right, she thought, so stared dead ahead, only to see that the bottomless, dark chasm turned ninety-degrees a few yards ahead of her. Just around the bend, a figure wearing stained, striped prison clothes stood on the far side of the void. He was flanked by two guards, one of whom roughly placed a noose over the prisoner's neck. As he pulled the noose tight it caused the prisoner to lift his head towards Bunny. It was Dietrich Bonhoeffer, who, on seeing her, opened his mouth to speak but before he could he was pushed over the edge and descended out of sight. Bunny screamed. The same fate awaited her. She looked down at her feet only to see that the crack beneath her feet was in the ice of a frozen lake. The crack was wide and ice-cold water was about to engulf her. Running towards her rescue she saw Dirk Willems, the Simonite martyr. It was too late, the final piece of ice holding her aloft splintered under her feet and she descended beneath the icy waters with a spluttering scream of,

"Help me, help me, please."

"I'm coming for you Bunny, I'm coming," Chris said, tears in his eyes and his heart racing.

The first rays of dawn were breaking as he sped along the route from Lane End Farm back to the hospital. He had snuck out of the rear door of the farmhouse when the police had arrived and, whilst their attention was on Rex, he had taken a dark circuitous route back to his car, hidden in the barn. The faint morning sunlight then helped him navigate his way back to the main road without the use of his headlights. With scant regard to either the speed limit or his safety he was intent on one purpose, on finding Bunny. It had taken him seconds to realise that the woman on the camp bed must be Velia Advowson. This fact made a lot of sense given that they had found photographs of her in the building. And his logic led him to the idea that if Velia was where everyone thought Bunny was then, just perhaps, Bunny was where everyone thought Velia was. He had no way to be sure, but it was the only hope he now had of finding his love.

"Hold on, Bunny. I'm coming."

The frozen water was cold. So cold! Bunny had never felt so cold in her life. Perhaps she would now have to accept that this was the coldness of death. As far as she knew, her eyes were open and yet everything around her was dark. Inky black... and silent. She had experienced these dark interludes earlier in her dream, and of late they had happened more frequently. Before, they only seemed to last a few moments before the lights would come back on. But this time it was lasting longer. She stared into the shivery darkness. Motionless. Silent.

"Help," she whispered. Not sure if the words were forming on her lips or were only audible in her head. She reached out,

"Chris, help me," she mouthed, hoping for rescue in the real world. Then she mouthed,

"Hegesippus?" appealing for a dreamland rescue.

No one was coming.

"God, help me," became her final plea.

Chapter 58

SLIPPING AWAY

By the time Chris arrived at the hospital, Ralph was waiting patiently with Thea against the far wall of casualty reception. His wound was little more than a deep cut, and had now been sealed with eight stitches and was buried deep within a sizeable bandage that looked so heavy it was no wonder that his arm rested limply in a sling. He was in good spirits but in Thea's opinion looked decidedly pale. The young man, Velia's boyfriend, was in a much worse condition and had already been taken to the operating theatre. Ralph had been formally discharged but as they had arrived together in the hospice ambulance they had no way of getting home other than with Rector Mashman.

The Rector was a few feet away, seated next to Lord and Lady Advowson, his lordship having agreed to, 'Sit down and stop shouting, as that wasn't helping anyone find his daughter.'

Chris's appearance was greeted by Thea, Ralph and Rector Mashman all rising to their feet, spontaneously but simultaneously.

"What are you doing here?" was the most obvious of questions and followed fifteen babble-strewn seconds as everyone spoke at the same time.

"I need to see Velia Advowson," Chris stated with a sense of urgency. The mention of the socialite's name was enough to bring her parents into the conversation, the Rector introducing them with his customary deference.

"We would *all* like to see her," Lord Advowson began, giving vent to his pent-up inner fury. Chris looked both agitated and confused. Thea came to his rescue.

"She's gone missing," she said in slightly hushed tones. "No one knows where she is."

Chris felt as though his legs were going to give way. He had pinned his hopes of finding Bunny on her being safely in casualty, mistakenly identified as Velia Advowson. He grabbed a nearby chair to steady himself. A movement that everyone could see.

"What's the matter, Chris?" Ralph asked.

Chris swallowed hard, realising he was going to have to be the one to tell Lord and Lady Advowson that he had just seen their precious daughter callously stabbed by her kidnapper. He sat down and suggested they did likewise. Lord Advowson was the last to retake one of the blue-plastic lightly padded chairs.

485

"Actually, I *do* know where your daughter is…" Chris said softly.

"Where?" her father demanded.

"She is at Lane End Farm… where she had been… kidnapped."

"Rubbish," the minor aristocrat rebuffed. "She's somewhere here in this damned hospital. It is just that these incompetent fools have misplaced her. Tell me, how do you misplace a patient?"

He looked in the direction of the rather flustered nurses manning the reception desk and thundered his punchline toward them,

"She isn't exactly a teaspoon!"

"I'm sorry, Sir… Madam," Chris faltered, "but you are mistaken." Lady Advowson could see he was being sincere and asked Chris to tell her what he knew.

"I've just come from the farmhouse and I promise you that she is there… was there… only she will be on her way here… to the hospital."

"Why?" Lady Advowson asked. Chris looked at his friends then into Velia's mother's eyes and could see years of love and motherhood now climaxing into an emotional pressure cooker about to explode. Chris couldn't be the one to tell her the awful truth.

"She has been injured… we called for an ambulance… so she should be on her way." That was the best he could offer. Lady Advowson clutched her coat together with both hands.

Lord Advowson dashed over to the desk, demanding to know of any ambulances that were en-route. His wife, before following him, had another question of Chris.

"Then why did you say that you 'Needed to see Velia' when you arrived here a few minutes ago?"

"Because the patient that they think is Velia is in fact…" he was too emotional to finish the sentence. Ralph stepped in and, having put two and two together, announced that the patient was,

"Bunny!"

Lady Advowson looked confused.

"I mean Miss Johan Elstow," Ralph clarified. "She's been missing all night."

Her ladyship turned to the Rector and asked him,

"Your secretary?" adding indignantly, "Did you know she'd gone AWOL, Vicar?"

Mashman gave his answer with a single nod of the head. The sound of her husband's bellowing voice drew Lady Advowson away with the promise that their daughter should be arriving in around fifteen minutes.

"Is it true?" Chris asked anxiously. "Has she really disappeared... somewhere in the hospital?"

The Rector couldn't answer Chris before releasing his signature expression which he had suppressed in the presence of his benefactors, for fear of offending them.

"Goodly heavens above!" he exhaled before addressing Chris. "It would appear so. For the last couple of hours they have been searching every ward, every corridor, every bed." He then relayed all that he had gleaned from his nursing confidants. Chris stood to his feet anxious to join the search.

"There's no point in you looking," Ralph interrupted, grasping Chris's sleeve with his unbandaged arm.

"Don't try to stop me Ralph," Chris snapped. "I know it might be difficult, but I have got to find her. I thought I had already."

Chris was confronted by the awful reality that he'd failed to protect her; then to find her only to discover that it wasn't her at all. Not for the first time that evening Ralph could see the passion and determination that was driving Chris's behaviour.

"I've got a second chance now and I am not going to waste it." Chris said emphatically. Rector Mashman pessimistically tried to explain to Chris the futility of his endeavours.

"But the place is full of locked doors, Chris."

It was true. All he could realistically achieve would be to charge around empty hospital corridors frantically grasping and twisting the handles of locked doors. Chris had to admit it, this was not a sensible idea. Ralph let go of Chris's sleeve, sensing that his quarry was not about to take flight. Chris sat down, conflicted internally, hung on the horns of a dilemma. On one horn was the need to do something, anything he could to find Bunny; but on the other the inability to identify anything that might work. All four sat silently. Chris, being the most agitated, drew the attention of the other three who watched as he finally closed his moist eyes and rocked his head backwards in despair. The motion of his eyelids caused two gathered tears to cascade down either cheek, washed away from their springs.

The sight of Chris's closed eyes prompted Ralph to offer a sympathetic prayer.

"Lord, help us. Give us the key to finding Bunny."

"Oh!" Thea interrupted. Chris pulled his head forward and opened his eyes to look at her. Ralph, who was still mid-prayer, suddenly stopped.

"Not a key as such," she said smiling. "But I do have a *pass* that will open any locked door."

"Behold, I have set before thee an open door, and no man can shut it," exclaimed the Rector.[1]

Someone must have heard her. The inky blackness faded into a seamless paper-white panorama that seemed to surround her.

"That's it, I must be dead," she said aloud as she pivoted around, subconsciously looking for Saint Peter standing at the pearly gates.

Suddenly her vision was pierced by a thin vertical black line, then another one slightly to its left. Then a third appeared, this one a little fainter and on the right of the original. A white circular line was then inscribed to one side, and within it a smaller circle in the centre and eight spokes radiating out forming segments. As she slowly rotated, more and more lines began appearing. They were not limited to her forward field of vision as lines, arcs and shapes were being drawn simultaneously all around her, above her and, causing her to reflexively step to one side, beneath her. She spun herself around more rapidly trying to make sense of the multiple lines and shapes forming around her. Then, as they began to connect and shading was added in parts, it became clear that this was an enormous three-dimensional line drawing.

"It's a sketch of a church," she said in enthralled, mesmerised wonder. "It's just like one of my sketches... but I'm inside it."

Soon the drawing was completed and around her was a perfect line-art depiction of her own church, All Saints'. It was familiar and yet seemed so fragile being made of no more than the strokes of an artist's pencil. But she could see no pencil, no hand, no artist. There must be an artist somewhere, she thought. Was it God?

She was surrounded by the comforting familiar landscape of the church she had called home for years and yet it seemed so transient, so ephemeral, the building was no more than a drawing and she was little more than detail upon

---

[1] The Book of Revelation: Chapter 3 verse 8

someone else's sketchpad. Suddenly she felt very small, very insignificant, very vulnerable, very... lifeless.

I'm definitely dead. She half expected to see a distant white light and hear the ominous tolling of bells.

But all she could see was a perfect three-dimensional depiction of her church, right down to the pews immediately next to her, each one holding the rectilinear depictions of a Bible, a hymn book and a kneeler. All were clearly line-drawn but seemed solid enough to pick up. She reached her hand towards the nearest wire-frame Bible to see if it had actual substance or was as ethereal as a mere drawing. Before she made contact, her attention was drawn beyond the pews to the lines and shading that had accurately depicted the north wall of the church. As she looked, they began to be erased and within seconds all the fine artistic detail had gone and a blank page loomed large. The rest of the drawing remained, surrounding her – it was just the north wall that was now blank. After what was little more than a few seconds, a new collection of lines, arcs and shading began to be etched where the north wall had been. Forgetting about the touch-test she had been about to perform, she instead walked over to the re-drawn wall, filled with curiosity.

"What is that?" she whispered as the drawing took shape. Where a wall once had been she found she could now step through and into another three-dimensional drawing as it was being completed around her. Shortly before the final pencil strokes were delivered she recognised it.

"C.R.F." she said in astonishment as she again revolved within the middle of the cinema-turned-sanctuary. Both C.R.F and All Saints' were now connected.

"There is no wall!" she exclaimed before walking quickly back into her Anglican domain, arriving just in time to see that the south wall was now mid-transformation. As she caught sight of the change her walk turned into a trot as she headed to where the south wall once stood. She braced for impact, still unsure if the drawing did indeed have substance, but there was no need. By the time she had traversed the knave the re-sketch was complete, and she found herself within yet another sanctuary: two aisles, crucifix and statue at the front. This was St Mary's, the very place where her journey had begun.

A journey that had undermined her previous surefootedness about what it meant to be a *church* person, which to her was, an *Anglican* church person. The neatly ordered boxes she had put those other church leaders into now seemed less important. Everything about Church had been tossed in the air and landed in places she hadn't expected. And to her amazement she found she had let go of her prior mono-denominational view of Church and allowed a whole new paradigm to form.

She looked over the landscape she had just crossed. She was inside a drawing of a Catholic church which connected to an Anglican one, and then into a Pentecostal one. Three very different churches and yet all inter-connected. The symbolism of erasing the physical divisions between each was obvious. This was a depiction of what she had come to realise. The divisions between each denomination were no more than drawn lines. Although not drawn by the hand of God.

She was settled in this understanding. And felt she was beginning to see Church through God's eyes, not the way that history had made it.

But something still wasn't right. Just *saying* that there should be no division between churches might be fine in theory, but the practical, obvious, reality is quite the opposite. This was the reality she could not escape. This was the reality that played out a month ago as blood was spilled on the All Saints' vestry carpet. If only she could reconcile the fact that there is so much division then she would be at peace. If she could find an answer to *that* question than she could close her eyes contentedly and allow herself to fall asleep.

Her thoughts were interrupted as she momentarily saw, in the corner of her eye, part of the St Mary's drawing move. She turned her head and saw that the lines depicting the curtain of the confessional had now been opened and were swaying slowly to a halt. She took it as an invitation to return to the start of her adventure, walked over and stood within its drawn space. She was tired and once inside, by reflex, went to sit down, before pausing as she realised that she hadn't tested whether the seat was really there and able to hold her weight. She tentatively lowered herself onto the shaded surface and exhaled contentedly as she felt it beneath her. The lines portraying the confessional curtain then re-closed.

The curtain has been *drawn*, she thought, enjoying the pun.

This was perhaps the most surreal moment in her whole lucid dream. She first set foot inside this confessional on a rainy October evening – that was in real life. Then somehow it became part of Martin Luther's church in Wittenberg in a dream that then later became a Nazi church; and now she was back inside the same confessional, but now it is no more than an Artist's Impression.

She shivered.

The last time she was here she had prayed. Now, that was all she could do.

"Dear Father. I've been on this journey; well, I guess you know that!" she started. "And I've seen first-hand how we have allowed, or encouraged, all sorts of division in your Church. Our motives have rarely been good." She then began to list some of the reasons that she had witnessed were at the birth of major denominations.

"Politics, jealousy, pride, anger, unforgiveness, greed..." the list trailed-off as she ended it with a resigned sigh. She couldn't skirt around it anymore. If she was going to be honest with herself, she was going to have to admit the truth; she was disgusted with her fellow believers, and that disgust included her own Church and, by extension, herself. Hundreds of years of infighting, suspicion, ostracization and strife had led to the unholy hotchpotch that the twenty-first century Church had become. Admittedly peace may now reign with no one baring arms against their fellow Christian, but conflict has been replaced by compromise.

"History has made every part of the Church trapped in their tradition. We are all stuck," she said exasperatedly. "No one is better than anyone else, we are all in the same boat."

As she said it the metaphor instantly formed in her mind.

"Every denomination stays in their own little boat, keeping away from every other fellow-*ship*. Admittedly, they approach those that appear to be similar, but then they frantically navigate away from those whose interpretation, or style, or dress code, or hymn book is different from their own. We all paddle around in circles, causing an almighty splash, whilst the world looks on and increasingly decides they would rather not step aboard." She reflected upon the boating lake image she had just concocted and closed her eyes to imagine each church as a faded blue moulded plastic boat, frenetically paddling about with nowhere to go, the far shoreline full of people watching on disapprovingly.

Closing her eyes was not a good idea. She may be within a dream, but her world was now cold, very, very cold. She could feel herself losing consciousness as her body began to shut down. She knew she had to do something to try to keep herself alert so clenched her fists and pulled herself awake, shouting out her angst.

"What an unholy mess we've made of it. We have managed to create an infinitely divided Church!" she declared as loudly as she dared. "I have lost count of how many. And they can't all be right, can they? Surely, wouldn't it be better if everyone believed the same?"

It was an obvious question and one which has been asked hundreds of times before. Over the centuries, ecumenical movements have earnestly tried to find the core truths that unite the diverse strands of the Christian Church, only to find that the common ground ends up being precariously thin. The exercise having failed to build unity, only succeeds in further exposing the gulfing differences. This was her key question. If she could answer this, she somehow knew she would be content enough to close her eyes once and for all.

At that point she heard a single bell chime from above her. She had no idea if St. Mary's had a bell tower. All Saints' had bells, though they were only rung on special occasions. As the bell tolled a second time a sense of ominous foreboding filled her. Was her time up? Should she ask for whom the bell tolls?

The bell rang out a third time, and was then joined by a second one coming, not from above, but from outside the confessional. She stepped outside and followed the sound of the second bell, back into the nave of All Saints'. Once there, a third bell sounded, this time it was coming from the direction of C.R.F. Bunny knew there was no bell in the former cinema. Three bells ringing was not only curious, but somehow she knew this was important.

The three bells continued to ring, each resonating at a different pitch. These weren't the familiar bells of All Saints', but these were chimes she had heard before. A fourth, then a fifth bell joined the peal. She *had* heard these bells before – on her time journey. One chime for each new denomination she met. What was at first an eerily single chime was soon becoming the pleasing sound of musical chords as the harmonics of the expertly tuned bells resounded together, each note accentuating the other.

Then she said it, almost without thinking.

"Live in harmony with one another."[1]

A smile lit her face for the first time in this pencil-drawn nether world.

"Harmony needs different notes! Different notes being played at the same time makes an overall better sound. If we didn't have different notes, there would be no harmony."

She had finally rung the bell of her own understanding as she realised that it is the differences that make the harmonics. You can't have *harmony* without *difference*. Suddenly it all made sense.

---

[1] Paul's Epistle to the Romans: Chapter 12 verse 16

"Yes, every part of the Church *needs* to be distinct, with their own purpose. It just won't work if they are all the same."

She made her way into the apse of pencil-drawn All Saints', and stood beside the altar as yet more bells joined the harmonic cacophony.

"I don't need to pretend that there aren't differences... I can do the opposite. I can..." The sound of bells was now so loud she needed to raise her voice to be heard. "I can celebrate them!" she shouted as she steadied herself with both hands on the altar.

She then did something that prior to her sub-conscious expedition she would have considered to be highly sacrilegious. She didn't know why, but in the stupor of her physical weakness she began to climb upon the altar. Throughout this... however long she had been dreaming, she had been inside many churches and discovered that most of them had no altar at all. It was just a *difference*, she thought as she sat on the middle of the sacramental table.

"Different. Different. And even if I don't understand them, or it is not my tribe," she said referencing the expression she had learned earlier, "I mustn't think of mine as better than theirs."

This was bold. Was she really saying that in accepting difference we could really live in peace with each other? This was huge. She looked up and saw through into the modern sanctuary of C.R.F. and, as far as she could make out, yet another sanctuary beyond that.

"There really is no division between us," she said, although too quietly to be heard above the chimes, adding, "If a house is divided against itself, it will not stand."[1]

Fatigue and cold were now extreme and she could do no more than allow herself to lie down, stretched out across the altar.

"I get it. I finally get it. It all makes sense," Bunny said as she lay looking heavenwards. "We are *meant* to be different; that is the plan, and difference is not division. And we can love those who are different."

The sense of satisfaction in Bunny was complete. She finally had the answer she wanted. Harmony needs difference. A body needs difference. Difference is good! Her journey was complete. Difference was not the same thing as division. We can be different without being divided. Difference is to be embraced, to be celebrated.

---

[1] The Gospel of Mark: Chapter 3 verse 25

Bunny felt her eyes closing. In her heart of hearts, she knew she didn't have much longer. The cold had now pervaded every sinew, every corpuscle, every breath and her heartrate had fallen desperately low. She relaxed and allowed her heavy eyes to shut as she listened in rapturous delight to the most beautiful campanological sound she had ever heard. There upon the altar she slipped out of consciousness.

Chapter 59

LAST BREATH

"When you said you had a pass that will open every door," Ralph asked Thea, "you didn't mean spiritually?" Thea laughed.

"No, I mean a real security pass that will open any real physical door in the building." She led the way to the administration desk opposite the WRVS café. Unlike earlier in the evening, the desk now had two people seated at it, one engrossed on her computer screen, the other finishing a phone call. Undeterred Thea continued towards them, side-stepped behind the desk, and thrust her hand deep into the CHAPL.IN pigeon-hole.

"Drat! It's not there!" She bent over to make a thorough visual inspection of the cavity. Her immediate thought was that the Rabbi must have tidied it away in his office, as she really ought to have done earlier. The sense of disappointment was palpable. Her three ecclesiastical colleagues, now standing beside the administration desk, just stared at her. Hope-deferred can be a crippling emotion. Thea began to turn her head and admit how sorry she was, but as she did her eye caught the end of a blue lanyard dangling out of the post box marked X-RAY. She reached for it and slowly pulled at the ribbon which came away easily. She took the few steps back to her friends, with the access-all-areas Chaplaincy Pass swinging between her fingers.

"Great, let's get looking for her," Chris said with haste.

"Wait a moment," Thea insisted. "This pass is not where I left it. Someone has moved it."

"Do you mean someone has *used* it?" Ralph suggested.

"Yes... well maybe." Thea admitted. "Someone could have taken it and used it."

"Can I help you?" The hospital administrator who had now finished her phone call asked the group, pointedly, wondering what they were doing loitering nearby. Thea turned to her, smiled disarmingly, and placed the Chaplaincy Pass around her own neck, signifying that she was part of the hospital *home team* and would not be in need of the suited lady's assistance.

"Yes, you can help us," Chris spoke up, and in so doing took the wind out of Thea's symbolic sails. Chris grabbed the pass and tugged it towards the desk, forcing Thea to follow.

"Are you able to tell us where this pass was last used?" he asked. The administrator looked at him, then back at Thea who nodded in agreement.

"I can just reset it," the administrator offered. "You don't need to go back to the last place, I can reset it." The blank faces of the four church leaders forced her to repeat her offer but this time with a more detailed explanation.

"If you don't swipe out of a zone when you leave it, the pass gets confused and stops working until you go back and exit properly. It happens all the time. We can reset it for you, do you want me to?" she asked holding her hand out to receive the offending pass and joining her colleague at the computer terminal ready to effect a reset.

"No!" Chris exclaimed. "Thank you, but I... we don't want it resetting. I just need to know where it was used last night."

Again, she looked at Thea for confirmation before agreeing to the unusual request. She then read the pass number, tapped it smartly into the keyboard, waited a few seconds and, following a couple of additional mouse clicks, gave a list.

"Okay, let's see. First floor room 316; that will be the Chaplaincy Office. Then Casualty Observation Ward. Then... Oh... that is most peculiar. That is the last place I would expect the need of chaplaincy," she said grinning.

"Where, where?" Chris pleaded.

"The mortuary," she said.

Chris, Ralph and Thea set off at speed leaving the Rector to thank the assistant and hear her strained witty punchline,

"Unless you are looking to raise the dead, of course,"

Around her she could hear the sound of singing. At first, she thought it was an angelic choir welcoming her into heaven, but no! These were human voices, both singing and praying. She was lying on a pencil-drawn altar within a frame-mesh church, but in her mind she was kneeling on a carpeted floor. Was this death or life? Was this madness? Was this a trick of the sub-conscious within her own sub-conscious dream? How many layers deep was she? No wonder she had no idea where she was.

The carpeted floor was in the midst of the twenty-four-seven prayer room in Herrnhut and passion and zealous prayer surrounded her. And there she sat on the floor, captivated by the overflowing joy around her. She tried to speak but could not. Then she felt a hand rest gently on her left shoulder. She slowly turned her head to see who it was, only to realise she was no longer in

Herrnhut but now was seated on the floor of Stones Folly, Topeka, Kansas, with the one hundred and twenty people desperately seeking the Baptism of the Holy Spirit. The hand on her shoulder belonged to a young Agnes Ozman, gently praying for her in Chinese. Bunny tried to raise a hand to thank her, but her limbs no longer moved.

Bunny looked away from Miss Ozman only to see the people in front of her were all crying. And once again the scene had changed. Now she was on Marham Mount, Bristol, and all the tear-stained faces belonged to a crowd of working-class folk all committing their lives to Jesus. Bunny lowered her head; she couldn't keep it upright any longer. As she did, she caught sight of a pair of black gentlemen's shoes, each sporting a vivid sliver buckle, to her right. Someone was standing next to her.

"Give me one hundred preachers who fear nothing but sin and desire nothing but God," the person said. It must be Methodist John Wesley. But then the voice changed direction, coming now from her left.

"Give me Scotland or I die." That was Presbyterian John Knox, she thought. Then he was followed by a cacophony of voices all of which she instantly recognised, and in so doing she recalled the positive impact they had had on her... and on history.

"Unless I am convinced by Scripture," that was Martin Luther, "My conscience is captive to the Word of God." Delivered with his usual bombastic confidence, contrasting markedly with the next voice, of St. Augustine.

"In essentials, unity; in non-essentials, liberty; in all things, charity."

Behind her, the French prophets of 1706 said in unison, "Thus saith the Lord." This prompted a declaration:

"A new sect of fanatics is breaking loose!" was the newspaper headline that Pentecostal William Seymour read aloud, and to which Puritan Praise God Barebone delivered a rapturous "Praise God!" closely followed by faith-healer Smith Wigglesworth who added, "They were *all* healed."

Bunny could feel herself smiling, although she suspected her facial muscles no longer responded. It may have been a journey where she had unearthed the dubious origins of whole swathes of Christendom, but nonetheless she had witnessed God at work, healing the sick, changing lives, saving souls. Regardless of which label they wore God was always at work.

Self-satisfaction released her exhaustion and permitted every muscle in her body to relax. As she lay upon the altar, she looked upwards, not knowing whether her eyes were open or not. There above her, her vision was filled with the image of Christ depicted in a blue robe holding a Bible and with a cartwheel-shaped halo. It was the mosaic from the apex of the Hagia Sophia. Staring at this image of Christ, Bunny remembered how she had first heard God's voice in the silence of the Quaker meeting.

She closed her already closed eyes.

"My heart was warmly moved," she heard a voice whisper in her ear.

"Into your care, Lord, I commit my spirit," she said although no audible words came out. Bunny's final mental image was of Chris, holding her arms and finally admitting,

"I like you."

She then exhaled her last breath, the cold having finally overcome her.

Chris was the first to arrive at the mortuary door but had to wait for Thea to arrive as she was still wearing the Chaplaincy Pass. In the moments it took for her to catch up with him, Chris realised that perhaps they should have asked the administrator to reset the pass after all, as there was a risk now that it might not work. Thea arrived and stooped slightly to allow the laminate to reach the electronic chip reader. Chris held his breath waiting for the red light to turn green. Success! Within seconds, they were inside. The motion-activated lights came on as soon as they entered. They were alone, well, so to speak. Chris had never been inside a mortuary before, but it was a scene he had witnessed several times on television crime shows. The floor was spotlessly-clean shiny grey epoxy, two hospital trolleys stood in the centre of the room, each devoid of any linen or pillows. These were austere trolleys for moving people whose need for comfort had come to an end. A single wheelchair stood to one side. There were no windows, as three of the four walls were taken up with what looked like industrial freezers. Indeed, that was what they were although with contents that were rather more sombre. The fourth wall, through which they entered, was peppered with notices, a wall-mounted telephone, a fire extinguisher and coat hooks from which three pairs of green overalls hung.

Rector Mashman arrived, having taken a somewhat more leisurely pace. When confronted with the solemn scene he whispered to himself,

"Goodly heavens above!"

The door to each cooler went from floor to above head height, enough to hold three bodies. There were at least ten doors on each of the three walls, so by a quick calculation that would mean Bunny could be in one of around a hundred places.

"Which one is she in?" Ralph asked the obvious question.

"Could be any," Thea admitted and approached the first door on the left side wall. "There are three names written on these," she said referring to the small whiteboards attached to the centre of each door.

"Hey, he wouldn't have written her name, would he?" she stated.

"No, you're right," Chris agreed. "Look for the blank ones." Sadly, a quick view of the name plates revealed that the vast majority were unmarked – the mortuary was barely at twenty percent capacity.

"We are going to have to open them all, guys," Chris warned his friends.

"Would you mind *awfully* if I didn't?" Reverend Mashman asked.

"No, you don't have to if you don't want to," Ralph said, then spotting the wheelchair suggested he sit down out of the way.

As Bunny's dead body lay motionless a woman reached out and lifted her cold lifeless hand, clasping it between the palms of her own.

This time Mercy Wheeler was standing beside Bunny as she lay, ready to replay the faith-filled moment when it was Mercy who had arisen from her bed after a lifetime of immobility. Mercy Wheeler was a woman of faith who, despite opposition, knew her God would heal her. Now, roles were reversed, but she nonetheless knew God could do it.

Mercy looked down at Bunny, her faith in God unshakable. She leaned over the unbreathing church secretary and whispered,

"Are you ready?"

Bunny's eyes opened as she met Mercy's stare. In an instant she too had faith for a miracle.

"Stop!" Chris arrested Ralph's suggestion, causing the Rector to immediately halt. "Why is there a wheelchair in a mortuary? No one comes in… in a chair!"

It was true. The stainless-steel trolleys in the centre of the room were for the purpose of moving the arrivals. A corpse in a wheelchair would be at the very least undignified, if not cumbersome. They each began to walk toward the wheelchair. It was pointing towards one of the doors with its brake on, and one could visualise someone being lifted from it and placed inside. Chris stood by the adjacent set of doors and, without hesitation, role-played lifting someone from the wheelchair, pivoting and laying them in a drawer. The bottom shelf was going to be the easiest to manoeuvre someone onto. He grabbed the shiny metal

499

handle, gave it a purposeful quarter turn, and pulled it open. The space was indeed occupied.

As the person-sized drawer slid out an empty intravenous bag fell to the floor with clear PVC tubing still attached to the arm. All eyes were on the body in the drawer covered by a sheet. Chris pulled it back to reveal Bunny still fully dressed but her skin almost blue. He placed his hand on her forehead.

"She's frozen," he said.

Thea lifted Bunny's arm and felt for a pulse. It was almost imperceptible – but it was there. She opened one of Bunny's eyes to reveal a widely dilated pupil.

"No, she's not frozen, this is hypothermia, and we'll have to act quickly to save her," Thea said calmingly.

"Well thank God we are in a hospital," Ralph said as he lifted the receiver of the internal telephone.

EPILOGUE

FOUR MONTHS LATER

Bunny couldn't remember the last time she had worn a brand-new dress, and certainly not one this expensive. But her parents had insisted she buy an outfit that was, in their opinion, 'befitting the occasion.' Despite her protestations on the unnecessary outlay, she had to concede that it wasn't every day one got invited to a formal civic reception at the Guildhall; and not only that, but one that is held in the honour of you and eight of your friends. So today, she had become a picture of English charm in a pale-blue silk pencil dress with a subtle pattern of delicate flowers and belt, together with complementary handbag, scarf, and shoes. The jewellery wasn't new but admittedly comprised only those items that she kept in the drawer of her late grandmother's jewellery box, those items she saved for best.

The reception was a formal luncheon which, after much internet research, she understood required 'an elegant and classy day dress and definitely not a cocktail dress or ball gown.' The men on the other hand were to wear 'dress suits or uniform, not black tie or medals.' The vagaries of English dress etiquette, whilst largely incomprehensible outside the echelons of the gentry and nobility, nonetheless established a calm, reassuring serenity in the setting where all had conformed to their constraints. Today was one of those days.

In addition to Bunny and her parents there were perhaps fifty people at the civic luncheon, which by all accounts was not only a formal occasion it was also set to be a sumptuous affair. This created secondary concerns in Bunny. Either she would spill food on the expensive dress or, more pressingly, the dress was so well fitting she was unsure if it would withstand the result of eating so much fine food. She knew she looked her best, but keeping it that way felt like it would be hard work.

Velia Advowson on the other hand not only looked elegant all the time, but she also carried herself with an air of confidence borne out of years of knowing that whatever happened she would still look good. Today being case in point. Velia looked every inch the model despite being wheelchair-bound and clearly unable to move her upper body freely. This was the result of three major operations that had managed to repair her abdominal wound, thankfully preserving her ability to bear children. Her fractured skull, inflicted with a full bottle of wine by her former boyfriend, gave the doctors more cause for concern.

Her full recovery, they said, was still months or even years away. But despite all of this, some ladies, Bunny thought, just seem to ooze sophistication. It must be in the breeding, she concluded.

The young socialite, who was staring somewhat vacantly into space, was being subtly and subconsciously guarded by her parents at the state end of the Guildhall, a modestly sized, but historically significant, room adjacent to the council offices. It was rarely used for such dining occasions, being more often the venue for musical recitals, art installations and the occasional high school debating contest. Thankfully, the council had other spaces for the more popular craft fayres and jumble sales, which helped preserve the ambiance of the Guildhall.

Lord Advowson, who was bedecked in his regimental mess dress uniform complete with epaulets that bore both a button and a crown signifying his rank of regimental major, stood behind Velia. He held a glass of champagne and orange juice in one hand, which sloshed about as his arms involuntarily punctuated his distant conversation. Bunny was sure that if the law had permitted it, he would have had a large cigar in the other hand. His wife, Lady Advowson, draped in an elegant pale red day dress and pearls, also stood behind their chairbound daughter.

His Lordship had been the visible face of the attempted kidnapping of his daughter last October. He had appeared several times in the national media and was presently urging the Government to add to their list of outlawed terrorists the Serbian group whose former national ringleader was Dragomir Bogdan Mecapovic – or, to use the now widely adopted tabloid shorthand, The Badger.

Lord Advowson had arranged for the regimental military band to play during the reception. They were ensconced in the front right corner of the room, their uniforms and instruments sparkling in the sunlight that spotlighted them through a nearby window. They had chosen to entertain the guests with a gentle background mix of classic hymns tunes, which most of those present couldn't help but hum along with.

Other than the musicians and his Lordship there was a small handful of uniformed people present. One of those was the Chief Constable in his dark blue dress uniform, his cap held securely under one arm. He was surrounded by an uncomfortably smart group of detectives. Bunny recognised two of them as those who had visited her to take her statement about the attempt to kidnap Velia Advowson. For her part, Bunny had no recollection of any of the events of that night and was as surprised as anyone to learn that she had been abducted

502

by mistake. Everything between knocking herself out in the confessional of St. Mary's and waking up in the hospital bed was, as she knowingly described it, no more than a dream.

It soon became clear to the detectives assigned to the case that Velia's pre-arranged head injury was to be the excuse needed to get her to the hospital and be transferred to the ambulance borrowed from St. Christopher's Hospice. This ruse would mean that the perpetrator of Velia's injury, her then boyfriend, would remain free to talk to her parents; the inside man making sure the ransom was paid. At least that was the plan. Bunny's arrival at the hospital at practically the same time as Velia was pure coincidence. Once The Badger realised his two accomplices had collected the wrong hostage from the hospital, in a fit of rage executed both in Sanguine Wood. He then returned to the hospital having re-stolen the ambulance and swapped Velia for Bunny, stashing her doped-up body in the mortuary. But no sooner had he returned to the farmhouse with his prey than a group of persistent church leaders turned up and foiled the plot.

Next to the detectives, Bunny could see a man standing with his wife. It was unclear if his ill-fitting suit was a result of a poor sizing choice or the necessities of accommodating the black neoprene sling that he had to wear until his shattered shoulder fully healed. The photojournalist had been invited, not in his professional capacity but as a fellow victim of Mecapovic. Despite that, he had brought his camera and had already taken dozens of pictures safe in the knowledge that today was going to be a healthy tabloid pay-day. The public had lapped up the Velia Advowson story. It had everything: kidnapping, murders, innocent victims, unlikely heroes and a double-crossing boyfriend who had become the target of much of the public's vitriol. That boyfriend, who survived his self-inflicted gunshot, was due to stand trial for several offences including kidnapping and attempted murder.

Over the months, once the core facts of the story had become exhausted, the thing that now generated more newspaper column-inches, airtime minutes and online posts than any other, said a lot about the public's priorities. As the kidnapping plot had been foiled before Mecapovic had issued his ransom demand, this meant that no one knew how much this ransom was to have been, and in essence how much Velia Advowson was worth. This was now the subject of several online polls, comparison pieces and tabloid speculation. There was even talk of her appearing on a TV special: 'The Top Ten Ransom Demands in History.'

Bunny wasn't the only one to feel decidedly uncomfortable with such speculation that trivialised the events of last October. Events which had resulted in the wounding of four people, the death of three and, had it not been for eight brave church leaders, a fourth – her own. Methodist Joel Whyens, Baptist Thea Howlsy, Lutheran Artur Thelmin, Quaker Rex Fogge, Presbyterian Jack Fort, Pentecostal Ralph Shafer, her own Rector Mashman and her dear Chris Palmer had all risked their lives to rescue her.

As she thought about it, she smiled. They had come to rescue her, *not* Velia. When it came to value, she knew exactly how much *she* was worth. Eight people who were willing to risk their lives for her; not only that but eight people who prior to that day didn't really get on with each other. This, she knew, was more than she could comprehend. Somehow, whilst she slept in her morphine enhanced coma, eight feuding people had chosen to work together to rescue her. She couldn't help but draw a comparison with Dietrich Bonhoeffer's Confessing Church in Nazi Germany which, despite being made up of several widely differing denominations, coalesced into a single group to oppose the oppression of the Jews. She didn't know how it had happened in her case, but it was as though focussing on helping someone in need was sufficient for Christians to put to one side their differences.

For her part, she now had a much more inclusive view of Church unity. She understood that difference was something to be celebrated – that without different notes you cannot have harmony. That each denomination, each 'tribe', is distinct and necessary. Every Christian needs to know where they fit in, to know the tribe that is *right for them* and more importantly to resist the divisive idea that their tribe is *the right one*. This was a huge change for a confirmed long-term Anglican.

Rector Mashman, himself in full clerical dress, was standing closest to the Advowsons, and was in deep conversation with Rex Fogge and his wife. Bunny knew she would have a job on her hands trying to explain that she now believes the Anglican Communion is just one of the equally valid parts of Christ's Church. When she brought up that subject with him previously, he didn't really understand and just repeated that he couldn't have rescued her on that night without everyone else. Perhaps that was as good a foundation to have laid, she thought. Maybe the Rector was too old to embrace a wholesale doctrinal re-emphasis. Only time will tell.

No one had seen much of Rex Fogge since that night. To be fair the Quakers did tend to keep themselves to themselves. But Rex had killed a man, an act which triggered much introspective turmoil within him. He fully expected to be prosecuted and was ready to take whatever punishment was due. Everyone who had witnessed the shooting had given their police statements, but it wasn't until Christmas Eve that Rex received a letter from the Crown Prosecution Service to say they would not be pressing any charges as 'Section 3(1) of the Criminal Law Act 1967 allowed a person to use reasonable force in the circumstances of the prevention of crime.' Rex was unsure that a fatal gunshot could ever be construed as *reasonable force*, but the letter went on to say they were satisfied that 'There was evidence he had only done what he honestly and instinctively thought was necessary,' and as that was the legal test, they had no grounds to pursue a case against him.

On hearing this news Bunny made a point of visiting Rex and his wife on Boxing Day. To her surprise, she discovered that they didn't celebrate what they considered to be the pagan Christmas festival. When she heard this something in Bunny's heart jumped in delight. The contrast between this simple view and the annual festive treadmill that was presently underway at All Saints' was indeed a joy. Whilst she didn't entirely agree, she had huge respect for their position. It was true, she felt, difference really was a good thing. For his part Rex admitted that the only other leader he had seen since that night was young Lutheran priest Artur Thelmin. Reading between the lines Bunny could see that to some extent Rex had taken Artur under his wing and without seeking to influence his Lutheran views was somehow providing pastoral support to the Austrian.

Bunny could see Artur standing a few feet behind Rex. In front of him, and in stark contrast to the formality of the occasion, Ralph Shafer was in a state of semi-undress. He had removed his jacket and rolled-up his shirt sleeve in order to show Artur's girlfriend the gunshot scar on his arm. This simple act was, itself, testimony to a change in Ralph. Being the pastor of the congregation with the largest attendance in the town had inevitably resulted in a subconscious attitude of superiority. Not that he would ever have realised it, but on the unwritten church league-table in his head he knew his would always be at the top. As a result of the events of that night, he had come to the realisation that he needed the other churches as much as he had previously assumed they needed him. He would have been unable to help his assistant pastor without the others. Without even knowing it, humility had kicked in and to be so freely disrobed today was part evidence of that.

The smile on Artur's face was a picture, Bunny thought. He was clearly pleased to be included. Four months ago he was an outsider, not dissimilar to how his whole denomination feels towards the rest of the Protestant movement. But on that night he found he had an important role to play. By using his analytical mind, and especially his language skills, without fear of being marginalised he had done his part. Whether it was acceptance that made him feel able to freely contribute, or that his contributions had made him feel accepted, was almost impossible to diagnose. What he did know was that these new friendships had been forged in adversity, and he wasn't going to let them go.

The next small group Bunny focussed upon stood towards the rear of the reception space, beyond some of the staff of St. Christopher's Hospice, and comprised Jack Fort, Joel Whyens and their wives. The sight of Presbyterian Jack brought a lump to Bunny's throat as she remembered the coffee she had shared with both Jack and Thea Howlsy in early January. Several of the group had begun to meet every week at Crossta Coffee at the open invitation of Ralph who had gifted them all Free Drinks for Life, itself another significant climb-down by the entrepreneurial Pentecostal pastor. On that particular Tuesday morning she, Jack and Thea were the only ones present. After a short catch-up on their mutual New Year festivities, Jack suddenly announced he had something important he wanted to say to Thea. Bunny offered to leave but he insisted that she stay as she was 'one also'. Bunny had no idea what that meant but nonetheless retained her seat around the circular coffee table. Jack then composed himself before delivering a clearly well-rehearsed apology on how he had been so rude to Thea, being a woman in leadership. Whilst he remained on the side of the Presbyterian Church that was opposed to the ordination of women, he said, he nonetheless could see that Thea was not only a strong woman, but also a Godly woman and as such deserving of his respect. When the burly Ulsterman then asked for Thea's forgiveness Bunny had almost released an involuntary vocal outburst of emotion. She kept it in. It was a beautiful moment. Thea said something about this being the second church leader she had had to forgive and tried to lighten the moment by joking that it was getting to be a bit of a habit. Neither Jack nor Bunny had any idea about her conversation with Joel back on that October night. When Thea saw his confusion, she stood up, stepped towards his side of the table and invited him to stand for a hug. Bunny wasn't sure if this was going to be one step too far for him, but she kept silent. He rose and embraced Thea with his two muscular arms that appeared to engulf her. Bunny couldn't see if either of them had tears in their eyes, all she knew was that she certainly had.

Mr. and Mrs. Whyens were a lively couple. In all the time that Bunny had known them she considered them to be a little too forward and vocal for her sensibilities, especially Joel. Previously, she had considered him to be someone who was never happy unless he was up at the front telling people what to do. Great for a preacher; somewhat irritating otherwise. But since that night she had seen a transformation. Joel was a regular at the Tuesday leaders' coffee and seeing his interaction with the others Bunny couldn't help but notice his default position had seemed to have been recalibrated into one of a team-player. It had taken Joel longer than the rest to realise that the events of that night were nothing to do with Kurdish relief and the Grey Wolves of Islam, but rather a Serbian terrorist looking to raise money for his cause. This confusion was something for which his fellow church leaders began to make fun of him; amazingly Bunny saw him take it in surprisingly good, and self-deprecating, humour. Bunny was convinced something must have happened which had allowed him to gain enough self-confidence to just be part of the group rather than feel he needed to perform and get noticed.

Bunny's room-wide survey scanned over a group of doctors, nurses and hospital chaplain Rabbi Tikvah, who made eye-contact with Bunny and nodded. Bunny smiled back before finally bringing her focus into the centre of the room where Thea Howlsy and Chris stood alongside her.

When Bunny had been found her body temperature was well below the 35°C that defines hypothermia. Her organs had begun to shut down and her comatose state was more a result of blood loss to the brain than all the morphine that had been pumped into her system that evening. The paramedics who attended to her in the mortuary said she was very lucky to be alive. The doctors later explained that the excessive morphine levels may have helped her body cope with the severe temperature reduction. She had just about made a full recovery, although still had no sensation in most of her fingertips. She was lucky, the doctors had told her, not to have frostbite in her fingers and to have lost some of them. She was indeed thankful for that.

Chris had remained at her bedside during the critical hours she lay unresponsive in the observation ward. He desperately wanted to hold her hand, but she was cocooned inside thermal insulation and he'd been warned not to interfere with it. So, he just sat there hour after hour, looking, waiting and praying. Praying that her body would regain temperature and that the morphine would release its grip on her. Praying she would open her eyes and that he would be her first sight.

Eventually his prayers were answered as consciousness returned and her vision slowly focused upon him. Feelings of relief and joy were then replaced by the realisation that he really ought to say something. Somewhat instinctively he joked,

"Well, I'm still waiting for your answer... do you like me too?"

A smile slowly grew across Bunny's lips and she, unable to speak, nodded her assent. Relief flushed through Chris prompting him to stand up, clumsily disturbing the aluminium-backed thermal wrap causing it to crackle and crinkle loudly. Thankfully, the nursing staff didn't hear. Both of their eyes were fixed on each other, each knowing what that precious moment meant. He slowly and quietly bent towards her, tenderly stroked her cheek with his fingers and placed a solitary kiss upon her cool forehead. As he pulled away, he saw her eyes were now closed as she slipped back to sleep. His eyes were filled with tears which he wiped way with the back of his hand. He knew she was back, and in time would recover.

Thea had visited Bunny in hospital perhaps as many times as Chris during her recovery in the first two weeks of November and she and Bunny had become the best of friends.

In hospital Thea had confessed to Bunny and Chris her feelings of guilt that she had met with Velia's boyfriend on that night but was more consumed with her own insecurities to detect there might be anything amiss, and that it was her hospital pass that had been used to gain access to the mortuary. Bunny had reassured her that it was fine, and Chris pointed out that without her intervention Ralph, as well as the boyfriend, might easily have both bled to death. We all did the best we could at the time, Chris assured her.

Rabbi Tikvah soon joined the group in the centre of the Guildhall, Thea making the polite introductions. Bunny was delighted to meet the Rabbi and immediately started asking him questions about the Jewish origin of the Christian faith. The Rabbi was surprised to find someone so knowledgeable on the subject, so too were both Chris and Thea.

"Is this something you have studied, is it so?" Tikvah enquired.

Bunny explained that a friend had opened her eyes to the subject and its significance to Church unity. She declined to point out that this friend, Hegesippus, had died nearly nineteen centuries ago.

When Thea started a new conversation with the hospital chaplain Chris took the opportunity to return to the subject that he had raised with Bunny twice previously. He was convinced that she must know something about the 'special announcement' that Lord Advowson had said he was going to be making today. But despite two glasses of buck-fizz it was proving near impossible to get her to admit it.

"I'm sure you know something."

"Maybe I do, but sometimes it's good to keep a surprise up your sleeve," she replied.

"We'll see about that," was the only answer he could muster. As he did, he unconsciously reached inside his jacket pocket for perhaps the fifth time since they arrived.

"Stop fidgeting, Chris," Bunny chastised. "You are making me nervous."

Chris immediately pulled his hand out of his pocket, apologised and slipped his hand into Bunny's. Thea couldn't help smiling at the fact that despite their gentle bickering Chris and Bunny were holding hands, like two teenagers in love she thought.

"Ladies and Gentlemen! If I could have your attention, please."

Lord Advowson's attempt to bring the room to order was punctuated by the gentle tapping of the back of a spoon onto the side of his now empty glass of champagne. The military band had already received the instruction to stop playing.

Rector Mashman immediately terminated his conversation with Mrs. Fogge. He always kept one eye on his Lordship whenever they were in the same room, for such an instruction as this. Rex took the opportunity to slip his hand into his wife's.

The tap-a-tapping of the empty wine glass continued as Artur nudged Ralph to quickly reverse his disrobing.

The final group who had failed to notice the crystal-glass reveille was the Fort's and Whyens' and a polite, but pronounced, cough was required to interrupt their merriment, Joel's laugh being the final sound heard before the room fell silent in anticipation.

"Thank you, thank you," he began. "Lady A. and I have invited you here for two reasons. Firstly, and most importantly is to say thank you. Your persistence, bravery and timely actions have meant that we have our precious daughter Velia alive with us today."

A spontaneous ripple of applause encircled the room.

"Our surgeon says that she was very lucky that the knife missed her vital organs and, three operations later, we are told she should make a full recovery." He placed his hand onto Velia's shoulder, an action which her mother replicated on the other. Velia didn't respond, continuing to stare ahead.

"And not only that. Our church secretary Miss Elstow was rescued."

This time, not applause, but a heartfelt cheer rang round the room. Bunny could feel her cheeks blush at the attention and squeezed Chris's hand tightly.

"Two lives saved! And there is more. The duplicity of a self-serving young man who had engineered his way into our family was exposed; and the evil plans of a kidnapper, whom we have all since learnt has carried out the self-same modus operandi several times in the past, has been once and for all terminated."

His Lordship may have expected a further cheer but only a solitary single handclap was heard. It wasn't clear as to whom it was, but it came from the direction of the detectives. Slightly taken aback by his audience's muted response, their host continued,

"Lady A. and I shall be eternally grateful to you," he said raising his still empty glass so as to punctuate his sincerity before placing it on the small circular linen-covered table in front of him. He lifted a pile of eight white envelopes next to the glass and quickly read out the elegantly handwritten names on the front of each.

"Christian Palmer, Ralph Shafer, Artur Thelmin, Ms. Thea Howlsy, Joel Whyens, Rex Fogge, Jack Fort and Rector Mashman."

Uncomfortable glances were exchanged between the addressees, no one knowing if they were expected to come forward to collect their envelope or not. Before anyone broke ranks Lord Advowson passed them to a nearby waiter with instructions to distribute them quickly. As the young server hastily ran between the recipients now signalling him, their host continued,

"In my capacity as Lord Lieutenant, I am Her Majesty's representative in the county. That position brings with it certain responsibilities, one of which is advising on the nomination of Royal honours. Never, in my opinion, has an award for bravery been more merited than in the actions of you eight, churchmen....and woman."

The room was stunned silence. Was he saying that these envelopes contained a note from the Queen?

"It is with pleasure that I can therefore advise you on behalf of the Crown..." he said gesturing to the recipients to open their envelope, "I can advise you that you have all been ..."

Envelopes were opened across the room to be greeted by gasps.

"... awarded the Queen's Gallantry Medal. And what you all have is official notification and invitation to your investiture at," as he described the Royal residence, "Buck House."

This was amazing news and came as such a shock to all, none of whom had any idea. Ralph looked across at Chris with pride and both of them laughed; Rector Mashman glowed with delight at being affirmed in his relationship with the Advowsons; Jack swelled with pride knowing his parents would be proud of his patriotism; Thea smiled in the knowledge that this was an award she had earned, in her own right; all Joel could see was the moment of fame it would give him; Artur smiled at the quaint Englishness of it, pleased nonetheless to be fully accepted.

"And thoroughly deserved by all," Lord Advowson ended.

A stunned silence filled the room for moments whilst the full implications of the letter were read. An invitation to Buckingham Palace for the investiture of a Royal honour; and that they would be entitled use the post-nominal letters of QGM.

Suddenly the silence was broken.

"I am sorry, Sir," Rex said as he walked towards the front of the room to hand his envelope, unopened, to the ceremonial Lord Lieutenant.

"But I cannot accept this," adding as he turned away, "I am no hero."

There was no need to ask why. It was obvious to everyone that Rex could not accept an award for having killed someone, no matter that the police investigation had already cleared him of any wrongdoing. Rex's faith dictated that he must be a pacifist and that one action had seared his conscience. He returned to the security of his wife's side, she grabbed his hand and kissed him sweetly on the cheek. Words were not needed.

Lord Advowson didn't know what to say, but before he took stock of the situation the sound of a letter being re-stuffed into an envelope preceded the footsteps of Jack Fort approaching the front. Ralph saw what he was about to do and began to slide his own letter back into its envelope.

"If my friend Rex can't accept it," Jack said boldly as he handed his letter back, placing it onto the white covered table in front of their host, "Then I too will, sadly, have to decline your kind offer."

"That goes for me too," Ralph added tossing his letter onto the table, next to Jack's, in front of a now bemused Lord Advowson. Within moments Artur joined them saying,

"Rex was a friend to me on that night, so I choose to stand by him today."

"No friends! You don't have to do this," Rex pleaded. "Take the medal, it is yours by right... it's just," he never finished the sentence as Thea stepped forward.

"It may be mine by right, but I choose friendship over rights," she said, adding impishly, "Anyway, it's my choice, and you cannot stop me."

Chris looked at Bunny for confirmation. The slightest twitch of her head was all that he needed, and his letter too was returned with a polite,

"Thanks, anyway."

"Do I want this?" Joel asked from the rear of the room in his usual obscure diction, only this time it was as much a heart-searching question, knowing that he certainly *did* want it. "Do I really want this?" he repeated, holding the letter aloft. Then, to everyone's surprise he said, "Yes I do!"

"It's fine Joel, you keep it, friend," Rex said reassuringly.

"But..." Joel teased, "I'm still handing it back. It is my sacrificial gift to you Rex."

Rex tried to speak to stop him, but nothing came out. Seven letters now adorned the table. The final one was in Rector Mashman's hand.

"Your Lordship," he began in his soft ecclesiastical tone. "I have served you and your father before you, always respecting your office and honouring you and your family." The Rector paused, waiting for a nod of agreement before continuing. It duly came.

"And I have rarely, if ever, done anything to displease you," again a pre-nod pause,

"But today I must tell you that my primary loyalty is to the Church."

"But!" Lord Advowson began, then much to everyone's shock the Rector lifted a finger to stop the aristocrat from interrupting him.

"As I was saying, my loyalty..."

"*Our* loyalty," Ralph added.

"Quite right! *Our* loyalty," the Rector continued, "is to the Church of Christ of which we are *all* part. Each in our different ways. So as much as it pains me to do this to you, I too must stand with my fellow Christian Soldiers." As he carefully laid his letter on the table, he delivered a most apposite biblical quote:

"We rejoice with those who rejoice," he said smiling at Miss Velia, "and we weep with those who weep," he shot a glance at Rex who had tears running down both of his cheeks.

The silence that followed was palpable ... eventually broken by the five-long followed by four-short taps of a spoon on a linen-covered table. Within seconds several others joined the impromptu percussive rendition of Onward Christian Soldiers, some clapping, others banging the table in front of them, and one tapping a full wine bottle with a dinner knife.

Lord Advowson gathered the letters and gave them to his wife, his face not one of anger as might have been expected but of bemusement. This was, after all, a time to thank those who had rescued his daughter.

"Well, I don't fully understand what has just happened," he began. "I am clearly out of touch when it comes to ecumenical matters. You all seem far more unified than I had given you credit for, which does make more sense of my second point." Everyone had forgotten that he had started by saying he had two points.

"And, I have to thank Miss Elstow for this," he began. Chris looked at her knowingly, he had suspected she was up to something. Bunny just smiled back. Then Lord Advowson coldly delivered a piece of information that shocked everyone.

"The upcoming inter-church event," he began.

"What?" everyone said in complete shocked unison, followed by a liberal dusting of "What event?", "But!" and "There is no event."

There it sat like a verbal hand-grenade spinning on the floor with its pin out, no one daring to pick it up. Everyone's mind flashed back to the meeting in early October and the fact that the only thing they had managed to agree was the date, Good Friday. Since then, despite their new-found friendships, the subject had not been brought up again. Best left alone in case it exploded.

Lord Advowson then explained that when he had visited Bunny in hospital, he asked her if she had any idea if there was anything he could do for the group of church leaders by way of a Thank-you. He stressed that the idea of the medal was his alone, an admission that now felt somewhat awkward. He was glad that he had another Thank-you up his sleeve, albeit he was a little nervous this too might be rejected. He explained that Bunny had suggested he might offer to host an inter-church gathering in the grounds at Brennan Hall – an offer he was only too delighted to make – and for the last few weeks they had been planning it in secret. The only thing he didn't understand, he went on to say, was her insistence that,

"It would be to mark the date of Christ's crucifixion," he said.

513

"Yes, Good Friday," The Rector chipped, adding with some satisfaction, "We all managed to agree on that."

"No, that is the thing. She insisted it must be a week later," the minor aristocrat said.

Furrowed brows looked at Bunny for an explanation. With glee she smiled and said,

"That will be Passover," she said as she looked at the person standing a few feet away, "Isn't it, Rabbi?"

The Hospital Chaplain could do nothing but nod in agreement, having suddenly been thrust into the middle of what felt like another controversial moment. All eyes were on the Rabbi, and as no one was speaking he had to say something.

"That is correct. The crucifixion happened at Passover with Jesus' body laid in the tomb before the start of the Passover sabbath."

Everyone continued to stare at him. Unsure as to whether those looks were accusatory or not, he quickly decided to pass comment on the core doctrine of the Christian faith.

"And the resurrection happened, three days later on..."

He paused, hoping to not cause offence. But before he could finish Bunny interrupted him saying with new-found glee,

"On the feast of First Fruits!"

Gasps filled the room. Bunny beamed with a huge grin. She knew she had received a divine revelation of a core truth of the Christian faith that had been abandoned only a century after the Church began. Having abandoned its roots, division began, and she was determined to play her part, in this small town in England, to wind that particular clock backwards. It took only a few moments for the silence to be broken.

"Well, we're up for it," Ralph said on behalf of his Pentecostal congregation.

"We are too," Baptist Thea quickly echoed.

Within moments the commitment to meet and mark the crucifixion, celebrate the resurrection and, most importantly, to demonstrate their unity was signalled by the leaders of the Methodist, Presbyterian, Quaker, Lutheran and finally Anglican churches.

"Well, on that optimistic note," Lord Advowson said pouncing upon the air of positivity, "I think it is time to eat."

The guests were then invited to find their allocated seats ready for what was destined to be a lavish meal. Napkins were unfolded, cutlery inspected, and wine bottles opened. As they took their seats Chris leaned over to Bunny and teased her. Referencing the carefully typed minutes she had made after the first inter-church planning meeting last October, he mocked,

"Date Agreed: Good Friday!"

Bunny laughed at the irony that even the one decision they had made had been wrong.

"To be able to find what you're looking for we first have to free ourselves from the constraints of the past," she replied thoughtfully whilst slackening the belt on her dress in preparation for the meal. As she did, Chris, once again, slipped his hand into his jacket pocket. Inside, he felt the velvet contours of the jewellery box containing the engagement ring with which he was going to surprise her later that afternoon.

"I couldn't agree more," he said.

END

For a more expansive exploration of the doctrinal basis of Church unity themes raised in this book, please read One Ancient and Modern Church by the same author.

Finally, I said there was a secret hidden in the names of each character. Let's start with our two main protagonists Johan 'Bunny' Elstow. Her first name and nickname are an anagram of John Bunyan. John Bunyan, author of *Pilgrims Progress,* the acclaimed story of a journey of discovery in the Christian life written in 1678, lived in the Bedfordshire village of Elstow. Talking of pilgrims, an alternative and less well-known name for a pilgrim is a Palmer. Hence Christian Palmer is himself on a journey of discovery. Now for the church men. I attempted to make their names each an anagram of one of the founders of their respective denominations. Joel Whyens (John Wesley), Artur Thelmin (Martin Luther) and Rector Mashman (Thomas Cranmer) were all particularly pleasing. Ms. Thea Howlsy (Thomas Helwys), Rex O. Fogge (George Fox) and Ralph Shafer M.A. (Charles F Parham) were all a bit of a stretch. But try as I may, I had to give up hunting for an anagram for Presbyterian founder John Knox. Instead, I made a simple substitution. John became Jack and Knox became Fort, as in Fort Knox. Not brilliant I know but you try and find one! I hope you enjoyed trying to decode them.